Fatherland

GINEVRA MANCINELLI

Book One of
Consecration

Copyright © 2021 Ginevra Mancinelli
All rights reserved.

No part of this book may be reproduced in any form by photocopying or any electronic or mechanical means, including information storage or retrieval systems, without permission in writing from both the copyright owner and the publisher.

This is a work of fiction. Unless otherwise indicated, all the names, characters, businesses, places, events, and incidents in this book are either the product of the author's imagination or used in a fictitious manner. Any resemblance to actual persons, living or dead, or actual events is purely coincidental.

This is for Nene and her unconditional support.

Prologue

Not a single breath of life made its way through the wooded meadow of Wilderose, the once protected land of the fallen and forgotten House Rosenfield, and yet, Patten could feel them getting close. The people who had tied his wrists and ankles to the branches and roots of the trees surrounding him. He had his shoes taken some time between the moment he lost consciousness after an entire day spent under the sun and the moment he woke up. His ruined garments, that looked like dirty rags more than clothes since he never had enough coin to afford anything new, were partially torn and hung loosely around his chest and thighs.

    Patten blinked then narrowed his eyes at the skies. No clouds layered the skies, which were dark blue. He didn't see any stars and that alarmed him. He should have been able to see them. The trees around him weren't that tall. The branches weren't entirely covered in leaves.

He should have listened to Old Martita, he told himself. "Pat," she called him after he delivered her some water from the town well. Fifteen liters she had wanted, the old hag. "Pat, go home, you lazy fleabag. The air smells of daisies. They are flowers for the dead," she insisted before carrying on with how her husband – whom everyone in Summerport believed to have never existed – used to bring her at least thirty liters of water every day. Fifteen liters in each cask snuggled under his giant arms.

Patten jumped slightly at the sound of fallen branches cracking under heavy feet. He held his breath, strands of brown hair clinging to his lips. "Who—who's there?" he croaked out.

A fire was suddenly lit before him and he saw her. A woman clad in a simple, sleeveless gown was holding the torch that lit the pyre in front of him. Long, chestnut hair slapped against her arms with every movement she made, but he couldn't see her face. It was covered by an iron helmet.

The woman soundlessly walked towards another woman behind her. Their figures seemed identical; tall, slender, and soft, although the second woman seemed slightly taller – Patten wasn't sure. The other woman's helmet suggested she was of higher importance. A shadow on the left side made it obvious that it was dented and a glowing, golden fabric adorned the top of the helmet and fell around the woman's shoulders as if it was her hair.

"Come forward," she ordered.

Patten's eyes darted around, only to notice that at least ten other masked maidens were surrounding him. They were all clad in white, walked barefoot, and dared not speak.

"What is your name?" the Golden Lady asked him in a soft voice.

"Pat—Patten," he blurted out. "Are you from Strongshore?" Patten panicked. "I swear to Lord Lionhelm, I did not borrow any coin for the taxes last moon—"

The Golden Lady clapped her hands and offered him a faint laugh. "You are severely mistaken, Pat."

The young man paled. Only Old Martita called him Pat.

"But fear not," the stranger continued. "You might be very lucky on this starless night." The woman walked up to him, swaying past the fire, and gently placed a hand on Patten's shoulder. "I see the tormented soul in you," she whispered. "Torn between fitting in a world that doesn't even know you and escaping every duty that weighs on you."

"I-I am a simple man," Patten's voice faltered. "What could you possibly want?"

The Golden Lady straightened her back, her hand dropping from where it rested on his shoulder. "It's your flesh I need."

She moved aside, giving him no further explanation while the maidens that remained silent crouched and fell to the ground, their slim fingers grasping the grass as they arched their backs. Screams and roars and moans escaped their lips as if the earth was swallowing their tongues and stuffing their throats with dirt. Patten's knees, which were already weak, began shaking, and his dull grey eyes stared at the Golden Lady who stood unflinching.

"What do you want?" he kept asking, tears of fear escaping the corners of his eyes.

He watched in horror as the helmeted witches arched away from the ground, throwing their heads back, chanting in a language unknown to him, and slamming the palms of their hands against the ground. They slammed and slammed again until Patten was certain he could feel the vibrations under his feet. It was all in his head, he tried to tell himself. The ground wouldn't shake so easily, he thought rationally.

Pain seized his right foot, and Patten began screaming as he felt a pointy end pierce his heel. With wide eyes, he stared down, only to realize it was one of the roots his ankle had been bound to. It was crawling under his skin, curling around his bones like a vine. His flesh was torn from the inside. He cried out, his vocal cords straining rapidly, but soon his left foot was pierced as well. His arms quickly followed, and Patten threw his head from side to side, shaking his shoulders as if to free himself.

Around him, some of the maidens sat with their thighs spread, others rested on their knees, and the Golden Lady watched the man. The wood that curled around his bones soon reached his back, his spine, and with each curl, they pierced his stomach, his chest. His bowels spurted out slowly, and his incessant screams turned into rasps.

Patten's bloodied eyes glanced down at the nearest witch he saw. She lifted the lid of her helmet, vivid emerald eyes staring at him. She was one of those who chose to sit on their knees. She had stopped chanting his death. He watched in horror as she lowered her dirtied hands and lifted her white gown to place both hands on her most secret place, cupping it and massaging it. One of the straps on her shoulders fell with her movements and unveiled a pale breast. Her hands moved faster, urging her hips to move as well. It wasn't long until she fell on her back, groaning loudly. Her hips arched off the ground, and she slid four digits inside her.

Her hips undulated and her back cracked, but Patten's vision was soon covered in red until he saw no longer. His jaw fell lax as if to let out a scream, but the vines that had dismembered him were clawing at his neck and piercing his eyes.

The largest animated branch twirled around the base of his neck and the Golden Lady raised her hands. Wilderose fell silent again. She didn't move, nor did the others, and they all stared at the fire, ignoring the sound of Patten's head falling to the ground. It was soon followed by an arm and one of his feet, but under her helmet, the Golden Lady was gritting her teeth.

The fire began dying out and soon the vines that held what remained of the dismembered man straightened and fell to the ground. No woman moved.

At last, the Golden Lady spoke.
"It wasn't him. Just another starless night."

Chapter I

Father's Will

Salty winds blew from the coast of Summerport up to the rocky lands of Strongshore and Tecla could taste them on her lips. Her bright hazel eyes looked at the blue skies for a few seconds, until the sun blinded her and she blinked away. She could hear the seagulls on the roofs of the villagers' houses – they jumped from barns to shops, flew from carts to carriages until they reached the top of the holy site she was about to enter.

It was just another mesmerizing temple, she thought upon gazing at the small pond covered in colorful flora. Bells rang for the mass, calling for the pious and the non-believers altogether. The entrance of the temple was lined with maidens who wore thin, almost transparent, golden robes that trailed behind them as they walked. Each carried a silver torch in her hands, their bare feet tiptoeing inside where a larger fire was lit in the middle of the room.

Tecla felt a hand wrap around hers tightly and the young girl looked to the side, where her servant was. Lyzon was a small woman with tanned skin and almond eyes, her incredibly long, black hair held together at the top of her head in what Tecla liked to call an overly complicated braid. The servant's large, beige gown hid her small figure, a fashion that the young lady always tried to mimic. Tecla's light chestnut hair cascaded down her back; it was tied near the ends just to avoid it slapping around her face as the spring winds blew. She knew her hair had to be properly tied on top of her head and that her large gowns were not the right attire for her social rank, but neither was the closeness with the woman next to her, whom she always regarded as someone between a mother and a sister. As long as Father didn't object, Tecla Lionhelm would continue living the way she wanted.

The two women were among the first to enter the temple once the procession was over, and another servant joined them – a man who had a smile full of teeth and many lines around his eyes. Fran was how he liked to be called, even though nobody knew if it was his real name. He tended to the gardens of Tecla's apartments at the Lionhelm palace and the young lady liked the man's presence and chatty personality. They were soon followed by other servants and nobles loyal to the Lionhelms. The warmth was replaced by chill air and scented smoke. Shivers ran down Tecla's spine as she adjusted to the temperature change and the atmosphere of the temple always brought peace, excitement, and, perhaps, a little bit of fear to her state of mind.

She looked up, the immensely tall cupolas of the temple making her dizzy. Sunlight pierced through the wide, tinted-glass windows, and as if more light was needed, chandeliers as wide as doors hung low from the ceiling. The fire maidens held their gaze low, looking only at the fire at the center of the room when they dropped their torches in it, then removed their thin garments to set them afire as well. They exited the holy room in two rows, one to the left and the other to the right, their bodies completely bare. Three men entirely clad in gold and iron stood behind the altar right above the fire, the stairs at their sides guarded by the military.

The man at the center moved forward, removing his sword from his side and uncovering his face. He was old and rugged, medium silver hair framing his face. He raised one hand before him, and the whole room proceeded to sit on their knees on the cold floor and hold their heads in their hands.

"Poor girls," Tecla heard her Lyzon say. "Poor girls," she whispered again.

She knew this wasn't Lyzon's religion, as the woman came from distant, unknown islands of the Zalejos Depths, located east of the Red Continent, places only her father had traveled to as a younger commander for the King's campaigns. However, Lyzon was pious and believed in the unseen. Whoever she believed in; she was praying to them in this temple.

"I wish to become a fire maiden too," Tecla admitted to her confidante, whose eyes widened in silence. "They are so beautiful."

"Behold the power of the Oracle and Her Angels of Steel," the Holy Commander began, his voice echoing throughout the temple. "For they fight the fay that waltzes with the dead."

"Burn fay," the crowd answered in unison.

Tecla's lips moved on their own as she knew exactly each piece of the action unfolding before her. She always found the mass beautiful because of the preaching that sounded like a poem and the distant chant of the maidens was a soft melody that would stay with her until the next religious event. Hazel eyes never focused on the Holy Commander who scrutinized every member of the Faith, as she was busy memorizing the scenes painted on the window glass.

Trees hugged clouds with their feathery leaves while their roots clawed at the earth; womanly figures were depicted in every corner – some slept, some wept, some seemed dead. Colors of blue and gold were used and reused in every corner, wherever skies and souls were painted. The windows themselves were majestic; hexagons divided in the middle, furtherly divided into more triangles. Each contained a scene from the Oracle's Memoir, the Oracle's portrait itself being painted on the central cupola of the temple. Tecla never looked at that one. She knew the eyes of the Oracle were cloudy and bore different hues and Her stare always made her feel hollow inside. Furthermore, she had grown up believing that the Oracle was of ethereal beauty, but when the ceiling of the cupola had been finished, her seven-year-old self hadn't expected the Oracle to share common facial traits. She could have been anyone, if not for Her eyes—midnight black fading into sky blue, mixing with fiery honey and scarlet.

"Where is the holiness in that?" the young lady whispered to herself.

"And it was in the moment the stars left the skies that the Oracle's eyes opened wide, black as the night, sucking in the light, that the seas were drained and birds rained down from their Heights," the Holy Commander continued what seemed to be the final chapter of the Memoir. "Remember, She spoke, blood condemns blood."

"May She find peace," the crowd recited.

"May She find—"

Tecla's right hip stung at that moment, and if it wasn't for the kneeling position she already was in, she would have fallen to the floor. Groaning, she held her side, leaning on one hand for support.

"Is everything alright, my lady?" she heard Lyzon ask.

The doors of the temple were abruptly flung open, the daylight floating in just as brutally. Tecla's ears were ringing, but she could hear the Holy Commander demanding an explanation.

"This mass ends here," a familiar voice spoke. "We need the servants to return to their duties and Lady Tecla needs to follow us, now."

Hazel eyes peeked behind, and she recognized him. It was Lord Angefort, Secretary of the Regency and Commander of the Lionhelm army. Tecla stood up with a little difficulty, even as she was helped by Lyzon and Fran. The holy room was completely silent, if not for the crackling of the fire.

"Lady Tecla, if you will follow us," Lord Angefort spoke politely, bowing his head.

"May I know what happened?"

"It is about Lord Thaesonwald."

Tecla frowned in confusion. Thaesonwald Lionhelm was her eldest brother, but they never grew up together. He was far older than her and had married before she was even born. She would see him every two or three months for official gatherings and ceremonies, but they would never exchange more than a couple of words.

Sensing her confusion, Lord Angefort added, "Something serious happened to your lord brother."

Truth be told, Tecla had always been a little afraid of her brother as a child. It could have been his thick, strawberry-blonde mustache, or his short and seemingly frail body, or maybe his little dark eyes peering up at everybody else in mischief – she wasn't sure. She walked silently past the gasping and whispering crowd, a sense of relief filling her chest.

✳✳✳

The ride from Oracle Hill to Strongshore lasted half a day, and Lord Arther Angefort led the Lionhelm knights through the clearings and forests beyond Summerport, up to the rocky lands where the palace would stand. Proud and bright, a sentinel of its own, the Lionhelm palace watched over the city-port of Edgemere from a distance and surveilled the decadent lands that once belonged to the Rosenfields, right before Courtbridge, which connected the Wilderose hills to the Regency and its capital city, Silverholde.

Lord Angefort quite often glanced at the carriage behind him, where Lady Tecla and her servants probably wondered about Lord Thaesonwald. It had not been her father's will to have her go back home so soon; it was, after all, her city day, but as soon as the news started spreading, Lord Angefort knew it would be Lord Tithan Lionhelm's wish to see all his children.

Arther Angefort had served Tithan Lionhelm ever since he was a boy. The Lionhelm in charge was the most respected lord of the Silver Lands, it was a fact well known amongst the Regency. Even as he was named Secretary of the Regency, Arther Angefort always sook for Lionhelm's guidance. The lord was old and wise and despite his eighty-three years of life, he was strong and sharp-minded. The entire southern region of the Silver Lands was under his firm control, and not even his spouse, Lady Voladea Lionhelm, born Terraward and of lesser origins, could reign over the household despite what the marriage laws dictated. The people of Summerport called her the Almost Lady Lionhelm, even though she had gifted her husband five children – Thaesonwald, Tylennald, Tesfira, Theliel, and Tecla.

Lord Tithan stood waiting at the wide-open doors of his palace as the carriage and his knights rode past the southern gate and followed the dusty path uphill. As they neared the entrance, the men lifted their weapons – spears, swords, longswords, bows – and their lord lifted his own broadsword before planting it on the ground before him with a flick of his wrist. It was a move that would upset his blacksmith, who always worked hard to make sure the blade was immaculate. Lord Angefort halted his brown, Wilderose horse, and the carriage stopped. Dismounting, he hurried himself to let the young lady out, helping her with her large, beige gown when it tried to get stuck on the doors. As if on cue, Lady Voladea appeared next to her lord, a displeased look on her face. The lines she bore spoke volumes about her worry, and Tecla knew it wasn't directed at her. Her parents were always an odd sight to her. Her father was tall, broad-shouldered, covered in indigo garments and a thick, amber coat that showcased his house's crest – three golden lion heads facing each other with long, snake-like tongues on a blue background. It was as simple as the Lionhelm's motto. Formed from many, now as one. His hair was always military trimmed, his face clean-shaven. Next to him, her mother looked like one of the Regency educators in charge of young nobles' knowledge. Her grey hair was tied into a tight bun, pearls on her earlobes and around her neck, her slightly puffy dress floating around her – a fashion Tecla had seen only in paintings older than her mother. Her eyes seemed baggy that day, a sign that she hadn't rested at all.

"Welcome, Lord Angefort," Tithan spoke solemnly. "Refreshment you will find in the hall, for our men and yourself."

"Thank you, my lord."

Ignoring the etiquette that her older siblings usually followed in such occurrences, Tecla gripped her father's arm, hugging his midsection. "Father."

"Tecla," the old lord acknowledged her with a smile he didn't try to contain. "Follow us." Glancing at the maid behind his daughter, he added, "Lyzon, you are welcome to wait for Lady Tecla in her bed-chambers."

The look he directed at her was intense but the woman bowed, her stare never leaving the young girl.

"If we are done with this circus," Lady Voladea butted in with anger, "your eldest son is in a critical state."

Lord Tithan ignored her manners and lack thereof, the couple walking together only for their common destination. The apartments of Lord Thaesonwald were located in the eastern wing of the palace, overlooking the coast. Only the ocean could be seen from there, and Tecla often wondered if it was somewhere there that her good friend Lyzon came from. The marbled floor and the stone walls made the temperature drop, and the girl found herself rubbing her arms. The elegance and opulence of the palace lacked the artistic touch, she believed. She used to tell her father about it often, only to be answered with a shrug and a chuckle. Tithan Lionhelm enjoyed good art, paintings, and sculptures most of all, but there were only religious artists that could be found in the Silver Lands and her father was most certainly not a believer of the Oracle. He had helped build the Regency and its scientific observatories. There was not a thing after death, he repeated to his children even when they were infants. Not a thing. Therefore, he had no interest in depictions of the afterlife. Instead, sigils, ancient and unusable weapons, fine silks, and rugs adorned every corner of the Lionhelms' vast settlement.

    The ivory and golden doors of Thaesonwald's bed-chambers were ajar, the corridor lined with his family and servants whispering and asking about his condition. Thaesonwald's wife, Lady Gwethana née Montel, was impeccably silent, her posture tall, while her eldest son could be seen praying to himself, his hands covering his forehead. Tecla was surprised not to see Thaesonwald's other children, for she remembered he and his wife had had two sons, but Thaesonwald often brought to the palace a good number of illegitimate children. The second-born of House Lionhelm, Tylennald, was missing as well, although his wife was there, having a hushed conversation with Tecla's older sister, Tesfira.

    As if on cue, the moment he was in sight, Lady Tesfira rushed to her father. "What now, Father? Half of Wald's body has been paralyzed. I heard the Secretary of the Regency is here. Always ready to spread some news in Silverholde, isn't he?" she commented with a hint of disdain.

    "Be quiet," Tithan spoke severely. "You always have to make a big deal of everything."

Turning to the other relatives around him, he cleared his throat. "Thaesonwald fell from his horse on his way to the encampment in Summerport," he informed them. "He was brought back here immediately, but on the way, he realized he couldn't feel the right side of his body. It started with his toes, and now it reached his face. Healer Martus is with him as we speak and he believes Thaesonwald is out of danger. However," he paused, swallowing for a moment, "we do not know whether he will be able to leave his bed ever again."

  Tesfira shook her head in disapproval, carrying on with her hushed conversation with her sister-in-law, Lady Wallysa. Tecla clutched the front of her gown, the plain fabric she wore in perfect contradiction with the fashion of the other ladies of the house. She stared at her sister Tesfira; whose long nails toyed with the ends of her long, curly, deep brown hair held together by several jeweled pins. Her straight dress was of a powerful red color, making her look even harsher than she was. Her thin eyebrows were framing her big, almost googly eyes. Wallysa, the wife of their brother Tylennald, was slightly bigger than Tesfira, but her long, straight blonde hair was a rarity in Strongshore. Pale hair was the hair of the people of the Sand Towers, all the way to the northeastern coast of the Silver Lands, but Wallysa's family, the Riverguards, always claimed to come from the crook of Courtbridge, where their fort was. Wallysa wore the Lionhelm colors more often than any other family member; her light blue and silver dress complimented her light eyes and matched the gold jewelry she wore on every occasion. She was more of a Lionhelm than Lady Lionhelm herself, the young girl noted as she kept staring. Tecla wondered if her children looked like her as well; she had never met Tylennald and Wallysa's son, nor their daughter, and a part of her was curious to see their facial features. In comparison to Lady Wallysa, Lady Voladea was very short and any trace of her past beauty had been lost, replaced by her signature frown, and her sandy-colored dresses almost made her look like an outsider. She oozed authority nonetheless, except when her husband was present. Lord Tithan was not a man who could ever be overshadowed.

  Tecla's gaze traveled to Lady Gwethana; whose son Tiran seemed to be praying still. She was the only one who didn't seem surprised at the news regarding her husband. Perhaps it was because her youngest son, Perren the Distracted, as he was nicknamed, had also had an accident when he was only a few months old, forever impairing his judgment and limiting his growth. Nevertheless, Gwethana kept her emotions to herself, even if the last time she was seen wearing a dark dress and headpiece was when she left, albeit reluctantly, the apartments she shared with her husband at the palace.

  "Can we see him?" Tiran asked his grandfather, emerging from his spiritual thoughts and looking balder and older than before if that was possible.

"You can," Tithan replied. "Make sure he does get rest though."

At the calmness of her husband, Lady Voladea's eyes twitched. "A word with you, my lord?"

Before he could reply, Tecla tugged slightly on her father's coat sleeve. "Father, may I go?" She didn't want to stay. She couldn't see her brother Theliel anywhere, and he was the only one she was comfortable around. She wanted to read the Oracle's Memoir or the chapters she found in the libraries at least, and maybe play in the gardens with Fran as well. Fran never said no.

Seeing her discomfort, Tithan nodded and motioned his spouse to follow him.

✷✷✷

"Are we not to discuss this?" Voladea complained, almost throwing her hands in the air the moment she and her husband were behind closed doors, in what Tithan called his observatory room.

The study was probably as large as the Regency's War Council room. Voladea wasn't sure; she had never been there, but there were seven tall windows on three sides of the room and a silver table that was three times Lord Tithan's bed. The concave ceiling was filled with what she believed to be millions of books, some probably even written in the old tongue of the Silver Lands. From the center of the ceiling hung a thin, long pendant which crystals reflected the sunlight across the room. A few candles were lit around Tithan's papers and manuscripts, and she watched him fix his round glasses on his tall nose, the copper-colored frame complimenting his hazel eyes.

Voladea held her hands together in a fashion that reminded her of her mother, Dayanna Terraward. It was a habit she had always disliked – she used to tell her mother that it made her look like she was always disapproving – but with time, she found herself doing the same. "Our eldest son may never recover from this sudden, inexplicable illness, and you announced it like a weather scribe observes the skies," she accused her husband, who raised both eyebrows at her before removing the glasses he had just put on.

"Inexplicable?" Tithan repeated. "Your son never took his role seriously. When he was born, I gave him quite the shelter and food; when he became a man, I gave him a good, smart wife who bore him two heirs," he reminded her. "Thaesonwald decided to poison himself with the wild plants of the Red Continent—"

"We do not talk about the Red Continent," his wife interrupted him with a whisper.

"Brought mistresses in Strongshore," he went on, "had one son with the first and two others with the current one and we've all been very accommodating. Were he to pass away, Tiran is his legitimate heir," the old lord concluded.

The greying mother locked her jaw, and with a clap of her hands, she asked, "Is that it? The boy trained under the best masters-at-arms of the continent and you more than I will have noticed that he isn't fit to lead any army; imagine a whole portion of the Silver Lands such as yours. And don't get me started on your poor description of Thaesonwald's life. You, of all people, can't make any comment on others' extramarital affairs." When she was met with silence, Voladea added, "You should reconsider Tylennald—"

Tithan slammed his hands on the table, causing her to slightly jump. "You have no say in what I can and cannot comment, Voladea," he roared. "Do not bring our second son into this. How many times need I repeat this?" he yelled. "Tylennald is off the list of heirs. The fact that I tolerate his and his wife's presence for the sake of daily family matters doesn't change anything."

"I can't believe you won't move on—"

"A son who attempts to write down his own father's last will before the latter's death is a depreciable act."

Voladea's brown eyes looked away and she held her breath for a few moments. Shaking her head slightly, she let her gaze drift to the scenery outside. While standing at the center of the room, she could still see the tall walls that protected the palace and its surrounding gardens, a thin, sandy path connecting the Lionhelm residence eastern gates to Edgemere's harbor. The bustling town was richer than most strongholds of the Silver Lands yet many left for the sunny, warm days of Summerport. These infinitely rich lands couldn't simply be taken for granted, Voladea thought.

"You can't treat everything as if it will always stay untouched," she insisted, her voice solemn. "Thaesonwald has his sons, no matter what happens to him—or you, but they are not reliable because you wouldn't grant me the right that is mine as a wife to educate the youth of this household."

"I have done everything in my power for my children," Tithan sighed out, shuffling the papers in front of him as he looked for a quill pen. "Thaesonwald had everything, and he turned it down with his behavior." Ignoring his second son, he carried on with his reasoning. "Tesfira wanted that commoner of a husband, so I gave him the title of Mayor of Edgemere but now, I hear rumors about her seeking a separation based on some religious grounds that I have yet to understand. Theliel is lucky to be part of the Regency's Treasure Council and he refuses to wed—which is fine, as long as he fulfills his duty."

"Tecla can be wed too," Voladea jumped in, taking a few steps forwards and resting her hands on the back of the chair across from him.

Tithan's glare was immediate. "She is fourteen."

"Only a year older than when I married you."

"It is out of the question."

Pushing the chair away and sending it flying across the room with a strength she didn't know she possessed, she hissed, "You owe me this, Tithan. I spawned heirs for you, I stayed silent for you when you came back with your bastard children—not only once, but twice. I kept them as my own and I am still thinking about them and their well-being. You may be strong but these are old bones. Don't you want to be the one deciding about her future?"

Tithan licked his thin lips, looking slightly hesitant. He briefly glanced at the chair made of solid wood and strengthened by iron and gold that his spouse had shoved away without breaking a sweat. "Tecla will join the Regency's Observatory Vault." His breath caught in his throat, and he added. "You may look for acceptable suitors but remember," Tithan said while standing up, "No marriage until she is seventeen years of age."

Voladea Lionhelm straightened her back and she bowed her head, part in respect and part in mockery. "My lord," she acknowledged him.

Never turning her back to him, she politely walked backward to open the door behind her and leave Lord Tithan to his calculations and other nonsense he had gotten into as an old lord. Her small heels clicked on the marbled floor as she slowly made her way back to her firstborn's bedchambers. She passed many guards holding their swords, ready to defend any member of the household but then she reached the wide, red corridor coated in carpets and curtains that connected Tithan's apartments to the common room. It was one of those areas of the palace that she called blind spots. Nobody ever stood in them for too long. A tall, strong figure walked towards her and she smiled faintly. He was the spitting image of his father. Chestnut hair with only one grey strand framing the right side of his face, big hazel eyes, and thin lips; every feature of his was an asset. Tylennald Lionhelm greeted his mother with a kiss on her forehead.

"Mother. You come from Father's apartments," he noted, offering her a toothy, charming smile.

"Through small victories, one perseveres," she answered, placing a hand on his cheek.

Chapter II

Writing of a Dirge

Gloomy, low notes escaped the violin played by the deaf and dumb boy outside the only tavern of Beggar's Pool. The insignificant town emerged from the shadows of Noirmont, the highest mountain of the Silver Lands that was located north of the Regency and its capital city. Every forest, every meadow, every fog-covered property belonged to the Rochelac family. That was until the headmistress of the family passed away a decade ago. The villeins of the Rochelacs swore that Lady Charlaine had had a son, but no one had ever seen the boy. The thick, never fading fog that engulfed the Noirmont and those who lived at its feet made it hard for anybody to reach the château. Loyal lords and servants kept bringing the harvested resources and the traded goods, for it was certain that someone lived in the castle carved in the mountain. The carts always returned empty to Beggar's Pool.

"Dark and steady, Loveleen walks," a girl not older than sixteen sang as the boy kept playing. "She has not seen daybreak yet.

"Loveleen tell me where he is,

"I know my boy surely lives."

As the patrons walked inside, a few coins were tossed at the pair's feet, but it wouldn't be enough for any kind of supper. The young woman resolved to hum when no one approached the tavern, and she didn't see the man towering over her until he was already there. Trying to remember where she left off, she didn't expect a full bag of silver to be given to her.

"T-too kind, Sir," she stammered, facing away.

"What song is it?" he asked her with a deep voice.

She peered up at him, the surprised look on her face turning into a slight blush when she realized it was a young, rather good-looking man talking to her. A rare sight for anyone born and raised in Beggar's Pool. "Awake My Loveleen," she answered; her northern accent thickening every vowel. "Are you a foreigner, Sir?" Before he could answer, she rambled, "Loveleen was the only daughter of Lord Zander Rochelac. She was wed to Lord Larcel Silenteye, who was from the Rain Lands, all the way from the western coast. They had only daughters, and Silenteye was rumored to have killed every boy of theirs by feeding them to the Beast of the Three Crosses town, and so the title passed on to Lady Charlaine."

The stranger nodded once, walking past her and the boy who never once stopped playing, lost in his trance as his lips moved but no sound came out. "Loveleen you have not seen me," he sang in a whisper, pushing the door open and studying the scene before him.

There were about ten tables total in that hole, and they were all full except for the one in the right corner. Two men sat there, discussing what seemed to be important matters as they wore the golden colors of the Regency. It was an odd sight to him; the Regency was never interested in the Fog Lands—the doomed lands, as they called them. They were either on their way back from the Sand Towers of the eastern coast or headed there. Moving closer to their table, he pushed back the hood of his dark brown cloak, revealing his medium-length, black hair. His black eyes were set straight ahead, waiting to be served. The two officials next to him scooched away from him and went on with their argument.

"What's it gonna be, lad?" an old woman asked him, carrying a tray with empty glasses and full of breadcrumbs.

"Just a stew, and a cup of wine."

"Look, I'm telling you, something is brewing out there," he heard the younger man on his right say in a hushed tone. "You can't tell me that these… oddities don't remind you of the Rosenfields' massacre."

"We do not even know the truth about the Rosenfields," the older one bit back while chewing on a rabbit leg. "Look, you are missing the facts here, boy. All we have is a series of murders of young men and the butchering of questionable young girls. There is no correlation between the two and let's not bring rumors about a dead family in the mix."

"Chief Eleres," the young official tried to insist.

"Hush now, Goldsnout. Eat your stew."

"That's a soup," the cloaked man who had been listening to their banter commented. The three men stared at each other as if trying to either remember or memorize each other's faces.

Chief Eleres was hunching over his meal, his greying beard and mustache dirtied by meat sauce and spilled wine. He wore no visible armor, only a uniform that suggested he was a high-ranking member of the Regency's Surveillance. The coat-of-arms of the Regency was on each piece of clothing he wore; a crowned golden owl shielded by one ivory rose and supported on each side by an azure lion and a black beast. Eleres kept chewing in a steady rhythm, while Goldsnout loudly slurped his soup. He was a simple boy, covered in armor, which made him look thicker than he was. His copper hair framed his round face, and his big, light green eyes scanned the attire of the man who sat on the same bench as him.

"What's your name?" Eleres asked him. "You don't seem to be from here."

"Jascha."

"Unusual name," the old man commented before spitting a bone and wiping his hands on the tablecloth. "Where are you headed?"

"You sure have a lot of questions," the black-haired man pointed out.

Unused to not being given the respect he deserved, Chief Eleres straightened up, ready to scold the insolent brat across from him, only to be interrupted by the old woman who had just dumped a tray on their table.

"Here's your cup of wine," she mocked, and Jascha stared down at the rusty, half-broken, and half-empty glass. "It'll be two silvers."

Jascha tossed three coins at her. Surprised and embarrassed at her behavior, the old owner walked away silently, wiping her oily hands on her dirty white headband. The two officials eating next to him remained quiet as well, finishing their meals without bothering each other. Eleres glanced now and then at the man who loudly rested his elbows on the table and took huge bites of bread with his very white and straight teeth. The mixture of commoner and noble manners had him confused, but the Regency's laws were strict and favorable to trade and exploration. No one was ever to be interrogated unless they were caught in illegal acts or suspected of such crimes.

The evening went on uneventfully for the two officials, watching as the tavern was slowly emptied, only a few men passing out of the wobbly tables. Goldsnout's eyes were full of sleep when Chief Eleres finally decided to walk upstairs, where the old owner kept a couple of rooms for traveling merchants and officers to rent. The melancholic sound of the violin that was now being played near the fireplace by the deaf and dumb reached their ears, the old woman who had served supper to the patrons shoving him to the side to let her guests pass.

"Hush now Derry," she scolded the boy, her large and round body limping upstairs.

"Your son?" Jascha heard Eleres ask.

"I'll be damned if any son of mine was mute. I have a daughter who takes care of all the cleaning at night."

"Why so?" Goldsnout argued. "The Angels of Steel of the Oracle were mute."

"The Oracle was from the Pit of Torture!"

"Such blasphemy…"

Their voices faded as they disappeared upstairs, and Jascha's unblinking gaze was set on the fire. The empty glass of wine on the table was untouched, and half the stew sat in front of him, cold and of a dull, green, and brown color. His dark eyes glanced down and he used his spoon to poke the lonely chicken bone in the bowl. It barely had any meat for him to eat. He stood up, looking back at the fire shadowed by the now unmoving boy who held his knees close to his chest. Jascha's lips twisted in disgust as he felt the taste of the stew in his throat, and he walked out. The icy winds that came from the North couldn't be blocked by Noirmont, and he promptly covered his hands with his thick gloves. He walked in silence near the tree where his ivory horse drank water and as he placed his right hand on the animal's nose, his black eyes were met with the sapphire stare of his mount.

The snow that had just started setting on the ground shifted behind him, and Jascha glanced around only to see a pair of bare feet nearing him. It was the girl who sang before, and her skin was turning blue from the dropping temperature. Wearing only old rags as clothing, he was surprised she could still move.

"Are you traveling alone?" she asked him in a curious tone.

"Why do you ask?" he retorted, with no intention of turning around to face her.

"Cold nights such as these can be very lonely for the explorer that wanders off alone."

Jascha turned heels at that, his black eyes filled with emotions that rivaled both fury and abhorrence put together. He took a step forward, the freezing girl in front of him barely reaching his chin. "Was the silver I gifted you earlier not enough?" he asked menacingly.

"That is not what I said," she defended herself, holding her own scrawny body as if to shield herself from the cold.

"I know what you said," Jascha cut in, sending his elbow against her stomach so she would fall on her knees.

The girl yelped, coughing and choking on her saliva as she tried to regain control of her breathing.

"You figured that I had more coin and that if you sold yourself to me you could leave this place while being fed and taken care of until the next idiot falls under your nonexistent charm."

"No, no!" she panicked, her greasy dark hair mixing with the dirt and snow she was shoved against as a fist collided with her now bare bottom cheek, and she screamed. "Mother, mo—" she yelled, her hand reaching out in the direction of the tavern that was so close to them, only to be silenced by the gloved hand that covered her mouth.

"Why are you being difficult?" the man who pinned her against the ground taunted, hissing against her ear. "Tell me," he ordered, "what about a good punch for every silver piece in that bag? Would your lower back resist?"

His glove was quickly coated with a mixture of the girl's heavy tears and the saliva that came out her mouth with each muffled cry of hers. Jascha tugged on the front of his cloak when it pressed against his throat, then punched her again. Her skin was red and bruised easily, her skinny body shattering quickly, just as her bones broke like branches of an old, dead tree. How old she was and how famished she felt were facts that mattered little to him as he repeatedly beat her bottom, her thighs, her spine. Could she still feel anything past her hips? He didn't know. As far as he knew, she still moved.

Her cries were duller now, and her whining had quieted down a bit. Perhaps she was cold, perhaps she was tired. Jascha opened the front of his britches, only to further part the girl's legs with his knees. Her inner thighs were coated in blood, either from his violent assault or from her sanguine days. His black eyes glanced down at his half-erected manhood and promptly drove himself deep inside the feeble girl who sobbed away against his hand. His hips moved frantically, the warmth of her blood and the dryness of her walls only further angering him. Dark strands covered his nearly pained face and he bit his lower lip, nearly monstrous sounds coming out of his mouth. He pushed deeper and deeper in, the thrusting resulting in a mere humping the more he went on. His hands tugged at her hair only to slam her face against the ground repeatedly. He emptied himself before he wanted to, breathing loudly. Jascha couldn't feel his lungs.

The inhuman noise of him breathing erratically was briefly interrupted by the words that escaped his lips, spit hitting her ears as he leaned in. "He has starved in your womb,

"Loveleen you have sent him to his tomb."

The girl's brown eyes widened for a second, before losing their spark again. "You said you didn't know the song," she whispered. "You didn't know. You didn't… know…

"You didn't know."

Jascha's own eyes were widely shut, the lost expression on his face twisting into a pained one. Silent sobs rocked his upper body, and the two of them stayed still in the snow, the icy winds blowing so hard that their howling was the only noise that could be heard. Desperate huffs and whimpers mixed with agonizing cries as Jascha reached for his sides with shaky hands. Sheathed against his right hip, a bright dagger shone with several colored jewels adorning its hilt. The crest carved in the pommel was hidden by Jascha's hand as he grabbed the weapon and plunged it in the girl's back, resting his forehead against the back of her head. He felt her constrict around him so he pushed her face deeper into the ground to silence her. The blade cut and stabbed again, and again, and with each plunge Jascha would scream in her place. The large, gaping wounds where he stabbed too many times were quickly filled with a mixture of blood, snow, tears, and saliva. He clawed and clawed again with his dagger, almost as if he was looking for something embed deep inside her.

With one last stab, Jascha dropped the blade, looking ahead, his arms halfway up in the air. His eyes weren't able to focus on anything in the dark, and he waited, his back straight. No more movement, he thought. He wasn't moving any longer, yet it felt as if something inside him was circling his spine.

The girl's spent body lifelessly remained on the ground, pieces of clothing scattered around her and tainted by blood. The winds that blew from beneath Noirmont engulfed her body with snow, leaving only a hand uncovered as if her corpse was still reaching out in the direction of the tavern. The icy winds circled and lifted the fog of the region even if only briefly. The moment they petered out, the dark fog settled again and the sun rose over Beggar's Pool. The surviving town emerged from its slumber, but Jascha had long disappeared and the first sound that was heard came from the deaf and dumb Derry who was shattering his violin against the stone path leading to the tavern.

It wasn't long until the old owner came out, strangled cries leaving her lungs as she found her daughter. Ignoring the two officials who soon ran towards her, awakened by all the noise, the woman dug inside the snow, her daughter's name on her lips.

Loveleen.

✳✳✳

The sound of hooves hitting the ground hard echoed through the mountains of Strongshore. It wasn't long until the gates began to open, the sound of buisines announcing the arrival of a Lionhelm. They sang the tune the family had adopted as theirs; a fast-paced, war-heavy melody in memory of the campaigns led by Tithan Lionhelm on behalf of the King of the Silver Lands and by his father before him, Theliel Lionhelm. As soon as the two riders were identified, the heralds switched with no transition to another hymn that was more solemn and moderately paced – the Regency's.

It wasn't long until the inhabitants of Strongshore lifted their heads and climbed the walls of the palace to better see who had just arrived. The members of the household themselves leaned against the windows and whispered to each other. The sight of Lord Lionhelm's fourth child answered many questions, but as soon as his light chestnut hair was recognizable, the curiosity vanished and the stares turned away. The workforce of Strongshore went back to their duties and the ladies who hoped to see lords from the inland of the Silver Lands turned heels.

Only a window was opened and it was the youngest Lionhelm's. Tecla had bounced from her chair, ruining Lyzon's braiding, and she smiled at the sight of her brother. The dark-skinned maid didn't need to see to understand that Lord Theliel had arrived. She knew her young lady and Theliel Lionhelm shared a special bond. Despite the fifteen years of age that separated them, they were closer to each other than any other pair of Lionhelm siblings. Lyzon didn't know if for some mystic reason, the two Lionhelms who were named after their paternal grandparents felt a connection to their ancestors or if they were simply the most genuine people of the household, given the fact that they were the youngest members and grew up with fewer responsibilities and expectations burdening them.

  Theliel Lionhelm was the tallest man in the family, despite not being the strongest. His shape was light and lean, which made him one of the best horseback riders of the Silver Lands, but not the strongest fighter. Theliel was a man loved by the simple people, but not welcome by the nobility. He was often rumored of bedding women with questionable habits, taking them from Egdemere's harbor and smuggling them inside the palace, but Lyzon knew the main reason was probably the fact that Theliel's mother had been an official mistress of Lord Lionhelm and while that was usually not something to be frowned upon, mental instability was.

  Theliel Lionhelm was not a man that was easily trusted, and his father had tried to give him a better reputation by appointing him to the Regency's Treasure Council at the age of eighteen.

Nevertheless, the young man would visit regularly, if only to hold his sister in his arms.

"Lyzon, I won't be long," Lady Tecla announced, rushing towards the tall and thin doors of her apartments.

"Educator Tomas will be here right after the Judgment Prayer," the maid reminded her.

"That gives me enough time," Tecla reasoned. "We just had our Praise Prayer."

Lyzon looked away, plucking the lady's strands that had collected in the silver brush she had been using until a few moments ago. The doors were quickly flung open and slammed back, and Tecla's small feet rushed past the guards and down the stairs of the northern wing of the palace where she resided. Her loose hair flapped behind her, her ivory, straight dress fitted under her small, round chest and trailing behind her.

She knew that by then her brother would be past the common room to try and surprise her at the next corner she would round. Only there wasn't anybody at the next corner. Catching her breath, her cheeks rosy, Tecla glanced around in confusion. She took careful steps, looking for her brother, even leaning closer to a few guards to check if he had decided to disguise himself for once. With less excitement filling her, Tecla reached the doors of the common room and a guard bowed to her before letting her in. It was empty, except for those few guards on top of the staircase that watched over the people who would come to eat and rest.

"Tecla," she heard her brother's voice. "Good day."

She turned around and Theliel was right there, looking like he had just come through the same door as she, a shorter, bulkier man at his side. The stranger offered her a smile as if to appear less scary to the young lady, but she stood frozen in place, eyeing his untamed, curly black mane and even bigger beard. The man wore no uniform and surprisingly enough, neither did her brother.

"You didn't come up to meet me," she said, her hazel eyes glancing back at her brother.

He brushed his hair to the side with his fingers, then leaned in to kiss her cheek. "I heard about Thaesonwald. I came as soon as I could," he explained. "I thought I would wait here for Father," he went on, slumping on the nearest bench, his Regency armor clinking.

"Where is your lance?" Tecla wondered out loud, looking for the weapon her brother usually carried along. It bore their family's crest with their motto engraved on it and no Regency colors.

"Left it with Master-at-Arms Fantine. It needs a little sharpening – she knows who to look for. Why?" Before his sister could answer, Theliel changed the subject. "This is my good friend Sarkis," he said, introducing the curly-haired man. "We met in Silverholde."

Tecla gave him a blank look.

"Riding is… a bit less dull when in good company."

"Your brother saved me from quite the tricky situation," Sarkis said with a hoarse voice. "You should be proud of him," addressed the lady with no manners.

Tecla narrowed her eyes. "I always am. And for your information," she turned to her brother with a bored, judgmental stare, "Thaesonwald is paralyzed. Half of his body doesn't respond and he's been stuck like that for days now. Relatives have been waiting in front of his doors to know if the line of succession is bound to change now," she blurted out, feeling disdain for the first time in her young adult life. "Isn't that what you are here for as well?"

Silence and disbelief filled the room, Theliel's lips parted until his mouth was half agape, and the man who had accompanied him whistled, seemingly amused. Blood rushed to Tecla's face as she realized the meaning of her words, but before she could speak, the sound of armor plates shifting in place reached their ears. The guards bowed deeply at the sight of their lord walking past them, his face set in a judging, almost disappointed expression.

Tithan Lionhelm looked with wrinkly eyes at his children and the man who had never been invited into his home. "What are you doing here, Theliel? And who have you brought this time?" he growled. "Wasn't I clear enough during our last exchange?" he went on, walking towards the young man whose stare had darkened into a defiant glare. "Your place is at—"

"I left the Regency," Theliel announced him. "I left the Treasure Council, I left it all," he repeated, almost reveling in his father's shock and standing up, the slight height difference between them working in his favor. "My place is here, Father. And if you'll have me explain—"

Tecla's sharp shriek filled the hall as her father's silver-plated hand collided with Theliel's face, sending him rolling on the floor, blood spilling from his nose and his cheek forever marked. She pressed her hands against her mouth to silence herself while Sarkis rushed to his friend, who pushed him away in return as he covered his nose and mouth with one gloved hand.

"Tecla." Tithan's deep voice left no room for doubt. She had angered him as well. "Walk with me, daughter of mine," he added in a slightly softer tone.

She raised her eyebrows at him, his hand on her shoulder shaking her from her stupor. She slowly dropped her hands to her sides, no longer needing to muffle herself. She nearly stumbled over her own feet as she tried to catch up with her father's pace, and they left the common room for Strongshore's gardens, Theliel's angered gaze fixed on his father's back.

He hadn't even been granted a breath for him to explain.

Chapter III

THE WILDEST ROSE

The Great Gardens of Strongshore were filled with labyrinths and harvestable fruit trees that were surrounded by other plants and flowers which seeds had been brought from all across the Silver Lands. Some even originated from the Red Continent thanks to Tithan Lionhelm's successful campaigns and exploration of the unknown depths that surrounded the Silver Lands. At times, even wildlife could be seen in the Lionhelm gardens, as the green scenery merged with the forests that surrounded the palace. Tecla's hazel stare fell on a deer that was enjoying the freshwater of the central fountain. She would usually have an eerie feeling upon being so close to animals that never let themselves be touched by humans, but her father's presence intimidated her.

Lord Tithan had her sit down on a stone bench close to the fountain, the clinking of his armor causing the deer to vanish behind the nearest trees. His serious expression and deep frown suddenly gave away his age and Tecla looked down.

"Forgive me," she whispered. "I shouldn't have spoken that way to Theliel."

"Is something worrying you?" her father asked; their identical gazes meeting. "The last time I heard you being that upset was when you were much younger and less educated."

Tecla shook her head, crossing her ankles and resting the weight of her upper body on her hands, her back stretching forward. "I just feel very different at times, Father. I know the other ladies, even Tesfira and Lady Wallysa… They call me the Mud Princess. Perhaps it is because of my light dresses and lack of jewelry, or maybe it is because the only people I can talk to are Lyzon, Fran, and their acquaintances." Shrugging to herself, she added, "I didn't mind, as long as I had Theliel, but today… Today, he seemed different too. He was preoccupied with things that he would never put before me."

Lord Tithan rested a hand on her head, gently tilting her towards him to place a kiss on her forehead. "Did you hear those comments about you, or was it Lyzon telling you?"

Tecla glanced at him before looking down again. "Lyzon told me, but some things I heard myself."

Lord Tithan nodded, resting his silver-plated hands on his thighs. "There is no shame in befriending the simple people," he spoke while staring at the peak of the tall trees ahead. "I wanted to live like them too." Ignoring the puzzled look on his daughter's face, Tithan went on, "Don't forget that your grandfather Theliel and your grandmother Tecla had two sons, my older brother Thaesonwald and myself. Thaesonwald drowned with one of the King's ships during the conquest of the Red Continent, and it fell upon my shoulders to carry on our father's legacy.

"I returned with success to Silverholde, only to hear about the news of King Helias Rainier, who had fallen ill with the Violet Delusion, and to learn that my mother had left my father sometime during the Great Conquest for reasons that I was never told. It wasn't long until my father found a new companion, but due to my mother's absence, it was never possible for him to legitimate his children without making it obvious that they were all bastards.

"At that time, the Oracle's Faith was widely recognized in the Silver Kingdom," Tithan reminded his daughter, his eyes filled with a certain sadness. "So, when one of my half-siblings died to this never-ending, dark cloud that sucked in the life of everything it touched, the Holy Commander refused to burn the body. Little Nall was only six months old, and he was wrapped in silk before being thrown down the cliffs of Edgemere, becoming food for the abyss.

"Simple people need no Holy Commander to burn their loved ones," Lord Tithan concluded, unclasping the plates that were making his hands sweaty under the bright sun of Strongshore. "If being with simple people brings you more joy, you shouldn't feel different, Tecla. You should feel proud."

A single tear ran down the young girl's cheek, and she looked to the side to wipe it away. She hadn't even realized how tight her chest felt as she listened to her father's story.

"As for Theliel," her father began, dropping the plates next to him on the stone bench. "I like to think that his appearance now is out of concern, considering Thaesonwald's state. I won't deny however that Theliel's impulsive nature always worried me to an extent that I cannot describe," Tithan admitted, squeezing his daughter's hand when she held his. "The Regency is the safest place for him, and I like to think it is yours too."

Her whole body stiffened. Tecla brushed away the hair that slapped against her cheeks due to the wind, and she asked, "Mine? Am I to join the Treasure Council too?"

"No," Tithan answered with a laugh. "The Regency's Observatory Vault is what I had in mind. Lady Lionhelm had other plans such as marriage but," he paused, looking at her flushed face, "what plans do you have?"

"Father, I…"

She was at a loss of words, the myriad of information being a little too sudden for her to digest quickly. The truth was that she had wanted to spend more time at the temple in Summerport to study the Oracle's Memoir, but after what her father told her about his half-brother, Tecla knew better.

"I have always tried to let my children make the first step," Tithan elaborated in a sour tone. "Perhaps I was wrong… but I like to think it somehow shaped their personalities, and that family remains their first thought."

"Do I have to answer now, Father?" Tecla asked; a gut-wrenching feeling in her stomach causing her to hunch her back slightly.

"No," Lord Tithan said as he grabbed his discarded plates and stood up. "But find an answer for yourself soon enough."

Tecla stood up as well, bowing slightly at him as he retreated. Lord Tithan stole another glance at his daughter, who was too busy with her thoughts to notice. With each passing day, her looks reminded him of his mother. From the hair to the paleness of her skin as well as her unpredictability, Tecla had always been his favorite child. He often wondered if others noticed as he would talk about her during his sparring in the barracks, like earlier that day. The girl used to be fierier and mouthier as a child, looking up to her sister Tesfira, but the more she grew up, the less she would spend time around the other Lionhelms, Theliel being the only exception. Tecla locked herself in a bubble made of religion and underworld tales, and the only person to have the key was Lyzon, even as he would ask her if she was happy to have him as a father.

"Yes," she would answer in her tiny voice. "If only you were younger, Father. So, I would have more time with you."

Tecla was the only one he had seen grow up without ever leaving Strongshore. The last thing he wanted was for her to not have what he could give her.

***

Shudders and spasms rocked his whole feverish body. He felt insanely hot while the rest of the room was freezing. He was running down the dark corridors of his home, looking behind him whenever he heard her voice or the music box that always played in the corner of her bed-chambers, right on the vanity. Right where she would paint her cheeks pink and her lips red. Right where she would stare at his reflection in the mirror.

Her pearly smile was directed at him, and the soundless call for him made his hairs stand. "My little, little boy," she whispered. "The first, the last, the only boy," she snickered. "Can that be?"

Her high-pitched laugh echoed in his head, the deafening sound causing him to stumble over his feet and roll face-first down the stairs.

"No, of course, it can't be," he heard her approach. "Where are you going?" she angrily shouted, before her voice switched again to a softer, motherly tone. "Would you leave me without a farewell?"

He felt her long nails rack down the back of his legs, pulling him towards her. His chin was bruised and his nose bumped against the stairs, a whine leaving his lips.

"I need you to be awake.

"I said, awake," she hissed before hitting the back of his head.

Jascha stiffened in his bed, sitting up immediately. His empty stomach rumbled and soon, he tasted bile in his mouth. He rushed to grab the water bucket next to his bed. It was meant as a refreshment for him to take during the night, but he emptied it all on himself, caring not one bit about the drenched bed and sheets. He held his face in his hands before rubbing his eyes, reminding himself that he was awake. He forced his black eyes open, only to realize that he was cold. His upper body was completely bare, his large back and defined chest covered in small scars. The odd pain in his spine had finally disappeared and he looked at his hands.

  His fingernails were still dirty with the blood that had drenched his gloves, and he had just wasted a lot of water he could have used to clean himself. He slowly got up, trying to dry himself with what was left of the clean, warm bedsheets he had used. He grabbed his large leather bag to find a change of puttees and a lighter shirt. He had ridden the entire night to reach Rainier's End, the town at the borders between the capital and the Fog Lands. The town was said to have been the last location where the King of the Silver Lands was seen before he fell ill and retreated in his dungeons, but to Jascha, these were only tales made to attract explorers and traders. He had paid for his one-night stay at the central inn, and given how bright the sun was shining, he had slept enough. His destination was still Silverholde, and he couldn't waste any more time.

He reached for the leather band in his pocket and tied his obsidian hair in a half-ponytail that he would then hide under the hood of his black cloak made entirely of bear fur. Jascha pulled the door open, ready to rush himself downstairs when he heard a familiar voice.

"We would like to spend the night here before we return to Silverholde," a man with a greying beard and mustache asked the innkeeper. "The Regency will pay you double."

Jascha's eyes narrowed. It was the man from the previous night in Beggar's Pool—Chief Eleres.

"We only have one room upstairs, and I'm afraid our current guest hasn't left yet. I will have to check and plop a new bed in there for you two," the old, decaying owner said with a trembling voice.

"Let us have a late breakfast first," the young man behind Eleres said, the one who went by the name of Goldsnout.

The innkeeper nodded, walking in the direction of the kitchen. Jascha rested his back against the wall, sliding down to sit on the floor and hide in the unlighted corner where the stairs met the door to the room he had slept in. The only patrons at that time of the day were the two Regency officials and their hushed voices reached his ears quite easily.

"I can't wrap my head around last night's murder," Goldsnout said with a sigh. "I simply don't understand. Other than you and I and a few drunkards who didn't move from their spots all night, there was nobody. No blood inside the inn— what are the chances that this girl, Loveleen, just took a stroll in the freezing night and angered a random freak?" he reasoned out loud, rubbing his hands together as if he was cold.

"Ah, stop it, boy," Eleres said, annoyed. "Didn't you see the state of her body? She was torn to pieces. She was probably mauled by a wild animal."

"I am convinced otherwise, Chief. Perhaps you didn't see it clearly because the mother rushed past you once the Derry boy began smashing his violin against everything, but I saw the girl's back. Those were stab wounds. Like the ones we saw on the dead girl in Three Crosses."

"The one allegedly killed by the Beast of Three Crosses?"

Goldsnout chuckled, earning himself a glare from his chief. His cheeks turned redder than his hair. "With all due respect, Chief, I don't think a mythological beast would stab anyone."

Eleres shook his head in an almost irritated manner. "It still doesn't matter, Snout," he concluded.

"But, Chief—"

"I don't know how many times I will have to repeat myself, Officer Opherus Goldsnout," he cut in, his voice louder. "To kill in cold blood is surely a crime under Regency laws, but we have no suspect and no way of bringing a corpse with us so that the Observatory Vault can draw some very logical conclusion as to what happened. I mean, have you seen the way that old woman cradled the body?" Eleres argued. "Simple people want no answers. They want to mourn in peace."

The smell of hot, vegetable soup reached Jascha's nostrils, and his stomach growled. He decided to stand up, glancing briefly at the two who were slurping away their meal way too loudly.

"Never forget what we are looking for," Eleres told his officer. "Cult murders. Beheaded-in-the-woods kind of victim, men with shattered spines, like we've seen at the border of the Sand Towers. We were given an assignment and we have to pull through. We are surveillants."

Jascha narrowed his eyes at that, only to go back to the room he had slept in. He would leave using the window.

✳✳✳

The sun was setting over Summerport, the bustling city never quieting down. The pale sand seemed to absorb the sun rays as it turned a vivid shade of scarlet. The calm waves that hit the harbor made the ships that had docked that day dance slightly, the sounds of children laughing as they bathed mixing with the chirping of the seagulls flying over their heads. The fishermen of Summerport hummed as they flung their full nets over their shoulders, taking home what they couldn't sell. Only a few brave men dared to turn the humming into singing.

Children sang along when the streets were filled with the song of the Lion of The Red Continent, the one that told the tale of Alatros the Red, a bandit that terrorized the Old City of Calaris, now buried under the Tinted Bay that surrounded the southern coasts of the Silver Lands. It was said that Alatros the Red was taller than two men put together and that his skin was as red as his hair. He was the first man to brave the waters that separated the Silver Lands from the Red Continent, named after him. Upon bringing back with him all the silver extracted in the Red Continent as well as new ships filled with delicacies, fruits, and plants unknown in the Silver Lands, exotic creatures such as tall felines he kept as guards, he was said to have married the warrior queen Aelneth, who had lent him her ships. Together, they founded the City of Drixia, where Strongshore rose thousands of years later.

  The late afternoon recreation was interrupted by several children running towards the armored man who wore the Regency's colors. Theliel waved and tossed a coin at nearly every little boy who clung to his boots, the girls being too shy and admirative to get closer. The people of Summerport nodded and smiled at him, greeting even Sarkis, whose silly smile never left his lips. No one asked who the man was, nor why his burgundy clothes were dirtier than theirs.

  "This place is a lot warmer than Silverholde—in every sense," the curly-haired man said, ruffling a curious boy's hair with his big, burly hands. "The people seem to be in love with you as well," he commented. "Your old man could've given you this city to manage instead of trapping you in the towers of the Regency."

  "Summerport is too important to be separated from Strongshore, in terms of rule,"

Theliel explained, leading Sarkis in a narrower, quieter street. "This is where ships depart for the Red Continent, for the islands of the East, for every other trade post in the Silver Lands. It will always be bound to the Headmaster of House Lionhelm and his Council of Steel."

Sarkis raised an eyebrow. "And you can't be that, because?"

"I've told you before. I'm Tithan Lionhelm's fourth child. I have two older brothers who have more rights than I. Not to mention they also have sons of their own. Plus," Theliel paused, stopping in his tracks to knock on a tiny door. "My mother wasn't my father's wife. Everyone knows it around here, and everyone believes I do not remember."

The door in front of them opened slowly, a pair of tired, wrinkled, hazel eyes peering at them. An old woman barely taller than a barrel of ale stood in front of Theliel and Sarkis, her body round yet strong, her hands swollen and marked by a lifetime of hard work. Her saggy, wrinkled skin was nearly frightening and her nose was as large as a man's. She hid her hair under a thick, clean foulard of white color.

She cleared her throat, which sounded like a gargle. "What brings you here?"

"Old Martita," Theliel greeted her with a polite bow as if he wasn't the richest of the trio. "This is my friend, Sarkis. He would require a place to stay, temporarily of course. And you might need the extra help, I figured."

The old woman sniffled at them, turning around and leaving the door open for them to scooch inside the small hut-like house. The two men hunched their backs to get in and immediately noticed that Old Martita wasn't alone. A big young man with common brown hair and light work clothes was lighting the fire for her. At the sight of Theliel, he bowed his head, but the nobleman's eyes rested on the woman who seemed to be sewing a new dress for Old Martita. Her emerald eyes were full of mischief and curiosity, and she offered the two a charming smile. Her dark hair was neatly pulled back in a low ponytail, and she was quick to get back to work.

"As you can see," the old woman sniffled again. "I got all the help I need. Pat here and his little friend Rosewillow are good children of the sea."

Theliel wasn't about to give up. "You must know of someone in need of a pair of extra hands. You are an institution here in Summerport."

She was quick to hit his forehead with the wooden spoon she used to cook dinner. "I said no, boy."

Sarkis pulled the younger man by the elbow. "Look, man, I don't think this is your day. We should—"

"You pulled me out of my mother's womb," Theliel spoke up firmly, shoving Sarkis behind him. "You did it here, in this house, in the heart of Summerport. I am a child of the sea as well, Martita; don't treat me like an outsider." Pointing at the burly man behind him, the hazel-eyed Lionhelm explained, "This man right here is suspected of illegal acts he did not commit. The Regency wants him and I can't just watch. Us being here means that I think this is the safest place I can think of."

Old Martita didn't seem impressed with the pleading speech she just heard, and she sniffled once more, eyeing the fish stew that brewed in her now burning fireplace. "After Strongshore," she pointed out. "And Strongshore didn't want him."

"My father helped with the founding of the Regency. I do not know what I expected," Theliel sighed out nearly dramatically.

"I think they do need help around the Seven Galleys," Rosewillow's soft voice cut in. She had set her sewing work aside, scooting near Pat to help him clean a few vegetables that sat waiting in a basket. "I heard so this morning. The tavern owner is full of patrons lately; he had to buy new tables to put outside, right in front of the docks."

Old Martita mumbled something inaudible to them, then gargled. "Well, you heard her. You can sleep on that," she told Sarkis while pointing at the wooden, overused bench where she usually sat to eat. "That is if it doesn't crumble under your weight."

"Well, it hasn't crumbled under yours," Sarkis automatically said with a silly laugh that was met with silence and one deadly stare from Old Martita.

Theliel eventually smiled at him and leaned in to whisper, "I will take care of things in Silverholde and meet you back here as soon as I can. Could be a month or two but, trust me, it will work out."

Rosewillow watched their exchange with a glint in her eyes, ignoring the way Pat stared at her from the corner of his eye. She cut vegetables without even looking, the even pieces of carrots and lettuce landing on the plate in front of her like raindrops in a pond. She watched Theliel Lionhelm leave the house while his curly-haired friend set his small bag that probably didn't even carry a change of clean clothes near the fireplace. Her long lashes grazed her cheekbones as she looked down to check if there was more for her to cut. When there wasn't, she turned to face the young man who had been talking to her all along, and she planted a chaste kiss on his cheek.

"I will fetch more of these," she whispered, offering him a charming smile.

Her bare feet soon found her little wooden slippers, and she walked outside Old Martita's house. Rosewillow's smile faded with each slow step she took, the evening breeze freeing her long hair from the ponytail she had worn all day. She walked past the little garden next to the old woman's house, disappearing in the alleys of Summerport with ease. Her sleeveless white dress caressed the walls of the small buildings and other huts as she walked past them. She rounded a corner filled with light, reaching a plaza overly filled with light and laughter. At its center, a tall statue of Alatros the Red climbing the infinite stairs of marble that disappeared in the clouds above Summerport shadowed an entire area of the city. He was fully armored and ready to attack with spear and shield, but his stare seemed void of any warring spirit. Rosewillow stood still in the crowd, her emerald eyes scanning the flock that moved all around her in a tornado of noise and figures until she saw her.

It was first the knight's helmet, then the golden fabric around it that covered the woman's hair that gave her away. Rosewillow saw her come closer in what seemed to be a blinking movement, as her steps were always hidden by the passersby and other groups that rushed from a corner of Summerport to another. The dent on the side of her helmet did nothing to diminish the aura that this woman carried with her wherever she went.

The Golden Lady brushed the tips of Rosewillow's chestnut hair, which turned slightly auburn under the large, warm torches that lighted Alatros the Red's plaza. The busy area seemed to bother neither of them as few stares were directed at them. They were completely unseen amongst the people who had opened their gates to the world in times of peaceful trade with every other known and powerful land.

"You have been quiet," the Golden Lady said. "Have you found our *Nakfèht*?"

"Possibly," Rosewillow answered. "He's no one's son and survives only thanks to the pity of an old woman who shows little respect for him. Violates the laws of Strongshore's Silver Master when it comes to coin. Was sold as a slave around the age of four to a sailor from the Red Continent and escaped only because the ship sank during a regular route and his body drifted to the shores of Summerport," she elaborated. "Will it suffice?"

"We shall not know until Her eyes will shut tight, Her pale lids white as day, letting out the light; until the seas will rise and birds take flight, reaching for the Heights," the Golden Lady replied, lifting her head as if she were looking at the great ascent of the statuesque stairs above her.

Chapter IV

Dawn of Faith

Located in the eastern wing of the palace, the narrow and rectangular room where Lady Voladea wrote undisturbed was poorly lit. Only a few candleholders were placed on the table that was almost as big as the room itself, the chandeliers above her head perfectly still and spent. The tall windows at her right and behind her did not help as it was a cloudy afternoon, and the thick, silver and sky-blue curtains blocked the faint sun rays.

Every inch of the walls that loomed over her was covered by portraits of the Lionhelms' ancestors and paintings of Old Drixia, which represented a less rocky, less cliffy, and much greener Strongshore. Each piece of art was carefully framed with silver and covered by glass. From Tithan's father to the discolored faces of those who ruled before him, every woman and man of the Lionhelm family shared either the large, hazel eyes or the wavy, light chestnut hair. The men let their strands graze their shoulders, their thin lips set in a firm expression, while the women with round, rosy cheeks braided their manes into crowns adorned with strands of gold and sapphires from the Zalejos Depths.

    The sound of Voladea's scribbling echoed in what usually was Tithan Lionhelm's Council of Steel's meeting room and Tylennald's index finger grazed the shelves that held a series of archive books up against the wall adjacent to the door. His feet made no sound as he walked on soft furs from Noirmont, and he silently wondered just how many other documents and manuscripts were stored above their heads. Most importantly, he wondered if his father's Council of Steel ever used any of those. His gaze lingered on the hatch above his head.

    A knock on the wooden doors interrupted his thoughts, and he heard his mother say, "Come in."

    It was Milefried, the Silver Master. The hunched, hairless man with a nose that resembled the beak of a crow kept his head low. "You called for me, Lady Lionhelm," he croaked out, permanently sounding as if he were sick. Despite his looks and quite obvious insecurities, the man never missed a line in his accountant books, and Strongshore prospered under his diligent calculations.

    "I sure did," the greying woman said, raising her head and removing the monocle she had tucked between her cheekbone and brow. "I will need five hundred thousand silvers for the ball that will take place three moons from now," Voladea explained, setting her quill pen to the side and letting the ink on her last invitation letter dry.

"Wh-what ball, Lady of Strongshore?" Milefried asked with a hesitant look directed at Tylennald, who ignored him entirely.

"Lady Tecla's ball. Lord Tithan has already approved of it, and I have carefully listed the most affluent and time-worthy families we will have as our guests. That includes their bannermen, their escorting armies as well as their advisors."

"Lady Lionhelm, we can have a hundred thousand silvers ready by then," the Silver Master informed her, his trembling hands toying with his simple grey robes. "Another two hundred thousand can be anticipated by the Regency's Treasure Council, but we are still missing a couple hundred thousand. This event is very close and there aren't enough moon days for us to collect taxes."

Voladea gave him a pointed stare, folding her hands on her puffy, tangerine dress. "Take them from Tecla's fund. You have my permission," she concluded, waving him away.

The mumbling man left in a hurry, his fingers spasming as he counted loudly.

"That is not a shy sum of money," Tylennald said with a smile, coming forward to sit next to his mother. He crossed his legs, drumming his fingers on the dark, wooden table. "Who are you trying to woo?"

"I am not wooing anybody," Voladea immediately said, standing up. The net that kept her dress wide and distended was beginning to hurt the back of her thighs. "We have not properly invited the other lords of the Silver Lands ever since Tesfira married Hamley Silverworm," she reminded him as she stood in front of the nearest window to catch the evening breeze. "And that was many years ago, considering her son Deril is older than Tecla by ten years."

"Does that mean there is not one invite that you wrote differently?" Tylennald insisted, raising an eyebrow.

"These are not easy times," she answered in a more serious tone. "If life had treated us differently, I would have personally sent one of our advisors to invite Lord Rochelac. The Fog Lands used to be the only military force that rivaled ours," she recalled out loud, "with their three hundred thousand men and giant striges ready to feast on the defeated. It is almost a blessing that the Violet Delusion won't leave Noirmont." Breathing in deeply and sighing out, she added, "But even then, we wouldn't want Tecla to hold such power, which is why I invited the Sons of Ferngrunn from the Sand Towers."

Tylennald tilted his head, his eyes darting around as he processed that information. "Their navy is strong," he pointed out.

"Not as strong as ours."

"But you do realize their culture is far different from ours, don't you, Mother?"

"What we want," Voladea cut in before he could argue anymore, "is for all of your siblings to be taken care of and to hold a certain position of strength, without minimizing yours." Stepping closer to her second born to hold his hand in hers, Voladea tugged on the front of his blue shirt to fix a small wrinkle. "Tecla might be a child now but it won't be long until she becomes a woman, and I have yet to understand where her loyalties lie, although her closeness to Tithan and Theliel gives me a good hint."

Her son placed a reassuring hand on her shoulder. "Do I sense regret?"

"My only regret," she turned to fully face him, her wrinkly lips twitching, "is to not have had a daughter of my own. Intelligence is wasted on men, but duty isn't."

Tylennald stared at his mother, his grip tightening around her shoulder. Her brown eyes defiantly scanned his face, taking in his aging traits and offended expression. He knew exactly what she was thinking. He could still feel the disappointment she voiced twenty years ago when he was caught with his father's last will in his hands. He had only acted upon his mother and his wife's wish, only to be on the receiving hand of his father's wrath and vindictive instinct.

"What do you think Strongshore was built on?" Voladea whispered, her eyes trailing back to the dark clouds that engulfed Edgemere in the distance. "Tradition? Good feelings between father and son? Bravery?" Before Tylennald could give his answer, she scoffed. "This land bathed in blood under Alatros the Red, and when there was nothing more to steal, no one else to flay, he took it to the Red Continent. And you know why?"

Tylennald shook his head, sighing out in a mixture of annoyance and ignorance.

"Because it was his duty to Warrior Queen Aelneth, who had given him all the resources to succeed. Their founding of Drixia was only the crowning of their initial agreement. The people sing of Alatros' success even millennia after his death in the Tinted Bay, but no one remembers that without Aelneth's strength and vision, the South would have succumbed to the northern tribes of the Avoryon Hills.

"Alatros and Aelneth laid waste to the Far North, but these lands don't understand the meaning of history," Voladea concluded bitterly.

Tylennald took his mother's hands in his own, bringing them to his lips. "I do, Mother. And Strongshore will stand for more centuries to come, I promise this to you," he solemnly told her, his hazel stare looking for her approval.

"No, Tylennald," she whispered to him. "I am the one who promises this to you."

✷✷✷

"Does your father know we are here?"

Lyzon's worried look caused Tecla to roll her eyes. She got off the carriage before her friend could say anything, receiving only a puzzled look from Fran, her gardener, and currently the man who escorted them both to Oracle Hill.

The young lady had dragged her two most trusted friends out of Strongshore at dawn, having overheard the night before that her father would be busy with Lord Angefort and her brother Theliel, probably to make sure they both returned safely to the Regency and to understand her brother's intentions. Between his duties and Lady Lionhelm's visits around Edgemere to evaluate Tesfira's husband's work, Tecla had found a safe window to leave the palace, only letting Educator Tomas know of her whereabouts. She trusted the burly, tanned man as much as any other person at her service. They would not alert anyone of the family as long as she returned before sunset.

Clad in a simple, deep blue dress that left part of her back bare, Tecla readjusted the grey shawl around her shoulders to cover her loose chestnut hair and with Fran and Lyzon in toe, she entered the temple. It was deserted at that time of the day. The armies of the Holy Commander patrolled the surrounding areas diligently, while his two captains were to be guarding the Oracle's Flame until the night mass.

The girl walked up to the altar where the three holy men would preach, only to realize the fire was out and the temple empty. It was only her, surrounded by tinted glass and scenes of the Oracle's Memoir. Distant murmurs and groans seemed to come from the adjacent rooms Tecla had never visited before, as they were part of the residential buildings of the site and reserved to the maidens of the temple and its holy forces.

Tecla could hear Lyzon and Fran whispering near the entrance. The door behind the altar was flung open, and she focused her attention on the silver-haired man who moved closer to her. He wore no armor for once, but his attire still spoke at length about his riches. The Holy Commander clad in deep golden robes looked wealthier than her father.

"Lady Tecla," he greeted her, a hint of surprise in his tone. "I am not used to you visiting the temple on dawn days."

"Holy Commander," she greeted back. "I come to you as I have found myself more interested in the Oracle's Memoir," she explained. "My interest reaches further than just traditional belief and practice."

The man in front of her offered her his arm, leading her to their right. "Does Lord Lionhelm know you wish to increase your knowledge of the Faith?" Nearing the doors that would lead them to the private chambers of the temple, the commander asked, "Learning more could be difficult for you; Strongshore is not exactly around the corner."

The room they entered was an immense library, one that was even bigger than the one held within the cupola of her father's observatory room. Books lined every wall from the floor to the ceiling. The sky above their heads was visible, and if it hadn't been for a sun ray reflection, Tecla would have never noticed the thick glass roof. Every step she took on the crimson and golden marble floor echoed through the infinite corridor, her hazel eyes looking past the shelves only to notice that behind some of them, narrow corridors met smaller doors.

"Where is everyone?" she asked plainly, her hazel eyes trying to read some of the titles in front of her.

"Entertaining the flame," the Holy Commander answered with a smile, handing her a copy of the Oracle's Memoir translated in the modern tongue by the commander that preceded him.

"But the fire was out."

He chuckled, pointing at the smaller cupola that could be seen outside. "You can't see it from here, but half of it is open, and that is where the real flame is. We wouldn't be as careless as to keep it alive around wooden altars and visitors," he explained. "The one flame that was lit by the Oracle is over there, in the Oracle Pillar. There was a time where it was the only standing tower of this site."

Tecla held the book in her hands. It had been written by a certain Frederyc Rosenfield, Holy Commander of the Angels of Steel and Ninety-Ninth Servant of the Oracle.

"You can take as many manuscripts and art collections as you can carry," the Holy Commander added. "You shall return them on your next visit, Lady Tecla."

Walking past her, the holy man rounded the shelf from which he had taken the book she tucked between her elbow and her right side, only to disappear behind the nearest door. Tecla took a deep breath and set the thick volume on the rectangular table between the shelf and what seemed to be the marble statue of a man pleading for his life in front of a half-bird and half-dragon creature that had planted its talons in his chest. Tecla paid little attention to it as she read the words written on the first page of the book.

"By the honor that has been granted to Us, We decided to translate the word *wūl* into 'memoir', for this is a collection of the messages She left Us and all that She saw. Sir Frederyc Rosenfield, Holy Commander of the Oracle's Angels of Steel."

A snicker reached her ears, followed by a thud, and Tecla frowned, craning her neck to see if someone had come in. Leaving the book where she had opened it, Tecla neared the door the Holy Commander had gone through only to realize it had not been closed properly. She moved to pull it but stood frozen in place. Through the slit, she saw a different room, one that looked like the living rooms in her apartments at the palace. Large pillows littered the floor, dim lighting causing the bright silks to look as warm as raw amber. The far end of the room was too dark for Tecla to see it, but soon her view was obscured by a woman who seemed to have just straightened up from the floor, her skin completely bare. Tecla held her breath, watching as the woman lowered her upper body on the very naked man beneath her.

It was one of the holy captains, she realized, her hazel eyes stuck on the motion the woman's hips were busy with. The back and forth she performed on the man's lap seemed to be causing him an odd pain, given the deep groans he emitted.

"What do you see?" the young woman pressed, planting her long nails in his belly.

The old man forced his eyes open, resting a hand behind her head and pulling her towards him to look into her eyes.

"You have not been graced with Her visions yet," he sighed out, his hands coming down to rest on her hips, tugging her forcefully.

Tecla nearly stumbled backward, swallowing hard. She quickly grabbed the book she had left on the table, her heels clicking fast against the floor as she fled the library.

✳✳✳

The streets of Rainier's End were dark and muddy, the heavy rains that flooded the town causing the villagers to rush in the direction of their houses, only to run and stumble into each other. Greetings and laughter were exchanged, silver coins were tossed; merchants urged to secure their goods under the thick, impermeable fabric of their coats while the children chased stray cats to play and hide. The sun had set a long time ago, but the bubbling town was filled with traders in the warm period of the year. Fair-colored, dark-colored, tall and menacing, short and quick – every person that roamed the streets at that time was a fat drop of paint in the canvas before Jascha's eyes.

His black eyes never blinked as he stared at the red-haired man clad in gold and covered by armor. He was clumsy and chirpy, tugging on the hood of his shining cloak to avoid being soaked. The owl of the Regency sewed on his cloak was big enough to be noticed even when the winds caused the garment to flap around like a flag. Goldsnout was buying what seemed to be pigeon tarts at the entrance of the marketplace, his freckles stretching across his nose with each exaggerated smile of his.

Jascha fisted the hilt of the dagger strapped against his side, his loose black hair clinging to his face and neck. The rain trailed down the dark skin under his eyes, falling on his lips and resting on the bump of his chin. It would take only one swift move on Goldsnout's way back to the tavern; one swing aimed at the neck and the officer would fall, dragging with him any thoughts on investigating the death of the girl of Beggar's Pool.

"Here is some extra coin," the red-haired youngster said, his arms full of treats.

"Hurry up, you're soaked, my boy!" the baker said with a toothless smile.

Goldsnout turned heels, his green gaze set on the pigeon tarts he bought for Eleres and himself, deciding that a couple of those he would keep for their travel days back to Silverholde.

Jascha watched him stumble over his own feet, only to be steadied by a passerby who chuckled at him. The black-haired man unsheathed his dagger, walking in his direction. It would be quick and soundless, he figured. The chaotic streets and turbulent weather caused enough confusion and whoever thought they could see him would lose sight of him quickly.

The water splashed around his dark, soiled boots with every movement, but his unblinking stare only cared about the exposed neck of the redhead that was now only a few steps away. Jascha's fist tightened around the hilt of the dagger, but when he was about to raise his arm and puncture the officer, a seizing pain hit his right side, and his breath hitched in his throat. He fell on one knee, pressing his left hand against the spot that hurt. It felt as if something was crawling inside him, tearing his flesh from the inside. He had felt it before, around his spine, but never had it been so real. Looking down at his hand, it was coated in blood. Jascha coughed, red droplets of saliva hitting the muddy ground. His heart was beating faster, and another slashing pain in his upper back caused his eyes to roll back in his skull.

"Help!" he heard a woman yell around him. "Someone, help me! This man is feeling ill!"

Her words were lost in the back of his head, replaced by a loud, incomprehensible chant that filled his ears and constricted his chest. Jascha fell flat on his back, his foggy eyes catching only a glimpse of a dark-skinned, dark-haired woman who leaned in with a worried look on her face.

"Hang in there," she whispered.

Near the woman, a man with a handcart halted himself to lift the unconscious Jascha and place him carefully on the wet straw he carried. He lost his hat between the tugging and dragging but he seemed not to notice. The woman's brown eyes landed on the dagger that was now covered in dirt and she took it immediately. She hopped on the handcart, sitting next to Jascha, and the farmer who had just helped her ran back to the front, ready to escort the pair to a drier location.

"To the Illusion Shelter," she told him, covering her head with an overused shawl full of holes. "I run it."

The ride was relatively fast, and upon reaching their destination, the farmer was offered food and a bed for the night. The wind blew harder at night and the rain didn't seem to be stopping anytime soon. Men and women rushed to the handcart to help. The Illusion Shelter looked like the other houses in Rainier's End and the only element that distinguished it was the sign at the entrance. The large rocks around the two-story shelter kept the mud of the streets away from the entrance, and the tall, dark-green trees that hid the roof glowed with a cold light. Their leaves were as large as windows and their thick branches remained unmoving through the storm. They looked immortal next to the decaying keep in the murky background, a small castle with narrow turrets forgotten by its owners, the Rosenbanes, and the simple people of Rainier's End.

"Rantha," a woman called her as they carried Jascha upstairs. "Do we start right away?"

The dark-skinned woman nodded, her plump lips smiling faintly at the skinny farmer who looked at her in confusion. "Thank you for your help," Rantha said. "We have soup in the kitchens."

"What are you doing to that boy?" the man asked, watching with wide eyes the sharp tools and baskets full of herbs that her helpers brought upstairs.

"We are curing him."

She went upstairs herself, watching each step her apprentices were taking. She evaluated every move they made and how tight their white bonnets and aprons were. It wasn't long until

Jascha's body was fully exposed, his clothes tossed in a basket. Rantha realized he didn't have a lot with him. No belongings, no coin – he probably left everything somewhere if not at his own house. She half-wondered if he had a horse to feed and where he was from.

His skin was fair and relatively smooth, if not for the cuts on his upper body. She saw no open wound, yet he had passed out in the middle of the street, holding his side as if someone had attacked him. Realizing that she still carried his dagger in her hand, Rantha set it on the end table, nodding away when the men began slicing his wrists vertically, letting the blood pour in the buckets they had prepared. The women started burning leaves and spices together, directing the smoke at the unconscious man using a large fan.

Rantha pinched her nose, the stench of bearpepper and greylemon mixing quickly becoming unbearable. She saw Jascha's toes twitch, and she frowned. Victims of the Violet Delusion usually wouldn't regain consciousness so quickly.

"Stop the bleeding," she ordered, taking herself some bandages to fasten around his wrists. She saw the muscles of his arms and leg spasm, and she narrowed her eyes. "Stop everything," she told the four other people in the room. She stood up slowly, eyeing the dagger on the end table.

The hilt was covered by jewels she could not even name, their colors shining bright in a mixture of crimson, amber, and wild green. Engraved on the small pommel was a black canine beast, the Beast of Three Crosses. The steel of his dagger glowed, the vivid yet cold pearly color a clear confirmation that this man was not someone she could treat as easily as the others.

"Stand back, everyone," she said in a softer voice, tucking a strand of curly hair behind her ear. "And grab the thickest ropes you can find. This man comes from the Fog Lands. We don't know how long he was exposed.

"Tie him up."

Chapter V

NAKFÈHT

The bright green light that hit his face was warm, too warm even. His skin felt like it was burning, and he could see the shadows around him even with his eyes closed. His mouth was dry and his throat itchy, but it was the cracking of the fire that forced him to open his midnight eyes. His wrists and joints were in pain, but whatever caused it had stopped. Jascha saw the rope that kept his upper body against the old bed. His wrists were covered in bandages tainted with his blood. He blinked then narrowed his eyes, shifting his weight only to notice that his legs too were tied.

A woman was leaning against the nearest wall and she silently studied him. She seemed to be hiding in the shadows and her features were like nothing he had seen before. She seemed to have escaped a painting of the Red Continent. From her black, curly mane to her brown skin, she was unique. Jascha eyed the bowl she held in her hands and realized that was where the smell came from.

"Untie me," he ordered her, his voice strained.

"I'm afraid I can't," Rantha answered. "Do you know what your name is? Do you understand where you are?"

Jascha's eyes glanced up at the wooden ceiling, feeling his blood boil. "Untie me. If you think bearpepper and greylemon are going to do anything to me, you are stupider than you think. Use them for the fever."

"You've been treated before," she concluded.

"This is not the Violet Delusion," he stated. "And even if it was, you would need wild pine berry juice, not the Dreamer's Root that grows around these," he added, his eyes glancing at the vivid light that the trees around the shelter emanated.

Her brow furrowed, eyeing the tree that was in sight. "Rosewillows have treated more victims than you can imagine."

"Did they survive long?" Jascha asked, coughing. When the woman remained silent, he shook his head. "My point exactly."

"How can you know all this?" Rantha came closer, setting her bowl on the end table, right next to the dagger she had found near him when he passed out.

Jascha's eyes followed her movements, her words lost in the back of his mind as soon as he saw his weapon being so close. The memory of the heavy rains clouded with the smell of hot pigeon tarts hit him in the face. His body jerked up, only to be restrained by the thick rope. Glancing at his right side, Jascha's alarmed expression turned into ire the moment he saw a fresh scar right where he had felt the invisible puncture from the inside. It had happened again.

The black-haired man tightened his fists, pulling his arms towards his chest only to let out a pained cry. He had forgotten about his injured wrists. "You drew my blood," he breathed out. "Ignorant troll."

"My name is Rantha, you ungrateful scum," she bit back. "You fell to your knees out of nowhere, held your sides while feeling imaginary pain; you are showing all the symptoms of the Violet Delusion. I just don't understand how you wouldn't stay asleep during treatment. Bearpepper usually quells—"

"It was not imaginary," Jascha interrupted her. "My right side was bleeding."

"All I see is a scar. No one can scar so fast."

Jascha's eyes met her brown stare, and they looked at each other briefly, an uncomfortable silence separating them. Her lips were plump and her nose small, but with each breath she took, he could see her chest rise and her throat pulse. His eyes lingered on her neck as his fingers twitched. This woman stood between him and his freedom.

"Bearpepper won't keep me asleep," he whispered in a calm, almost frightening tone. "Nothing can keep me asleep." His nostrils flared with his next breath. "Untie me. I will not repeat myself."

He felt her cold hand on his shoulder and he nearly jumped at the sudden contact. He hadn't realized she sat down next to him. "Let me help you," Rantha insisted. "You seem to know a lot about the Violet Delusion, and I vowed to find a cure for it," she explained, her hands moving closer to wrists, reaching for his dagger to cut through it. "I lost everything to it—my parents, my mentor, the kind knight we served… They all succumbed to it, losing track of everything, no longer understanding their reality," she went on, her brown eyes filled with determination. "They harmed themselves, burned themselves—my mother threw herself down the staircase, screaming how 'it' wouldn't stop and that 'it' was chasing her.

"I never knew what she referred to. Initially, I thought she meant the fog that surrounded the castle, but even as it faded, nothing would change nor improve."

His hands broke free and Jascha sat up almost immediately, black strands falling between his eyes. His back was hunched and he felt dizzy. It clouded his vision and for a moment, he saw double.

"Careful there," Rantha whispered, steadying him by putting her hands on his bare shoulders. "I should probably bring you some food."

Jascha glanced at her with hooded eyes. "My horse is at the central inn," he told her.

She offered him a polite smile and a nod. "I will take care of everything. Rest now," she said, her expression giving away her satisfaction upon hearing that he might have to stay longer.

    The moment she left the room Jascha fell back on the bed, holding his stomach. His entire body felt on fire, and the pain from earlier that day wouldn't stop. It traveled from his side to his back, tore his insides, and stiffened his legs. It had never been that violent before. Rantha's words echoed through his mind as he tried to clear his mind, only to scoff at the thought of the Violet Delusion, the illness that had decimated more than half of the Silver Lands, long before he was even born. It was said that the dark, purple clouds had gradually descended from the Heights, trapping the Silver Lands in a fog that killed whatever it touched, causing severe burns and long-term symptoms, including sudden pain and hallucinations. The King himself was said to have been touched by it, and before disappearing from the public eye, he had asked for help from Lord Lionhelm to establish an entity that would rule in his stead following only his will even when it would be too late for him—the Regency.

    But Jascha knew; he wasn't suffering from it. The Violet Delusion had dissipated when he was just a boy and the thick clouds were concentrated around Noirmont. The last person to have died from it in Noirmont was his mother. This was different. This was real, he thought to himself over and over again. The scars were real.

    His eyes fell on his dagger, and he exhaled slowly. If he hadn't felt so weak and if his belongings were with him, he wouldn't have had to stay with the nosy healer. He fisted the hilt of his dagger, his thumb tracing the biggest ruby. The guard of the dagger was made with the fangs of the Beast of Three Crosses, and the jagged steel reflected the green light from outside. Jascha figured that the sheath had been tossed somewhere with the rest of his clothes.

    Jascha closed his eyes, his hand clutching the blade only to feel it pierce his skin.

✳✳✳

    The audience room where Lord Lionhelm sat was of inhuman proportions. It was rumored to be larger than the throne room in Silverholde, and on its own, it looked like it was half the palace. The marble floor looked like a vast mosaic, the many shades of every color intertwining to create the history of Old Drixia. Theliel entered the room, his booted feet following the path painted under him. He walked the Bloodied Road of Alatros the Red who razed every corner of the Silver Lands, back then known as Asarul. First, the tribes of the Far North, the Avoryon Hills, fell under his mace and fists; then, it was the turn of the eastern coasts, run by mercenaries and merchants who paid them well enough to defend their harbors. The red, white, and sandy marble felt like it was shifting with every step Theliel took, but soon it turned blue, signaling Alatros' crossing of the Tinted Bay. The blood of the once peaceful, Red Continent, was shed and drank by the giant bandit who had been painted with red lips. Whether Alatros did or did not feast on the defeated was a mystery, but Old Drixia liked to think he did.

  The more he came close, the more Theliel's eyes narrowed. His father sat on a wide, cushioned chair with a backrest that bore more depictions of Strongshore's legacy. At Tithan's feet, the history of the modern era laid undiscussed. War was waged between the crystal blue spears of Strongshore against the crimson bows of Noirmont, swallowing the Silver Lands in a war that lasted until the surroundings of both regions were turned to ashes and one wise mind quieted them down. Aleyne Rainier was crowned King of the Silver Lands in 1500 BCR. His family ruled for centuries until Helias Rainier and the Regency.

  The man who stood next to Tithan Lionhelm stepped down and walked up to Theliel, halting him in his tracks. He held his helmet under his arm, and his looks reminded him a lot of Lord Lionhelm himself, with his military trimmed hair, greying looks, and serious stare. Lord Angefort was a clement man, everyone in the Silver Lands knew that. Born and raised in Limemeadow, on the eastern coast, he had served the Headmaster of House Lionhelm as a commander until the Regency was created and Tithan granted him lordship over his homeland.

  "Second dawn day of the fifth month of year sixty-two After the Creation of the Regency," a deep, female voice spoke. "The first audience is granted to Theliel Lionhelm, son of Lord Tithan Lionhelm and former member of the Regency's Treasure Council."

"Thank you, Fantine," Lord Tithan spoke just as seriously.

The red-haired woman clad in armor from her chest down to her shins bowed her head. Theliel nodded at her as well, feeling slightly out of place. Fantine was the master-at-arms of House Lionhelm; he had trained under her for as long as he could remember. She was old enough to have been his mother and never had she introduced him so formally. Theliel's hazel eyes drifted to his father's solemn, no-nonsense expression.

"You will travel back to the Regency tonight, alongside Lord Angefort here," Tithan ordered him, his gloved fingers tracing the veins of the wooden armrests of his chair. "You will beg for the Treasure Council's forgiveness and will be granted another chance at fulfilling your duties for the Regency. You will be reinstated as a member of the Regency's Treasure Council within a month, relinquishing once again your potential claims and titles bound to Strongshore."

Theliel saw red instantly. "Is that it, Father? We are not going to discuss anything? You will just give me orders to follow as if I was a foot soldier of yours and not your son."

"Did you ever think of discussing it with me before you deserted the Regency?" Tithan accused him in return. "Of course not. You are impulsive, irrational, and arrogant, and you have certainly not inherited these traits from me."

Theliel ran a hand through his medium-length, light chestnut hair. "No, Father, it was all my mother's doing." Glaring at the guards that silently lined each side of the room, he raised his voice. "Let's not keep up with the masquerade, Father. Everyone here knows who my mother was." When no one reacted to his outburst, Theliel shouted at the guards. "Don't you know?"

"Theliel," Tithan called him, standing up. "That's enough."

"No, Father, it's not," the young man seethed. "I fail to understand why out of all your children, I am the one who gets punished. When Thaesonwald, Tylennald, and Tesfira conspired against your legacy, I warned you despite the fact I was only a child. Everything you wanted me to do for you, I did."

"The Regency is the top of the known world," Tithan reasoned, shaking his head. "It holds the power of the Silver Lands. The best healers, observers, commanders are in Silverholde. Why you treat this as punishment is beyond me, son."

"It is not what I want," Theliel answered. "It is as simple as that. No offense to you, Lord Arther," he said, glancing at the one man who had remained silent.

"None taken, Theliel."

"When Tesfira decided to marry a man of the simple people, you didn't mention anything about the top of the known world," he kept arguing. "What is the difference between her and me? She as well came from the womb of Emelyne the Demented, or are we going to keep pretending she didn't?"

Tithan's glare turned into a look of pity mixed with sadness and disappointment. He could hear the guards around them whisper; he could feel Arther Angefort's confusion as he glanced back and forth between father and son. Licking his thin lips, Tithan whispered, "Tesfira is very sane. Her lack of empathy has nothing to do with Emelyne's folly."

Theliel gritted his teeth at his father's stubbornness. "The Regency is a lie. The Kingdom is a lie, and if you would just listen to what I have to say—"

Tithan shook his head, raising his right hand at his son to have him stop talking. "Take all the belongings you can carry and leave. There are two hundred people after you waiting for an audience and I don't have time for excuses."

✷✷✷

Old Martita puffed at the fly that was buzzing over her head as she skinned the rabbit she bought from a merchant at Summerport's marketplace. It was an incredibly hot day, and it was impossible to stay indoors to get lunch ready. The steady hammering behind her reminded her that she was no longer alone all day waiting for Patten to come back with that day's earnings, and Martita glanced at the chubby man who sweated more than a pig in heat. She hung the skinned rabbit over the small fire at the center of her garden, letting out a series of curses as she stood up, pressing her swollen hands against the small of her back to stretch.

She limped slowly towards Sarkis who tugged on the hem of his shirt to use it and wipe his forehead. His big belly was in sight and Old Martita sniffed with disgust. "Did you repair it?" she asked, eyeing the door that connected the garden to the kitchen.

"It's all good now, Tita," he answered with a goofy smile. "See?" He opened and closed it a few times, a proud look on his face.

"Is this what you used to do in Silverholde?" the short woman asked, nodding at the good work. "Apprentice carpenter?"

"No, Tita. I was an actor."

Martita raised an eyebrow at that and scoffed. "You mean, one of those degenerates who sing and shout in the main plaza?" She shook her head before he could answer. "Your talent was wasted. All that is useful in this world can be touched," she rambled, knocking on the repaired door for good measure. "Can art be touched? I think not."

"That's just practice, Tita," Sarkis countered, furrowing his brows. "Art is what requires talent."

Old Martita sniffed again, studying his seemingly saddened face. "Your front teeth stay past your lips even with your mouth shut," she noted. "Reminds me of those rabbits we should eat. Come."

They walked together near the bench that Sarkis had dragged out of the house earlier. The two of them sat in silence as they watched the meat being roasted, and Martita occasionally spat in the fire, watching the flames spurt and graze the little legs that turned a dark shade of brown. Sarkis scratched his head, his curly, greasy hair falling back on his forehead. In the back of his mind, he wondered how long it would take Theliel to come back, or if he would come back at all. Summerport didn't seem like a bad place, but repairing houses and being at the service of old, mean women wasn't exactly what he aspired to do in life. Not only that, but they also had an agreement.

It wasn't long until Martita handed him a stick with the biggest rabbit impaled on it. He figured it was her way of thanking him for his help.

"Take that one," he heard her say. "It's pretty obvious to me that you like stuffing yourself."

"Did you always live here, Tita?" Sarkis asked, his mouth full of flesh and bones, juice coating his fingers.

Before she could answer him, a third voice chirped in. "Old Martita was born and raised in Summerport. The lands you see behind the house were hers until her husband passed away. She now rents most of it to the nearby villagers so they can work on it."

Sarkis glanced up, spotting the broad-shouldered young man who just set down two huge buckets of water. Sarkis watched Patten as he wiped his hands against his dirty pants before sitting down next to Martita, smelling the rabbits before snatching a leg.

"My husband was a legend," the old woman said with a hint of pride.

"So much of a legend that no one around here seems to have ever seen him," Patten told Sarkis with a toothy smile, the two of them breaking into a fit of laughter.

"Hush, you two fleabags," Old Martita scolded them, throwing the bone she munched on at the one she called Big Boy Pat. "If it hadn't been for the Violet Delusion, he would still be with me. A strong man he was, my Gerd."

"Oh well, thank you Old Martita for the food," Patten said, squeezing her hand before standing up. "I have to hurry back to the harbor. Rosewillow is waiting for me."

"It is dawn day today," Sarkis mentioned. "I thought fishermen came back on dusk days."

"They do," Patten nodded at him. "But I have to stop by the marketplace for dinner tonight and they don't need me in the fields today, so Rosewillow and I are going to defeat this warm weather with a swim." Staring at the burly man who looked at his feet out of shyness, Patten asked, "Sarkis, do you wish to join us? It will be fun."

The dark-haired man shook his head. "I am not a good swimmer," he admitted. "Maybe some other time, in some other place."

"You should listen more to fat-face," Old Martita butted in. "Pat," she spoke seriously. "Go home, you lazy fleabag. The air smells of daisies. They are flowers for the dead."

Sarkis giggled at that. "What are you on about, Tita?"

She pushed herself up, fixing the foulard around her head. "You probably can't smell a thing other than your stench, but the air carried petals of yellow daisies this morning. I know death when I see it," she muttered, putting out the fire that was causing her to sweat even more. "The air smelled of daisies on the day Lord Theliel Lionhelm died, and again when his son Thaesonwald died, and when Gerd left me forever, daisies bloomed in our garden.

"Go home, Pat," she repeated, waving in the direction of the small house squeezed between Martita's and the neighbors'.

Patten smiled at her retreating figure. He knew it was that time in the afternoon when Martita would nap the heat away. Light on his feet, Patten ran in the direction of the docks, the sun rays grazing his hair making it look more golden than brown. His fair skin was tanned after hours of hard work under the sun, and he couldn't wait to jump into the fresh waters of the Tinted Bay, right under the cliffs. Merchants and sailors always advised not to jump in there, as it was too close to the Dented Reef, where fanged fish bit at human skin and wild seaweeds clung at any limb within reach to drag their victims into the abyss, but Patten figured it was just another tale meant for children to stay safe.

Perhaps if he had heard such tales as a child it would have spared him quite the trouble. He would have stayed away from the sea and not been sold as a slave by a ruined merchant who baited him in his home with the smell of fresh pigeon tarts and lamb kidney pies. Hopping past the carts and discarded barrels of ale, Patten stood near the largest rocks of the harbor, ignoring the kids that bumped into him or ran past him to throw themselves in the salty waters of the bay. A hand grazed his shoulder, and he immediately turned around, his cheeky smile directed at the dark chestnut-haired woman who peered at him with emerald eyes.

"You were here before me," he said, holding her hand to pull her in the direction of the water.

"Maybe I was," Rosewillow said, smirking at him. "How are things going with Old Martita and Sarkis?" she asked.

"I don't want to think about them now," he laughed out loud, holding her by the waist and jumping in immediately, quickly followed by the children who leaped from the small cliff above his head.

They emerged with their eyes covered by hair and their clothes dragging them into the water, laughing and splashing at each other. This was where he grew up, Patten reminded himself. Swimming with slaves and playing with orphaned children, just like he was. He watched with bewitched eyes as Rosewillow wiped the water away from her eyes. It was always hard for Patten to believe that she was just another orphan of Summerport, earning little coin by sewing clothes and cleaning taverns. Her demeanor was almost noble, and her looks were too refined for her to be just another fisherman's daughter.

She swam backward, away from him, her emerald eyes always set on his face, beckoning him. Rosewillow seemed to be looking for more shade and less noise, her feet splashing away to inch herself further and further away from people. Patten followed her easily, even when his soaked clothes dragged him a little down into the deep waters.

"Why don't you come closer?" the green-eyed woman asked with a chuckle, throwing her arms around his neck.

Patten held her by the waist, inching their bodies closer. "Is this what you had in mind when you said to go for a swim?" he asked, glancing at her plump bottom lip. "I planned on taking you to the Seven Galleys for dinner, too, got some extra coin after today's work. For once I won't even have to borrow silvers from Old Martita for the next moon. You know, it's kind of illegal too—"

Rosewillow planted a kiss on his lips, her tongue grazing his skin. "You ramble, Patten. You are a cute boy, but you ramble."

He gulped, licking his lips as if to taste her. Their lips met again, slowly, and she parted hers. Patten's tongue found its way to hers, albeit clumsily, his breath hitching in his throat when he felt her legs wrap around his waist and her hand clawing at his bottom cheek. Rosewillow pressed her chest against his, her full breasts teasing his hardened nipples. It wasn't long until she took control of their kissing, teeth biting and lips pulling. The discomfort he felt in his pants underwater was becoming more obvious with every second that passed and he hissed upon feeling her hand grabbing between his legs.

The two stared at each other, and she smirked at him, her hand stroking down. "Do you want to play a little game, Pat?" she whispered against his lips.

His hands gripped her hips, nudging himself closer to her. "What kind of game?" he breathed out, feeling her skin against his as she wrapped her intimate folds around his stiff, engorged manhood. Rosewillow groaned, closing her eyes and tightening her legs and arms around him.

Patten stared at her ecstatic face with lidded, lovestruck eyes until his heart skipped a beat and the heat was drained from his body as he shivered and jumped. Rosewillow had opened her eyes, the green hues of her irises replaced by complete and utter black. Her lips parted and her face twisted into a feral expression. Patten could see the blood inside her eyes and the pulsing veins of her brain.

"The one where you tell me what you see, *Nakfèht*," she snarled, her once sweet voice replaced by a deep, otherworldly sound that chilled his bones.

Where her pink lips once were, a wide black hole threatened to suck the air from his lungs. Patten wanted to scream, to push her away and beg for someone, anyone to help him, but all he could feel was her nails on his right side and her arm around his neck. Patten shut his eyes the closer she leaned in, the pain in his stomach coursing through his entire body.

Chapter VI

THE DARLING IN MIND

The rain had finally stopped in Rainier's End, the faint sun rays slowly replacing the dark clouds that had previously plunged the town in complete darkness. Rantha walked down the mudded streets with a thoughtful look marking her features, careless of the dirt that would splash against the hem of her cloak and soil her boots. Her wild, black hair puffed up with the humidity, and she scrunched her nose at the smell of waste and excrements that had invaded the town with all the flood and wind.

The central inn wasn't too far from the shelter, and when she spotted the innkeeper talking to two gentlemen, Rantha went straight for the barn where she figured her uncooperative guest's horse was. Her boots kicked the straw that blocked the door from opening correctly, and her brown eyes widened as she stepped inside. There were only three horses in there, and it wasn't too hard for her to guess which one she had to take. The two black horses on the far right were saddled properly, with light golden skirts and darker golden cantles. The stirrups seemed new, and the horn was shaped in an owl. The third horse, however, which stood on the left side of the barn, was completely white, almost silvery. Its eyes were deep blue, and the simple, yet polished crimson saddle made the mount look quite intimidating and otherworldly. A leather bag had been left on the wooden planks behind the horse, and Rantha grabbed it quickly before she untied the horse and stroked its side. The white creature let out a neigh, and Rantha smiled.

"You," a masculine voice startled her. "Is the Avoryon horse yours?"

She turned around, only to face two Regency surveillants and a very confused innkeeper. She shook her head, but when she was about to explain, the three of them got caught in a messy conversation.

"The man from the previous night left it here," the old and frail innkeeper said. "He paid to have the horse fed for another day but he never returned for it."

"Chief Eleres, I saw this horse before," the red-haired official said, "in Beggar's Pool, when I was the one watering the horses. You can't just miss an Avoryon mount when you see one."

"So, what, Goldsnout?" Eleres snapped at him. "We should have left a long time ago, but this weather stalled us. We need to get back to the Regency."

"But Chief, what if this man saw the girl who was attacked? What if there is any clue that we might have mi—"

"Are we seriously going to talk about this again?"

Rantha cleared her throat, tugging on the reins to get closer to the exit and speak with the innkeeper. She took a silver coin from her pocket and handed it to the old man with a faint smile.

"For the extra food," she said.

The innkeeper took it without hesitation, bowing his head to her shyly.

She was nearly out of the door when an urgent "Miss!" reached her ears. The red-haired officer, Goldsnout, directed a toothy smile at her. "Would you mind if I stopped by your place to talk to your friend for a moment?"

"Snout."

"Chief, please," the young man begged. "I will be quick and join you on the Red Road before sunset."

Rantha stared at him in confusion. "I—sure," she replied. "I take care of the Illusion Shelter," she explained. "I am curing the owner of this horse," she added. "If you don't mind being quick with your questions… He needs rest."

The two of them walked side by side, their horses in toe, Rantha having explained that she wasn't comfortable with riding someone else's mount. Goldsnout had acquiesced in silence, his lush armor shining under the sunlight as they walked to the shelter. From there, the forgotten keep of the Rosenbanes in the distance looked a little less blood-curdling despite the tree branches growing on its walls. Rantha stole quite a few glances at the young man, wondering what had happened in Beggar's Pool to make him go against his chief's orders only to talk to a sick man. Her gaze lingered on Goldsnout's ginger locks, and she noted how even the color of his lashes was fiery. His green eyes looked back at her, and she looked away immediately.

"I didn't mean to stare," she whispered, slightly embarrassed.

"Ah," he sighed out, "it is my fault. I am still new to this; I've been assigned to a few missions under Chief Eleres' guidance only some months ago. I haven't even properly introduced myself." Stopping in his tracks, he faced her and brought her hand up to his lips. "I am Officer Opherus Goldsnout of the Regency's Surveillance."

She laughed at that, offering him a clumsy bow as she failed to bend her knees properly. "I am Rantha of Rainier's End, trying to find a cure for the Violet Delusion."

"Wow," the redhead chuckled. "Your job is more important than mine."

They smiled at each other, the faint blush on Goldsnout's cheeks more obvious than Rantha's flush. The woman cleared her throat, tucking her hair behind her ear. They were almost there, and she realized she still didn't know exactly what this officer wanted.

"Officer—"

"Please, call me Opherus."

"Opherus, what… What exactly happened in Beggar's Pool, if you don't mind me asking?"

"Well, a girl was killed. It was," he paused, collecting his thoughts, "a massacre. I don't even know how to describe it. She was barely recognizable; she seemed to have been stabbed to death and the Oracle knows what else. There was no suspect, no trace of anything, really, probably because of the snowstorm that night. Chief Eleres believes a wild bear did it, but—"

"But you don't," she concluded. With dread on her face, she asked, "And this man you want to question, do you think he—"

"He might have seen something, you know?" Goldsnout rambled. "He left before Chief Eleres and me. What if he saw the girl speak to someone on his way out?"

Rantha nodded slowly, her brown eyes glancing at the window on the second floor of the shelter as they stopped in front of it. The soft wind caused her curly locks to slap against her forehead, hiding the furrowing of her brow as she saw the mysterious man stare right back at her through the window, his upper body bare and his black hair around his shoulders. The fury that marked his features was not lost on her.

✳✳✳

Lyzon tugged at every ribbon dangling from her young lady's back, securing them to have the dress fit perfectly. Her movements were quick and strong, and Tecla's body often jerked backward with every knot. The dark olive-skinned woman had a blank stare on her face as she worked, moving from the straight, sky blue dress that showed more skin than it should have, to the wavy hair of the young girl who proceeded to sit in front of her vanity. Lyzon's dark eyes glanced at the crimson book with golden angles that Tecla held in her hands as she read in silence. Shaking her head, she began braiding her young lady's long, light chestnut hair from the back of her head.

Ever since they came back from the holy site in Summerport, Tecla behaved in strange ways. She didn't talk to her nor Fran and spent most of her time reading the Oracle's Memoir, almost as if the book had bewitched her. It had been going on for days, and Lyzon wondered if the young lady even paid attention to Educator Tomas whenever it was time to study. The maid's fingers worked swiftly through the combed strands, reaching the end of the braid in just a few minutes before lifting it and rearranging it into a crown on top of Tecla's head. It was the first time in her life that Tecla had asked for a traditional, southern hairstyle.

"Young lady," she said, signaling that her work was done.

Tecla's hazel eyes glanced up at her reflection in the mirror. She quietly set her book on the table, between her brush and hairpins, and tilted her head a few times to see how she looked. The blue dress was sleeveless and showed a certain amount of cleavage. It wasn't as large as her previous dresses, having requested the newest silks to be sewed to fit every curve or her body. She could feel the air on her exposed back.

"The back necklace," she reminded Lyzon. "Where is it?"

"The one your father gifted you?"

"Yes, the long one—the Darling Mind. I could never wear it when I was younger, it just slid over my shoulders. But I would like to try wearing it now; I am much older and it was given to me when I was born."

Lyzon reached for it on its stand next to the vanity and proceeded with her young lady's wishes. She let the long, silver pendant tickle Tecla's lower back and she stepped back, folding her hands behind her. The blue-green jewel encased in the swirling frame shone brightly against Tecla's fair skin.

"Young lady," Lyzon repeated.

"I look ridiculous, don't I?" Tecla asked.

"You look like a Lionhelm," Lyzon replied, her gaze never meeting Tecla's.

"Mother said there will soon be a ball in my honor," the young girl sighed out. "I am trying to figure out what I like and what I should wear for the occasion. What do you think, my friend?"

"I think that you won't find answers in that book."

Tecla turned around at that, glaring at the maid. "Why are you angry at me, Lyzon? It's been a few days since you started acting this way. There is nothing wrong with the Memoir. Educator Tomas praised me for my interest in religion."

"Educator Tomas will approve of everything you do and will cover you with the guards when you leave the palace because he works for your father," Lyzon explained, brushing invisible dust off her beige, loose dress.

"And you don't?" Tecla asked, befuddled. "I don't underst—"

"The ball was not organized in your honor, Lady Tecla," the dark-haired woman went on. "Lady Lionhelm wishes to find you a husband, Fran heard it in the kitchens. As for the Memoir," Lyzon said with a dark stare, "I fail to see its usefulness. Faith comes from within yourself and as beautiful as the ceremonies are at the temple, I don't think you should spend more time there. A lady doesn't preach."

"Then what do ladies do, Lyzon?" Tecla asked in an exasperated voice. "They don't marry and they don't follow the righteous path in your vision of the world. So, what do ladies do?"

The maid seemed to be at a loss for words. Her hands toyed with the ends of her loose, side ponytail, and she shrugged. "I don't know, my lady. You once told me your father wanted you to join the Regency's Observatory Vault. That doesn't sound like a bad idea," she answered meekly.

Tecla remained silent, walking up to the tall windows that offered a view of the rocky cliffs of Strongshore and the vast forests that preceded Wilderose. She leaned against the frame of the window, the feel of the cold marble of the wall and the warm wood of the frame causing the hairs on her arm to stand. Her hazel eyes looked green and amber at the same time due to the sunlight that hit her face.

"Did you know that when a man becomes Holy Commander, he renounces to all the titles and lands he possesses?" she asked softly. "He even renounces to his name. But Sir Frederyc Rosenfield didn't, and after completing the translation of the Memoir, he left his position in favor of the current Holy Commander.

"The Oracle was born a simple girl named Kothore. She and her twin sister Kashezeth grew up in Old Calaris to serve as healers; back then, it was thought that fire purified every sickness, healed every wound, so they would soon keep a fire lit at all times for the next person to help as it was not uncommon during the Warring Tribes Era," Tecla told her, with a distant look in her eyes. "But one day, the armies of Alatros the Red arrived in Calaris, razing everything that was in sight, pillaging the merchants, and stealing their daughters.

"Kashezeth was taken, and Kothore never knew what happened to her. One of Alatros' generals tore her clothes away from her while his subordinates cheered him on. Some say Alatros himself attacked the girl," Tecla went on, and Lyzon listened in horror at the tale the young lady had been busy reading. "They held her arms and legs for the general, but he had barely started breaking her body when Kothore spoke in a calm voice, her body seized by spasms and violent shivers.

"She told them that Warrior Queen Aelneth would attack them at dusk with a horde of fifty-thousand men from the east coast while they would be busy destroying the northern areas of Calaris, but they ignored her, using her body until the next day. When Queen Aelneth beheaded all of Alatros' generals, the bandit demanded that the girl was brought to him.

"He told her that Aelneth had offered him a deal in exchange for his life; conquer the unknown lands across the bay for her, and she would spare him. Alatros asked Kothore to tell him if the warrior queen was telling him the truth and if there was anything across the salty waters, but Kothore remained silent, for she would be granted visions only in the presence of the fire she kept alive and cured the damned with."

Lyzon moved from her spot slowly, reaching out for the open book on the table, her long fingers brushing against the old pages that made cracking sounds whenever she touched them.

"Alatros the Red took her to his encampment at the gates of Calaris and locked her in a cell where she was told to light the fire, right where the Oracle Pillar stands today in Summerport. Every night, one of his soldiers would visit her and force himself on her as Alatros believed that she wouldn't tell him anything unless her body was seized by another rapture, and he thought the odds would be in his favor if he just replicated the previous events.

"It wasn't long until his wish was fulfilled, and Alatros built the Oracle Pillar for her, consulting her before every expedition of his."

"I thought the ancient tribes only believed in the Gods above the Heights," Lyzon whispered, closing the book only to trace its title with her fingernails.

"They did," Tecla answered. "Alatros believed the Oracle spoke their will through her visions. After he wed Aelneth, the two appointed an entire army to protect the Oracle Pillar. It is said that Kothore had an indefinite number of children and that every girl she had was raised to tend to the fire they would keep using for their duties as healers and potential oracles."

"What about the boys?" Lyzon asked in a worried tone.

"They joined the ranks of the military, and Alatros named them the Angels of Steel. Their only duty was to protect the Oracle Pillar and generate more oracles and more angels."

"We are all children of the Oracle," Tecla concluded, glancing back at her maid.

Lyzon's mouth was agape, her lips twisting in a mixture of shock and disgust. As if to keep her mind off of it, she began tidying the vanity, cleaning Tecla's brushes, and putting the hairpins back in the drawer.

"This is why I can't take any of this seriously, my lady," she admitted, slamming the drawer into place. "It upsets me that you would believe such tales, as it upsets me that you seem to agree with Lady Lionhelm's wish to sell you so easily. I know that me being born and raised in islands unknown to you in the Zalejos Depths make me some sort of savage," Lyzon reasoned out loud, speaking words that had probably been directed at her before. "But we do not assault girls to know the

Gods' will and base our entire religion on it and we do not marry for lands if we have any."

Tecla turned around to face her, frowning at her words.

"What happens between a man and a woman is out of care for each other; care and respect, young lady."

The chestnut-haired girl walked up to her with careful steps. They stared into each other's eyes for a moment, and Lyzon hoped that she had been clear enough to convince the girl she had nursed ever since she was born, and was now taller than her. Tecla placed a hand on her soft, round shoulder covered by plain fabric and leaned in.

"I will read now," she whispered. "Please close the door as you leave."

✳✳✳

The sound of the hooves echoing through the forests that were once the Rosenfields' kept Theliel company as he rode in silence next to Lord Arther Angefort in the direction of the Regency. The sun had set a long time ago, but Angefort wasn't one to tire easily. They hadn't once stopped since they left Strongshore, and were already entering Wilderose. Between the virgin grass and the empty fields past the forest, it was hard to believe that anyone had lived there for thousands of years. Theliel figured that at that pace, they would be reaching Silverholde in less than five days when it usually took two long weeks of horse-riding. The

Rosenfield castle was in sight, even if Theliel had to narrow his eyes to see properly.

 The skies above were dark blue, almost black, and not a single star was visible. The only light was provided by the soldiers that rode on each side of Lord Angefort, their torches showing them which path was the Red Road.

 "I apologize for my outburst earlier," Theliel told the Secretary of the Regency. "It was not something I should have done in the publicity of the audience room."

 The fatherly look Angefort gave him almost reassured him. "As the Commander of the Lionhelm forces, I must tell you, you shall never voice your thoughts to someone who is, by all means, your superior. Your father didn't achieve success by throwing tantrums in regal halls. But as a friend of the family," he went on, his body leaning towards Theliel without losing balance, "I can't say I don't understand you."

 "Really?" Theliel asked, surprised. Running a hand through his messy, medium-length hair, he added, "So, you do think it was unfair."

 "Don't get me wrong, son. I think Lord Lionhelm did the best he could with every child of his. It is not easy to fill his shoes; he had to marry in a hurry to make sure he had at least a couple of heirs was he to perish in the King's campaigns across the Tinted Bay, not to mention the Violet Delusion still made a rampage in the Silver Lands; it wasn't as contained as now.

 "Your mother was an incredibly beautiful woman, Theliel; tall, with mahogany hair and marble grey eyes," Angefort went on. "I often blame myself for what happened, as I am the one who introduced her to your father."

"You did?" Theliel asked, flabbergasted.

"I suggested Emelyne became the new lady-in-waiting of Lady Lionhelm; Emelyne had lost her family to the Violet Delusion and was afraid she would have to work in a pleasure house. She didn't know anything to the point where she could have used her skills to earn some silvers, and even if she did, very few places offered honest work. She had visited Summerport's encampment out of desperation.

"It was good timing, I must say. Lady Lionhelm was looking for a fresh face after her old lady-in-waiting passed away, but your father was enamored with her. It wasn't long until she gave birth to Tesfira, and Lady Lionhelm decided to take the girl as hers. The lord's affair was known by everyone, but aside from a few trusted people who knew the details, no one suspected your sister and you to be Emelyne's children." Arther paused, eyeing the young man who was drinking his words.

"I didn't know you knew," he whispered.

A question, in particular, was burning Theliel's lips. He pulled the reins of his horse, and Angefort did the same, raising a hand to signal his men to stand back.

"Do you know what made her lose her mind?"

"No, Theliel," the old man answered, his wrinkly eyes looking at him with sadness in them. "I just know it happened some time while she was pregnant with you. She left the palace and began roaming the streets of Edgemere, and became wildly impulsive.

"A few members of the Observatory Vault are looking into what they call behavioral changes, as they believe it is not always caused by diseases like the Violet Delusion but, to be honest with you, I don't know much about that. You should look into it yourself," Angefort advised him. "If you wish."

The young adult beside him looked dejected. "Lord Angefort, have you ever walked past the secretary quarters to meet King Helias?"

The old man didn't expect that question. Puzzled, he answered, "The orders are to not disturb King Helias unless he summons you."

"But have you been summoned recently?"

The commander scanned his face as if to understand what he was getting at, but their exchange was interrupted by a deafening cry. The riders behind them whispered to each other, hushing their horses when the animals began moving away in panic, and Lord Angefort turned around in the direction of the sound. More cries reached their ears, the utter pain and agony chilling their bones.

"You," the silver commander ordered to the first soldier on his right. "Scout ahead."

"It could be a boar hunt gone wrong," the scout said, earning himself a glare.

"Who hunts at this time of the night?" Theliel retorted, urging his horse in the direction of the victim's screams.

He rode quickly, pushing himself up and balancing his feet on the stirrups to have his horse run faster. His armor and heavy uniform of the Regency made him not as light as he wished to be to gain speed. He didn't have his lance with him, he realized when it was already too late, but Theliel figured – and mostly hoped – that the bow and arrows strapped against his saddle would be enough against whatever he was about to face. A part of him did hope it was only a wild boar.

He was soon surrounded by Angefort's men, some brandishing their weapons while the others lighted the way. The screams never relented, only supported by the heavy vibrations of the ground underneath their feet and a haunting chanting made of inaudible words. The cavalry lost its organization pretty quickly, the men falling soundly off their horses, hurting themselves with the heaviness of their armors.

"Easy, boy, easy," Theliel tried to appease his mount, urging it forward.

Lord Angefort flew past him, and the two of them quickly smelled smoke. Right behind the pine trees, a faint light indicated a fire. Theliel was quick to catch up, his horse only a few feet away from the commander's. Angefort came to a halt suddenly, and Theliel nearly fell off as he pulled on the reins. An empty meadow stretched before their eyes, with a burning fire at the center of it. They rounded it carefully; the screaming had just ceased. Theliel neared one of the trees of the Wilderose forest, swallowing hard.

"By the Oracle and all of Her children," he heard Lord Angefort whisper in horror.

Blood coated the ground, spilling from the insides of a man shattered to pieces. His arms and legs had been pulled apart and pinned to the roots of a tree that looked more like thick thorns, leaving his midsection flat against the trunk where he was impaled. Bowels spurted and hit the earth, his intestines unrolling slowly and reaching Angefort's feet the moment he dismounted. The man's head had fallen near his left arm, his eyeballs glassy and a thick branch piercing the back of his head only to come out from his mouth, causing his tongue to loll out. Theliel glanced around as if to catch the sight of whoever had done this to the poor man, but all that surrounded them was the night, the smoke of the fire behind them, and the doomed, haunted land of Wilderose.

Chapter VII

No Lips to Kiss

"Take note of his looks if you can and burn the body," Lord Angefort had ordered his men before silently leading everyone where they would spend the night. The initial plan was to ride until they reached the Rough Rill river, and seek refuge at the gates of Courtbridge, but the unexpected events of Wilderose had not only sent a wave of fear among the ranks; they had lost their momentum, and their clouded minds felt the need to rest.

Angefort had decided to stop at the abandoned Rosenfield castle, but those who escorted him didn't feel like they would get a lot of rest. The imposing structure proudly stood on the highest hill right outside the Wilderose forest, overlooking the Rough Rill and offering a clear view of Courtbridge. The castle itself wasn't very large in Theliel's eyes, but its three watchtowers were tall enough to make him dizzy. The dark grey stone looked black in the night, and all that could be seen was the keep. The Rosenfield castle's drawbridge was permanently down and the portcullis had been left open. Ever since House Rosenfield's disappearance, their residence had been free to visit, like a mausoleum.

"We will warm ourselves in the great hall," Angefort had announced as they passed the lower bailey, the curious stares of his men jumping from the outhouse to the temple, almost as if they expected to see someone.

Theliel had been too busy warming his hands near the small fire that lighted the great hall to listen to the tales the soldiers told each other, sharing Edgemeran wine and handing each other brown bread and dried meat. The glassy eyes of the poor man in the forest were still fresh on his mind, and as much as he was hungry, he felt as if the smallest bit of meat would make his stomach churn. The last thing he wanted was to empty his stomach on Angefort's feet. Theliel's hazel eyes glanced up at the paintings that decorated the great hall, surprised to see that none of them portrayed any member of House Rosenfield. They were all still life paintings; from fruit to flowers, the young man realized that most of the plants he saw he didn't recognize. The more he looked, the more he noticed that some fruits in the transparent bowls had faces on them – Theliel blinked, and they seemed to disappear, only to reappear in landscapes with trees of shining green.

"Enjoying the rosewillows, Theliel?" one of the foot soldiers asked him, chewing on a piece of ham.

"I was just looking for the portrait of someone," the young Lionhelm replied, rubbing his hands above the fire. "I have heard of the Rosenfields, but never have I seen their faces."

"I saw Sir Frederyc once," an older rider said, coming closer to the fire as if to roast his piece of meat. His green eyes peered at Theliel as he added, "He wasn't the friendliest of men but I was still a child, so I could have just been scared of him."

"What did he look like?"

The green-eyed man shrugged, scratching his black hair. "I don't know what to tell you. He was pretty average; big beardy mustache, brown hair, and brown eyes. He wasn't that tall either. His only mission was to become Holy Commander, and no one saw him after he abandoned the Oracle Pillar in Summerport. His daughters, though… They were fine ladies.

"They wore their long, reddish-brown hair loose, aside from the twin braids on the back of their heads that they twisted into roses. It always fascinated me; not to mention their warm, goldenrod eyes."

"How many daughters did Sir Frederyc have?" Theliel asked out of curiosity as the others around them quieted down to listen.

"If I'm not mistaken, he had three—Breonna, Reanna, and Deanna. Quiet ladies, they were; they were said to be extremely pious and reserved, and never attended any public event. Some argue that it was because they were meant to be betrothed to Lord Lionhelm's sons, but who knows anymore."

Theliel had heard about that too when he was still a child; fortunately for him and unfortunately for their house, the three Rosenfield daughters had gone missing and their entire staff butchered. The people of Summerport would tell him stories of witchcraft and madness; some would say that the three daughters were sacrificed by a secret circle of heretics, others that Sir Frederyc had lost his mind and refused to see his household being absorbed by the Lionhelms', therefore preferring to end his legacy the way he saw fit. Tithan Lionhelm never commented on the event in Theliel's presence, and all that was clear was that the Rosenfields' territory was being surveilled by the Regency.

Theliel was lost in his thoughts when a resounding knock on the great hall doors silenced everyone. The men exchanged confused glances, and Lord Angefort himself raised an eyebrow, his eyes scanning the room as if to see whether someone was missing.

Pointing at the man who had just spoken with Theliel, Lord Angefort ordered him, "Gulmont, see if it's Stez. The man tends to wander off on his own."

The green-eyed soldier nodded, rushing towards the doors while the others whispered that Stez was there, that he wasn't, that he passed out under a bench and other theories. Gulmont pulled the heavy doors open, exhaling loudly, narrowing his eyes to try and see outside. No one was in sight, not even near the portcullis. He took another couple of steps outside but saw nothing.

Shaking his head, the soldier turned heels. "My lord, no one—"

An arrow hit him straight in the head, piercing through his skull and coming out of his left eye. Gulmont fell with a thud and his companions were quick to react. Spears, crossbows, and broadswords were readied, and Theliel immediately rushed towards his spear. It wasn't ideal considering that he was trained to use it while charging with his horse, but Theliel's sight had never been great, and he wasn't about to use any bow in the middle of the night. Shields in place, a few foot soldiers marched towards the entrance, expecting more arrows to rain from the skies. Angefort dragged the fallen Gulmont's body away, whispering a few prayers.

"Show yourself!"

Theliel watched carefully from where he stood beside the crossbowmen, but there was not a single noise, nor a single shadow to confirm that someone was indeed attacking them. The screeching sound of the portcullis reached their ears, and Lord Angefort came forward, elbowing his men to let him pass. Agonizing cries became louder and louder, and Theliel spotted one of the shield-wielders wet himself. He moved forward himself, only to widen his eyes in horror.

The portcullis was being closed, the spikes closing down on several people who screamed in pain. Their spines cracking and their bones breaking were sounds accompanied by the raw sight of their blood coating the ground. They spasmed and begged for help, for pity. For forgiveness.

Bodies fell from the windows of the outhouse; heavy with armor, their bodies splattered near the well, but the sound was covered by the yelping and crying of a woman from the ladies' apartments, right beside the keep. Theliel felt a tug on his boot and he looked down while the soldiers around him tried to push the doors close, failing miserably as they seemed to be stuck. More arrows were shot from the battlements, but his hazel eyes were focused on the auburn girl with dust on her face under the wooden bench.

"Please, help me," she whispered pleadingly.

"There's a child here!" he shouted, but no one paid attention to him. Angefort's forces were busy trying to fight the unknown or smashing the windows open in an attempt to escape from the back of the great hall. "There's a—"

"Please," the girl repeated, crawling near the staircase wearing only a dirty, brown dress.

Theliel chased her as she ran upstairs and disappeared behind a door that led to a dark, narrow corridor. As fast as he was, the little girl was a lot faster than him. Her twin braids began to loosen, slapping against her back, and whenever she glanced back at him, her topaz eyes sent jolts through his body. The corridor seemed to never end, and Theliel bumped into several empty armors and statues made of hard, cold stone. His breathing became more erratic and his chestnut locks clung to his sweaty forehead.

"This way," the auburn girl indicated, her hand reaching out for what seemed to be a door. "Help Reanna," she begged.

The young man stumbled forward as a rush of wind pushed him through the open door, and he found himself on the battlements. Catching his breath, he looked around, distracted by the sounds coming from downstairs. Theliel leaned against the crenels to see what was going on, but the entire hall had caught fire, and even the commander was running outside, turning into easy prey for the invisible archers. Theliel's head jerked upwards as a deafening cry hurt his ears, and he saw her. The little girl was staring at him with a blank expression, pointing at the woman on top of the keep who stood barefoot, covered by half-shredded pieces of white lace. She swung a little too close to the edge, her head slightly bent as she looked down.

"Reanna?" Theliel called her, a part of him wondering if it really was her, as she was supposed to have disappeared a long time ago, but the blood of the Lionhelm infantry was real, and the fire too. "Reanna Rosenfield?"

The young woman raised her head, her skin much paler than the little girl's. Her chest was bloody and her cheeks sunken; she stood like death hovering above a pyre, with no eyes to look into and no lips to kiss. Her bones were visible just as her skull while her hair was slowly stolen by the wind. A sharp tug on his pants startled him, and the girl who had led him there was pulling him towards her.

"Can you help?" she asked, her own eyes falling out of her head, worms feasting on her tongue.

✷✷✷

Jascha watched with weary eyes as Rantha and the Regency officer walked up to the entrance of the shelter. From the way they talked, they seemed to know each other, and that was not something in his favor. The last thing he needed was for the red-haired man to see him once more and start asking questions, but he figured there was little he could do in his weakened state. Jascha stood in his birth suit by the window, slowly reaching for the clean clothes that one of Rantha's apprentices had brought him earlier. She had left them on the dresser across the room, right next to an old, iron-framed mirror. Jascha took in his appearance for a moment, noting how he was less muscular than he used to be. His midsection was thinner, and his thighs lighter. Between his sick and starved face on top of the scars that covered his back and chest, he felt like he had become a stranger to himself.

He heard the wood crack under the heavy steps that neared his door, and he slid into the loose shirt of someone who, he figured, died at the shelter. His hair, greasy from the rain and mud of the previous day, clung to the back of his neck. Jascha tugged the pants up, and the door was flung open. Goldsnout looked at him with a neutral expression, while Rantha seemed uncomfortable. She set his bag on the floor, tucking her hair behind her ear, which she often did when thoughtful, he noticed.

"I apologize for the disturbance," the officer said with a polite smile. "I am Officer Goldsnout; I believe we met each other in Beggar's Pool. At the inn, to be precise." Scanning Jascha's face, he nodded to himself, as if to confirm that they had indeed met each other before. "I am sorry, I am afraid I don't remember your name."

"Jascha," was his answer.

"Ah, yes." Goldsnout came closer, glancing at the shelter owner as if to ask for permission to question him more. "I have a few questions if you are not too tired."

"I am," Jascha replied instantly, "but I doubt that will stop you from asking."

Deciding to ignore that bit, the officer went on. "Did you talk to the inn owner's daughter, a girl named Loveleen? She used to sing to the deaf boy's music."

"I did."

"And what did you talk about?"

"I gave her thirty silvers for her song, and asked her what it was about," Jascha said plainly, sliding his hands in his pockets. "She rambled a bit about it and we never spoke again until I left."

Goldsnout nodded, his green eyes darting around as he registered the information. "Your last words to her?"

Jascha's lips curved up a bit, and his face relaxed as a pleasurable feeling filled his chest and trailed down his entire body. "He has starved in your womb; Loveleen you have sent him to his tomb," he answered. "As the song went on."

Goldsnout furrowed his brow, exchanging a confused glare with the woman beside him. Toying with his gloves as if he was unsure as to whether he should remove them or not, he sighed out. "Alright, and did you see her talk to anybody else as you left?"

Jascha's smile widened slightly, and he shrugged. "No."

Disappointed with his answers, Goldsnout forced himself to nod. "Well, thank you for your time, Jascha. May I have a word, Miss Rantha?"

The two of them exited the room as quickly as they had entered it, exchanging hushed words and puzzled looks. Jascha watched them in silence through the door left ajar, but as they neared the bottom of the stairs, their voices no longer reached his ears.

Goldsnout ran a hand through his messy ginger hair, scratching his scalp. He stared at Rantha as she straightened her dress and folded her hands behind her back. Jumping out of his reverie, the young officer pulled what looked like a coin out of the purse attached to his large belt and placed it in her hands. Her brown eyes stared curiously at the round piece of silver with an emerald owl on it. The bird was partially covered by the engraving of a shield with an eye on it. It was the first time she saw this type of silver.

"With this, you can reach the Regency's Surveillance quarters without having to request an audience with the chief," Goldsnout explained. "In case Jascha remembers anything or tells you something unusual, please stop by." Placing a hand on her shoulder, he asked, "You have your horse, don't you?"

Rantha nodded fervently. "Yes, I do, but what do you mean by unusual? This man could very well be sick and you know how people are when they are hit with the Violet Delusion. They talk a lot of nonsense, harm themselves, kill themselves—"

"Rantha, I don't think he has it."

The two remained silent, looking into each other's eyes. Rantha's lower lip trembled as if she was profoundly disappointed in herself, trying to understand what the officer was telling her.

"I am not that experienced; I will admit that. But usually, when I question people, they first ask me why and what happened. Your guest up there didn't seem to care, almost as if he knew."

"That doesn't exclude that he—"

"Yes," Goldsnout chimed in. "Listen," he said, gently grabbing her elbow to walk further away from the staircase. "I could be wrong here but something is off. Before the girl in Beggar's Pool, Chief Eleres and I walked into other disturbing cases on our way back from the Sand Towers. Some of them involved very brutal deaths of girls and women about your age, all around the Fog Lands, the first one being in the town of Three Crosses.

"If you hear anything about it from that man, please, come to the capital," Goldsnout concluded before politely kissing her hand and promising to see her soon.

A smile grazed her lips as she watched the young officer leave the shelter so soon but as much as she wanted to have kind words to say to him, all she could think of was Jascha's dagger, its jeweled hilt, and the Beast of Three Crosses engraved on the pommel. Rantha glanced upstairs and saw Jascha watch her as he leaned against the wall next to the door of his bedroom.

Frowning, she tightened her fist, feeling the Regency's pass press against her palm. "You should rest," she told him in an authoritative tone before turning heels and heading for the kitchens.

✳✳✳

The fat raindrops that trailed down the windows of Lord Lionhelm's observatory room completely clouded the view of the coast and Tecla felt like the entire study was submerged by water. She sat still on the wooden steps that led to the cupola where all the books her father owned were lined on round shelves and looked like they as well would fall like raindrops on the golden and blue marbled floor. She peeked down, toying with her pendant, memorizing every line of the family's coat-of-arms painted right at the center of the room.

Tithan Lionhelm could be heard whispering the letters he was reading, and Tecla smiled, resting her chin in the palm of her hand. It wouldn't be long until her carriage would be ready to take her to Summerport. It was her city day as well as mass day, and she had just finished reading the Oracle's Memoir, much to Lyzon's disappointment and her father's disapproval. Her left leg kicked the air as she looked at the Darling Mind in the palm of her hand, the blue and the green of the pendant mixing like opposite winds. The surface of it reminded her of the tall windows of the temple; her fingers could trace the triangular lines that formed a hexagon.

"Why did they call it the Darling Mind?" she asked her father, who simply hummed and held the letter in his hand a little closer to his face. "Father. The stone?"

"Some say it was one of the stones on Queen Aelneth's crown and it had been found by Alatros himself for his bride," he explained in a monotone. "In my opinion, it was just a lie told to add value to the jewel. It belonged to my mother, who received it from my father's mother and it has just been in our family for a very long time, although originally, the stone was much bigger."

Tecla frowned at that. "What happened to it?"

"I just had it split in two," Tithan said, reaching for his quill pen and signing his letter.

"And where is the other half?"

There was a brief moment of silence, and Tithan put down his paper and pen. "Sadly, I lost it."

The young girl nodded absentmindedly, her foot still kicking the air as she went back to staring outside the windows. Tecla's unblinking gaze seemed mesmerized by the pattern the heavy rain made on the tinted glass, and her foot slowly stopped moving. She felt the steps underneath her bend and she lost her balance. Gripping the sides and opening her mouth in a silent scream, she felt a sharp pain on the side of her head and her ankle stung as if she had twisted it.

Before she could realize it, Tecla said, "I don't want you to die, Father."

Tithan frowned at that, standing up to walk up to his daughter, watching her carefully. She sat perfectly still, staring in the distance, with her hands holding the sides of the wooden steps as if they were the ropes of one of the swings in the Great Gardens. The old lord placed a large hand on her knee. Her hazel eyes blinked, and she placed her hand on top of his, her fingernails tracing his swollen veins. His skin was soft despite his age and warrior past and Tecla smiled faintly.

"I don't want to die either," he replied, helping her get down without stumbling on her indigo dress. "Sadly, we are not given a choice as humans," he added, circling her bare shoulders with his arms.

Tecla put her slender arm around his waist, her small form nearly disappearing in her father's embrace. There was a quick knock on the door before Master-at-Arms Fantine entered the room, bowing to her lord. The woman's dark red hair barely reached her shoulders, and her sober, black uniform distinguished her from the rest of Tithan's Council of Steel. Black had been the color reserved for the best warriors of the South since Alatros the

Red commanded it. Some traditions were undiscussed in Tecla's eyes, just like the Council of Steel that took care of the ordinary matters of Strongshore and the Lionhelms' vastest lands.

"As you requested, I brought Lord Tylennald," Fantine announced.

The youngest Lionhelm glanced up at her father in confusion. As far as she knew, the two hadn't spoken to each other in years, if not required to during public gatherings.

"Your carriage is ready, Lady Tecla," Fantine added, showing her profile and bowing her head, signaling that she was ready to escort her. "If you will follow me."

Tithan motioned her to leave, the young girl raising her eyebrows and not exchanging a single word with her older brother as he came inside. The doors closed behind him, the sound of them being locked echoing through the halls of the palace. Tithan didn't greet his son nor did he offer him to sit down, preferring to go straight for his chair.

They held their gazes, and Tithan felt like looking in a mirror that showed him a younger version of himself. Only age separated them, and the old lord felt a bitter taste in his mouth at that thought. Age, and cunning, he figured. Not to mention the polished and overly expensive sense of fashion that was Tylennald's; Tithan had always preferred his choice of clothing to be military but his son basked in the glory of his last name, the splendid silks and soft furs that covered his body a feeble attempt at overshadowing those around him.

Tylennald sat across from him, crossing his legs and leaning back into the chair. His posture was straight and his expression composed. As it was usual for him, the second-born didn't speak first. Tylennald always let the others do the talking, only to hiss later.

"We haven't talked in quite some time," Tithan began, clearing his throat and folding his hands over the stack of papers he had been working on.

"Twenty years," his son answered. "That was your wish."

"At least for once in your life you respected one of my wishes," Lord Lionhelm pointed out stoically. "When your brother Thaesonwald had his accident I immediately summoned Lord Angefort, who has so far kept in a safe place the last will you tried to write in your favor.

"Now, I have thoroughly revised it, which is something you and your mother will probably be happy about."

Tylennald leaned in slightly, his eyes narrowing into a doubtful look.

"Shall Thaesonwald not regain full consciousness, my title will directly be his son's, Tiran," Tithan elaborated, occasionally glancing at his papers. "If Tiran passes away without an heir, his brother, Perren the Distracted, won't be able to inherit it due to his condition.

"Considering that Tesfira can't inherit as she already settled in her husband's name for the position of Mayor of Edgemere, and Theliel is bound to the Regency and off the list of heirs for behavioral reasons that we all understand, that leaves you and your sister Tecla."

Tylennald's raised eyebrows failed to hide his satisfaction. "Tecla is a child, and if she was to marry, let's say, a lord of the northern lands, that would quite compromise the strength of the South. We are the descendants of Alatros the Red, according to history," he argued with wit. "We need to preserve that integrity."

"There is a good chance that Tecla herself might join the Regency," Tithan conceded. "However, if she does not marry nor swear on the Regency's laws, she would inherit the title of Lady of Strongshore and have full control of the southern coasts, therefore bypassing you, which she doesn't know yet."

Tylennald's feelings of disappointment, anger, and confusion caused his face to twist into an outraged expression. He stood up, the single strand of grey hair that clashed with his chestnut mane falling between his eyes, and he fisted the front of his light blue jerkin. "So, you are putting your youngest bastard daughter before your only healthy legitimate son?" he asked out loud. "What about my son Terrel, and my daughter Elva?"

"I am putting the interests of Strongshore before your mother's, as she has no idea, after all these years, of what it means to look at the bigger picture," Tithan's answered bluntly without a blink nor hesitation. "Neither do you."

"And a child does? Where are we going with this insulting conversation, Father?" Tylennald roared for the first time, slamming both hands on the table in a fashion that reminded Tithan of his spouse.

"I am telling you because tonight you will take your belongings with you and escort your spouse to Courtbridge, where you will reside and possibly rule after Lady Wallysa's father passes away. You will rekindle your relationship with your children at last and learn how to lead in case the tides shift in your favor one day," Tithan ordered him with a calm, severe voice, wrapping his revised last will in hardcover for later binding at the Regency. "You may leave, now," he said dismissively, never looking back at his son.

Tylennald turned heels, his jaw locked and his lips thinning into a repressed snarl. As he neared the door, he reminded himself that it had been twenty years; twenty years of humiliation and repudiation, only to be furtherly shunned for wanting to secure his family's honor and name. He gripped the door handle, squeezing tightly as if he wanted to break it, and his knuckles turned white. Upon opening it, two guards stood in front of him as if they had been waiting for him all along.

"Needless to say," he heard his father's voice, "from now on all forms of communication between you and your mother are forbidden until I say otherwise."

Chapter VIII

The Faithful

Fran's warm brown eyes glanced back and forth between the two women that sat across from him. The carriage they sat in had just finished wobbling its way down Strongshore and would soon arrive in Summerport, but both Lady Tecla and Lyzon were silent and looked outside. It was not an ordinary sight to him. It had been about five years since he joined the Lionhelm household; his father had served as Lord Lionhelm's stableman until his last breath, but Fran wasn't as good as him and a terrible friend to horses. The Great Gardens were partially his creation though, and Tecla's gardens were, humbly and truthfully, the best-looking gardens. They were home to a thousand different flowers and plants, with tall, orange-colored trees from the islands of the Zalejos Depths and dark purple fruits from the northern coast of the Red Continent. Warm and cold hues danced around the many paths inside the gardens, enveloping the young lady's apartments in a colorful bubble meant to keep her away from the merciless winds of Strongshore.

Fran's big fingers toyed with his untrimmed, brown beard. "You are quiet today," he pointed out, lines all around his eyes as he smiled. "You usually don't even let me say a word with all your chatting."

Lyzon shrugged at that. "Lady Tecla has other interests now."

Hazel eyes glanced at her annoyingly. "Lyzon here doesn't understand the religiousness of the Oracle and Her story. It makes me wonder why she is even coming to this mass," Tecla chimed in with a hint of arrogance in her voice.

"I am at my young lady's service," Lyzon replied in a monotone.

Tecla let out an aggravated, forced laugh. "I don't understand you sometimes. You are the same age as my brother Theliel; can't you act more like a sister?"

Fran and Lyzon's eyes met briefly before the maid looked away almost sheepishly. The temple was soon in sight, with its bright golden cupolas. The Oracle Pillar was smaller and made of stone; it was old and less captivating to look at, reminding everyone how at times, holiness shined in the simplest places and people.

The mass was different that day; it was a moon day, and it was widely accepted that moon days increased not only the sea and the tidal range, but also the connection between the earth and the Heights. For three moon days, the Holy Commander and his holy captains would expect prophecies and visions from their maidens, who would dance around the fire and let the doors of the temple open for every woman and man in need of healing, food, or shelter. It was the time of the month that the simple people preferred, although Fran was more of a dusk day person. Anything between dawn days and moon days was about duty and reverence to Alatros the Red, but dusk days were Aelneth's gifts and rewards. They were days of abundance and feasting.

  He wasn't sure when exactly, but Lady Tecla left him and Lyzon sometime after the first reading of the Memoir's fifth chapter, where the Oracle had warned the warriors of Calaris about their imminent loss. Lyzon looked unfazed, but the anger in her dark eyes told him otherwise. As they stood up from their praying position, the gardener placed a hand on her upper arm.

  "You can't react like that," he whispered. "I can imagine how you feel but she is Lady Tecla to you."

  She shrugged his hand off and sighed loudly. "You can't imagine anything. My father used to tell me that if you keep looking inside a well, the water will eventually flow out," she said, a worried look on her face. "It's a saying in our language."

  Fran's thick eyebrows nearly grazed his hairline as he raised them. "You mean, if you look for trouble, it will eventually find you?"

  Lyzon nodded, chewing on her lower lip. "Our beliefs include many spirits. Illnesses and death are for us caused mostly by spirits and sorcery, which doesn't happen very often unless you poke around too much," she explained in a hushed tone, straightening her back when she thought those around them were listening.

    Fran didn't seem convinced. He scratched his head, waiting for the row behind them to exit the temple before he answered, "You think Lady Tecla is poking around… what, exactly? I don't think we have many spirits around here. Our baddies are very real and when they get angry, they use swords."

    Lyzon's eyes were wide open as she stared at the tinted glass windows and paintings retracing the life of the Oracle. As peaceful as the art was, she could sense the violence in every scene too. "Young girls around a fire capable of draining the seas and sucking in the light by just opening their eyes — doesn't that sound like sorcery to you?"

    Deciding to ignore the feeling of dread in his stomach, Fran tugged her towards the entrance. "It's just a story, Lyzon. It's a story written by humans, to find a reason as to why they suffer so much," he repeated. "I find it peaceful here. It is a good break from our daily duties. Don't look too much into it," he spoke in a gentle tone.

    He caught the glimpse of blue in the corner of his eye but decided not to tell Lyzon. Lady Tecla's long dress waved behind her with the airflow due to the open doors. The temple emptied gradually, and the young girl was speaking with the Holy Commander, handing him a thick, crimson book. It wasn't long until the two of them moved to the adjacent room, followed by the holy captains that went wherever their commander wanted. Tecla's shawl fell from around her shoulders as she walked with them, never glancing back at Fran and Lyzon.

Tecla watched intently as the Holy Commander placed the copy of the Memoir back on one of the shelves in that immense library with the glass roof that let the light in. She half wondered who the commander had been and what his name was before he gave it all up to join the ranks of the faithful. Tecla's hazel eyes peered at one of the barely visible doors behind the shelf on her right, and she remembered the woman straddling the captain that stood at her right at that moment. As old as he was, he was still younger than the Holy Commander and her father. His expression was cold and composed, contrary to what she had witnessed last time.

Clearing her throat, Tecla told them, "I would like to speak with one of the maidens." At the commander's startled face, she added, "They carry out the Oracle's words and adopt Her way of life. I have a few questions about what I have read so far."

"Lady Tecla," the captain at her right said in an almost mortified tone, "they don't speak with anyone. The only words that must come from their mouths are the visions granted by the Heights. That is all they are allowed to tell us."

Her eyes narrowed, and she licked her lips, thinking of her next move. "Are there other oracles?" she asked. "If what the Memoir states is true, then those women are Her descendants, but what visions do we know of? And what if they don't have any? What about their children, where are they?"

The Holy Commander placed a reassuring hand on her shoulder. "Your genuine interest and curiosity are certainly admirable. Never would I have imagined finding support from the Lionhelms under Lord Tithan," he praised. "We would gladly discuss everything with you, my lady, but all in due time. The Oracle's legacy is much more than premonitions and memories painted on the windows." Glancing at the captain at Tecla's right, he added. "Captain Rainbeard will show you around. I believe many answers can be found in the architecture of this holy, eternal site."

Unsatisfied with his answers, Tecla reluctantly followed the man who led the way to the opposite side of the room, where another set of double doors separated the library from the Oracle Pillar. The tower was sober from the outside, she recalled, but inside every inch of stone was covered by creeping laurel vines. Yellow flowers that looked like daisies, if not for their spiky petals, littered the windowsills. The Oracle Pillar was less of a museum than the rest of the temple as it emanated the feeling of home and the only paintings that had been placed on the floor or small pieces of furniture, alongside other plants Tecla could not name, portrayed views of the Silver Lands. She recognized Old Drixia, the Ancient City of Calaris, a more flowery landscape that she thought was Wilderose, and the bare, castle-free, black shadow of Noirmont.

"The Oracle's residence," Rainbeard spoke behind her. "There are thirty floors, and each is home to at least three maidens. Some girls truly are the descendants of the Oracle," he explained, recalling Tecla's questions, "but many of them are orphaned girls of Summerport. Offering a shelter to these girls is more important to us than gathering visions the Good Gods are willing to share with us."

"So, you holy captains and your commander lead the ranks of the Angels of Steel but I assume they are no longer descendants of the Oracle either," Tecla reasoned out loud. "What about Sir Frederyc Rosenfield?"

The old captain raised his eyebrows. "Lady Tecla, I don't know many descendants of the Oracle. Many of them died during the wars that opposed Strongshore to Noirmont. After King Aleyne Rainier's coronation, it took centuries to recover from the devastation that was left all around the Silver Lands," he told her mournfully. "Not to mention the Violet Delusion that plagued us when your grandfather was still Lord of Strongshore; it killed millions."

The young girl's fingertips poked the fabric of one transparent golden robe that had been discarded on a rusty iron chair. "Why is this here?"

"One of the maidens caught a terrible fever."

Tecla felt a lump in her throat as she took in the captain's words. She felt as if she had been lied to, yet at the same time, she was mad at herself for believing that things had remained the same as when the Oracle was alive. Educator Tomas had spent enough time teaching her the history of her lands, the blood that was shed, and all the sacrifices it had taken her ancestors to build the peace that now reigned in the Silver Lands. Still… She wished. She wished she could see as well. She wished that all the tales she read were true; they had to be, otherwise, Lyzon would have been right and her father as well, and the whole meaning of her future was to comply with her mother's wishes and find a good husband, with good land, and reduce her moon day prayers to wishes for better harvests and acceptable health.

    Tecla put her shawl down, right next to the robes. Her light blue dress felt too tight, almost constricting, or maybe it was her breathing that became erratic. She tugged slowly on the side laces for release, almost as if she had forgotten that a man who was nothing more than a stranger stood behind her. Her luxurious garments fell to the floor in no time, and she stood only in her pale underdress. It was quite easy to remove, sliding the loose silk down her body. She was completely bare, aside from the fact that she still wore her black heeled shoes. She slid into the golden robes as soon as her clothes were off, the material so light she felt as if she was surrounded by a soft breeze that never went away. Her light chestnut hair was still braided on top of her head, and the Darling Mind hung past her hips, the pendant tickling the small of her back.

    Her small, supple body was vulnerably exposed, and Captain Rainbeard caught himself staring at her lean calves and round butt cheeks. Her hips were wide for a girl, hinting at the fact that she had already bled, and if he didn't know her, he wouldn't be able to assume her age. Tecla Lionhelm turned around slowly, her eyes widening slightly when she realized that he was studying her body. However, she didn't flush, and her gaze showed no trace of shyness. Her stare darkened and she didn't even seem to be looking at him when she stepped closer.

"I shall leave, Lady Tecla," he told her with a polite bow.

"I saw you," she whispered, "with that girl. What did her eyes tell you?"

Rainbeard stuttered for a moment, his eyes darting around in order not to look at the very naked chest of the lady who just pressed her body against his. "I—nothing—"

"Try mine," was her firm order.

✷✷✷

The kitchens of the Illusion Shelter were quiet although five people sat around the table, waiting for the stew to be ready. Pots and rags were scattered wherever there was a spot left to use, the fairly big room bubbling with books, dried leaves and roots, half-torn manuscripts, and sheep meat left to bleed out above the sinks. Rantha seemed to be engrossed in the reading of a guide, while her apprentices sewed dolls made of leaves and smashed roots that released a horrid stench with each press. The brown-eyed woman glanced at the shaking lid of the cooking pot, but her thoughts were elsewhere.

Jascha had been with them for a few days already, and even though he seemed to be regaining his strength, she didn't feel like he was responding to any of the brews she would sneak in with his dinner. She had tried Sandy Tea, Mellow Stargazer, and other concoctions that were used in the Silver Lands, from the Sand Towers to Founder's Breach on the southwestern coast, but he was still the same. She was beginning to believe that he was right and that the Violet Delusion had nothing to do with what caused him to fall unconscious. Did that mean that there was another illness she didn't know about? The Guide to Drixia's Unnamed Misfortunes wasn't giving her any answers.

Her youngest apprentice, a little blonde woman who went by the name of Yenny, noted her deep frown. "Miss Rantha," she spoke softly. "Have you considered letting him be on his way?" she asked.

"I did," Rantha sighed out, running both hands in her wild mane to push it backward. "But you know me; I can't simply risk the man's life. There has to be an explanation."

"I saw something similar before I was bought by the merchants of the Tinted Bay," the young man sitting next to Yenny said as he put down his doll. "My mother was one of the best healers of the Zalejos region," he told them. "The little culprits… were the little ghosts, she would say. They would play with your soul, well with one of your souls, causing an imbalance of your spirit and therefore causing illnesses and hallucinations, if not death." He took his doll again and waved it at them. "This is why we use *wiigbaa fuk'uwe*, the infants, to give the little ghosts a shell and leave us be," he added with a smile that caused his almond eyes to appear even smaller.

Rantha offered him a smile, closing her book. "I know, Zurzon. But we tried the infants on Jascha and still…"

"What about curses, Miss Rantha?" Yenny suggested. "Have you considered witchcraft?"

The healer looked at her as if she had just said the silliest thing she had ever heard. "Witch is just a broad term to designate everything man does not understand," she answered.

"No offense, Miss Rantha, but you come from the Red Continent," Yenny went on. "Witchcraft has deep roots in our history, even though nobody talks about it.

"Some say that it originated from Kashezeth, the Oracle's twin sister. She was taken by Alatros the Red's men and sold to a pleasure house as they saw no use of her since only Kothore had premonitions, but Kashezeth had them too when she slept. She was called Kashezeth the Dreamer."

At that, Rantha's eyes glanced at the freshly smashed roots Yenny had placed on the table. The Dreamer's Root, she remembered, just as Jascha had named them.

"Kashezeth's visions were not as imminent as her sister's, so she was rarely believed. Yet, they helped her escape the pleasure house and find a haven in the Ancient Forest of Soleba, today's

Wilderose. It was said that in one of her visions she saw the Oracle bring doom to Drixia.

"And it was in the moment the stars left the skies that the Oracle's eyes opened wide, black as the night, sucking in the light, that the seas were drained and birds rained down from their Heights," Yenny recited, recalling the last chapter of the Memoir. "Kashezeth had warned the Angels of Steel about it, and as they feared for their lives, they trapped the Oracle at the top of Her Pillar, their hundred swords plunging into Her body before it was too late.

"It wasn't long until their actions were condemned by Alatros and his queen, accusing them of succumbing to the makings of witchcraft, and the warrior army of Aelneth set fire to Soleba in hopes of decimating the followers of Kashezeth."

Rantha sighed out, wondering how that was supposed to serve as an explanation. "Old Drixia was still destroyed," she pointed out, "by what we believe was an underwater fire. The Observatory Vault is still studying it. And I don't see what the followers of Kashezeth if they still exist, would want from a man like our guest."

Yenny was about to go on with her theory, her little green eyes sparkling with interest, but the door was flung open and a fully clothed Jascha walked in. They all fell silent, eyeing the way he seemed to be interested in the food that was still cooking and Rantha tried hard not to smile. Appetite was always a sign of recovery.

Jascha's black gaze scanned the messy room, his lips tightening slightly. He clutched his leather bag in his left hand and looked like he was about to say something when his gaze met Rantha's and went blank.

 Her breath hitched in her throat as she witnessed his eyes roll back, a trail of blood escaping his left nostril and the corner of his lips before he passed out in front of them, knocking a series of pans and books as his body hit the furniture around him. The apprentices shrieked and gasped before rushing to his side, and Rantha held his head as he spasmed. His chest felt incredibly hot, she realized as she tried to drag him out of the room with the help of Zurzon. She rested his head on her lap and ripped his shirt open, only to see his bones while his skin burned right where his heart was, it's beating visible to her between layers of decaying flesh and imploding veins.

✳✳✳

 Captain Rainbeard's hand rested on Tecla's hip, his forearm circling her waist as she forced him to lie on the floor with a gentle, yet decisive push. His light armor clinked against the cold stone and Tecla's eyes were focused on his chest piece and pauldrons, noting how trained the man was despite his age. His beige britches were soft against her skin, and she watched the plates come off with ease once they were unclasped at the sides.
 He sat up to remove his ivory shirt and push her golden robes apart, his lips coming closer to her small, yet full breasts. His lips closed over her brownish nipples quickly, sucking on them with his

tongue lapping at the soft skin. Tecla's lips were slightly parted as she watched the silvery man work on her body, but her unblinking stare seemed unfazed, almost as if she was studying him. Her hands found their way in his trimmed hair when he pulled her lower body towards his, and she felt the hardness in his pants.

    Tecla's lower parts were tingling with a sensation she hadn't felt before, almost as if all her nerves were on fire. The pendant she wore felt heavy against her back when Captain Rainbeard tugged on his pants, his erected manhood soon pressing against her slightly hairy, tight folds. She held on to his broad shoulders while he lifted her hips, her eyes searching for his when he pulled her down in a swift move. Tecla gasped loudly, feeling as if her insides were being split, wondering how far it would go. She felt something wet between her legs, but she wasn't sure of what it was.

    The stinging sensation felt like a burn or an itch, and she soon lifted her hips, pressing her hands against Rainbeard's shoulders, for it to go away. He was quick to pull her back down, earning another surprised sound for her, and he repeated the motion. The stinging was still present, but the itch seemed to be scratched away. Fluids still pooled from between her legs, and soon the silver-haired soldier lied flat on his back, lazily guiding her hips back and forth on top of him. Her sensitive areas brushed against his skin and her movements became faster. She spread her legs a little more, recalling that other woman's position when she had spotted her straddling this same man.

Tecla heard him say something to her, but she didn't pay attention as she leaned in, her long necklace falling between their bodies. Her hazel eyes looked into his, only to see the ecstatic look in his brown eyes as he pulled her by the hair and used his other arm to secure her hips against him. He moved his hips fast and pushed into her with violence; grunts and moans escaping his lips and teeth looking for her bouncing breasts.

"Who would have thought," his raucous, exhausted voice reached her ears, "that this young lady is not worth more than a pleasure house kid," he taunted her, his hands gripping her bottom and spreading it.

Tecla's hand clawed his cheek when he tried to look away from her, ignoring his words. "What do you see?" she asked in between ragged breaths.

He seemed to be laughing, his hardness filling her to the hilt with each move before one of his hands gripped her breast and he went silent.

Tecla felt the heat between their chests, ignoring the way her pendant glowed. His eyes became the mirrors of a dark room, and outside those windows, she could see thick, purple fog. She saw a boy run from a very skinny woman; their cries inaudible to her. She saw the boy fall down the stairs, only to be dragged back up by the leg. His eyes were too dark and soon, they blended in with his dark surroundings. There was a fire in the corner of the room where she last saw the boy, but it wasn't bright and warm; it was green and pale. Tecla soon realized that it was no longer a fire after a few cracking sounds. They were eyes; and they seemed to be looking past her, not even acknowledging her presence.

A woman stood in front of her, her dark brown hair clinging to her sleeveless white dress. She was covered in blood that seemed to be hers as she whispered a single word in a language Tecla didn't understand. The woman talked to someone else, but Tecla felt like she was frozen in place, and couldn't turn around to see who it was.

"The Quiet Tear," Tecla heard the person behind her repeat, unable to identify the voice.

The smell of burning flesh caused her to jump, realizing that the man under her was screaming at her. His chest was red and charred, and his face looked like he had seen a monster. Blood spilled from his mouth and nose, but Tecla couldn't speak. Her lips weren't moving, and she couldn't tear her eyes away from his face.

Captain Rainbeard's chest melted, exposing his beating heart and swollen veins, but all he could see was the bright, blue-green light the woman's necklace blinded him with. As his heartbeat slowed and his mouth was filled with a metallic taste, he found himself unable to beg for help or mercy. The woman above him was no woman anymore; her eye sockets were empty and her jaw had disappeared.

Where her mouth once was, he saw only a hole and the nothingness it offered him as the afterlife.

Chapter IX

Red Summer

His back was hurting and he soaked in his sweat. His bright hazel eyes blinked when the sun blinded him, and Theliel raised his arm to shield himself from the sunlight, only to hiss in pain when his elbow throbbed and his shoulder muscles burnt. He narrowed his eyes to try and take note of his surroundings. Everything was moving and wobbling; he was on the back of a cart. He looked up, only to see the bloodied, tired face of Lord Angefort who was chewing slowly on what looked like a piece of dry, brown bread.

Around them, a few soldiers rode on their equally tired horses, and Theliel's heart skipped a beat when he realized that two-thirds of the men who escorted them were not present. Flashes of the last evening he remembered clouded his mind, and he realized it hadn't been a simple nightmare. The pain that rocked his body was real, and more than a hundred soldiers were missing.

Theliel remembered the little girl he had followed, the one who had requested his help; he remembered the young woman on top of the keep. Their putrefying bodies had fallen apart before his eyes and everything else had gone black. He could still hear the screams in the background and smell the smoke from the great hall. Lord Angefort's eyes were on him, but his stare was blank and he seemed to be either in deep thought or lost in his shock.

The young Lionhelm tried to push himself upwards, only to be stopped by Angefort's firm grip. "Don't move. I think your left arm is broken and I am not sure about the rest of your body. We are almost at the Regency; the physicians of the Vault will take a closer look," he said sternly.

"I hate to ask this," Theliel croaked out, licking his dry lips, "but what happened?"

"I don't fucking know," was Angefort's answer. Theliel had never heard him curse before. "I don't fucking know." He threw the dry bread over the cart and wiped his hands on his pants, his jaw locked as he glared in the distance. "I didn't see you until you fell from the battlements; I had no idea why you were there or what you were doing. But you were screaming nonsense I couldn't make out, and you fell on top of the men who got attacked and killed by invisible crossbowmen, only to be bitten, eaten, and pulled by these... monsters," he explained in disbelief. "Corpses that crawled from the portcullis up to us... I pulled you out only because you seemed alive and were still blabbing about little girls needing your help."

Theliel remained silent. Reanna was the name of the woman he saw, but Reanna Rosenfield had died years ago or at least disappeared. Was she to be alive still, she would be much older, and in any case, the being he had seen didn't seem alive nor human at all.

"We pushed through the undead with all we could, slashing our way to the portcullis as the fire expanded and started burning down everything around us," Angefort went on with a bitter voice. "Sir Geoffroi and Sir Jeanna fought all the while trying to lift the portcullis back up, dying in a manner no knight should ever die just to make sure a few of us got away."

Theliel's eyes searched for his, but the old commander avoided his stare. "Arrows?" he whispered. "Fire?"

"Suffocating," Angefort replied, his tired look finally meeting his. "They were pulled down by these monsters that crawled on top of them, their arms extended towards the skies as if they were begging for mercy themselves, and the smoke engulfed them all.

"But their eyes… Their eyes were always wide open. The fire kept burning, but the Rosenfield castle is still in a perfect state."

"This is unheard of," Theliel mumbled. His empty stomach churned as the cart came to an abrupt halt. The flags of the Regency were hanging above their heads from the tall stone walls of Silverholde. They had reached the southern gateway of the city. "What are we going to say to—"

"To the Regency? To your father, after his elite got slaughtered and cooked like pigs?" Angefort cut in. "The Regency has no army of its own," he reminded Theliel. "Our forces are the forces of the Silver Lands put together, and if word spreads, I doubt the lords will keep sending us their best men," he admitted.

"Halt," a third voice ordered. Theliel heard the hooves of a horse stomp their way closer. "Regency's Surveillance, I'm Chief Thierry Eleres. State your names."

Lord Angefort turned around slightly, and Theliel craned his neck to watch. "Chief Eleres, I am Lord Arther Angefort, Secretary of the Regency and Commander of the Lionhelm armies for the Regency. I travel back from Strongshore with Theliel, son of Lord Tithan Lionhelm and Member of the Regency's Treasure Council. We are escorted by the fifteen men you can see," he replied in a monotone that spoke volumes about his current focus and his distaste for exaggerated formalities.

"Welcome back, Lord Angefort," Eleres greeted him. "I am back from the Sand Towers. We were expecting your return this morning," he pointed out. "The reports we have, however," he paused, and Theliel heard the sound of papers being unfolded, "state that you left with more than a few men and that there is a pending report for Lord Theliel, who is no longer, to my knowledge, a member of the Treasure Council."

Lord Angefort stood up from where he sat on the cart and jumped off with ease to face the Surveillance chief. "They perished," he whispered.

When Chief Eleres remained silent for too long, the Secretary of the Regency ordered, "I want everyone in the Regency's audience room. I want you as Head of the Surveillance, Sir Ferrand of Founder's Breach as Head of the Treasure's Council, Sir Sybbyl of the Sand Towers as Suppressor of War, and Grandmaster Rodbertus of Three Crosses as Grandmaster of the Observatory Vault. Is that clear to you, Chief Eleres?"

Theliel propped himself up on his good elbow, only to see the bald man in front of Angefort pale and frown.

"With all due respect, my lord, only King Helias can summon every head of the Regency. This is why we always send in reports to you; so that he can decide what matters need to be discussed by everyone."

Theliel wanted to speak up as soon as the monarch was mentioned, but Angefort was quicker. "I am the Secretary of the Regency. I am King Helias' spokesperson." With a hand gesture, he let every horse pass the arches of the city entrance. "Be in the audience room at sunset, Eleres."

✸✸✸

The bed-chamber was too dull. It was what Voladea had always thought ever since Thaesonwald's apartments were finished. The blue, silver, and gold of the Lionhelms were present in every corner; the fine rugs and, light, endless curtains that grazed the floor were more elegant than the ones in her apartments. It was certainly fit for the firstborn of Tithan Lionhelm, but it didn't please her. Everything that had been done for her son had been etiquette and protocols; it was what had to be done, and not what Tithan wanted for him. The bed-chamber was sterile. There was no warmth anywhere, and none had been given to her child either.

Voladea sat at her son's side with her elbows pressed against the mattress, holding her hands together as she studied her eldest son's resting expression. His beard and mustache had been trimmed regularly even as he slept. He hadn't woken up since the accident, and his chest heaved faintly. Voladea's lower lip trembled as she realized that her son was old, that she was old, and that their lives hadn't been what she expected. His strawberry blonde hair was like his uncle's, but it turned greyer with each passing day.

She placed a wrinkled hand on his cheek, forcing a smile on her lips. She knew that side of his body would never respond again, nor feel her touch, and tears formed in her brown eyes. "Son, have you heard the lions roar," she sang for him in a whisper. "Their heads were chopped and their meat sold,

"But then the Reds shaped their armor,
"And lion skulls their heads now wore.

"Red Summer. It used to be your favorite bed song, remember," she told him, brushing her fingers through his locks, "when you wanted to be a warrior, not a little lord. And I would just tell you all about Alatros the Red and the gifts he brought from the Red Continent. Mama, you would call me;

Mama, why can't we talk more about the Red Continent, you would ask."

"History doesn't allow it," a tired voice said behind her.

Voladea straightened up immediately, wiping her tears away with the side of her hand before turning around to nod at Healer Martus, who had just entered the room with a tray full of medication and plants to infuse.

"Forgive me for the interruption, Lady Lionhelm. Around this time, I fill the room with the Dreamer's Root smoke and wet Lord Thaesonwald's lips with Wilderose water for—"

"For better sleep and recovery," she finished for him, standing up. "I know, Martus. I should have come later."

The old healer walked up to her, bending slightly to leave the tray on the still mattress. His pristine, white robes hugged his round but strong body, but his eyes were kind, as always. Voladea politely smiled at the man who had been her family's healer ever since she was a little child. He had helped her give birth to her two sons, and he was the only person in the household's staff that she trusted blindly.

"I am sorry, my lady," he whispered. "I saw Lord Tylennald leave in the middle of the night."

Voladea's saddened look turned into one of anger. "My lord Tithan has his vindictive way of educating his children," she replied. "His expectations are all that matters. Our sacrifices, our concessions—they are taken for granted.

"Does it matter that I held his bastards in my arms? Of course not. As long as the child is his and he can place them around the board that is the map of the Silver Lands, he wins the game," she explained bitterly. "That is all he needs; an heir in Strongshore, another in Courtbridge, and a third in Edgemere. Protect the Lionhelms' interests in the Regency too, and whoever is left to secure that there will be a bit of his blood in the northern regions.

"And then, there is me. The Almost Lady Lionhelm," she laughed at herself. "What a life, Martus."

The healer narrowed his eyes as he tried to understand. His tired hands worked on the plants he would soon burn, separating the dark leaves and bending the roots to make sure they would fit in the small red censer he brought.

"Your children all get their share of the power meant for them to inherit," he commented. "You are one of the luckiest ladies of the Silver Lands if we put things into perspective."

"Wald and his son are not suitable for Strongshore," Voladea admitted out loud. "It pains me greatly to say this, but it is the truth. Tylennald would have made a great ruler. His mind is sharp and has his father's charisma."

"Tylennald alienated his children," the old healer pointed out. "And Lady Wallysa doesn't seem to be… much more fertile," he added in a whisper. "Considering Tylennald's age, that doesn't leave him much time to prepare his children to succeed him."

"Terrel is in Founder's Breach," Lady Voladea said about Tylennald's son, her puffy dress swinging with each step she took as she circled the bed and reached the closest window to open it. "Elva, I am not sure. Wallysa believes her daughter left for the Rain Lands; that is if she made it safely past the Fog Lands. Neither Tylennald nor Wallysa talks much about her; no one is ever proud of rebellious children.

"In any case, it is not a hard task to find Terrel again. Lord Tithan simply does not believe the man to be a fitting heir; Terrel is a lot like his grandfather and was raised with the same freedom as my husband."

Martus nodded. "The freedom of those whom no one expects to see as rulers because of their place in the line of succession," he concluded for her.

A knock on the double doors interrupted their discussion and it wasn't long until the hairless, hunched Silver Master came in, bowing deeply. Healer Martus greeted Milefried before he returned to the plants he dropped in the censer, and Lady Voladea looked at him without emotion, waiting for the little ugly man to speak.

"Lady Lionhelm, the ball expenses have been paid and we have received quite a few replies to our invitations," he said, pulling nervously at his fingers. "We might be expecting slightly more guests."

She furrowed her brow and lifted her chin slightly. "The Rochelacs of Noirmont?" she asked, secretly hoping for a negative answer.

"No, my lady. We don't even know if the Rochelacs have received your letter. However, all three Sons of Ferngrunn confirmed their presence."

Voladea's lips nearly twitched upwards. "All three, you say," she repeated.

"Yes, my lady. Thaum, Remm, and Mokr seem to have taken a slight interest in Lady Tecla," Milefried elaborated. "They will be our guests with their entire… court," Milefried elaborated, nervously glancing back and forth between the two people in front of him.

Healer Martus glanced at him. "Court? You mean—"

An all-too-pleased Voladea interrupted him. "He means with their generals."

❋❋❋

Tecla's leg was shaking.

She bit hard on her fingernails as she sat on the windowsill, her eyes darting around every few seconds. She held a round mirror in her other hand, checking her reflection just as often.

Her once hazel eyes were tainted with hints of sky blue.

The moment Captain Rainbeard fell backward, his body burnt and the cavity in his chest exposed, Tecla jumped away, muffling her screams with both hands. She killed him, she kept repeating herself. She murdered him, and she didn't even know how she did it. One moment she saw images of a boy she didn't know, and the next the captain was screaming at her. Tecla had no idea if anyone heard them, but the second part of the mass had been going on and no keeper of the fire had been seen since the beginning of the ceremony. Tecla had put her dress on in a hurry, her teary eyes never leaving the agonizing face of the man who died in her arms. She watched his face even as she tugged his clothes back on. She had rushed back to her carriage, where she waited for Fran and Lyzon, whom she asked not to talk to her until they arrived in Strongshore. Her heart had never slowed down as she waited, wondering if the Holy Commander or anyone else would come to find her before she had a chance to leave.

Upon arriving in Strongshore, she explicitly requested to be left alone, and she didn't see Lyzon nor any other maid for days. She spent her days in her bed-chambers and begged Educator Tomas not to ask her anything that wasn't related to their lessons. Tecla bathed and ate alone, although she often left the meat and beans and nibbled only on a few berries.

She had no idea what she was supposed to do or say.

Her door opened slowly, and she jumped. With eyes wide open, she held her breath, only to frown at the sight of her older sister Tesfira walk in with a worried look.

Tecla looked away immediately, putting down the mirror in her hand. "I thought I asked the guards not to let anyone in," she said, her voice upset.

"I told them Father wanted to see them," Tesfira said with mischief filling her voice. "I just came to check up on you."

"I thought you were busy in Edgemere," Tecla replied, ignoring the rest of her sister's words to her. "As always."

"Mother talked to me about the ball. The one for you."

When her sister remained silent, Tesfira closed the door behind her and walked up to her. Tecla watched her reflection in the window. Her sister's long, curly locks danced around her shoulders with every step, and her bright, tangerine dress hugged her curves perfectly. Her arms were completely bare, if not for the jewelry that squeezed her biceps and wrists. She was always very flashy with every style she decided to try, from classic to contemporary, but Tecla didn't find any of it fitting. In a way, Tesfira seemed as out of place as their mother, or herself. Silks were revelatory of one's position in a family, in Tecla's opinion, and so everything that came out of her sister's lips, Tecla couldn't take seriously.

Tesfira stood behind her, her long nails toying with Tecla's wavy hair. It wasn't long until she began braiding it rather clumsily. "You know, they hosted a ball for me too, when I was your age. It is not only out of courtesy for the other nobles, but it's also—"

"It's for marriage," Tecla said, unfazed. "I've studied enough history with Tomas to know that. A powerful man invites other powerful men, offers them a banquet they won't be able to forget as well as one of his women as a token of a meaningful, silent agreement on united forces and whatnot," she recited sourly. "I know all of that, but you ended up with a simple man from Edgemere with no name, no land, and Father gave him both things by the time you were seventeen."

Tesfira's thin eyebrows went to her hairline. "Well, I knew Theliel shared a lot with you but I didn't expect him to tell you about my husband too. I guess nothing can stay secret too long." Her fingers continued working on Tecla's hair. "Do you know what happens after marriage? Did you and Educator Tomas—"

"I know what isn't supposed to happen," Tecla whispered. "I meant to say that I think I will be alright," she quickly added, shivering at the mere thought of Oracle Hill.

Tesfira stopped braiding her sister's hair, reaching for a pin in between her tresses to secure the twists on top of Tecla's head. Her hands rested on the young girl's shoulders and she whispered, "Look at me." When the light-haired girl didn't, Tesfira placed a finger under Tecla's chin and gently turned her head. "Marriage isn't easy but it is one of those things in life that no one in our position can avoid," she explained, looking into Tecla's grieving eyes. "It will be good in the beginning, it will be great after your first son, and then you realize you are tied to someone you haven't known enough time. And it will be alright."

"What can be wrong with Hamley Silverworm?" Tecla asked with a raised eyebrow and a defiant look.

Tesfira frowned at the much younger girl and offered her a small shrug. "Different views on a few things," she answered. "He thinks our society is built on the wrong values and a series of lies. He thinks the Dreamer's visions were the guidance we mere humans should've sought, not the Oracle's."

Tecla blinked in confusion. "The Dreamer?"

"It doesn't matter," Tesfira went on with a sigh. "You know our father's views on religion. He wouldn't take this seriously so I will stay with Hamley until fate decides otherwise." Glancing back at her sister's face she broke into a smile that Tecla couldn't decipher. "Your eyes are prettier with each passing day. They were always gracefully shaped, like almonds, you know. Our grandmother had gorgeous blue eyes. Yours seem to keep changing the more you grow up. That isn't very common."

Her words lifted a weight off Tecla's chest, and the young girl stiffened when her sister placed a chaste kiss on the corner of her lips. Tesfira had never been affectionate with her, not that she recalled.

"I know you only have eyes for Theliel but let me know if you need anything," the older woman said, walking away. She was almost at the door when she stopped in her tracks and said, "I'm sorry, by the way. I heard one of the holy captains passed away from heart failure. I know you spend a lot of time at the temple, so you probably knew him."

Tecla's startled expression turned into a confused one. "Heart failure?" she asked.

Tesfira nodded. "That they say. He was found lying on the floor with no trace of blood or anything. The man was old; if he didn't slip on anything, his heart must have stopped."

Tecla stopped breathing, nodding at her sister's words. "Thank you for telling me," she forced herself to say, her glance falling back on her reflection on the mirror she had placed next to her.

Her eyes still sparkled with blue hues.

❋❋❋

Fair skin met dark silk, and Lyzon sighed out, letting her naked body fall on the sky-colored sheets of the mattress. Groans and moans had filled the palatial room all evening, echoing sounds bouncing against the ivory walls and faint lighting coming from outside through the oriel windows. The only witnesses had been the grim faces that hung from the walls and the warriors of Old Drixia that were trapped in a perpetual tribe war in the painted ceiling above her head. Lyzon tried hard to catch her breath after that encounter, but her mind was quickly going places again and the excitement slowly left room for the anxiety that filled her since she had come back from Summerport days before. Lady Tecla had kept her away at all costs and she didn't understand why. Perhaps it was because of their clashing points of view about faith, but Lyzon wasn't convinced. She had been with Tecla since she was born. Since Lyzon was fifteen.

The muscular arms that hugged her waist brought her back to reality and she snuggled against her man's side, nuzzling his chest as she overthought the situation. She recalled that Fran didn't seem to have noticed anything different about Tecla, but she didn't blame him. The girl was good at shielding herself from others, but not from her, and that was probably why, Lyzon concluded, Tecla refused to see her.

"Are you still thinking about Tecla?"

Lyzon's dark eyes peeked up at the one who held her, and she smiled, her perfectly straight teeth showing. A hand brushed her long, black locks before resting on her caramel skin again.

"I am sorry," she whispered. Hazel eyes looked into hers and Lyzon's slender fingers brushed his silver hair. "It is hard not to, Tithan."

"Kids her age think of all sort of things and get utterly confused with themselves," Tithan told her with half-lidded eyes. "She will come around. You've always been a great mother."

Lyzon's melancholic stare wasn't lost on him. "Does she know that?" was her rhetorical question.

"Haven't we talked about it enough times?" Tithan groaned, tightening his arms around the young woman and trapping her in a warm hug. "We are lucky she took my looks; otherwise, it would have been too obvious to everyone. We had a deal when we came back from the islands of the Zalejos Depths."

"I recall it perfectly," she answered. "You arrived in the region under the Regency's flag for those campaigns of theirs and nine months later, you smuggled me and Tecla on your ship under the condition that I would not let anyone know the truth. It is not my intention to break any deal," Lyzon said firmly, holding her gaze. "It is just not easy. I want to help her but have no authority to do so. Not to mention that your wife wants to send her off with some stranger, away from me," she argued.

Tithan laughed at that, shaking his head. "No strangers. And no wedding talk until she is older, I said." He sat up, kissing her lips gently. "All I wanted was for you to raise your daughter, Lyzon, but keep in mind that she will eventually have to grow up, and I will leave this world one day too. I don't want you to stay alone in that situation." When she remained silent, Tithan asked, "What about Fran? I appointed him to Tecla's service to keep you company."

Lyzon shrugged, pursing her lips. "He's kind to me, but don't push me into others' arms. It makes me uncomfortable."

Tithan nodded at that and brought her hand to his lips. "Fair enough. I need the lavatory."

Lyzon tried to contain her smile at the sweet gesture, and she sat up too, watching him get up from the bed, naked from head to toe. Her firm, large breasts bounced with her movements and she kept her eyes on his still muscular back. Tithan disappeared behind the curtains that separated his bed-chamber from his private lavatory and Lyzon's smile never faded, until she heard him cough.

Tithan coughed repeatedly, sounding as if he had a fit, and he cleared his throat as he tried to catch his breath. She heard the water splashing and more coughing.

"Everything alright?" she asked with a small voice, ready to get up if he hinted at any type of help needed.

"Yes, love," was his strained answer, followed by wet coughing.

Lyzon's heart sank, and she looked down at her bare lap. If she had been worried before, she was even more concerned then.

Chapter X

CHILD OF THE SEA

The look in Rantha's eyes was a mixture of disappointment and pity. The healer was sitting on a wobbly wooden chair next to his bed, her fists tight against her knees. She looked as if she hadn't gotten any sleep for days, and Jascha wondered just how long he was out. Rantha's earthy orbs were surrounded by red and the eyebags that rested against her cheekbones were not a sight he was used to. Granted, she never looked well-rested, but perhaps it was the thoughts swimming in her mind that caused the added fatigue.

Jascha tried moving his legs, only to feel a stinging pain in his chest the moment he took a deeper breath. He remembered the burning feeling inside him, the one that felt like his heart had been surrounded by flames; he recalled the blood that had collected in his throat and escaped his nose and lips. He remembered the voices that whispered foreign words in his ears. They had been distant, yet familiar, and then nothing. The emptiness that accompanied every moment that followed had him wonder if that was death. No windy Heights, no shaky Pit of Torture. Just the feeling of nonexistence, and fragments of his fading conscience.

"I am leaving," he breathed out, talking to himself more than to the dark-skinned woman who watched over him.

Rantha nearly stood up. Her hands found his wrist and she squeezed. "Don't. What if this happens again? Who will look after you?"

"You are a slave," he stated plainly, causing her eyes to widen. "An insignificant, ignorant slave," the black-haired man emphasized, his equally dark eyes scanning her face. "This goes beyond your comprehension and I don't have the time to wait for you to get some form of education." Jascha sat up slowly, wincing at the pulsating pain in his core. Swatting her hands away, he ordered, "Get my belongings. You can take twenty silvers for my extended stay."

Rantha stood up, an outraged expression marking her features. She straightened her cream-colored skirt, paying no attention to the wobbly chair that had lost its balance behind her due to her sudden movement. "I don't need your money. All I wanted was to help you; I was so close to—"

"What did you find, then?" Jascha's calm tone surprised her. He was on his feet in no time, narrowing his eyes at her. When she failed to reply, his lips twisted into a mocking smirk. "Rantha."

Her name on his lips felt like a death sentence. She felt the chicken skin all over her body and in no time, his large, pale hand was squeezing her neck, pinning her against the nearest wall. The color drained from her face, and she parted her plump lips to try and breathe in. She failed.

"I left my home to find the bastards who did this to me," he whispered at her, leaning in until their noses touched. "This is not an illness; this is someone's doing," Jascha added, his fingers tightening around the woman's throat. "Do you think a single day passes by without me feeling it inside me? The way it curls around my bones, tears my flesh from the inside?"

Rantha coughed and gagged, a faint "please" lining her lips.

Their eyes connected briefly and Jascha's breath hitched in his throat. He relinquished his hold on her almost instantly, as if her skin had burned his hand, but his glare was still in place. "Fetch my belongings," he ordered her again. "Take twenty silvers," he repeated, "and vanish from my sight. You make me sick."

His words cut through her like a thousand knives, and Rantha's feet moved on their own will as she rushed outside the room and into the stair railing, the wood pushing hard against her stomach as she nearly fell over. Rantha coughed and coughed again, spitting on herself as she tried to clear her mind and calm her senses. She rested her right hand on her chest, breathing slowly, the other hand reaching inside her pocket for a vial she always kept with her. The lavender concoction would help her calm down, she figured, but she couldn't find it anywhere. She patted her other pockets, only to realize that her vials had never been refilled when she was in the kitchen; Jascha had felt ill right when her apprentices were working. Instead, a hard, cold piece of silver met her fingertips.

Rantha took the coin out of her pocket and stared at it until her heart rate went down. The Regency's crowned owl and its eyed shield was the pass she needed to speak with Opherus in the capital. Never had she believed the man in the adjacent room to be a threat. All she knew was that he was ill, and apparently, she was wrong. Rantha had seen her share of dangerous men during her years at Sir Loys Rosenbane's service; men so greedy for power that they rode from the Wilderose forest up to Rainier's End to convince Sir Loys to succeed the Rosenfields and tried to defeat him when he refused to gain power for himself. Yet, none of them had ever turned her blood into ice by simply calling her name.

She had never tried to ask him where he was from nor where he was headed, as he spent most of his time resting, and now any thoughts of doing so were quickly discarded. "Yenny," she called out when she spotted the blonde mop of hair downstairs. "Collect our guest's belongings," she said in the most neutral tone she could muster.

The confused look on her apprentice's face caused Rantha to sigh out loud. "Are you sure, Miss Rantha?" Yenny asked, putting down the buckets of water she carried. "Sanson, Maryell, and I were just getting started on these recorded cases of witchcraft."

"Do as I say, please."

"Yes, Miss."

The sound of steel sliding against leather caused her to jump, cold sweat trailing down her back. Her heart rate increased once more, the warning bells in her head going off out of survival instinct. Rantha turned to the side, only to see Jascha's indifferent stare directed at the girl downstairs as he fixed his dagger at his side. His demeanor had changed completely, and he seemed to have reverted to his usual attitude.

Rantha's brown eyes were fixed on the hilt of the dagger, memorizing every color of every jewel that adorned it, its shape and guard, as well as the length of the blade. If asking Jascha wasn't an option, researching weaponry was. She still had access to Sir Loys' libraries and if they happened to not contain any valuable information, she could very well travel to Silverholde and ask Opherus Goldsnout for a tour of the Regency's Observatory Vault.

Jascha caught her staring at his side, and Rantha looked away. Her feet neared the stairs when she heard his low voice. "Don't fall, Miss Rantha."

Her eyes shut tight, and with a steady breath, she walked away from him.

✳✳✳

The smoke that escaped the small fireplace inside Old Martita's house reminded Sarkis of the nights he would spend in different taverns in Silverholde. A little food and nightly shelter in exchange for a couple of songs and impressions of nobles that the simple people rarely saw in the flesh, often followed by snarky remarks and not-so-friendly jabs by the innkeeper. Artists were never regarded as more than buffoons, at least in the capital. Yet, he had heard of the times of Aleyne Rainier's rule, many centuries ago, where the arts were part of daily, cultural life in the Silver Lands. The Violet Delusion had left no place for joy and light entertainment in the hearts of the people.

Old Martita was shrugging old fur rugs and coats, preparing for the chill weather that was knocking at the door, as she said. She had spent the last couple of days repeating how old bones needed more warmth, often changing subjects whenever he asked if Patten would show up anytime soon. Without the big boy around, Sarkis found himself dealing with housekeeping more than he wanted to, and he wasn't strong enough for all the trips to the well that Martita required. The woman always cooked, washed, and requested services. Between her and his work at the Seven Galleys tavern, he was exhausted.

Slumping on the wooden bench he used as a bed, the curly-haired man gulped down a glass of bad, sour wine. "Say, Tita," he called her, "how much do you know Theliel?" he asked. He heard Theliel say that the woman helped the Lionhelm's mother give birth, but the two seemed closer to each other, given the way he saw them behave.

The old woman peered at him, folding a cloak. She didn't seem to be in any mood for chatting. "Not much," she replied bluntly. "I knew his mother. I know his father."

Sarkis' thick eyebrows went up to his hairline in surprise. "You know Lord Lionhelm? Stop pulling my leg," he laughed, emptying his glass.

"I'd pull your tongue out of your mouth if that would make you stay quiet." She came to sit next to him, the way she hunched her back and her tired face making her look older than she was. Sarkis didn't believe the woman to be older than sixty, but what did he know. "Theliel is a good boy," she added in a softer tone, "but he is not as strong-willed and quick-witted as his father.

"Lord Lionhelm was always good to us simple people; especially after the Dark Clouds decimated his lands. But even before that…" She paused, spitting in the fire when too much saliva collected in her mouth. "Even before that, he always made sure everyone could work a piece of land. He is one of us, Lord Tithan. A child of the sea."

Sarkis frowned at the woman's words. He closed his mouth, any retort dying on the tip of his tongue, and the woman laughed at the way his front teeth still bit into his lower lip.

"I don't know how you and Theliel crossed paths, but believe me, boy; you be on your way. Let Theliel on his."

The two of them sat in silence, and Sarkis' dark eyes looked into Martita's. With the light that shone from the fireplace, her hazel eyes seemed almost green. "Do you have any family left, even though your husband passed away?"

"A sister," was her plain answer. "But she does not live here in Summerport. That is if she is still alive. My other younger sister and my older brother both perished a long time ago."

Before he could ask her more about her life, the loud banging outside interrupted their casual conversation. Old Martita's glare was back in place as she realized that whoever pestered them that late in the evening was inelegantly knocking on either her neighbors' door or Patten's. And considering that her neighbors would have answered already if their door was shaking, it meant only one thing. They were looking for Big Pat.

Standing on her feet with ease, Martita limped her way to the door, pushing it open with ease since Sarkis had repaired it, and she whistled. She couldn't properly see in the dark distance, but two shadows had moved from Patten's door, whispering to each other as they neared Martita's house. Sarkis was right behind her, clumsily pushing past her, in an attempt to intimidate whoever was coming their way. The burly man pumped his chest, only to deflate at the sight of armor and sky-blue cloaks. He had seen this attire when Theliel took him to Strongshore. They were Lionhelm soldiers, although their chest plates suggested they rode under the Regency's banner.

Old Martita scanned their faces; both were young and dirty, almost as if they had seen battle, which made little sense considering the current times of peace. The shorter soldier had a head bandage and he carried a rather large, wooden box that was unsealed.

"Pardon for the noise," the taller man said, bowing his head. "We are looking for the family of a missing young man. What we know about him is that he was rather tall and muscular; brown hair, grey eyes. The traders in the marketplace said the only recently missing individual they could think of is someone named Patten and that he lives around here. Do you know his family?"

His words had Sarkis' brain get into gear. Patten hadn't returned in days, but he assumed that he had been busy with the green-eyed woman he followed everywhere. He didn't believe the man to have gone missing and that no one around Summerport had seen him either. He began formulating a reply in his head when Old Martita was already done processing the soldier's words. Her eyes were set on the wooden box the most injured of the two was carrying, and she glanced at the little house squished between hers and the neighbors'. Damn the old couple for not hearing all the ruckus, she thought to herself. She didn't want to deal with this.

"Patten has no family, like every child of the sea," she stated bluntly. "He stayed with me."

The way the two soldiers looked at each other was the confirmation she didn't need.

"Our sincere apologies. We didn't get there in time…"

Old Martita snatched the box from the young man's hands, opening it with ease, only to find dirt and remains of Pat that were slowly being eaten by worms, one of them crawling out from an empty eye socket. There wasn't much left of his body, almost as if the soldiers hadn't been able to find all the pieces of Pat's torn shell. Martita stared at the decomposing flesh and broken bones without blinking. Without breathing. The faint sound of Sarkis gagging and emptying his stomach behind them didn't faze her. Her swollen fingers clutched the box even tighter, ignoring the men's voices when they suggested she closed the box until cremation.

She had to burn Patten's remains, she repeated in the back of her mind.

Pat was dead.

Old Martita sniffed in her usual fashion and directed her staring at the two disgusted men before her. "Have you found them?" she asked in a commanding tone. When they just glanced at each other, she added in a cold tone, "The women who did this to him. Have you found them?"

"The… women?" the bandaged soldier gasped out. "What are you talking about?"

"Tita, please close it," Sarkis pleaded behind her when the stench of the remains became too much for him to bear.

"Fools," she hissed at them before setting down the box. "Fools!" she screamed, her voice echoing around them.

They didn't get the chance to retort as she rushed inside the house, only to reemerge with a torch she had probably lit in the fireplace. She threw it inside the box with ease, the rising flames nearly burning the already injured soldiers. Old Martita's eyes were glinting with a mixture of anger and sorrow, and Sarkis tried to pull her back when the burning remains nearly harmed her legs.

"The Circle, the Rosencircle," she muttered.

"Tita, be careful," Sarkis insisted, his fat hands clinging to her arms. "What about the girl?" he asked the Lionhelm soldiers in a panicky tone. "The girl who was with Patten—where is she?"

"There was no one with him," the taller soldier replied, covering his mouth when the smoke reached his face. "He was found in Wilderose alone and dismembered, clearly," he explained without an ounce of tact as he grew annoyed at them. "Let's go," he whispered to the man beside him, his eyes staring at Old Martita as if she had turned mad.

"There will be more," she whispered to no one in particular, her balled fists shaking at her sides. "There will be more starless nights until the *Nakfêht* is found and his body flayed; for only he, under the Darling's eye, will cry the Quiet Tear."

Sarkis swallowed hard, coughing and his eyes tearing up when the smoke clouded his vision. He pulled Old Martita harder from the growing fire, the meaning of her words lost on him. All he knew was that he had to get them away from the fire that was now swallowing a good part of the garden. Sarkis ran towards the entrance, where he found the last bucket of water he had carried earlier that day and promptly emptied it to put out the fire. This was not how cremation was done, he wanted to point out, but something told him that cremation wasn't what had been on Old Martita's mind when she set fire to the remains.

She had been scared of something, and that was not a sight he would ever forget, nor understand.

※※※

The circular hall of Rainier's Pavilion was not a place Theliel had missed. Shielded from every side by the mountains that surrounded Silverholde, the royal palace resembled the Lionhelms' if only in terms of architecture. Eleven cupolas rose from the ground; five on the eastern side, five on the western side, and the biggest one shining at the center of the condescending, intimidating structure. The Pavilion embodied the personality of every Rainier, in Theliel's eyes. The monarchs that succeeded one another were not known for being practical or down-to-earth. They had always believed to hold more spiritual than temporal power, and the palace itself shadowed the center of Silverholde like a king holding their scepter above the people's heads.

The entryway was a long corridor of water, and Theliel followed Lord Angefort as they walked next to it. The sun peered at them as it filled the hall with light, the round ceiling completely open. Theliel's wet footsteps echoed through the hall, and every twenty columns, side corridors that were not filled with mountain waters led to a wing of the palace that was reserved to a specific order of the Regency.

The light yet warm colors of the walls looked plain to Theliel, as every painting and statue that was related to the Rainiers had been removed long before he joined the Regency. It was meant as a statement of King Helias' will to have the Regency fill in his shoes with neutrality and fairness and a long time ago, Theliel did believe in it. Eleven years had passed since he first walked these steps.

Contrary to what he was used to in Strongshore, no guard lined the hallways of the palace. As they reached the heart of the Pavilion, the throne room, Theliel readjusted the arm sling that prevented him from getting even more injured, courtesy of the Surveillance that had escorted him, Lord Angefort, and the survivors of Wilderose inside the city.

The throne room was open on every side, or at least seemed to be. There were more windows than walls, and two large fountains burst with life as they made their way inside. Creeping laurels and other flowers that Theliel swore he had seen in the Great Gardens of Strongshore littered the floor around the empty, silver throne with armrests shaped in the form of owl wings. The headrest itself looked beaked, but the many spikes around it made it look more like an ancient, tribal crown. Behind the chair, two statues faced each other; the serpent-tongued lion of Theliel's own house, and the canine, human flesh-eating Beast of Three Crosses. The roses made of silver that rested on the throne were the only reminder of King Helias' presence, for only daisies were flowers for the dead.

As they reached the center of the room, another set of footsteps reached their ears. Lord Angefort bowed his head at the sight of Grandmaster Rodbertus of Three Crosses, a man as old as him and the Head of the Regency's Observatory Vault. The man had come from the Fog Lands as a boy, escaping the Violet Delusion and looking to train under a known knight of Rainier's End, back then known as Bane's Keep, only to end up fueling his thirst for knowledge.

Wearing his longest crimson robes, the old master extended his hands at Lord Angefort, greeting him. "Arther," he spoke. "I heard you wish the Regency to meet in the audience room," he immediately said."

Angefort nodded his head, glancing around. "Where are the others?" he asked, his voice low.

"Eleres is still at the entrance, I'm sure," Rodbertus answered, his grey stare fixed on Theliel's tired face. Brushing his long, silver beard, the master explained, "The meeting will commence as soon as Lord Theliel finds his way to his bed-chambers."

Theliel frowned at the man who kept his long white beard in a tight braid. "I saw what happened to the other soldiers. I knew them. I trained with them," he argued calmly.

"If we need witnesses, we will make sure to call you," Rodbertus concluded, resting a hand on Angefort's shoulder, leading him away from Theliel and closer to the doors where he had come from.

"Does it not matter?" Theliel butted in, taking a step closer to them. "Does it not matter that I came back here? All these years of service," he pointed out, quickly running out of breath from the tiredness. "And you dismiss me from a meeting this important. A meeting where the best men of my father's lands were slaughtered."

Lord Angefort sent him a compassionate look, but Grandmaster Rodbertus seemed displeased. "They do matter to us, son," he conceded. "If they didn't, we wouldn't have agreed upon receiving a large sum of money from Lord Lionhelm as an apology for your missing days and incomplete tasks that were temporarily shuffled to others.

"It seems to me that said years of service don't matter to you, Theliel, as you left us without an explanation."

The light chestnut-haired man fell silent, licking his lips. Rodbertus smiled faintly at him, before resuming his hushed conversation with Lord Angefort. The dismissal hit Theliel in the guts harder than when his father ordered him to return. He felt like the sick kitten of the litter, the one the mother promptly killed before tending to the healthy felines. The analogy sounded bad in his head, but it was all he could think of as he dragged his feet in the direction of the stairs, at the far right of the throne room. He had to go all the way up to cross the bridge that connected the center of Rainier's Pavilion to the other ten wings, even though in eleven years, he had only known his.

The Treasure Council and everyone at their service spent most of their time under the far eastern cupola, where one small, quaint bedchamber was reserved for him. Theliel's arm hurt from all the climbing and walking, the arm sling doing a poor job at keeping it in place. If he knew how to take care of a dislocated arm himself, he wouldn't have to wait for someone from the Observatory Vault to visit him, but he was born in times of peace, and no one during training purposefully broke his body just for him to learn what to do in such scenarios.

Theliel scratched his head as he neared the corridor that would take him to a comfortable, albeit small bed. The opposite hallway led to a study room only he used. Glancing around, he was not surprised upon finding anyone else. Sir Ferrand, the Head of the Treasure Council, was probably joining Lord Angefort, while the other members of the council would be working until dusk.

He entered the cold, stone room, only to realize everything had been left untouched. Either that or whoever had been in charge of cleaning and rummaging through his work was good enough to not let a single trace. Theliel's hazel eyes rested on the stack of missives and rolls on top of the mahogany table. The daylight filled the room with an orange hue that made him feel slightly nostalgic, and he sat down, eyeing the green scenery outside. The royal gardens of this royal cage.

"The top of the known world," he whispered his father's words with a grim smile.

Opening the first letter on the stack of papers, his assignment was the same as the others that awaited him. The tax collectors of Rainier's End had sent him their numbers for him to report on the Regency's records. It was a simple task, one that any man with a semblance of education could have done. Pulling the drawer to his right open, Theliel grabbed a sheet of paper and his quill pen, his fingers copying the letters and the numbers his hazel eyes were memorizing on the original letter.

A hundred thousand silvers, the tax collectors had written.

From the tips of Theliel's left-hand fingers, the sum turned into fifty thousand.

Chapter XI

THE FAY THAT BURNS

The scent of lemon was fresh and stingy. He remembered his mother telling him how death wore the scent of lemon and grass as if it was only waiting to take souls down a bright, sunny path until it was decided whether the dead would be granted the towering Heights and their freedom, or the stone-cold ground of the Pit and its endless years of torture. He had always believed it to be a tale told to those who neared the end to appease their torment. However, he could smell it.

His greying, strawberry blonde eyebrows furrowed, and his wrinkly eyelids blinked open. Bright hazel eyes glanced around, taking in the familiar surroundings. He felt the silken sheets of his large, soft bed, and saw the canopy above his head. He was home. He tried to reach for the covers with his right hand, only to realize it wasn't responding. The accident on the way to Summerport had been real.

Thaesonwald Lionhelm cleared his throat, his left hand coming to rest against his right cheek, but he couldn't feel it. His vision became clouded, and his body felt overly tired. He closed his eyes, and the breeze that hit his skin was cold. One of the windows of his room was open and he heard the door open, followed by a loud thud and the sound of breaking glass.

"Lord Thaesonwald?" Healer Martus' voice reached his ears. "Quick!" he heard the man tell the guards. "Lady Lionhelm needs to know."

"No," Thaesonwald croaked out. "No," he repeated. "She knows," he told no one, as Martus had left the bed-chamber.

"She did it."

✷✷✷

The coughing wouldn't stop. From her perch on the ladder underneath the cupola where her father's books were nestled, Tecla watched him rub his neck as he busied himself with more documents and scribbling. She never really understood what had him so engrossed every day after his sparring in the barracks but whenever she asked, Tithan would smile at her fondly, promising that one day, she would know. The young girl sighed, her eyes falling on the book she had placed in her lap. Her father's observatory was the first place she had wanted to be after she emerged from her apartments. The news Tesfira shared the previous day had soothed her nerves, if only a little, but it hadn't been enough for her to visit the temple. She wasn't ready. Her father seemed to not have noticed that she was not leaving for her city day, but Tecla didn't mind. She preferred not to be asked questions.

"Did you find the book you were looking for?" Tithan asked her, never glancing up at her as he readjusted his copper-framed glasses.

Eyeing the title of the one she now held in her hands, she shook her head, even though she knew he couldn't see her. The Tales of Old Drixia & The Ruination of Calaris by Grandmaster Rodbertus of Three Crosses offered no answer to the many questions she had. Ever since her sister mentioned the existence of the Dreamer and the cult associated with her, she had been curious to find out more. The Oracle's Memoir told no tale about Kashezeth, at least not the version translated by Sir Frederyc Rosenfield. Tecla had hoped one of the history books would contain at least a clue about this parallel faith. The Oracle's Memoir said nothing about visions that caused men to die in atrocious circumstances. Perhaps, the Dreamer's followers knew something the holy men in Summerport didn't.

"No," she told her father as she left the book on the closest step. She wasn't about to climb to the top again; a servant could do it for her. "It doesn't matter," she quickly added.

"It is your city day today," Tithan pointed out in a monotone, sitting back in his large, cushioned chair and grabbing the glass full of black, Noirmont wine that rested between two stacks of books.

"Father, I... I have thought about what you said to me. About what I had in mind, and... I would like to try and see what the Regency's Observatory Vault is all about," she admitted, partially to change the subject, and because she had little to no intention of returning to Summerport.

She had Tithan's full attention. The old lord whipped his head around, removing his reading glasses. "Why is that?" he asked calmly. "Don't get me wrong, Tecla. I am pleased to hear this; however, I was under the impression that you were not ready, given the amount of time you spend at the temple."

The chestnut-haired girl nodded at that. She couldn't deny it. "I still believe, Father. I have strong reasons to believe in the Oracle, in Her message," she voiced her thoughts out loud. "I also think that there are more answers out there and, as much as I try to find them here, I can't."

Tithan watched the way her stare fell on her lap, where her balled fists rested, and his strong features softened. Brushing invisible dust off his warm, silver fur coat, he answered, "I can't just send you over there. You are too young." At the sight of her dejected expression, he almost chuckled. "How about we let you stay at the Regency for dawn and moon days, and then on dusk days you come back home?" he offered. "We can proceed this way until you are ready to join the Observatory Vault and serve the lands. And, if you won't, Strongshore will still be here."

Tecla's face beamed, causing him to smile right back at her. The coughing fit came back with the next breath he took, and Tecla rushed down the ladder and up to him, resting her small hand on his back as she kneeled to his side. "Father," she whispered. "Are you sure you don't need water? Or Healer Martus?"

"I would rather die than let him lay his hands on me," Tithan glared in the distance. "I am well," he tried to reassure her. "Cold days can cause this."

Tecla frowned, standing up only to cross her arms under her chest. "It surely does not help that this room is so dull," she told him, her eyes scanning his large desk. "Instead of this," she ranted, picking up the almost empty jug of wine, "we could have some fresh flowers from the Great Gardens, especially before the winds get colder."

Smiling faintly at her antics, the silver-haired lord nodded away. "Would you bring me some, daughter?"

Bending to kiss him on the cheek, she asked, "What would you like?"

"You know yellow daisies are my favorite."

Tecla nearly sauntered her way to the double doors, but they were quickly flung open, a rather impatient Lady Voladea pushing Master-at-Arms Fantine out of the way. Her mother seemed particularly angry that day, Tecla figured, frowning upon catching the sight of her sister down the hallway.

"Tecla, if you'll leave us," her mother ordered her, never once greeting her nor looking at her.

Bowing her head, Tecla offered a small smile to the red-haired fighter that guarded her father's doors every day after encampment training. Fantine bowed deeply in return, her serious expression never faltering.

Tecla's heels clicked against the marble floor, her frown intensifying as she realized Tesfira was talking to her maid, Lyzon. Before she could hear their conversation, Tesfira turned around with a toothy smile gracing her features.

"Good day Tecla," the curly-haired woman greeted her. "Is Mother already inside?"

"Yes," was the youngest Lionhelm's answer. "I shall not make them wait for me."

The way Lyzon glared at her sister's back wasn't lost on Tecla. Inhaling deeply and forcing a smile on her face, a part of her ashamed of the way she had kept her friend away for days, Tecla hooked her arm around Lyzon's, ignoring the maid's slight jump upon contact. Tecla tugged her forward, mentioning news she could not wait to tell her.

※※※

"I do not think this is a good idea."

Lyzon's midnight eyes glanced at the man sitting across from her with a sour look. They had been finishing breakfast earlier than usual, as it was the only time the kitchens of the palace were mostly empty, aside from the cook, Charity, who walked back and forth from a counter to another, but the middle-aged woman was too busy working on the buffet for the Lionhelms to pay attention to Lyzon and Fran.

Fran's warm brown eyes studied her face in a way she disliked. He almost looked judgmental. She hadn't expected him to agree with her, but the criticism wasn't needed.

"I think you need to set boundaries for your own sake," he added, running a large hand through his short-trimmed hair, the haircut making him look older than he was. "You have to remember that she is a young lady and that you can't barge in with the freedom you think you have."

"But I have it," Lyzon countered, only to be shut down.

"You think you have it," the gardener insisted. "You share the same apartments and you've been with her since the very beginning. However, you have to respect her orders, otherwise, she will start having doubts as well."

"It is easy for you to say," she replied quietly, poking the bread crumbs inside her soup with her rusty spoon.

Her long and slim fingernails pushed the bowl away, her hands coming to rest on her lap, toying with the beige fabric of her simple dress. She had let her long, straight black hair down, save for the top half of it, which was pulled back into a braid that joined the rest of her tresses as they cascaded down her back. Her full lips thinned against her front teeth as she bit back the words she wanted to direct at Fran. Lyzon knew he wouldn't deserve her wrath. The man wasn't at fault, quite the contrary.

Fran was the only person who was allowed into the secret she shared with Lord Tithan, and that was only because his father had been one of the closest, if not the closest friend Tithan had ever had. There were not many people with a heart as kind as Fran's, her lord would often repeat. The mere thought of his daughter growing up in her mother's care and surrounded by trustworthy people brought more joy to Lord Tithan than anyone could imagine, but the silence was too heavy to bear, especially in times like these, with Tecla being so isolated.

Lyzon knew very well that she could not push her luck, that the guards could see or hear, and whilst Lord Tithan's affairs were rarely the subject of scandal, it was one thing for the mistress to be talked about, and it was another to have her raise her child when the same right had been denied to Lady Lionhelm.

Fran's hand grazed her shoulder and she peeked at him, wondering when he had gotten up from his seat.

"Come on now," he spoke softly. "We have work."

Her hand rested on top of his as a silent thanks.

The maid walked back to Lady Tecla's apartments without even bothering to look around, knowing her feet would take her there even if she was blind. Her flat shoes made no sound with every step she took, and it wasn't long until she and Fran parted ways. He worked outside, while she cleaned the bed-chambers and washed the young lady's silks.

Lyzon was nearly at the double doors when the sight of a woman she did not want to see blocked her path. Lady Tesfira stood by the small balcony that overlooked the Great Gardens, her fiery red dress moving behind her as the wind blew. Her curly, dark chestnut locks flapped around her neck, and Lyzon forced herself to bow politely.

"Lady Tesfira."

"Lyzon, walk with me," the woman who was older than her by at least ten years ordered. "Tecla is not in her bed-chambers; she left early to be with our father," she informed the maid.

Lyzon did a poor job at hiding her surprise, and Tesfira laughed coldly. "My little talk with her yesterday must have convinced her to not fear her impending matrimony."

"I doubt the young lady is worried about a marriage that will not happen until she is older," the dark-skinned woman replied, keeping her stare low.

"You can doubt," Tesfira conceded. "In silence."

She straightened her back and raised her chin even more as they continued their ascent to the highest story of the palace, where Lord Tithan's observatory was. The silence Lyzon did not mind as it took a lot of willpower to not pull the curls out of Tesfira's skull and set them on fire every time she spoke. If she had to choose, she would rather spend time with Lady Voladea herself. As Tithan often said, Tesfira was confrontational for no apparent reason. It was her way of asserting the power she never had over anybody, not even over her son Deril, who was only seen in the company of his father. The boy was too shy to keep up with his mother's behavior.

As they made their way down the hallway that led to Tithan's observatory room, Lyzon heard the double doors being opened, but Tesfira suddenly stopped and turned around to face her, blocking her view.

"One more thing, Lyzon," she said in a hushed tone, her hazel eyes piercing through her skull. "When you visit my father, try not to do it when Belvadair is on guard duty. He works for me, but a couple of silvers and a glass of ale would be enough for Mother to extract any information she might want on her spouse's private hours. Tecla does not deserve this."

Lyzon's heart skipped a beat, but before she knew it, the youngest Lionhelm was near them, being greeted by the woman who had just threatened both of them. She jumped slightly at the contact Tecla made with her. She let out a breath she didn't know she was holding, and her heart suddenly beat faster at the realization that Tesfira was truly holding a sword over her head. Lyzon did not want Tecla to learn anything about her and Tithan from someone else.

"I have great news," Tecla's chirpy voice filled her ears. "Father agreed on letting me go to the Regency, that is, for a little while, until I decide."

Lyzon nodded quickly, trying not to make it so obvious that she had missed her.

"I am sure you are happier this way too. You never seemed to like our days spent in Summerport."

"You are young, Lady Tecla," Lyzon whispered. "It is normal if you wish to experience different settings."

Ignoring her comment while she rambled, Tecla went on, "Have you ever been to Silverholde? Do you think we will like it?"

Lyzon smiled, reaching out to hold the young lady's hand. "I am sure we will, young lady."

✳✳✳

The seal of his house secured the letter with one reptile-tongued lion head. The wax was quick to dry in place, and Tithan Lionhelm dropped the result of his work for the day in the rectangular-shaped box in his top drawer. He would have Fantine deliver it herself to the Regency; the confidentiality of his writing could not fall in someone else's hands. Tithan wasn't arrogant enough to believe that what he spent hours on was worthy of the public's eye, but he found himself to be more and more reserved as the years passed by, and there was only one person he wanted the message to reach, Grandmaster Rodbertus of Three Crosses.

Tithan felt Voladea's stare as she stood across from him, her long fingernails drumming against the hard fabric of yet another expensive dress that seemed to have been sewed in lands different than his. The metal that lined the sewing made her look rather terrifying. The last time he had seen such fashion was during the years of the Great Conquest in his father's era, and back then it made sense for the noble ladies to seek refuge in the thicker, protective materials.

    He hadn't had the time to speak as the double doors opened yet again, his eldest daughter making her way inside with that strut of hers. Tithan eyed the ceiling, a part of him wishing it would crumble on their heads in that instant. "What did I deserve to have my two favorite women together in my apartments?" he wondered out loud, his tone heavy with sarcasm.

    His spouse repressed a scoff, exchanging a look with Tesfira, who pursed her lips as she sat down and properly folded her hands on her lap.

    "Father, I think you know," the curly-haired woman spoke first. "We are here for Tylennald."

    Tithan wasn't surprised. Reaching out for what was left of his black wine, he took a sip, waiting for one of them to elaborate. He couldn't argue too much with Tesfira. The woman had a way with words that made his blood boil with ease. He could not blame her either; Tesfira was incredibly attached to her half-brother Tylennald, almost in the same way Tecla loved Theliel, but less adorably. Tesfira listened to Tylennald as if silver rained from his lips, and never questioned him, never sook better advice or different views, which was probably why Voladea tolerated Tesfira more than any other child he had had with other women.

"Isn't it delightful, the way you greet us?" Voladea pointed out, taking a seat herself across from her husband. "But when it is about Theliel, you have him stand in line in the audience room."

"Theliel's problems I wanted to address personally," Tithan replied bluntly, more wrinkles forming on his forehead as he frowned at them. "I didn't know you both had problems that needed my attention. Every time one of you visits me, it is rarely about me solving what troubles you. It is more about the claims and complaints you wish to formulate."

Ignoring her father's witty comment, Tesfira leaned in. "We simply want to convince you to have Tylennald come back to Strongshore. Think about it, Father. Wald and his family are not suited for succession, whilst Tylennald is more like you than anyone else."

"We are just worried. What would happen if Tiran was to run Strongshore?"

Tithan inhaled deeply, feeling the itch in his chest that signaled he needed to cough. "The same thing that would happen if Tylennald was in charge," he whispered. "No man of this family has what it takes to carry on with the legacy of our ancestors." Before either woman could interject, Tithan added, "It is not because they are not capable. It is because they have all lived the quiet lives of those born in times of peace. They know nothing of the ruthlessness of unknown illnesses that decimate entire towns, they cannot fathom the reality of having to swing their weapons through a foe's body. They have seen little of the Silver Lands, and nothing of the Red Continent. They haven't crossed the Tinted Bay, nor swam for their lives in the Zalejos Depths.

"The future lies not in the strength a man can showcase. There will be no lord, no lady, no monarch by the time we all leave," he elaborated calmly, one of his gloved hands resting on his chest as if to prevent another fit from bursting. "The Silver Lands cannot survive long with such traditions. The Regency is a good step ahead with their methodical ways of administering the capital, and their research vault."

He saw Voladea's grey eyebrow twitch at his words, and he understood that she hadn't. "Is this your way of disregarding the South in favor of the central powers?"

"No, Voladea," Tithan sighed out, clearing his throat. "This is my way of saying that we are not to be considered the masters of the universe. The southern lands now thrive with the exchange agreed upon with the other lands and with the Red Continent after the King's Campaigns. Trading and freedom of simple people.

"One day, it is all we will know. I can't stop that; you can't stop that."

Voladea remained silent, her retort dying in the back of her throat as she reminded herself that Tesfira was present and that she did not want to bring up Tecla's future into the conversation, not with another child of Tithan's present. Lady Lionhelm believed that her husband had spoken his true intentions but there was more. There always was with him. She hadn't had the chance to speak with Tylennald since he had to leave Strongshore, but as much as every Lionhelm heir's future seemed clear, Tecla remained the exception. She didn't know what Tithan had in mind for her, but she was the youngest child of his. From her own experience, she could say that the youngest was always the one on a parent's mind.

"Why are you here?" Tithan asked Tesfira, interrupting Voladea's thoughts and breaking the silence that was cluttering around them. "You spend a lot of time in Strongshore lately, for someone who is supposed to supervise the daily matters of Edgemere. I thought the harbor needed repairs; isn't that why your husband asked for more silvers this month?"

Tesfira fidgeted in her seat, nodding. "He is supervising, not me."

Tithan's hazel eyes saw perfectly the way her lying face twisted and flushed. Hamley Silverworm didn't even know how to count, as far as he knew, yet somehow, he was able to supervise the repairs of a harbor as big as Edgemere's. "Very well," he conceded for the time being. "What I cannot see, the Silver Master will," he reminded his daughter.

The resounding knock on the double doors caused Tithan to slam his gloved hands on the desk. Standing up, his deep voice roared, "What now?"

Fantine's red hair appeared for a second, but Healer Martus quickly stumbled inside the room, nearly tripping over his robes. He was out of breath, sweaty, and fumbling with words.

"Lord of Strongshore, Lord Thaesonwald is awake. The Oracle and Her Angels of Steel granted us this moment," he cheered with a tired smile, "for they fight the fay that waltzes with the dead."

"Burn fay," Tithan heard the two women sitting across from him whisper to themselves.

"They granted no such thing," he cut their antics short, his thoughts going over the possibilities of his son to be fully conscious.

✹✹✹

The central inn was too busy that night. The frail, old innkeeper looked like he would pass out with every step he took around the tables he served, but Jascha preferred it that way. He didn't want the old man to take the time to recognize him. He knew the innkeeper talked to the two officers he came across in Beggar's Pool, and Jascha wasn't sure how much information they shared and if he happened to be the subject of their conversation. He wasn't too worried about the Chief of the Surveillance; the man seemed to have his agenda and orders to follow that didn't include countryside mishaps. The officer who seemed to be training under him, however, was too happy to indulge in side missions.

Jascha hadn't thought too much about the girl of Beggar's Pool, Loveleen. It all happened before he could realize anything, just like it did before, in Three Crosses. He hadn't wanted her dead, nor had he wanted her at all when he first laid eyes on her. The mere thought of her skin made him feel extremely soiled, and only her blood quelled the urge to skin his limbs.

His bear fur shielded him from the cold winds that came from the North as the innkeeper kept the door open to let some of the smoke out, as many patrons were indulging in the wild plants of the Red Continent to dull their senses. Jascha run a hand through his freshly washed and brushed black hair. He had decided to stay in Rainier's End for one more night just to wash off the dirt that had collected in his hair and the dry sweat that made him smell like a swine. He could have done it at the Illusion Shelter, but he had been in a hurry to leave the forsaken place. Jascha didn't want to have another incident over there, as they would simply claw at him like beasts, pretending to be looking for answers, invading the privacy of his mind and body.

There was no cure for him, for he was not ill, he repeated himself.

"It is you," a high-pitched voice interrupted his musings.

Setting down the glass of Summerport ale, his black eyes glanced at his side, where a small, blonde girl with eyes as green as wet grass stood. It was Rantha's mouthy apprentice, Yenny.

"So, you are feeling better," she noted, reaching for one of the dried meat sandwiches on the counter of the wooden bar.

"Ecstatic," Jascha commented dryly, gulping down the contents of his glass.

"I was surprised to hear that you left so suddenly," Yenny said while chewing on dry meat, causing the man next to her to wrinkle his nose. "Miss Rantha and I were about to get started on those documented witchcraft cases. You know, Miss Rantha herself decided to discard the theory of you coming down with the big delusion," she rambled carelessly, a hint of rudeness mixing with the chirpy tone she used with him.

Jascha's fingertips tugged on the ends of his hair that reached past his collarbone. "Witchcraft?" he whispered, arching an eyebrow. "As in, witches, ghosts, and whatnot?"

"Witches, as in fay. Burning fays of Soleba," Yenny corrected him. Noting the way her words didn't ring a single bell in Jascha's mind, she grabbed a jug of wine for herself, dropping a few coins for the bartender that was busy serving a group to her left. "You don't believe in it," she stated.

"I know nothing of it," he said plainly, standing up to end their conversation.

"I wanted to suggest Miss Rantha map out the scars on your body."

The offending suggestion caused him to narrow his eyes at her. "Why?"

"Witches is what the religious people called the fays after King Aleyne Rainier's ascent to the throne. They are merely followers of a different faith. Do you know anything about the Oracle and Her mortal life?"

Jascha nodded faintly. He had a holy captain visit his home as a child quite often since his healers had all died the way his mother did after they tried to cure her of the Violet Delusion. He wasn't pious himself, but the holy captain had carried a copy of the Memoir with him, and he recalled reading it as he tried to block out his mother's pained cries during treatment, one that was very similar to what Rantha herself had tried on him, the main difference being that his mother hadn't been unconscious.

"The Oracle's words were not as widely followed as Summerport wants us all to believe. Many others thought the Dreamer's message to be the Good Gods' will. Their practices weren't any less controversial though, and that included a set of rituals for the new fays to perform. It was their consecration, their entrance into the faith."

"You believe I'm part of a ritual," Jascha concluded for her when their conversation wasn't evolving into anything interesting to him.

"Perhaps. That is why I wanted to map out the scars on your body. Rituals are not casual, so if there is no pattern, then we could rule that possibility out."

His black eyes stared into her green hues for what felt like an eternity to her, and he eventually relented. "Map them then."

Yenny's eyebrows shot up in surprise, glancing around. "Where?"

"They have a room upstairs. My bag is still there," he told her.

Jascha had left his belongings in the room after washing himself earlier that evening. The innkeeper had been busy with the opening for the night, but the bartender hadn't complained about the extra silvers he had been given to leave the room for him for the night. Rooms were usually left for traders and Regency surveillants who hadn't planned on staying, while the patrons who were too drunk to remove themselves by the time the place was closing would simply pass out on the tables.

  Yenny held tight on her leather bag as they squeezed their way upstairs, already pulling out a piece of paper and a small bottle of ink. Jascha studied the way she fumbled with her belongings as he closed the door, and she simply explained that she was still training with Miss Rantha. Writing down information and drawing the plants that were deemed useful for their craft was her way of memorizing valuable things.

  Jascha's cloak was quickly discarded, and his brown shirt doubled with a black jacket were next. The garments were thrown on the floor without care, and he stood in front of her with an impossible look on his face, the marks on his upper body causing the blonde girl to narrow her eyes and chew on the inside of her cheek as she quickly focused. She sat on the bed, placing her small bottle of ink on the end table, dipping the tip of her quill pen to get started. Jascha's scars didn't seem to be part of a ritualistic pattern, but she wasn't that well-versed in any type of research to know for sure. It would take her many hours and many books to find out.

  The most significant scar she started with. It was right above his heart, and it was large. She figured that if it had been an open wound, she could have slipped her hand in there. The thought of it made her shiver, and she shook her head. The silence around them was at times broken by Jascha's loud breathing, but he stood perfectly still. Yenny couldn't believe the man was that compliant; Miss Rantha always seemed anxious when it came to him.

Green eyes glanced up, only to draw a messy representation of one last little scar, one above his hip. She scribbled a few words next to it, figuring that it would have been easier if she had taken her pencil out of her bag. She had been too excited, rushing to get started. It was the first time she did anything without Miss Rantha's indications.

"Alright," she whispered. "Can you turn around? If you have any on your back," she said, looking for another piece of paper in her bag, hoping she still had some. She hadn't planned any of this, so she hadn't taken any more paper with her. She was supposed to just grab dinner in the city.

"Get up," Jascha commanded her.

Startled by the order, Yenny looked at him, only to realize he stood much closer to her than before. His hands were balled into fists at his side, causing his biceps to swell slightly and the veins in his forearm to stand out. Frowning, she did as he said. She barely reached his neck. Jascha's dark stare wasn't on her but her notes and inky sketches. His index finger traced the letters he read, staining himself with the still fresh, blue ink.

"So, you were serious," he noted.

Yenny felt slightly offended. "I am not one to joke."

"I am not often asked to undress for a couple of sloppy drawings."

His gaze was directed back at her, and as much as she wanted to call him colorful names for suggesting she had been lying to him, the feel of his breath on her face froze her in place. He didn't seem angry at her, but his straight posture and locked jaw suggested otherwise.

"Tell me," he spoke, his voice barely above a whisper. "You drew my scars all over that piece of torn paper, but not my body. Why?"

The blonde girl flushed, her hands fisting the front of her pale grey skirt. "It is improper," she pointed out, her stare falling to the tip of her shoes.

"And asking me to undress is not?" A laugh escaped his lips, and it was a cruel one. "What a little stupid thing you are. Does it disgust you?" he asked, his voice rising.

"What? N-no—"

The first slap came crashing down like the roof of a burning house. Yenny felt blood fill her mouth, and she fell back on the bed, holding the side of her face. Her body temperature rose, and she felt her heartbeat in her ears as tears collected in her eyes, failing to understand what just happened.

"I hate," Jascha's muttered words filled her brain, "I hate all of you," he hissed, forcefully pushing her head against the mattress as he pulled her skirt up and used his right knee to part her legs.

Yenny tried to resist, kicking his thighs and pushing his hands away from her petite frame.

Jascha's quickest reaction was to reach at his side, unsheathing his dagger to plant it inside her left thigh with a swift movement. His left hand immediately covered her shriek, and he removed his weapon from her body, only to push it again inside the same spot until the tip of the steel met a hard surface. Her bone.

The girl writhed beneath him, and Jascha felt her hot breath against his hand, which was quickly coated in spit. Yenny moved a little less with her injured, bleeding leg, and his right hand left the dagger deeply inside her thigh to avoid blood spilling all over bedsheets that weren't his.

"Be quiet," he whispered against her ear as he undid his britches. "Or you'll have more scars to map out."

His hand curled around his half-hardened member, the head pushing through her hairy folds, finding her entrance rather quickly. Yenny mumbled something against his hand, and Jascha removed it, wiping it on her now wrinkled skirt.

"Please, don't," she begged him with big, red, and teary eyes staring into his. "I will just leave," she promised with a nod of her head.

His thumb rested on her cheek, the one that wasn't bruising, and he pinched it. "You slit my wrists," he reminded her with a gentle voice.

He pushed in with one buck of his hips, promptly covering her mouth again as she screamed. She was dry down there, so he retreated for a moment, stroking his length for a few seconds before ramming inside her once more. He repeated the motion, and again, until he was covered with her fluids and blood, and probably piss too, he figured, but he cared not as he plundered her into the wooden, half-broken bed of the central inn. His mind was blurry and his breath ragged. Her folds were tight and her body colder than what he expected. Jascha rested his forehead on the crook of her neck as he bit his lower lip, releasing a load of himself inside her intimate parts.

His manhood fell limp within seconds, and his hand looked for the hilt of his dagger, still rooted inside her thigh. "Stand," he rasped, tightening his hand around her neck to drag her upwards.

Yenny gasped and coughed, yelping at the pain that jolted through her leg, her inner thigh dirty and destroyed by the forceful motion of his hips. Jascha pulled her away from the bed he did not want to stain and closer to the window, pushing her against the windowsill. He needed air. He felt like he was suffocating.

His hands fumbled with the lock on the window, and the small blonde seemed to regain full control of herself. She was breathing heavily, and each time she exhaled, a whimper made it past her lips, her eyes widening at the realization of what had just happened. The whimpers turned to faint screams, but Jascha rested his left arm against the wall, closing his eyes as the cold wind soothed his nerves.

"Quit it," he ordered when her voice became louder. "I said," he paused, moving to grab her, only causing her to stumble away from him, "quit it."

His large hands were on her shoulders in no time, but Yenny pushed hard against him, setting him off balance for a split second, and Jascha backhanded her with a force he hadn't meant to use in that precise instant. The girl's back hit the windowsill and she found herself hanging halfway out the window, the hit and the cold wind causing her to cough when she wanted to scream for help. Jascha reached for the dagger still embedded in her thigh, and he pulled it out, his other hand stopping in mid-air as he reached out to tug her up. She yelped at the feeling of steel leaving her body.

    With a sob and a fading cry, Yenny's body fell. Jascha's fingers tightened around the hilt of his dagger, and he leaned forward, catching a glimpse of the girl's body on the dirty ground at the back of the inn. His long black hair slapped against his face as the cold wind blew softer. Droplets of Yenny's blood fell on his boots, but his eyes, as black as the starless night, focused on the crimson pool that collected around the blonde's head.

Chapter XII

GUARDS OF THE RIVER

Mud slapped against the hem of his long, ivory, and blue cloak as his Edgemeran horse galloped its way towards the bridge that ran over the Rough Rill, the watercourse that separated the southern coasts from the river lands, drawing a clear border between Strongshore and Silverholde. The travelers that would keep traveling to the West, following the river, would reach Founder's Breach within a week, while those headed to the East wouldn't be far from Limemeadow. Tylennald Lionhelm tugged down the sash that covered half of his face, protecting him from the cold, his eyes blinking at the sight of his wife's homeland.

Wallysa rode next to him, her deep indigo cloak bearing the crest of her father's family; a large, winged sea-horse rising from the waters. Tylennald exchanged a look with his wife as they approached the walls of a castle-city that had been meant to separate the southern lands from the rest of the continent. Horns in the distance signaled their arrival to the current lord of Courtbridge. The lion heads of Strongshore flew high in the sky as the bannermen that escorted Tylennald sped up, nearly riding past him. Soon, the portcullis was lifted.

The villeins of the local lord stopped working, just like every other villager and guard that stood at the entrance of the castle-city. Their faces were coated with dirt and sweat, probably even excrements, and Tylennald scrunched his nose at the stench. The men removed their hats, if they wore any, whispering a faint, "Lady Wallysa," at the sight of Tylennald's wife. She nodded at each one of them, while the women at work bowed their heads in respect. Tylennald's hazel stare was directed at what was right ahead of him, the Riverguard castle.

The putrid smell that filled Courtbridge was one of the reasons he had always refused to move in his wife's household to take over her title, even if he had every right to do so. Crossing the Rough Rill felt as if he had gone back in time, to places that knew nothing of sewers and basic hygiene. The mere fact that the walls of the castle-city still stood was an offense. His father was the lord half the continent obeyed to. The Angeforts of Limemeadow, and, long ago, the Rosenfields of Wilderose had all started as vassals of Lord Lionhelm, and soon, House Riverguard would succumb to the Lionhelms.

"Not vassals," his father would tell him when he was a young boy. "Family. In a way or another, you will always find us tied in blood."

And he had been right. Tylennald himself had to wed a Riverguard, and if Tesfira had been born sooner, she would have probably been betrothed to Lord Angefort, but all wasn't lost since it seemed that Wallysa's younger sister, Meryld, was seeking an arrangement with the eastern lord.

The hood that covered Tylennald's light chestnut hair fell back, and the one grey strand of hair on his head grazed his forehead. At the gates of the castle that looked like a dark grey stack of spikes with only a few tall windows to let the sunrays in, Lord Lovel Riverguard and his wife, Eloisa Riverguard née Rosenbane, stood waiting underneath a large, beaked gargoyle with three reptilian tales above the entrance. Their sober, dark attire suggested this was no special occasion for them, and it was furthermore confirmed by the stoic looks they directed at the couple.

"Wallysa," Lord Riverguard greeted his daughter, who kissed his knuckles in respect and kneeled before her mother, an unacceptable sight in Tylennald's opinion.

They were by law superior to them.

"Lord Tylennald."

"Father-in-law," Tylennald replied bluntly, ignoring the honorifics.

The great hall of the Riverguard castle was nothing Tylennald hadn't seen before. His very first meeting with Wallysa had taken place in that very same place, only his father had been present, accepting the invitation of Lord Lovel. It happened over thirty years ago. He had been just a boy, but his father had come back from the King's campaigns in the free cities of the Red Continent, and the future of the kingdom had been unstable as plans for Regency to come alive were discussed in Founder's Breach. Tithan Lionhelm hadn't known if he had to cross the Tinted Bay again in King Helias' name, and he had wanted both his sons to settle down in case anything happened to him.

    Lord Lovel Riverguard hadn't changed one bit since the last time he saw him on the day of his and Wallysa's wedding. His shoulder-length, straight blonde hair was neatly kept, and the black, warm wintry clothes he wore were only highlighted by the indigo and purple of his coat, closed around his midsection by a large belt. His blue eyes were identical to Wallysa's, and his hairless face was barely wrinkled. Eloisa Riverguard, on the other hand, showed many signs of aging, from her greying, mahogany mane pulled into twin, cone-shaped buns at the top of her head, to the lines on her forehead and around her thin lips. Dressed in a fashion that mimicked her husband's, the woman was quick to excuse herself.

    The drapes that hung low from the balcony above their heads showcased not only the Riverguards' crest but the Lionhelms' as well. It was certainly not a pleasing sight to the man who had been granted no male son, but he as well as Tylennald knew that Courtbridge was Tylennald's for the taking the moment Lovel passed away. The long dining table at the far end of the hall was full of delicacies of the river lands. The smell of mulled wine and trout broth reached Tylennald's nostrils, and his stomach rumbled.

"Would you take refreshment?" Lord Lovel asked, moving to sit at the center of the table.

Wallysa silently sat a few chairs from him, and one of the maids behind her promptly served her.

"Gladly," Tylennald answered, coming to sit right next to him.

"Judging by the pieces of luggage you brought with you, I expect this to be a rather long visit."

"Father seems to believe now is the time for me to learn from your wise rule," Tylennald suavely replied, indulging in the slices of bacon and duck breasts before him. A maid appeared to his side to fill a small bowl with trout broth, and the Lionhelm added, "I fail to believe he has not told you anything."

"What good would it be for us, if I were to teach you anything?" Lovel mused out loud, his knife cutting through his meat. "Your bones are aging, and my piece of wisdom should directly pass to Terrel, but you seem to have failed not only at believing in my words, but also as a father."

Tylennald dropped his knife, swallowing carefully as the comment caused his chest to tighten. Snapping at the man was not an option. Snapping at anyone wasn't an option, for someone in his position. "My son is in Founder's Breach. If you wished to share your wisdom with him, you could have summoned him a long time ago," he pointed out sharply, pushing his plate to the side.

"Are you no longer hungry?" Wallysa asked him, arching an eyebrow.

The faint smile that grazed her father's lips caused her to stand up before she finished her meal herself, and Tylennald was quick to follow. Grabbing her cup of wine, the long-haired blonde woman who still wore her braids in the southern style neared the fireplace and leaned against the wall while she stared outside. She could see the muddy streets of Courtbridge. It just started raining.

Her husband rounded the long dining table to look straight into his father-in-law's eyes. "I am afraid we will have to get along a little better than this, for I will have to stay for quite a while and you are loyal to my father ever since our families were joined by marriage."

Lord Riverguard stood up slowly, his cold stare rivaling Tylennald's demanding attitude. "Of your father," he repeated, needing no other words to make his point across. "I have never seen you so… unsettled, Tylennald. You are a rather charismatic, poised man. However, your attitude makes it obvious that Courtbridge is not your idea of a fine reward. And yet," the older man paused, rubbing his chin as he pretended to be looking for the right words, "Courtbridge is the one place that separates the southern lands of your father from Silverholde and the North. History was made here long before Strongshore gained any meaning."

"You and I know that is a lie," Tylennald quickly retorted, raising his eyebrows at the delusional man. "Calaris was home to the greatest civilization known to us, and the City of Drixia founded by Warrior Queen Aelneth and Alatros the

Red carried on with its legacy for centuries. Such are the lands that today belong to my father, and they have expanded throughout the years. Aside from the Regency and what little is left of the North, the Lionhelms have deep roots everywhere in the Silver Lands.

"Truthfully, the Regency itself stands thanks to my father Tithan."

Lord Riverguard clapped his hands slowly, amusement written all over his face. "I thank you for the history lesson, Tylennald. It is true, your family's ancestry is magnificent, enviable even. However, we are far from the sea," he pointed out, "and what makes you Lionhelms strong as you are is your navy. Your army is partially the Regency's, and quite frankly, I doubt any army could breach the walls of Courtbridge. They were raised before the destruction of Old Drixia, which is today just a good-looking cliff for Strongshore, and no war has ever seen Courtbridge taken by anyone."

"Father," Wallysa sighed out from her corner, growing tired of their banter.

"I doubt it has anything to do with the walls," Tylennald nearly laughed. "The Riverguards have always been good at switching sides. Besides, is treachery on your mind, Lord Lovel? Why would you even entertain the idea of seeing my father's men at your doors?"

"I would never, but would you?"

The question made way for a comfortable silence to settle between them, and Wallysa turned around to look at them with glinting eyes and doubts on her father's true intentions. While the two men in the hall had never been close nor accommodating around each other, she hadn't expected their conversation to take such a wild turn. However, her father was a man who had always lived up to his reputation. As much as he could not be deemed to be a threat, given the scarce number of men in his armies, Lovel Riverguard's knowledge of the human mind bypassed the logic of steel and strength. Wallysa wasn't surprised to find her husband tricked by the manipulating insinuations her father made. Whether he was serious or entertained was a matter she would rather not address.

"After all," Lord Riverguard thought out loud, "Tiran Lionhelm lacks the training that is expected of him. Tell me, Tylennald. If Tiran was to step back, does Strongshore fall under your command?"

His blue eyes were scanning every little movement Tylennald made. Nostrils flaring, his son-in-law forced his shoulder to relax, his head twitching to the side slightly as if to regain composure. "I suppose," he lied through his teeth.

"You suppose."

"No," Tylennald corrected himself, his hazel eyes looking to the side. "Not if my sister Tecla is in Strongshore. Father has favorited her," he admitted, loathing the disappointment in his voice.

Lovel Riverguard nodded slowly, sitting back into his chair and resting his forearms on the armrests. He watched with curious eyes the way his daughter neared her husband, resting a hand on his shoulder as if to comfort a man who wanted none of it.

"Little Tecla is certainly not a concern," the woman spoke, glancing at her father from the corner of her eye. "The day Tiran becomes Lord of Strongshore, he can always name us his successors. The man does not seem to find an interest for any woman he could wed."

Lord Riverguard burst into laughter, his gargling sounds filling the great hall for several moments, earning the confused looks of his guests as well of his servants, who stood still in the shadows, waiting to be ordered around or dismissed. Lovel coughed a few times, resting a hand with too many rings around his fingers on top of the table.

"I missed these pearls of wit, Wallysa. You are both fools who deserve no better treatment than the one that was served to you by Lord Tithan," he commented dryly, his wide smile never leaving his lips. "Here we have Lord Tylennald," he presented, extending his arm in the man's direction, "soon to be an oldster, and his wife, who is not getting any younger, wishing to become the heirs of a nephew who is a weak warrior and a celibate.

"Wallysa," he called his daughter, clasping his hands together in delight. "I know for a fact that this entire predicament could have been avoided if you hadn't tricked the thick mind of your husband into forging a will that did not belong to Lord Tithan."

Wallysa shook her head at that, the anger and disdain that filled her eyes begging to be released. "I have had enough of that story," she spoke in a low voice. "I do not know how many times I had to repeat myself, but neither Tylennald nor myself have ever forged anything."

"Was the document not found in your husband's private chambers? Are you not interested in the least in your place in the line of succession?"

She was about to answer when Tylennald held her back, gripping her shoulder. "Don't," she heard him command her.

Lovel Riverguard studied their expressions, nodding to himself. He knew liars when he saw them; however, their body language failed the checkmarks he mentally listed for himself when assessing such a situation. He laced his hands together, his index fingers resting against his lower lip.

"Unheard of," he said with another short laugh before rising to his feet. "You two get the rest you need. Ninette here will escort you to your bedchambers," Lovel dismissed them as a maid came forward, bowing her head. "Do not bother unpacking too much; I know in a few days we are expected in Strongshore for Little Tecla's ball.

"And regarding what you said, about the walls of Courtbridge," Lovel recalled, glancing back at Tylennald, "you were right. They have little to do with the fact that wars never destroyed them. They were never built for that purpose.

"The walls of Courtbridge were erected before Soleba's fire, Wilderose's fire. There was a time where the walls lined the Rough Rill, stretching from the East to the West. It is said every inch of the walls were wet with Quiet Tears, to keep at bay the fays the river lands did not wish to see. It is a shame that these stones can no longer be found. Their value would be greater than silver itself.

"Courtbridge does have its share of history."

Without excusing himself, the Lord of Courtbridge left the great hall, taking his musings with him, lifting the invisible fog that had been weighing on the Lionhelm couple since they arrived.

✳✳✳

The heels of Lord Angefort's boots hit the stone floor with every heavy step of his. He marched inside the audience room of the Pavilion like a man who just left his home to go to war. His face was still bruised and dirty, and the cut on his upper lip pulsated, but the possible infection was not his main concern as he reached the round table at the center of the room. Never one to be easily mesmerized by his surroundings, Arther Angefort thought to himself that the audience room was a mere copy of Lord Lionhelm's observatory, with the exception that the cupola above his head hosted fewer books, the shelves alternating with glass that let the sun rays light the room. A circular chandelier still hung low from the center of it, the spent candles reduced to pools of wax that had dried around the metal bars.

The walls were of a deep, emerald color lined with golden hues that created rectangular patterns around the edges, a clear contradiction to the round shape of the entire audience room. A single painting stood at the foot of a small secretary desk. The portrait of a young, platinum-haired king stared back at the people who just entered the room. The standing figure was slim, fair-skinned, with eyes as grey as the wintry skies and a small, elegant mole on his right cheekbone. The young King Helias was dressed in garments that were not common for royals, looking as if he was just about to head out for a sporty hunt, a silver owl perched on his left shoulder. Lord Angefort diverted his gaze from the painting that was created several decades ago, choosing one of the seats as his own while the rest of the Regency followed him.

    Sir Ferrand Nickletail of Founder's Breach sat next to him, his signature brown ponytail cascading down his skinny body clad in white. The man's mustache wiggled with the way his lips twitched now and then. The man of forty years of age and Lord Arther had always been on amicable terms, despite the cultural differences that separated them. The people of the Breach were usually wary and tactical, while Angefort had been taught the southern boldness from his years spent with Lord Lionhelm. To his right, Sir Sybbyl Nobleleaf of the Sand Towers plopped down without an ounce of grace, the woman too muscular and heavy to care about the lady-like manners that were expected of women. Her short blonde hair and tanned skin were common features of those who came from the northeastern coast. She crossed her arms on top of the table, her armor plates scratching against the surface of the wooden table covered by thin glass.

It wasn't long until Grandmaster Rodbertus of Three Crosses joined them, sitting across from Arther with Chief Thierry Eleres right behind him. The two of them were the only low born, head members of the Regency, but their wisdom and prowess were highly regarded by their peers as well as the lords of the Silver Lands. Lord Angefort scanned the faces of the people around him, smiling inwardly at the choices Lord Lionhelm and King Helias had made over sixty years prior. Simple people and noble people, women and men, young and old, southerners and northerners; the Regency had been founded with care and in hopes of continuity. He only hoped they would listen to what he had to say to them.

"My lords," Arther spoke first, resting his palms on the cold surface of the table. "I know this meeting might cause you to think that I overstepped my functions as Secretary of the Regency. King Helias Rainier did not order this," he told them with sincerity. "However, a tragedy hit my men and me on our way back from Strongshore, and the events must be discussed immediately.

"As you may already know, I had left Silverholde for Strongshore as I must return to Lord Lionhelm on every first dusk day of the month for my reports."

The middle-aged Sir Ferrand next to him grunted, "You were, after all, a vassal of Lord Lionhelm."

"His best men are the elite fighters of the Regency," Sir Sybbyl, the Suppressor of War, joined in, her thick eyebrows knitting together. "I can't help but wonder what happened to more than half of those who escorted you. Security is lax already in the capital," she commented, eyeing the Chief of the Surveillance, "we certainly cannot afford to leave our best armies in the South. You lead them in the Regency's name."

"Wait right there—" the bald man known as Eleres butted in, only to be quieted down by Angefort, who raised his hands at them.

"My lords," he spoke with authority. "Lord Lionhelm appointed me with the task of returning his son Theliel to the Treasure Council, and we rode as soon as arrangements were made. Unfortunately, as we reached Wilderose, we walked into an execution that we could not comprehend.

"A man had been torn apart, quite literally, his insides spilled all over the ground and his limbs were attached to roots and branches."

Rodbertus, the Grandmaster of the Observatory Vault, who had been silent until that very moment narrowed his left eye and asked, "I have heard of this before, from you Eleres. Is that correct?"

The Chief of the Surveillance rested the palm of his hand on his smooth scalp, nodding. "Indeed. The Surveillance was summoned upon request by the Sons of Ferngrunn, in the Sand Towers." His brown eyes met Sybbyl's blue ones. "Several similar occurrences have plagued the northern coasts. What I have uncovered so far, with the help of Officer

Goldsnout, is that these murders are part of a ritual, but no trace of those who conduct them can ever be found on site. It is almost as if it was the earth itself swallowing these men after chewing them up."

His choice of words made Arther's skin crawl.

"These men," Rodbertus went on. "Who are they? Is there anything that ties them together?"

Chief Eleres shook his head. "No. They are usually simple people with small law-breaking records, but they do not seem connected in any way."

"What stands out here is that most occurrences have taken place in the North," the Grandmaster concluded out loud, toying with his long silver beard. "If it also happened in Wilderose, then it is a net of individuals acting behind the scenes. For all we know, they might be in Silverholde as well." Nodding at Eleres, he added, "A cult, a society, anyone able to perform, as you said, rituals unapproved of."

Seemingly bored at their reasoning, Sybbyl drummed her fingernails against the surface of the table. "It does not explain where our men are now, Angefort."

The old lord felt her concern. The people he lost had trained under her as well, not only him. "Having been stalled in the forest, we decided to not ride to Courtbridge during the night for a comfortable stop the following day at the Guards of the River's," Arther went on with his explanation. "We decided to stop at the Rosenfield castle, where we…" He swallowed slowly, licking his lips and shaking his head to himself. "Where we were attacked."

He heard whispers around him, and a wave of incomprehension hit him in the chest.

"For the Good Gods' sake, by whom?" Sir Ferrand asked.

"I have no idea," Lord Angefort admitted. "Bolts came flying at us from the battlements, and before we knew it, the portcullis was being closed on what seemed to be crawling corpses of men who appeared from the ground, sprouted from the well. The great hall took fire as if the fireplace had exploded on us, and soon, we were outnumbered," he explained with a strangled voice. "Our men," he stated, looking straight into Sybbyl's eyes, "perished right at that moment. Those who returned with me and Lord Theliel are the only ones who survived."

"Ridiculous," the young woman beside him whispered. "No owl has reached the Pavilion with a message saying that the Rosenfield castle has been burned down. Lord Lionhelm himself would have reported it; doesn't Strongshore rise high above the Wilderose forest and its wooded meadow?"

"The castle is, in fact, intact."

The heavy silence that filled the room was only background noise for the loud thoughts of those who stared at him with wide, confused eyes. Angefort confided in the fact that they believed him, but he couldn't blame them for the discomfort and dread they felt at that moment. He had shared the same feelings as well.

"Perhaps," Grandmaster Rodbertus suggested with a serious tone, "we ought to inform Matillis."

The other members of the Regency gasped around him, and Chief Eleres promptly waved his hand at him. "Mad Matillis? No," he shook his head several times at the idea. "We secure the area around Wilderose and prohibit the entrance to anyone who dares walk inside the castle. As for the incident in the forest, I will scout ahead myself as it is already part of what I investigate."

The Suppressor of War seemed to agree with him for once, which was not a usual scene to be seen at the Pavilion. "If supernatural rituals are involved, I believe that finding the culprits will bring more answers as to what happened in Wilderose. In the meantime, I suggest we do not let this information spread," she said, looking intently into Angefort's tired eyes.

"And how do you expect us to do so?" was his retort. "I can't just tell Lord Lionhelm that his best men vanished, a good portion of his cavalry. I swore to him as well as to the Regency. It can't be one without the other. I can't discard the friendship that ties me to that man."

"You will have to," Rodbertus confirmed with an authoritative tone. "Until we know more, it is not necessary to report these losses to Lord Lionhelm. The man is older than all of us here and as strong as he may be, the news could instigate the desire of riding to Wilderose himself. That cannot happen."

Chief Eleres glanced at the dejected-looking Secretary of the Regency, adding a plain, "The King must not know either, for very similar reasons."

Repressing the urge to dryly laugh at him, Lord Angefort nodded. "Fear not about that, Eleres."

"Now," he heard Sir Ferrand say, "about the Lionhelm boy, I suggest we let him pursue his activities for a couple more moons without reinstating him in his position. The way he abandoned the Regency was… unsettling, to say the least."

Lord Angefort sat in silence, his gloved hand toying with the hem of the aquamarine undershirt that peeked from under his plates, paying little attention to the conversation that carried on without any intervention of his. Theliel was not a problem in his eyes; Thierry Eleres' decision to wander off on his own to find out more was. However, there was little he could do to impede him. The Surveillance was not his to command. Only King Helias would have the power to tell him to stay clear from Wilderose, and the monarch's judgment was not, sadly, an option to be taken into consideration.

Arther Angefort felt older than he was, he realized, his other hand tracing the engraved words on the edge of the round table. One right, our fatherland.

Chapter XIII

EYES OF FAWN

"Where is it?" the young lady pressed. "By the Oracle, Lyzon! My heels."

Tecla Lionhelm stared at her reflection with panicked, yet excited eyes. Her blue-stained, hazel orbs took in her reflection in the mirror that was almost as tall as the walls of her bed-chamber. She stood straight with her hands on her hips as the maids adjusted her dress around her body while she tormented Lyzon with every little request she could think of. To say she was nervous was an understatement. She had never had a ball in her honor. Never before had so many eyes been eager to see her, the last Lionhelm, the little child of the family, the one her father's knights and their ladies called the Mud Princess, the simple people's shy friend.

One of the maids secured the iron-braced corset around her with sharp, quick tugs on the long laces at the back. She felt her chest constrict with each movement, the thin fabric of her underdress clinging to her pale skin. Another woman promptly came up to her with a net underskirt and Tecla held on the other maid's hand for balance as she slipped into it. She had just started getting dressed and she already felt hot, courtesy of the thick garters that squeezed around her legs. Lyzon came back with a pair of short-heeled, black shoes with flowery-laced patterns that soon hugged her small feet. The maid that had been lacing her corset proceeded with draping the layers of her skirt on top of the net, the light golden color complimenting Tecla's eyes. The girl straightened her arms behind her as the maids slid the top part of her dress over her arms, carefully buttoning it over the corset, and pinning it against the skirt and underskirt. The light blue fabric was highlighted by the white daisy pattern all over it and the loose, three-quarter sleeves lined with pearl-colored lace. Around her cleavage, more lace fluttered against her skin, connecting with the front part of the dress to form a perfect triangular shape and run down her waist, where the top piece flared and cascaded down her skirt, the hem of it coming half-way down her legs and making her backside look rounder.

  Tecla wore no jewelry aside from the Darling Mind that had been braided into her hair earlier. Donning a less conservative hairstyle, her long, light chestnut hair had been divided into two parts, the top one braided around the back of her head and the lengths cascading around her shoulders, with yellow daisies made of amber raining down her locks. The pendant her father had gifted her sat on top of her crown of braids, the green and blue colors shining under the candlelight.

    Lyzon applied a light, rosy powder on her cheekbones before taking a small brush wet with what smelled like lavender oil and carefully applied it on the girl's eyebrows and curly lashes. Tecla could already feel herself relaxing thanks to the soothing scent.

    "How do I look?" she whispered. "Is it time?"

    The black-haired woman smiled at her and placed a reassuring hand on her shoulder. "It is. The young lady looks like a grown lady."

    The distant music playing in Strongshore's ballroom reached Tecla's ears as she walked carefully and slowly from her apartments to the Great Gardens. Violins and cellos played tunes she had heard only at others' official ceremonies and promises of holy matrimony. The musicians who had been invited were from Silverholde, from Rainier's Pavilion. They were the King's masters of strings, the ones whom she thought to have been part of a tale from another era, with their mechanical instruments that ticked like clocks and filled the rooms with melodies that made her chest grow tighter.

    Tecla walked alone, the chill breeze that gave her goosebumps accompanying her until she crossed the Great Gardens, following the stone path, and went straight into a much larger room with walls that were painted in House Lionhelm's colors from floor to ceiling. Depictions of nature and the Silver Lands covered every inch of the walls where they were not interrupted by rows of tall windows that let the starlight in. A few tables had been readied for the supper of the noble lords and their advisors, while the other guests were welcomed in the great hall and all around Strongshore's encampment.

The master of the ceremony called for attention the moment Tecla walked in, her eyes searching for her father's. Lord Tithan was seated with the rest of their family at the central table, the biggest round table in the room. The lords of the Silver Lands who had been invited stood behind their chairs, as they were not allowed to sit until the opening ceremony was over.

"Lady Tecla Lionhelm," the man behind her who wore more layers of lace than she did announced.

Tecla wet her lips, reminding herself that she had rehearsed for this. She could feel her mother's stare in the distance.

"Ladies and Lords of the Silver Lands," she timidly spoke, raising her voice with each syllable. "I welcome you to Strongshore on behalf of my father, Lord Tithan Lionhelm, and humbly thank you for your presence."

Sitting next to Tesfira, she saw her brother Theliel wink at her, his way of telling her that she had done it right.

One of their guests moved to stand next to his table, and the master of the ceremony announced, "Lord Arther Angefort of Limemeadow."

"Lady Tecla," the Regency commander greeted her with a fatherly smile. "It is an honor for my house to be present tonight. May I introduce my nephew?" he spoke solemnly, extending an arm in the direction of the young man who stood next to him, "Jarvis Angefort, son of my younger brother Amaud."

A boy of her age bowed his head at her, messy brown bangs falling over his forehead. He looked as shy and uncomfortable as she was, and he directed a meek smile at her.

"It is my pleasure to meet you, young lord Jarvis," Tecla said.

"Lady Tecla," the young man spoke. "To thank you for your hospitality, the people of Limemeadow offer you silks and pearls from our coasts, praying that they suit your liking."

At that moment, Tecla realized that lined up against the wall adjacent to where the master of the ceremony was, every lord's steward stood quietly with presents in hands. The man who wore the black and grey colors of House Angefort came forward, placing a glass box on the marble floor and opening it for her.

Before she knew it, the master of the ceremony had already introduced the next guest. "Lord Destrian Snowmantle of Founder's Breach."

A man who had to be Tylennald's age came forward with a mature and serious look on his face. "Lady Tecla, the portraits of you that reached the West pale in comparison to your beauty. Your lord father told us that you are a woman of wisdom as well, so we offer you our original collection of hand-written songs and poems of Old Calaris, which were in our custody for centuries."

Her eyebrows shot up in sheer interest, finding herself at a loss of words. A part of her wanted to snatch the books and run into her father's observatory to read, but she settled for a polite answer instead.

The introductions went on for several moments, and Tecla realized just how many minor houses served the major ones she knew, but much to her disappointment, she saw no one from the distant Rain Lands.

"Lord Ja—" the master of the ceremony behind her cleared his throat, his googly eyes going over his list of guests, frowning as he got lost. "Lord Sóley Rochelac of Noir… mont…"

The ballroom fell silent, a couple of whispers reaching Tecla's ears. She scanned the crowd of guests from where she stood, near the center of the room, only to notice that no one moved.

"Pardon," the man behind her muttered. "A terrible mistake on my part." Moving to the next name, the master of ceremony announced, "The Sons of Ferngrunn of the Sand Towers; Thaum, Remm, and Mokr."

Three men emerged from the table behind Lord Angefort's. They were tanned and sunflower blonde-haired, Tecla noticed as they walked forward. Their locks were longer than hers and matted, something she had never seen before. The older two were taller than any other man in the room, and the youngest of the three reached Lord Tithan's towering height. Their formal attire was unlike the other lords' chosen garments. Their warm jackets with snow-colored fur collars were open and reached only above their waists. The leather brown and bright yellow colors they displayed gave them an almost tribal look, but what caught Tecla's eye in a way that caused her already pink cheeks to flush was the fact that they wore nothing under their jackets. Scarred skin and defined muscles were showing and for a moment she wondered why she seemed to be the only one surprised by it.

She had no idea who these men were.

"Lady Tecla," the eldest of the three brothers spoke with a raucous voice and an accent so heavy it was difficult for her to decipher her name. "My brothers and I have heard of your pious heart. We bring you the Leaf of the Serpent, from the Vale of the Gods."

When Tecla saw the contents of the small wooden box she was shown, her brow furrowed. The scent the dried leaves emanated was inebriating, but she failed to see their use. Glancing back at the master of the ceremony who gave her a lopsided smile, she sent him a questioning look.

"For smoking, my lady."

"Excuse me?"

"The people of the Sand Towers worship ancient, mysterious beings that live under the sand. The Leaf of the Serpent is a plant that grows only in the Dark Barrens, the vast desert that surrounds their lands. It is said to have miraculous, healing properties."

Smiling back at the eldest Son of Ferngrunn, Tecla apologized, "Pardon my lack of knowledge, Lord Thaum, and thank you for the sacred leaves. I would love to hear more about your beliefs and culture. It is not often that we meet northeasterners in Strongshore."

Thaum offered her a nod, his bright honey eyes glinting. "Not lord," he rasped. "Only son."

Tecla bowed her head in false understanding, deciding that she needed to ask Educator Tomas more about the Sand Towers. She hated feeling so ignorant.

Her hazel eyes lingered for a few more moments on the Ferngrunn man as she walked to her table, taking the seat that was hers between her brother Theliel and Tesfira's son, Deril. Her father sat across from her at the round table, whose content smile had never left his lips. Tithan Lionhelm stood up, acknowledging their guests and bringing his silver chalice up.

"Enough with the etiquette," he spoke loudly, exchanging playful smiles with the lords he had known for a lifetime. "Is it not the time for us all to feast?"

Cheers and laughter erupted all around him, followed by clapping and the sound of chairs being dragged.

"To Lord Lionhelm!"

The musicians who had never stopped playing a soft tune moved on to a more joyful one, and soon the maids dressed almost as finely as the Lionhelms entered with large trays of food.

Tecla felt a warmth she had never experienced before fill her chest, and her eyes trailed from the laughter that left his father's lips, to the serene expression on her mother's face. Thaesonwald hadn't been able to join them, as he felt too weak still, or so she heard. His eldest son Tiran sat next to Lady Voladea instead. Tylennald and Wallysa, who had traveled alongside Lord Angefort, sat in silence, sometimes whispering to each other before exchanging pleasantries with her sister Tesfira, who often pursed her lips together as if to feel her bright red lipstick. Her son Deril ate quietly next to Tecla, and Theliel gently nudged his little sister with his elbow.

"Not bad, Tecla," he praised her. "You did better than Tesfira."

She chuckled at that. "How so?"

"I remembered she showed up a little late, and well, she lacked in the smile department."

Tecla wanted to ruffle his medium-length hair. "That's not nice to say."

"I meant no offense," Theliel added, looking at Deril.

The black-haired young man answered with a small shrug. "I cannot disagree, uncle Theliel," he said with a lopsided smile of his own.

Tecla paid no attention to the rest of their conversation, her focus solely on the music that played and on the rather candid, peaceful atmosphere that surrounded her family. She wasn't familiar with it, as her older siblings were always preoccupied with other matters that never involved her, and she was rarely interested in their lives. Her father seemed to be feeling well too, having not heard him cough at all. She took a mouthful of the stuffed, boiled ostrich egg in her plate, silently entertaining herself by watching the other lords and the company of their choice. She noted how Lord Angefort's nephew looked a lot like him, with their tall noses and square jaws, but it was Thaum's long locks that truly intrigued her. Tecla didn't catch herself staring at the man until her hazel orbs connected with his youngest brother's fawn eyes; Mokr flashed her a mischievous smile.

"Anyone caught your attention?" she heard Lady Voladea ask her.

"Don't push it," her father instantly warned, his voice void of any meaningful threat.

Her lady mother ignored him, awaiting an answer from her as she brought her glass of wine to her lips.

"I am afraid not, Mother," Tecla replied, her knife poking at the large slices of mushroom inside the egg.

"There will be plenty of time to get acquainted with most of them," Tesfira chimed in, brushing a curly lock behind her ear when it got slightly stuck in her large, round earring.

Theliel clicked his tongue against his teeth, leaning back into his cushioned chair. His mind seemed to be elsewhere, and Tecla placed her hand on top of his.

"How are things in the capital? I know you didn't want to go back."

"I didn't," he admitted, leaning in and hunching his back a little due to the height difference. "But Father tells me you will soon keep me company. I might lose my mind without you," he joked half-heartedly. "Honestly," he said in a more serious tone, moving his hand to hold hers, "I wish for you to stay at the Regency, with me," he confessed. "No offense to these folks," Theliel added with a glance at the tables behind theirs, "but your place is not in one of their castles."

    The young girl remained silent, a part of her swelling with pride. Thoughts of marriage had never been pleasant to her, especially after what happened in Oracle Hill, but it was too soon for her to decide. She hadn't even been to the capital yet. If she had to choose at that precise moment, surely spending the rest of her life somewhere close to her brother sounded more agreeable than following the rules of a hypothetical husband.

    The clinking of the cutlery and the chatter soon made room for louder strings and stronger beverages, a cloud of smoke rising from the tables of the lords who so indulged in the wild plants of the Red Continent and their dried leaves.

    Tecla found herself spending more time talking with Theliel and Lord Angefort, whose nephew turned out to be pleasant to be around. She marveled at the way her brother seemed to know every guest of theirs, aside from a couple of exceptions. She figured that it must have been his years at the Regency, where he dealt with lords from all over the continent, but there was probably a hidden social talent of his. Theliel introduced her properly to Lord Snowmantle of Founder's Breach, telling her how the man had been supervising the education of Tylennald's son, Terrel. They shared tales of the Breach and its history before the creation of the Regency, explaining to her that the name didn't come from the Rough Rill's dividing streams at the edge of the western coast, but because it was the only location where the tall walls made of Quiet Tear stones had been broken in, centuries and centuries ago.

Tecla's head soon reeled with amusement and too many cups of wine, but her father's voice quickly interrupted her laugh and loud chatting. "I shall not stay much longer, Tecla," Tithan told her quietly. "But before I go, I must ask you to honor your old father with a dance."

Her father led her to the center of the ballroom, the other merry participants stopping in their tracks and making room for them. Tecla wanted to laugh at the fact that she barely reached her father's collarbone. The towering man who wore soft furs and all his military medals on his chest, from conquests and campaigns she had only heard of, held her hands high above her head, waiting for the five-man orchestra to play the one song that would truly get the ball started, The Birth of Loveleen.

The quick pace of the ticking violins and mechanical cellos had Tecla twirl only half-way, first left and then right, her palms coming to rest flat against her father's before Tithan hooked one strong arm around her waist, walking her backward before spinning her around briefly. He continued to lead the dance with her back against his chest, their joined hands reaching out towards the crowd, who quickly joined in one of the most famous couple dances of the Silver Lands.

"I picked this one for you," Tithan told his daughter, his thumb grazing her round cheek before they both took three steps away from each other then joined hands again several times to the tempo of the music. "It may not be a melody of our lands, but Loveleen Rochelac reminds me of you."

Tecla tilted her head, resting her back against her father's chest once more. "I have studied the Rochelacs' ancestry," she told him. "But Loveleen Rochelac was an only child. I can't say the same for me."

"She was the only child Lord Zander had ever wanted, and the one he changed laws for so that her descendants would remain Rochelacs," Tithan corrected her. "Every day I convince myself more that if there was such a thing as a true Lionhelm, that person would be you."

His daughter frowned at his words, craning her neck to take a look at the old lord's determined face.

"You are curious, you care not about what others plan around you, you follow your instinct to choose your path," he elaborated, slowing the pace of their dance. "You may be young, Tecla, but you are more man than woman in this world," he told her, his eyes never leaving her face. "You only surround yourself with those you value. You must not change," he all but commanded her, tightening his hands around hers. "And you will never yield."

Tecla came to a halt, sliding her arms around her father's shoulders as she embraced him, pressing the side of her face against his chest in a silent promise.

Tithan Lionhelm excused himself first, leaving the ballroom with no one following him. Tecla had no time to think about the meaning of the words he just spoke to her, as Jarvis Angefort invited her for the next dance, only to be followed by Theliel himself who abhorred the idea of having to dance with Tesfira instead or one of the ladies that accompanied their guests.

It was only in the middle of the night that Tecla decided to rest, her feet hurting and her throat dry. She excused herself from a dull conversation with her sister and other women whose names Tecla could not remember, grabbing her refilled cup of wine before heading towards the terrace. The freezing wind was the reason no one else had been spending time outside, but Tecla didn't mind the quiet. She was certain it wouldn't be long until her legs wouldn't be able to hold her up anymore. She would enjoy one last drink before retreating herself, she figured silently as she stared at the calm sea. It was so dark that it became one with the sky.

Soft footsteps came up behind her, and a voice she had not heard before reached her ears. "I was told the palace on the cliff would be covered in auburn vines and green branches. I am disappointed to see plain, ivory columns with no mystic cascade over them."

Tecla spun around, her darkened eyes meeting the genuine sand stare of Mokr of Ferngrunn, the youngest of the Sons. "How old are you?" she asked him bluntly, taking in his youthful face and overly muscular body.

Mokr laughed. "Thirteen."

He was only a year younger than her. "Impressive," Tecla commented. "You have the physique of a grown-up soldier." Shaking her head at herself, she addressed his comment. "Strongshore was the way you described many centuries ago. I've read about it, seen paintings about it, but sadly, the only greenery we have now is in the Great Gardens and every apartment's gardens."

Mokr nodded, his short, matted hair tickling his broad shoulders. "I am under the impression that you do not know much about the Sand Towers, is that correct?"

Tecla acquiesced slowly, realizing that contrary to his eldest brother, the boy before her spoke without an accent.

"We received an invitation from Lady Lionhelm, but her insistent tone is not the reason why we agreed on coming," the young man explained, walking up to the railing of the terrace and sitting on it. "The elder worshippers of our temple in Hvallatr told my brother Thaum that the Sand Towers were to emerge from the Dark Barrens at the hands of a woman born in the heart of the sea, from faraway, southeastern lands," Mokr admitted to her with a faithful tone. "Our lands haven't been the subject of any good omen since the Crimson Crystal Wars, before the crowning of Aleyne Rainier."

"You think I match the description," Tecla concluded with an arched eyebrow.

Mokr let a canine tooth graze his lower lip as he stared at her. "I didn't think I also needed to list the many political reasons that would make the union between our lands a profitable agreement, but if you insist…"

Tecla waved at him, discarding that thought. "I appreciate your honesty, kind Mokr. I am sure the long way to the South has not been an easy one. The least I can do is take your offer into serious consideration," she told him as diplomatically as she could.

"The Sons of Ferngrunn don't make offers," Mokr corrected her promptly. "Thaum, Remm, and I are the leaders of the one tribe named to rule all the others. We can do so because we follow the will of the Deities, and if the Deities inch us in a particular direction, we will not relent until we reach it.

"It meant more than you can imagine, for my brother Thaum to leave the Sand Towers to personally meet you. He even learned the modern tongue while we were on our way to come here," he added with a lighter tone, causing Tecla's lips to curve up.

"As I said before," the young Lionhelm cut their conversation short, heading inside, "impressive.

"You Sons of Ferngrunn truly are."

✷✷✷

Ragged breathing filled the otherwise quiet bed-chamber, the candlelight on the closest end table flickering with every exhale. Thaesonwald Lionhelm awoke before dawn, feeling his throat dry. His left hand reached out for the tray that had been left there by Healer Martus, a faint groan leaving his lips when he realized that the jug of water was empty. The single light only showed him the portrait that hung above the table, a poor depiction of his younger days at the side of his wife, Gwethana. Thaesonwald's saggy eyelids felt heavier, and his hazel eyes took in his younger appearance. He had been donning the military armor of the family, a silvery gold helm tucked between his side and the crook of his elbow as he stood next to Gwethana, her dark hair safely hidden under a headpiece. She held their newborn son, Perren, in her arms, while a three-year-old Tiran clutched her arm.

The double doors of his room were opened, and Thaesonwald tried to sit up, using his left arm for support but failed miserably. "Hello?" he croaked out.

"Wald," his father's voice tried to reassure him. "Don't move too much."

Blinking at the darkness, the eldest Lionhelm son let out a breath he didn't know he was holding until his father sat down next to him, propping his elbows on his knees.

"You took your time," the strawberry-blonde man chuckled.

"It is not easy to visit you in private when all your mother does is fret about you," Tithan joked in return, a large hand of his resting on his son's still leg. "Then your sister was here, then Tylennald was here… I figured visiting you at this hour would be best."

Thaesonwald's lips curved up but only the left side moved, never the right side. "It is around this time that I used to get up for the early encampment training. I fear that is the only habit I took after you."

"One is better than none."

A silence that lasted for quite some time settled between them, neither of the two knowing how to speak with the other. Thaesonwald had spent most of his younger days without his father's attention and care, being looked after by educators and master-at-arms who would try to make him a man before the time was right. Tithan Lionhelm had been focused on the establishment of the Regency, following King Helias' orders, and by the time Tithan started spending more time in Strongshore, he had met Emelyne, the woman who brought Theliel into the family. Thaesonwald held no grudge against his father and was rather fond of all his siblings, even those he spent little time with, but staring at the old lord before him, he realized the two of them didn't truly know each other.

"How was the ball in Tecla's honor?" Thaesonwald asked. "I am sure she was beautiful."

"She was," Tithan answered with a nod and a smile. "I feel she was happy to spend a family evening before she has to go to Silverholde."

"Is Tecla joining the Regency?"

Tithan only shrugged. "Perhaps. One day."

Thaesonwald closed his tired eyes. "You must be proud," he said with a hint of pride himself. "She is a good child. I regret not being half the man you wanted me to be."

Lord Tithan stood up, walking up to the tall windows. It was still dark as night outside. "Don't be," he commanded. "You have the name of my brother. He had a kind heart, a shy personality, and a body too frail for battle. When I heard that he had drowned on his way to the Red Continent, to fight off the coastal tribes that attempted to cross the Tinted Bay and reach the Silver Lands, I believed the men who told me he had been refused a safe escape on the boat after their ship sank. Too many men on a boat too small." Tithan glanced back at his son, the resentment clear in his eyes. "When I was back myself and my father passed away, I sentenced them, but one of them told me, before I severed his head, that Thaesonwald had never made it to the boat. He swam too slow and the waves were too big."

"Did you believe him?"

"Men who are about to die would tell you their deepest secrets and the ugliest truth if it would save their lives. Regardless, such a tragic fate suited my brother more. He was loved by his men and he loved them in return; he would have left his spot on the boat in favor of anyone else. I can't imagine anyone denying him a spot on a lifeboat."

"Some of us are not meant for harsh positions like ours."

Thaesonwald's eyes searched for his father's. "I wasn't half the man my uncle was either. I have been a poorly skilled fighter, a terrible husband, an absent father. You were right, you know? I drank too much, smoked too much, and cared too little. And here I am today; a cripple has better chances of survival than me. I can't even pour myself a glass of water."

His father moved closer, his hand squeezing his left shoulder so he could feel it. "You are my son," Tithan told him with a warm tone. "You have lived as freely as it was allowed. I have no regrets, and neither should you."

Thaesonwald wet his lips, but before he could come up with a reply, his father left his side, telling him to rest some more. The strawberry-blonde man felt tears prickle at the corner of his left eye, and he let his heavy eyelids flutter close. The silence that filled his bed-chamber once more made him feel as if he had dreamed the entire conversation as though his father had never been there in the first place. The emptiness inside him reflected the void around him. He realized that this what was he deserved; for no one to be waiting at his side. No woman, no son, no one. Only the ghost of his father.

The candlelight vanished with a whiff of air, and Thaesonwald glanced to the side. He didn't recall his father open the window. "Father? Are you back?"

Someone was standing next to him; he could not see them, but their presence was as real as his father's had been. The skies were still dark and the palace asleep. Yet, someone very awake was beside him, and Thaesonwald's tired old eyes could not make out who they were.

"Father?"

The soft and light fabric that covered his face he didn't expect, and soon the pressure that was applied against him made it extremely hard for him to breathe. His left arm slapped around his side, reaching out to grab the person who had just pressed one of his pillows against his face. He felt furs and silk, and his fingers curled around what seemed to be a large belt. His vocal cords were strained and his body too weak to scream and fight. Thaesonwald tried to push the pillow away, but a hand stronger than him pinned his wrist against his stomach. His mind became foggy and his throat hurt. His left leg kicked under the bedsheets, only to convulse.

"It pains me more than you can imagine," were the last words he heard as his fingers twitched.

Chapter XIV

THE SOUND OF BONES

The Regency's Surveillance's headquarters were filled with soft chatter and clinking sounds as the officers that entered for their shift exchanged words with those who brought reports from all over the continent. The golden drapes that hung from the wall and bore the coat-of-arms of the Regency swung slightly as doors swung and windows were opened, and sitting at his desk near the entrance, Opherus Goldsnout felt a little chilly despite his heavy clothing. It snowed the previous day, and the skies were still grey. He had lighted the oil lamp on the table, narrowing his emerald eyes at the report he was reading. He pursed his lips as he focused, the dimples on his chin deepening.

The report came from Rainier's End, and he was growing concerned. A large number of people seemed to not be paying the taxes they should have, yet at the same time, the poorer areas of the town claimed to have less and less coin to spend.

Pickpocketing cases had increased by six times in the last three months, and the most violent inhabitants even indulged in burglary and brawls in public. It made little sense to Goldsnout since he read the Regency's reports on increased profit from trade routes, so he wasn't sure what conclusion he could draw for Chief Eleres. A part of him wanted to inspect the town himself if only to stop by Miss Rantha's shelter to see how she was doing, but his chief was going to demote him on the spot if he mentioned adventuring on his own once again.

Goldsnout scratched his unruly red mane with a gloved hand, his armor clinking with every movement he made. Another officer walked up to his desk, wearing the same armor and golden colors as Goldsnout, and cleared his throat. "Opherus, there is a woman at the entrance asking to speak with you," he whispered. "She has your pass."

The redhead blinked at him, dropping the report. He stared at his peer, Officer Gulmont, and asked, "Are you sure? What does she look like?"

Before the black-haired man in front of him could answer, said woman peeked inside through the door left ajar, her big eyes looking at Goldsnout in a mixture of fear and relief. "I apologize," she whispered.

"Miss Rantha," Goldsnout almost gasped at the sight of the young healer. Turning to Gulmont, he said, "I'll be outside for a few moments."

Ignoring the whispers that he was the subject of, the man strode past the doors, making sure to close them before bowing his head. "Miss Rantha," he greeted her once more. "Is everything alright?"

Noting the distraught look on her face, he nearly chastised himself. "You wouldn't be here if it were," he whispered, gently placing a hand against her back to take their meeting to a more private room.

Rantha kept her head low, the slump of her shoulders indicating that she was deeply worried, if not worse. She barely looked around the meeting room Goldsnout had picked and simply followed the officer who offered her a seat at the long, rectangular table. The shelves around them were full of folders and manuals, but her mind was elsewhere. Goldsnout sat next to her, their chairs turned so that they faced each other.

The redhead searched her eyes in silence. "Would you like something to drink? Red Edgemeran tea, perhaps?" he suggested, given the cold weather.

"Opherus, I…" Rantha swallowed hard, her eyes swelling with tears. "Yenny was murdered," she whispered, instantly covering her mouth as a sob pierced her throat. "My apprentice," she cried out, "Yenny, she—"

"Easy, easy," the officer spoke softly, placing a steady hand on her shaking shoulder. "Tell me everything from the beginning, otherwise it will be hard for me to help you."

Rantha looked at him, the anger and confusion twisting her face. "I don't know what happened," she confessed. "She went to the town center to have dinner at the central inn, and the following morning she was found dead. It looked like she had fallen from the highest story of the inn," she explained between choked sobs.

Hating himself for suggesting it when it was mandatory, Goldsnout said, "Most deaths are the results of accidents, Rantha."

"It was not!" the woman snapped, her fists clenching the fabric of her brown skirt. "I saw her body. She was wounded, with a deep gash on her thigh, like a stab wound. Her skirt was coated in blood coming from…" Rantha swallowed the bile that started collecting in her throat. "Coming from her inner thighs."

The description sounded too familiar to Goldsnout. Whilst he couldn't be sure about the inner thigh area of the girl from Beggar's Pool due to all the blood that he saw on and around the corpse, the stabbing part was undoubtedly a pattern. He and Chief Eleres had come across a similar situation in Three Crosses as they returned from the Sand Towers. Whoever did it was traveling to the South, but there was one issue; he couldn't investigate.

Rubbing her shoulder, Goldsnout asked, "Does Yenny—did she have any family left?"

Rantha shook her head. "No, not that I know of. Why?"

With an apologetic stare, the officer explained, "I can't start anything without the family's consent. Especially if no one saw her interact with a possible suspect; you know the law. Unless you are caught red-handed, the simple people—"

"She was at an inn," Rantha cut his babble short. "She could have talked to an indefinite number of people," she said, repeating the same words the innkeeper had spoken to her when she found out. "Yenny lived with me. She lived with me since she was twelve years of age. Don't I count as family?" the curly-haired woman all but pleaded.

Feeling like the scum he didn't want to be, Goldsnout's stare fell on her hands. Her very dark hands. "Rantha, you are… You are—"

"A slave?" she scoffed, more tears running down her cheeks. "I can't believe it—I served Sir Rosenbane since I was a girl. He never treated me nor my family any differently than he treated his equal; and yet, without him, I am just…" Standing up abruptly, Rantha wiped her cheeks with the back of her hand. "I am sorry. I shouldn't have come here."

"Hold on," Goldsnout stopped her from leaving, tugging on her wrist and blocking her path. "You need to calm down. I never said I wouldn't help you and just because I must follow some rules, it doesn't mean I consider you inferior; I thought that much was clear," he said in a serious tone. "I haven't forgotten about the two girls who got mauled in the Fog Lands, and I won't forget about Yenny, either. I simply can't work on it officially," he spelled out for her. "I need to find the beast who did this to them and only then the Surveillance can act."

Inhaling deeply, Rantha nodded at his words, her left hand toying with the pass he had given her.

"Are you sure Yenny is all that is on your mind? You seem frightened, or worried about something else."

She looked straight into his light green eyes. Yenny wasn't the only person on her mind, but she couldn't bring herself to voice it. Jascha's words and behavior were still fresh on her mind and skin, and hearing Goldsnout tell her that she didn't have any right to summon the Surveillance because she was not related to the girl who was assaulted, coupled with her lesser and foreign origins, was a blow she was unable to parry at that moment. She had always known the law, but for some reason, something had been broken inside of her, and she was having a hard time keeping it together.

"Everything else is regular," she told Goldsnout.

The redhead didn't seem to buy her answer. "What about the man in your care, Jascha; did he get any better? And your other apprentices, how are they?"

"Jascha left on the same day Yenny was killed," Rantha replied without batting an eyelid. "We never managed to find a cure; he wasn't ill. Yenny theorized that he might have been —" Sighing at her rambling state, the curly-haired woman shrugged. "It doesn't matter."

"On the same day," Goldsnout repeated.

Their eyes met, and they thought in silence for what felt like a whole day and a whole night. It was a bold suggestion, the Regency officer realized, but the man had already been present in Beggar's Pool, where Loveleen was killed outside her home.

He even admitted speaking with her. However, Rantha didn't seem as convinced.

"Jascha left hours before," she explained. "He wanted to be as far from us as possible, so I don't think he stopped at the inn and happened to meet her."

The young man nodded faintly. "I understand."

He wasn't about to exclude the possibility that Jascha was the assailant, but at the same time, he couldn't let his judgment be clouded by assumptions caused by what looked like a series of coincidences. Chief Eleres' input would be incredibly fruitful on this, but Goldsnout was sure that if he mentioned these incidents once more, the chief would have his head, at least figuratively speaking. The old man had told him the previous day to get his brain into gear, for they would leave in three days for Wilderose. This was not the moment to upset him.

Then again, Rainier's End was only a day away from the capital. "Miss Rantha," he decided. "If you will wait till noon when my shift ends, we can ride to Rainier's End together. I won't be needed in the capital for the next couple of days; that leaves enough time for me to speak with some potential witnesses and be back for duty," he offered with a slight bow of his head.

At a loss for words, the dark-skinned healer nodded watching him search the pockets of his cloak.

"Kindly wait for me at the Shattered Ambry. Here," he handed her a bag of silvers, which she politely refused. "I insist. The tavern behind the Regency's Athenaeum is quite pricey."

Opherus Goldsnout watched the woman walk out but his mind was already full of thoughts. He had partially lied to her; he wasn't exempted from work until he and Chief Eleres would leave for the South, but he had to find someone to cover his shift for him. He had promised her that she could reach out to him if need be, and he wasn't about to let her down. Besides, he had decided long before they met that the butchering of these girls couldn't be left unpunished. Cold-blooded murder was not something that he could just ignore; that, and whatever other torture had been inflicted on the victims.

Goldsnout entered the room filled with other officers and sat at his desk. His hands rested idly on the surface, the reports he had been reading completely forgotten. Two officers sat across from him, Gulmont and another dark-haired male who went by the name of Longspire. The three of them had been falling in the same ranks since they joined the Surveillance, but the red-haired officer never truly bonded with anyone.

The shorter of the two, Longspire, rested his chin in his hand. "So, who was that?"

"Just a friend," Goldsnout retorted absentmindedly.

"Like so," Gulmont joined in. "She must be a close friend for you to hand her your pass. Does Chief Eleres know?"

"Obviously," the other man replied for Goldsnout. "This is Eleres' golden boy we're talking about."

Goldsnout glowered at the two, failing at being menacing. "Quit it, you two."

"But you know it's true," Longspire argued. "He commands you to follow him everywhere and it has been this way for nearly a year. I wouldn't be surprised to see you become a senior officer before we do."

There was little he could retort to contradict him. Opherus had been traveling and training alongside their chief for so long, he hadn't been able to return home. He had sent many owls to his mother in Limemeadow, but he had yet to visit her. His family had never been a big one; it had always been him and his mother since his little brother passed away due to the fever. He often wondered if his mother felt lonely or worse, abandoned, but he couldn't step down just now. She wouldn't want that; he was sure of it. With the silvers he would earn by ranking up, he was sure he could afford a little house in the capital for them to live closer to each other.

Interrupting his thoughts, Gulmont asked, "Hey, do you know if some of Lord Angefort's men stayed in Strongshore?"

Frowning, the redhead shrugged. "I haven't heard anything of the sort. Why?"

"My brother hasn't returned yet and I received no message from him. It is unlike him."

Longspire leaned back in his seat, crossing his arms behind his head, his double chin coming forward. "Lord Lionhelm probably removed some of his best soldiers from the Regency's army. I wouldn't put it past him to pull a stunt like that until our King names him his successor."

Two pairs of green eyes widened at his words, and Gulmont slammed his fist on the table, causing Goldsnout's ink bottle to fall on the floor. "Watch your mouth, Joss."

"Had Lord Lionhelm wanted to become King Helias' heir to see his family rise to power, he wouldn't have invested so much in building the Regency."

The chubbier man snorted. "Back then the Rochelacs hadn't lost their mind yet. They would have fought the bastards without any second thought, just like during the Crimson Crystal Wars. Now the Rochelacs are either dead or about to die, seeing how no one has seen a living soul in Noirmont for ages. Reminds me of our own King," he disdainfully commented. "What's stopping the cats from eating mice?"

"Disrespectful brat," Gulmont hissed.

"Ignore him, Theod," Goldsnout sighed out as he glanced out the window.

Lords' feuds were none of his concern. He very well knew that some sympathized less with the Lionhelms than most did, but as far as he was concerned, he would support anyone and any institution that would keep prosperity and order in place. The Silver Lands had seen no war on their continent for nearly five hundred years, he reminded himself as he watched the snow coat the streets once again.

✳✳✳

As Jascha neared the northern gate of Silverholde, his Avoryon mount neighed and took a few steps backward. Pulling on the reins, the man who hid underneath the hood of his bear fur cloak whispered to the horse, his right hand patting its neck.

"It's alright. You can soon rest."

His gloved hand kept petting the animal as his black eyes stared at the two guards at the entrance of the city. He had known about them, but he hadn't quite decided what to tell them. He had studied the city long before he even began to ride south. If the underground tunnels that connected his home to the Pavilion hadn't been blocked, Jascha wouldn't have found himself in this type of situation, he inwardly told himself. A part of him wondered if the tunnels had been barred on the southern side as well, from Silverholde to Summerport, but ultimately, it was none of his concern. There were four main areas in the capital; Jehanel's Forum, Melisentia's Opera, Maugre's Arena, and Danyell's Athenaeum, the latter being his destination. Every area had been named after a Rainier, and they all had been built around the statue that rose from the center of the city. Paintings of Silverholde always featured the towering sculpture of Aleyne Rainier, the first King of the Silver Lands, often nicknamed the Founder of Silverholde, the Builder of the Pavilion, the Peacemaker of the Silver Lands. He had chosen to be depicted as the strong, bare rider of a half-dragon and half-bird creature also known as Iathienar. Jascha had grown up listening to the tales of the monster that opened its eyes and beak to swallow all light. To imagine that someone would be narcissistic enough to envision riding a dragon bird with feathers of steel without wearing any armor made him laugh.

Kicking his silver horse into motion, Jascha neared the gate. He had no other option. The two guards didn't acknowledge his presence until he was literally in their faces, ready to cross the entrance, but they lowered their spears, crossing them together to block his path.

"State your name," the one on his right ordered.

"Jascha, of Three Crosses," he half lied, his black eyes glancing back and forth between the two men who acted as if they hadn't heard him.

The guard on his left circled him in silence before returning to his spot. "I don't see any goods. You're not a trader. What is your business in the capital?"

"I thought the laws facilitated access to traders and explorers," Jascha pointed out.

"Northern dog," the guard on his right spat. "Trying to pass off for an explorer? What tells us that you aren't here to spread one of your nasty diseases?"

Jascha's eyes narrowed, his lips forming a thin line under his scarf as he bit back the nasty retort that tickled his lips.

"Even his horse is from the Avoryon Hills. These shits are usually packed with all sorts of illnesses. Too many centuries of inbreeding for a species that was already in a bad shape," the other guard joined in the dissing. "Maybe this scum too is a pile of shit to throw in the Rough Rill."

The two men laughed at that, their raspy voices echoing through their helmets and sounding like metallic gargles in Jascha's ears.

"Get lost," the one on the right ordered him. "Before I make you."

Tightening his grip on the reins, Jascha refused to obey. "You can't make me, as it is against your law," he retorted. "Chief Eleres has met me before. He will let me in."

The guard on the right was quick to react. With a deft move and a flick of his wrist, the spear hit Jascha straight against the back of his head before the flat end collided with the side of his face, successfully sending his head reeling. Jascha tasted blood where his teeth lacerated his tongue, and he counted the seconds till he could slice the man's throat.

"You think you can feed me lies to look like someone with connections?" the guard snarled. "I will not repeat myself. Remove your filthy asshole from Silverholde."

Jascha's hand was on the hilt of his dagger in a heartbeat, but the neighing of a horse that wasn't his stunned his impulse, and the two guards who blocked his way instantly backed off.

"What is going on here?" the bellowing voice of a woman asked with an authoritative tone. "Since when do we beat people at our gates?" she accused the two guards, her blue eyes scanning the bruise that was forming on Jascha's cheek.

"Sir Sybbyl Nobleleaf," the two men whispered their greetings, bowing deeply. "This man—"

"I don't want to hear it; it's the streets that should be kept under control with firmness and strength. Assaulting people who try to legally enter the gates is not what the Surveillance taught you, or is it?" the muscular knight reprimanded, the snow starting to cover her short blonde hair. "You," she addressed Jascha with a quick nod. "Any weapon to declare?"

Jascha wrinkled his nose. "No." Kicking his heel into the sapphire-eyed horse's side, he slowly strode past the two guards, unprepared for Sir Sybbyl's next words.

"Very nice dagger," she whispered, leaning in. "I'd better not catch you using it, northerner."

His black eyes glanced down at his side. The hilt was showing where his cloak had moved when he tried to reach for it.

❋❋❋

The scraping of Tithan's boots as he stopped on his way down the ladder of his library was louder than nails on a chalkboard. He quickly adjusted his glasses that threatened to slide down his nose before tightening his fingers around the step before his eyes. In his other hand was a copy of Grandmaster Rodbertus' 100 Untreatable Ailments of the Silver Continent, but he was quick to note that he hadn't grabbed the correct edition. He had meant to take the most recent one, but the spine of the tome stated this was the second to last version of the grandmaster's findings.

Tithan grunted, whispering to himself that he needed to focus, his heavy foot coming to rest on a higher step as he climbed back up. He paused for a moment, feeling the need to clear his throat a couple of times. His eyes looked at the floor underneath him; he was at least five feet above his desk, and he realized this was where Tecla would usually sit. A smile crossed his face, his features relaxing. Of course, she would like this perch, he figured. She could see everything from there; the vastness of the room, the painted marble floor, the heights from outside the tall windows. It also made sense that she nearly lost her balance once, although he wondered whether it was solely because of the towering point. She had seemed lost in her thoughts and daydreaming, her eyes unblinking.

And she was gone. Tecla left Strongshore and her father's lands for the first time since she was born, right after the ball held in her honor. She had decided she would prefer to travel with Theliel, who had to return to the Regency as soon as possible given his undefined position in the Treasure Council. Tecla would be gone for the next dawn and moon days, and she departed with an overly tired Lyzon and an all packed-up Fran, who had gathered Tecla's most used belongings and favorite silks in a rush.

Tithan pushed his weight upwards when his master-at-arms and guard entered the observatory room. Fantine stood at the doors with a frown marking her features and a worried, mournful look in her bright eyes.

"Lord Tithan, forgive me for the abrupt interruption."

"What is it, Fantine?" he asked, turning his head to the side but not quite facing her as it would prove to be difficult to not lose balance. "Remind me I still have a message I want you to deliver soon."

"My lord, how can I—" Tithan heard her bite back her words, and his frown intensified, creating more lines on his forehead and around his eyes. "Lord Thaesonwald has been found inanimate in his bed-chambers."

She must have noticed his slight jump or heard his breathing stop because within a blink she was at the bottom of the library's ladder, arm extended.

"Care, my lord, let me help you."

"It's alright, Fantine," he tried to reassure himself more than her. "It's alright," he repeated.

He stepped down slowly, his heart rate increasing with every beat. His breathing was more erratic as the news settled in his brain. He had to have misheard the warrior. He spoke to Wald only a few hours prior, and he had been fine. He had been lucid, talkative even for someone who had been out for many moons. Tithan dropped the book he was holding, the cough he was forcing down seizing his chest and making it impossible for him to breathe. He felt his saliva go down the wrong pipe, impeding him to swallow to try and calm his body down. He felt the ladder shake as Fantine tried to reach for him to help in the best way she could, her strong arms circling his chest from behind. She was talking to him, but he couldn't hear her properly.

    With the next fit, his foot slipped and his jaw collided with the wooden ladder. His bottom teeth hit the top row hard and fast, the gritting sending shivers down his entire body, and his full weight fell backward, trapping Fantine behind him and the floor as they collapsed down with a heavy, resounding thud and the sound of bones cracking.

Chapter XV

Ecliptic

The strangled sobbing of Lady Lionhelm filled the hallways of the palace. Muffled words and pleas mixed with the cries of a mother who had outlived her son. Tylennald walked in silence across the balconies that connected the different wings of his home, his black fur coat covering his otherwise light blue garments. His breathing came out in small puffs of air, reminding him of the winter that had just come to the southern lands. Wallysa walked behind him, equally silent, but his deep hazel eyes were focused on his brother's family. Lined up outside his bed-chambers, Lady Gwethana and her sons didn't acknowledge the presence of the three younger boys who remained at her side, confused and sad.

Tylennald stopped near them, his large hand resting on the youngest's shoulder. "Your father was a good man," he told him with a gentle smile before glancing at the other two. Turning to face the estranged wife of Thaesonwald, Tylennald asked, "What will happen to them?"

The widow merely shrugged; her hands folded in front of her. Her dark hair was tucked under a black and grey veil, making the harsh features of her face stand out. "What will happen to us?" she asked in return, her sons weeping in silence.

Tylennald nodded faintly. Gwethana had never had any form of relationship with Thaesonwald's family, the only man she respected, and perhaps even feared, being Tithan himself. But his father had had an accident and the news spread like wildfire within a few hours, sending both the household and their servants in a state of utter panic and shock. His sister-in-law's position could either be strengthened or weakened without her husband and Lord Lionhelm. On one hand, her son Tiran could prepare himself to take over, but without his mother's support and with the frail bond that connected them to the rest of the family, the attempt could easily prove to be a failure.

"You could return to Three Crosses," Tylennald offered.

For the first time since he met her, Gwethana smiled. Her upper lip curved up, but the glare in her eyes made it clear to him that she was not about to do just that. "That would please you greatly, wouldn't it, Brother?" she rhetorically asked. "Would you also suggest that I return alone while my sons stay with you?"

Tylennald peacefully raised a hand. "You are still the Lady of House Montel," he reminded her.

"Tiran, on the other hand, is very close to becoming the next Lord of Strongshore. We would all be happy to have you here as well, but you never seemed pleased to stay in the South."

Gwethana stepped closer, either to avoid the others listening to her hushed words or to properly make her point across. "My house swore allegiance to the Rochelacs long before your father united half the continent under his banner. Yet, I left my homeland to comply with my father's wishes. I did what was expected of me; marry your brother, raise his children, respect his family.

"All I received in return were his excuses as he bedded other women, but I refused to do what your mother did," she spelled out for him, glancing at the three boys who seemed distraught. "They will bid farewell to their father, then return to their mothers in those expensive, lavish mansions by the sea that Wald gifted them. But I will stay right where my sons are," she concluded with a firm tone. "I will die before I let you and your mother maneuver them as you please."

The bed-chamber doors were flung open, revealing a red-eyed, swollen-faced Lady Voladea. Her greying hair was in disarray, and the front of her tangerine dress completely wrinkled. "Guards," she ordered the men who lined the corridor. "Arrest this woman for the murder of Lord Thaesonwald."

Gwethana's eyes widened, and her look of anger left room for confusion. Tylennald raised an eyebrow at her, the confident expression on his face igniting the hatred the woman felt for him. Tylennald moved to the side, blocking the view for his brother's youngest sons, figuring that boys that young didn't need to see this. His cold stare met Tiran's desperate eyes that were filled with unshed tears as he hugged in place his younger brother, Perren the Distracted. The strawberry-blonde man was speaking inaudible words, the only sounds that came out of his mouth resembling those of a child in the process of learning how to speak.

Voladea walked up to the woman who was grabbed by two guards, the fury that filled her brown eyes solely directed at Lady Gwethana. "You can wait for your trial in the keep," she hissed. "It is rather cold and humid, but I doubt it will be much different from your inland home."

"What is going on?" Tiran's shattered voice reached her ears.

"Nothing, Tiran," his mother answered, trying to wiggle her way out of the guards' grasp. "Your grandmother is trying to accuse me of sins I know nothing of."

"You see," Tylennald began, his arm coming to circle Voladea's shoulders. "When my brother woke up, he told us that before his accident, he visited you. He went to his spring residence in Summerport, where you have been living, and spent the night there. Thaesonwald usually heads to the Summerport encampment directly, waking up in the middle of the night to ride from Strongshore to Summerport. However," he said as his eyes scanned the faces of the witnesses around them, "that one time he decided to spent the night with you, and you had dinner together, isn't that correct?"

"Are you implying that I poisoned my husband?" the widow hissed at him through clenched teeth. "Or did he accuse me himself? What were his lying words?"

"Thaesonwald was confused for days after he opened his eyes again. But there was one sentence he kept repeating." Leaning in closer to her ear, Tylennald licked his lips. "She did it." He felt Gwethana freeze in place, and wasting no time, his bright eyes stared into the nearest guard's. "Take her."

The protests and insults that left Gwethana's lips were ignored by all and covered by the even louder sobbing of her eldest son, who rested his hand on his bald scalp as he tried to contain the tears that ultimately ran down his cheeks. Tylennald exchanged a look with Wallysa, who had watched the scene with an immutable expression on her face. Voladea's trembling hands fumbled with the handkerchief she had used to wipe her tears; the sight of her daughter-in-law being dragged away doing little to quell the anger that consumed her insides.

The bed-chamber doors were closed behind them, Healer Martus glancing at the backs of the Lionhelms. The many wrinkles on his face were showing even more as the tiredness consumed him. He was the one to find Lord Thaesonwald that morning. It had been an odd sight to him; he had helped Lady Voladea deliver her first boy and it had seemed as if only a day had passed since then. Declaring the death of the man who once was a newborn his younger self cradled in his arms made

Martus imagine just how cruel it was for the mother to see the still body of a being she had been protecting all her life.

"My lady," he whispered. "I understand your feelings but Lady Gwethana's charges are…" Clearing his throat, the old healer sighed out. "I am afraid that Lord Thaesonwald was smothered, not poisoned."

Wallysa's blue eyes narrowed, and she stuck her chin out. "How do you know?"

"Bloodshot eyes, bruising inside the mouth as if the lord's lips were forcefully pressed against his teeth," the old man began listing his findings, only to be interrupted by Voladea.

"Gwethana wanted to finish what she started." Rubbing her left temple, she dismissed him. "The Regency will judge her actions. I will now visit my lord husband." Her stare softened as she turned to face the grandchildren who still waited outside the bed-chambers, the distinct "momma" that Perren blurted out causing her throat to tighten. "Bid farewell to your father before his body is taken," she whispered. "He sure loved you with all his heart," she added, her fingers brushing against the right cheek of the youngest illegitimate son, a small chubby boy with sandy hair and deep blue eyes. "I want their mothers to come here," she told Tylennald, who raised both eyebrows at her.

"Mother?"

"We have much to discuss with those women."

***

As the carriage made its way through the cobbled streets, swinging and wobbling, Lyzon felt like emptying her stomach. They had been traveling for five days straight, perhaps even more, she wasn't sure. She had counted up to five until the day she woke up destroyed by the slow pace of the trip. It was as if Lord Theliel wasn't in a rush to arrive at their destination, and Lady Tecla was all too happy to stop every time the scenery around them resembled a painting.

Tecla didn't sit in the carriage with her and Fran, leaving room for Educator Tomas, who had joined them upon Lord Tithan's request. The young lady rode next to her brother, with her legs swung over to one side. Lyzon glanced at her now and then, part of her worrying that she would fall off the horse at any moment. Lady Tecla had been instructed properly, but she rarely rode, and the maid didn't feel comfortable.

Next to her, Fran was having a deep conversation with the educator who filled two seats on his own. His little burly hands were on his large belly, his vivid green robes and purple turban covering him from head to toe. His skin was several shades darker than Lyzon's, and his big, round nose was all she could see whenever the man spoke. He was a well full of knowledge, and the gardener that Tecla was happy to bring along was lost in the tale Tomas was entertaining him with.

"So, the Sons of Ferngrunn are the descendants of the warrior who defeated Alatros the Red," Fran summarized, his thick, brown eyebrows raised so high that his forehead was covered in wrinkles. "That is history older than ours."

Tomas nodded at him fervently. "Fascinating, isn't it? It is known that Ferngrunn's ancestors left the Avoryon Hills long before the birth of Alatros, settling near the coast in hopes of trading with the continent of Driazon, across the Zalejos Depths."

His words instantly piqued Lyzon's interest. "My people never knew about building big enough ships," she said, leaning forward.

Educator Tomas wiggled in his seat, smiling. "The islands of the Depths are nothing more than the highest peaks of the mountains of a continent that was swallowed by the seas thousands of years ago, my dear. Driazon was inhabited by women and men who knew more technologies than we do today." Switching to the previous topic, Tomas looked back at Fran. "Ferngrunn defeated Alatros the Red after the latter sacked and razed the Avoryon Hills, Ferngrunn being favored by the harsh weather that had decimated a good number of Alatros' troops. The Avoryon Hills were always covered in snow and ice, but the Dark Barrens surrounding the Sand Towers are never-ending pools of scorching sand, and no man can cross them unprepared.

"It is only thanks to the Barrens that even the armies of Emperor Mosse Rochelac didn't conquer the Sand Towers in 1500 BCR. Grow strong, die free, the Sons of Ferngrunn say."

Fran nodded again, his nails scratching his hairline. "I heard of that. The Empire of the Rochelacs once extended from the West to the East, or would have, if the Sand Towers had crumbled."

Tomas shook his head at him, raising an index finger. "The Rochelacs never conquered the Rain Lands," he corrected. "In their attempt of expanding in the same fashion as the Lionhelms, the Rochelacs failed to breach the walls of the City of Rockfall, renamed that way to spite the Rochelacs. At once our enemies rest is the Rochelacs' motto. Imagine being able to defend against them. The Rain Lands are the smallest region of our continent, and yet, they are well-versed in defensive tactics. They shot down the striges of the Fog Lands without breaking a sweat, aiming at the beasts with darts just as large as them."

"Striges?" Fran and Lyzon asked at the same time.

Tomas nodded, closing his eyes dramatically. "Imagine owls bigger than palaces, with eyes so small that you can only see a glimmer of yellow light as you stare at them. Their feathers are grey, white, and black at times, but their talons can shatter hills and the bat of their wings can wipe a city with a gush of wind."

"My people call them *nyitute*," Lyzon told them quietly. "Messengers. They are the messengers—"

"The messengers of the Pit," Fran finished her sentence. "I thought your people had different beliefs."

Tomas laughed. "Ah," he clapped his hands together, "part of our beliefs come from Driazon and the Red Continent. The Observatory Vault is studying the traces of civilizations that preceded ours; not only fauna but flora as well seems to have come from the lands across the seas, long before Alatros the Red brought seeds and wild animals from his conquests."

"But," Lyzon frowned, crossing her arms, "if that is true, then what were the Silver Lands before the known history? Before Alatros the Red, the Oracle, and Ferngrunn?"

"That is a good question and many have theorized and terrorized others with all kinds of tales. However, there is still no proof."

"Tales such as?" Fran asked.

"It is believed that the Silver Lands were one big forest, populated by fays, the spirits of the dead. The corpses that had been thrown in the sea by the people of the Red Continent and Driazon would land here if their spirits sook revenge, or so the legend goes, but that would be ignoring the fact that the body deteriorates after death and that the beings of the sea feast on the corpses," Tomas concluded.

Lyzon sat back, her dark brown eyes glancing back at the young lady outside, who seemed just as engrossed in her conversation with Theliel as she had been upon hearing Tomas' words. The blasting sound of buisines reached her ears, but even as Tecla heard them, the young lady didn't look away from her brother.

Tecla was still taking in her brother's confession about what happened at the Rosenfield castle, and although the hymn of her house was being played by the heralds who spotted her arrival at Rainier's Pavilion, she couldn't look away from Theliel's genuinely scared face. She couldn't recall her brother being scared before that day, but he still couldn't understand what happened, and it didn't sit well with him.

Theliel had told everything to his sister. He hadn't planned on doing it, but she had asked him all kinds of questions about the Regency and how they treated him to prepare herself for what was in store for her. It had been stronger than him; the feeling of being utterly ignored in such an important matter was still fresh. He halted his horse at the entrance of the Pavilion, having seen Grandmaster Rodbertus walk towards them.

"Do they do this every time?" Tecla whispered; the music that echoed around them being a deafening kind of loud.

"No, this is your first welcome," Theliel told her, his stare never leaving the silhouette that approached. "It is to woo you a little bit, to have you tell Father that the Regency treated you well. After all, he pays for the training, and it is not a shy sum of silvers."

The resentment in his voice was heavy, and Tecla's fists tightened around the reins of her mount. It wasn't long until her brother dismounted, walking around his horse to come up to her and help her. He grabbed her by the waist, holding her like a small child as he put her down, mindful of her dress around the saddle.

    Grandmaster Rodbertus bowed his head at the two, a faint smile attempting to cover the sourness in his eyes. "Lady Tecla, at last, you have arrived. I am Grandmaster Rodbertus, Head of the Regency's Observatory Vault and your mentor for as long as you will have me," he greeted her.

    "It is my pleasure to meet you, Grandmaster," she said in return with a bow of her own. "My brother Theliel has told me about you and your valuable wisdom."

    "I am afraid that what you will remember of our first meeting will quickly overshadow the good your brother speaks of," the grandmaster apologized. Reaching inside the front pocket of his robes, the grey man took a message that had flown across the Silver Lands. "Lady Tecla, Lord Theliel," he spoke in a low tone, "Your brother Thaesonwald passed away." Ignoring their gasping sounds and whispered words, he added, "Lord Lionhelm himself had an accident but it seems that nothing serious is compromising his recovery. His fall was cushioned by his master-at-arms."

    Theliel took a step forward, and it was hard for him not to grab the old man by the shoulder and yank him forward. "Fantine? How is she?" he promptly asked when Rodbertus mentioned nothing about her well-being.

    "She is being taken care of as well."

    Tecla's eyes were full of tears, and her mouth was covered by a shaky hand. "We should probably head back," she suggested, her other hand grasping Theliel's.

"My lady," the grandmaster shook his head at her, "Healer Martus has assured me that your father is not suffering from any consequences. But if it will please you, I will travel to Strongshore myself on the next dusk day, when you are supposed to return as well," he offered as a compromise. Bowing deeply, the man brought a hand to his chest, where his heart was. "My sincere condolences about your lord brother."

Tecla's shoulder shook as a sob racked her body. Right as she thought that it was ill of her to be thinking only of her father and Fantine, her brother's words cut through her brain.

"Thaesonwald was doomed for a very long time."

Walking past them, Theliel tugged his horse in the direction of the stables.

✳✳✳

Danyell's Athenaeum stood proudly between the marketplace and Maugre's Arena. The outside of the building looked a lot like the Pavilion that Jascha had seen in many paintings, with its large, emerald cupolas, and tall columns of an ivory color. He climbed the steps that led to the entrance, blocking out the chatter of aspiring educators. The iron doors were open, and his boots dragged some snow inside as he reached the counter in the hall. A woman stood behind it, engrossed in her work, and his black eyes quickly glanced at the paper in his hands. He knew Yenny's sloppy drawing by heart, but it remained his compass. Jascha stared at the woman who didn't seem to have seen him. Her emerald robes were covered by a white fur cloak to shield her from the icy winds, and her light brown hair was carefully pulled back in what looked like a braided headband.

Jascha stood in front of her, clearing his throat. "I am looking for a book," he told her.

"You've come to the right place," she said in a bored tone. Her grey eyes glanced up at him and she frowned. "What book is it?"

"I don't know."

"Look, don't waste my time," she sighed out, dropping her quill pen. "Reading is free of charge, but if you need to take something with you, you have to come back here and pay thirty silvers. If you return the book within three days, you get fifteen silvers back. Understood?"

As she went back to scribbling, Jascha eyed the long table at the center of the room. A dozen chairs lined both sides, like a lord's dining table. There was a crimson rug under it, and five large candleholders had been placed on the table for the readers to light in case of necessity. A circular staircase started at the far end of the table, and Jascha noted that each circle it made mirrored the size of the cupola above their heads. Shelves covered every wall of every story, the banners hanging from the balconies coming from every corner of the Silver Lands. Jascha saw the lions of the South, the owl of the Regency, the chalice of Founder's Breach, the hammers of the Sand Towers, the clockwork of the Rain Lands, and the canine bear beast of his lands. The roots of a massive tree served as walls where the stone met wood, and Jascha realized that the athenaeum had been built around an old rosewillow. The wood shone a bright green, and yet some people leaned against it as they read.

Jascha glanced back at the rude woman. "On which floor can I find anything about witchcraft?"

She raised an eyebrow, the boredom vanishing from her face, replaced by curiosity and, Jascha felt, a hint of suspicion. "What do you mean by witchcraft?"

"Rituals, mostly."

"On the last floor," she told him without batting an eyelid. "The Occult Vault has sealed most records though," she informed him. "If you need them, you will have to file a request that I will forward to the Regency's chancery."

"The Occult Vault?"

She shrugged, grabbing her quill pen to get back to work. "It used to be an order of the Regency."

Jascha nodded, licking the inside of his cheek. "Thank you…" He paused, realizing he had never asked for her name.

"Rosaleah," she said with a small smile.

"Thank you, Rosaleah."

He walked his way upstairs, the light fading the more he climbed, almost as if no one had wanted to make it obvious that there was a tenth floor inside the building. The chandeliers hung low until the eighth floor, while the last two were dark.

A few torches were lit around the shelves, but the floor was completely deserted. Jascha had little clue as to where he should begin searching, a part of him wondering if there was even anything worth his time, considering that some information had been sealed away. He let his fingers brush against the spines of a series of books, his eyes quickly scanning the titles. It seemed to him that most of them were about ancient folklore and faraway legends, and he balled up the drawing he carried before shoving it in his pocket. It was stupid of him to believe in what Rantha's apprentice told him; the woman had no idea of what she was doing, yet instructed others. Still, he was having a hard time letting go of the possibility that he had been part of a ritual.

There was a thump behind him, and Jascha's senses were on alert. He turned heels almost instantly, looking around to catch a shadow moving, but there was nothing. His heavy boots made no sound as he rounded the shelf behind him, black eyes darting around. He fisted the hilt of his dagger, going around another shelf, but found no trace of another person on the same floor as him. He stepped closer to the railing of the stairs, looking down to see if someone had been there and was leaving, but to no avail.

Jascha let go of his weapon, scanning the books on the shelf he previously walked past. A series of small guides were lined before his eyes, but one tall, brown tome stood out in the middle. Rituals and Unbinding, by Grandmaster Matillis of Summerport. He slid the book out, holding it with both hands due to its weight. Jascha flicked the first few pages, licking his fingertips to grab the next page. The first few words he read didn't register as he realized that he had tasted no dust. Either someone read the book right before him, or it was recently placed there. Putting the thought aside, for the time being, Jascha took the book with him, throwing it on top of the nearest single table he found.

    The first couple lines of the book were introductory, but he quickly found himself engrossed in the terminology that was being used. Grandmaster Matillis immediately underlined the fact that she would not be using the words witch and witchcraft, deeming them to be inaccurate and degrading. The rituals themselves were described as either summoning, celebration, or even formality for a distinct group that was recognized by neither steel nor faith, a group that existed before lordships and civil laws, a group that could be divided into other subgroups but remained united under one name.

    The Rosencircle.

Chapter XVI

First of Many

The northern encampment was not far from the entrance of Silverholde. Sybbyl rode effortlessly through the setting snow, feeling the chill weather crawl inside her bones with every hop of her blonde horse. The encampment was protected by walls as tall as the city's, and considering how high in the sky the sun shone, albeit weakly, she figured that the military training was done and over for the day. A couple of surveillants nodded at her as they exited the structure. Chief Eleres often had his men spar with the armies of the Regency, to keep them in shape and ready for any form of combat. Sir Sybbyl disliked the man, but she had to admit that his methods were effective. Not that she would ever say it out loud; she still believed that the capital wasn't safe enough and that the Surveillance needed more men, but part of the problem was the resources they lacked. There were not enough people to mine iron in the Fog Lands after they were devastated by the Violet Delusion, and there was never enough money in Silverholde.

Sybbyl dismounted quickly at the entrance, leaving her horse in the care of the stablemen, her heavy armor clinking with each step of hers. Her emerald and golden cape bore the coat-of-arms of the Regency, but the chest plate she wore proudly showcased the burning rosewillow of her house. It differentiated the members of the Regency, who welcomed both nobles and simple people in times of recruitment. Chief Eleres, for instance, didn't have any symbol on his chest plate when he wore one, but Sybbyl's distaste for the man went beyond his lesser origins; Thierry Eleres always acted as if he knew more than she did. Was it because of the age gap between them or plain arrogance? Sybbyl didn't know. What she knew, however, was that his men misbehaved in front of her, and she wouldn't let it pass so easily.

The men inside the Suppressor of War's tent scattered quicker than wild cats at the sight of her, leaving Eleres to wrap up his report as he sat at Sybbyl's table. He bowed his head at the sight of her, then proceeded with the scribbling.

"Sir Sybbyl, I don't normally see you on the Surveillance's training days."

The tall woman rested her left hand on the hilt of her broadsword, her chin sticking out. "I spotted two of your guards harming a civilian who was legally entering the city."

"I reckon you sanctioned them already; it would be unlike you to let me decide on their punishment." ·

He was already grating on her nerves. "Eleres," she spoke seriously. "I am not here to discuss the guards' behavior." Grabbing the nearest chair, she placed it across from him before sitting down. "I would like you to have the man followed, the one they assaulted."

Never once looking up as he wrote down his evaluations, the chief asked, "Wasn't he a civilian entering the city legally?"

"He carried a dagger forged in Three Crosses."

Chief Eleres glanced briefly at her. "And?"

"When is the last time anyone from the Fog Lands entered the capital?" Sybbyl pointed out. "Let alone someone from Three Crosses."

"You know, just because the Fog Lands have suffered the most from the Violet Delusion, it doesn't mean that no one survived."

"The simple people who survive generally have little food left and surely no horse or dagger. You should have seen the hilt of that weapon, Eleres," Sybbyl went on with a confused look. "Stones that shone brighter than silver. Are we to believe this commoner stole it?"

"Are you telling me he is no commoner?"

The two stared at each other as they thought about the implications of what that meant, but Eleres was quick to shrug at the woman sitting across from him. His gloved hand scratched his bald head before his fingers traced his thick eyebrows as if to brush the hairs back in place.

"Sir Sybbyl, I am afraid you are letting prejudice have the best of you. I know half your family was slaughtered by Mosse Rochelac during his wars, but that was at least fifteen centuries ago," he reasoned out loud. "This man is probably not a commoner, but I doubt he is here on behalf of the Rochelacs or the Montels."

Her icy eyes narrowed at him. "You believe the Rochelacs are gone."

"I believe," Eleres wanted to correct her as he stood up to gather his belongings while the ink dried on the paper, "that they are probably in the same state as our King. No one survives the Violet Delusion without some serious deficiencies. So, why would they, or their advisors, send one of their men without making it known to the Regency? They can't possibly attack us. We've had a defensive pact with all the overlords of the continent for the past sixty years.

"The only Montel I know of is Lady Gwethana, who married Lord Tithan Lionhelm's firstborn. It is safe to assume the Montels are loyal to their overlords as much as to their newfound family, and the Lionhelms have been more than supportive of the Regency as an institution."

Sybbyl drummed her fingers on the wooden table, blankly staring past him. Eleres was voicing out what she had tried to convince herself of, but she couldn't forget the nature of the lords of the Fog Lands. They were ruthless and powerful, and she doubted their armies had suffered from the Violet

Delusion as much as the Regency believed. The Rochelacs were one of the most ancient houses of the Silver Lands, and they had dominated their portion of the continent long before the Lionhelms rose to power in the South. They had effortlessly annexed territories with anti-cavalry and air attacks, and her own house survived only because they fled past the Dark Barrens, her ancestors seeking protection from the Sons of Ferngrunn. She didn't trust the reports that were sent to the Regency years before she was even born. Sybbyl knew history well enough to remember that Noirmont was a natural shield for the entire infantry of the Rochelacs, and she couldn't shake off the feeling that the man she spotted was, at the very least, one of their servants.

  Sensing the mixed feelings she had about the whole ordeal, Chief Eleres exhaled slowly, rolling his report before sealing it with a few drops of wax and the Regency's sigil. "I will send more men out for patrol if that helps," he offered, his dark orbs searching for hers. He didn't expect her to refuse.

  "I want it to be you," she declared, standing up herself, towering over him. "I trust you with the training of your men; I do believe you teach them to use their instincts before they unsheathe their swords or brandish their spears. However, most of them are still boys, and if I happened to be correct, this man is more dangerous than what he appears to be."

  "I can't do that, Sybbyl," Eleres almost pleaded. "You know I have to leave very soon. At best, I can leave Goldsnout in the capital; consider him to be me, only with fewer lines and more hair," he attempted to joke.

The blonde shook her head vehemently. "I shall do it personally, then."

"Sybbyl," Eleres called the moment she turned heels, ready to leave.

"It's Sir Sybbyl to you," she spat, pushing the curtains of the tent aside as she walked out, adding their conversation to the list of reasons why she disliked the man with everything she had.

✳✳✳

The central inn of Rainier's End was filled with more people than Goldsnout had ever seen. Many patrons enjoyed their drinks outside, mindless of the fact that it was still snowing. Small pyres had been lit outside for warmth, and the loud chatter that was giving him a headache was exclusively about rumors and grim stories of what happened in that same inn.

It seemed as if Yenny's death was on everyone's lips, and that was not good at all. The confusion that rumors fueled would only make his job harder; he already knew he would be hearing made up stories and theories that had nothing to do with the truth. He wondered if anyone had reported the events to the local surveillant, but he too would probably deliver him farfetched stories about who killed Yenny and how. Goldsnout wished Chief Eleres would implement a strict protocol for Surveillance reports, but the man was hung up on his own mentor's teachings, and they did not include the daily safety of the simple people, let alone immediate reports of findings and minor crimes.

His light green eyes were on Rantha as she scanned the crowd. Goldsnout had tried to convince her that she didn't have to follow him, figuring that hearing all kinds of things about her apprentice would only hurt her, but the woman was insistent and stubborn, and she wouldn't take no for an answer. Rantha had been mostly silent during their trip, only acknowledging his words with a nod and a faint smile. Goldsnout had wanted to hold her hand even if for just a moment, to let her know that he understood her feelings and that he wouldn't relent until he reached the bottom of the story, but he couldn't bring himself to do it. It was as if an invisible veil hugged the woman, blocking him out.

"Where do you even plan on sleeping?" she asked, eyeing the inn that had exceeded its maximum capacity. "I doubt they have any room left."

The red-haired man stood with his lips parted, failing to find an answer. It was indeed a good question. He had been so focused on Yenny that he hadn't thought of where he would spend the night if the central inn was full.

"Come at the shelter," Rantha told him with a flat tone. "We have no one to treat at the moment."

"Miss Rantha, I couldn't possibly."

She arched an elegant eyebrow at him. "Why is that? It is just one night. It's better than to freeze outside."

"I don't think it's proper for me to accept a lady's invitation into her own house."

"It's not my house," she breathed out, looking away. "The Illusion Shelter used to be a portion of the kitchens of Sir Loys Rosenbane's Illusion Lodge." Sensing his questioning stare, Rantha furtherly explained. "Sir Loys had… an obsession for men younger than him," she whispered. "He built the Lodge to host gatherings where he would find men of his liking. I sometimes worked in the kitchens when I was small. It was all very quaint and Sir Loys was never inappropriate with anyone but, one day, there was a fire. Sir Loys used to say that it was an accident, but my mother and I never believed it. Nothing that night could have led to an accidental fire.

"When the Violet Delusion reached Rainier's End, even though it was thought to have ended in Beggar's Pool, Sir Loys fell ill. He allowed me to continue using the remaining areas of the Lodge as a shelter for anyone who needed it. Risen to the Heights, Sir Loys would repeat. He said helping others brought us closer to the Good Gods.

"You can have the room Jascha slept in. It's the warmest," she concluded, tying the reins of her house to the fence outside the inn.

They elbowed their way through the crowd with ease, but the only person Goldsnout was interested in meeting was the innkeeper. He remembered the frail old man he once spoke with, and a part of him doubted that the man would recall anything in particular, but he had to start somewhere. Rantha pushed herself up at the bar counter, waving at the bartender and telling him to serve them two pints of ale. Before Goldsnout could reach inside his pockets, the woman dropped two coins in front of her. Begrudgingly, Goldsnout let go of his silvers, deciding that they seriously had to talk about her manners. He hadn't been able to thank her even once for her company and hospitality. He felt as if he was being paid for services he had taken an oath for.

"Piper, where is the owner?" Rantha asked the man who set the pints in front of them, the ale slightly pouring out as the counter shook under one of the patron's weight.

"He'll be here any moment now. He grabbed some more tarts from the kitchen."

Goldsnout felt his stomach rumble. "Pigeon tarts?" he asked. He remembered those he bought in Rainier's End the last time he was there. He had rarely tasted tarts that good. "Can we have some?"

The skinny man behind the counter shrugged, pushing his greasy hair behind his ears. "Sure, whatever you need." Leaving them to their drinks, Piper walked in the direction of the kitchens.

It wasn't long until the innkeeper came into view, and both Goldsnout and Rantha followed his every movement. They saw the bartender whisper something in the old man's ear, who looked dejected. Walking up to them slowly, the owner leaned against the wooden bar to keep his balance.

He flung a dirty rag over his shoulder, his baggy eyes scanning Goldsnout's face as if to figure out whether they knew each other or not.

"What can I help you with, Officer?"

"I think you know," the redhead instantly replied. "I am here to investigate the death of a woman called Yenny."

"I have been asked the same questions all day," the innkeeper sighed out, grabbing the rag to wipe the counter. "I didn't see her and I didn't talk to her."

Goldsnout took another sip of his drink. "Is there anyone who did interact with her?"

"Probably Piper, since he serves everyone. But because he serves everyone, I doubt he remembers them faces all the time."

Rantha and Goldsnout exchanged looks that spoke volumes about their expectations for the night. If the innkeeper had seen nothing and the bartender was too busy to remember anything, the entire investigation would undoubtedly lead nowhere. Still, Opherus Goldsnout wasn't about to forfeit. Piper soon came back with steaming pigeon tarts that he placed in front of them, and this time, Goldsnout was quick to pay, hearing none of the complaints Rantha had in store for him.

The Regency officer took a large bite, nearly burning his tongue, before addressing the bartender. "Do you mind if I check upstairs? I know the girl fell from the top floor."

Piper shrugged at him again, emptying a few glasses that had been left half full on the counter. "There is only one room anyway," he informed them. "The others have some cracks in the roof and other problems that need fixing, so I doubt the girl was anywhere else."

Rantha finished her meal before Goldsnout, who promptly shoved the remaining tart in his mouth, caring little about the fact that he must have looked like a glutton with his mouth full of food. He chugged his ale just as quickly before hopping off the stool, waiting for his companion to walk upstairs first. They had to push through the patrons even there, and soon they were covered in spit and smelled of wine as the crowd didn't care about them and kept eating, drinking, and yelling at each other.

Goldsnout tugged his cape from where it got stuck under someone's foot, sending the man rolling down the stairs and taking with him half the people who cluttered the staircase. Shaking his head at them, the officer walked up to the closed room from where a series of sounds came out. He heavily knocked three times on the wooden door, only to hear curses and fumbling.

"Fuck off," a man grunted from inside.

"Regency's Surveillance," Goldsnout announced. "I am walking in."

A sight he wasn't expecting blinded him, and behind him, Rantha gasped, and if he wasn't mistaken, even laughed. Leaning against the window frame, a man stood with his britches in a pool around his ankles, two hairy butt cheeks on full display. A woman who wasn't any more gracious than him was bent over the window, her dirty rags pulled up and exposing her lower parts, which were entangled around the man.

A beardy male glowered at him with an unmistakably southern accent. "What the fuck? Go the fuck away!"

Goldsnout scratched the side of his head before he took two long strides towards the couple, yanking the man by his ponytail and bending his back at a painful angle. "What is wrong with you freaks?" he bellowed. "A girl was murdered here, and you just get your rocks off from it?" Pushing the man away, he grabbed the woman by the arm to help her up. "Get out, now."

The half-naked male stumbled backward on his pants, falling on the floor with a loud thud, his family jewels jiggling before the woman helped him up, earning only a handful of insults in return. Rantha watched with an overly amused expression the way the couple rushed outside, only to stop once she realized it was the first time she smiled after learning about Yenny's death. She shook her head, entering the room her apprentice had been in only a couple of nights prior, and she looked around, finding nothing worthy of her immediate attention.

Goldsnout leaned against the windowsill, inspecting the ground below. It was where Yenny's body had been found, so there was no doubt about the fact that she had been standing near that window before falling. The floor had been cleaned, and his green eyes found no trace of blood, although Yenny had been stabbed in the leg. Opherus circled the bed, inspecting every inch of it, only to find it immaculate. Perhaps he had arrived too late, he thought to himself.

  Rantha sat down on the bed, her eyes scanning around as she tried to imagine what Yenny had been doing up there. There was nothing that could have harmed her; only an end table stood next to the bed. It had to have been someone. Could it be that she had just wanted some private time like the couple who left? Rantha nibbled on her lower lip. It wasn't impossible that what could have been a friendly, intimate meeting turned out to be a violent one, but that didn't explain why the man would have pushed the girl out of the window.

  "Maybe she walked in on the wrong person and saw something she shouldn't have," Goldsnout whispered, standing closer to her.

  The curly-haired healer remained silent, one dark hand resting on the surface of the end table as her index finger traced the lines of the light wood. "Why would she walk into a room on her own? I think she was invited here."

  "I am sorry to go there again but I think she met Jascha," Goldsnout tried to reason with her with a deep frown marking his features. "Think of it this way; Yenny rarely leaves the shelter, and the only people she truly knows are you and the other apprentices. If she came here alone and agreed on coming upstairs with someone, it must have been a person she knew on some level. Unless there are other acquaintances of hers that you haven't mentioned—"

  "Opherus."

He glanced down, only to find Rantha completely entranced with a piece of furniture, her fingers tracing what seemed to be a stain. He doubted she had heard any of his words.

"It's ink," Rantha told him. "What if Yenny came up here to write something?"

"The stain could be older than we think. It's not necessarily her ink that was dropped." Sighing at the fact that they weren't going anywhere, Goldsnout offered her his hand to have her stand up. "Let's go get some rest," he whispered. "But I ask you to consider what I just told you if you were listening."

Her eyebrows knitted together, and she followed him outside the room. "I was," she told him. "But I don't think Jascha would harm someone who actively tried to help him. He had a lot of problems, that much was obvious, but murder?"

Goldsnout stopped in his tracks, turning to face her fully. His gentle look and friendly demeanor had been replaced by a character Rantha had never seen before. He gazed at her coldly, with his shoulders back like a trained soldier. "Are you sure about that, Rantha?"

Her plump lips parted to furtherly convince him, and herself, that Jascha had left long before Yenny walked out of the shelter, but she held back. She recalled his hand around her neck all too clearly, remembered the way he had spoken to her because she was a low-born. After all, she had failed him, and Jascha held her accountable for what he was still going through. Had Yenny received the same treatment? Did Yenny fight back, and was killed for it? Her mind went in several directions at the same time, and Goldsnout could see it.

Placing an arm around her shoulders, the Regency officer led her down the stairs. "Until I figure this out, promise me to not let the man in if he ever shows up at the shelter again," he said calmly, his hand protectively tightening around her shoulder. "Please, Miss Rantha."

The woman nodded, staring at her feet as they left the inn and found themselves in the cold weather again. They walked in silence towards the horses, and Rantha wasn't sure why Goldsnout wasn't relinquishing his hold on her, but she minded not. She felt less cold with him keeping her close to his armored body, or perhaps it was something else.

Suddenly, the man beside her yelped, and she jumped in his grasp. He brought a hand to the side of his head, where something snowy and sharp just hit him.

"You're bleeding," she gasped, looking around. A few drops of blood tainted the snow where a rock had just landed. Rantha turned heels, glaring at the group who stood next to one of the pyres, the ire in their eyes directed at Goldsnout.

"Fucking piece of trash of the Regency," she heard the shortest boy mutter. "Look at him, all covered up in warm clothes just to collect some extra taxes."

Wiping his forehead, Goldsnout took a step forward. "I am no tax collector," he informed them.

"I am a surveillant, and this is insubordination to a uniformed officer," he warned.

An older boy spat at his feet, yellow mucus mixing with dirt. "Think you can scare us?"

"I think you should stop before it's too late," Rantha raised her voice, only to be ignored by the group who drank by the fire.

A third person pushed past the boys, and Goldsnout's eyebrows shot up. He recognized the man he had thrown out of the room, and he was holding what looked like a steel glove with spikes on the knuckles. "You interrupted me rudely," the beardy man pointed out with a cold glare. "It winds me up, boy. I think I should take it out on you directly unless you hand me your slave right this moment," he sneered.

Goldsnout's look darkened, and his hand reached for the sword at his right. "Try and say that again," he defied the drunk.

The man bared his brown teeth at him, "Come at me, red squirrel."

The two boys at his side ran in his direction and Goldsnout braced himself, refusing to take his sword to fight two kids way younger than him. His heart skipped a beat as they rushed past him, tackling Rantha into the ground and pulling her curly mane. She screamed and kicked at them; the shorter boy shoved her head into the snow.

"Stay still ma'am, my brother needs a moment with you," he laughed in her ear.

Goldsnout was about to leap at them, when the man behind him pulled him closer by grabbing the sash around his neck, an armed fist colliding with the officer's cheek. Goldsnout felt his teeth break and his cheek being pierced by the spikes on the glove, and he fell heavily. Rantha's screams filled his ears as she fought the two boys climbing on top of her, the youngest straddling her upper body to keep her from moving. The man who hit him stood above him; a foot pressed against his plated chest.

"Now this gets my rocks off," he laughed out loud. "Do you like it?" he asked, raising his armed fist. "I had it forged in the black market just to take care of you greedy harlots from the capital."

Goldsnout's breath came out in short puffs, white clouds of air altering his sight. He felt a wave of anger that had never possessed him before, and his left hand reached for the smaller sword at his right, pulling it out silently before planting the steel in the man's calf. The moment his assailant screamed, stumbling backward, Goldsnout pushed his weight upwards, ignoring the metallic taste in his mouth. He shot up faster than he had been taught, grabbing one boy by the back of his coat and sending his head colliding into the other boy's. They rolled in the dirt, ready to fight back as the older one pulled a rusty knife from his pocket.

Rantha immediately crawled away, tears rolling down her face, only for them to be replaced by the sudden warm blood that splashed against her face. Her big brown eyes glanced up, only to see that Goldsnout had unsheathed his broadsword, driving straight into the beardy man's belly. The red-haired man pulled back his weapon, kicking his foe away, and staring at the blood that pooled all around the latter. The patrons of the central inn gathered behind them, whispering at the scene before their eyes. Their words never reached Goldsnout's ringing ears.

    The two boys rushed to the man's side, their threats being replaced by fat tears and sobs, but Opherus only clenched the hilt of his sword, hitting the still armed boy in the back of his head, knocking him unconscious. Droplets of blood trickled down the tip of his steel, and the officer dropped to his knees, his bright eyes solely focused on the face of the man who bled out with his mouth agape and terror-filled eyes. Goldsnout spat the gore that had collected in his mouth, standing up only to help Rantha do it as well. He felt her arms circle him, tugging him away, whispering words inaudible to him as he grimly realized that he had never killed a man before.

Chapter XVII

Yard of Willows

Goldsnout hissed at the sudden burn. Rantha sighed softly, pressing the cloth soaked in acid vinegar against his forehead. The cut caused by the sharp rock that had been thrown at him wasn't too deep, so there would be no need for stitches. The bleeding, however, hadn't stopped, so the two young adults sat in Rantha's kitchen in silence. They hadn't uttered a single word since she patched his cheek where the gauntlet tore his skin.

"Hold this," Rantha told the officer before her, her hand pressing a little harder. "No, no. Harder," she ordered him before gathering her pieces of cloth and other medication tools.

She stood up rather abruptly, her elbow nearly colliding with Goldsnout's face. Rantha shut the lid of her kit, promptly shoving it on one of the upper shelves. She pinched the bridge of her nose, recollecting her thoughts and trying to stay calm. They were supposed to be looking for answers regarding Yenny's last moments, but the violent attack had completely changed the meaning of Goldsnout's visit. The tension in the room was palpable, and the man who was sloppily removing his armor seemed more than upset. Her tired stare fell on his trembling limbs, and she wondered if he was cold, if she needed to add more wood to the fire. She wasn't even sure she had more wood; her apprentice Zurzon usually took care of such things, but after Yenny's death, no one acted the way they used to.

  Rantha ran her fingers through her locks, pushing the hair away from her face. She came to sit across from Goldsnout again, and her brown stare lingered on his pale lashes that tickled his cheekbones. His fingers had just finished unclasping the shin plates, and with a lazy kick, he got them out of his way. He relaxed in the chair, stretching his legs and resting his heels on the nearest bench. They remained in silence for what felt like an eternity until Rantha suggested they drink something warm, but a resounding knock on the front door startled them.

  Goldsnout sensed the agitation and figured that the earlier incident was still too fresh on her mind. Hissing as the sudden movement caused his knees to crack, the officer ruffled his mane, a part of him wondering if that gesture hadn't simply made him look even more terrible. He wiped the side of his head with his white sleeve, wincing at the sight of blood. He figured that he should have listened to Rantha and pressed the cloth against the cut a little longer, but the stinging coupled with the smell of the vinegar was getting to his head. Pulling the door open, his green eyes narrowed.

A man not much taller than him gazed at him with a stoic expression. It was raining heavily outside, but the man was fully clothed in his winter uniform, the Regency colors hugging his bulky frame. His hood was drenched, but the man didn't seem to be in discomfort. His light brown eyes were hosts to an intimidating stare.

"Officer Opherus Goldsnout?" he asked with a deep voice. "I am Senior Officer Saer Dunac," he introduced himself. "I was told by the villagers you left in the company of the woman who lives in this shelter."

"Her name is Rantha," Goldsnout cut in. "I am sure the villagers know her name, and so do you."

Ignoring his words, Dunac went on, "You and I need to talk about what happened. I am the surveillant assigned to Rainier's End and I have more than thirty men at my command. If we had known an officer from the capital was coming, we would have certainly offered him to stay with us in Rainier's Fort."

Reluctantly, Goldsnout took a step forward, closing the door behind him. He stood in the rain without his cloak, waiting for his superior to skip the formalities.

"I am not here on duty," the redhead said. "If I was, I would have informed the local surveillants. Then again, I don't plan on staying very long, so there is no need for me to stop at the fort."

The senior officer nodded at him. The forts built for the Surveillance were usually far from the center of the town or city they belonged to, and although they were initially military castles, under times of peace they became the Surveillance's meeting points. It would make sense for a younger officer to prefer the bustling center for a short stay, but it wasn't enough of an explanation as to why the Surveillance hadn't let Dunac know about Goldsnout's presence. It mattered little that the latter wasn't on duty, for he wore the uniform of the Surveillance, and represented the Regency in the simple people's eyes.

"What happened at the central inn is a problem, I hope you understand that," Dunac explained, relieved to see Goldsnout hold his stare. "I can't avoid reporting it."

"Chief Eleres doesn't know I am here," Goldsnout confessed. "The man at the inn attacked me and Miss Rantha," he added, his fingers circling the bandage on his mauled cheek.

"With or without my report, Chief Eleres will understand something is off since half the side of your face is covered."

"What do you want me to say, Senior Officer?"

Dunac eyed him briefly, pursing his lips. "I have a feeling you were at the inn because of that dead girl who is on everybody's lips. I can report you were violently interrupted during your search or, I don't know," the senior officer cleared his throat, "I could say you were being robbed while in sweet company."

Opherus' stare darkened instantly. The man before him would lie about Miss Rantha without any second thoughts, given the fact that a former servant's honor mattered little to the likes of him. Surely, such a report would leave not even a stain on the timeline of Goldsnout's promising career, but it was a lie that tarnished someone else's reputation. Not to mention that Chief Eleres knew him well enough to not believe that he rode to Rainier's End just to find himself a harlot. Saer Dunac had perfectly guessed that Goldsnout's presence hadn't been requested by anyone and that he wasn't there on behalf of the chief. He couldn't have any report mentioning his unofficial investigation when Chief Eleres expressively told him to keep his priorities straight. Goldsnout knew that Dunac was offering him a way out without prying, though it was not an option.

Fat raindrops ran down his face and neck, trailing underneath his shirt and causing him goosebumps. "You can report the truth," Goldsnout whispered. "You can tell the Regency I was attacked by a man ready to kill me and everything I stood for because of his utter distrust and hate for us, for the Surveillance, for the Regency. The man spoke clearly.

"You can also report that he had a weapon forged in the black market because he was ready to take down the next Silver Master who would attempt to collect taxes from him. Perhaps this is where Rainier's End begins to starve."

Dunac straightened his back, clenching his fists at the brash tone the younger officer was using with him. "Careful, Officer. You can't know that," he pointed out.

"Oh, but I can. I was raised in streets like these," Goldsnout argued, extending his arms as if to make the brown-eyed man look around. "It begins with the drinking, the brawling, the people gathering at the inn or some other tavern because they can't afford wood anymore and don't own land to chop it and use it to warm themselves.

"It doesn't take long to switch from hot pies to roasted mice, Senior Officer Dunac."

"Winter is harsh on the population, it always was."

The two of them looked at each other in silence, the heavy rain turning Goldsnout into a dripping mess. His shirt clung to his body like a second skin but he didn't feel it. He couldn't feel anything as he wondered if the man before him was the author of the report he read the day before.

Licking his lips and tasting dirty water, the younger officer asked, "Why did you mention in your reports the rising violence in Rainier's End if winter was always harsh on the population?" Reaching behind him to open the door, Goldsnout bowed his head deeply in respect. "I wish you a good sleep," he whispered before stepping back and disappearing inside the shelter without taking a look at the man who remained silent. Goldsnout could feel his heart hammering against his chest, and he wondered if the previous agitation he sensed was truly Rantha's or if it was his own.

He rested his back against the door, staring with a pair of unblinking eyes at the puddle that formed around his boots. He was drenched from head to toe, something that last happened when he was, perhaps, a boy playing in the mud of Limemeadow's outskirts. Goldsnout sniffled, feeling his body turn cold. He still didn't know what had gotten into him all night; he felt as if his body had been possessed while he was still conscious. He felt like the spectator of his own life since his blade disemboweled the drunk who wanted his blood.

  Goldsnout walked soundlessly inside the kitchen, ignoring Rantha's questions and panicked demeanor as she ushered him near the fireplace, suggesting that he take off his wet rags while she fetched something dry for him to wear. She blabbed on as she wanted to know who he talked to and what they wanted, but all he could think of was Chief Eleres and the infinite amount of cussing that would be directed at him. He had left the capital to help a friend, only to end up sentencing a man with his sword and act disrespectfully to a superior of his. Although he had properly phrased his point of view, Goldsnout doubted that Dunac would simply shrug off the insinuations that were made. The young officer was treading on dangerous waters, testing the limits of subordination, and a part of him wondered if that was the reason why Eleres always kept him around. Was he not to be trusted? He wondered. Was he too impulsive, too careless of the rules of the Surveillance?

  Would the drunk be dead if Chief Eleres had been with him?

"Opherus," Rantha's voice snapped him from his thoughts. "Wear this before you come down with the fever." She pushed a pile of clothes in his arms, as well as a thick cover that looked like it was made of wolf fur.

The redhead's hand reached out for her arm, tugging her in place when she tried to leave to give him some privacy. "I'm sorry, Miss Rantha," he told her shamefully. "I came because I said I would help you, but I fear that after tonight's events, it will be hard for me to find a way to leave the capital and continue looking."

The disappointment in her eyes was crushing him. "Of course," she nodded, "I understand. Your injuries are too obvious," she reasoned out loud. "Is it safe to assume it was another surveillant at the door?"

It was Goldsnout's turn to nod. "A report will be sent to the Surveillance's headquarters. Chief Eleres will have my head, and I don't know if it is just a figure of speech."

Her expression softened, and she placed her hand on top of his, leaning in. "You did more than you should have," she reassured him. "I don't think I will ever find the truth about Yenny, but I will try. You have given me a path to follow, Opherus. I just need to figure out if she had acquaintances I didn't know of, and see from there," she told him, her hand tightening around his so that he would finally look at her. "I doubt your chief will punish you for doing the right thing; honoring a promise."

"You are right," he whispered back before straightening up. "And I should probably change," he chuckled at himself, letting go of Rantha to place the new clothes on the nearest chair.

The curly-haired woman turned heels the moment Opherus' shirt was off, hastily dragging her feet towards the door to respect his privacy. Her fingers grazed the door handle when she heard the man behind her ask her a question. She could feel the smile in his voice.

"I am sure you've helped other men change, or am I wrong?"

Her lips curved up, but she refused to turn around. "You're not my patient, Opherus," she reminded him as she left, repressing the urge to laugh as her cheeks felt a little warm.

✳✳✳

The feel of cold water splashing all over his feet caused Jascha to frown and curse under his breath. The horse standing next to him came to an abrupt stop as he pulled on the reins, muddying his boots even more. A few people collided around him in the busy marketplace of Silverholde. The stands had been placed all around Jehanel's Forum, and one of the nearby twin bridges that separated the plaza from the main areas of the capital was being threatened by the overflow of the Restless Channel.

As he waited for his turn at the fruit and vegetable stand, the inlander mentally summarized his less than fruitful research. He had spent the past few days skipping through the pages of Grandmaster Matillis' book, but none of the rituals she described came close to what happened to him.

He figured that the grandmaster had been mostly theorizing and collecting testimonials because had she seen anything that happened to the participants, she would have gone deeper into detail. Jascha had instead found information on a group that called themselves the Rosencircle, one that had seemingly dissolved over the centuries, subdivided into other unnamed groups. They claimed that they were the descendants of the First Wardens of Asarul, the first people to walk the earth renamed as Silver Lands, and they recognized no other civilization that originated from Alatros the Red's conquest. Each generation chose a matriarch that they called their Mastria, and their society followed the strict rules of a faith unknown to mankind. The members of the Rosencircle were often called witches and fays who believed in the Dreamer's message and denied the existence of the Oracle's power of premonition. As much as they were believed to have perished in the fire of Soleba, subgroups were said to be crawling the earth still, but none of that was useful in Jascha's eyes. There had been no mention of sudden pain, blood, and visions.

    Yenny had mentioned recorded cases of witchcraft, and Jascha figured it was probably what he should have been looking for instead. However, he couldn't shake off the feeling that Matillis' book had been placed there for a reason. There had been someone else with him on that floor; he was sure of it. For a brief moment, he thought that Rosaleah, the bookkeeper at the entrance of the athenaeum, had been the one to sneak past him. She seemed intrigued by his piqued interest in witchcraft, or perhaps he was getting more paranoid every day.

"So, you're not reopening Ye Jazzy Mole?" he heard a man behind him ask another. "That sucks more than your momma in Jamys' Yard."

"Watch your dirty tongue, ya fucker," an older voice retorted, the annoyance in his tone being all too clear to everyone around them. "That fat face, Sarkis, completely bailed on me; some actor he was. We had the entire play written out; it was going to be something new. Satire, ya know? We even had costumes with them real crests of them nobles, and we had wax seals of the Regency forged," he grunted loudly. "Ya have no idea how much I invested in this, and one day, this fucker is gone. Even my shit is missing; I bet ya he sold it all to some other playwriter."

Jascha glanced behind him, eyeing the two burly men who yapped around in their dirty clothes.

"I told you, you should have kept it as a tavern. I mean, I am sure everyone enjoyed the entertainment, but pies and wine are easy money; you never know if what you put in those plays is ever coming back," his friend smugly advised.

"I know it's not coming back, fuckers."

Jascha walked up to the stand the moment the lady before him walked away and merely nodded at the skinny, hairless man behind the counter. He pointed at a couple of items without really thinking about what he wanted, but he figured a few pears would do for breakfast. The inn he stayed at, behind Maugre's Arena, only offered onion soup and chopped carrots. Having them every day was slightly depressing.

"What a stallion you got here," the greengrocer commented with a toothless smile.

"It's a mare."

The skinny man laughed loudly at that, placing Jascha's items in a paper bag. "These Avoryon mounts are so tall and strong, you'd assume they're all male."

"I don't."

"What's this beauty's name?" the greengrocer asked, wiping his hands on the front of his coat. "Special beasts usually have special names."

"Arora," Jascha simply replied, fishing inside his pocket for a silver. "What are you doing?" he asked with narrowed eyes as the man added vegetables he didn't ask for to his food.

"It's celery, for the lady. It makes horses go faster."

Jascha raised both eyebrows, resisting the urge to smirk. "Really?"

"No, I'm just messing with ya. Ya seem to be a good lad. And this celery would rot anyway with this weather."

Jascha reached out for the bag he was handed when he felt a tug on his pants. Glancing down, he spotted a boy who couldn't have been older than four years of age, his round face coated in dirt. His wet black hair clung to his scalp and he wore nothing that would have shielded his small body from the harsh winter. He raised himself on his tiptoes and extended a hand, his tiny blackened nails trying to grasp Jascha's food.

The man kneeled, offering the bag to the boy. "Take it," he told him, but before the boy could, a woman's voice scolded him.

"Josclyn," she called her son. "I told you not to do that," she roared, tugging the boy away. Her grey-blue eyes peered at Jascha; the shame written all over her tired face. "I apologize."

Jascha's dark stare fell on the woman. She looked as old as his mother before she passed away, with crow's feet spreading out from the corners of her eyes and lines framing her lips. Her hair was covered by a rag she probably used as a shawl when it wasn't raining, and her dirty blue dress spoke years of poverty. The woman was dangerously skinny, and the small bag she carried probably contained food that wasn't near enough for her and her son. Jascha stood up, offering his grocery bag to her.

"I insist," he said plainly.

The woman's tears were not the reaction he expected. She sobbed and covered her eyes with her forearm, holding back as much as she could. The dark-haired man tilted his head in sheer curiosity, letting the little boy between them reach out for the pears inside the bag. The fruit disappeared in his mouth after two or three bites, and soon the two men who had been waiting behind Jascha started complaining out loud.

"If ya done, move the fuck aside!" he heard the play writer growl.

Jascha tugged his horse back into the muddy puddle, effectively dirtying the burly and rude man's cloth shoes, moving to the side slowly to send a cold glare his way. He motioned the woman to follow him in the direction of the street, but she wept inconsolably, limping beside him.

"I am sorry, I don't usually overreact like this," she said with a ragged voice. "It's just that it's been three days since our last meal."

Jascha caught the boy munching on the leaves of the celery, and he glanced back at the greengrocer's stand. "Do you need—"

Before he could even offer it, the woman shook her head vehemently. "You're too kind, but we will be fine. I received some silvers for my work at the baker's."

Turning to look at the boy, Jascha asked him, "More pears?"

The child immediately disappeared behind his mother, peeking at him half-hidden in her dress.

"Josclyn," the mother scolded him again. "At least, thank the kind man." The boy disappeared behind her once more, and she sighed out. "Forgive him. He doesn't talk much." She placed a cold hand on his upper arm. "Would you have breakfast with us? I bought a few slices of bacon. We also received some eggs and soup from our neighbors, that is, if you don't mind walking down Jamys' Yard."

"Why would I?"

"It is not the safest of areas."

Jascha shrugged, patting the side of his Avoryon mount. "Need a ride?" he asked the woman.

The woman hoisted herself up awkwardly before Jascha lifted the boy, the mother and her son clutching the horn while Jascha walked beside them, tugging the reins in the direction he was told. The boy fell asleep against his mother's chest in no time, and as it rained harsher than before, Jascha covered his head with his hood. They exited Jehanel's Forum rather quickly. Soon the streets were empty, as if the population rushed to the capital center, avoiding the residential areas, and Jascha quickly understood why.

The cobbled streets were replaced by dirty pathways and small patches of grass. He spotted many tents around the buildings that fell apart, and people with more diseases than teeth glared at him as he entered the Yard. Tall, dying trees dangerously leaned towards the small houses and huts crammed together on each side of the pathway, and the stench that arose was a clear indicator that no sewers had been constructed in that area of Silverholde. Rats as big as cats ran from house to house, some of them feasting on the corpses of the homeless.

The road went slightly uphill, and in the distance, he could see cupolas between the thick clouds. "Rainier's Pavilion is on the other side of the Restless Channel," he heard the woman say. I am afraid it is the only great sight of this part of the city."

He could understand why. The emptiness of Jamys' Yard was in clear contrast with the cries that emerged from the houses and abandoned huts, the yelping of women in pain mixing with the strangled whining of starved infants and suffering old men who waited to die in their beds before being thrown out. None of them could afford cremation, none of them believed in the Heights' redemption. Neither did he, he thought as his gaze fell on the sight of a woman rummaging through the open-air garbage museum before him.

"Jamys' Yard was named after Prince Jamys the Doomed," the woman told him. "Prince Jamys was the second-born of King Renfry Rainier, and he had made it his cause to build safe homes for the entire population. However, the expenses were so high that after a couple of solid buildings, he had to resort to lesser materials, until the day King Renfry put a stop to it.

"Prince Jamys hoped the people would support his claim as king once his father passed away, confiding in the admiration they nurtured for him, but spending so much time with the simple people only caused Prince Jamys to come down with the fever. He died a few months after his brother's coronation."

"King Phorbas the Devoted," Jascha finished for her. "The one who built more temples than proper housing," he added in a whisper.

"Stop here."

Jascha helped her dismount, offering his hand, which the frail woman only took after her ankle nearly gave way under her weight. The child was quick to rush inside the small, thatched-roof house, leaving the door open behind him. The woman's shawl fell around her shoulders, revealing short and matted black hair.

"This is where you live."

"I-I am sorry, I realized I haven't even… I haven't properly introduced myself," she stammered. "My name is Mawde."

"I'm Jascha," he said in return, the left side of his lips curving up. "Is there somewhere I can leave my horse without her freezing to death?"

Mawde nodded, pointing at the stable squeezed between her house and another. "It's been unused for quite some time since we had to sell everything… the horses first, then the cattle, then…" She paused, forcing herself to smile. "There is a hole in the roof but there are dry spots as well." She dragged her feet as she made her way inside, and Jascha hurried his mount to the stable, a part of him wondering if this short trip had been a good idea.

He formed a loose knot with the reins, knowing that the animal wouldn't just run away on its own. He decided he would leave quickly enough, knowing full well that if he didn't, someone would attempt to steal his mount and resell it. The whole place stank anyway, and he wanted to be at the athenaeum the moment it opened.

Jascha tapped the front of his boots against the wooden floor as he walked in, trying to shake off the mud before he dirtied everything. Mawde and her son were living in a single room, with a lit fireplace in the far corner, and the few belongings they owned stacked on the opposite side. He spotted a covered chamber pot that emanated a smell just as foul as the stench of the entire area, and he wondered when was the last time they had washed it. Little Josclyn was already opening the small bag that contained raw bacon, and his mother was quick to snatch the food away to cook it. Mawde removed the lid of a pot to check its contents before hooking the pot above the fire. Perhaps, even she wasn't sure the soup was still edible.

What Jascha hadn't expected, however, was the young woman who quietly sat in front of the fireplace, staring at him the moment he stepped in.

"Jascha, come closer to the fire," Mawde said while his eyes were focused on the woman who arched an elegant eyebrow at the mention of his name.

Her hair was dark chestnut, and her eyes as green as spring. Her skin was fair and her cheeks slightly flushed from the cold, although her body was entirely covered by white fur that must have belonged to an Avoryon bear. She looked too clean for a woman who lived in Jamys' Yard, that much he could tell. He hadn't spotted not even one bucket of water inside the house, figuring that bathing was the least of Mawde's worries.

He walked up to the older woman, his eyes as black as raven feathers glancing at the eggs the woman was boiling in a smaller pot, ignoring the younger woman who was being hugged by the silent boy. "Your daughter?" he asked her, although their facial features differed too much for the two to be related.

Mawde smiled at him again, shaking her head. "No, Rosewillow is my daughter's friend. She came here for a visit."

"So, you do have a daughter."

She nodded, adding a little salt to the soup she just tasted. "Leah has been extremely busy at the athenaeum. She rarely comes home as it is a long walk from there. She and Rosewillow met at the temple some years ago, is that correct?" she asked, briefly glancing at the green-eyed woman who played odds and evens with the child. "The temple offers temporary shelter for those who work in the center."

Jascha had never heard of temples welcoming the workers for extended periods, but he wasn't about to contradict the woman who wouldn't stop talking.

Before Rosewillow could answer, Mawde introduced him. "Jascha here kindly offered us some food at the marketplace. I invited him to have breakfast with us."

"I am afraid I won't be able to stay, Mawde," he quickly told her, ignoring the dejected look on the woman's face. "Thank you for the offer."

"Oh." Removing her wooden spoon from the pot where she stirred the onion juice, she offered him a polite smile. "Feel free to visit anytime."

Rosewillow stood up, her fingers brushing against little Josclyn's cheek. "Heading to the center?" she asked him bluntly. "Would you mind if I join you?" she asked as she stepped closer to him.

His black orbs looked into her unblinking eyes. The woman barely reached his chin, but she carried an aura bigger than the room. He wasn't intimidated, but his insides were churning and the only thought that filled his mind was to leave. Perhaps it was the green of her eyes or the familiar, yet uncomfortable feeling that sent shivers down his back. He tried to remember whether or not he met her before, failing miserably at the task. She was an average woman in terms of looks and clothing, and he was certain that many others looked just like her, but no one came to mind as he tried to remember her face. Concluding that he was, indeed, getting more paranoid by the day, Jascha stuck out his chin a bit before turning heels.

"You're walking," he told her.

Chapter XVIII

The Devoted

The sweet acidic smell that permeated the room made Fantine's head reel. Her stomach churned, and she felt the bile collect in her throat as she kept her eyes tightly shut. The back of her head felt extremely heavy, and she wondered if the swelling still hadn't reduced. The master-at-arms had no idea how long she had been out, but if the hard mattress of her single bed was any indication, she assumed it had been at least a day or two. Her deep blue eyes glanced around. Her foggy vision still allowed her to recognize the dull bed-chamber that was hers. Soon, the shape of someone's head hovered over her, partially hiding the wooden ceiling.

"Easy, easy," she heard an old person whisper. "Don't try to sit up, Fantine. Your body is still weak."

"Martus?" she whispered, coughing when her tongue felt dry.

She was offered a glass of warm water that smelled of rosemary and lemon, and she involuntarily made a face. Forcing herself to take a sip, the seasoned warrior felt her arms shake under her weight as she leaned on her bent elbows. She promptly fell back down, sighing loudly. Her back hurt as well, and she felt her chest tighten.

She had fallen from the library stairs trying to help Lord Tithan, and his body had completely crushed hers. Sitting up instantly, nearly retching from the sudden movement and the realization that Lord Tithan had been harmed, Fantine reached out for the end table to try and stand up, using it as support. Healer Martus' reaction was quick as he placed his swollen hands on her shoulders.

"Please, you need more rest."

Eyeing the bowl full of Dreamer's Root dust, she scowled. "Get that away from me. I need to check on Lord Lionhelm." The sudden understanding that she had been kept asleep sent her into a panicked state. Had they not woken her because her lord's fall had been fatal? Her lips parted slightly, and she immediately covered her mouth with one hand. She couldn't have failed Lord Tithan, could she? A million questions invaded her mind, and she couldn't help but feeling both ashamed and at fault.

"It is because of me, isn't it?" she whispered. "I told him about Lord Thaesonwald, and he wasn't—it wasn't my place to—"

"Calm down, dear," the old healer interrupted her, his thick, black eyebrows knitted together. "If it wasn't for you, Lord Tithan would be in a critical state if not worse," he reassured her. "His coughing worsened, and he's been in bed just as you have. I have requested a consult from the physicians of the Regency."

She nodded at his words, her short hair tickling her round chin. Fantine tried to steady her breathing, but Martus noted the paleness of her face and he lifted a small, empty bucket he had used to bring the water he needed for his remedy. Fantine immediately grabbed it as if her life depended on it, dry heaving and spitting bile. Her strained body was at its limit, and tears prickled her eyes. She had never felt this weak in over thirty years of service. She had been at Lord Tithan's side since she was twelve years of age, followed him on every campaign assigned to him, trained with him, and trained his men, his sons, his guards. And yet, that fall had rendered her useless.

"Who is guarding him now?" Fantine asked with a faint voice.

"Our best guards are at his doors day and night."

Her blue orbs peeked at Martus, and he could see the uneasiness in the look she was giving him. "I can't stay here and you know it.

"Lord Thaesonwald's death was not due to his accident, you told me. What if the person who murdered Lord Tithan's heir is still around?" Lord Tithan hadn't felt safe in years, she knew that much the moment he appointed her as his guard instead of relying on the palace security. She wasn't about to tell Healer Martus just that, but it was clear as day. "Just give me a stick, Martus. I've seen worse," she lied, stubbornly convinced that no matter her health condition, she needed to be by her lord's side.

"Lady Gwethana was arrested for what happened to Lord Thaesonwald. It is Lady Voladea and Lord Tylennald's belief that she is involved. The guests from Lady Tecla's ball have also left; the palace is only filled with trustworthy family members," the healer argued, sliding his hands in his large sleeves.

Fantine nearly snorted. Her muscles twitched as she forced herself up, leaning against the edge of the bed as she stumbled forward in an attempt to walk. "Lord Tylennald is still here, isn't he?"

"He and Lady Wallysa are staying to comfort Lady Voladea. Lord Riverguard won't leave without them either."

"Arrange bedding in the antechamber of Lord Tithan's apartments. I will not leave him," Fantine ordered him, reaching for her broadsword by the door. She painfully leaned to the side as she used it as an ineffective crutch. "I can't stay in these barracks, they are too far from the palace," she added in a strained voice.

Healer Martus stood up as well, a serious look on his wrinkled face. With a tone void of his usual friendliness, he stoically pointed out, "No one has ever been granted the privilege of sharing Lord Lionhelm's apartments. I understand that you take your duty seriously, even more so than anyone at the lord's service, but you have no right to make such decisions."

"You are Lady Voladea's family healer," Fantine argued without even looking back at him. "Yet, you have treated Lord Lionhelm, fully knowing that he never allowed you to throughout the years."

"His life—"

"—is mine to protect," she barked. "You will not approach until the Regency's physicians reach Strongshore." Glaring at him as she opened the door, she asked, "Is that clear, Healer Martus?" When the old man didn't answer, his fists clenching and unclenching inside his sleeves, she repeated, "Did I make myself clear, old man?"

"I shall convey your words to Lady Voladea. As her husband is incapacitated, she has the authority to decide for her household."

The glowering glare he received didn't make him falter.

"I pray for your good recovery, Fantine," he concluded, moving to gather his plants and herbal infusions.

✷✷✷

"Have you not recovered yet?" Old Martita's voice bellowed.

Sarkis was curled into a ball by the fire, entirely covered by the red fur blanket Martita had given him. The burly man was sobbing silently, poking the fire with a stick, occasionally lifting the lid of the pot where the steaming broth was being cooked.

The old woman grunted to herself, sharpening the broadhead of another arrow against her lime. She sat on a short stool with her legs parted and her back fully hunched, the wood cracking under her weight with each movement she made. The toothy boy had been crying over Big Pat's death for days, and after they buried his ashes in Old Martita's yard, the weeping only increased. Sarkis had rambled about the injustice and the atrocity of what happened to Patten's body and complained about the way Martita dealt with his remains. He asked her over and over why she hadn't shed a single tear and how she was able to just burn the remains as if they were waste. He asked her why they hadn't prayed, not even in silence. Martita never answered him, preferring to spend every day in silence.

"You didn't even know him," she pointed out coldly. "Get it together, Sarkis. You won't find food by sitting around."

"I am a very bad hunter," he sniffled, a hand coming to scratch his face and wipe the tears away. "I can't even aim; I don't know why you're sharpening your arrows," he whimpered. "Maybe I can work at the Seven Galleys tomorrow, if they need me, and buy something… Rice maybe? Do they even have rice at the market?" he sniffled again.

"You airhead, these aren't for you to use," Martita scolded him. "You need to feed yourself for the next few days. It's time you get your fat, stinky ass up, Sarkis. I am serious," she told him, throwing her last arrow in the pile of sharpened blades. "I am going."

Sarkis blinked a couple of times before turning around, clutching the blanket. "Going where? Tita," he called, staring as the old woman stuffed a bag with dry food and flasks that contained either acidic wine or water. She had enough sharpened arrows to take down someone's army, he thought, only to realize he had never seen a real army. "What are you doing?"

"I am going to terminate the witches who did that to Pat," she answered plainly as if what she just said was as natural as telling him she would be out for work.

"Terminate? T-the w-witches?" Sarkis stammered. "What are you talking about?" He had heard her mention witches in front of the officers who brought Patten's remains home, but he thought she was just name-calling the boy's butchers. "Tita, please," he pleaded, standing on wobbly legs. "I am concerned."

Old Martita froze for a moment, her lips thinning as she thought. She put her bag down, her eyes never meeting Sarkis' stare. The many lines across her face seemed more accentuated than ever, and her hazel eyes turned a darker shade of brown. "You are from the capital, I don't expect you to understand," she muttered.

Sarkis swallowed the sob that threatened to choke him. "I can try to," he told her.

"Before the Silver Lands were the Silver Lands, the forest of Wilderose was part of a region known by all as Soleba. It was said to be populated by the First Wardens, the first women and men to have walked on the continent, Asarul.

"The First Wardens claimed to be the incarnations of the fays, the spirits of the dead that drifted to our shores from faraway lands. Contrary to what history claims, the First Wardens were never conquered by Alatros the Red, who was said to be very superstitious himself; either that or the sight of the never-ending forest deterred him from crossing it, settling instead for the western paths that eventually led him at the doors of Old Calaris, a city that back then included today's Summerport and other territories that later sunk in the sea.

"When the Faith of the Oracle was born, it was widely embraced by the lands conquered by Alatros, but Soleba's people remained true to themselves, worshipping deities we know nothing of, until the day the Dreamer's message was found, and the First Wardens began to come out in the open, declaring that the Oracle's words were lies.

"They successfully convinced a large number of the Angels of Steel that the Oracle was to be eliminated, and the mortal woman Kothore was murdered in the Oracle Pillar. Her daughters, who entertained the flame on top of the pillar were shown no mercy either."

Sarkis listened carefully, occasionally licking his lips and swallowing. "I've heard legends about the Dreamer," he said. "They say she was an imposter who claimed to be Kothore's twin sister."

Martita nodded curtly. "So they say. However, following the massacre, Alatros the Red and his queen proceeded with the arrest of the

Angels of Steel who had plunged their blades in the Oracle's body, crucifying them to the trees of Soleba, before burning them alive. Nearly the entire forest disappeared in the fire, and the vast majority of the First Wardens perished as well. Alatros called himself the Potentate of the Salurites after this.

"It was meant as a warning, as well as an opportunity to eradicate the First Wardens' beliefs from the continent. However, those who survived are rumored to be acting in the shadows still. Many centuries later, in 956 BCR, King Phorbas the Devoted passed a law that allowed only his builders to construct temples. His ministers convinced him to not raze any previously built temple, to avoid rebellions in the North. To be more precise, to avoid the rebellion of the people of the Sand Towers. They never flinched under Alatros the Red, and therefore still follow different traditions in the holy city of Hvallatr. However, any other religion practiced in the shadows of the realm was deemed to be witchery and treachery," Martita concluded.

Sarkis walked up to her, only to kneel in front of her, his eyes searching hers. His protruding front teeth stabbed his lower lip as he spoke. "Are you saying that Patten was a victim of said fanatics? How do you know all this? You are as educated as Theliel, you know, Tita."

She flicked his forehead. "Not everyone is as dumb as you, boy."

"I am just—"

"I told you I had a younger sister," she reminded him. "A sister who might be alive, and two younger siblings who were not as lucky. My younger sister was wed to a man who believed in the Dreamer's message more than in common sense. Her name was Briar," Martita whispered. "She had daughters, two or three I think before she disappeared at the hands of the fays."

"How do you know it was the witches? And what about your brother; was he a victim of theirs as well?"

Shaking her head and picking up her bag, Old Martita rummaged through it to check if she had forgotten anything. "My brother died shortly after his birth." Grabbing her quiver from where it hung on the wall, she put her arrows in it, her small eyes darting around to check where her bow was. "Pat was found dismembered in the Wilderose forest. I've seen Briar do it in the same location," she said, answering his previous questions. "I was too late to save her from that life, and I was too late for Pat," the old woman angrily stated. "I am not too late to end those women's plans."

Sarkis blocked her way to the door, waving his hands in front of him. "You're crazy!" he exclaimed. "You can't be serious, Tita. You are telling me that you've seen them butcher people before, and you just want to find them. You're out of your mind." When she stared at him unfazed, Sarkis panicked. "You're older than Alatros the Red's breast milk, and you want to take down those... those bitches! On your own!"

With a flick of her wrist, Martita shoved the tip of her bow in his bouncy stomach before slamming it against his throat, knocking the air out of him and sending him to his knees. She ignored the way the man gasped for air.

"I think I will be fine, fleabag."

"Tita…" Sarkis coughed out.

"If Theliel shows up in the meantime, tell him to stay out of trouble," Old Martita said, pulling the door open. "And you too," she added with a less harsh tone.

The slamming sound startled Sarkis, but when he finally stood up, the old woman was gone. A part of him feared that she would not return. Bringing both hands to his head, Sarkis nearly tugged his locks to the point of hurting himself. The smell of burnt meat reached his nostrils and he cursed loudly. He rushed to the fireplace, burning his fingers when he forgot to grab a rag before touching the lid. Peeking inside the pot, he noticed that most of the broth had been absorbed by the overly cooked meat.

Grabbing the long-handled shovel by the fireplace, Sarkis promptly put out the flames by scooping up the ashes. Food could wait, he figured. He had to find Tita, he told himself, despite the fear that caused him to feel weak in the knees. Sarkis absentmindedly glanced at the ashes in the fireplace before leaving, reminding himself of what happened to Patten.

❋❋❋

Rubbing her arms and hurrying next to the fire that burned on top of wood and ashes, Tecla smiled to herself. She had expected her bed-chambers to be as plain and straightforward as Theliel's, only to discover that her brother had requested for her the largest and most recent apartments at Rainier's Pavilion. Her bed-chambers were located on the middle floors of the Observatory's wing, the surrounding rooms being occupied and warm, keeping Tecla's apartments at a cozy temperature, although the southern girl wasn't used to the harsh winter of the inland and still felt chilly.

    Wearing a coat dress of a silver color lined with faint, pale blue streaks that reached the floor and with a dark blue scarf hugging her neck, the youngest Lionhelm left the warm spot to walk up to the nearest window, gazing at the snow outside. She could see down below the busy streets of the city, and the emerald cupola of the athenaeum. Theliel had promised he would take her to the city soon enough, as they would spend a few days exploring the capital before the next dusk days. It wouldn't be anytime soon, however, she agreed with Theliel that a change in scenery would benefit them both before they visited their father.

    Tecla found Silverholde to be quite colorful, from the buildings to the bustling sounds, but in the distance, she could see a much greyer, less than lively area. On her way to the Regency, she had been too enthralled with Theliel's story to pay attention to what little she saw in the cobbled streets of the capital.

    "Young lady," she heard Lyzon speak somewhere behind her.

Tecla turned around, watching as the maid unpacked her belongings. She figured she might have brought too many things.

"You are to meet with Grandmaster Rodbertus," the older woman reminded her.

"Do you know what that place is?" Tecla asked, ignoring her friend's words and pointing at the darker area.

"I believe Educator Tomas mentioned Jamys' Yard," Lyzon said as she carried a pile of warm blankets to one of the many dressers of the room. "It is where the poorest people live, my lady."

"I see."

The girl frowned for a moment before turning around to stare at the room, coming to rest her hands on the backrest of a large, golden, and emerald chair set in front of a tea table made of crystal. The canopy bed looked plush and warm, and the colors of the sheets were the hues of her house. Tecla was content with the fact that the painted walls displayed the many sceneries of Silverholde, from the tall, vivid green rosewillows of the outskirts to the coronation temple. A part of her wanted to visit it, wondering if it was as majestic and intimidating as the temple in Oracle Hill.

A knock on her door caused Lyzon to rush to open it, and she bowed her head before turning to face Tecla. "Young lady, Educator Tomas is here to accompany you to the Vault."

"Thank you, Lyzon."

Before walking past her, Tecla affectionately squeezed the woman's upper arm. She greeted

Tomas with a warm smile, hoping that at least the educator would be thrilled about being back in Silverholde, where he had trained. Lyzon had seemed out of place and extremely tired since their arrival, while Fran had been eager to tour the indoor gardens of the Pavilion alongside Tomas.

"How do you feel about being back to the Regency?"

"Quite excited, my lady," the tanned man beamed, folding his hands together on top of his belly as they walked. "It has been ten years since I was here."

"Since you were appointed to my service," Tecla added.

The man nodded, his purple turban moving slightly due to the motion. "I will miss the warm days in Strongshore," he admitted. "The humidity in the air is so high. I can feel it in my bones."

They walked down the endless corridor with hanging portraits of every Rainier's coronation, and Tecla was sure she could name each one of them. Tomas had always been strict about the royal genealogy and remembering every ruler born since the coronation of Aleyne Rainier in 1500 BCR was no easy task. The kings and queens of the Silver Lands were always crowned in Summerport until King Phorbas' reform and building of the many temples across the continent. Staring at the history that coated the walls of the Pavilion almost made Tecla feel like she lived on a different continent; gone were the endless depictions of Alatros the Red and the Oracle as they were replaced by the many faces of a dynasty that wasn't even as old or as powerful as the Lionhelms or the Rochelacs. The Sons of Ferngrunn's ancestry had roots that preceded the birth of Alatros the Red, Tomas had told her.

    Tecla had read a lot about the ancient times of Asarul after Destrian Snowmantle of Founder's Breach gifted her songs and poems of Old Calaris. The coasts had been the main settlements of many civilizations, from the people of Warrior Queen Aelneth in the South to the Sons of Ferngrunn in the North. Founder's Breach had been the home of the Sacred Sea Folk, a pacific tribe that consumed no meat from the Tides of Aelneth and the Rough Rill river and that quickly joined Warrior Queen Aelneth's people with the southern unification treaty she passed in 3306 BCR. On the other hand, the inland territories were divided into warring tribes from the Avoryon Hills to Noirmont, although all of them shared one common ancestor according to the Regency's Observatory Vault's research; Rohdron *vek' julpur*, or Rohdron the Skeleton, the one man said to have been born on top of the black mountain and to have fought all those who tried to claim Noirmont and its surrounding lands for themselves. Only after his first grandson's death, Gholl, did the tribes fall back into endless eras of war and starvation. And yet, despite the rich history of every territory that surrounded Silverholde, it was the Rainiers who kept the continent at peace and were celebrated through arts. Tomas once told the young Lionhelm that history and dynasty often became meaningless when one could grasp power without drawing blood. Aleyne Rainier had been but a noble lord of the northwestern coast, born in the city of Rockfall, the place that put an end to Emperor Kester Rochelac's violent territorial expansion and the formal war against Tecla's ancestor, Warrior King Raulyn Lionhelm. After Rainier had brought down the striges of the Fog Lands and allied with Lionhelm and the Sand Towers, the peace treaty signed in Flatgrave – the only standing city between the two warring forces – designed Aleyne Rainier as the First King of Asarul's Children and Defender of the Oracle. Flatgrave was rebuilt and renamed Silverholde and Aleyne Rainier married his cousin, Roesia Rainier, in 1503 BCR.

    As they rounded the corner, two sets of double doors were pushed open, and Tecla gawked. Grandmaster Rodbertus stood at the center of a round room with only one large window. Its painted glass was visible behind the Head of the Regency's Observatory Vault. The pillars that held the room together were engraved with old alphabets and ancient carvings, but they were split in the middle and rendered transparent, shining liquids of different colors flowing through them. Glancing around, Tecla realized that the room wasn't that round as the sides flared like sleeves, libraries taller than her father's shielding every desk where a member of the Observatory Vault worked or read. There were no stairs anywhere, and the observers simply used what looked like an automated, elevating platform. Gone was the emerald color that could be found in every corner of the Pavilion as it was replaced by the topaz hues that surrounded her.

Rodbertus walked towards her, bowing his head to her slightly. "Lady Tecla, welcome to the Regency's Observatory Vault."

Her eyes trailed up to the ceiling, where the Regency's motto had been written on the round frame. "One right, our fatherland," she whispered.

"And as such, we must preserve it," Tomas recited beside her.

Noting how the girl wasn't looking back at them, Rodbertus' smile widened and he bent down slightly to pull the lever by his feet. The ceiling immediately began turning like a clockwork of the Rain Lands, which she had only heard of, and the skies were soon exposed in all their cloudy glory, a long, retractable object unfolding its way down. Tecla moved, with eyes wide open, as the massive tool dangled its feet until they touched the floor.

"You seem surprised, my lady. I thought your father had a telescope of his own."

"My father—a telescope?" Blushing vividly, Tecla politely bowed at the grandmaster. "Forgive me, I haven't even addressed you properly," she said, blinking back up.

Rodbertus laughed at that, exchanging an amused smile with the educator. "Lord Lionhelm's observatory room has an identical telescope, Lady Tecla. This one was donated to the Regency by your lord father."

At the mention of her father, Tecla's excitement and awe quickly dissolved to be replaced by worry. It didn't go unnoticed by the two men, and Rodbertus quickly changed the subject. Guiding her through the room, he tried to be as concise as possible.

"These are the main libraries of the Regency. Our observers tend to spend most of their time memorizing these books, depending on their specialty fields. Some train to join the Regency as resident observers or future masters and grandmasters, while others, like Tomas here, are to become educators for the noble families of the Silver Lands.

"The Observatory Vault's goal is the research of both old and new technologies, as well as the discovery of forgotten populations. I won't deny that most of this is possible thanks to your family's patronage and Rockfall's contribution.

"Normally, what can't be found here is stored in Danyell's Athenaeum, as it is our King's wish to share as much knowledge as possible with the educated people of the land."

Tecla nodded; her full attention directed at him.

"For example, these," Rodbertus placed a hand on the glowing red column beside him, "are the result of a recent experiment. We have always known that rosewillows emanate a natural, green light, and we managed to extract the sap and give it different colors to create light without the use of fire."

"That's incredible," she whispered. "It's revolutionary."

"It is indeed." Grandmaster Rodbertus fingered his long braided beard. "Is there any area that particularly interests you?"

"I don't know, I…" She gulped; her smile uneasy. "I have always been more of a history person, Grandmaster. But there is so much more…"

A man clad in amber robes approached them hastily, bowing at Tomas and Tecla before whispering to Rodbertus, "A message for you, Grandmaster. It is from Strongshore."

Tecla frowned, her hazel eyes staring at the small scroll the eldest man was handed. "Is it my father?" she bluntly asked.

Rodbertus gave her a sympathetic look. "If it is, I will make sure to inform you. If you'll excuse me."

Tecla's gaze never left his figure as the man walked away and out of the room, and she almost didn't hear Educator Tomas' words had he not placed a hand on her shoulder.

"These rosewillow lights are astounding, aren't they?"

Before she could answer, the young man who had brought Grandmaster Rodbertus the message from Strongshore butted in. "Would you like me to show you the process? We documented it."

"If you don't mind, I'd be honored."

Their voices disappeared in the background as she walked around the main room, analyzing every corner and every map framed and hung on the walls. Tecla walked aimlessly through the libraries, where she found books about saddles for the disabled as well as incomplete deep-sea research and the so-called underwater fires. As her heels clicked against the floor, Tecla found herself in a corridor lined with drawings of the Red Continent and drawn trade routes connecting her homeland to the red shores. One of the maps was titled, "King Helias Rainier's Second Campaign: Flesh of The Lower Race – Campaign Leader: Lord Tithan Lionhelm." Several territories had been named on that map, but only the northern coast was readable, Kingbridge Hall. Tecla frowned at the wording, inwardly searching for the meaning behind it before something else caught her attention. There was a door, a much smaller one compared to the others, at the far right. Walking up to it, Tecla felt disappointed when it wouldn't open. Shrugging, she turned heels but stopped dead in her tracks as she heard it being opened.

    Glancing back, she saw a short, old woman cloaked in brown. Her grey hair was short and messy, looking like a turnip on top of her square face. Her bulky nose stood out, and her hazel eyes narrowed at Tecla. "Who are ya," she said. It wasn't a question. "Come 'ere."

    Tecla looked around and took a hesitant step forward. Her chin was immediately grabbed by the woman, who pulled her down forcefully. "I could recognize this face even blind. You're Tithan's daughter."

    "It's Lord Lionhelm," the girl huffed, pulling back. "Who are you?"

The short woman ignored her question. "You've got foreign eyes though. Another bastard child, aren't ya?"

Tecla felt the blood run straight to her face at the offense. "Excuse me?"

"Little bastard, don't ya try to open this door in the future. Ya listen?"

She moved to close and lock the door, but Tecla stuck her foot between the wooden door and the frame. "Who are you?" she repeated in a lower tone.

"Matillis," the woman grunted. "Haven't they told you?" Pointing behind her, she added, "The Occult Vault is no more. Ya listen? Go away." Kicking Tecla's foot out of the way with her own, the old woman slammed the door in the girl's face.

Tecla let out a silent exclamation of pain as she grabbed her foot and tried to balance herself on her other leg. Damning all old women to the Pit, for the time being, she limped her way back to the main room.

Chapter XIX

Return to Dirt

The ride from Courtbridge to the entrance of Wilderose had been silent. Goldsnout and his chief had been traveling for quite some days. They had readied their weapons and gathered a few essentials the moment Goldsnout returned from Rainier's End. Chief Eleres had been oddly silent about the officer's whereabouts, yet Goldsnout knew that if Dunac sent an owl after their exchange, his message reached the Surveillance in no time. Goldsnout's injuries were healing properly, however, his cheek was still bandaged and had caused the headquarters to be filled with rumors about what happened to him. Some believed that Goldsnout had acted on Eleres' behalf, while others were sure that the red-haired officer would be demoted rather than promoted. Despite all that, they still traveled together, and Thierry Eleres' thoughtful look was becoming unsettling.

Opherus' lime eyes glanced at the skies, watching the sunset in the distance as they approached the hill where the Rosenfield castle still stood proud. To believe that flames had engulfed more than half the Regency's elite fighters was harder than he thought. The castle was perfectly intact and even years of abandonment didn't make it look any less pristine and functional. Perhaps, that was just as unsettling as Eleres' silence.

They stopped in Courtbridge the previous night, but Lord Riverguard hadn't been present. They were still granted bedding and food at the barracks and a meek greeting from Lady Eloisa. The only words Goldsnout and the bald man riding beside him exchanged then were about Lady Eloisa's family, the Rosenbanes. Opherus had been surprised to learn that the Rosenfield family had a minor branch, the Rosenbanes, which originated from the attempt at legitimizing of one the bastard sons of Lord Karolus Rosenfield, a great-grandfather of Sir Frederyc Rosenfield. Unable to claim the child as his own for his wife had passed away, Lord Karolus gave his son Wilkie the surname Rosenbane. Backed by the friendship he shared with King Maucolyn, Wilkie Rosenbane was granted his land and a castle outside Silverholde, which had been used as the capital's main prison, Bane's Keep. Goldsnout had wondered out loud if the Rosenbanes had clues as to what happened to the Rosenfields, but Eleres had merely glared at him.

"The two families have no ties with each other since Lord Karolus passed away," he had said. "They do not want to have any. The late Lord Rosenbane passed his title and his lands to Lady Eloisa, for his son, Loys, had refused to take a spouse and lived as an estranged knight."

"But Lady Eloisa has two daughters herself," Goldsnout had argued, poking at a dry piece of bread.

"And one of them is married to Lord Tylennald Lionhelm. You put the pieces together, Opherus."

He tried, he did. As they approached the entrance of the castle, eyeing the lifted portcullis, Goldsnout couldn't help but wonder whether Officer Longspire had been right that day he argued with Officer Gulmont over history and politics. What if the Lionhelms had been the reason for the Rosenfields' demise? Lord Tithan Lionhelm was the overlord of the South, but one of his children was part of the Regency for a decade already, and another would inherit Courtbridge and the territories surrounding Rainier's End. Surely, Bane's Keep was in such a poor state no one ever thought of it as a castle anymore. Only the dungeons were somewhat being looked after, but Lady Wallysa was the eldest daughter of Lady Eloisa, and Lord Tylennald could easily take over Rainier's End and the keep, perhaps even restore it to its former glory.

With the Rosenfields' disappearance and the Rochelacs' hiding after the Violet Delusion, no one could oppose the Lionhelms, not even diplomatically. The Regency itself survived with Lord Tithan's patronage. Shaking his head,

Goldsnout tried to focus on his current mission. After all, would it be that bad for the Lionhelms to take over the continent? He wondered in silence. The South had been nothing but peaceful and prosperous under their rule.

Eleres trotted past him, a hand on the hilt of his sword as he scanned the entrance. It seemed that nobody was present, not even on the battlements. He believed in Lord Angefort's words, yet, at the same time, there was no evidence of the episode the old lord spoke of. The castle was deserted. Dismounting with ease, he nodded his chin in the direction of the gates behind the portcullis.

"Come here and let's close these before anyone else attempts to sneak inside," he ordered.

Goldsnout nodded and flung his leg backward, hopping down like a feline. Grasping a door handle, the officer pulled, releasing a deep breath when the heavy gate door wouldn't move. Eleres found himself in the same situation, and the two exchanged an embarrassed look. Neither of them had ever tried to push nor pull a gate door before.

"Get behind it and push it while I pull," Eleres suggested.

The redhead nodded, breaking into a light jog. The two grunted as they pushed and pulled, and suddenly, the gate felt a lot lighter, the door nearly slamming into Eleres' face. With the second one, Goldsnout decided to push with a little less force, not wishing to be locked inside. As soon as they were done, Eleres rubbed his gloved hands together before resting one of them on the iron door handle. He nodded to himself, nostrils flaring as he took deep breaths to recover from the short exercise.

"Alright," he whispered. "Let us inspect these woods before the sun completely disappears."

"I don't think we have enough time, Chief."

"That's why we brought torches."

Goldsnout hopped back on his horse the moment Eleres did, frowning at the man's back. "Chief," he called. "I am not sure this is a good idea given what you've told me."

The man halted his mount, his mustache moving when his lips curved down. "Lord Angefort was clear. The curiosities he spoke of happened after sunset, and if we are to replicate that evening, there are bigger chances of us walking straight into the monsters who dismembered that man," he reasoned.

Goldsnout shook his head, his wavy hair slapping against his cheeks. "If we were to replicate it, then tonight is not the right night. It is the first moon day today, but Lord Angefort came back on a dusk day. What he spoke of happened on a starless night, Chief Eleres."

"Son, I have no intention to argue with you. You will follow me now, or stay here."

The two of them rode in the direction of Wilderose without further ado, their flamboyant Regency capes flapping behind them. Goldsnout had never been in Wilderose before, and the wooded meadow they soon found themselves in was a beautiful sight to him. Trees of inky green towered all around them, reaching for the darkened skies. The bright grass and the colorful flowers their horses stomped were unnatural. It seemed as though the wintry weather hadn't reached Wilderose at all. There were no sounds of wild animals, not even the chirping of birds. They followed a soft stream, looking around for anything that could have given them an indication as to whether or not someone lived nearby. If they did, they would settle for a location near freshwater, Goldsnout thought. However, the deafening silence was heavier than the gate doors they just closed.

"Chief, what if the people we are looking for live in the castle?" he suddenly asked, his voice slightly echoing through the wooded meadow. "We could be looking in the wrong place."

"I don't think they live anywhere."

Goldsnout was taken aback.

"What do you see?" Eleres said out loud. "I see only nature, as pure as it gets. No trace of hunting, and tall grass everywhere, as if nobody ever walked through it," he reasoned in a dark tone.

The two glanced behind, taking note of how their path had been cleared. Where their horses had stomped their way, the grass was intact.

"We should head to Edgemere as soon as possible," Eleres prompted, the urgency of his tone sending shivers down the officer's back, "and come back with more men. We need to send an owl to the Regency."

Goldsnout nodded, his hands tightening around the reins. "Will we manage to do it without anybody alerting Strongshore?" he quickly asked.

"You said Lord Lionhelm cannot know of what happened until we find answers."

"We will manage," Eleres reassured him. "The Mayor of Edgemere is his daughter's husband, and I was told he is a reserved man. We might not run into him straight away."

They ushered their horses in the southeast direction, riding at a fast pace until the meadow was entirely replaced by pine trees and the sky was no longer visible. They slowed down the moment they began hearing gentle cricket sounds and the flapping wings of invisible birds. They hunched and dodged the lowest branches of the looming trees, short puffs of air clouding their faces as they exhaled in the chilly evening. Chief Eleres seemed concerned, almost frightened, and it was the oddest of sights for Goldsnout. The man had always been stoic, precise, organized, and well prepared for everything that was assigned to him, only this time, it seemed that his personal beliefs shattered his composure.

Stuck in his thinking process, Chief Eleres' question took him by surprise. "So, how is your friend in Rainier's End?"

"P-pardon?"

For the first time since they began working together, the bald man let out a hearty laugh. "I am not a fool, Goldsnout. You've stayed longer in Rainier's End before after we came across that woman. I received a report from Senior Officer Dunac; it was not difficult to guess what truly happened. The woman felt in danger, didn't she?"

Wondering what exactly Dunac had written, Goldsnout decided to go along with it. "Miss Rantha is doing better."

They remained in silence, both keeping their eyes on the city-port below. It was still far, only the lighthouse could be seen, but they would make it before the wee hours. "Have you asked for her hand?"

Goldsnout nearly fell off his horse. "Chief Eleres!"

The older man waved him off. "Don't waste your time, Opherus," he ordered him with a stern look. "Our lives are not easy. We spend our younger days training and the rest of our lives serving the people, the institution, a ruler we did not even meet," he spoke softly. "Take a bit of advice from an old man. I wish I had more time for my loved ones."

The red-haired officer frowned. He didn't know Chief Eleres had a family. "Where are they?" he softly asked.

"Behind the central inn in Rainier's End."

"What? But we were so close, and you didn't—"

"It's complicated, and I have no wish to talk about it. All I want is to return to them before I return to dirt," he solemnly stated before craning his neck to better look at the young man beside him. With a fatherly smile on his lips, he told Goldsnout, "If that woman truly caught your interest, let her know."

With a rising blush, Opherus looked down. "Yes, Chief Eleres."

***

Rounding the corner that brought him to the back of the inn he stayed at, the Wild Rock Skunk, Jascha came to a stop. He had been musing about the green-eyed woman he met at Mawde's little house, persuaded that he had seen those eyes before. Was she from one of the visions that plagued him? He didn't know, but the woman gave up the idea of walking back to the center of the capital when he made it clear that he wouldn't share Arora with her. It was one thing to help a starving woman get home, and another to allow a stranger who seemed perfectly fine to approach him. He had wanted to spend a little more time with the one who reminded him of his mother, perhaps out of nostalgia or curiosity, or both, but ultimately, he was better off on his own.

For that reason, he disliked being followed. "Show yourself," he spoke in the deserted alley cluttered with garbage and infested hounds.

The clicks of an armored body caused some stray dogs to growl around him, and Jascha turned around with narrowed eyes. The tall, blonde woman who had stopped him at the northern gates stood before him, her blue eyes piercing through his skull. The burning rosewillow on her chest plate was enough of an indication. She was a Nobleleaf, a vassal of the Sons of Ferngrunn, and the Regency colors of her cloak spoke for her.

Sir Sybbyl rested her hand on the hilt of her broadsword. It was of an onyx color with dozens of holes that had been filled with ruby-colored stones of little importance. The pointy pommel was equally red, a color that fit neither the Regency nor the Nobleleafs. Jascha had seen the sword being held by the lords of his homeland, in paintings that portrayed them during the Crimson Crystal Wars. Decimation was the sword's name, having bathed in more northeastern blood than other weapons.

"Is there any reason for this meeting?" Jascha asked with a hint of boredom. "I am fairly sure you haven't seen me unsheathe my dagger yet."

"Yet," Sybbyl emphasized. "I have some questions to ask you. But first," she said, walking forward. "You will give me your weapon."

To her surprise, Jascha looked amused. "On what grounds?" he asked, crossing his arms over his chest. He had little time for this; after the day he spent unsuccessfully finding information in the athenaeum, all he wanted was a bit of rest and to feed the horse that waited for him at the Wild Rock Skunk. When the Suppressor of War didn't answer him, Jascha saw an opportunity he hadn't thought of before. "Here is what will happen, Sir Sybbyl Nobleleaf." He saw her right eye twitch at the mention of her name. "You can have my weapon if you defeat me in a fair duel. If you fail," he offered, staring at Decimation, "you will hand me yours."

Her scoff was predictable. "Do you think yourself to be above the law? When a high-ranking member of the Regency, or the head of an order, commands you, you obey. Your dagger bears the head of the Beast of Three Crosses, which makes you either a thief or a servant of House Rochelac," inching closer, she opted for a menacing tone. "You can imagine my surprise upon seeing the symbol of a house that is rumored to have perished in the purple fog of Noirmont."

"No law allows you to disarm me when I harmed no one," Jascha pointed out. "You are the one who thinks to be above the law, Nobleleaf, not me. Are you afraid you wouldn't win?"

She shot him an incredulous stare. "I am armored from head to toe," she pointed out.

"Think of it this way," Jascha reasoned calmly. "We duel, I lose, you get both my weapon and the chance to interrogate me as we could consider the whole ordeal as me wielding my dagger to harm you. As you said, you're clothed in armor; that puts all the odds in your favor."

"Then, why would you do it?"

Jascha politely smiled, his white teeth showing. "See it as a friendly sparring session," he said. "As long as you stop following me, we have a deal."

The man had cunning written all over him, but Sybbyl unsheathed her broadsword, revealing its curved double edge. He said it himself; the odds were in her favor, and she wasn't about to hold back.

"A volcanic hilt and sand steel," Jascha noticed with glinting eyes. "Did you inherit the sword from Lord Ansketel Nobleleaf?"

The man knew his history, she realized. "My grandfather died before I was born," she retorted. "My brother Aslac gifted it to me when I was knighted by Sir Ferrand Nickletail at the age of fifteen."

"Quite the prowess, Sir Sybbyl."

Standing in a guarded position the blonde held her weapon, pointing it at his face. With a flick of his wrist, Jascha unsheathed his dagger, throwing it above his hand before catching it in mid-air, the end pointing between Sybbyl's eyes. Without a warning, her gaze holding Jascha's, Sybbyl went in with a horizontal slash, forcing the man into a deep backbend. Planting his foot forward, he came back to her side, nullifying her second blow. His dagger rested on her wrist, pointing at the exposed flesh between her plate and her glove, knowing full well that the mail would block his blow. He smiled at her again, reveling in Sybbyl's confused expression. With a roar, she stepped back, swinging Decimation straight in his face, but Jascha came forward and hit her hand, eliciting a yelp from the fighter, before aiming the dagger at her, yet again, covered neck. Keeping his last three fingers together, the black-haired man twirled his weapon, aiming at the back of her neck.

Inhaling deeply, the warrior held her broadsword with both hands, clutching the blade with her metal gauntlet to press the attack into her opponent, who didn't circle her at all and evaded her bursts while standing in front of her. Catching the way his body moved from side to side, she kicked him straight in the chest, only to stare at him wide-eyed as he crouched down before jumping over her head with ease, landing soundlessly behind her. Sybbyl swung her broadsword as she turned around, only to slice air since she blindly moved.

Jascha stared at her with hungry eyes before throwing his dagger in the air again, clasping the blade in his hand and cutting his skin while the opposite leg faced Sybbyl. He turned his upper body, throwing the weapon above from his shoulder. Quicker than wind, the dagger impaled itself in the wooden pile of discarded boxes behind Sybbyl, missing her barely. They stood in place for a few moments, catching their breaths and staring at each other in both horror and satisfaction.

The black-eyed man swallowed soundly, straightening his back. "Battle helmets still leave the eyes exposed," he pointed out. "Opting for a closed one would be a good investment on your part." Nodding his chin at her steel, Jascha added, "You lost."

"Bastard," she hissed, throwing Decimation at her feet before pulling at the sheath plastered at her side and discarding it as well. "Your moves," she breathed out. "Who, in the Oracle's birth name, are you?"

Folding his arms behind him, Jascha bent into a bow. "It was an honor dueling you, Knight of the Silver Lands," he said so seriously it nearly hid the mocking that lingered in the air.

Walking backward, out of the alley and into the main streets, Sybbyl tried to conceal the hatred and disappointment in herself. Her chest felt like it was about to implode as she aimlessly walked among the simple people, their fighting stuck in a loop before her eyes.

Staring at her fading silhouette, Jascha picked up the broadsword, eyeing the sharp blade before sheathing it, and retrieved his dagger. He scanned the deep cut in the palm of his hand, figuring that he would have to take care of it before it caused a bad infection. Glancing back at his newly acquired weapon, he broke into a faint smile.

"Welcome back," he whispered.

❋❋❋

The change in the wind felt like an icy rainfall. Goldsnout tugged on the reins of his horse even as Chief Eleres kicked his horse into a steady trot, only to yell at the officer who wasn't following him. The blasting wave that hit them straight in the face caused their horses to rear up, their ears flicking back and forth. Goldsnout was quickly thrown off the saddle, landing on the ground with a resounding thud of his armor. Eleres managed to dismount, albeit with a little difficulty, before rushing to the younger man's side and help him up. It wasn't long until their mounts ran away with all their might, leaving the two surveillants alone at the edge of the forest. Rubbing the back of his head, Opherus grunted a few curses, blinking around in the darkness.

The sound of Chief Eleres readying his weapon rang through his ears, and Goldsnout was quick to mimic his actions. They stood back to back with their knees bent and their swords stretched out like another pair of arms. The crickets and the owls had gone silent. Light rainfall quickly wet their heads, and Eleres dug the ball of his foot into the ground, readying himself to parry any sudden attack with a swing.

"Chief," he heard Goldsnout whisper behind him.

"Hush and keep your eyes open."

There was a faint light ahead of him, and Goldsnout narrowed his eyes to take a better look. Among the pine trees, a wider trunk stood out, fire all around it. It was a chestnut tree and its body looked like it had been parted, flaring into a round shape. The young man's face relaxed at the sight of it and its lighter green leaves. It would have remained unseen hadn't it been for the pyres around it. Goldsnout had heard legends about it, and he had always believed it to have been just his mother's invention when she ran out of bedtime stories to tell him. She called it the umbrella tree, or the Lioness' Shield, telling him how in 1220 BCR, on her way to wed Lord Thorkel Lionhelm, the youngest daughter of King Hendry, Ailith Rainier, found herself stuck in a terrible storm. She and the thousand soldiers who escorted her discovered the chestnut older than mankind, and sook refuge until the storm passed.

Eleres moved behind him at the sight of the umbrella tree, whispering a distinct, "May the Angels of Steel have mercy on us."

Looking away from the Lioness' Shield, Goldsnout's breath hitched in his throat. White shadows surrounded them. They were women, he realized. Barefoot women with sleeveless dresses of pure white. Every one of them held a torch in one hand, and their faces were masked as they wore soldier helmets over their heads. They stood silent, forming a circle around them. For a brief moment, Goldsnout wondered how they managed to ambush them without making a sound and light fires just as instantly. Was this how Lord Angefort found himself trapped in the Rosenfield castle? Were these the people who caused death in the most mysterious circumstances all over the Silver Lands? Were they the ones Chief Eleres had been looking for, for months?

"Chief, are we to… to…" Clinging to his sword, Goldsnout couldn't bring himself to speak the words.

"Annihilate these women?" the older man behind him finished for him. "If we must."

"But they're not carrying weapons."

The ground shook underneath their feet, and they both nearly lost their balance. It was as if something was trying to crawl out of the deepest recess of the earth, and before they could make a decision, three large roots emerged from the soil, nearly impaling them if it weren't for Eleres' push. One of the roots still pierced through the chief's foot, shattering his shin plate as it curled around his leg.

Eleres screamed, dropping to one knee and relinquishing the hold on his weapon, while Goldsnout took a swing at the growing roots. His blade vibrated as if it hit cold stone walls, and he rushed to the man's side, trying to free him.

"Stupid boy," Eleres groaned through pained lips. "Get out of here!"

"I will not!"

A clap caused the roots to fall back to the ground, and Goldsnout turned his upper body around, all the while keeping his chief's arm around his shoulders to help him up. A woman emerged from the old chestnut tree, a dented helmet hiding her identity and golden lace falling around her shoulders like hair. Unlike the other women, she wore a silver cloak to shield her body from the rain and cold weather. She stepped forward, but not close enough for Goldsnout to identify any particular feature of hers.

"What are you looking for, stranger?" she asked him. "Soleba is no one's to claim. You shut the gates of the respectful," she reminded him.

"Soleba?" Goldsnout repeated, taken aback. "The Rosenfield castle and its surrounding lands are under the Regency's supervision." Beside him, Eleres was groaning in pain and having a hard time keeping his eyes open. "State your identity!"

The woman laughed behind her masked face. "You stand in the presence of the Descendants of the First Wardens, and you are only allowed to know that because you will not leave alive."

As she unfolded her hands, the roots that trapped Chief Eleres moved again, slamming down Goldsnout's back and sending him face-first into the ground. He felt the wound on his cheek reopen as he gritted his teeth and tried not to let go of his weapon, but the weight of the haunted wood felt like a pile of bricks. Goldsnout stared in horror as Eleres' head was being pushed into the earth; his body being swallowed entirely. He saw the chief's shoulders shake as he tried to breathe, the dirt filling his nostrils and mouth to suffocate him.

  With a deep scream, Goldsnout balled his hands into fists, using the strength of his upper body to counter the flattening of the roots above their bodies, screeching and hollering as he tried to free himself. From the corner of his eye, he saw that the Golden Lady had disappeared from his view, yet the women that watched in silence stood unmoving. Tears clouded his vision as Opherus realized that he wouldn't last very long and that there wasn't enough time left for him to crawl out of the roots' grasp and free his chief. All he could hear was the thundering of his heartbeat in his ears and the rasped breathing that came out of his lips and nose. The fact that his foe was not even directly attacking him enraged him more. It was cowardice to him, and he refused to succumb. He refused to see his mentor die in such conditions. Eleres brought him because he trusted him, and he couldn't fail the man because of the strength he lacked. The Golden Lady said that Soleba was no one's to claim, and they were right. But Goldsnout repeated himself that he was just as right for defending the Surveillance's actions, for these women killed in the lands that had been united by Aleyne Rainier. It was Chief Eleres' right to hunt them down, it was the chief and Goldsnout's right to protect the Fatherland.

  A sudden scream that wasn't his broke him from his resolute thinking, and he watched an ivory maiden fall to her knees, an arrow piercing her chest from side to side. He blinked, looking from side to side until he spotted a short, greying woman drawing another arrow. Dumbfounded at the sight of her perfect stance with her feet shoulder-width apart, he watched her let another arrow loose. It flew over his head, killing another woman. As the two victims' torches fell along with them, the nearest bushes and tall grass caught fire, minimized only slightly by the light rainfall.

"Mastria!" Goldsnout heard the third woman scream as an arrow pierced her stomach.

He saw the Golden Lady reemerge from the shadow of the chestnut tree, which was void of any light now, and she extended one arm towards the sky, her slender limb and delicate fingers pointing at the moon. Goldsnout felt the weight of the roots being lifted off his body, and as he coughed to catch his breath, he pulled Chief Eleres up, who spit the dirt that had collected in his mouth. The two gasped for air as the old woman aimed yet another arrow at the Golden Lady, never faltering at the sight of the possessed roots. The moment she let it loose, her target lowered her hand and her earthly weapons stretched in the archer's direction, destroying the arrow as it collided against them and diving straight for the woman's head. Goldsnout sprung in her direction, only to see another man jump at her from behind.

"Tita!"

The old woman was pushed out of the way as she and the curly-haired man who emerged from the shadows of the pine trees rolled together on the ground. The roots met the ground before falling flat and turning into quivering masses, and Goldsnout realized that the other women had taken that moment as an opportunity to flee. The Golden Lady herself was no longer there, and the chestnut tree couldn't be seen anymore. They had all left the scene to avoid the risk of being unmasked, Goldsnout told himself, feeling the rage building inside his chest.

Eleres coughed incessantly, his eyes blinking open as he regained his senses. The root that had armed his foot was gone the moment the attack was redirected at the person who saved them, and blood flowed freely from his limb.

"Chief," Goldsnout whispered, helping him sit up. "It's over."

"It is not," Old Martita cut in when she stood up, but not before glaring at Sarkis, who still lied on the ground. The fire around them was slowly being quelled by the heavier rain. "Those women didn't want to be found, and now, they'll be after us."

"Thank you for what you did," Goldsnout said, ignoring her words. "You saved us. You saved Chief Eleres when I couldn't."

"Saving your lazy ass was the least of my worries," Martita said. Looking at the pool of blood under Eleres' feet, she sniffled. "Come now. We need to take care of that wound before it gets bad. Edgemere is close."

Goldsnout nodded, helping his mentor up, wondering how he would manage to carry the man to the city-port with their horses missing. As he scanned the area in hopes of seeing a trace of their mounts, Goldsnout tried to remember in which direction the horses had run for their lives. It wasn't until the chubby man screamed at him that he saw one of the quivering roots crawl in their direction, plunging deep into Eleres' neck, blood splattering all over Goldsnout's armor.

  The strangled sound the chief made turned his whole body into stone as Goldsnout watched with horrified eyes full of tears as the Chief of the Surveillance collapsed into the ground. The root melted into his neck, before dissolving completely. The incessant screaming of Sarkis didn't reach him, nor did the words Martita spoke to him as she fell to her knees to put a hand on his shoulder. It was only in that moment that Goldsnout realized he had fallen to his knees, soaked in his mentor's blood.

  Of all the words the chief had spoken to him that day, the only ones that echoed through his mind were, "Take a bit of advice from an old man. I wish I had more time for my loved ones."

  "There is no more time," Goldsnout whispered in shock and disbelief. "No more time."

Chapter XX

THE TERROR I SEE

Their horses had been eating grass at the edge of the cliff that overlooked the city-port of Edgemere. With a little help from the curly-haired man who seemed to know his savior, Goldsnout placed Thierry Eleres' body on the mount that had been his for years of service. He let Old Martita ride his, while he and the other man who seemed to be roughly his age, if not a little older than him, walked in the direction of the city. Goldsnout tugged gently on the Eleres' horse reins as they came to a slope that connected Wilderose to Edgemere. Little rocks rolled down the side of their path as they traveled in silence.

   The events that took place in the woods were so unreal that Goldsnout decided to bottle up the tears in his eyes and the ire he exuded despite his attempt at keeping calm. He asked himself if he could have been more persuasive earlier when he tried to convince his chief not to venture through

Wilderose the way Lord Angefort did, but the decisive tone Eleres had used with him beat his arguments even in his mind.

It seemed that Edgemere was lit up with lanterns and overall lively even during a rainy night of winter. The city reminded Goldsnout of Jehanel's Forum in Silverholde, and it certainly was as big as the capital's area, with its oval meeting points and the bubbly chatter of the Edgemerans. He saw many taverns serve outside their halls, and the homely feel of the scene was only overshadowed by the E-shaped palace of medium size that could be seen behind the forum and past the harbor. It was difficult to make out its colors and notice its gardens at such a dark hour, but Goldsnout imagined it to be silvery and flowery, for he knew that Lord Lionhelm's daughter, Tesfira, lived in the palace with her husband, Hamley Silverworm, Mayor of Edgemere.

"We can't go any further," Opherus whispered, halting Eleres' horse. "Chief Eleres couldn't let Lord Lionhelm know of Wilderose. We can't ask for a funeral in a city governed by Lord Lionhelm's daughter."

He didn't hear Martita hop off his horse, but suddenly, she was standing beside him. "Won't he learn about Chief Eleres' death once the news reaches the Regency?" she pointed out. "Or are you going to keep it a secret from them as well?"

"I will tell the Regency," Goldsnout answered, never directly looking at her. "They will decide when to inform Lord Lionhelm."

"What about the body? You can't travel back through Wilderose," Martita reasoned, sniffing at the sight of the corpse. "You will have to go to Strongshore and then reach Summerport before traveling to the West until you arrive at the ruined walls of Courtbridge and cross the Rough Rill again.

"By the time you set foot in the capital, the body will be in such an ugly state of decomposition that you will catch some sickness. Not to mention it would be highly disrespectful towards your chief and whatever family waits for him at home."

"I know that," Goldsnout snapped, tightening his fists. "I haven't—I don't…"

Thierry Eleres' family. He hadn't known they existed until that very day. The chief had always seemed so engrossed in his duties that Goldsnout had always assumed that the man was a surveillant first and foremost. He couldn't imagine the man as a father, as a husband. What would he tell them? That he had failed to protect the man who always had his back? What would Miss Rantha think of him? Mentally scolding himself for thinking of a woman when he had more pressing matters to attend, Goldsnout let a single tear run down his left cheek as he finally looked into Old Martita's eyes. The gaping hole in Eleres' throat was not something he wanted the man's family to see.

"Come here," she ordered the burly man that followed her around. "Help us get this body out of its clothes."

"Tita?"

It wasn't until the man spoke that Goldsnout realized how shaken he was. He was trembling from head to toe, a horrified expression painting his face. The man's front teeth were chewing away his lower lip and it seemed that the mere thought of undressing a cadaver made him sick.

"You completely ruined my chance of getting rid of those witches," Martita scolded him. "Now, get your fleabag butt moving and help us."

"What do you plan on doing?" Goldsnout asked as they put Eleres' body on the sand.

His eyes were closed and his face relaxed. If it wasn't for the blood that soaked his clothes and the vicious gash in his throat, one could have believed the man to be sleeping.

"We will take his uniform," Martita said as she untied the man's cloak around his neck. "You will bring it back to his family as a sign of respect. We will burn his body here unless you prefer his body to be returned to the sea. What were the man's beliefs?" she asked him, pausing in her movements.

Goldsnout sat back on his heels, a faint, bitter laugh escaping his lips. "I have no idea. But I doubt Chief Eleres would want his body to return to the sea; it is a practice of the Sand Towers, and he was born and raised in the capital."

They fell back into an oddly comfortable silence as they cautiously removed each piece of the Regency uniform, almost as if they didn't want to wake Eleres from his slumber. Goldsnout made sure to search the chief's pockets to avoid losing something his family might be interested in keeping. Soon, the body laying before him looked like it belonged to somebody else. With only his undergarments left, Chief Thierry Eleres looked like an exhausted farmer who had been attacked by a group of angry and hungry homeless boys to be ripped of his silvers. Goldsnout rose to his feet with the folded uniform and Eleres' weapon in his arms to secure the items on the back of the chief's horse. He pulled out a bit of rope from the bag nestled under the cantle of the saddle. The rope was meant for potential arrests, and Goldsnout hoped he wouldn't have to bring anybody to Silverholde with him on his way back to the capital. He doubted that the rope that was left would suffice.

  He was left to say his goodbyes to Eleres in silence as he watched the people who had saved him walk in the direction of the city to bring back enough wood to build a small pyre. Goldsnout would have gone with them, but he wouldn't risk leaving the chief's body at the mercy of hungry, wild animals, or even stray dogs. He offered Old Martita his horse, but she waved him off, saying that she was stronger than she looked and that a properly saddled horse of the Regency would raise unwanted questions. Refusing to argue, Opherus sat down with his elbows resting on his knees as he stared at the first glimpse of the moon.

  "I did not deserve your training, Chief Eleres," he whispered. "I was supposed to have your back, and yet, I didn't see the attack until it was too late," he admitted. When the roots came out from the ground, separating them, Goldsnout wasn't at fault. However, when they quivered and plunged in Eleres' direction the second time, he should have seen them. The old woman and the other man had been on the ground before rushing to their side to help them; still, Goldsnout didn't look behind them. "You should have been accompanied by Gulmont, or even Longspire," he added, biting back a sob. "Anyone in the Surveillance was certainly a better choice."

Pressing his fingertips against his temples, Opherus let the tears stream down his cheeks in silence. A part of him thought that the self-pity was out of place and uncalled for; Thierry Eleres died fulfilling his duty. He had been looking for those women for so many moons they had both forgotten what the Surveillance's headquarters looked like. Eleres found them and perished fighting them. It was not a dishonorable death; it was the opposite, Goldsnout tried to convince himself. Still, he felt like this death could have been avoided, either by using the right words or through the right actions.

He lacked judgment for both.

※※※

"It will be twenty silvers."

"I eat for six moons with twenty silvers," Martita argued as the woodcutter tied their order together. "Since when are sticks, logs, and bark this expensive? You walk outside and you're surrounded by the forest."

The boy who was barely taller than her spit at her feet before wiping his mouth with his dirty yellow sleeve. "Listen, woman, things have become a tad complicated out there. They say a man died not so long ago in Wilderose and not by accident. It is hard to find other woodcutters who are willing to help me bring enough wood for Edgemere. Imagine having a random old hag come up to me and ask me this much wood when she does not even reside here," he rudely explained before dumping the pile in Sarkis' arms.

Sarkis stumbled trying to find his balance, disorientated at the sight of the boy who went back to grab his ax, which had to be heavier than him. "H-how old are you?"

"I'm nine; what does it matter?" Grabbing another log, he split it in two with ease. "My old man is an old man. And he is at the mass. Someone needs to work."

Martita quirked an eyebrow, moving to carry her wood on her back when Sarkis failed to take a step in any direction. "A mass? Now?"

The boy shrugged, focusing on the pile of logs behind him. "Don't ask me. If you're into that, head to Aelneth's Plaza."

Old Martita and Sarkis left the boy's yard after paying him. Thankfully, the Regency officer had handed her a bag of thirty, otherwise, she would have never been able to cover the cost of the wood needed for the small pyre. Sarkis panted like a stray dog behind her, and part of her wanted to get back to the beach as soon as possible, but the mention of the night mass caught her attention. There was a small temple in Edgemere, nothing as intimidating as the one in Summerport, but the woodcutter specifically said that the mass was taking place in Aelneth's Plaza. Did something happen to the temple? She wondered silently. And why would the gathering take place under the moonlight?

Ignoring the mumbling sounds of Sarkis, Martita hastily walked in the direction of the center. Edgemere was only half as big as Summerport from what she knew, and it wouldn't be such a long walk from where they were to the main plaza.

"Wait up!"

Rolling her eyes, the short woman turned around. "You have completely ruined this hunt, let me tell you," she accused him. "I don't even know why or how you followed me, and you can't even carry half of what we need."

Sarkis looked bewildered. "Tita, they almost killed you with—with those—I don't even know where to start," he caught his breath, leaning forward due to the weight he tried to strap on his back in the same fashion she did. "I was right behind you the moment you left," he admitted. "I was worried, and rightfully so after I saw how they killed that man."

Old Martita remained silent, only to nod her chin in the direction of the center. She had been traveling for quite some days, with a bag full of dry food and enough silvers to afford a night in Strongshore's citadel and another in Edgemere to properly rest before venturing in Wilderose. She noticed that Sarkis carried nothing with him, and she understood.

He had been exhausted, and starved, surviving only out of concern for her. "Let's grab some food in the city before we return. That young officer may need some time to fully process what we witnessed."

They walked in silence through the empty streets of the city-port, and Martita couldn't help but notice the decadence that surrounded them. The tall lanterns that lighted their path only stressed the absence of a population known as cheerful and easy-going. The clinking of cups and the loud conversations seemed to be concentrated in the heart of the city, where the statue of Warrior Queen Aelneth was erected thousands of years before, after the creation of Old Drixia. The short, sinewy woman was sitting on an elaborate chair with a round backrest and two large armrests shaped in the skulls of identical lions. Her axes rested at her feet, larger than her and probably heavier as well. On her armored lap, the teeth of her defeated enemies had been carved like the jewels of a dress, and her crown full of gaping holes bore no stones.

Sarkis was quick to drop his package on the ground to rush in the direction of the tavern, undoubtedly to relieve himself and eat until he couldn't stand up anymore. Martita remained nearby, claiming a spot for herself behind the last row of people who seemed way too engrossed in what the man perched at the feet of the statue was saying.

He was short and rather chubby, thin black hair cascading down his shoulders while the top of his head was bald. His squinty eyes stared almost maliciously at the crowd before him, a torch in his right hand held up high to make sure he could see them and they could see him in return. His dark blue garments looked black, and if it weren't for the large silver belt around his belly and a necklace just as wide around his collar, Old Martita would have never recognized him. Mayor Hamley Silverworm looked nothing like he used to. She had seen him on the day of his wedding when he and Lady Tesfira Lionhelm exited the temple in Oracle Hill. He had been slim and rather charming, with glee written all over his face.

"Lies, I tell you; lies!" the man roared at the crowd, who cheered him in return. "Are we to believe, after centuries, that the Oracle was gifted with the power of foreseeing? If she could predict the future, our future, why did she not warn her queen that Alatros the Red would invade the South?"

Martita felt the goosebumps on her arms the moment the crowd cheered him again.

"And it was in the moment the stars left the skies that the Oracle's eyes opened wide, black as the night, sucking in the light, that the seas were drained and birds rained down from their Heights," Hamley recited the last chapter of the Oracle's Memoir. "Is the message of destruction the one we shall believe in? Is this why we wait for another Oracle, when the real one, the one who promised us the light, was brutally murdered?

"Even in death, the Dreamer kept Her promises to us, for Her eyes were shut tight, Her pale lids white as day, letting out the light. The seas rose and the birds took flight, reaching for the Heights.

"Edgemere shall not endure the same fate as Old Drixia and the City of Calaris, both destroyed by the fires of the depths and swallowed by the tinted waters because of an impostor who did not warn the population that worshipped her!"

A man who stood right next to Martita shouted his approval, pumping the fist that held his ale, letting the alcohol splash around him. "Death to the impostor and all who follow her!"

Hamley's smile turned into a grimace. "I promised you last moon that I will not tolerate the infamy that once brought our ancestors to their knees. Not anymore." Turning his body to the side, looking in the direction of the small temple that rose between Aelneth's Plaza and the Edgemere palace.

The crowd fell into a deep silence, their eyes trailing in the direction of the temple, and Martita failed to notice Sarkis, who had just returned to her side, handing her what smelled like mulled, black wine of the Fog Lands. A collective gasp echoed through the city as the temple was suddenly on fire, screams of people burning alive filling the air. At that moment she saw the holy captains and the Angels of Steel appointed to the city tied to the pillars of the burning temple.

"We need to leave," she whispered urgently, watching the faces of the Angels contorted in pain as they could not scream, for their tongues and vocal cords had been removed, as tradition commanded.

"What is happening?" Sarkis asked, feeling his back break under the weight of the wood he hoisted on his shoulders. "Has everyone gone mad on this side of the Rough Rill?"

"Shut your mouth before they make you join them," Martita ordered, rushing in the direction of the beach, ignoring the cheering of the people who watched men burn and rejoiced at the idea of ending a faith that had lasted longer than any family's reign until that very night.

They wobbled their way back with difficulty as more people exited their homes to see what was going on. Sarkis repeatedly fell to his knees, earning himself more curses for Old Martita, who tugged him back up before the curious children and worried mothers stumbled over him and scattered the wood logs he carried all around them.

"We must inform the Regency surveillant," Martita decided as they dragged their feet past the city entrance.

"About that," Sarkis coughed out, running out of breath once more, "can you do it on your own?"

She flicked her fingers against his forehead. "We build the pyre, pray for that good man's soul, and then maybe, only maybe, I will not throw you into the sea."

"Tita," he pleaded with big, round eyes. "The Regency is after me, remember? I would rather not spend too much time around their surveillants."

Aggravated, Martita rested her fists against her sides. "What did you do that you must go into hiding? And since it's so serious, why did you not stay in Summerport?"

"I didn't know we'd run into their chief!"

"What happened?" a third voice chimed in, freezing them both on the spot.

Old Martita unfastened the ropes that kept the wood strapped against her back, mindless of the way it sloped down noisily. Officer Goldsnout shot them a worried look, the circles around his swollen, red eyes, a clear indication that he too was exhausted and had spent the whole time crying over his loss.

"You two were taking a lot of time, I was thinking maybe something came up." Facing Sarkis to help him with his straps, he repeated, "Why would the Regency be after you?" When the burly man didn't answer, Goldsnout tried to offer him a reassuring smile. "What is your name?"

Sarkis wouldn't have answered if Martita hadn't thrown a log at him. "Sarkis. My name is Sarkis."

Goldsnout nodded, bending down to collect some of the logs. "I read all the reports sent to the Surveillance's headquarters in Silverholde. I have never read your name in any of them."

Startled, Sarkis stammered, "B-but h-how—"

"Whatever you may have done is probably not classified as an offense. There must have been a misunderstanding."

He watched in silence as the red-haired officer walked back to the idle body of Chief Eleres. Martita shook her head at Sarkis, who remained dumbfounded.

"What did I tell you?" she scolded him. "You be on your way and let Theliel on his."

The Tinted Bay seemed tormented as the three of them placed the wood all around Chief Eleres' body before covering his body as well, leaving only his face intact. Sarkis shivered in the cold night. Goldsnout pulled a small box from his bag, along with what looked like burnt garments. Unboxing a fire striker that he slid over his fingers, Goldsnout grabbed a light-colored stone and approached Old Martita, who was busying herself with the rearrangement of the wood, making sure that every layer faced the opposite direction compared to the other layers cushioning it. She filled empty spots and lined each layer of the pyre with the bark the woodcutter had provided them with, quickly turning it into small bouquets she secured with the wooden sticks to avoid it all flying away due to the wind. Soon enough, Goldsnout held the charred cloth on top of his flint, bashing quick and hard against the sharp edge of the rock with his fire striker until sparks set fire to the cloth and he let the ember grow, consuming both the cloth and the first layer of bark.

The whistling wind spread the fire in a heartbeat, and both Martita and Goldsnout took several steps back to watch the pyre come alive. Goldsnout's wavy red locks slapped against his cheeks while he prayed in silence for Eleres, finding himself unable to voice his thoughts and recite a chapter of the Oracle's Memoir. Old Martita's narrowed eyes were set straight on the pyre as well, but it was not Chief Eleres she saw, nor the monsters who did this to him. She saw the temple of Edgemere and heard the crowd that cheered loud enough to mask the cries of those who burned.

"You must not stop in Edgemere," she whispered to the grieving young man. "The city-port is no longer under control. They burned the temple of Edgemere following the Mayor's command. They believe in nothing; they will hear nothing from you."

Goldsnout's shaky voice barely reached her ears. "I can't deal with anything or anyone right now," he confessed.

"That is good," Old Martita told him while beckoning Sarkis to come closer to at least catch a little warmth from the burning pyre. "Heresy has consumed Edgemere and I am afraid you would risk your life there. We should all travel back to Strongshore as quick as possible, perhaps you may want to speak directly with Lord Lionhelm."

"I already told you," Goldsnout said through gritted teeth, partially wishing he could shove the old woman away. "The Regency decided not to tell Lord Tithan. Not until we know more."

"These events are not disconnected from each other," she argued.

"Quiet, please," he pleaded. "Tonight is about Chief Eleres. I would like to honor him with silent prayers and your words are distracting."

Old Martita sniffled, reaching inside her bag for a piece of salty meat wrapped in paper. She knew not a single prayer for the man and preferred to not interrupt. Words had been her way of coping with what reminded her of the day Big Pat died; she remembered his kind face and that smile that was always plastered on his lips to the point it was contagious for those around him, except her. She had never returned one of his smiles. She hadn't even built a pyre half as decent as the one this officer paid for. She had simply burned the box with Pat's remains in it, out of rage, out of despair.

When they least expected it, Sarkis kneeled before the pyre, his calm voice emptying their minds and filling their hearts with a chapter of the Memoir. "When the child came to this world, it was the twentieth of Her womb, but She, who had seen all and touched our souls to bring light into our paths, knew that child to be Her last, for it had been conceived on the day the Sun married the Moon and plunged the Heights in unforgivable darkness.

"She held the girl with stretched arms for the Good Gods to see, before releasing the tiny body and watch it fall down the Pillar and into the Bay, for that was the fate of the unworthy.

"Release me from this life, She cried."

"Release me from this bane," Opherus joined in with a hushed voice. "Release me from the terror that I can see but cannot change."

Chapter XXI

King of Heights

The muddy streets of the capital were just as busy and noisy as on a sunny, summer day. The heavy rain that melted the snow around the stone houses turned the white scenery into a messy painting of brown and grey. Carts and carriages that wheeled down the crowded areas splashed dirty water over the soaked feet of the less fortunate. As most day time activities were concentrated around Jehanel's Forum and Danyell's Athenaeum, people rushed to the northeastern parts of Silverholde, but not Jascha. Rounding the statue of King Aleyne and the Iathienar, he headed in the direction of Melisentia's Opera. He could see the bright purple, circular building rise above the rest of the area, but his destination was another. His boots and pants were covered in dirt as he made his way through small pools of water where the Restless Channel flooded the city, filling it with a good number of dead mice and excrements.

An abandoned tavern sat between the opera and a two-story house in front of which an old, skinny and barely clothed old man was emptying his bowels. Jascha pulled the front of his cloak a little higher as to cover his nose, hoping the split open roof of the forge behind the tavern wasn't any indication that it had been abandoned as well. Rounding the corner, Jascha glanced inside the shop where he was surprised to find only a broad-shouldered man hunched in front of the farthest fireplace. Puffs of smoke came out of his mouth as he indulged in the wild plants of the Red Continent. A mop of dark hair covered his ears and tangled with the curls on his neck and back. The man glanced at Jascha before his face disappeared behind another cloud of sweetly scented smoke.

"What ya want?" he asked, sticking his little finger in his ear to scratch it.

"I'd like to commission some work for you."

"And I'd like to fuck a girl half as pretty as ya."

Ignoring the crass words, Jascha unstrapped the sword around his waist before placing it on the table, next to the blacksmith's tools. The man didn't budge, the nostrils of his square nose flaring as he let the smoke out. The moment Jascha unsheathed the sword, pointing at the ceiling with it before holding it horizontally, the man spit his smoking tube and stood up, scratching his stomach.

"Sand steel," he noted.

Jascha handed him Decimation. "Volcanic stone hilt, steel of the Barrens. I was told at the Wild Rock Skunk you knew how to work it."

"Aalart surely can," the blacksmith said, speaking in third-person as he smirked at the weapon. "They tell thousands of legends on sand steel," he mused. "They say this steel comes from the iron feathers that fell from the defeated Iathienar."

"Chapter one of the Memoir," Jascha nodded. "Gods, have you seen the King of Heights?"

Aalart licked his lower lip. "He stole the moon's eyes and the sun's breath, but as He dived for Mother's Lands, the Mastria arose and lifted her hands. She had His sight and His talons' fire, and soon melted his whole attire."

"It rained feathers on Mother's Lands, but His fall hid them under golden sands."

"Where'd ya get this?" Aalart asked, running his black nails on the flat side of the blade.

"It's too heavy," Jascha simply told him. "I can't move properly with one sword shifting all my weight to one side." Staring into the blacksmith's blue eyes, he added, "I want you to make two blades out of it."

Aalart nodded at him, slowly, as if he was hesitating. "That'll cost you lots."

"Very well."

"A hundred silvers."

Jascha narrowed his eyes at the bold request. "Make it two hundred if you deliver the work in three days," he said before turning heels, knowing full well that the blacksmith would be too entranced with the weapon to retort.

Heading back in the direction of the athenaeum, Jascha walked past the forum, where an almost empty marketplace had left room for less honorable activities. A couple of stands were being tended to by greengrocers and silk vendors who never glanced up at the people who stood close only to find shelter from the rain. A small group of children played under the rain, singing songs about the thousand knights of Princess Ailith who perished under an old tree Jascha had never heard of, and how they were brought back to life to become Executors of The Collapsed. The children played pretend as they brandished invisible swords and fought each other, rolling in the mud like skinny, famished piglets. Jascha's eyes scanned the scene, void of any emotion until he saw the toothy smile of the small boy named Josclyn. He was tackled by another boy who playfully swished his nonexistent blade above his head. Looking around to see where his mother was, Jascha spotted an even more weakened Mawde being led into a nearby alley by a man who looked just as foul, a hand grabbing her backside almost urgently.

  Diverting his gaze from them, Jascha reached the athenaeum feeling utterly nauseated by his stench. He would have to buy a new pair of pants after that stroll in the open-air sewer, but the price of his new weapons would render him silverless sooner than he expected. He climbed the steps to the entrance quickly as the rainfall turned into a storm, but at the counter by the doors, there was no trace of Rosaleah. Instead, the woman with the white fur cloak stood waiting, her hood still covering her dark locks. Her emerald eyes peered at him, her expression remaining neutral.

Deciding that he didn't mind the absence of the nosy girl who would ask him again about the books he was looking for, Jascha moved in the direction of the stairs, only to hear Rosewillow right behind him.

"Rosaleah isn't here," she told him. "I know this place well if you need any help."

He came to an abrupt stop at the end of the staircase but never faced her. "I need nothing from a person like you," he stated.

"A person like me?" she repeated as if to better grasp the meaning of his words. "From what I gathered you come here often. I thought I could be of help since you can't find what you are looking for."

"I will know what I am looking for when I find it," he told her. Jascha wanted to roll his eyes at the obviousness of his own words, but he figured this was the only way to make his point across. "Leave," he ordered her.

"You sure know how to make friends," Rosewillow said, her laugh so light it was void of any meanness as she walked back to the counter to wait for the other girl.

Jascha swallowed a lump in his throat, climbing to the top floor of the Regency's open library, refusing to acknowledge her existence.

✺✺✺

The noise that Lyzon made as she folded the thick covers Tecla had scattered all over the bed was faint, yet the thundering in the young lady's head created the illusion that the fumbling was louder than the storm outside. Tecla leaned on her elbow as she sat on her chair, massaging her temples with one hand and holding her book with the other. Educator Tomas had given her the assignment of memorizing several pages about medicinal plants used to treat the Violet Delusion, but she had spent the entire morning listening to Grandmaster Rodbertus as he explained the process of making the weapons that had been used during the Crimson Crystal Wars. None of these subjects interested her, but it was part of the education her lord father had ordered her to get, and so Tecla let the mixture of boredom and exhaustion consume her.

She briefly glanced at Lyzon, whose frown had yet to leave her face. She watched the maid's calves as the woman bent and hopped from a corner of the bed to another, and Tecla shook her head. She watched her friend stumble over one of the covers as she stacked them in her arms, only to realize that it hadn't happened. Tecla smiled to herself, thinking that Lyzon was quick and agile and that she shouldn't deem her clumsy. Her hazel stare fell back on the page she was reading about the rosewillow trees that grew around Silverholde and part of Wilderose. She found herself stuck on the same line for a long time, wondering why it seemed so vital for her to remember that the frequent consumption of rosewillow sap caused patients to have difficulty breathing and that as much as it was often used with the Dreamer's Root to alleviate pain, the lack of proper breathing during sleep could cause more hallucinations to take place. Tecla figured that it would probably be of as much use as the warfare knowledge the grandmaster had shared with her; none whatsoever. The Crimson Crystal Wars had opposed the Lionhelms and the Rochelacs for centuries, neither family ever succeeding in defeating the other. The crimson coats of the mountain people had built breaching towers tall enough to threaten Summerport, only to see them destroyed during the Battle of Everspring, a militaristic city build between Courtbridge and Summerport. The city fell during a second battle, when the Riverguards shifted their allegiance in favor of the Rochelacs, lowering the bridge that connected the now ruined walls of Courtbridge to Everspring. Yet, after many attempts, the Rochelacs failed to establish their forces around the coasts of the Silver Lands, for the Lionhelm's navy was always ready to take them down with their ranged ships, and the strongest striges of the Rochelacs had perished in Rockfall, in the Rain Lands. With the menace of the air attack gone, Strongshore was unattainable, and the silver coats of the Lionhelms countered every attack with spears, shields, and coursers too fast for the Rochelacs' rain of arrows.

   Tecla nearly fell asleep as she skipped the following line about creeping laurel aphrodisiac properties when she heard Lyzon curse under her breath and apologize. The woman had dropped half the covers, her feet getting caught in them.

"Lyzon."

"Forgive me, young lady. I didn't mean to say these words in your presence."

"I was just going to ask you to wake me up before Theliel comes," Tecla told her. "I need to close my eyes for a bit."

Lyzon chewed on her lower lip, her dark eyes glancing around. "Is it wise to go to the city, young lady? The rain won't stop."

"Theliel wanted us to go to the Shattered Ambry. He says they serve food like no other tavern in the Silver Lands."

"A tavern?" Lyzon's eyes widened. "Young lady, this is not appropriate."

"You don't have to worry," Tecla smiled at her. "It is right behind the athenaeum. I was told it is mostly where the future members of the Observatory Vault spend their time. I doubt we'll see brawls in there.

"You, Tomas, and Fran can come as well," she added to soothe Lyzon's nerves before she closed her eyes and leaned back into the cushioned chair.

She felt Lyzon drape furs over her body as to not have her feel cold, and it wasn't long until she fell asleep.

It was no soundless sleep as her breathing became heavy and her eyebrows twitched. Tecla could hear the cracking of the fire behind her, and she felt as if she were on a boat caught in a tempest, swinging dangerously to one side then on the other.

She wanted to roll off the chair and empty her stomach, but she couldn't. Tecla felt as if her arms and legs were paralyzed as her eyes shot open, her blue-stained, hazel orbs replaced by a glowing green light. She felt extremely cold as if the fire in the fireplace had vanished; as if her surroundings had faded and she was left in a dark, humid place. She felt the wet earth under her feet. Where were her shoes? She wanted to ask no one, but her lips were sealed. She tried to move them but felt how tightly sewed they were. Tecla tried screaming, but her cords didn't vibrate. Visions of hands clawing their way from under her feet and out of the ground tried to grab her; she saw faces, empty stares, and the sunken cheeks of a woman so skinny that her tiny wedding robes looked too big for her. Her auburn hair slapped against her face, covered her plucked eyes, though there was no wind.

"The Tear," she heard her say. "Give me the Tear."

A small hand finally caught Tecla's and the young girl jumped, only to catch the sight of a little child looking at her with pleading eyes. "Can you help my sister?"

"Where is your sister?" Tecla thought she replied, but her lips were still clasped together.

The little girl pointed behind Tecla, who craned her neck to see a fire. It was her fireplace, she realized, the one in her bed-chamber at the Pavilion, but the flames quickly turned a vivid shade of green. She had been there before, she thought, but she couldn't quite recall when exactly.

It was like a word on the tip of her tongue. She knew the answer, but she couldn't say it.

She heard drums and a tune that was almost a warring one. A voice sang to it, but it was neither male nor female. It resembled a dead language; one she would imagine people from either Old Drixia or Calaris to speak. There were women around her, but they did not seem to notice her. Helmets were at their feet as they touched each other, pouring what looked like oils over their bodies. They were injured, Tecla saw. Others bathed in steaming water that was dark blue and the faint smell of flowers reached her nostrils. The walls of the wide, circular room were woodsy and dark as if the place had burned a long time ago. A pyre that reminded her of the fire inside the temple of Summerport lighted the entire room, but no one entertained it. A woman with a silver cape that trailed behind her almost endlessly had her back to her, but her hair was covered by a veil. Another woman stood beside her, clad in only a sleeveless ivory dress and a helmet over her head.

"The Tear," the veiled woman repeated. "I need the Tear."

"No documented trace of the Tear, I'm afraid, Mastria," the other woman whispered.

"Curiosities?"

"Leah requested Willow's assistance due to the presence of the Darling. Hard to locate."

The veiled woman turned around, revealing her golden helmet. "Is the Darling one of our worries?"

"She says a man has been researching the occult."

Tecla tried to move as the Golden Lady fully turned around, a hand holding her side. She watched the woman's skin go from smooth to scaled, her fingernails flashing from rosy to yellow.

"I need Willow to find the *Nakfèht*," she answered in a hiss. "Else all would have been in vain."

The other woman bowed deeply. "Mastria, forgive me for asking, but wouldn't the Darling bring us closer to the *Nakfèht*?"

The Golden Lady gave her no warning before she curled her fingers around the woman's throat and pushed her backward, forcing her to bend her back at a painful angle, the tips of her hair nearly grazing the fire.

"Are we not blessed with the King of the Heights' sight?" she breathed against the woman's helmet, right where her lips would be.

"M-mastria—"

The Golden Lady silenced her before releasing her neck and pushing her to the side. She walked forward, in Tecla's direction, stopping only a footstep away. Tecla watched her without breathing, failing to see her eyes through the golden piece that covered her entire face.

"She's here," the Golden Lady spoke. "Right here."

Tecla's heart began beating so fast it threatened to jump out of her chest.

"Tecla," she heard her name being called. "Tecla."

"Young lady?"

The girl nearly fell out of the chair as she jumped, steadied by the firm grip of her older brother. Her heart was still thundering, and the back of her neck felt sweaty. Her clammy hands were shaking and she stared in panic at Theliel and Lyzon who exchanged concerned looks. Theliel's hair slid from behind his ears as he bent, helping her stand up slowly. Tecla grasped the fabric of his emerald coat, and she felt him rub her back.

"Are you feeling ill? You seemed to be having a nightmare," he told her quietly. "We don't have to visit the athenaeum area today."

Lyzon nodded at that, offering a glass of root juice to the girl. "Your brother is right, my lady."

Tecla shook her head at their antics, taking the glass to sip the juice. "I was tired," she told them. "The things I read and the stories I heard just turned into a dangerous mixture my mind wasn't prepared for," she explained, looking intently at Theliel, who nodded in understanding.

"Shall we, then?" he asked her, offering his arm.

Tecla nodded, extending her arms behind her as Lyzon slid her coat over her body before tightening the front laces. She was quick and careful as to not ruin her lady's long braid, making sure that the girl's favorite jewel was neatly secured against the back of her head between the layers of hair. Lyzon waited for the Lionhelms to exit the bed-chamber before disappearing silently through the door that connected Tecla's room to her smaller one to grab her cloak.

The young lady watched the tip of her shoes as she walked and the way they disappeared under her long, pale blue dress. Theliel was oddly silent that day, and the lines under his eyes were a clear sign that he hadn't had much rest either. Perhaps she should have listened to Lyzon and decided against their early evening in the center of Silverholde, Tecla told herself.

"Is everything alright?"

She glanced up, and her brother was looking at her with one of the kindest looks he had ever directed at her. "Yes, I just need to properly wake up," she replied with a blush.

"They won't let you rest until you soak up all that knowledge," he laughed. "At least the Observatory Vault is more interesting than the Treasure Council," he mused as they went down the stairs that led to the ground floor of the Pavilion.

"The main hall of the Observatory Vault is like the base of a very tall mountain," Tecla told him. "You can't see its peak. I feel that way when I think of all the information that place contains. A lifetime wouldn't be enough to discover it all."

"What they couldn't store in there is in Danyell's Athenaeum," her brother said, fighting the shivers that ran through his body as the cold air from outside the Pavilion found its way through the watery corridors of the entrance.

Tecla was imagining the libraries of the athenaeum when she remembered the shelves of the Observatory Vault and the woman behind the small door. She furrowed her brow at the words she could still recall, and she halted her brother. Mustering the courage she didn't think she had, Tecla stared straight into his eyes that were so much like hers, and yet so different.

"Theliel, do you think—am I—your mother isn't our mother, is she?" she asked him, her voice so low she wondered if he heard her.

His expression softened, a quivering smile on his lips. "My mother was a woman named Emelyne," he answered. "I thought it was a well-known fact."

Ashamed for bringing up a subject he didn't want to discuss, Tecla held his hands in hers. "Am I also the daughter of another woman?"

Theliel's eyebrows shot up, and his lips parted and closed a few times before he could formulate an answer. "Tecla, that is something you should discuss with Father," he whispered. "Why are you asking me this, why now?"

"I met a woman," she admitted. "A woman named Matillis," she added, missing the way Theliel stiffened. "She said something about my eyes. I was just wondering who she was, and what the Occult Vault was, but she just slammed the door in my face."

"They call her Mad Matillis," Theliel explained, walking her towards the carriage that awaited her. "She once was the Head of the Occult Vault at the Regency, but that didn't last very long."

"Why?"

"Many reasons," Theliel sighed out. "You know our father; anything he deems as superstition is not worth his silvers. Matillis herself wasn't very inclined to recruiting members for her studies, and then there was the problem of the Edict of Three Crosses."

"The Edict of Three Crosses?"

"King Phorbas signed a law where he built his last temple, allowing no practice that would go against the Oracle's Faith. Lord Angefort tried to have the edict modified by King Helias, but that wasn't possible. By the time the Regency started governing the Silver Lands, King Helias was no longer capable of judgment, or so they say." Theliel helped his sister get inside the carriage before covering his head with his hood to shield himself from the rain. "These matters are not important," he concluded, cupping her cheek. "You are my sister. The rest is a pile of frivolities that are not worth our time."

Tecla watched him hop on his horse with ease, paying little attention to Lyzon, Fran, and Tomas as they took their seats around her. She watched her brother ride alongside the two guards that escorted them to the city. Raising her arm, she wiped the fogged window of the carriage to peek outside as they made their way to the center. She heard Tomas tell another tale to Lyzon and Fran, who seemed vaguely interested in it. The largest cobbled streets of the city were parallel to the tunnel and secret passage underneath Silverholde and they connected both Noirmont and Strongshore to the Pavilion. They were said to have been built by the armies of the Rochelacs and Lionhelms while they were at war, but Tomas refuted that possibility, deeming it impossible to have a tunnel stretch under the Rough Rill. Such secret gateways would also render the existence of Courtbridge pointless, he said.

"What if it's just another buried city?" Lyzon suggested.

"You did say Driazon was swallowed by the Depths," Fran added, nodding at his own words. "Perhaps another ancient city was buried under this one."

Before Tomas could answer, the carriage stopped, and Tecla narrowed her eyes to try and see past the fog. She saw only children gather around the carriage before being pushed back by the guards. Their faces were brown, covered by dirt. Their thin garments were of no help against the cold weather, and many of them shook from head to toe as they peered at her with curious eyes. She had never seen poorer faces.

"Why did we stop?" Lyzon asked.

The door opened, and Tecla heard her brother's voice. "The Shattered Ambry seems full. Let me talk some people into leaving," he told them with a grin.

He was about to slam the door shut when Tecla held out her hand. "Wait!"

Her brother was gone, but Tomas held the door open for her. Lyzon shivered at the sudden gush of wind, and Tecla's eyes marveled at the sight of the huge, emerald cupola that hid the dark skies.

"Is that the athenaeum?"

Tomas bent slightly forward before letting out a chuckle. "Yes, my lady."

"Do you think we can go in?"

"Surely. It is open until the last person walks out."

They both got off the carriage in a heartbeat, reluctantly followed by a very cold Lyzon and a famished Fran. The guards stood by the carriage as Tecla followed her educator, who took her directly to the back entrance of the Regency's libraries instead of going round the athenaeum to use the main entrance. They spotted other educators go in and out the same doors, bowing their heads at the young lady and their fellow educator. Tecla blocked out the incessant babble of Tomas, taking in her surroundings with her mouth agape and her eyes wide open. A faint light shone through the circular glass at the top of the cupola, and an endless staircase curled around every floor made of shelves and little study tables. The heels of her boots clicked against the floor as she rounded the roots of a massive tree that held the place together. Her fingers brushed against the wall, and she saw a long, rectangular table at the center of the room where many educators in training seemed to be studying. Large plates filled with fruit, brown bread, and dry meat were placed here and there on the table, and Tecla tried not to snicker at the sight of Fran rushing to grab a bite while Lyzon snatched an apple from the fruit basket.

"Tomas, I can't believe it's you," an old man said behind her as he stole the educator's attention.

Tecla noticed that the other educator was the first one she saw who wore robes of vibrant colors such as Tomas'. Resting her hand on the stair railing, Tecla began her ascent. She quickly noticed how a sign had been placed at the foot of every shelf to inform the visitors of what they would find on each floor. The history of every noble house was on the first floor, followed by healer manuals and botanical knowledge. Between naval tradition and explorer findings, Tecla saw the encyclopedias of arts and the codes of lawful men. She climbed the stairs until she noticed that the lighting was dimmer, and she had to glance down every time she took another step to avoid stumbling.

    A few paintings lined the walls of the last floor, but they were still-life ones, although for a moment she thought she saw a face on one of them. She walked in silence, glancing at the very dusty library that seemed abandoned, but every title she saw piqued her interest. Agrestal magic was a recurring theme, along with rituals and ancient ceremony codes. Tecla ran a hand over her light chestnut braid, stopping in her tracks when she saw a large, mahogany book. Stones and Songs of Aelneth, she read silently, wondering what the warrior had to do with what was the world of the occult.

    Her small fingers traced the spine of the book from bottom to top, curling them around it to grab it. A tiny cloud of dust arose as she slid it out, only to instantly drop it. Tecla's breath hitched in her throat and she stood in place with her arm extended before her. There was a space right behind the spot where the book had been placed on the shelf, and a pair of black eyes were staring straight into hers. The person on the other side of the shelf didn't move nor blink, and she wondered if it was truly a person or just another trick of the mind.

"I didn't know anybody was here," she whispered, quickly dropping to her knees to grab the book she dropped.

When she stood up, the pair of eyes was gone. Tecla closed her eyes, inhaling deeply, only to be startled again.

"What do you have?" a deep, steady voice asked her.

A man stood beside her; his stare focused on the item she held in her hands. He was much older than her but not as old as Theliel, she thought. His hair was straight and as black as his eyes; as black as a starless night. He was wearing equally dark clothes, save for the brown bear fur that kept him warm. His skin was pale, not as much as hers, but still very light. His nose was straight and tall, while his jaw was square and a faint dimple parted his chin.

"Stones and Songs of Aelneth," Tecla answered.

He looked at her, scanning her round face and noting the lion heads embroidered on the front of her thick coat. He licked his lips slowly, running his tongue on his lower lip first then over the curve of his nonexistent smile before glancing back at the book. "May I?" he asked.

Tecla was quick to nod her head, handing it to him.

He stood still in front of her, and although he received the item he wanted, he didn't budge. Tecla swallowed, wondering if it would be appropriate for her to ask if he needed anything else, only to remain silent. A wave of sadness hit her straight in the chest, and she felt a chill in her bones for the second time that day, just like in the dream she had. She heard no more sound, smelled no more scent. She felt lonelier than ever before. Tecla's lips moved but nothing came out. She saw his shadow move on the adjacent shelf; did he lean in? She looked up, and he only slightly bowed his head.

"My lady," he politely whispered before rounding the shelf and disappearing from her sight.

Urgent footsteps echoed through the floor, and soon, Tecla spotted the top of Lyzon's head. "My lady, your brother is waiting for us at the entrance," she informed the girl. "I couldn't find you anywhere."

Tecla moved from where she had been frozen in place, taking Lyzon's hand as the maid helped her down the stairs. The girl stole a glance behind the shelf before walking down, but to no avail. That person seemed to have vanished as quickly as they appeared.

Chapter XXII

Good Fortune

The cup of mulled Noirmont wine in his hand was getting slightly cold. The Shattered Ambry served the best poison, he had to admit that much, and the entire tavern was warm, not only the area that was closer to the kitchens. There were three fireplaces lighting and warming the tavern, and although all the tables were taken, Jascha felt comfortable resting his back against the cozy wooden wall adjacent to the entrance. It was the first time he entered this place, preferring to stay at the Wild Rock Skunk in Maugre's Arena. The storm had gotten a little too violent for him to walk across the city.

The past few days had been more fruitful when it came to the time spent at Danyell's Athenaeum. It turned out that the last shelves he searched through did not contain books but archives full of documented cases and practices about what common men called witchcraft. Never officially allowed, they were tolerated until the reign of King Phorbas the Devoted, leading to several ceremonies that had welcomed outsiders eager to produce drawings and take notes of the proceedings. Rituals often included many devout people. Women and men who were allowed to wear only a layer of Drixian silk would gather three times a day to fulfill the Applaud, the Perception, and the Reconciliation. They were similar, if not identical, to the three prayers of the Oracle; the Praise, the Judgment, and the Subjugation. However, whilst the followers of the Oracle reveled in the dusk days and awaited Aelneth's rewards after weeks of labor and duties, the people who claimed to be the First Wardens dedicated their starless nights to the awakening of the *Nakfèht*. Who the *Nakfèht* was remained unclear to Jascha, as the few mentions of them were only about the first *Nakfèht* who was said to be a man who left the First Wardens on a moonless night to join the new Sarulites, the population that walked the same earth as them but mingled with those who came from Driazon and another continent named Ephyron, across the Tinted Bay. The *Nakfèht* fled his people, but not before stealing their most valued treasure, which was never described over the centuries. Some suggested it was a manuscript while others claimed it to be a stone, but as Jascha thoroughly read the book about Aelneth's stones, no particular jewel was said to have been tied to the First Wardens.

   Jascha's stare left his drink to drift to the table placed right next to the fireplace across the room. From where he stood, he stared at the girl who had handed him the book. She sat with her back to him, laughing loudly at something the man next to her was saying. From her coat, Jascha had understood that she was a Lionhelm, but the man who very much resembled her was wearing the Regency's colors. Across from them, a large and round educator was feasting on a kidney pie while the two servants next to him seemed just as captivated by the man's tale as the Lionhelm girl was. Jascha watched as the girl rested her hand on the man's forearm. Every time she spoke, he noticed the way her eyebrows would move and her head tilt to the side. He felt an odd sense of peace in her presence at the athenaeum, and he found himself unable to leave straight away, almost as if she had been absorbing his thoughts and stealing the air he breathed.

"Have you found what you've been looking for?" a female voice asked him. The woman rested her shoulder against the wall, her body facing him while he stood unmoving.

"Is this another fortunate coincidence, or are you following me?" Jascha asked Rosewillow, turning his head in her direction.

The woman let out a tiny chuckle. "Well, I am glad you consider me a fortunate coincidence."

"That is not what I said."

"I believe it is."

Jascha set his empty cup of wine on the windowsill to his left, briefly glancing at the woman in the ivory coat before his gaze shifted again to the table he was watching. Rosewillow glanced in the direction he was looking, and her smile slightly widened.

"Do you know who they are?"

"Do I care?" was his retort.

"I come from Summerport," she told him in a suave voice. "Their family rules the southern lands. They are quite impressive; all of the Lionhelms have a certain charisma that draws attention," she commented, looking back at him. "As you can see for yourself."

Ignoring the second half of her sentence, Jascha fixed his gloves and covered his head with his hood. "It is quite interesting that a simple woman from Summerport is the longtime friend of a simple woman of the capital," he commented dryly before storming out of the tavern.

He knew the ivory woman was behind him. He rounded the first corner, pressing his back against the wall, and the moment she appeared, he grabbed her by the neck, sending her straight into the surface he leaned on. He tightened his hand around her throat and banged her head once against the wet wall. Rosewillow gasped for air, her hands immediately covering his as she glared at him. He was much taller than her, but his feet were sinking into the mud, just like hers.

Jascha inched his face closer to hers to the point she could feel his breath against her skin. "Start talking, now," he ordered her. "Your little friend at the library was quite the nosy goblin, but you are deranged," he hissed, pressing her further into the wall.

Rosewillow gritted her teeth. "Why," she whispered against his lips. "Do I make you uncomfortable, Jascha?"

The moment she said his name, he relinquished his hold on her, partially turning to the side. He breathed heavily as if to hear his own inhale and exhale. He brought a hand to his mouth, balling his fist against his lips. Rosewillow fixed her cloak, taking a step away from him when his hand came crashing down against her cheek. She nearly fell to the ground due to the impact, but she leaned against the cold wall behind her, bringing a hand to her rapidly bruising cheek. An angry, surprised laugh escaped her lips, and her stare darkened. He looked at her with unspoken fury as she laughed. He was disturbed by it, and she noticed it.

"Prying eyes do not stay open for long," Rosewillow warned him. She placed a steady hand on his shoulder, and he watched it trail against his neck until she cupped his cheek. "I am the first and last warning you will receive," she added in a firm tone. "The First Wardens do not mingle and they certainly do not share, no matter what the laws others may dictate. You may think knowledge is within your reach because it resides in a place you are allowed to enter, but it is not."

Jascha was quick to grab her wrist, tugging her forcefully to hold her shoulders. Glaring down at her, he stated, "You're one of them. And tell me, what is it you do to your *Nakfèht*? Flay him? Slaughter him? I saw all the drawings. I saw the body parts that were mutilated."

Rosewillow parted her rosy lips, her face contorting into a grim smile. "Do you care?" she mimicked his previous words to her. "Do you want to see?" she asked, her emerald eyes staring into his dark orbs as she leaned in.

He pushed away brutally, and Rosewillow hit the ground. Her ivory coat was covered in mud, some splashing even against the side of her face. "I want you gone," he answered.

Turning heels, Jascha headed in the direction of the inn he stayed at, never looking back at the offending woman. He could feel the blood rushing to his head, and the last thing he wanted was to strangle the one person who could give him answers. Jascha wasn't convinced he wanted to hear those. He half wondered what it would take for it all to end. How many First Wardens would he need to eliminate to stop the visions, to stop the bleeding? What if it didn't stop at all?

The rain kept pouring over his face, but even the cold droplets against his boiling skin could not come close to the sense of peace he decided that he only imagined earlier that day.

✻✻✻

The sails were raised high by the halyard, the bright blue color of the tensile only highlighted by the ivory crest of the Lionhelms. The three lion heads that faced each other and their serpentine tongues screamed in the horizon the arrival of overlords chosen by their king. Their campaign across the Tinted Bay had been a long one. Years had passed since Tithan last saw his family home. He had begun to forget what his father looked like. His usually short, military-trimmed chestnut hair reached his shoulders, and his beard needed a shave as well. He was exhausted, but the harbor of Summerport was in view. The lighthouse called for his five hundred ships, and the heralds already announced his arrival.

    The Red Continent had proved to be harder to handle than what he'd been told. The northern coasts were chaotically split between free cities, and the recruitment of young men was no longer seen as an opportunity for the red people. Tithan had been welcome, however, and treated with respect; the hospitality of the people of Khar'had was unique. He had found himself with a smoking tube in his mouth more often than with a sword in his hands, until he moved to Al Siger, in the western desert. The seven governors of the largest northern free city had given a new meaning to the Red Continent, using slaves from the southern lands as their currency. When Tithan tried to restore the use of the silvers, the Al Siger governors would remind him that the mined silver went straight to Summerport and that they would trade flesh with flesh. Tithan had been on the verge of drawing his sword and commanding his men to do so as well, but this was not the way of King Helias. Mildly offended at their ways, Tithan decided to appoint an ambassador to Al Siger, the young cousin of his commander Angefort, a boy by the name of Almeric, and the governors gifted him a boat full of virgin slaves, women with a skin shade darker than the Pit and covered in gold. Many of his men bedded the women, but Tithan refused to, until Yesiantha. He remembered her soft cheekbones and big amber eyes all too well. She had refused every other man and spent her days staring at the sea, showered with gold and eyes full of sorrow. It was on one rare rainy night that she told him with a heavy accent that the governors had kept her locked away for years, deeming her luscious straight hair a bad omen because she was desert-born. They shared a rather gentle night, but she refused to follow him to the Silver Lands. Tithan left her at the harbor of Khar'had the following year, but not without a token dear to him.

Arther Angefort stood next to him, his long brown hair cascading down his back and his thick beard covering even his neck. "We are home, my lord."

"That we are," Tithan replied, placing a hand on his commander's shoulder. "Although I am afraid I will be needed in the capital sooner than I would want to."

Angefort tilted his head before nodding. "Khar'had heard of the Violet Delusion spreading around the capital. If that is true, King Helias will have other issues to deal with than the blatant rejection of his campaigns in the Red Continent."

"He can't expect to mine their silver without repercussions for the rest of eternity. The slave trade turned the simplest of men into powerful governors. The free cities are bigger than any stronghold of the Silver Lands, and we, as well, can find slaves disembarking on our shores."

Preferring to change the subject, Angefort asked, "Eager to meet your second-born? When we left, he still nursed."

Tithan broke into a smile. "I am, my friend. Voladea named him Tylennald after my favorite uncle. I wish for my son to become at least half the man my uncle was."

"I heard your uncle was the one who invented the repeating crossbow with poisoned darts," Angefort recalled.

"I wouldn't give him that credit," Tithan laughed, shaking his head. "Uncle Tylennald was a man of knowledge. The repeating crossbow was said to have been a commonly used weapon in Driazon. Pieces of these weapons were retrieved along with antiquities during the discovery of the islands of the Zalejos Depths."

"Which another one of your ancestors conducted."

Tithan's expression darkened at that, his beaming smile dulling down. "If discoveries and diplomatic campaigns were all we Lionhelms did," he quietly spoke. "Perhaps the Violet Delusion will one day cross the Rough Rill, and at that moment, we will get a glimpse of the damage we have caused to others," he told Angefort without an ounce of regret tainting his tone.

"Yes, my lord."

Tithan closed his eyes, deeply inhaling the scents that reminded him so much of his homeland. The faint scent of lemons, the overwhelming perfume of the yellow daisies he so much adored, the hot smoke that carried the smell of baked pastries. It was all gone. He could only see the purple fog. It was everywhere, tickling even the base of Strongshore. No one waited for them at the harbor; the villagers were suffering, others were dead. Entire towns became ghost settlements, void of any form of life. The southwestern lands were no more, every minor house vanishing from the continent as if they never existed; the Rain Lands of the northwestern coast became inaccessible. The Rochelacs never exited Noirmont anymore. His father spoke incoherently, repeating over and over that Thaesonwald was dead.

"Thaesonwald is dead," he whispered.
"Yes, my lord," a woman whispered.
"Thaesonwald."
"Lord Tithan, I am so sorry."

He opened his eyes again, his vision foggy, and the clouded silhouette of a woman hovering above him. "Thaesonwald," he called.

"It's me, my lord. Fantine," the woman repeated.

Tithan blinked a few times, recognizing the fiery red hair of his master-at-arms. It was not the strawberry-blonde mane of his brother. "Fantine," he repeated. "Look at you; all grown up. How long has it been?" he asked, wetting his lips as he closed his eyes again to regain control of his thoughts.

"You have been unconscious for some days now. Healer Martus requested the Regency's physicians' presence for a consult."

Tithan smiled at her, his large hand searching for hers on the bed. The woman immediately grabbed it, squeezing it. "So grown up," he repeated. "Did the second campaign last that long?" he asked her. "You were only a child when we left Strongshore for the Zalejos Depths."

Confused, the warrior replied, "I was. I was only twelve years of age. A long time has passed."

"I see." Lord Tithan coughed a bit, and he was immediately offered some water. Waving it away from his face, he breathed steadily. "I had a weird dream, Fantine," he whispered. "I dreamed that Thaesonwald was dead."

"I am afraid it is not a dream," she told him with a pained voice, the lines around her eyes deepening every time her face twitched.

"My brother isn't dead," her lord repeated, drifting back to sleep. "I must tell Father that my brother isn't dead.

Covering her face with her free hand, Fantine swallowed the sob she didn't want him to hear. "I will tell him myself, Lord Tithan," she said in a soothing tone. "Lord Thaesonwald lives."

"He must," Tithan replied tiredly. "He is Lord of Strongshore. I don't want to be Lord of Strongshore.

"Lordship means a long life but only a few days of good fortune."

✳✳✳

The audience room of Strongshore was filled with the echoing sound of Lord Riverguard's boots as he made his way inside, ignoring the loud screeching of the double doors behind him as well as the stares he received from the Lionhelms present and the few minor lords that assisted. Lovel's bright eyes fell on the two women who stood before Lady Voladea, her son Tylennald and her grandson Tiran. They were accompanied by three young children, and Lord Riverguard came to stand next to his daughter Wallysa, at the base of the steps that led to the tall chair Lord Tithan would sit on. With it being empty, the cushions of the chairs were visible to all, and so was the history embroidered on their fabric. From the foundations of the southern history painted on the floor to the peak of their known civilization on the unofficial throne, the Lionhelms remained the family whose power never faltered. From Alatros the Red's conquest from the Avoryon Hills to his ascent on the throne of Old Drixia, from the independent kingdoms that fought the northern empires to the stable alliance between Silverholde and Strongshore, from Asarul to the Silver Lands, it mattered not if the chair was lined with emerald hues and golden tones. The King's justice was Lord Lionhelm's justice, and the latter's counsel was the former's decision.

    Lady Voladea wore a straight, dark brown dress and a black coat that covered only her upper body, revealing the incredible amount of weight she lost in a short period. Her hair was neatly collected around a tall headpiece that resembled a crown. Other than the silver nestled in her greying curls, she wore no jewel and sprayed no pink dust on her pale, sunken cheeks. Her son was dressed in black as well, his single grey strand grazing his cheekbone while his chestnut mane was properly brushed back and oiled. Contrary to Tylennald, Tiran had been asked to wear the colors of his house, his light britches stressing his visible lack of training and his blue waistcoat clashed with his medium complexion. His bald head was covered by a simple wool hat and his shoulders were slightly hunched. He was shorter than most Lionhelm males, but that was not the reason why he felt utterly out of place and showed it to the world.

Lady Voladea spoke first, addressing her grandson of over forty years of age. "Dear Tiran, the women your late father bedded stand before you," she reminded him. Looking at the woman with very short dark hair holding the hand of the eldest boy, she told him, "this is Miss Annot, a simple woman of Summerport, and her son Anfroy. They both were gifted a piece of land as well as a decently big house overlooking the bay. They receive a thousand silvers every six moons." Moving to stand closer to the second woman, she went on, "This is Miss Esabell, lovely little thing; she could be your little sister. Her sons are Launce and Theodric. Your father had for them three thousand silvers every six moons to ensure their needs are taken care of as well as the mansion where they live in Edgemere."

Tiran timidly looked at the two women in front of him, who dared not return his gaze. "Yes, Lady Lionhelm," he replied.

"Given the circumstances, with your father's death and your grandfather's accident, I think there is no better way for you to start learning about your responsibilities as Lord of Strongshore," Voladea explained calmly, returning to her spot next to the empty chair and leaning in, her hand resting on Tiran's shoulder. "You would have to decide whether to revoke these women's allowances, take their homes from them, or keep everything intact," she paused, "or modify the terms.

"It is no longer about your father's silvers; it is about yours."

Tiran straightened his back, his ignorant stare scanning the small crowd before him as if to find the answer hanging in the air. Lord Riverguard narrowed his eyes at him, awaiting his answer almost excitedly.

"I-I can't take their homes," Tiran said, his eyes connecting with Miss Esabell's.

Voladea's lips curved up slightly, exchanging a look with Tylennald, who played the part of the impartial witness almost as perfectly as Lord Riverguard. "That is fair," she reassured him. "After all, these boys are your half-brothers."

"I-I don't know about the allowance," Tiran went on hesitantly. "I would need to ask the Silver Master."

His grandmother nodded once. "The allowances have been estimated accordingly," she told him, offering him a warm smile as if to praise his common sense. "But what about the boys?"

"The boys?"

"Well, forgive me, dear, if I bring this up now, but you chose no wife; you have no heir. If you were to inherit the southern lands today, or tomorrow, or in a few years, what happens to your legacy?

"Do you wish to keep your half-brothers in this household," she offered, her eyes widening slightly at the sight of the two mistresses hugging their sons tighter, "and educate them and take them as your heirs, or do you wish to nominate someone else?"

Lord Riverguard took a step forward, politely bowing his head. "My apologies for interrupting, Lady Lionhelm, but I think such matters have probably been handled already by Lord Tithan. Surely, if Lord Tiran were to leave no heir of his own, there is already an established line of succession."

Lady Voladea clasped her hands together, stepping down to come eye-to-eye level with Lord Lovel. "Of course," she conceded. "The hypothesis is based on the premise that my lord husband's line of succession couldn't be respected for the conditions Lord Tithan laid down were not met."

The blonde lord folded his hands behind his back, turning to face Tiran. "Well, then what is your answer, Lord Tiran?"

The man stared at his half-brothers again, boys he had never met before and that he didn't think he would ever meet, not in such a context. "I do not take them as my heirs," he whispered.

"Wiser words have never been spoken in this room," Lady Voladea praised him again, nodding her chin at the nearest guards so they would escort the women and their children outside. "May our dearest family members be our witnesses," she added, extending her hand in the direction of Lord Riverguard, his daughter, and the rest of their household, including Lord Jarvis, the nephew of Lord Angefort who had been invited by

Lady Voladea to stay longer in Strongshore after the ball held in Tecla's honor.

Lord Lovel eyed the young man with glinting eyes before he reminded himself to smile and bow his head at the lady of the house. "Since we are your witnesses, Lord Tiran," he spoke, earning himself a curious stare from both Voladea and Tylennald. "May we know about the line of succession? I am sure Lord Jarvis here would need to report to his uncle, the Secretary of the Regency, if he witnessed any changes that could, I dare say, clash with the dispositions Lord Lionhelm left in Lord Angefort's care."

Before Voladea could respond, Tylennald held her wrist. "Of course, you may, my lord," he replied with a genuine smile that fooled the rest of the crowd. "My father's wishes were to see his son Thaesonwald rule over Strongshore and Tiran after him. Were my nephew not have any children, the title would be mine to share with my lovely wife, your daughter," he replied, "for Theliel is a member of the Regency and my sisters will both be married to men that do not belong to our lands."

Lord Lovel chuckled before he inhaled, looking intently at the future Lord Angefort who had participated in the ball just like many other young lords. "Will they?" he asked his son-in-law. "Has Lady Tecla chosen a husband?"

"The Sons of Ferngrunn have made an offer we cannot ignore," Voladea replied sternly. "It seemed that our little Tecla spent quite some time exchanging pleasantries with one of them during the ball." Hushed words instantly filled the audience room. "However, it will be my husband's duty to make a decision," she confidently explained.

"Are there not better chances that Lady Tecla stays in Silverholde?" Lord Riverguard pressed with an amused smile on his lips. "I hear she has yet to return."

Whispers filled the room so quickly that even the guards seemed to be leaning into each other to discuss the future of House Lionhelm. Voladea's eyes darted in every possible direction as she suddenly felt constricted in her corseted dress, disliking the smugness that defined Lord Lovel Riverguard's face. She saw Healer Martus among the crowd, his guarded expression signaling her that whatever words were being hushed were not in her favor. She felt Tylennald stiffen by her side, his secretive stare directed solely at the man who tried to force the truth about the line of succession past their lips, for everyone to hear.

Lord Lovel shifted his weight to look at his ever-silent daughter next to him, taking pride in the glare she was gracing him with. "Wouldn't it be quite the fortunate coincidence for Lady Tecla to find out about her father's will during her stay in Silverholde?"

"You are my father," Wallysa hissed at him. "Aren't you supposed to stand by me?"

"I am," he told her in a serious tone. "I am, dear daughter," he repeated, cupping her chin.

When they least expected it, Tiran cleared his throat, his shiny eyes reflecting the apprehension that filled his tone. "May the Oracle and all of you present be my witnesses," he spoke, silencing the audience room. "I shall hereby name Lord Tylennald, my uncle, as well as his descendants my rightful heirs if the Good Gods decide against my lord grandfather's established line of succession."

The crowd roared again, incessant chatter filling Strongshore from the audience room to the hall. Voladea exhaled faintly, almost failing to believe his words, and she felt her son's hand against her back. Her eyes met Tiran's, who then promptly looked into his uncle's eyes. There was a shift in his attitude, it was barely visible, but it certainly was palpable. The tips of his ears were turning red, and his round eyes narrowed. His cheek twitched, and the next words he spoke were not the ones Lady Voladea imagined.

"And now," he whispered. "You will release my mother from the keep."

Chapter XXIII

Days of Dusk

"One more," Tecla cheered, raising her chalice of black wine. "One more, Tomas."

Lyzon and Fran's laughter caused Theliel to break into a burst of his own, partially spilling his drink over his food. Her brother coughed as the ale hitched in his throat, and the two siblings stared wide-eyed at the educator who stuffed the fifth tart in his mouth. His cheeks had doubled in size, and he couldn't properly say the Lionhelm's family motto anymore. Tecla leaned against Theliel, placing a hand on his forearm, as she tried to catch her breath. The broken syllables of "Formed from many, now as one" sounded like an insult as chunks of meat and chewed bread fell from Tomas' lips. The educator chugged some of his ale to swallow the food he could, and Tecla watched Fran wipe away the tears that prickled his eyes due to all the laughter.

"My lady," Tomas sighed out, wiping the beads of sweat on his forehead, "that was evil. And you too, my lord."

Theliel ruffled his medium-length hair before leaning back in his wooden chair. "It's just a game my father told me he would play with his men at sea," he explained. "I think ten tarts was his personal best. Or Lord Angefort's, I'm not quite sure."

"Father played this?" Tecla asked in sheer surprise.

"Imagine this, sweet sister; it takes about two moons to reach the Red Continent on a Lionhelm ship, and three to reach the Zalejos Depths. A man must vanquish boredom at night."

"One can only imagine what those men did once they found land," she heard Fran say.

Tecla straightened up in her seat, poking at the chicken bones in her empty plate with her fork. She saw Lyzon stare darkly at the man beside her, and Tecla understood. After all, her brother was the product of an affair, and perhaps she was too. Had his father taken liberties with other women in faraway lands, it wouldn't change the way she saw him. He had been a good father to her and her siblings; no law and no faith forbade the bedding of multiple women and men, although it was fairly common to hear more about a lord's affairs than those of a lady. The latter was usually frowned upon and kept a secret.

Deciding that a change of subject was needed, Tecla cleared her throat, glancing at her brother, who was picking his teeth with the tip of his knife. "Are we to visit more places tomorrow?" she asked.

Theliel winked at her. "I am afraid not. I heard Sir Sybbyl Nobleleaf requested a meeting with Lord Angefort; usually, Sir Ferrand Nickletail likes to keep his afternoon clear of any duty when such meetings take place, just in case he is summoned too. And that," he sighed, brushing his knuckles against Tecla's cheek, "means that I get to do his work."

The girl pouted, earning herself a soft chuckle.

"You could always spend some time around the marketplace, but with guards, Tecla. Or you could attend the mass at the Temple of Phorbas." Theliel stood up, eyeing the man behind the bar counter. "You go ahead and wait for me inside the carriage while I pay the owner."

Tecla watched her brother in silence while the others gathered the few belongings they had brought with them. She knew it was whimsical of her to wish that her brother spent less time in the dull confines of the Treasure Council's quarters, although it was his duty. Educator Tomas had spent the entire evening telling her and Lyzon and Fran about Maugre's Arena and the winter fights that took place in there. The complex would be open to both nobles and simple people, allowing them to entertain themselves with winter sports. Tomas spoke of snowy races where the finest breeds of Noirmont hounds would drag sleds to the finish line. It surely wasn't the way Tecla had hoped to spend the winter, but she figured it would do until she could finally see Melisentia's Opera in the spring. The amphitheater was said to welcome performers from all across the continent to play the Oracle's Memoir and the greatest battles of the Silver Lands. As Tecla neared the exit of the Shattered Ambry, she fell into a sullen mood. The following day would be the last moon day; she would have to travel back to Strongshore for the dusk days to come and worry quickly filled her heart. She truly hoped that Grandmaster Rodbertus had been right and that her lord father would be recovering quickly from his fall. She imagined that arrangements were already being made for her brother Thaesonwald's funeral; she surely wished that such arrangements wouldn't also be made for Lord Tithan.

    Theliel leaned against the wooden counter as he waited for the patrons standing next to him to leave. He ordered another warm drink for himself as he and the tavern owner exchanged a silent glance. The Lionhelm slid a few silvers his way, more than what was needed to cover for the meal. He sipped his hot brew in silence, the liquid gracing his thin lips with a purple tint due to the flowery ingredients. It tasted bitter, but it made Theliel feel a little more awake after the heavy supper. The owner's eyes were staring straight ahead, and Theliel glanced around out of curiosity. He saw a man clad in black clothes rush outside the tavern, a woman with an ivory dress right behind him.

    "Am I missing something, Rollant?" Theliel asked the chubby adult who wiped chalices across from him.

"I know many faces around here, Lionhelm," the tavern owner replied, clicking his tongue. "Those two in the corner I did not recognize. I like knowing who my patrons are."

"Perhaps your fame has attracted more travelers," Theliel said with a glint in his eyes.

"Quit the horseshit, will ya, Lionhelm," Rollant told him as he set down the chalice and flung the rag over his shoulder. "I got your stuff stashed in my shop behind the stables, and it's been there for longer than it should have. My wife is starting to ask questions; questions I do not know how to answer. She knows we don't make that much profit," he explained, lowering his voice. "Not when half the city is starving."

"My apologies for the extended custody," Theliel replied, reaching inside the pocket of his cloak. Sliding a small envelope towards Rollant, he whispered, "It took me a while to identify the correct ship. You can send everything to Limemeadow; at the harbor, the captain of Lion's Glory will be waiting for the shipment under Sarkis of Silverholde's name.

"Once the ship arrives in Summerport, you will receive compensation within three dawn days."

Rollant shook his head, his brown eyes staring straight into Theliel's hazels. "That's too long of a wait. What if your ship sinks?"

Theliel laughed lightly, his pearly teeth showing. "Worry not, my friend. Lion's Glory is Terrel Lionhelm's ship. It was a gift from my father for his grandson's birthday. Lionhelm ships do not sink, even after many moons of sailing."

"There's a first time for everything."

"If you attended a naval battle, which ship would you place your bets on?" Theliel argued in a serious tone before emptying his mug. "Some would try to cheer the movement of a Sand Tower ship, but many would still put all their silvers on the robustness of a Lionhelm ship. Do you know why?"

Rollant narrowed his eyes before shrugging. "The bigger the better?"

"The bigger the more men on board," Theliel nodded. "Once they harpoon the enemy ship, it's an entire army assaulting its foe. This is why our ships are never attacked by mercenaries. The Lionhelm navy is made of men who live at sea and train on their way to trade. And once they reach a harbor, they repair the ship before they even think of visiting the local brothel," Theliel boasted. "We're not just some coastal raiders, Rollant."

The tavern owner didn't seem convinced. The nostrils of his large nose flared and his jaw twitched, but eventually, Rollant grabbed the silvers in front of him and tucked the envelope between his belt and his britches. "Three dawn days," he reminded Theliel.

"Thank you for the fog tea," the young man concluded, pushing against the counter before turning heels, hoping his sister hadn't been waiting for too long outside the tavern.

✳✳✳

Tecla's half-lidded eyes looked away from her book and outside the tall window of her bedchamber. Her lips curved up slightly at the sight of her gardener friend trying to shield his plants with his body as he worked on a creeping laurel vine with another Regency gardener instructing him. Fran seemed to be paying little attention to the man wearing a large, round hat made of straw that clashed with the emerald hues of his uniform. Sighing as she tried to focus her attention back on the subject Tomas told her to study, Tecla tried to memorize the names of the cities and towns that were reduced to ghost lands after the Violet Delusion. Bouldershell by the southwestern coast, Glimmerforest around Summerport, and Madmire before the ruins of Everspring were only the territories that her father once ruled over. Lands that had seen the end of minor houses such as the Dawnshields of Everspring or the Sunhorns of Bouldershell; lands that no one cared to remember anymore. Tecla let the book fall on her lap before she closed it on the tea table next to her, smiling faintly at Lyzon, who seemed busy knitting a shawl for herself.

"Lyzon."

"Yes, young lady," the maid instantly replied, her fingers freezing.

"You have been very quiet since we arrived," Tecla noted. "Is there anything bothering you?"

The tanned woman mimicked her smile, bowing her head. "I am not used to the capital, my lady. For decades, all I've known was Strongshore.

And to know that Lord Lionhelm may not be well has me wondering if we will ever go back to the life we had in Strongshore," she admitted.

Tecla stood up, causing the maid to rise to her feet as well as a sign of respect. The young lady's gentle expression turned into a frown as Lyzon's words sank in, and she walked up to the servant to rest a hand on her shoulder. "I don't think we will," she whispered. "We will probably stay in Silverholde for many years, and I will visit Father on every dusk day as he and I agreed."

Lyzon didn't look up, her small almond eyes fixed on the floor.

"Have faith, Lyzon," Tecla told her. "Father will be well and Silverholde isn't so bad, after all, is it? Days may not be as sunny as at home, but the livelihood of the capital is refreshing."

"Of course, young lady."

Lyzon watched her lady exit the bedchamber in silence, although she only wanted to scream. She reminded herself of the boundaries Fran suggested she respected, and it only made her lonelier. As she put down her needlework to clean the room now that her lady had left, Lyzon questioned if following Tithan to the Silver Lands had been a wise choice. It had been a selfish one, as both had refused to bid farewell to each other, and she couldn't imagine abandoning a newborn to picture the little being raised and educated by another person. However, Tecla was a woman now, or close to being one at the very least, and her father was dying. Lyzon knew he was; she hadn't wanted to mention his coughing to Lady Tecla for she wasn't sure the girl had noticed it, and she didn't want to alarm her young lady. As she heard the echoing of the girl's heel fade down in the hallway, Lyzon closed the doors, almost as if she were afraid that her thoughts could fly out of the bed-chamber and reach Tecla's ears.

    The youngest Lionhelm walked in silence in the direction of the Observatory Vault's main room, even though she knew Grandmaster Rodbertus wouldn't be there. He told her that very morning that he would spend the afternoon selecting the explorers that were in charge of finding the artifacts and sites that could rewrite the history of the Silver Lands. Tecla's only comment had been about the explorers being all male. She had pointed out to him that many knights and overlords were or had been women, and Grandmaster Rodbertus had agreed with her, only to reply that the ability to defend themselves in dire situations was not the reason why male explorers were usually chosen. It was because of the noble families who prioritized female educators that ultimately, the exploring was left to men. Shrugging the thought away, Tecla simply reminded herself that it wasn't Rodbertus she wanted to see.

    As she passed the first couple columns lighted with red rosewillow sap, Tecla went over what Theliel told her about her father and her birth. He didn't seem to know whether Lady Voladea was her mother or not, as he was more preoccupied with making sure she didn't feel like she wasn't his sister and a true daughter of the parent they had in common. Tecla knew that perfectly, however, what she didn't understand was how the woman everyone called Mad Matillis seemed to know more about her than the rest of her household. Tecla walked past the last row of shelves, nodding her head at an educator who bowed at the young lady.

Firmly balling her right hand into a fist, Tecla knocked three times at a fast, impatient rate. When nobody answered the small door, she repeated her motion. "Open the door, Grandmaster Matillis," she ordered.

The wooden door cracked, and a pair of small hazel eyes peered at her. "What ya want, runt?"

Tecla's arm dropped and she stared at the short woman with resolution. "I need to talk to you," she answered, a part of her wondering if she should be straightforward about the matter. "You called me a bastard child."

Mad Matillis simply rolled her eyes at the young lady. "You should speak with Tithan, not me."

"My father is ill."

A wave of sadness seemed to soften the old woman's face, only to be quickly replaced by her usual scowl. "Ah, well, nobody is eternal," she whispered before pushing the door closed.

"Wait," Tecla pressed, holding the door open. "Please."

The short woman leaned in slightly, scanning the girl's face. Her burly fingers curled against the door frame and she said, "I know nothing of your mother. I know these eyes are not Sarulite eyes," she commented. Grabbing Tecla's chin, she pulled her closer. "You," she whispered. "Your eyes are tainted like your soul is."

Swatting the woman's hand away, Tecla glanced around. "My grandmother Tecla had blue eyes," she repeated Tesfira's words. "I don't see what the problem is."

Matillis sneered. "In that case, we have nothing to discuss."

Tecla pushed against the door again when the woman tried to block her out.

"Blue is the stain of the Iathienar's eyesight," Matillis told her. "The eyesight is granted only to the Holy Ones. Your hands have claimed the life of a servant of the Good Gods, haven't they?"

Tecla didn't respond. She had no idea what to say; Tesfira told her the holy captain died of heart failure, and it nearly convinced her that she had only dreamed about the man's charred flesh, but Matillis was right. Her eye color was stained since the event and the smell of burnt flesh wasn't a memory easy to erase.

When Tecla remained silent, Matillis took a step back, allowing the girl to enter her vault. The young lady hunched her back to slip through the door and found herself to be slightly disappointed at what seemed to be the Occult Vault. It was a mere room that resembled one of the athenaeum's floors, with dusty shelves and wooden colors. A messy table was pushed against the only window available, and it was full of manuscripts and overused books with yellow pages. The air was humid and the smell quite hideous. Mad Matillis didn't seem to be the kind of person who would think of letting the window open from time to time. She watched the old woman walk up to her desk; her black robes so long Tecla wondered how the woman managed not to stumble over the hem.

"Speak up, child," Mad Matillis ordered, hopping on the wooden chair as she resumed her work without paying much attention to the uncomfortable and utterly confused lady behind her.

"My soul is indeed tainted," Tecla whispered, a shiver coursing through her body as she admitted it. "I have taken the soul of a man in the House of the Oracle. It was not my intent—"

"It was," Matillis cut in, resting her elbow on the backrest of the chair as she twisted her upper body to turn around and stare at the lady. "The sooner you admit it, the better for you."

"I didn't know—I still don't know how it happened."

The greying woman narrowed her eyes as she tried to assess the situation. Tecla didn't seem to be lying, yet she couldn't be so sure. "Come closer," she ordered, flipping the pages of her tallest book, causing some dust to fly in her face. The woman sneezed loudly before wiping the slime with her sleeve. "Do you know what this is?"

Tecla bent forward, her right eyebrow twitching. "It's a crown."

"This is Warrior Queen Aelneth's crown," Matillis corrected her. The crown drawn on the left page of the book had no cap but a thick, golden band with three major sections that arched upwards. The massive stone at the center was painted of a color that swirled from green to honey, its hexagonal shape standing out between the three ruby sun crosses that framed it; one to its left, one to its right, and one above it. The rest of the band was lined with the different stages of the moon, but right under the biggest stone sat a black one of an identical shape. "This," Matillis pointed at the black stone, "is the Quiet Tear. This one," she slid her finger over the honeyed blue-green stone, "is the Darling Mind. And these," she circled the sun crosses, "are the Gifted Crosses."

Tecla shook her head, reaching around her neck to sling her braid over her shoulder. Pointing at the pendant tangled in her tresses, she said, "This is the Darling Mind; it's a lot smaller."

"Because it's incomplete. Where is the other half?"

Tecla's eyes darted around as she tried to remember. "Father... Father said he lost it," she answered.

Matillis flicked her fingers against Tecla's forehead. "Tithan doesn't lose anything unless it's his pants in front of a pretty creature."

Tecla made a face. "Will you tell me how do you know my father?"

"Pay attention," the grandmaster scolded her. "Warrior Queen Aelneth didn't bring half of Asarul to heel only because she could; what she wanted weren't lands or power. She wanted these," she went on, her short nails scraping at the drawing. "The Quiet Tear is the gateway to the past; the Gifted Crosses are the path to the future and the Darling Mind is the key to the present. With the stones of Aelneth, there is no limit to what one can see," Matillis concluded, turning the pages of her book until a very familiar portrait caused Tecla to gasp. "But the price is high."

Tecla stared with unblinking eyes at the Oracle's face. It was the same face painted on the ceiling of the temple in Summerport. Matillis traced the Oracle's eyes, her index finger tapping around the irises that spun with green and blue hues before they turned honey and sunset, ultimately fading into black.

"Every vision you get, you steal a soul," Grandmaster Matillis whispered.

"That's not…" Tecla cleared her throat. "That doesn't make sense. Are you saying the Oracle used the stones? That she was never blessed with the Good Gods' will?"

Matillis stood up, closing the book. The golden title, Stones and Songs of Aelneth, was just another book authored by her. "Premonition is not a gift from the Good Gods," she revealed. "There is a thin line between the research one can conduct in the Observatory Vault and the practices you can follow in the Occult Vault." Rubbing her round nose, Matillis looked out of the window. "Every human can sense other people's energy, and feel the impending changes before they occur; I am sure you went through it before. It is a common sensation," she reasoned, looking at Tecla from the corner of her eye. "However, these stones convey the energy of the human mind in precise directions."

Tecla's head was spinning. The short woman before her managed to do in a heartbeat what her father could never accomplish in fourteen years; shake her beliefs and make her question her faith. Mad Matillis was listing facts that caused the Oracle to sound like a fraud that lasted for millennia. Tecla wanted to argue, to ask for further proof, but she couldn't form a single sentence.

"Queen Aelneth received the Gifted Crosses from her first husband, Rathdron the Tall, a warrior of the inland who claimed to be the second grandson of Rohdron the Skeleton. His tomb is still worshipped by many in the Fog Lands, in the small town of Three Crosses, which took its name from the warrior's legend.

"Rathdron might have been tall, but strength wasn't a quality of his. He died against Alatros the Red's troops after the first assault. Alatros wasn't able to cross the Rough Rill immediately after his victory, for the river flooded, and brought to the river's bank plenty of small, black stones that shone brighter than silver.

"Have you read songs or poems of Old Calaris?" Matillis asked although she didn't wait for an answer. "And the brave men arranged a bedding of dark pearls, for only the Good Gods could be the ones allowing the Red to cross the waters of ire," she recited. "After being flanked by Aelneth's warriors, Alatros decided to fuse the quiet tears and create a stone to offer to the one woman he wanted to marry; quite romantic, if you ask me, for a man whose odds to win had been evened out with one battle, courtesy of the years spent warring others before Aelneth," she snickered. "Aelneth took the Quiet Tear, and for all we know, she possessed the Darling Mind already. The early carvings of Old Drixia that the Observatory Vault found around Edgemere depict a queen with a very large pendant around her neck. And the rest is history," Matillis concluded.

"Aelneth was the one with the visions," Tecla whispered, raising her eyebrows as she diverted her gaze and leaned against the sturdy chair. "But all the stories about Kothore and the warning she gave Alatros the Red… What about those?"

"What Kothore wrote in her memoir might be true," Matillis conceded. "She warned Alatros about the attack that would end his conquest, and he didn't listen. That doesn't mean Kothore wasn't sent by Aelneth or that she wasn't simply a harlot who serviced a warrior a little too eager to discuss war tactics. In any case, Aelneth wore the stones; everything that was prophesized after the founding of Old Drixia either came from her or the Oracle was given the stones."

Tecla ran a hand over her braid before pressing her thumb against the stone her father gifted her. "Anyone with these jewels can see," she whispered almost disappointedly.

Matillis hummed. "Perhaps, although I am sure these stones are bound to the blood of those who used them first. Binding isn't uncommon in the world of the occult," she quickly added, pushing a few manuscripts away until she found the one she was interested in. "It is a bit like the laws of succession in a noble family."

Tecla unfolded the manuscript, dropping it at the sight of a drawing of a human body being pinned by wide pieces of wood that looked like the roots of an ancient tree. Markings on several parts of the man's body made him look like a living map, but one large mark above his heart stood out.

"This is a binding ritual, for example. The body hosts a stone for an extended period until it only recognizes the blood it is bound to. Unless this happened to the Quiet Tear and the Gifted Crosses, I would say their powers are still tied to Aelneth's descendants." Matillis sighed, taking the manuscript away from Tecla's hands. "Ya don't look so pleased."

Tecla shot her a glare. "Forgive me for being slightly confused," she sarcastically said, running out of patience at the woman's antics. "I have just discovered a world I didn't think would exist, and you stepped all over my beliefs—"

"I did?"

"—and I just have more questions. You said the Holy Ones are blessed with the Iathienar's eyesight, but then the stones are bound—"

"These are two different things."

"—and how do I use the Darling Mind correctly?" she ranted, her cheeks flushing at the memory of the first time she had a vision.

Matillis remained calm and composed, her voice dropping a little lower. "You don't," she answered. "You take it off and store it away in a closet, or you let it be swallowed by the sea—I do not care. You don't use it. It is a dangerous stone," she warned the girl. "Many will lust after it and if they don't kill you to get their hands on it, it will end you."

The green fire, Tecla remembered. The voices by the pyre, the masked women; were these the people Mad Matillis was hinting at? Could she ask her? She wanted to know who they were and what their interests were, but Matillis had already turned her back to her.

"Who would—?"

"Get out, will ya," Matillis growled. "You've taken my time, now make sure you take my advice as well and get rid of it."

Tecla hesitantly took a step forward.

"I am serious, you little idiot," the grandmaster snapped, grabbing the girl's forearms to push her out of the room. "Throw it and never think of it again. And send my regards to Tithan."

Before Tecla could argue back, her head bumped against the door frame as she was inelegantly expelled and the old wooden door was slammed in her face, again.

✳✳✳

Supper was slowly coming to an end in the Lionhelms' great hall. Lord Tithan's seat at the center of the long table was vacant, but Lovel Riverguard noticed how Lord Thaesonwald's was quickly filled by his brother's mighty posterior. Lovel Riverguard heard several servants and minor lords such as Jarvis Angefort repeat the new nickname Lord Thaesonwald was granted shortly after his death; the Almost Lord of Strongshore, to mimic his mother's moniker. Fitting, Lord Riverguard thought, but not as fitting as the self-claimed role of regent Lord Tylennald seemed eager to fulfill. Neither he nor his mother seemed able to physically detach from Tiran Lionhelm's side, and for someone as proud as Lovel Riverguard, it was a pathetic scene to witness. "To the skies, we rise," Lovel would say, but rise Tylennald never did.

Standing with his chalice in hand, the Lord of Courtbridge requested everyone's attention. The great hall quieted down, and the confused stare his daughter was giving him he ignored. Lovel bowed his head at Lady Voladea as he spoke, "My ladies, my lords, I wanted to thank House Lionhelm for the extended welcome many of us here have received."

"To the Lionhelms," he heard the others cheer.

"However, I recall Lord Tithan request of me that I instruct Lord Tylennald and my dearest daughter Wallysa about the future of Courtbridge," he went on with a sly smile. "I was wondering if time hasn't come yet for us to return across the Rough Rill."

Tylennald smiled back at him. "My lord, thank you for your kind words," he promptly replied. "You can imagine how hard it is for us to leave in these days of mourning. The funeral will take place as soon as my brother Theliel and my sister Tecla arrive in Strongshore. And what kind of son would I be if I left home while my father is ill?"

"I have yet to see you visit Lord Tithan," Lovel cut in.

"I am sure Lord Tithan needs to rest, Father," Lady Wallysa answered for her husband.

Whispers surrounded them as Lord Lovel tried to think of his next move, wondering if Tylennald's intentions were as transparent to the other lords as they were to him, but the sudden sound of horns reached their ears, and soon the entire household stood up, rushing towards the doors. The deafening conch horn was never used to summon the overlords outside of events related to either war or religious emergency, and since the first hypothesis was improbable, Lovel wondered what could have happened.

Tylennald rushed in the direction of the gates, which were being opened as two people escorted by a small number of Angels of Steel made their way to the palace. His heart rate went up as soon as he saw his sister Tesfira's pale face, her normally cheery expression replaced by fear. The Holy Commander of the Oracle's Faith himself looked upset and beyond worried, and out of anxiety, Tylennald clutched Wallysa's hand in his. He watched his sister dismount with the help of a guard, and she quickly ran towards him, her curly locks bouncing against her body.

"What happened?" he heard Lady Voladea ask numerous times.

"Lady Lionhelm," the Holy Commander greeted her with a deep bow. "Forgive us for the unannounced visit."

Tylennald held his sister close, and Tesfira hugged him tightly before falling in Wallysa's embrace. "I was in Summerport today," she told them, explaining her absence during the hearing of Thaesonwald's mistresses earlier that day.

"I sent an owl for Lady Tesfira yesterday," the Holy Commander explained. "I needed to talk to her about the growing fears I had about our religious community in the city of Edgemere, but we were interrupted by the most terrible news we could ever receive," he said, running his gloved fingers through his short silver hair. "Where do I begin?" he asked himself out loud.

"Hamley burned down the temple in Edgemere," Tesfira cried out, clinging to her brother's shoulder. "He has always been very vocal about his rejection of the Oracle's Faith, especially for the past few years, but he burned them alive— the holy captains in charge, the Angels, the other believers," she sobbed. "Tylennald, what do I do? Deril is with his father right now."

"Has he ever been violent to you?" Tylennald pressed, holding his sister's face. "We should march to Edgemere straight away."

"No," Voladea interrupted them, stepping forward with a stoic expression. Placing a hand on the Holy Commander's plated arm, she stopped their plans before they even formed. "It sounds like Hamley won't follow reason. He is acting based on his feelings and to blatantly contradict him would be too dangerous since Deril is with him. We do not march on someone who keeps one of us as a hostage," she told them fiercely. "Tesfira, dear." She paused as the woman failed to hold back the tears in her eyes. "You need to go home."

"H-home? But—"

"Get it together and go home. The best guards will escort you, but you shall pretend you either don't know what happened or that you think nothing of it," Voladea elaborated. "Hamley needs to believe that his wife stands by him. Otherwise, it will be difficult for you to bring your son back here."

Tesfira nodded, the woman's steady voice soothing her distress. Tylennald didn't seem to be agreeing with their mother, but he remained silent.

Voladea leaned in, placing a soft kiss on Tesfira's forehead. "Convince your husband to come here as well to honor Thaesonwald's memory. At that moment," she said as her gaze trailed back to the Holy Commander, "we will let him explain himself."

Tesfira inhaled deeply, and Lovel Riverguard watched in silence as their conversation was being heard by all and in particular by Tiran Lionhelm, who failed to appear shocked and whose mind seemed to be focused on other matters. Soon enough, both Tesfira and the Holy Commander were accompanied inside to shield themselves from the cold, and the once lively supper turned into a sullen, meager feast as if it was the prequel of a darker play Lovel Riverguard was all too thrilled to watch.

Chapter XXIV

Death Beds

The smell of feces was not what Lord Angefort's usually liked to begin with on a working day. Although many would leave their duties for the first dawn day, the Secretary of the Regency knew no resting day other than the few he allowed himself to take. As he entered the owl post, he was not surprised to see so many birds sleeping in their cages or eating from their trainer's hands. With fewer people working, fewer messages were being sent.

The owl post was the Regency's, even though Silverholde had its centralized owl post across the entrance of Jamys' Yard. The owls transported to the capital were naturally homed in the main strongholds of the continent, from Noirmont to Strongshore, from the Hvallatr of the Sand Towers to the distant city of Rockfall. The other towns sent their owls and sometimes ravens to the central post of Silverholde, but what mattered to Lord Angefort were the birds homing in the capital. He looked around, ignoring the curious stare he received from the trainer, but found the Regency cages to be empty.

Arther Angefort scrunched his nose at the growing stench and nodded at the short, red-haired man who served as a living perch for the feathered creatures. "Good day," he said. "No messages from the South?"

The trainer shook his head. "No, my lord. Should I alert you in case an owl returns?"

"Yes, anything from Strongshore or sent by Chief Thierry Eleres needs to be brought to my attention immediately."

"Yes, my lord."

Angefort excused himself, exiting the owl post faster than he could say his Praise Prayer. He stormed out of the small building, ready to walk across the Pavilion's gardens to reach his area, only to spot a furious knight march his way with no intent on letting him carry on with his daily duties. Sir Sybbyl looked like she hadn't slept for quite some days, the dark lines under her dull blue eyes clashing against her tanned complexion. Her usually sleek and short blonde hair was growing in all kinds of directions, and the fury she transpired successfully had the Secretary of the Regency on edge. The lord halted himself, taking in the quick and almost dismissive bow Sybbyl greeted him with. Large snowflakes fell from the thick grey clouds above their heads, and they didn't seem ready to melt once they touched the cold ground. Even as Sybbyl's hair was being covered in an icy ivory cap of snow, Lord Angefort's attention was solely focused on the woman's waist and the absence of the weapon usually strapped around it.

"Sir Sybbyl," he greeted her. "What brings you to the Regency at this time? I'd expect you to be at the barracks or the Surveillance, given Chief Eleres' absence."

Sybbyl wasn't sure what displeased her the most, the fact that she was expected to fulfill Eleres' duties in his absence or Angefort's obvious attempt at covering his confusion after seeing her disarmed. "I need to speak with you, my lord," she answered in a commanding tone. "I am afraid my lack of judgment brought shame to the Regency," she added through gritted teeth.

Her choice of words was unexpected. "What happened?" he asked in a gentle tone. "Surely, you were only acting based upon the information you gathered."

"I lost Decimation, the sword that has been in my family for many generations," she admitted, trying her best to hold the lord's gaze. "I lost it in a duel."

"A duel? I didn't think you would duel anyone; no one duels anymore."

"I was talked into it by a man of the Fog Lands, someone I suspect to serve House Rochelac. He didn't seem to be any high-ranking officer of sorts, but he did carry a dagger with the Beast of Three Crosses carved into it.

"He was fast, that I must admit. And he showed me how quickly he could have killed me, had he wanted to."

Lord Angefort's discomfort was rapidly showing. "What are you saying, Sir Sybbyl?" he pressed, taking a step forward. As they stood face to face, their eyes staring into each other on the same level, he rephrased her words. "A man unknown to us can take down the Regency's Suppressor of War? And he is freely roaming the streets of our capital without any of us knowing neither his motives nor his destination?"

Sybbyl remained silent, the occasional twitching of the left side of her face giving Angefort the answer he did not wish to hear.

"Do we have a name?"

"He told the guards at the northern gates that he was named Jascha. The name could be fake, for all we know."

Lord Angefort exhaled loudly, moving to walk past her. "The man didn't break the law, did he? He drew his weapon because you allowed him to," he reasoned. "Keep a close eye on him if you know of his whereabouts. I have to think of Chief Eleres and Wilderose. Grandmaster Rodbertus has already left in the company of the Lionhelms and the physicians who will examine Lord Lionhelm. There is only so much I can take care of," he told her dejectedly.

"Grandmaster Rodbertus left although we have no news of Eleres?" Sybbyl scowled.

"Worry not," Angefort quickly retorted. "They are headed to Limemeadow, where they will board a ship and sail for Summerport. It seems the harbor of Edgemere has yet to be repaired," he informed her. "They will not cross Wilderose."

Before the Secretary of the Regency could walk away, Sybbyl licked her lips and requested his attention once more. "My lord, with all due respect, if King Helias would permit us I could arrest the inlander to interrogate him. Only the King's wishes bypass the laws of free movement—"

"That cannot be done," Lord Angefort interrupted her. "King Helias doesn't hold audiences anymore."

"You have been granted permission to speak with him directly," Sybbyl insisted. "My lord, I ask you—"

"Sir Sybbyl Nobleleaf," he cut in again, raising his voice. "There have been several matters over the years that I wished for King Helias to address and, believe me, if that was possible, I would do it." Lowering his gaze as a sign of respect for the fierce warrior, he concluded, "It disheartens me to hear about Decimation, but I am sure you will find a proper replacement to empower your talents.

"May the Oracle and Her Angels bless your day, Sir Sybbyl."

✷✷✷

A closed athenaeum and a thick carpet of snow that covered the steps awaited Jascha as he reached the entrance of the building where he spent his days since he arrived in Silverholde. The faint laughter of children running through the streets was no longer accompanied by the thundering hooves of the merchants' horses and Jascha realized it was the first dusk day of the month. He arrived a little later than usual since he spent part of the morning making sure his mount was being taken care of at the stables of the innkeeper. His horse came from the harsh North, and he knew the winter weather wouldn't be much of a problem for Arora, but he still preferred to feed her himself whenever he could. Avoryon horses were smarter than the average ride, but they were also particularly attached to their owner.

  Reluctantly, Jascha hopped down the steps, only to hear the bells of the temple ring in the distance. Figuring he had nothing better to do that day, he walked in the direction of the Temple of Phorbas, also known to all as the coronation temple. It was quite easy to spot, with its tall pillars circling the building. Contrary to most temples, the main cupola of the Temple of Phorbas was not of a golden color. The resplendent red tint that shone under the faint sunlight was a welcomed change in the otherwise grey and emerald scenery of the capital. The pathway to the entrance was marbled and clean with the Angels of Steel lining each side with their swords extended above their heads. Behind every guard, statues of cloaked womanly figures with a burning candle in their hands lighted the way. Adjacent to the main building, a smaller portion of the temple seemed to be welcoming the followers of the Oracle's Faith for the Praise Prayer, although Jascha didn't see many people enter. Above every hexagonal window, the owl of House Rainier proudly extended its wings. Jascha pushed back the hood of his fur cloak before entering the sacred site. The sound of water filled his ears, and he turned around, his lips parting at the sight of an artificial waterfall parting the temple in two and pooling down the main entrance as if to block out anyone who dared approach.

Inside the small chapel, rows of wooden benches awaited the faithful. It was an odd sight to Jascha, who had always known the followers to pray on their knees. As opposed to the plain, light floor, the ceiling was coated in gold and painted from side to side with visions mentioned in the Oracle's Memoir. Jascha didn't recognize any, aside from the darker scene of dry seas and rotten carcasses. The last chapter of the Memoir was the only one he truly remembered, for goals were more important than the journey that led to them.

He sat on the far end of a bench on the right row, his black eyes scanning the faces behind him. He saw the girl who usually stood at the entrance of the athenaeum, Rosaleah, in a deep conversation with the woman he couldn't quite decipher.

Someone moved in front of him, and before he could turn around, he heard his name being pronounced. "Jascha?"

A middle-aged man in full armor and with a pure golden cloak over his shoulders was smiling at him. Carved in his chest plate was the brandished sword engulfed in light that distinguished the holy captains from the Angels of Steel and their Holy Commander, but even as Jascha stared into the man's warm eyes, he couldn't place a name on the stranger's face.

"You don't remember me," the holy captain noted. "It was to be expected. The last time I saw you, you were a child, soon to become a man. I am Captain Chadras."

The words came out before Jascha could realize it. "By your standards or my mother's?" This man was the holy captain who came to treat his mother when she fell ill with the Violet Delusion, he thought to himself. No other member of the faith had ever entered his home before his mother lost the little reason she had left. "I am afraid I don't remember you," he quickly added.

"I understand." The holy captain licked his lips in discomfort before he asked, "And the baby? Your little sister, how is she? Have you received any news?"

Jascha felt as if the walls of the temple disintegrated and debris fell all over his body. He didn't recall having a younger sibling, and yet the holy captain's words seemed so familiar, a part of him wanting to answer that the little girl was well, but he didn't see her face in the memories of his childhood.

"Forgive me, it is not my place to ask. I am surprised to see a face like yours in the capital; the people of the Fog Lands don't tend to leave their mountains."

"I don't mind you asking," Jascha quickly replied.

"Is there a reason you left home?"

"I just came for answers," he said bluntly. "But all I've found are more questions."

The sandy-haired man nodded at him, glancing behind Jascha. "Perhaps it would have been wiser to stay hidden in the fog," Captain

Chadras whispered. "I smell death beds littered with roses, and it is your limbs they await."

Jascha's eyes darkened, the two of them exchanging a silent look. The man was mentioning the light brown-haired female seated a few rows behind him and Rosewillow, and Jascha didn't know what unsettled him the most; that the holy captain knew them or that the two women were indeed following him, invalidating his thoughts about him being overly paranoid and wary of strangers.

"Who are they?" the black-eyed man pressed.

Captain Chadras rested a hand on the hilt of his sword as he straightened his back. "Your mother's sins have been forgiven," he answered, "but the other sinners do not forget. Your mother has left you with your bane and I, for I have brought her back into the arms of the Oracle, have also been left with fays that are mine to burn." Bowing his head, the holy captain excused himself. "The time has come for us to pray."

Jascha twisted his upper body to look behind him, however, the rows had been quickly filled and he could see neither Rosaleah nor Rosewillow. He didn't last long, sitting through the ceremony that breathed life into the ember on the altar, with women in translucent robes dropping their torches in the Oracle's flame. Captain Chadras had just begun reading a chapter of the Oracle's Memoir when Jascha slid past the guards that lined the walls and hastily made his way outside, ignoring the angry glances he was receiving and the accusations of blasphemy other followers hissed at him.

The moment the cold air hit him in the face, he felt his stomach churn and his head reel. The change in temperature from the warm confines of the chapel to the blowing winter wind made him want to empty his stomach on the marbled path. Jascha walked fast, ignoring the way his hair slapped against his cheeks and panting loud. His feet took him away from the scarlet temple and further into the hidden areas of Silverholde, his mind going over the words the holy captain had spoken to him. His life had always seemed like a blur to him, but he knew who he was. He knew where he came from; he remembered his mother's name, his mother's face. He recalled the colors of the walls of his bed-chamber, the music that played from the carillon on his mother's vanity. He remembered the straw dolls and the wooden soldiers scattered on the rugs around his bed. He heard his mother's singing and his mother's screaming; he recalled a holy man who tried to heal her, but she had never been well, to begin with. And yet, among all the memories he had, there was no trace of little girls, no women who lurked in his mother's shadow, so why would his mother be related to those who followed him?

Soon, the streets were no longer clean and his boot got stuck in a muddy pile of stickiness. Jascha glanced down, kicking at the air to free himself from what seemed to be waste and rotten food at the entrance of Jamys' Yard. He had no idea how long he had been walking, but he was out of breath. He brought a hand to his chest as though it would slow his heart rate down, but it wasn't working. He felt someone approach him, and from the corner of his eye, he saw a beggar extend a hand in his direction. Jascha roared, feeling a stinging pain on the side of his head, and he pushed the man away with brute force. The beggar stumbled backward and crying ensued, but no amount of begging stopped Jascha from ramming his soiled boot into the man's stomach. He did it once, twice, three times, and he lost count as the frail body shattered under his ire.

  Others yelled around him, and he saw a little girl just as weak as the man he had just destroyed. Her pale blue eyes looked at him in a mixture of horror and resentment as she cradled the man's face in her tiny arms. Jascha covered his face with a gloved hand, releasing a pained roar in his fist before he walked away at an even faster pace, only to round the first abandoned house he saw on the left and slumped against the cold stone surface, his body sliding down until his bottom hit the ground. There was something wrong with him, he told himself, and it wasn't simply the convulsions and the visions he had.

  He sat frozen in place with his forearms shielding his head as he buried his nose between his knees. He felt hot streams of tears run down his cheeks, but only a couple of sobs racked his chest. The faint tug on his sleeve was the touch that brought him back to reality, and his reddened eyes caught a glimpse of a boy he had seen before. Jascha sat up, gazing at the worried face of Mawde who hugged a bag full of food and held the other hand of the little boy.

"Would you like to come inside?" she offered, nodding her chin in the direction of her house.

The single room house hadn't changed in the least. It was slightly cleaner, Jascha noticed, as the foul stench of excrements no longer permeated the air, but other than that, the bed was still a pile of straw and the cooking pot was tainted with food stains. Mawde went through the bag in silence, handing a couple of pastries to the ever-hungry Josclyn before taking the ingredients she would use for her stew. Jascha wondered if the little boy was mute or simply shy since he never heard him say anything, but he preferred not to ask. He sat on the floor, pinching his fingertips, trying to find comfort where there was none.

The inviting smell of leek mixed with onions, turnips, and other vegetables soon filled their nostrils, and Mawde stirred the stew, adding breadcrumbs as the ingredients boiled in the chicken bone broth. Jascha's eyes followed her movements, his stare lingering on her frail limbs. He saw many scratches on her forearms, as well as bruises around her neck, and he remembered the last time he saw her at the marketplace, in the company of a man who was paying for his lustful desires.

Reaching inside his cloak, he grabbed a small bag attached to his belt and dropped it on the floor. "I would like you to keep these," he whispered.

Mawde's eyes widened, and she dropped her wooden spoon. "Jascha, you don't have to," she quickly told him, eyeing the bag of silvers. "I'm not an innkeeper; the meal is free."

"Just take them."

She smiled at him; the kind of smile that spoke volumes of sadness and caused the lines on her face to appear more evident. "Your mother must be proud to have such a good man as her son."

"She is dead," was his plain reply. "Your daughter," he mused, staring into space, "works at the athenaeum you said. Her name is Leah, is that correct?"

"Yes, it is."

"Does she ever help you out? The Regency surely pays her every moon."

Mawde exhaled loudly, shifting her weight on her left leg. "I don't blame Leah for her absence. I have never been very present for her myself."

The ghost of a smile grazed his lips. "I wish I could say the same about my mother."

She chuckled at that. "Overbearing parent?"

He wasn't sure the word was appropriate to describe his mother.

"What was her name?"

"My father called her Karleen," he whispered. "But I think it's because he was from the northwestern lands and never quite adapted."

Mawde nodded, reaching for the shelf on the adjacent wall and taking three small bowls. She carefully filled them with hot stew before setting them down, calling her son and Jascha to join her by the fire so they could eat and warm themselves.

"Is your father alive?" she asked him, handing him a piece of bread and a slice of salted cheese. "Josclyn's father left a long time ago. Starvation is worse than the Violet Delusion, no matter what others think," she confessed sourly.

Jascha winced at the extremely salty meal. "No," he answered, letting the child grab his bread and cheese after he saw the way Josclyn stared at the slices. "My father passed away when I was still very young. He was pretty old."

They ate in silence, and as he sat with his stew growing cold, Jascha tried to remember his father's face. He couldn't, but somehow, he didn't miss him. The word father only made him think of old bones and charred flesh rotting in a cushioned chair, images he sometimes saw when he closed his eyes at night, although the correlation was lost on him.

✳✳✳

Opherus lied on his back with his arms crossed behind his head as he stared at the moonless sky above. Right after sundown, Martita decided to start a fire in the woods beneath Strongshore to avoid getting hit by the cold sea wind that would have grasped them anyway had they stopped by the beach. They shared some of her dry meat and equally dry bread, but it wasn't enough for Sarkis, whose body seemed to suffer from the lack of food the most. He was balled in his thin cloak, inching as close to the small fire as possible while the old woman poked at the wood with a stick. Neither said much since the prayer by the funeral pyre, and Goldsnout was left to ponder his choices. The scene of Chief Eleres' death played in his head over and over again, the words the Golden Lady had spoken echoing through his mind. They shut the gates of the respectful, she told them. She had been referring to the gates of the Rosenfield castle since those were the only gates he and Eleres had closed, but that meant that these women were truly related to the events Lord Angefort mentioned to the Regency. However, the multiple sacrifices that took the lives of men from the Sand Towers to Wilderose were the acts of a cult or a society unapproved by the laws of King Helias and the Regency; Goldsnout didn't understand why the Rosenfields were named the respectful. Had they always been tied? He wondered in silence. Were there more cases he and Eleres had been unaware of? Who dealt with them before the creation of the Regency?

A small rock hit his cheek and Goldsnout sat up, rubbing the side of his face. Old Martita hit him right where his previous injury was. "What is it?"

"I can hear you thinking," the old woman pointed out in a bored tone. "You need to rest. You haven't slept since that night. If you pass out, you are dead; Sarkis here can't carry himself. Do you think he can fling your body over the saddle of your horse?"

"I am not tired," Goldsnout retorted. "If you are, just lay down." His eyes fell on the bow by her side, and his lips twitched. "I meant to ask," he said as he brought his hands closer to the fire. "Where did you learn archery? You seem like a simple woman, yet your skills are better than most men's at the Regency's barracks."

Old Martita wasn't fazed by his comment. "I grew up in barracks," she told him.

Sarkis looked up, his interest growing. "Are you the daughter of a soldier?"

"My father wasn't married to my mother. They had me, my twin sister, our younger sister, and our youngest brother. My mother passed away shortly after my little brother's death. He wasn't even one year of age when he left us. She never really recovered," Martita went on, her gaze still focused on the fire. "Father could have taken us to his residence but he was unsure of how his wife felt about it. I doubt she would have minded; she wasn't very present, nor that interested in her husband after she bore him two sons.

"My twin sister hated the barracks, the encampment, and the little house nearby which we shared. She liked her books a lot more, so I was the one who was taught how to craft arrows. When Father died, his second-born offered to let us live with him. He said we were his sisters and that we could be whoever we wanted to be. My sisters stayed with him, for a while, but all I wanted was to live my own life.

"I met Gerd, my husband, shortly after settling in Summerport, and that appeared to be that."

Goldsnout reached inside the bag by the fire to grab another piece of dry meat, and he almost broke his teeth trying to take a bite.

"What happened after?" Sarkis asked her, his body still quivering.

"My youngest sister, Briar, was married to a man a bit too passionate about his religious beliefs." Looking at Sarkis, she added, "If you think what Mayor Hamley Silverworm did in Edgemere is frightening, you wouldn't have wanted to meet Briar's husband."

Goldsnout furrowed his brow. Old Martita did mention the events of Edgemere the moment they rode in the direction of Strongshore, but as much as he wanted to intervene, it was the Holy Commander's duty to report to Lord Lionhelm and the Regency. After all, Silverworm was Lord Lionhelm's son-in-law and the Regency's Surveillance wasn't allowed to deal with religious emergencies unless the overlord or the Regency themselves appointed the surveillants.

"Briar vanished," Martita went on, her voice faltering. "Our brother tried to bring her back but she wouldn't listen and her husband's clear intent was to hide the fact that his bride was born out of wedlock and that she wasn't the person he claimed she was.

"My other sister, Tyllis, never forgave our brother. She left for the capital and I never heard from her again," Martita concluded, throwing in the fire the stick she held. Her hazel eyes met Opherus' light green orbs and she knew that he understood.

"Those women," she spoke in a quieter tone, "will not stop until we make them."

"Who are they after?" Opherus pressed, strongly hoping she knew the answer.

"You mean, what are they after?" Old Martita shook her head, staring at the dark skies. "I wish I knew." She slid down against the trunk of the tree she rested her back against, shifting her weight in an attempt to find a comfortable position. "Let us rest, for now."

Sarkis quickly imitated her, closing his eyes, a pool of drool quickly forming around his chin. Opherus stared at them in silence, wondering where in the Silver Lands he could ever find the answers to his questions. Still, he believed the old woman across from him knew more than she let on. Old Martita was educated, and she trained in the past; surely, she would know more than just local legends or whatever her sister Briar told her before disappearing.

"Your name," he whispered as to not disturb Sarkis, who was fast asleep. "Isn't Martita, is it?"

"It's Tamar," Old Martita replied. "Gerd called me Martita," she admitted, never opening her eyes.

Opherus smiled. "Your birth name is very ancient," he noted. "I read a book once about a southern princess of the independent Kingdom of Drixia. Chief Eleres made me read it, to be honest. I had joined the ranks of the Surveillance and I was just a simple boy of Limemeadow; the chief believed only those who knew their history well could build a better future.

"They say Princess Tamar Lionhelm was a leading conqueror in one of the Crimson Crystal Wars."

Martita snorted, waving a hand at him. "Compare me to a princess again and I will roast your face against this fire and turn you into a squirming piglet," she warned him light-heartedly. "Get some rest, will you? Otherwise, you won't live long enough to help me end the pathetic lives of the Rosencircle."

Opherus' smile faded instantly. She had never put a name on these helmeted ladies before, but the Rosencircle wasn't a name he was about to forget. He would go through every manuscript stored at the Regency and Danyell's Athenaeum if he had to, return Wilderose to the dirt and find the remains of the Rosenfields if any of it meant bringing a form of justice to honor his chief's death.

Chapter XXV

LITTERED WITH ROSES

The blacksmith shop was colder than the last time Jascha visited it. The snow had collected in a corner, the hole in the roof above still gaping and letting the icy wind in, along with all kinds of garbage and the occasional bird dung. Aalart sat by the forge, chewing on wild plants that tainted his already yellow teeth with a hint of dirty green. Jascha walked in silently, knowing that the smith was aware of his presence. His gloved hands traced the blunt edge of the bench, his black stare lingering on the variety of tools and jigs. A small hammer sat on the anvil, and two swords lied on top of the table, a soft-looking cloth cushioning them.

The larger blade was a one-handed sword, the sand steel polished and sharpened to the point it reflected the dark light of the room. The hilt was fairly similar to the original, the obsidian color mixing with the night undertones of the sword. Gone were the crossed hammers of the Nobleleafs, replaced by a fanged pommel that reminded anyone of the feral beast of the Fog Lands. Jascha's lips curved upwards at that, pleased with the fact that Aalart's eye was sharp enough to realize where he was from.

The other blade was shorter and thinner, the slightly curved edge making it look more like a dagger than a sword. Its hilt was made of regular leather, but a volcanic ring decorated it. Jascha spotted a dual sheath resting against the table foot. He slowly picked it up, inspecting the fine leatherwork covering the metal. The scabbard was lined with scarlet jewels that were used to decorate the original hilt of the sword. Jascha tied it quietly so that the sheath would rest comfortably against his back, and grabbed the two swords to check their weight. He held the shorter blade in his left hand and gripped the long one with loose fingers.

"You are on time," he told Aalart, who simply grunted.

"The Haunting Sisters. Beautiful, aren't they? Price hasn't changed."

Two hundred silvers, Jascha remembered. The problem was that part of his money went to Mawde and her son, and the rest he needed if he wanted to stay away from home for at least another year. Jascha swung the blade to test it, unhappy with the slashing of air. Never diverting his gaze from his new weapons, he decided that he first would have to try them.

"Pick up a sword," he told Aalart. "I want to see if this shatters or if you truly were able to work sand steel."

Aalart spat the herbs in his mouth, glaring at the younger man who insulted his craft. "I am a smith, boy, not a fucking knight."

"We don't need to fight," Jascha countered. "Just take a swing or two at me with whatever you have." When the big man didn't move, he reached for the purse attached to his belt and threw it on the bench.

Aalart stood up, reluctantly reaching for the only sharp weapon he had. It was a regular two-handed sword, one he kept in case someone decided to try and rob him, but he wasn't an experienced fighter. He knew a few moves, and he hoped they would be enough for the impertinent boy to get out of his shop faster than lightning. He worked hard to shape the rare steel into what Jascha requested, and he wasn't about to let anyone comment on restless nights of perfectionism that made it possible for Decimation to be turned into what he named the Haunting Sisters.

The blacksmith stood in front of Jascha with his arm extended before gripping the hilt with both hands and pointing at his opponent's head. He went straight for Jascha with a firm blow, but as he expected the young man to block his blade with crossed weapons, his eyes widened. Jascha stepped to the side, parrying the blow with the longer blade while attacking Aalart's shoulder with the shorter one. The steel didn't puncture him, but that wasn't what Jascha looked at, his gaze focused on their touching weapons, as if to make sure that his Haunting Sister wasn't damaged.

Aalart stepped back, taking another swing at Jascha, who again parried it in the same fashion, this time aiming his shorter blade at the man's stomach with a thrust. "You satisfied, now?" he asked as Jascha's expression didn't change; he seemed bloodthirsty or, at the very least, eager to see the limits of his new weapons.

As it was Jascha's turn to strike Aalart, he attacked the smith, who blocked his blow quite easily, only to see the shorter blade point at his chest. Aggravated with the fight, Aalart pushed him away. Jascha smirked at that, reeling backward and repositioning the longer sword across his body, resting it on his hip, while the other blade aimed behind his shoulder. He came forward quickly, and Aalart was only able to parry the shorter sword's attack while the other threatened his throat.

"Alright," he breathed out. "Will ya fuck off now?"

"No," Jascha replied with a satisfied smile. His blades didn't collide; the length difference was correct.

"You had it coming."

Aalart reared back, letting out a roar before raising his longsword and striking downwards, going for Jascha's head. His opponent didn't budge; Jascha's stare was solely focused on the longsword, and in an instant, he caught the blade on the guard of his two Sisters. They looked at each other just to catch their breaths, and Jascha's toothy smile showed. Easily manipulating the longsword from where he caught it, his left blade slid smoothly against it, pushing it to the side with ease while the other pointed straight at the smith's neck.

The steel plunged into Aalart's throat, cutting through flesh like it was made of paper, and the smith choked once, twice, his eyes nearly bulging out as they widened fully. Jascha retracted his weapon, now coated in blood, watching the man fall backward as his life essence left him to collect around his head in a crimson pool.

"Your work was surely worth more than two hundred silvers," Jascha whispered, wiping the blade with the cloth that was still on the table.

He sheathed the longer blade above his head and the other one around the small of his back and then kneeled by the smith to snatch the keys of the shop that hung from his belt loops. Jascha looked around then back at the corpse, sighing softly. Lifting the man wouldn't be so easy, he figured as he walked towards the door to lock it.

✳✳✳

The heavy knocking on the front door startled her from her reverie. She had been sitting by the fire, documenting herself with ancient cures tested throughout the centuries, hoping to find something remotely close to the Violet Delusion and see what was used against it. However, nothing proved to be satisfying enough for her to delve deeper into it; most records were lost during the wars, and she figured what remained was safely stored either at the Regency or in its athenaeum. Rantha wasn't about to leave Rainier's End to spend an indefinite number of days in the capital; she couldn't afford it, and she needed to take care of the shelter in case someone showed up, like that night. Tossing the book against the pile she brought from Sir Loys Rosenbane's library in the abandoned keep, she rushed towards the entrance, rubbing her arms when the warmth of the fireplace was replaced by the chill air of the corridors.

"Coming," she told whoever was on the other side of the door.

A part of her hoped to see Opherus, but it would be too soon. She knew the officer had to go all the way to the Wilderose forest, and that was no easy ride, especially given the harsh weather of the past days. She highly doubted he would be back so soon, but the hope was still there. The days that followed Yenny's death and the incident at the central inn had been dull, quiet, almost depressing in a way that made her want to leave the Illusion Shelter, beg for Sir Rosenbane's forgiveness and maybe sail back to the Red Continent. Rainier's End felt less and less like home, and she wasn't the only one who thought so. Zurzon, her apprentice who came from the islands of the Zalejos Depths, had been badly shaken by Yenny's death. They were the only two who came to Rantha with a specialty; Maryell and Sanson, the other two who lived with her, were there to follow in her footsteps. Yenny treated soldiers and common wounds before her arrival, while Zurzon believed in the exorcism of the spirits that played with one's soul through what he called the infants. However, for Rantha, it was less about the companionship; she felt as if she had let it happen, as if she hadn't told the young girl to be careful enough, as if, somehow, she was responsible. And that was a feeling she couldn't shake off.

"Yes?" Rantha sighed out as she opened the door.

Before her, an old man shorter than her left his handcart right in front of the shelter. His skin was saggy just as his clothes were loose. He wore black rags and what looked like a fisherman's hat, but behind him a woman just as old cried silently, clutching the hand of a woman who lied in the cart, her skinny body convulsing on top of their light luggage and straw bedding.

"Please, we don't know where to go anymore," the old man whispered. "Our daughter…"

"Wait here," Rantha ordered, closing the door.

She rushed back to the kitchen, grabbing a white apron while asking her apprentices to prepare a room as quickly as possible and help her get the young woman inside. Maryell was quick to go upstairs, tying her loose brown hair into a ponytail, while the men grabbed their clean gloves and coats to carry the woman. Rantha led the old couple to the kitchen, offering them to sit down and eat something warm, but the woman cried louder. The healer wrapped the woman in a thick blanket and grabbed a chair to sit closer to the man. She offered him a polite smile, hoping he would be easier to talk to for her to get the information she needed.

She pushed a bowl of soup in his hands, and asked, "Where are you from?"

The old man peered at her with grey eyes. "Three Crosses."

"That's a little far away."

"We walked for days and days," he rambled. "The only healer left in our town passed away and we were told the closest shelter would be in Rainier's End. My wife… she tried to medicate our little girl but, how can we? We don't even know how to cauterize wounds."

Rantha frowned, pursing her lips. She thought they came so she would treat the Violet Delusion. "What is your daughter's name? What is your name?" she asked.

"I am Peares, my wife's name is Iseuda and our little girl is Irryelda," the old man answered, wiping his large nose. "She has it, you know? The fog engulfed her."

Rantha nodded, watching him sip the onion soup. "What about you and Iseuda?"

Peares shook his head. "No, no. We had it before when we were young and the fog was thicker."

"And you survived?" Rantha's heart was beating fast. She had never seen anyone survive the Violet Delusion, not to mention the old couple didn't seem to bear any visible scar or suffer from other consequences. It surprised her greatly, as most people who fell ill harmed themselves. "How?"

Iseuda looked at her with sorrow in her eyes. "It was never that severe," she answered. "Our parents had us tied to our beds to prevent us from harming ourselves or each other, but even as we shook from head to toe, we were still aware of our surroundings. We knew what was happening; our baby doesn't. She…" The woman paused, never finishing her sentence as she broke into tears again.

"We were exhausted," Peares continued. "We fell asleep and we forgot to tie her ankles. The villagers outside Three Crosses woke us up in the middle of the night; it felt like a terrible dream.

"They led us uphill, where the Restless Channel meets the foot of Noirmont. Nobody goes there, you know?" he went on, his hands trembling. "Nobody goes to the Black Cave, where the Beast resides. It is forbidden, oh Good Gods, it is forbidden. Every lady and lord of Noirmont forbade it.

"But Irryelda crawled there, they said. She said her lady went in once. From the flesh of the Skeleton we were made, she repeated, and through the blood of the Beast can we be reborn. Oh, the villagers, they stayed away from her, afraid of contamination. They said she repeated those words and that she told them her lady was right."

Rantha ran a hand over her forearm where the chicken skin was showing. "Her lady?"

"Irryelda was one of Lady Charlaine's maids when she was still a child. She came home after Lady Rochelac passed away, saying the mistress' heir dismissed nearly all the help."

The dark-skinned woman was beyond shocked. She still couldn't wrap her head around the fact that she stood in the presence of two survivors of the Violet Delusion, and now they told her that Noirmont wasn't as deserted as she thought it was. Someone still lived in the castle behind the fog, although they never made a public appearance.

"Miss Rantha," she heard Zurzon call from upstairs.

"Please, try to eat," she told the old couple. "I will now attend to your daughter's needs."

She ignored the louder weeping of the woman who refused to feed herself and rushed upstairs, anxiety pooling in her stomach. She saw a pale-faced Maryell sit against the wall adjacent to the door of the room the woman had been brought in, and Rantha wasn't sure she wanted to take a closer look. She had to, she reminded herself, stepping inside. Zurzon and Sanson hadn't tied the woman to the bed, pressing a translucent fabric against Irryelda's left shoulder and around her inner thighs. Rantha felt the bile in her throat, watching with horrified brown eyes the deep gashes that marred the woman's body. She had been bitten where her shoulder met her neck, and her inner thighs were bloody, bruised, and utterly destroyed. She saw part of her insides peek between her legs.

"How is this woman still alive?" Rantha gasped, her hands reaching for the surgical kit her shocked apprentice had left by the bed. "How is this possible? What happened?" she asked herself out loud, ignoring the two men who tried to stop the bleeding despite their obvious need to dry-heave.

"She won't be for long if we don't stop the bleeding," Zurzon commented. He saw the woman open her eyes, her head lolling from side to side. "She seems to be having visions still," he informed Rantha.

"Did she," Sanson muttered, swallowing back the contents of his stomach. "Did she mate a wild animal?"

Rantha shook her head, fighting the shivers that ran across her body. "I don't need to hear that," she told the blue-eyed boy.

Out of nowhere, the woman on the bed arched her back, heavy moans and even deeper groans escaping her lips. Her breathing was ragged and her eyes rolled in the back of her head as her hips undulated. She spoke broken words that Rantha couldn't make out, but it was the incessant moaning that sent her over the edge.

"Knock her out," she ordered Zurzon. "She can't be awake if I'm going to cut her open," she explained, grabbing a sharpened obsidian knife. "Dress the minor wounds in black wine, or she'll die of infection before I can even repair the damage."

"If you even can," Zurzon whispered, soaking a clean cloth in a basin full of purple-black liquid.

Rantha ignored the tanned man, her stare fixed on the woman's lower body, the old man's words echoing through her mind. From the flesh of the Skeleton they were made, and through the blood of the Beast could they be reborn. Perhaps, it was all in the blood, she reasoned. Maybe something in the old people's blood made it possible for them to survive the Violet Delusion and major wounds. Her thoughts drifted to Jascha's wounds for the first time since he left, and she tried to remember. He was from the Fog Lands too, and he pulled through the most inexplicable events as well. What if he did share the same illness, but survived the same way this family seemed to be surviving?

Placing the tip of her knife under the woman's belly button, Rantha figured that the only way to find out was to try and save this woman to better study her.

✱✱✱

It wasn't until the sun slowly set that Jascha returned to the Temple of Phorbas, the orange hues that painted the sky shining down the snow-covered city. The holy area basked in the crimson reflection of the temple cupola, and the faithful who attended the Subjugation Prayer left to return to their homes. Jascha waited by the open gates before the marbled entryway, leaning against one of the stone columns with his arms crossed and his head bent forward. His hood fell past his forehead, nearly hiding his eyes as he scanned those who went in and out of the temple. He would occasionally glance at the main street ahead, waiting patiently.

She appeared from the corner of the left building; her light brown hair still wrapped around her hairline in a loose braid. She wore simple clothes; the robes of the Regency having been discarded for the dusk days. Emerald and gold turned into dull, almost dirty brown, and Rosaleah resembled her mother more. Her thick black boots splashed against the melting snow, her eyes widening slightly at the sight of the man who stood by the entrance. She was quick to recompose herself, he noted and she was about to walk past him, had he not opened his mouth.

"Mawde did mention you live at the temple."

The young woman stood still, her eyebrow twitching. "You know my mother?"

Jascha shrugged. "Casually so. She wanted me to show you something."

Rosaleah's lips curved up, and she fully faced him. "I don't think so," she replied. "I haven't seen my mother in quite some time. She knows where to find me if she needs anything," she explained.

"She sells her body," he told her, pushing himself away from the column he leaned on. "Did you know that?"

Her smile faded quickly, and she glared at him. She didn't know, but she had yet to understand what he wanted from her.

"Follow me," Jascha ordered, turning heels.

He knew she was hesitant, as she should have been. He heard her light footsteps behind him as they walked down the main street until they reached the statue of King Aleyne and the Iathienar. The plaza was mostly empty as activities quieted down, the workforce who could afford it spending time in the warm confines of their homes, with their families, as tradition commanded. A couple of street artists sang the song of Queen Aelneth's revering gifts, but Jascha dropped no coin at their feet. He and Rosaleah walked in the deserted direction of Melisentia's Opera, and the woman felt less confident about her choice the more they isolated themselves from the busy areas of the capital. Jamys' Yard was in the opposite direction, and she couldn't comprehend why her mother would want to meet her in another place unless something happened to her.

Jascha could feel her stare against the back of his head, but he knew he had piqued her interest. She had always been curious about his reading, and he saw her roll the pages of the books he returned every time he returned to Danyell's Athenaeum as if to see if he spent more time on certain pages or left notes here and there. He wasn't sure she knew he was aware of her antics, but it mattered not. The blacksmith shop was in sight, still squished between the abandoned tavern and the shattered house, and he pulled out the keys from the inner pocket of his cloak.

Rosaleah narrowed her eyes, her heart racing inside her chest. "Is this where you live?" she asked, reading the sign that indicated the shop belonged to a man named Aalart.

"No. A friend lives here," he answered. "Come in."

His tone was calm and nearly soothing, but Rosaleah still didn't feel at ease. She was the one who asked Willow to travel to Silverholde after the man showed up at the athenaeum, sticking his nose in books only a few people knew of, and somehow, he came across her mother who seemed to be using him as her messenger. Something about the whole ordeal didn't feel right, but she held her ground. She wouldn't stay longer than needed.

The inside of the shop was clean and properly taken care of. A soft ember burned inside the forge, leaving most of the room in the darkness. There was a hole in the roof, covered only by a thin piece of fabric that left the faint skylight in. No one else was there, and that was enough to make Rosaleah doubt his words.

"Alright," she spoke. "I don't see your friend and I don't see my mother. This is not funny."

Jascha broke into a smile, sitting on the smith bench swinging one of his legs. "Fine," he conceded. "You got me. I just hoped I'd speak with you," he told her, arching an eyebrow at the now flustered girl. "I normally stay at the Wild Rock Skunk and that place is crowded these days. So, here we are."

Rosaleah felt her cheeks burn. "What is there to talk about?" she prompted.

"You see," Jascha sighed out, pushing the hood backward. "I can't help but feel like I was being guided in my findings. First, a book about a society called the Rosencircle, then one about rituals, then when I thought I had read everything about the so-called witchcraft, I find a manuscript about stones," he went on, never looking at her in the eyes. "Was that you?"

She cleared her throat, shaking her head at his question. "You said you know my mother. I am a low-born, the daughter of a whore and I am certainly not that educated to guide anyone through anything," she reasoned as calmly as he did, straightening her back as if to give herself more self-confidence.

He nodded briefly at that, hopping off the bench and walking closer to her. "Fair point," he whispered. "But you did call that other woman, didn't you? The one who is everywhere, all the time."

Rosaleah remained silent, feeling her blush evaporate from her face and her heart sink in her stomach.

"I mean, it is obvious at this point," he laughed quietly, even though his face showed no sign of amusement. "The Rosencircle," he quoted, folding his hands behind his back. "Your mother calls you Leah but you introduced yourself as Rosaleah. That woman's name is Rosewillow. You don't need to be that educated to figure it out," he reasoned, leaning in. "What I didn't figure out, however, is what in the Pit you want with me."

"Absolutely nothing," she spat at him, stomping her way towards the door.

Jascha's arm was around her waist in a blink, curling around her body and holding her against him in a tight, painful squeeze. "Ah, ah, ah," he scolded her. "Wrong answer. You might want to think twice before you lie to my face again," he breathed against her ear.

"You used my family to lure me in here," she said through gritted teeth. "Let me go or I start screaming."

He nodded at that, agreeing with her plan. "We will get to that point, eventually."

"What?"

"It's either you or your mother. Or your little brother," he threatened her. "He already doesn't speak so I don't think he'll miss his tongue."

Her retort died in her throat as she was flung backward and dragged into the darkness of the shop. Rosaleah clawed at him, her hands fisting the front of his cloak and hitting his hard chest with the little strength she possessed. She kicked his thighs as he hoisted her up against the wall, his knee connecting with her stomach when she began screaming at the top of her lungs. She fell forward, her forehead meeting his upper body as she tried to catch her breath, numbly feeling his hand tighten around her wrist. She blinked as she tried to move again, only to release a high-pitched scream when she felt a stinging pain pummel into her palm. Her head shot up, and her eyes nearly fell out of their sockets. He just stuck a large nail into her limb, pinning her against the wooden wall.

"Let me go," she yelled at him. "Let me go, you sick bastard!"

He ignored her words, his face falling into a cold, stoic expression as he grabbed her other wrist while his free hand aimed another large nail at the center of her palm. Rosaleah writhed and cried, and the hammer pounded against her hand. She felt her nerves on fire and her bones crack, and as Jascha threw the hammer back on the bench, she realized he had sat on it just to sneakily grab his tools. His hands had been folded behind his back only to fool her, and a fool she had been. Their eyes met for what felt like an eternity, and Rosaleah's silent tears streamed down her cheeks. She watched him walk towards the bench once more, grabbing more nails before rubbing his square chin as he pondered where to stick them next.

"Please," she whimpered in the corner. "Let me go."

"I need answers," he retorted as he crouched before the fireplace to light it. "But it's a bit cold in here if you don't mind waiting a bit."

"What?" she whispered; her vision foggy with tears.

She watched him bring the fire to life and even warm his limbs, completely ignoring her presence. Rosaleah felt sick. She felt her stomach churn and her arms go numb with the loss of blood and the pain that scratched her bones from her hands down her arms. Jascha rose to his feet shortly after, grabbing a torch that had been leaning against the fireplace and sticking it into the fire. He slowly made his way towards her, pausing as he stood a step away from her body, and gloved fingers cupped her round chin.

"I want you to tell me what this means, and if you won't we'll just have to wait for your friend to show up," he whispered against her lips, his nose brushing against her runny one.

He slid the torch inside the holder on the wall, and Rosaleah screamed louder. A man was pinned to the wall right next to her, his fresh corpse bleeding out still, several nails embedded in his hands, arms, shoulders, knees, and feet. Even his throat hadn't been spared, although the large gash suggested the nail wasn't what killed him. His eyes were wide open, and his head lolled to the side, facing her.

Her grey eyes looked away from the man's face, but the rest of his naked body was an even worse sight. Rosaleah's body shook and the balls of her feet pressed harder into the wooden floor as she tried to hoist herself up when she felt the palms of her hand being slowly ripped apart due to her weight. The man beside her had been cut entirely, a massive wound above his heart exposing his flesh. Another one was on his right side, and other minor cuts turned the man's upper body in a disturbing, circular drawing. Every wound was connected to another by superficial cuts, forming a hexagon and leaving only the man's stomach intact.

Jascha leaned against the edge of the blacksmith's bench, toying with the nails in his hand while the other one reached for the drawing he always kept with him. The piece of paper was completely crumpled and turning yellow, but the inky lines were identical to the ones on Aalart's body. Unaware of the horrified stare directed at him, he took in his work, nearly pleased with himself as he shoved the drawing back inside the outer pocket of his cloak.

Black connected with grey at last, and Jascha told Rosaleah, "I want to know," he told her again, his voice reverbing through her body as if it was going to be the last sound she would hear. "And you're going to tell me."

Her knees almost gave way under her weight, and she swallowed hard. "As revolting as this is, don't think you can scare me," she hissed.

Jascha raised his eyebrows, his lips parting as he exhaled softly. "You think I want you to be scared?" he asked her. "I don't.

"I want you to feel every moment, every sharp tug, every stinging pain and repressed scream I felt; every burn on my skin and every scratch at my bones. I want you to know what happened to me during whatever ceremony you or your little friends performed. It won't be that hard with all the tools our good Aalart left behind," he spoke softly, running his fingers over the curve of one chisel that rested on the bench. "And if you're still alive by the end of it, refusing to tell me the truth, I will take that other woman and do even worse," he went on, his teeth grazing his lower lip. "I will go after each one of you until there is no one left and I, at last, find peace."

Chapter XXVI

THE SCENT OF DAISIES

The view of the snow-covered palace left Tecla with a feeling of dread and sorrow pooling in her stomach. She had never seen Strongshore that way. She always spent the cold days of winter in the warm confines of her apartments. As her horse trotted up the rocky path, the fur covering her shoulders tickling her cheeks, she felt like an outsider in her homeland. She had yet to recover from the days spent on the waves from Limemeadow to Summerport, and she wondered why they weren't able to travel through Wilderose to shorten the trip. On their way to the capital, they traveled through it without any problem, but Grandmaster Rodbertus insisted they boarded a ship of the Lionhelms instead, Lion's Glory. To Tecla, it meant that something had happened in the lands that surrounded the Red Road, or the Regency suspected it at the very least. Why they hadn't stopped in Edgemere was another question left unanswered; the city-port was closer to Strongshore than Summerport. With most dusk days spent traveling, she and Theliel had less time to spend with their father before they would have to return to the capital.

Theliel rode closer to her, his bangs grazing his long eyelashes as the wind blew harder. "I will stay in Summerport," he whispered, halting his horse.

She mimicked him, giving him a confused, almost angry look. "You can't," she replied.

"I have to," he insisted. "Don't worry, dear sister," he immediately added with a warm smile, leaning in to place a kiss on her forehead. "I can be pretty fast on a horse. I just have something to do first, and since we're already here…" he elaborated, his big eyes glancing around as if to make sure no one heard them. "I'll be there before sunset. Stay with Father."

Tecla watched him kick his horse into a fast pace the moment the men escorting them went past her, some of them looking behind to make sure she was catching up. She heard whispers about her brother, but it was not their place to question him. The carriage Grandmaster Rodbertus traveled on was way ahead, and she reminded herself that at that moment her father and his health were more important than whatever Theliel wasn't willing to share with her. It was still fairly early in the morning, she noted as she looked at the timid sun in the dark skies above her, so Theliel would indeed make it before sundown. And yet, the air was filled with a little something she couldn't name that didn't make her feel at ease. Slowing the pace, she rode closer to the carriage where Lyzon, Fran, and Tomas were probably asleep, and inhaled deeply.

✳✳✳

"Thank you, for everything."

Old Martita shook her head, handing food wrapped in paper to the young officer who stood at her door. They had made it from Strongshore overnight, after a quick stop to rest their minds and bring water to their horses. Sarkis had promptly wrapped himself in layers of blankets as she lighted the fireplace and heated the soup that would have gone stale had it not been winter. They had eaten in silence, for the most part, Martita occasionally giving Goldsnout the indications he needed to travel back without crossing the forest of Wilderose.

"Stay out of trouble," she told the face full of freckles. "I mean it," she added in a serious tone, her small hazel eyes glaring at him.

"I can't promise you that," Goldsnout retorted before lifting the food in front of him. "Thank you again, Martita."

She stood by the door as she watched the young man hop on his horse and guiding the other to follow. His golden and emerald uniform was slightly ruined and mostly tainted with blood, but Goldsnout sat with his back straight and his chin up. He waved back at her before he left the alley and disappeared in the main streets, and the ghost of a smile graced her lips. The wind had stopped blowing, she noticed quietly, and the scent of flowers that couldn't bloom filled her nostrils. The clouds above were thick and the skies dark, almost as if it would be snowing again soon. They would need more wood.

"Sarkis," she called.

The curly-haired man blinked several times. "Yes, Tita?"

"Why don't you get us some more firewood?" she offered gently. "You're strong now. And we're out of it."

Sarkis sniffled before wiping his runny nose with his dirty sleeve. "I don't know about me being strong," he countered. "I need some silvers."

She gave him a small pouch, her hands resting against his biceps for a little longer as he fastened his thin cloak around his body. She watched him smile at her with his large teeth poking past his lips before he walked out, nearly slipping on the frozen ground when he clumsily left her house. Old Martita closed the door slowly, walking towards the fireplace with her hands folded behind her back. She never liked winter. It was a season that reminded her of the evenings spent looking for her younger sister, of the empty southern lands during King Elias' campaigns, of the plague that consumed her husband's body and mind. The cold seasons had been more bearable after she took in Pat, but Pat was no more, and she was the only one to blame for it.

Old Martita narrowed her eyes when her vision became a little clouded, and she glanced at the window, only to realize that the skies had turned a darker shade of grey. "So, it is snowing," she muttered, poking the fire with a stick as her thoughts took her back in time.

A shadow covered her window, and she abruptly turned around, only to see nothing. Sarkis had improved a lot but he sure wasn't that fast, she mused. Another shadow dimmed the already faint light coming from outside, and Martita stood up, cautiously walking closer to the opposite window. She took a better look at her yard and the growing dead weeds in her garden before grumbling to herself and walking back to the wooden bench Sarkis usually slept on, as close as possible to the fire. Her door was flung open before she reached the bench, and Martita stumbled backward when the wind knocked over several pieces of wobbly furniture.

"For the love of the Good Gods," she complained out loud, hurrying to close the door.

The shadows hovering over her windows appeared again, and she stopped in her tracks. She saw the white fur cloaks and the iron helmets. They were all around her house, she realized, her mind already trying to remember where she put her bow and arrows the moment she got home. It was useless, she concluded as the woman behind the golden helmet walked inside, her feet making no sound against the wooden floor. Behind her, the young women stood patiently outside while their Mastria walked closer to Martita, her slender, pale hands reaching for her helmet.

"You and I need to talk," she said calmly, unclasping the protection that covered her head. "I am surprised you still live here."

"Why would I leave?" Martita grunted. "You mean no threat to me."

"You tried to kill me," the Golden Lady pointed out, removing her helmet.

Martita watched as the face she already knew was revealed to her after years of absence. Long, golden-brown locks cascaded down the woman's upper body in soft waves. Her high cheekbones and pointed chin made her round face look slimmer, and in over thirty years, she hadn't changed. Even the cold look in her hazel eyes stained with green was the same. A silver rose adorned her leather collar, and as she spoke her upper lip looked thinner than her lower lip.

"It's not the first time," Martita replied. "And you killed Patten. Why are you back? Why now?"

The Mastria offered her a lopsided smile. "I never left, sister of mine. There is just something I need now more than ever."

Martita frowned. "From me?"

The woman laughed. "No, silly." Shifting back to an expressionless façade, she added, "But you are becoming very problematic. I told you to stop before and you didn't listen."

The older, shorter woman repressed the urge of rolling her eyes. "Shame on me for trying to bring you home," she sarcastically said. "Had you listened your daughters would be well and alive," Martita accused her.

"They were no daughters of mine." The Mastria walked closer, coming shoulder to shoulder with Martita despite being taller, and leaned in to whisper, "I have explained this to you, Tamar. I am not Briar of Summerport, not anymore. The feelings Briar harbored for her family are still anchored in this one's body, but that will never stop me from finding what doesn't belong to the Salurites."

Martita licked her lips, her eyes fixed on the women waiting outside. "I don't believe you came all the way here only for the friendly reminder. You killed them all," she replied coldly. "You killed your husband, you killed your children, and then you killed others' children. Be quick, now, will you?"

The Mastria placed a hand on Martita's shoulder, softly biting her lower lip. "No," she said. "No, I didn't."

"Oh, yes you did," Martita hissed, whipping her head to stare at the face that once belonged to Briar. "My only regret is that Frederyc didn't put his hands on you before you did what you did."

The Golden Lady removed her limb from the old woman instantly, as if she had been burned, and her face twitched. "Farewell, Tamar," she whispered before her long fingers curled around a loose grey lock and forcefully pulled the hair out.

Martita instantly pushed her away, bringing one hand to the side of her head where it stung and whispering curses directed at the intruder. The Mastria stared at her, kissing the oily lock in her hand before throwing it in the fireplace. The two looked at each other for what felt like an eternity before low cries erupted from the house. Martita's eyes widened in horror as she felt a burning sensation crawl up her legs and her body slowly caught fire. It was a fire she couldn't extinguish, she realized as she grabbed every bucket of water she could find and emptied it on her body. When it didn't work, she swatted the flames away, strangled cries seizing her throat as her clothes vanished and her skin turned a darker shade of brown. She called for Briar once, twice, but the Mastria covered her head again, and her silhouette disappeared as the flames burned stronger. Martita's screams were filled with names but no Gerd, no Pat, no Sarkis, and no Tithan answered her pleas.

Her body fell to the floor like a broken vase, her charred body a smelly mess of ashes and bones but her eyes were intact. Big, round white balls with hazel hues gazed at the void surroundings that Martita once called home before said home turned into her grave.

✼✼✼

The ticking violins played the music of a triple-time dance that he knew all too well but never truly liked. It always felt anachronic, as if it belonged to a past era he had never known, but if Tithan had to name one tune that took his mind away from his current predicament, he couldn't find any. His feet moved on their own accord as he spun the blonde-haired woman in his arms, her vivid blue eyes looking at him as if he were the most precious man to her, but he wasn't. Tithan knew that Lady Tecla's boy hadn't returned from the sea, and he was the only one left. His mother's hands were covered in transparent lace and the smile plastered on her face was only there to reassure her lord husband who watched them dance across the ballroom. The ever-frowning Lord Theliel, she liked to call him. Tithan wanted to talk about his brother Thaesonwald, but he couldn't bring himself to do it, as if the name alone would permanently erase the serene expression that marked her features so graciously.

"Your dancing skills have improved, son," she whispered.

His lips parted, but no sound came out as her body became smaller, her silver dress turning blue and her sapphire eyes fading to reveal a hazel shade.

"Do you hear me, Father?" the young Tecla asked him with a toothy grin.

The room spun around them, the bright colors of the wall becoming a whirlwind pool of leaves that fell on the first day of autumn. His long chestnut hair flew around him as he spun in his arms a toddler who squeaked and gargled at him, laughing and chewing on her little fingers. Tithan put the little girl down, slumping on the ground. He watched in silence as the builders of Summerport shared ideas on the ongoing construction of the encampment and its barracks. A woman with golden-brown hair sat beside him, cradling a baby boy close to her chest as she told the two little girls beside her to finish their meal. Tithan leaned back, resting the weight of his upper body on his elbows. His father was nowhere to be seen, and he hoped the physicians of the capital hadn't kept Lord Lionhelm in the confines of his apartments once more. Some said it was the Violet Delusion, others spoke of the fever. He smiled at his father's woman, Marion the Kind, as they called her in the hallways of the palace ever since his mother left Strongshore.

Tithan brushed his knuckles against the baby's cheek. "Nall seems to be doing better," he commented.

"Yes, young lord." Narrowing her eyes at the twins who pulled on Tithan's sleeves to have him get up and play, Marion scolded them in a tone so light they didn't take her seriously. "Tamar, Tyllis, stop it."

"Let them," Tithan shrugged off, crawling on all fours to pretend he was about to attack the two children. "Did you hear the story of the Lions of the Red Summer?" he menacingly asked, the least credible roar escaping his throat.

The children screamed at the top of their lungs, running in circles around their mother as their imagination filled the gaps between Tithan's impersonation and the tale they couldn't focus on. They ran a little faster, their identical grins making it harder for him to tell them apart. The sound of their little feet stomping the grass mixed with the resounding thud of hooves against the hard ground and he wasn't prepared for Arther Angefort's worried look as Tithan found himself sitting in the audience room of Strongshore. The friend of a lifetime bowed deeply in his presence, seeking refuge behind rigid etiquette as his lips spoke words Tithan would never forget.

She fell, they said. She fell from a horse, but Tithan knew Emelyne didn't ride any horse, she didn't know how to. But Arther explained she was riding with her son, and let go. The halls of the palace were filled with comments on Emelyne the Demented, on Theliel the irresponsible Lionhelm, and Arther spoke in a voice that wasn't his.

"Father, forgive me, for I can't forgive myself."

Tithan stood on top of the highest cupola of Strongshore, where the view was known to no one until that moment. His third son still wore his training garments, his unruly mane making him look like a simple man rather than a Lionhelm. He stood on the railing of the small balcony on top of the cupola, the wind threatening to push him off any moment, sending his body to roll down the curve of the roof and shatter on the cold ground of the Great Gardens.

"Step back, son," he said softly. "It wasn't your fault."

"It wasn't hers either," Theliel's voice broke.

Tithan's stare fell, and he whispered back, "No. It wasn't."

"Catch me," he read on his son's lips.

"Theliel?"

"Catch me!" a feminine voice ordered him, and laughter filled his ears.

Tithan could see himself run after a young girl who had barely come of age. Her dark hair slapped against her back, tickling her upper thighs before she fell down a small slope, laughing and rolling down, sweat coating her forehead. The summer heat was scorching. His younger self rolled next to her, the two of them staring at the clear skies as they tried to catch their breaths. She wore a sleeveless, light brown dress that reminded him of her eyes. She was a playful girl, but Tithan knew the muddy games would soon end. He was expected to set sail for the Red Continent very soon, as much as he didn't want to follow his older brother in the expedition. Their father commanded them to go.

"Say, Dea," he sighed out. "Would you marry me?"

The girl laughed, her lungs threatening to explode. "You know I don't see you that way," she teased him, nudging him with her elbow. "You're kind of skinny."

"You're not that good-looking either," he retorted with a frown, gently slapping her hand. "What if I die?"

The girl snorted in a very unladylike manner. "You won't," she told him, kicking at the air barefoot. "We can always talk about it when you come back."

"If I come back."

"Father, I came back," he heard in the distance.

It was the voice of a woman, but he couldn't quite recognize whose voice it was. The light blue color of the summer sky dimmed into a deeper shade, one that was tainted with crimson and steel, one that looked oddly like the paint in the ceiling of his bed-chamber. Tithan closed his eyes again. He remembered now. It was the ceiling that told an endless tale of war and conquest, a conquest that was never truly achieved yet shed unnecessary blood. It was a painting of war framed by light and embraced by the representation of the Oracle's supple arms and resting face. Tithan never considered himself to be a believer of any sort, but if he had to choose, he guessed he would rather lay his body to rest in the shadow of the Oracle and not in the light of the Dreamer. Religion had taken too much from him; from the soul of Little Nall to the living memories his father cherished.

"I am sorry," he whispered, his voice strained. "Tell them I am sorry."

Tecla leaned in closer, hugging her father's hand to her chest. Her eyes were filled with tears as she sat next to him alone. She had rushed to his side the moment she arrived home, wasting no time in greeting neither the rest of her family nor the devoted master-at-arms who guarded the doors. She had ignored Grandmaster Rodbertus' pleas to have his father visited by the Regency's physicians and himself as soon as possible, for she saw her father was speaking incoherently. Just a few moments, she had asked them.

She kissed his cheek softly. She saw him shiver, and Tecla guessed it was because her nose was still cold from the ride. "Are you awake?" she whispered.

His eyes opened again, his tired hazels looking into hers. "Tecla," he recognized her with a smile. "When did your eyes turn blue?"

She broke into a smile, choking back a sob. "They are not. Grandmother had blue eyes," she reminded him.

"She lives in you," Tithan told her, tightening his hand around hers. "That is what I like to believe." His head lolled back against the cushions and he coughed. "Wald," he called. "Wald."

Confused, Tecla held his hand up when she felt his arm lose its strength. "Wald is—"

"Wald, why did you leave that boat?" he asked no one as his eyes softly closed again. "Why did you leave me?"

Feeling new tears roll down her round cheeks, Tecla quickly wiped them away with her fingernails. Perhaps, it was time to call Grandmaster Rodbertus, she thought.

"Tell them I'm sorry," Tithan rambled. "If you see them; if you see Father, Marion, and Little Nall, tell them I'm sorry. I should have fought better for Briar; I should have done more for Tamar and Tyllis. I should have killed Frederyc Rosenfield with my own hands but I…

"I am…" his voice faltered. "I am a weak man."

Tecla dropped her father's hand, watching his chest rise and fall until it didn't. His lips were parted, his cheeks sunken, his skin dry. She didn't sob, she didn't utter a word as she let the tears run freely down her face, fall in the creases of her lips. More streams left her eyes with every blink, and she could only shake her head. No, she wanted to tell him. No, he wasn't a weak man. He was a great lord, an even greater father; someone who had made sure that every member of his family would be well and taken care of. She wasn't sure who the women he mentioned were, but she knew of Little Nall, so Tecla could only imagine that he was referring to the bastard children her grandfather had after her grandmother left Strongshore.

  She brought his hand to her lips, kissing it briefly before placing it on his chest. She rested her head between her arms as she lied her upper body down, next to him, causing her to sit at an awkward angle. It wasn't fair, she told herself. Her father was old and tired, but it wasn't fair. If they had come sooner… If she hadn't listened to Grandmaster Rodbertus… If she had argued to take the shorter route… Many ifs filled her head, just like rage filled her chest as she remembered that Theliel was late. Theliel should have been with her. Everyone should have been there, Tecla told herself as she wondered where the rest of her family was. Why was her father alone in his bed-chambers, aside from Fantine's guarding presence?

  Tecla didn't hear the doors open behind her. She cried in silence, repressing the urge to scream her anger at the world and beg the Good Gods to return her father's soul, and was unprepared to feel a warm hand on her back.

  "Stand up, dear," Voladea whispered.

  "No," was her muffled reply.

  "It wasn't your fault," the woman spoke, rubbing Tecla's back. "Come with me. You can't stay here."

"I have to, Mother," Tecla told her in a tone she found to be more aggressive than she intended. The word mother didn't roll off the tongue the way it used to, not since Matillis called her a bastard child. "Tyllis," she whispered, her pounding headache growing.

"What?" Lady Voladea asked, removing her hand. "Tecla, your father—"

"Is dead," Tecla finished for her. "I wish to stay a bit longer," she added in a quieter tone.

"My lady, only we can state that," a third voice chimed in.

Tecla looked up, and she realized that Lady Voladea had come in with the group of physicians from the Regency. They wore white, pristine robes, and she could see Grandmaster Rodbertus stand by the doors next to Fantine, both waiting with saddened, nearly blank expressions on their faces. Feeling ashamed for her behavior in front of all these people, Tecla swallowed hard, standing up slowly and keeping her head low. Lady Voladea escorted her out of the bed-chamber, walking side to side as they crossed the antechamber and stopped at the entrance. Tecla then saw the people lining the corridor in the same fashion they did when her brother Thaesonwald had his accident. She saw Tylennald and Wallysa waiting for their turn to enter the bed-chamber, she spotted Lord Riverguard leaning against one of the columns, exchanging words with Jarvis Angefort. At the far back, she could see the weeping servants of her father, his favorite maids, his cook, his shoemaker; she saw Fran hold Lyzon in his arms as she cried hard, and Educator Tomas blow his nose with a green handkerchief.

      Tecla felt her throat tighten. Theliel was nowhere to be seen. Tesfira seemed to have spaced out as she watched the others around her, and Tiran paced next to her with shaky hands. "What will happen now?" she asked Lady Voladea. "Will there be a joint funeral, for Father and Thaesonwald? How long are Theliel and I staying before we travel back to the capital? I should ask Grandmaster Rodbertus if he minds us staying longer."

      "You are not going back to Silverholde."

      Tecla's eyebrows knitted together. She stared at the woman beside her, who impassively looked back at her. Lady Voladea wore black from head to toe, in a fashion close to how Lady Gwethana dressed, and her hair was pulled back in a tight, braided bun. In the back of her mind, Tecla wondered where Lady Gwethana even was, but Lady Voladea's words still echoed through her mind.

      "I know your father treated you like a child whose whims needed to be attended. I don't blame him," Voladea told her. "You were, after all, his youngest child. But it is time to grow up now," she stated. "You will embark on a ship as soon as possible and leave for the Sand Towers. Strongshore has accepted the alliance with the Sons of Ferngrunn."

      Tecla opened her mouth to protest, but no sound came out.

      "The preparations for the funeral will take several days," Lady Voladea went on. "There will be a private ceremony and a public one in Summerport. You can't stay here until next moon when the Sons of Ferngrunn are already preparing for your arrival."

"You can't do this," Tecla finally answered in disbelief. "You can't send me away before the ceremony; you can't send me away from my home," she exclaimed with a louder voice.

"As your mother, I very well can."

Tecla stepped forward, raising her chin. "No, you can't."

Lady Lionhelm's eyebrows shot up, her face relaxing in understanding. "Very well," she conceded. "How do you plan on opposing my will?"

Tecla sprung into a fast walking pace, her small heels clicking against the marble floor. She held the front of her dress to avoid tripping on her way to Theliel's apartments, ignoring the curious looks she was receiving from the rest of the household and the way her servants trotted behind her. She wasn't going anywhere, she repeated to herself. She certainly wasn't about to be sent to unknown lands where a group of strangers waited for her without her even knowing about it. Some of the guards turned their heads as they saw her walk down the hallways that lead to Theliel's apartments, fully knowing that their young lord wasn't in there. Voladea followed Tecla at a much slower pace, her fingers laced together.

"Open the doors," Tecla ordered the two guards standing next to the chamber doors. She saw them exchange a look before reluctantly pushing the doors open.

Tecla walked in slowly, her heart pounding wildly against her rib cage, and her eyes darted around. The bed-chambers were empty. She never expected them to be full of Theliel's belongings because he lived at the Pavilion, but his most private room was deserted. The bedsheets were still light and soft and not suited for the cold weather. It was as if Theliel never gave any order to have his room ready for his return. Tecla stopped breathing, and the tears stopped flowing. Theliel wasn't coming back, she concluded. He wouldn't come back for her, she reasoned inwardly. He already tried to leave the Regency once, who was to say he wouldn't do it a second time?

"Young lady," Lyzon's voice reached her ears.

Tecla turned around slowly; dread written all over her face. She felt ready to fall on her knees, but Lyzon threw her arms around her, holding her firmly as they cried. She felt the maid's hand rub the back of her head, and though her vision was clouded, she could see Fran and Tomas shed tears as well at the loss of their lord.

"He's gone," Tecla whimpered. "They're all gone," she crumbled down.

"It's alright, my lady. It will be alright."

Tecla didn't know how long they stayed in that position, but from the corner of her eye she saw the hem of Lady Voladea's black dress, and her hands turned cold.

"Guards," Lady Voladea ordered. "Kindly escort Lady Tecla's educator to the guest apartments."

Tecla blinked the tears away, watching in silence as Tomas was forcefully shielded by two men who didn't seem willing to wait for him to be ready. Her swollen eyes met Lady Voladea's hardened expression and the next words the woman spoke engraved themselves in her brain like carvings in the stone.

"Take the help."

Two other men left their spots in the hallway, grabbing Fran by the arm and ripping Lyzon from Tecla's embrace. The two women wailed in opposition, and Tecla ordered them to stop, but they didn't listen to her. Lyzon fought unsuccessfully against the guard who wouldn't relinquish his hold on her, and her long, straight black hair that was so neatly brushed back messily slapped around her body. Lady Voladea didn't bat an eye as the two servants were taken, her glacial stare halting Tecla's movements as the girl tried to follow them.

"You will find better help in the Sand Towers," the grey woman concluded before turning heels.

Tecla felt her swollen eyes burn. She wanted to rip that bun and pull the woman's hair out; she wanted to run after her and tackle her against the railing of the balcony before pushing her down. She wanted many things at that moment, including ramming her fists into Theliel's chest to knock the air out of his lungs, just so he could feel the way she did, although she knew her little hands would do no damage to her older brother. In the cold and abandoned bed-chamber, Tecla oddly felt at her place.

Chapter XXVII

BLACK WINGS

Tall pyres were placed down the main streets of Summerport in front of every tavern, inn, and building of importance for the southern people, especially those who couldn't keep themselves warm because they had no home to return to and no coin to afford a shelter. Theliel pulled on the reins of his horse as he neared the Seven Galleys, the tavern Sarkis worked at if he recalled correctly. His fur cloak was covered in snow and his bangs were wet, but he didn't feel cold. He couldn't stay in the city for long, he reminded himself as his eyes trailed to the statue he saw in the distance. Alatros' ascent to the Heights was partially clouded by the thick grey coat of clouds, the chatter echoing through the plaza being the only music that kept everyone with their feet on the ground, as one could easily get lost in the veil of mystery that enveloped a statue so big it could have only been forged by giants.

Ignoring the greetings and the smiles directed at him, the man whistled at a waiter in light clothing who scrubbed the tables outside the tavern with a soapy sponge and salt crystals. The balding man raised an eyebrow at him and continued working.

"I am looking for a man named Sarkis," Theliel told him.

"Haven't seen him."

Reaching inside his cloak, Theliel was quick to toss a coin at the sour worker.

"It's been some days since Sarkis was here," the waiter said. "I don't know where he went. It's a shame, the patrons liked him."

Theliel seemed surprised. "Is that so?"

"Yeah," the man answered, scrubbing a little faster. "He made people laugh. They liked him and came back."

"Thank you for your time."

Theliel kicked his horse, deciding that the only place Sarkis could be at that moment was Old Martita's house. He had hoped to find him at the tavern instead, for he didn't wish to speak of some matters in front of the old woman. Granted, she had helped them quite a lot even though she didn't have to, but some things needed to remain between him and Sarkis.

He trotted down the street that connected the center of Summerport to the wheat fields of the more fortunate, and Theliel couldn't help but notice the sullen mood of the southerners. Perhaps it was the weather, or maybe they heard of their overlord being bed-ridden. Either way, Theliel needed to be quick; he too wanted to see his father and be present for Tecla in case the situation worsened. Theliel didn't want to consider that though; his father had been there his whole life, and as much as they seemed to get less and less along with each passing day, he couldn't imagine a world where Tithan Lionhelm no longer existed. The man had never been gentle with him; from the harsh training he had to endure in the southern military to being forced into the Regency's Treasure Council, Theliel wasn't as lucky as his siblings, who always seemed to get at least part of what they truly wanted. Thaesonwald's less than honorable behaviors had never been frowned upon, and aside from the supervision of the Lionhelm forces, not many duties had burdened him. Tylennald was rarely punished for his ambitions, and even when he was accused of attempting to change Tithan's line of succession in his favor, he was allowed to stay in Strongshore. Tesfira ran from a marriage she didn't want, refusing to become the lady of either an Angefort or a Nobleleaf and eloping with a simple man with no consequence. Tecla herself could afford to decide whoever she wanted to be, and as much as Theliel loved her, jealousy often crept in the back of his mind. And still, Lord Tithan Lionhelm was a part of him he didn't want to let go of. He wasn't ready to do it.

  Sarkis was spotted with ease. The chubby man wobbled in the direction of Martita's house, a pile of firewood secured by large laces in his arms. Theliel smiled faintly at the sight of his friend's nearly losing his balance, but as he hurried his horse and thought of what to tell Sarkis, he missed the way the burly man dropped the wood in front of the open door.

"Sarkis," Theliel called, quickly hopping down his mount. "Sarkis, I came back. I don't have much time; you need to get your things."

The black-haired man didn't acknowledge him. His stare was solely focused on the scene before him, and Theliel cleared his throat to try and get his attention. He noticed that Sarkis' beard had grown a lot in his absence and that his clothes were dirtier than ever. Some mud stains on his clothes looked more like blood, and Theliel felt utterly confused. Old Martita wasn't one to not have people freshen up and wash their garments.

"Sarkis," he tried once more.

His friend finally diverted his gaze from the house with the open door, only to look at Theliel as if he had seen a ghost. "Theliel, I... You can't—you won't believe…"

Theliel's smile widened. "Look, I told you I would fix it, didn't I? A ship is waiting for us at the harbor," he explained. "I've got enough for us to live a life without worries, but we will have to lay low for a while. Listen," he ordered in a lower tone. "You need to wait for me on a ship, Lion's Glory, the captain's name is Wulfscoe. Ask for him. I need to get my sister first; I'm not leaving her behind."

Sarkis frowned at him, his front teeth biting into his lower lip harder than usual. With a firm grip on the tall man's forearm, he tugged Theliel forward, forcing him to take a look inside. Old Martita's body lied on the wooden floor in a pile of dark ashes that the wind slowly scattered around the otherwise clean place. Her round, strong body was just melted skin and bones, bones so small they could have belonged to a child. Her arms were bent forward as if she had tried to bring her hands to her face while she burned. Theliel took a hesitant step inside the house, his eyes scanning for anyone's presence or for a reason as to why it happened, but there was nothing. Pots and pans still hung from the shelves mounted on the wall, clean linens were folded on a stool and the faint smell of onion permeated the air. How Old Martita caught fire while the rest of the house was intact he couldn't explain; the floor was even wet in several spots as if she had tried to save herself. But her eyes… Her eyes staring right at him in their dark sockets was the indication she didn't die in an accident. Theliel had seen enough oddities to know that something inexplicable and most certainly inhuman happened. He heard Sarkis cry behind him, muttering words inaudible to Theliel. He was trying to talk to him, but the words wouldn't register in Theliel's mind.

"We need to leave, now," the young Lionhelm stressed. "Quick, Sarkis," he pressed, grabbing one of the folded linens to drape it over Old Martita's remains. "We need to leave before anyone pins this on us."

"We can't leave her just like that," Sarkis argued, reluctantly holding his bag that Theliel picked up from where it leaned against the wooden bench and shoved it in the burly man's arms. "This woman—she treated me better than anyone else out there," he elaborated. We can't just leave without giving her proper sepulture." When Theliel dragged him outside with no second thoughts, Sarkis shoved him away. "What is wrong with you? Where is your compassion?"

"Compassion?" Theliel roared back, a droplet of spit hitting Sarkis straight in the eye. "That woman was my aunt. Do you think I want to leave like the ungrateful bastard everyone in my family thinks I am?" Ignoring Sarkis' look of complete shock, he repeated, "Wait for me at the harbor. I am taking Tecla and we are leaving this forsaken place. You have no idea what I went through to make this possible."

Sarkis still didn't understand and his shoulders slumped. "Your—what? What did you do?" he whispered. As his brain kicked into gear like a ticking violin, Sarkis told Theliel the truth. "A Regency officer was here, Theliel. He said no one was ever looking for me."

Theliel shook his head in disbelief. "I am not discussing this now. We have to get moving." He threw his leg over the saddle of his horse, refusing to hear more. Seeing Old Martita reduced to ashes with her eyes still intact only reminded him of the Rosenfield castle, but he couldn't afford to analyze that, not when his father was ill and his sister alone by his side. "Remember, ask for Captain Wulfscoe."

Before Sarkis could reply, the sound of bells filled the city, freezing its movements, and causing Theliel to look in the direction of the temple and the Oracle's Pillar. When his eyesight failed him, Theliel narrowed his eyes, only to see a cloud of a black color flutter from the eastern coast, where Strongshore stood less proudly than usual.

Sarkis watched as the dark wings filled the skies and he asked, "Ravens? Why ravens?"

"My father died," Theliel whispered, the words sounding ridiculous to him. "They free the ravens from the bird post when an overlord dies," he explained, tightening his fists around the leather reins.

"So, your eldest brother is Lord of Strongshore now?"

"My brother died too. Hop on," he said softly, earning a blink from Sarkis.

"What about your sister?"

"Strongshore is going to turn into the Pit of Torture within the next few moments. If I go back I surely won't be able to leave, let alone bring Tecla without raising suspicion." Swallowing hard, Theliel bit back the tears that threatened to spill any moment. "I will send her an owl before we head to the harbor."

Theliel extended a hand to help Sarkis up, the burly man quickly hanging on the cantle of the saddle to avoid falling from the horse the moment it started moving. With the crowing of the ravens filling the air, Theliel took one last glance in the distance, telling himself that he was doing the right thing enough times to convince himself. He had gone too far now; all he could hope for was Tecla's positive reaction to the message he planned on sending her. Without Tithan Lionhelm as Lord of Strongshore, there was no reason for neither of them to abide by the rules the Regency used to hide their truth or even worse; the rules Voladea and Tylennald would now be free to lay down.

***

It was the first dawn day of another cold month of winter and Jascha stood at the foot of Danyell's Athenaeum with his dark gaze fixed on the clouds above that ran at a fast speed to bring even colder winds and coats of snow to cover the city. The Rippling Run was already frozen in some areas, allowing only shy streams to flow past the city bridges. He saw many handcarts transport the bodies of those who didn't find refuge and died before being hidden by the snow, only to be dumped in mass graves dug outside the city walls. The least damaged bodies were carried to the Regency's Observatory Vault for the sake of research, and sometimes Holy Captain Chadras was seen honoring the dead with a brief ceremony that consisted of lighting pyres where the bodies had been buried. Jascha saw another wave of black wings fly above Silverholde, signaling the death of a major lord of the Silver Lands. Some patrons of the Wild Rock Skunk said Lord Lionhelm of Strongshore passed away, but Jascha paid no attention to the theories that followed such declarations. That girl's father, he thought to himself, was dead.

Glancing back at the closed doors of the athenaeum, Jascha wondered why it hadn't reopened already. It was way past midday, and yet, the doors were locked. Fewer surveillants roamed the streets as well, and he hadn't caught Sir Sybbyl Nobleleaf trying to follow him yet. He doubted she would sit still after losing her weapon, but the Suppressor of War was nowhere to be seen. Jascha turned around, his nostrils flaring in annoyance, as he decided that he would spend the rest of the day at the inn. He spun around, only to come face to face with a woman he hadn't seen in some time.

Rosewillow was looking at him with a look colder than winter, and for a moment he wondered if she knew about Rosaleah. Her harsh traits instantly softened, and her half-lidded eyes took in his appearance. "I was thinking of paying my friend a visit," she told him quietly.

He remained silent, moving past her.

"Just in case you think I'm following you," she added with a smile.

Jascha glanced behind him, and he saw her bright green eyes stare at his back. "I don't think anything about you."

Rosewillow laughed lightly. "Are you sure about that?"

No, he thought, but he wasn't about to tell her the truth. The last time he saw her he tried to understand what she was after. She was part of the Rosencircle, but what his ties to that society were she wouldn't say. Perhaps, he was another man she tried to lure in as a *Nakfèht*; he couldn't say for sure. She told him she was the first and last warning he would receive, and he doubted that was how she approached those whose blood she lusted for.

"The last time we spoke you offered to show me," Jascha reminded her. "Show me what it is you do."

Rosewillow tilted her head as if to figure out whether he was bluffing or not, but his serious expression nearly convinced her otherwise. She followed him without saying a word, memorizing every street they walked down and every alley they crossed. She didn't know where he stayed nor if he resided in Silverholde, but she was about to find out. Rosaleah had been missing for days, but as much as she wanted to believe the man she followed was involved, she didn't know enough to come up with a theory that would connect all the pieces of information she had. Jascha met Rosaleah's mother once, but the woman didn't mention anything about him when Rosewillow visited her in hopes to find Rosaleah. Mawde and the athenaeum were the only reasons that could have brought Jascha and the girl together.

The thought of him killing Rosaleah crossed her mind as they reached the abandoned areas surrounding Melisentia's Opera; Jascha did treat Rosewillow callously at the Shattered Ambry. She wouldn't put it past him to get even more violent, but what was the point of ending Rosaleah's life if he used it as a warning to neither her nor anyone else from the Rosencircle?

Jascha pushed the door of the blacksmith shop open, making sure to lock it behind him after Rosewillow stepped in. The only source of light emanated from the forge, and Rosewillow scrunched her nose. The hint of a foul smell permeated the air as if dead mice filled the corners of the shop.

"Interesting place you chose," she commented. "Something died in here."

Jascha got rid of the blades strapped against his back and unfastened his cloak, hanging it on the door handle. "The previous owner was a mess," he told her. "But I don't plan on staying here for long."

Rosewillow removed her hood, freeing her dark chestnut hair from where it was stuck between the hood and the collar of her white fur. "So," she said, looking at him in the eyes. "I think you know where Rosaleah is. You tell me where and I show you what you want to see."

Jascha took a step closer, removing his gloves and throwing them on the floor as he pressed his lips together, thinking, calculating. "You always think you make the rules, don't you, Willow?" he whispered, hooking his long fingers around the knot that kept her cloak in place. With a tug, the wolf fur fell, leaving her in a pale dress with sleeves patched around the loose fabric of her underdress. "I don't play by them."

Rosewillow's eye twitched, and she tried her best not to seem pleased. He was making it a little too easy for her. "There is no rule," she whispered, straightening her back as if it would make her reach his height. "Only a deal."

Jascha nodded slowly, his dark gaze leaving her green pools to fall on her own parted lips. He could feel her breath. The quietness of the room was deafening and only the whistling wind from outside seemed to try to cut through the silence like

Jascha's blades cut through flesh. The fingers that touched her cloak found her chin, and he realized how cold her skin was. His lips were on hers with her next inhale, their eyes wide open. They remained still even as their lips parted, flesh resting against flesh. Rosewillow licked her lips, the tip of her tongue grazing his skin. His hand fisted the hair at the nape of her neck and he took two long strides, sending her against the nearest wall. He felt his knuckles collide with the wood, and their mouths bit at each other again. It was quicker this time, and Rosewillow's hands quickly found his mane, fisting and tugging the dark strands as she sucked on his lower lip and licked the roof of his mouth.

    Jascha grabbed her by the waist, and he felt her ribcage, then her round hip before his hands traveled further, down the swell of her bottom. He held on the back of her thighs as he slid her up the wall, and as she bent her legs around his body, he scratched his way under her dress, leaving red marks on her skin. She sighed against his lips, leaning back to watch as he brought one of his hands between the mounds of her chest to pull at the front of her dress. Rosewillow leaned in at the feel of his teeth scraping the side of her neck while his hands found her legs again, his thumbs pressing against her inner thighs before brushing against the smooth lips hidden under her dress.

    His jerkin was quickly discarded and Rosewillow pulled at the wool tunic that covered his upper body while Jascha carried her to the blacksmith bench with one arm. He dropped her uncerimoniously as he removed the shirt in a swift move, his scars quickly catching her eyes. Her long fingernails traced them, and her stare darkened. His pupils were dilated, but before his hands could move from where they rested on her hips, Rosewillow unfastened his loose britches, which pooled around his ankles, leaving him erect in front of her. Her swollen lips found his again, tugging him closer with her legs clasped around his hips. He held his rod with one hand, guiding it through her soaked folds, rubbing the head up and down her entrance.

 Jascha jerked himself away from her, grabbing her left leg and crossing it over the other before driving himself inside her. The tight, unusual angle caused her to yelp, and Rosewillow adjusted her body by turning her upper body in the direction of her bent leg, mostly lying on her right side. It was a problem, she realized as she couldn't grab him, let alone look into his eyes. His hips pounded against her in short, forceful thrusts that elicited a series of moans and pained yelps. She scratched at the wooden workbench, her inner muscles clenching and unclenching with each thrust of his, and she watched with knitted eyebrows as his face contorted in an expression of anger rather than one of enjoyment. Rosewillow forced her upper body up by resting her weight on her elbows, but one of Jascha's hands left her hips to grab her shoulder. He had her flat against his chest quickly, and his fingers tugged on her long hair again to properly bend her back, allowing him better access. Her eyes were shut as he hit her womb, high-pitched cries of pleasure that turned into pain filling the shop.

"It doesn't work if you can't look me in the eyes, does it?" he whispered against her ear, his hips fully slapping against her bottom.

Rosewillow felt her heart skip a beat. "How—"

"Maybe it's you who should keep them open."

With a harder trust that sent her further up against the wooden surface, Jascha tore himself away from her, waves of hot seed splashing on the floor as he tried to regain control of his breathing. Rosewillow felt her thighs shake and her insides were on fire, but as her emerald eyes opened slowly, a strong, deep-throated sound escaped her lips in terror. She saw a dark pool of dry blood coat the floor and two shadows above it. She caught the sound of rustling fabric as Jascha pulled his pants up, shortly coming to stand in front of her with his chest still bare, holding a torch in his hand, while she quivered.

The light hovered over the body of Rosaleah, and Jascha's breathing was ragged as he watched Rosewillow flushed face pale at the sight of his work. Horrified groans mixed with the sobs that rocked her chest as she tried to push herself up, but the stinging pain in her lower body made it a hard task. Rosaleah's corpse was nailed to the wall next to another decomposing body that was no longer recognizable. Her flesh had been cut through repeatedly. Gashes all over her upper body were connected by cuts to form a symbol she knew all too well; the six sides of Aelneth's stones. But Rosaleah's body hadn't simply served as proof that Jascha understood the search for the *Nakfèht*; he had sought revenge. He had cut through the girl's flesh wherever he could find a hard surface. Her arms, her legs, her ribs, and even her face had been scratched with a blade so sharp it carved her bones. Rosaleah had ended up telling him, Rosewillow realized. Knowing her, she doubted Rosaleah told him everything she knew, but enough for him to trick Rosewillow.

"Is that what you wanted to do to me?" Jascha asked her, his eyes hungrily trailing to the body that had the green-eyed woman's full attention. "She held on for some time," he told her, running his tongue over his lower lip.

"You are no *Nakfèht*," Rosewillow hissed at him. "But I wouldn't have minded either way," she spat.

Jascha walked over to her, grabbing her by the chin to plant an emotionless kiss on her lips. "I bet you wouldn't have, you demented wreck." Holding the torch closer to her face, he asked, "So, what did you both want from me?"

Rosewillow eyed the fire that was too close to burning either her skin or her hair, perhaps even both. Forfeiting the round, her lips trembled and her body shook violently. "Nothing," she whispered bitterly. "Your curiosity and your face were the alarm," she told him.

Jascha let go of her, rearing back as if he had been the one burnt. "My face?"

"You look just like her," Rosewillow told him, failing to sit when her womb still screamed. "The woman who left the Rosencircle without permission. We know she had a son," she explained. "We just never met him."

He felt his heartbeat in his ears with every word she spoke. "My mother was part of nothing. She lived in a world of chimeras without the need for your intervention."

Rosewillow shook her head at him, her stare lingering on one of Rosaleah half chopped breasts. "Rosaleen was her name. I remember her very well; I remember her voice, her straight black hair, and her blue-grey eyes. I remember her slim, tall nose and her thin red lips. And I remember the day she left. She said she was with child for the second time and returned to the Fog Lands."

Jascha dropped the torch, paying no attention to the way it rolled closer to the corner of the wall. "You're wrong," he retorted, his voice barely above a whisper. "That wasn't my mother's name."

And his mother couldn't have been with child again; he didn't remember it. His father died when he was only a small kid, and Rosewillow was roughly his age. If she could remember the woman clear enough, then when she allegedly saw his mother for the last time, she had been too old already for the events to have taken place before his father's death. Not a person came to mind when he tried to remember the face of the one who could have fathered the child. Then again, Holy Captain Chadras did mention he had a sister.

"That doesn't explain why everything you perform is embedded in my body," he pointed out. Jascha could feel the acidic taste of bile in his mouth.

Rosewillow gave him a blank stare. "We didn't even know whether you were still alive or not. We could have never willingly targeted you for anything."

That was not the answer he wanted to hear. He could not be back to the point of departure again.

"Perhaps your mother—"

"She was not my mother," he stopped her right there, collecting the pieces of clothing he had discarded around. He refused to hear more nonsense that would lead him to nothing more than ifs and maybes.

"The Mastria could know," Rosewillow insisted, a part of her chastising herself for trying to bring answers to a man who had tortured Rosaleah for days. "If you would—"

"Come with you to see the revenge your people are going to seek for whatever my non-mother did?" he finished her sentence, laughing spitefully at her, tying his cloak around his body after he fished for his gloves on the floor. Feeling the fury that made his entire body shake, he glared at the woman who slowly stood up. "Go fuck yourself for the next hundred years, you and all your kin," he snarled before grabbing his Haunting Sisters and shutting the door behind him.

Chapter XXVIII

Living Memory

Glimmerforest was a sea of fat wet leaves and narrow paths that zigzagged between tall, thin trees that threatened to break at any moment. Goldsnout had serious trouble finding his way out of the ghost town that nature was busy reclaiming and guiding Eleres' horse through it was particularly hard when he was forced to hunch his back to avoid low branches and crumbling roofs. He wasn't even sure how long he had been stuck in Glimmerforest since he left Summerport. The sky was invisible to him. The only streams of water he found were tainted purple, and dead carcasses could be found where wild animals had tried to hydrate themselves.

He checked his waterskin and felt it was nearly empty. He couldn't take a sip before he got out of Glimmerforest, not when he wasn't sure if the situation was any better around the ruins of Everspring. Goldsnout had never traveled on this side of the southern lands before, and without the

Red Road to guide him, he was certain he was lost. It could have been a day or two since he left Old Martita and Sarkis. His light green eyes scanned the funerary view of what used to be a hunter town. The abandoned slaughterhouses and their blood-coated walls were nothing compared to the desolation of the entire place. The dark fog had laid waste to Glimmerforest, returning it to the dirt faster than any war. Many houses fell to pieces without proper maintenance, and only the stone ones seemed intact, but no one was left to inhabit them. Not even mice could be seen roaming the dirtier streets. Goldsnout tightened his sash around his mouth and nose just in case.

  The sun had already set by the time he found the northern entrance of Glimmerforest, the gates entirely covered in rust and vines. Bones were scattered outside, and he wasn't sure he wanted to know whether they belonged to humans or animals. Goldsnout took a deep breath as he saw the shadows of the ruins of Everspring in the far distance. The Rough Rill wasn't too far, and neither was the capital. Unless he got lost again, he should be able to make it back to the Regency within a few dawn days. Deciding to set up a small camp away from the open-air grave, Goldsnout wondered where he could find water safe to drink in these lands. Engrossed in his planning, he was completely unprepared as Chief Eleres' horse let out a faint whine before collapsing to the ground, its body shivering.

  Dismounting quickly, the red-haired officer kneeled beside the animal, placing a hand on its neck, stroking it gently. "You're exhausted too, aren't you," he whispered sadly. Seeing Eleres' mount leaving him only added to the feeling of foreboding that chased him since the events of Wilderose.

Goldsnout stroked the animal's light fur until its eyes stopped blinking and its body no longer spasmed. His throat tightened and his eyes burned as he retrieved Eleres' uniform from where he had strapped it on the saddle. He walked back to his horse with a sour expression, forcing a smile on his lips as he secured the items on the saddle of his mount.

"I guess it's just you and me now," he whispered.

Starting a fire at the foot of the tallest tree proved to be a challenge. Most of the wood he found was wet or covered in snow, and his own hands felt cold as he tried to use his fire striker. The small ember quickly died several times before he managed to get it to turn it into a flame that would last long enough for him not to freeze overnight. Goldsnout reached inside his bag, every fiber of his body feeling the tiredness and his muscles cramping due to the lack of hydration. He chewed on a piece of dried pork, wishing there was anything he could hunt nearby, even a squirrel for what it was worth, and roast it. He rested his back against the trunk of the tree, the piece of meat still dangling between his lips as his tongue lapped at the salt, and closed his eyes.

The rustling of leaves and the sound of humming interrupted his trance. The hair at the nape of his neck stood faster than him, and his right hand was on the hilt of his sword. He looked around, but the darkness of the night made it impossible for him to see past the fire. Goldsnout circled the trees that surrounded him, leaving footprints in the snow. He unsheathed his sword as the humming became louder. It was the voice of a man.

"Son, have you heard the lions roar,
"Their heads were chopped and their meat sold,
"But then the Reds shaped their armor,
"And lion skulls their heads now wore."

Goldsnout narrowed his eyes at the brush, making as little sound as possible as he approached.

"But when the striges came from above,
"A storm of fire killed my love,
"To end the skeletons, I swore—wooo—!"

Goldsnout jumped backward, nearly landing on his bottom, and a man who wasn't quite his age quickly fastened the front of his pants. His face was flushed and he looked as startled as the officer.

"F-forgive me," Goldsnout stammered, turning around to give the man some sense of privacy. "I didn't think anyone was here."

"It's alright; I didn't think others traveled around here either." The man cleared his throat and soon placed a hand on the officer's upper arm to tell him he could turn around now. "I am Jarvis Angefort, son of Amaud Angefort, the Lord of Limemeadow."

Goldsnout took a better look at the young man. He didn't look particularly strong and was shorter than his uncle. His messy brown hair partially covered his dull blue eyes, but his strong jaw and square forehead were typical traits of the Angeforts.

Bowing his head, Goldsnout introduced himself. "Officer Opherus Goldsnout. May I kindly ask why the young lord travels alone and away from the Red Route?"

Jarvis nodded. "I left as soon as Lord Lionhelm passed away and his daughter, Lady Tecla, embarked on a ship," he replied. "I believe that my uncle, the Secretary of the Regency, needs to know this before the news spreads. Avoiding the Red Road was the only way I could get away without being questioned," he reasoned. With a meek smile, he added, "I didn't expect to run straight into a surveillant; my plan wasn't as flawless as I thought."

Goldsnout looked away immediately. As he thought, he had been wandering through Glimmerforest for far too long. He wasn't sure what tied the young lord to the Lionhelms to the point he felt that he needed to reach the capital before the official news reached the Regency, but it wasn't his place to ask. He knew the Angeforts had started as vassals to the Lionhelms and that Lord Tithan and Lord Arther were closer than brothers; perhaps, young Jarvis himself had a connection with Lady Tecla.

"Would you like to travel together?" Jarvis offered. Before Goldsnout could answer, he pointed behind him. "We could share some water and food. My horse is loaded."

Goldsnout laughed in relief. "I would very much appreciate it, my lord."

***

Under the dim lighting of the Council of Steel's meeting room, Lady Voladea ran her nails over the dry ink of a message that didn't belong to her. The narrow room she sat in alone was empty, the paintings of sceneries that no longer belonged to Strongshore being the only company she was granted. Her brown eyes scanned the faces of the Lionhelms that lined the tall, looming walls and she realized that soon, her husband's portrait would join them. They would hang it right next to Lord Theliel Lionhelm's, and their similar faces would be staring at her back for the rest of her life.

She wasn't sure how to feel about her husband's death. She didn't feel freer nor more powerful; she just felt. Lady Voladea knew perfectly that the Council of Steel would organize a meeting soon and possibly summon Lord Angefort for the will reading before addressing Tiran Lionhelm as the new Lord of Strongshore. As she sat at the head of the ebony table, Lady Voladea couldn't recall the last words she spoke in the presence of her husband. They had never been very happy; they never had the chance to try after they were married. Tithan was often away and came home only with other women's children, and by the time he settled in Strongshore, she was no longer the lively and sometimes muddy girl who played in the wheat fields of the Terrawards, just as Tithan was no longer the second-born of an overlord who could let go of responsibilities that weren't his, to begin with.

 A guard opened the door of the council room, and a man she didn't expect to see entered to interrupt her musings. Her eyes fell back on the message Healer Martus handed her the moment it arrived, and she reminded herself that at least two of her problems were taken care of. Theliel seemed to have left the Silver Lands and according to his words, he had wanted Tecla to follow him. Rolling the message to slide it in her sleeve, Lady Voladea considered herself lucky enough to have sent Tecla to the Sand Towers before Theliel's owl reached Strongshore.

 Lovel Riverguard rested his hands on the backrest of the nearest chair, leaning his body forward with a sly smile on his face, one that Voladea abhorred. He wore his signature black coat lined with hints of dark purple, and he even seemed to have trimmed his shoulder-length, blonde hair. How he managed to look as young as ever was still a mystery to her. They were, after all, about the same age.

 Folding her hands on top of the table, she asked, "To what do I owe this pleasure, Lord Lovel? Can't a widow mourn in peace?"

 "I wanted to ask you where I could find Lady Tecla," Lovel replied quietly. "She seemed particularly shaken by the disappearance of her father."

 "She was," Voladea conceded. "Can you blame her? They were extremely close." Standing up, she told him, "I am afraid that if you want to communicate with the young lady you will have to travel to the Sand Towers." Her stare lingered on Lovel's relaxed face, and he didn't seem surprised at all. It unnerved her.

"For a daughter who was so close to her father, it frightens me to see how quick she was to leave. The funeral didn't even take place."

It only took two sentences to remind her why she loathed the man. Tangling her fingers together, Lady Voladea circled him. "Strongshore was no longer home after my lord husband's death and the inexplicable cowardice of her favorite brother." She made her way towards the door when Lovel's next words halted her.

"I feel terrible for assuming the worst," he sighed dramatically. "For a moment, I thought your motherly instincts dissipated, when truly all you wanted was to appease her and not, I dare say, send Lord Tithan's heiress as far as possible while you find a way to dispose of Tiran."

She turned heels, her long, pearly earrings hitting her cheeks when she whipped her head around. "These are some heavy accusations that can't go unpunished, Lovel."

The fair-haired lord held his hands up defensively. "Tylennald told me the truth about the will. He and Wallysa are also claiming to be innocent when it comes to the incident of twenty years ago. I was thinking," he paused in his reasoning, walking up to her, "what if Lady Lionhelm was the one who tried to alter Tithan's last wishes?"

She laughed dryly. "Believe me, I did want to make him see reason. But I would never go against the laws of our family and the laws of the Regency. Tiran is Tithan's heir and our household will now follow his rule." She knocked on the door to have a guard open it, and she whispered, "As for Tecla, her marriage to the Sons of Ferngrunn will benefit us all. They are the best option for her and the Lionhelms. Don't think it was easy for me to rip the girl from her mother's arms."

Lord Lovel arched an eyebrow, his smile widening slightly. "Wasn't it something you longed to do since Tecla arrived in Strongshore? I wouldn't judge."

Lady Voladea stuck her chin out. "It wasn't," she firmly stated. "Tecla is a sweet child, but what benefits the family can't be cast aside for the sake of affections. It was a hard lesson Tithan taught us all, for lineage is the only warranty that keeps these lands together. The moment it no longer is, even the worthless will be able to claim lands as their own."

Lovel bowed his head at that, bending his left arm behind his back. "Your words fill this one's heart with warmth like the poems of Old Drixia," he confessed in a tone that wasn't quite as sarcastic as usual. "And She opened Her eyes,

"Turning the Hammers of Sand to rust,

"Freezing the Clockwork of Rain,

"Appeasing the Beast's Pain,

"Alas the Lions were still not covered in dust," he recited. "A true lioness you seem to be, Lady Voladea."

The grey woman tightened her lips, holding the front of her dress. "You'd be wise to spend less time reading and try to figure out how your grandson's ship, Lion's Glory, seems to have disappeared alongside Theliel Lionhelm," she told him before exiting the Council of Steel's room.

✳✳✳

The ride past the ruins of Everspring had been silent, for the most part. Goldsnout felt less tired than when he made it through Glimmerforest, thanks to the water Lord Jarvis had provided him with and the cooked food that certainly rivaled Old Martita's survival meal. They both managed to have their horses drink clear water and rest as they spotted the Rough Rill, staying for a day in the shadow of what was left of the foundations of the encampment. The military city felt primitive, with very little housing and a small well for its long-gone population to use. Goldsnout and Jarvis took a brief walk through the ruins, sat on the northern walls to glance across the Rough Rill, where the remains of walls as black as the night were proof of Courtbridge's past defenses. They crossed the river the following day, both deciding to avoid stopping at the stronghold of the Riverguards, for Lord Jarvis informed Goldsnout that Lord Lovel hadn't left Summerport and that he wasn't sure if it was wise for the Riverguards to know that the young Angefort wasn't headed back to Limemeadow. Between less important topics and the casual exchange of pleasantries Goldsnout found himself in, he managed to avoid being questioned about his situation. He felt ashamed for thinking that perhaps, the death of Eleres' horse had been a blessing, otherwise the young lord would have been more inclined to ask him where he was going, avoiding the Red Road with two horses. Lord Jarvis never commented on the second uniform Goldsnout carried around, and for that, the officer was glad.

Courtbridge was far behind them, but the dark clouds that chased them from the coast up to Silverholde seemed to announce the arrival of a snowstorm that only added to Goldsnout's morose mood. His scalp felt itchy and his once clean-shaven face was now sporting a hint of facial hair that grew unevenly. He wasn't sure this was how he wished to appear in front of Lord Angefort, but he couldn't return to the Surveillance's headquarters before he managed to speak with the Secretary of the Regency. Goldsnout found himself smiling bitterly. The mere idea of speaking with Lord Angefort meant that it had all been true. Everything that happened wasn't just a nightmare; the chief was killed and he didn't know much about the Rosencircle. What could he tell the secretary?

"Officer Goldsnout," Lord Jarvis' voice interrupted his thoughts.

They stopped halfway up the Red Road as the southern entrance of Silverholde came into view. Every entrance was normally guarded by two men, but this time, only one seemed to be on duty. It was one that Goldsnout didn't know, and judging by the relaxed stance of the man, he could only assume the guard just completed his training.

"State your names," the young guard ordered.

"Jarvis Angefort of Limemeadow, I have come to speak with my uncle, Lord Arther Angefort, Secretary of the Regency. This is Officer Opherus Goldsnout."

The young guard seemed to nod as his helmet slightly bobbed. "Welcome to Silverholde. I am afraid no guard can escort you to the Pavilion, my lord."

Goldsnout narrowed his eyes. "Is everything alright?"

"It is not my place to cast judgment, Officer."

"I will escort Lord Jarvis myself," he promptly said to save himself the trouble of having to answer potential questions about his absence, although he doubted the new guard even knew he had left with Chief Eleres.

As they entered the capital, however, the feeling of homecoming was absent and Goldsnout's detached stare fell on the covered bodies that littered the sides of the main streets. He had spent many winters in Silverholde since he was recruited by the Surveillance at the age of eleven but never before had he witnessed so many people perish outside of Jamys' Yard. It seemed that Lord Jarvis himself didn't feel at ease, and Goldsnout could easily understand why. He came from Limemeadow too, and although his family was all but wealthy, the small settlement took good care of both the lords and the simple people. He watched as some slumped against the nearest building to cough blood or hold their pained stomachs, while others offered them warmer linens to drape their bodies with.

As they rode towards the statue of King Aleyne and the Iathienar, Goldsnout sensed Lord Jarvis' discomfort. Silverholde seemed to have turned into a living memory of Glimmerforest, minus the Violet Delusion. The once busy population of the capital was sick and strained, but the oddest part was that no guard and no surveillant seemed to be on patrol.

"Days like these make me realize how grateful I am to be a southerner," Lord Jarvis whispered with a sad smile. "These men don't have it easy."

Goldsnout wanted to argue that this sight was unnatural, but he refrained. The last thing he needed was an alarmed young lord. He smiled inwardly at himself; once he would have had no qualms in telling the truth, and Chief Eleres would have scolded him for it. They headed to the northern areas of the city without stopping at any tavern for refreshment, following the direction of the Temple of Phorbas and its crimson cupola. Rainier's Pavilion could be seen miles behind it. The golden palace was coated with thick snow, and although Goldsnout had never been there before, he rode into its shadow with the frosty wind biting at his skin.

They were not allowed inside the Pavilion. It seemed that the surveillants had all been assigned to the palace to guard every entrance, and the fully armored soldiers that stood at the gates in a defensive stance were the confirmation that there was more in the air than just the death winter brought with itself. Lord Angefort appeared from behind the gates after several moments spent in one of the most awkward silences Goldsnout had ever experienced. His and Lord Jarvis' horses were taken to the stables and the three men walked away from the Regency soldiers, but not quite closer to the entrance of the Pavilion.

The snow made the Secretary of the Regency's hair look even whiter than it was, a clear contrast to the black he wore in memory of his late overlord. "Jarvis," he spoke first. "I wasn't expecting you."

The young man bowed his head in respect. "Uncle, there are matters I must discuss with you in private."

Lord Angefort nodded briefly, his gaze traveling to meet Goldsnout's. "Jarvis, will you give me a moment with the officer first."

The brown-haired man was quicker to obey than a surveillant was, and Goldsnout held Chief Eleres' belongings closer to his chest. "Lord Angefort."

"You must be Opherus Goldsnout."

"Yes, my lord."

"You came back alone," the Secretary of the Regency noted. "And these must be…"

"We stopped by the castle of the Rosenfields first," Goldsnout reported with his head held high. "We closed the gates and entered the forest of Wilderose. As we neared Edgemere, we were attacked by a group of women who hid their faces behind heavy helmets. They told us we shut the gates of the respectful and they attacked us," he went on in a formal tone. "Chief Eleres' throat was pierced by animated roots and he died shortly after," he concluded, licking his lips when they trembled. "A woman who seemed to know about them saved me and told me it was the Rosencircle's doing."

Lord Angefort took in his words, but his stare eventually fell on Eleres' folded uniform. "Do you know what to do with his belongings?"

"Yes, my lord," Goldsnout replied. "If you'll allow me, I can immediately ride to Rainier's End. I also heard of unsettling events in the city-port of Edgemere but I would like to meet with the chief's family first."

The silver-haired man placed a large hand on Goldsnout's shoulder, squeezing slightly. "Please, do so. I will inform the other members of the Regency and we will honor Thierry Eleres for his bravery before we find out more about the wrongdoers," he reassured the officer. "Make sure you rest, Officer Goldsnout."

Goldsnout bowed deeply before he excused himself. Lord Angefort watched him walk in the direction of the stables to ask for another horse, and all the secretary could think of was that another dutiful man had left this world. Had it been any other moment, he would have run himself to find the so-called Rosencircle, without even trying to find more information about them, but his spirit was free of any anger as it had already been consumed by the loss of Tithan Lionhelm.

Walking up to Jarvis, who waited for him under a rosewillow to shield himself from the snowfall, Arther threw an arm around his nephew's shoulders. "What brings you to the Pavilion?"

"Uncle, it has been brought to my attention that Lady Tecla Lionhelm left Strongshore immediately after her father's death. I can't help but feel that she left against her will," the young man explained shamelessly. "Our family has always been faithful to the Lionhelms and I must tell you, uncle, that you should disclose Lord Tithan's will before others are forced away as well. Lord Lovel Riverguard himself has hinted at preoccupying matters."

Lord Angefort frowned, staring at his nephew in bewilderment.

"We could leave—"

"No, Jarvis," he cut in firmly. "You need to do something else for me if what you say is true.

"And no one can know."

❋❋❋

She sat on an old cushion, squished between the frame of the fireplace and the old chair Maryell slept on, cradling in her arms a rather large book she was able to hold only by resting the spine against her bent legs. Between the cracking of the fire and the heavy snoring of Zurzon, Rantha found it hard to concentrate. Sanson was a heavy sleeper instead, and as he lied on the floor next to the louder apprentice, he rested undisturbed. Rantha pressed the palms of her hands against her eyes, drumming her fingers against her forehead before running them through her curly hair. She chewed on her ample lips as she tried to focus on the last sentence she read, but to no avail.

Ever since Irryelda and her family showed up at the Illusion Shelter, she had gotten no rest. She had managed to repair most of the damage, but the woman seemed paralyzed from the waist down. They had moved another bed in Irryelda's room for her parents, but often she would spend the night alternating between screams and groans. Not that night, however. The shelter was silent, and that was the main reason why all her apprentices fell asleep in the kitchen right after supper.

Rantha closed the book written by a certain Healer Colley of Founder's Breach. "Of Blood and Lineage," the cover read but she had yet to find something that would confirm her theory or expand it. Healer Colley was convinced that the inhabitants of the Silver Lands either had the blood of the Salurites or the blood of Rohdron the Skeleton, for the First Wardens were not to mingle with the other two groups. Colley seemed convinced that over time the two types of blood mixed to the point they made the human body too frail and unable to fight many illnesses, such as the fever and the Violet Delusion, but even less serious conditions often led to death, like the berries that covered people's skin, turning them into swollen, itchy creatures filled with pus. Colley's theory didn't sit well with Rantha as the book seemed to have been written after the Crimson Crystal Wars, a period where many wished to believe in the existence of an upper group or at least avoided reproducing with those who lived across the Rough Rill.

The ebony woman put the book down, stretching her legs to hear her knees pop. She was ready to try and catch some sleep when she heard soft knocks on the front door. Rising to her feet, she made sure not to step on cracking wood to let her apprentices sleep. Engulfed in a wool shawl, Rantha slowly opened the door, holding her breath at the sight of a man she didn't think she would see for a long time.

Opherus Goldsnout exhaled softly, his breath coming out in a large puff of air that clouded his vision. His short beard framed his blue lips, and his skin looked so translucent, his freckles disappeared.

"Opherus, come in," Rantha pressed. "You're going to freeze in this weather."

He walked in immediately, bringing some snow inside when he tapped the front of his boots against the floor. His back hurt from the cramps caused by the cold.

"I thought you would be gone for much longer," Rantha whispered as she locked the door. "The way you phrased it last time made me think so. Not that the past moon wasn't a long period," she caught herself rambling.

Opherus turned around the moment she placed a hand on his shoulder, and his once lively eyes were void of any emotion.

"Is everything well?"

She thought he was falling forward when he hunched his back and threw his arms around her skinny body. Rantha held her breath again, slowly inching her arms around the man's shoulders. Opherus clung to her as though his life depended on it, and she cupped the back of his head. He was cold, extremely cold. His clothes were coated with a thin veil of frost, and the plates he wore felt like ice against her body. She felt something wet where her neck met her shoulder, and she realized that Opherus was crying.

"I'm sorry," he mumbled, letting go of her but not quite looking at her face. "It was out of place."

Rantha's lips parted but she couldn't find the words. Her hands found his cheeks, frozen to the touch and wet by tears. Opherus finally peered at her in shame, and she offered him a small smile. "It was not," she whispered back.

She rose on her tiptoes, and her lips brushed lightly against his thin ones. She closed her eyes at the feeling, wondering if he closed his too. It didn't last very long, but her heart thumped inside her chest, and as their lips parted, she rested the round tip of her nose against his cheek. Rantha felt his hands tighten around her waist, and the following hug he tugged her into felt more intimate than the first one.

Chapter XXIX

Powerless

"The soup is good." Rantha put her empty bowl on the night table, offering him a small smile. It was his third serving already. Opherus hadn't said much since his arrival, and she wasn't sure he wanted to talk in the first place. She brought him upstairs to avoid waking up the others, offering him a small room with no window. The single candle that served as lighting cast flickering shadows around them and made him look paler than he was. His large eyebags suggested he hadn't slept much lately, but she couldn't judge him for that.

She picked a glass of water from the tray placed on the floor, and he drank it all quickly. "There is a family here," she spoke. "They are from Three Crosses. The woman was touched by the fog but she seems to be showing signs of recovery. Fewer visions." Opherus didn't look at her. "Her parents survived from it too," she added. "I am trying to find out if their blood is what makes them more resistant." She licked her lips, frowning at his lack of response. "Opherus."

"Forgive me," he whispered, lifting his head to finally look at her. "You must think I came here only to seek refuge from the snowstorm and for the free food."

She placed a hand on his. "That is not what I think."

"We rode into Wilderose. I don't know where they came from exactly, I don't know why we didn't see them but they were there. Those women… I don't know what to believe in anymore," he admitted, never looking away. "Witches, fays, whatever they are, they killed him and the only reason I am alive is that a woman who knew about them was on a hunt and more prepared than we were.

"I don't think I've ever felt this useless, Rantha," he told her as his voice faltered. "I keep repeating myself that I did all I could with the information I had but it's a lie. When we train to become surveillants, the first rule you have to remember is that you don't go anywhere on your own. You must be two when you're on official duty. And if you sense danger, you fight with your back against the other's back because only then do you have full vision, full control. I turned my back, Rantha; I hoisted him up, tried to drag him away when I should have told Old Martita and Sarkis to take him while I covered them.

"I failed."

She felt her eyes sting with tears the more he went on. Her other hand cupped his cheek. "You wanted to save him. You acted upon instinct. You are good," she insisted, emphasizing every word.

Opherus squeezed the hand on his cheek hard. "I am a mess. I wanted to find the person who butchered those girls, and I didn't. I wanted to find the one who killed Yenny, and I didn't. What do I do now?" he asked with a raucous voice. "Do I go after the chief's murderers? Where do I find them exactly? Who do I bring along?" he ranted. "I am clueless. Powerless. I do want to be good," he told her as an angry tear escaped his right eye. "I wanted to come back here and ask you to spend the rest of your life by my side but there is no reason as to why you would accept, is there?"

Rantha choked on a sob, wet lips briefly grazing his. "I can't," she breathed out. "I want to, but I can't."

He laughed dryly. "See? I was right. For once."

She shook her head vehemently. "You don't understand. Sir Loys wanted me to stay here, to find a cure," she explained, sniffling. "He might have treated me as a person but I am a slave bought by the Rosenbanes and if one day Lady Eloisa, or her children after her, decide to take over Bane's Keep, I am not sure the Illusion Shelter will still stand. I have to do my part before that happens. I owe Sir Loys that."

He turned his head to plant a kiss on the palm of her hand. "You don't owe anybody anything. You are a human being, not cattle," he insisted. "You can't be sold; you can't be bought. Do you understand?" Opherus retorted, his narrowed eyes glaring into hers when she didn't seem to agree.

Rantha gifted him a grateful smile. "Let me find a cure, Opherus. I know I am close. And then I will be more than delighted to spend the rest of my life by your side and have…" She laughed out loud. "And have dozens of kids with freckles with you."

His face relaxed at that, and he found himself laughing at the idea as well. He pulled her into a hug, his hands cradling her head under his chin. Opherus held her tight against his chest, so tight she could feel his heartbeat against her skin. He brushed her mane with his fingers as his back rested against the overused pillows on the bed. He wished he got to that every night, but that wasn't quite alright. Before his hands could wander down her back, he gently pushed her away, kissing her forehead.

"You should go get some rest," he whispered.

Rantha scanned his face, her fingers tracing the hem of the bedsheets. "I could stay if you want."

The officer pursed his lips and took both her hands in his. "That wouldn't be wise, Miss Rantha. If you were to do that, I doubt I'd be ever able to leave your side again."

Her cheeks suddenly felt wildly hot, and she pulled away to grab the tray on the floor. She stood up slowly, a feeling of excitement and anticipation fluttering inside her chest. "Goodnight, Opherus," she said quietly.

He looked calmer, and he inhaled deeply. Opherus tilted his head to the side, his light green eyes fixed on her. "Goodnight."

Opherus Goldsnout left the following morning. He found out that Rantha hadn't gone to sleep at all, preferring to tend to his horse and pack some heavier clothing for him as well as food, as if he wouldn't get either by the time he reached the Surveillance's headquarters. They enjoyed a simple, silent breakfast in the company of her remaining apprentices, and she accompanied him outside to watch him leave on his horse at a slow pace. The only words he said to her were that they would see each other soon enough, and Rantha remained by the door even long after he left. She perfectly knew that Zurzon was watching her from where he stood in the hallway, although he should have been changing Irryelda's bandages and checking on her.

Rantha turned around cautiously, disliking the smug smile on the tanned man's face. The man's long straight hair was pulled back in a low ponytail, and his arms were crossed over his chest. "What is it?" she finally asked, shutting the door.

"You know what," Zurzon replied with a raw accent.

"I am afraid I don't," she insisted, rubbing her arms as she felt shivers course through her body.

"You should leave with him. He loves you and you love him," he stated plainly. "Leave this shit place and go to the capital."

She lowered her gaze almost instantly. "I can't do that."

"You can," he insisted as Opherus would. "There is nothing here since Sir Loys passed away, only death and crazy people moaning at night. I would understand if you left. Everyone would," he added before turning heels, heading straight upstairs.

✳✳✳

If there was one thing Fantine had always abhorred, it was the lighting in the meeting room of the Council of Steel. She wished the chandelier was replaced with a bigger one that could hold more candles. The room faced away from daylight and having to squint her eyes to properly see the people sitting at the rectangular table quickly gave her a headache. She took her seat next to the head of the table, across from Milefried, the Silver Master. Next to him, Healer Martus was staring at her, looking more displeased than ever. She guessed it had something to do with the way she ignored his advice last time, but the blue-eyed warrior couldn't care less at that moment. Her lord's portrait had been hung earlier that day next to the previous lord's, and as she sat straight in her black armor, Fantine silently convinced herself that Lord Tithan's death would not diminish her authority in the council.

The seat next to her was empty. It was reserved for the Mayor of Edgemere, but Hamley Silverworm never arrived in Strongshore. Tesfira

Lionhelm could fill his shoes in such meetings, however, the curly-haired woman was nowhere to be seen. The three members of Tithan Lionhelm's Council of Steel sat in silence as they waited for two other people to make their presence known, ignoring each other profusely. Fantine's right leg was shaking and her back still hurt from the fall. She glanced at the door impatiently. She truly hated the lighting, she thought again.

The door was pushed open by a guard, and the three councilors exchanged surprised glances upon seeing Lord Lovel Riverguard enter, followed by the one man who always presided the council yet didn't reside in Strongshore. Algar Irwine wasn't a tall man, and his simple garments were a clear indication of his lowborn status, but he carried himself in a way that suggested otherwise. He was neither lean nor chubby, and the mop of grey hair on top of his head was of the same color as his eyes. His large, flat nose was bigger than his mouth, and his very tanned skin suggested he spent a lot of time under the sun. A thick silver chain hung from around his neck, an even thicker key being the pendant that meant more than all of the councilors' roles in the Lionhelm household.

Irwine sat at the head of the table, while Lord Riverguard took a seat with nonchalance next to Milefried, whose eyes twitched uncomfortably. "We shall begin," Irwine announced, resting his palms on the surface of the table after arranging several sheets of paper.

"Excuse me," Fantine interrupted him straight away. "But why is Lord Riverguard here? If you don't mind me asking, my lord," she said, directing her glance at the blonde man.

Lord Lovel mockingly bowed his head at the warrior, although she should have been the one showing him respect. "The Holy Commander escorted Lady Tesfira to Edgemere to attend matters of high importance that I was asked to discuss in your presence," he explained. "As of today, I will be representing the Mayor of Edgemere and the Faith." Pleased at the councilors' aghast expressions, he drummed his fingers on the table to display his many rings. "Please, consider me as a mere colleague and not a lord for the duration of this meeting. I can't outvote any of you," he elaborated. "The master-at-arms, the noble healer, and the silver genius count as three votes, and Surveyor Irwine of Summerport counts as two."

"We don't need you to remind us of our procedure," Fantine pointed out, looking away.

Surveyor Irwine watched the exchange with little interest, nodding at Lord Lovel. "Very well. This is not a meeting I thought we would be holding for the next ten years but Lord Lionhelm passed away and we have yet to read his will. I sincerely hoped we'd only talk about regular administration," he began formally. Picking the quill pen near the center of the table, he was quick to take notes. "On the first dawn day of the eighth month of year sixty-two After the Creation of the Regency, Lord Tithan Lionhelm passed away," he spoke as he wrote. "The present meeting is taking place three days after the event.

"As Surveyor of Summerport, my report consists of the assessment of a peaceful situation and renowned prosperity in the city. Silver Master?"

Milefried's body shook nervously as he tried not to stutter. "The southern lands count a working population of six million lives," he said without needing any notes, knowing his numbers by heart. "As the regulations state, we split the ten months of the year into four instances of tax collection, every two and a half moons. As of today, the working population deposited a total of eighteen million silvers in the Lionhelm's Treasury. It has always been Lord Tithan's wish to transfer eight million silvers to the Regency's Treasury. That duty can be fulfilled."

"Healer Martus?" the surveyor went on without looking up to keep writing.

The round man's thick eyebrows knitted together. "No owls from the southern cities have reported any illnesses that would be of great concern," he answered. "House Lionhelm has been faring well, aside from Lord Tithan's cough. It is Grandmaster Rodbertus' opinion, backed by the physicians' statements that Lord Tithan's condition could have been a consequence of his extended stay in foreign lands."

Irwine raised an eyebrow at that. "After so many years?"

Martus nodded briefly. "Lord Tithan left a message for Regency. We found it in his observatory room. It seems he was researching his condition lately. The physicians seemed to agree with the theory that the symptoms of certain ailments can be experienced over time."

"That isn't reassuring at all," the surveyor commented. "Master-at-Arms?"

Fantine cleared her throat. "The Lionhelm forces are in a deplorable state," she said flatly. "Lord Tithan had Lord Thaesonwald in charge of supervising the encampment of Summerport but Lord Thaesonwald himself wasn't a great fighter, let alone an acceptable teacher. His son, Lord Tiran, is even worse in that aspect. I was in charge of forming the elite myself, but every good fighter was sent to the Regency to follow Lord Angefort's commands. Truthfully, many moons have passed since the Secretary of the Regency's last report." Her eyes met the malicious stare of Lord Lovel, and Fantine held her head a little higher.

Irwine stopped scribbling to take a better look at her. "That is not good news at all."

"The understatement of the century," Lord Lovel butted in. "Gladly, these are times of peace."

"Do I sense a bit of sarcasm, my lord?" Fantine asked.

"If I may," Lovel said, earning a nod from the surveyor. "The Mayor of Edgemere has made it his mission to eradicate the Oracle's Faith. He burned the temple of the city-port along with all the Angels of Steel and the holy captains assigned to it. The Faith is most undoubtedly worried and I fear that Edgemere is less inclined to follow the rule of Strongshore."

"Thank you all," Algar Irwine said, carefully choosing his next words. "It is under this premise that I must ask you what the Council of Steel thinks of suggesting to the new Lord of Strongshore. Once Lord Tiran holds a speech at the feet of Alatros the Red's statue the council needs to provide a plan of action to tackle these issues, mainly the military one."

"The new lord," Lovel cut in. "Or lady."

"I beg your pardon?"

His eyes sparkled. "What if Lord Tithan's last will surprises us all and Lady Tecla turns out to be his chosen heir?"

Fantine's lips curved up slightly at the idea. "Lady Tecla was always our lord's golden child. But she is a child." Before he could add anything, she went on, "I am sure we would all be delighted to serve Lady Tecla, but quite frankly, it seems unlikely that she will succeed him. With Lord Thaesonwald's death, Lord Tiran is the first in the line of succession. Lord Tithan never mentioned anything that would go against this."

"Not to mention Lord Tiran named Lord Tylennald his successor, were he not to have children of his own," Healer Martus reminded Lovel. "If Lord Tithan's will were to state otherwise, we would find ourselves in an unpleasant situation."

"Not quite," Irwine argued. "I was told by Lady Voladea that Lady Tecla is betrothed to one of the Sons of Ferngrunn. If she could and wanted to contest the current line of succession, the southerners wouldn't agree so easily with the idea of being ruled by the Sand Towers." Frowning at

Fantine, the grey-eyed man asked, "The state of our navy?"

The red-haired warrior exhaled loudly. "I would have to speak with the captains, although I doubt that they are in a worse state than our foot soldiers," she commented dryly.

Lord Lovel leaned back in his seat. "There is one part that doesn't convince me," he told the councilors. "Lady Tecla was, as you said, Lord Lionhelm's golden child. Yet, she left Strongshore immediately after his death, almost as if she was forced to." Sensing their discomfort, he continued, "Isn't that a clear indication that someone in this palace knows something about our late lord's will?"

Healer Martus made a noise in the back of his throat. "Accusations."

"Suggestions," Lovel corrected him with a suave voice, rubbing his chin.

"We shouldn't be envisioning little girls plotting wars against their homeland," Martus pointed out offendedly. "And even if it were to come to that," he paused, leaning forward on his elbows, "we have more ships and can sink their fleet. And if they were to travel by foot, the ridiculous infantry of the Sand Towers can't cross the Fog Lands without perishing, and even if they managed to, the Regency and Courtbridge stand in the way; unless you decide to change that. It wouldn't be the first time a Riverguard turns his back on the Lionhelms."

Lord Lovel laughed to himself, glancing at the ceiling.

"Enough," Surveyor Irwine ended their banter. "Silver Master Milefried, kindly send a formal invitation to Lord Angefort for the will reading. If he doesn't answer within the next dawn days, Lord Tiran will be officially invested with the powers of the Lord of Strongshore."

Milefried nodded frantically, and Fantine watched him hurry out of the meeting room. While she agreed with the surveyor, Lord Lovel's words were deeply ingrained in her brain, and the more she thought about it, the more it seemed likely that the young lady had been forced away from her home. She hadn't seen Lady Tecla's servants either, as if they all vanished with Lord Tithan's last breath.

She heard Algar Irwine speak, but she couldn't focus. She had sworn an oath to Lord Tithan, and she wasn't sure whom her loyalty belonged to anymore. As Fantine raised her head, she noticed that Lord Lovel's lopsided smile was solely directed at her.

❋❋❋

The cell was constantly dark. There was no way of making anything out. The permanent darkness was enough to drive anyone mad, coupled with the stench, the humidity, and the haunting noises that could be heard in the recesses of the keep. Lyzon had never been there before; she had only heard of where offenders were sent after thievery or assault. She never thought she would ever end up in a cell herself. She knew there was someone else behind the same bars, but it wasn't Fran. He would have said something already, instead of staying silent for so long. It was someone who breathed heavily and never moved. It made her feel uneasy and anxious; she could never sleep. And she was hungry. Licking her chapped lips, she wondered if she would have to drink her urine before someone decided to bring her water.

Her mind could only focus on one thing; Tecla's crying face as Lady Voladea ordered the guards to take her and Lyzon to the equivalent of the Pit of Torture. Lyzon screamed as she was dragged to the keep. She tried to fight as well but to no avail. The guards were too tall, too strong, or maybe it was her who lacked the strength to bite their ears off and run back to her little girl who was being shipped away like a slave.

A flame burned in the distance, and she heard two guards walk down the stone steps. Lyzon crawled towards the bars, curling her fingers around the lock. She winced as light filled the narrow corridor, and she watched as one of the guards used his torch to light the others before they rounded another wall.

"They are about to torture someone," the prisoner she shared the cell with spoke. "Don't mind the screaming. These two you just saw are the most degenerate of all guards. They have nothing better to do."

It was a woman, Lyzon realized. Moving to take a better look, her heart nearly stopped. The woman's pale face was as white as snow, and her ebony hair looked a lot like Lyzon's. She wore expensive silks of a black color, but she was dirty and dangerously slim. If it wasn't for the seal on her necklace, Lyzon would have never recognized her. The glaring strige was the clear indication that she was Gwethana Lionhelm née Montel, Lord Tiran's mother.

"Is it Fran?" Lyzon dared ask.

"No. They don't harm those who served the Lionhelms," Lady Gwethana replied. "Why are you here?" Before Lyzon could answer, Gwethana waved at her dismissively. "So, they got rid of Little Tecla and sent her mother to die. It seems to be a pattern these days."

"You know?" Lyzon asked in disbelief. "And to think that I lied for fourteen years while everyone knew."

"I don't know about everyone," the Lady of Three Crosses retorted. "I am a mother. I know how mothers look at their children, and you are bad at hiding it. Did Lord Tithan die? I can't imagine another reason why they managed to send you down here unpunished."

Lyzon nodded, her eyes dropping. "Lady Tecla was sent to the Sand Towers. Why are you here?"

"I am a hostage," the lady answered. "With me here Lady Voladea and her favorite son can manipulate Tiran however they like. They pinned the murder of Thaesonwald on me."

"Murder?"

"They say someone smothered him. To be honest, I wish I was the one who did it. That man was a bastard."

Lyzon scooted back towards the lock. Her eyes were fixed on the light the torches emanated as if to suck in the flames. "There has to be a way out," she whispered, staring at the dirt under her fingernails. "There has to be."

"There is one," Lady Gwethana acquiesced. "Death."

The two women stared at each other, and Lyzon wasn't sure what the older woman meant. She swallowed hard. Lady Gwethana hadn't mentioned death in a resolutive manner, and that confused her. A loud shriek of pain echoed through the keep, and Lyzon jumped, her eyes darting in the direction the guards walked in. Lord Tiran's mother wasn't lying about the torture part.

"I need to get out of here, but they will never let me unless they believe I am you and that you are dead."

Lyzon wasn't following. Narrowing her dark eyes at the woman, she asked, "Do you plan on killing me, my lady?"

Gwethana's trembling hands reached behind her back, and Lyzon heard the sound of laces being tugged. "We trade places, Lyzon," she said, running her hands over the dirty floor and smearing dirt across her face. "You wear my clothes and I wear yours. Once we pretend you died of either starvation or something else, they will throw your body in the sea. They don't bother with simple people. This is the lowest level of the palace; I can swim to shore but not in these clothes. Yours are lighter," she reasoned in a hushed tone.

It was ridiculous, Lyzon thought. "You seem to forget that we look and sound very different, my lady."

"We have time to fix that. The Montel accent isn't that hard. After some days, we'll be so dirty and dehydrated that they won't be able to tell us apart. Once I find Tiran I can get you out of here," she promised, looking Lyzon in the eyes. "Can you trust me?"

Lyzon's entire body was shaking. "I can trust you; I don't think I trust your plan, my lady. How do you know they'll even keep us in the same cell?"

Gwethana smiled faintly, shaking her head. "The other cells are full and they're all men. They put us here because they have no other choice. Let us hope the two demented guards don't torture anyone to death before we are done." Extending an arm, she asked, "Agreed?"

Lyzon held the lady's hand, bringing Gwethana's knuckles to her forehead as a sign of submission. "Yes, my lady," she answered.

Trying was better than withering away powerlessly, wondering what would happen to Tecla on the northeastern coast with no one by her side.

✳✳✳

Chief Eleres' house looked nothing like Goldsnout would have imagined. He wasn't even sure this was ever the chief's house, considering the poor state in which the house was kept. There was no other property behind the central inn of Rainier's

End, so the little stone hut had to be the one Eleres mentioned to him. Goldsnout kicked the muddy pile of snow in front of the half-broken wooden door, and he knocked three times before shoving his gloved hand under his cloak. The snowstorm had passed, but the freezing wind still blew.

No one answered, so he knocked again. He wondered how many years had passed exactly since the chief visited his family. Surely, they couldn't be all dead, the young officer reasoned. The chief's belongings were tucked under his left arm, weighing on him more than the feeling of guilt he had yet to shake off. Goldsnout waited in the cold, wondering if he should just head back to the capital when his impulse kicked in. Pushing the door open as he tried his best not to further break it, Goldsnout wasn't prepared for the scene that awaited him.

The single room looked like the one he grew up in back in Limemeadow, only dirtier and darker. He thought such houses existed only in Jamys' Yard. "Hello?" he breathed out, scanning the poorly lit room. "I am Officer Opherus Goldsnout, Regency's Surveillance," he introduced himself.

"Come in," a weak voice answered. "Oh, you already have."

Sitting in front of a nearly spent fireplace, a frail man wrapped in bandages from head to toe didn't even bother looking at him. Goldsnout could barely see his eyes, the only visible feature being his thin, wrinkled lips. He closed the door behind him, taking a hesitant step forward.

"I was told this is where Chief Thierry Eleres' family lived. Forgive me if I was mistaken."

The man craned his neck slowly, his glassy eyes looking in the direction Goldsnout's voice came from. "Thierry? What happened to Thierry?" he asked, his voice cracking.

So, it was the chief's family house, Goldsnout thought. He took a long stride towards the bandaged man, carefully placing the chief's folded uniform in the relative's lap. "Chief Eleres died fulfilling his duties as the Head of the Surveillance. May he find peace in the Oracle's arms."

The man's glassy eyes never looked down, and Goldsnout realized he was blind. Covered hands patted the fabric of the emerald uniform, fingers tracing the embroidered coat-of-arms of the Regency, and soft, pained sobs escaped the man's lips. He repeated the chief's name several times, cradling the clothes as if he were holding an infant, and his body rocked back and forth. Goldsnout looked away, finding no more tears to shed.

"What happened to him?"

Clearing his throat, the red-haired officer settled for a plain response. "An ambush. The mission was to identify the authors of unnamable crimes but we were outnumbered."

"Thierry," the man whined painfully. "Nothing was ever spared. They took even him."

"I reckon you were very close," Goldsnout whispered, kneeling before the man and placing a hand on his forearm. "I wish I had done more to save him."

"Don't," the man reassured him. "Thierry was always stubborn and hot-headed. And I loved him for it."

His words left Goldsnout speechless. His mouth opened and closed a few times, patting the man's arm.

"Thank you, Officer, for bringing back his uniform."

"May I ask your name?"

"I am just an old blind man who is too old to be alive still. My name is Loys," the man answered. "Loys Rosenbane."

Goldsnout nearly fell flat on his bottom. "Sir Loys Rosenbane?" He couldn't believe it. Rantha told him the man died a long time ago due to the Violet Delusion and yet, the nearly mummified man before him claimed to be the knight of Bane's Keep.

"Once they called me that." Sir Loys ran his hand over the emerald fabric again, as if to find some comfort.

"You were supposed to be dead," Goldsnout whispered, flabbergasted. "Miss Rantha said—"

"You know Rantha," the old knight said with the hint of a smile. "What a sweet little girl she was, just like her mother. Oh, I loved them both so much, as if they were my children," he rambled nostalgically, tilting his head back. "Her mother tried everything to cure me, but it left only scars all over my body. I was afraid to scare the little girl away and what kind of knight can a man be if he can't see nor wield his sword? It was better to leave me here."

Rising to his feet, Goldsnout held the man by the shoulders. "You have to tell her you survived," he pressed; his grip firm. "She is still looking for a cure. Survivors are precious to her research."

Sir Loys shook his head weakly. "Leave an old man to die, will you?" he spoke breathlessly. "Memories are all I have left. Good memories. With Thierry, with Rantha; I don't want these memories to be ruined. I don't want anyone to see me like this. It would ruin their memories of me as well, and that is an awful way to leave this world."

Goldsnout let out a deep breath. His throat tightened and he felt the tip of his ears burn. Stepping back, he walked away in silence, shutting the door before he dropped to his knees and scooped some snow in his gloved hands before splashing it over his forehead and cheeks. He pressed a trembling fist to his lips, fighting the urge to run back to the shelter to tell Rantha everything. He couldn't, he repeated over and over again in his head. Chief Eleres had respected Sir Loys' wish to not be seen in such conditions and he had to do the same.

Ignoring the curious stares he received from the people in the streets, Goldsnout looked up at the skies with swollen, red eyes and his lips stretched into a toothy smile as he laughed loudly and nervously, tears running down the sides of his head and past his ears. The sobs mixed with the spams of laughter he couldn't control and his voice broke.

"May you be damned, Chief," he whispered heartfully. "May you be damned."

Chapter XXX

Hues of Purple

Lion's Glory was a massive, fully-rigged ship with three masts. The sails were all of a light blue color that mirrored the clear sky, the flying jib, as well as the inner and outer ones, displaying the Lionhelm arms. It was a well-known fact that the ship belonged to Terrel Lionhelm, as it had been Lord Tithan's gift to his grandson when the latter came of age, but ever since Terrel left Strongshore for Founder's Breach, the ship had become another trade vessel of the South, often found navigating across the depths that separated Summerport from the Red Continent and the islands of the Zalejos Depths. Theliel had decided to keep that information to himself when he convinced Rollant, the owner of the Shattered Ambry, that Lion's Glory was as good of a bet as a southern warship. The captain set sail three nights ago, much to Theliel's disappointment. The harbor of Summerport was no longer in sight. Theliel leaned against the railing of the main deck, ignoring the dubious stare of Sarkis, who sat on a barrel of ale left behind by one of the crew members. They had just returned from the hold below the orlop deck, and saying that Sarkis wasn't pleased by what he saw was an understatement.

Theliel bit hard on his lower lip before glancing at the man he considered a friend. "Are you going to say something?"

Sarkis held his hands together, never diverting his gaze from the endless sea ahead. "When you said you'd fix everything, I didn't expect any of this." With a judging glare, he asked, "What is going to happen now?"

"That's a lot of questions for someone who should be glad we finally left," Theliel pointed out with a sigh.

Sarkis rubbed his nose nervously. "I know you lied to me," he muttered. "I met a surveillant."

"What? I told you to lay low."

"It's not like I wanted to," he quickly countered. "You don't know how much crap I went through in your absence. For starters, you could have told me Tita was your aunt, or whatever she was. But you refuse to tell me how we ended up with all those silvers in the hold, so why do I even expect you to tell me anything at all?" he commented bitterly, looking away. "That officer told me there was never a report about me. And yet, when you showed up at the tavern in Silverholde, you told me all the material for the play was requisitioned."

Theliel's face softened. "You can't honestly forge the seals of the Regency for a play without authorization," he reasoned. "The whole play couldn't possibly take place; you would have simply gone through a lot more trouble." When Sarkis remained silent, Theliel walked up to him. "I didn't think telling you about Old Martita was necessary. She doesn't consider herself a Lionhelm."

"Didn't," Sarkis corrected him. "She is dead."

Theliel nodded slowly, coming to sit next to Sarkis. "I am sorry."

"Look, I don't want to pry, but I'm not sure leaving was a good idea. Tita mentioned a lot of weird stuff about those women, the Rosencircle, and I can't think of anyone else doing that to her. She tried to hunt them down after they butchered Pat, the big man who lived with her, you know? That's how we met the two surveillants in Wilderose; they were being attacked too. The chief died," Sarkis revealed, his voice pained. "And then, in Edgemere—"

Theliel frowned. "Chief Eleres is dead?"

"—your sister's husband, I don't remember his name… He burned a bunch of religious people alive. What's going to happen now? Your father is dead."

Sarkis watched in silence as the young Lionhelm's hazel eyes became clouded with a million thoughts. He knew very well that Theliel was thinking of either his older or younger sister, perhaps even both. Sarkis himself was worried about them, and he didn't even really know them. He placed a chubby hand on his friend's shoulder, fingers squeezing. Theliel had wanted to wait for Tecla to show up at the harbor in Summerport, but they waited and stalled the captain with no result. The youngest Lionhelm never joined them, and they left Theliel's homeland in the middle of the night. It hadn't been an easy choice, but Sarkis understood Theliel's urgency the moment they climbed down the ladder that took them to the hold. He had never seen so many silvers. A part of him wondered if that was Theliel's inheritance or personal fund, or if the man's reluctance in riding back to Strongshore was because he may have stolen the money from his own family. Then again, it made little sense. As far as Sarkis knew, Theliel spent most of his time in the capital and not in Strongshore.

    The sound of footsteps approaching the main deck interrupted his thoughts, and Sarkis turned around to see the captain of the ship nodding at them. He had never seen a more intimidating man before, aside from Lord Tithan. Captain Wulfscoe was a towering human with broad shoulders and thighs so strong that his pants clung to his body like a second skin. A golden saber was strapped to his waist and an even brighter eagle was perched on his right pauldron. The bird's feathers were deep ebony that faded to ivory around the tips, but what mesmerized both Theliel and Sarkis was the metal that shielded the eagle's head. It was a jeweled crown that made the bird look like it had horns, and the rubies that adorned it were as red as the eagle's eyes. Captain Wulfscoe himself had bright crimson eyes and dark skin, his textured hair staying perfectly in place as the wind blew and inflated the sails.

"Captain," Theliel greeted him politely.

"Lord Theliel, I came to inform you that Lion's Glory is no longer headed to Khar'had." His voice was a growling one. "Word has spread about your father's death and it seems that the northern regions of the Red Continent are experiencing some turmoil. Trade ships from the Silver Lands can no longer deck."

Theliel paled, licking his trembling lips. "What's the plan?"

"East is the plan."

"The Zalejos Depths? Is it safe?"

Wulfscoe made a chirping sound, and he glanced at his eagle. "Veadecta," he called. The eagle flapped its wings, taking flight instantly. "Worry not, my lord. This one has enough friends to know trouble before it occurs."

The moment he was out of sight, Sarkis leaned in. "Where did you find such a scary captain?"

Theliel stood up, rubbing his forehead and ignoring Sarkis' question. The islands of the Zalejos Depths were not part of his plan. Khar'had was the place where he planned on bringing his idea to life. He didn't expect his father's authority to be the only thing that kept the Red Continent and its northern regions at bay, and Tiran wasn't about to step up, Theliel knew that much. He only hoped the red troops never crossed the Tinted Bay like they tried to in the past.

"Theliel?"

"I wanted Khar'had to become another seat of power for my family," he whispered with a downcast expression marring his features. "That is what the silvers are for," he admitted. "I had great plans; you know? Khar'had is wealthy and welcoming, my father told me. They are very much dedicated to the arts as well; you could have had your opera."

Sarkis' eyebrows shot up, and a warm feeling filled his chest at the revelation. He walked up to Theliel and rested his back against the railing of the deck. Truthfully, he had never sailed before, and he was starting to get a little sick, but his friend seemed too worried for Sarkis to be thinking of himself at that moment. "You saved all that money for this, didn't you?" he asked quietly.

Theliel held his breath, feeling the salty wind on his face as the ship moved faster. "I wish I did, Sarkis."

✳✳✳

"Back for the celery, aren't ya?"

Jascha looked up, catching the greengrocer's toothless smile. "Pardon?"

"I gave you celery last time, for your pretty mare."

He offered him a small smile. "Sure."

He watched as the old man stuffed a paper bag with the fruits Jascha requested and the celery he never wanted in the first place. His feet were cold from standing outside for so long; the snow never seemed to stop falling in Silverholde. Jascha walked away from the stand, his mind going over the events in the blacksmith shop. He was right back at the beginning, or somewhere close to it. He wanted to blame both Rantha and her little apprentice, but he knew he couldn't. He walked towards the only fountain that had been built in the forum and sat on its steps. Crows were perched on top of it, but no water flowed from it. The vase was filled with frozen water and a few cracks could be seen where the birds tried to beak at it. Jascha watched the simple children roll in the snow, but there weren't as many as before, and he could only guess it was because of all the bodies that were transported outside the city walls daily. Winter claimed many lives, and it didn't discriminate.

  Biting into an apple that wasn't ripe at all, Jascha chewed on it for a moment before spitting it out and throwing the fruit away. It was disgusting, he thought to himself before looking in the distance, nearly missing the little girl that ran in his direction to pick up the apple and cradle it against her chest. Jascha put the paper bag down, reaching inside his pocket to throw a silver at her.

  "What's your name?" he asked plainly.

  "Mott," the amber-eyed girl replied shyly.

  "Will you do me a favor?" Jascha asked her, diverting his gaze to nod at the two young surveillants who stood by the entrance of the forum. "Will you tell the men over there you heard a noise in Aalart's blacksmith shop? It's behind the opera," he told her, handing her the groceries he just bought. "You can keep it," he added softly, watching the way her eyes widened and she smiled with rotting teeth at him.

 Little Mott quickly walked up to the two surveillants of the Regency, waving her hands and pointing in the direction of Melisentia's Opera, just as she was instructed. Jascha's nostrils flared as he watched the two young men immediately hop on their horses, their emerald capes flapping against the back of their mounts as they trotted away. Jascha followed them in silence, ignoring the way the little emaciated girl waved at him while hugging the food he gifted her. He hadn't returned to the shop since he left Rosewillow in there, but he doubted she took the time to retrieve Rosaleah's body. He had used over twenty nails to keep her in place. Jascha had been tempted to just retrieve his horse and either ride back to Rainier's End or leave for an entirely different place. He doubted there was anything useful he could find about the Rosencircle in the capital and if they weren't even targeting him, he didn't know where to go from there.

 By the time he arrived near the shop, the two officers were already inside. Jascha stood quietly around the corner, leaning against the door of the abandoned tavern. The loud noises coming from inside and the flow of curses he heard could only mean that the officers found the bodies and weren't sure how to unpin them. Jascha rested the back of his head against the wooden doorframe, waiting.

"By the Good Gods, what is this?" he heard one of them say. "Who would do this?"

"Shut it, Gulmont," the other chastised. "Aalart was one of the best blacksmiths in the city, if not the best. I can't believe this happened to him."

"What about the woman?" When the other officer didn't reply, Gulmont asked, "Longspire. Do you know her?"

"I'm not sure. She looks like the girl who works at Danyell's Athenaeum, but she's covered in so much blood… Wait, are these her clothes?"

Jascha heard more noise, and he figured they were going through the tools on the blacksmith bench. He had left Rosaleah's belongings on top of the utensils on purpose.

"There is a Regency coin in her leather pouch. Shit, Gulmont, it is her."

"Do you think they were lovers or something? I mean, this murder looks like some jealous suitor's doing."

"I need to get out of here," Lonsgpire decided. "This stench is making me gag."

The two officers stood outside the blacksmith shop, their faces pale and their knees shaking. The man who had to be Longspire held the Regency coin in his hand, taking deep breaths while his green-eyed colleague paced beside him, often glancing inside the shop as they left the door open.

"Does she have any family?" Gulmont asked. "Because, you know, they could receive a pension from the Regency."

"I don't know, maybe," the shorter officer replied, running a hand through his oily dark locks.

"We'd have to ask the Observatory Vault. Let's get these bodies out of here before they get completely disfigured by crows," he said, eyeing the dark-winged birds that sat on the roof.

"Let's hurry," Gulmont added, walking inside. "The new chief will be at the headquarters after midday and I don't want to leave a bad impression."

"I still can't believe that little prick is the new chief. Dunac, of all people?"

"Better than having Sir Sybbyl Nobleleaf as Chief Eleres' replacement. That woman breaks my back in training."

Jascha didn't need to hear more. Exhaling loudly, he walked away from Aalart's shop, dragging his feet through the snow as to not leave clear footprints. Unless another snowstorm was brewing, he was ready to leave the capital after getting some warm food at the Wild Skunk Rock. Perhaps, it was time to head back home, he thought bitterly. Home never truly felt like it, though he didn't have many options. It was either the Fog Lands or a warmer place to spend the rest of the winter at. Jascha knew that nobody expected him to return nor missed his glaring face. That alone was enough of a deterrent. A third option was to keep his promise to Rosaleah and find every fay he could to slaughter them, but that would mean roaming the lands aimlessly. Grandmaster Matillis wrote that the First Wardens were killed in the fire of Soleba; however, Wilderose still existed. It wouldn't be too farfetched to assume it was still where they gathered, Jascha thought to himself. Glancing at the faint sun rays that pierced through the grey clouds, he decided that he still had time to make up his mind.

Jascha looked away, missing the hues of purple that peeked through the smoky-colored coat that shielded the Heights.

✳✳✳

Purple clouds, Tecla thought as she looked in the direction of the black chain of mountains. The boat she sat on caressed the soft waves as the sailors and guards that escorted her rowed towards the shore while the two-masted ship of the Lionhelms was anchored in the distance. She didn't know how much time she spent at sea, but for someone who wasn't very used to it, she only felt sick enough not to consume the nutrients she needed. Her once round, rosy cheeks were sunken and pale, and her body had slimmed down notably. Tecla had been thrown in a luxurious cabin that she still hated, and she couldn't recall getting any real sleep in the bed that was big enough to accommodate three people. Every day and night she spent with her hands and face plastered to the window that faced the coast, watching as Strongshore became a faint dot in the horizon until it completely disappeared. Many other ships sailed from Summerport on the morning she was sent away, but hers was the only one headed for the northeastern coast.

Tecla glanced at her hands and touched the tresses that cascaded past her shoulders. Her nails were much longer and so was her hair. She could have been traveling for a month for all she knew. She never bothered to ask. The crew members who served her breakfast and supper never tried to be talkative, but in any case, all she could think of was her father. She hadn't even been allowed to attend his funeral, and then, there were Lyzon and Fran. Tecla didn't want to imagine what happened to them after they were taken. Were they prisoners? Were they sold? Could she even send an owl to find out? Would anyone answer? What about Theliel, did he come home looking for her? What happened when he didn't find her? She had so many questions she dared not to ask, and as the boat hit the shore, she jumped slightly.

  She fisted the front of her light, pale tangerine dress and looked at the small crowd that awaited her. The only familiar face was Mokr's, the youngest Son of Ferngrunn. He politely smiled at her, surrounded by bulky soldiers who wore only a short piece of pleated fabric around their lower bodies. Shield and spears and helmets completed their attire, but Tecla noted that some of them also wore pauldrons with the crossed hammers of the Sand Towers carved into them. She could only imagine that these men were generals, hence the slight difference. A large litter covered in colorful silks and large cushions waited for her, and Tecla frowned at the sight of almond-eyed slaves chained together who stood around the transport. They were supposed to carry her.

  One of the generals walked up to her, offering his forearm to help her climb out of the boat. She directed a confused glance at Mokr, who was quick to answer her silent question. "Men are not allowed to touch women or offer them their hand." Mokr's smile widened and he bowed his head in respect. "Lady Tecla, it is a pleasure to welcome you to the Sand Towers. I hope you traveled undisturbed."

She wet her lips, clearing her throat. "Thank you for your hospitality."

Mokr snapped his fingers, and one of the slaves promptly reached for the tray on the litter while another opened a casket of water and poured some in the chalice he was handed. Tecla accepted to take refreshment, wondering how they managed to keep the water from boiling under the scorching heat. The youngest Son of Ferngrunn accompanied her to the litter, and Tecla didn't mind the shade created by the tall, arched backrest. The slaves that didn't lift the litter stood close to her with large fans in their hands, creating a soft breeze. Mokr returned to his horse, a rather large ivory beast with big blue eyes. He kicked his mount into an easy pace to ride beside her, but Tecla didn't feel like exchanging words.

"May I ask what made you choose the Sons of Ferngrunn over every other house?"

"I didn't," she retorted.

"You will have plenty of time to adapt," the young man reassured her. "My older brothers are delighted to have you here. There are three handmaidens assigned to you, waiting for you in your bed-chambers. Our servants come from the islands of the Zalejos Depths, but I was told you were already used to them. They are quiet and work quickly."

Tecla's back stiffened, but she remained silent. She wanted to tell him that no one would replace Lyzon, but she doubted he cared about what she wanted.

"There are thirty guards on your floor and we purchased a cook who knows how to prepare southern meals. You can rest today as the ceremony in Hvallatr will take place only in the evening."

"The ceremony?"

Mokr's fawn eyes peered at her. "The Mothers of the Sanctified City perform a ritual called the Rebirth. Consider it to be a conversion. Your past sins are erased and you adopt the religion of the Sand Towers."

"Which is what, exactly?" Tecla asked in an offended tone.

"It's not too different from yours, except that we don't rely on an intermediary to spread the will of the Deities. No Oracle, nothing."

"And these Mothers? What are they, then?"

The blonde, tanned boy laughed at her boldness. "Our lawmakers, my lady."

They ascended the Sand Towers through an endless set of stairs that began at the wide gates on the shore and went all the way up the promontory. Tecla often heard the sound of a whip cracking whenever one of the slaves carrying her litter nearly missed a step, but whenever she tried to offer them a sip of water, she was glared at by the generals that followed Mokr, and the slaves kept their eyes glued to the steps shamefully. She saw what seemed to be a large city on top of the promontory, and given the size of the stone walls and the way they stretched behind the visible parts of the cliff, Tecla assumed that the Sand Towers were nearly as big as Summerport. Two towers, one being shorter than the other, poked at the clouds like Driazon pyramids she read about in one of Tomas' books, and their rust color reminded her of the Sons of Ferngrunn's skin. Plants of a vivid green shade rained down the towers, and exterior stairs connected the floors. Large torches lined the railings of the balconies and bigger pyres burned on each side of the tall metal doors.

Tecla's breath hitched in her throat as she looked away from the city and in the direction of the Dark Barrens. The desert looked infinite if it hadn't been for the large pool of black she saw, and the snow that kissed the skies in the distance. "What is that?"

Mokr followed her gaze. "That is the Sanctified City, Hvallatr. It's entirely built with volcanic stones, hence why it looks like a huge stain from here. Past the Dark Barrens, where you can see the snow, are the Avoryon Hills. The best mounts of the continent come from there."

"Does anyone live there?"

"Who knows anymore. Maybe some tribes survived after your ancestor butchered most of them. We don't usually venture that far. The horses themselves reproduce here."

She nodded, her stare already traveling to the purple hues she saw before. "The Violet Delusion."

Mokr looked at her uneasily. "Yes, Lady Tecla. Where the fog meets the clouds. Noirmont is visible from here."

"I wonder if anyone survived there. Where I come from, they say the fog destroyed nearly everything and everyone," she mused, realizing that she had been talking more than she intended.

"I'm sure they did survive, especially the Rochelacs. Why they lay low is a mystery to me," he admitted. "Those bastards are hard to kill. We would have already disposed of them otherwise. Everyone would have."

Tecla hunched her back, leaning in out of curiosity. "Because of their armies?"

"No," Mokr answered with a stern look. "Because they are a disease."

Mokr wasn't lying about the numbers when he mentioned her servants and the guards on her floor. The meeting with his older brothers, Thaum and Remm, was brief. The eldest Son of Ferngrunn spoke a few words in the modern tongue to her, then asked his youngest brother to translate his greetings and other polite sentences that Tecla was too tired to hear. She appreciated his kind approach; despite being a mountain of a man with piercing blue orbs and long matted locks, he didn't seem rough at all. His brother Remm, on the other hand, was the only one who never smiled and never addressed her properly. Tecla figured that the man probably didn't speak a word of the modern tongue. Just like the first time she saw them, they wore open jackets with snow-colored fur collars and bright britches. She wondered if this was their formal attire, or if they hadn't even bothered when they visited Strongshore. Either way, there were other questions she wanted to ask, but she wasn't sure the handmaidens would be able to answer them all.

After a steaming hot bath, the three women who looked nothing like Lyzon made her sit on a short wooden stool, her body covered only by a white sheet. They were indeed silent as each worked on a different part of her body. The eldest was busy at her feet while the youngest, who was probably Tecla's age, took care of the lady's nails. The third woman was trimming Tecla's hair and oiling it with calming scents. Tecla never smelled anything that sweet; she was curious to know the names of the plants that grew in the Sand Towers, but her eyelids fluttered closed with the soothing attention she was getting. Out of nowhere, the handmaiden at her feet part her legs gently, and Tecla jumped at the feeling of something extremely hot being spread over her leg.

"What are you doing?" she asked, panicked.

The handmaiden blinked at her. "Wax, my lady."

"Stop it," Tecla ordered her after the handmaiden peeled away a lot of hair.

The three women exchanged worried and confused looks. "My lady, we have to," the one who filed her nails whispered. "It is rule."

"It is rule," the one behind her repeated.

Tecla was instantly angry. "Who told you to do this?"

"No one," the handmaiden beside her replied. "It is rule, for Rebirth."

"Yes, Rebirth is possible only if we bring back your body to…" She paused, searching for words. "To when my lady was baby."

Tecla felt her stomach churn. They planned on applying wax all over her body. She stiffened as she felt more wax sliding on her right leg and she shut her eyes tight before the handmaiden ripped the hardened wax away. Exhaling loudly, she peeked at the most talkative of the trio and asked, "Is this going to happen often?"

"What my lady mean?"

"The waxing," Tecla said, wincing at another tug. Her skin was reddening by the minute. "Is it going to happen often, for example, for the wedding? Do you know when they plan on celebrating it?"

The almond-eyed woman frowned as she massaged the sweet oil on her nails and hands. "I not know ceremony. Sons of Ferngrunn have marriage very late after first child is born."

Tecla felt her heart stop. Gulping, she asked, "What do you mean?"

The handmaiden who was done brushing her long hair came into vision, and she put her hands on her hips. "Tradition, Lady Tecla. Only Son of Ferngrunn who puts baby inside has right to marry."

"You are saying…" Tecla couldn't believe her ears. With a frightened stare, she continued, "You are saying I am to sleep with all of them?"

"Maybe. Maybe not," the handmaiden replied. "If Thaum of Ferngrunn puts baby inside you he will be husband of my lady. We know after moon if my lady has no blood."

If she didn't bleed, Tecla thought. She had to bleed, she had to bleed, she had to bleed. "When?" she croaked out. "When are they going to start taking turns like animals?" she asked with a trembling voice.

"When Mothers of Hvallatr say time is right. Mothers know."

"Mothers know," the other two repeated, continuing to work on her appearance. "Mothers say the moon of woman shows when woman is ready."

The moon of the woman, Tecla repeated in her head. She glanced out of the window, watching the once calm waves become more violent. She wanted to go home. She wanted to swim home or drown; even begging Lady Voladea sounded better than going through what tradition in the Sand Towers commanded. She would crawl on her knees and kiss Lady Voladea's feet if it meant being betrothed to anyone else than those who based their unions on fertility. In the back of her mind, she could understand why they thought that way. A fertile couple meant the survival of their house; it was no wonder that the Sons of Ferngrunn still had the blood of Ferngrunn himself. Why no one told her about their ways was beyond her. As the handmaiden pulled the light cloth up to reveal her moon of the woman, readying more wax, Tecla refused to cry. She felt humiliated enough.

Chapter XXXI

Hope for Death

The water in the oval pool was scorching. It was all Tecla could think of as the wooden platform she lied on was lowered by rattling chains and she was dumped into the flaming breaths of the Sanctified City. She wanted to scream, but she reminded herself not to open her mouth as to not inhale and fill her lungs with scalding water. She wondered if her skin would be burnt; if she would be able to move after the ceremony. Tecla shut her eyes, letting her breath come out in small bubbles, as she tried to focus on something different, but everything around her faded to black; from the chanting of the Mothers to the cheering of the children and the generals, they were all too distant for her to hear. She felt the platform sink even further and her lips parted.

The deep green hue of the water surrounding her reminded her of the streams that escaped the eyes of the face carved on the entrance wall of the Sanctified City, Hvallatr. The city was small and built at the center of the Vale of the Gods, another wasteland of the Dark Barrens, where monstrous skulls would sometimes poke their heads out of the sand. The black walls that protected Hvallatr were lightened only by the two fighting statues above the main gates; Alatros' mace clashing against Ferngrunn's hammers, the symbol that remained throughout the centuries. But Ferngrunn was the only one revered as his old, beardy face and curl-framed forehead watched anyone who dared enter Hvallatr. He cried, he always did, as the streams filled a bigger pool, one held together by the skeleton of one big creature with no legs and no wings. The Serpent was said to have been a protector sent by the Deities against the Iathienar, for it would curl its entire body around the lands of sand, and the Iathienar would never be able to plant its talons in the Serpent's flesh. The Serpent was made of fire and thunder, as it was nothing more than a dragon of the Heights whose legs and wings had been removed as punishment for its rebellious and chaotic nature.

    Tecla heard the words that were spoken to her, but she couldn't understand them. It was the ancient tongue of the Sand Towers, she guessed, or perhaps it was even older. It could have been a dead language for all she knew, but the womanly voice was talking to her. Was it the Mother who performed the ceremony? She wasn't sure. The sound was all too clear in her ears. The water seemed greener, she thought as bigger bubbles of air escaped her nostrils until there was no more water. It was fire, one she had seen before. Gone were the pale women who guarded it, and her hands felt suddenly cold, as well as her feet. She blinked slowly as the crowd around her dissolved, leaving her in a cold forest engulfed in deep blue hues. The fire still burned, she could hear it, but it was no longer in sight. Embers flew past her, some even grazing her bare skin, though Tecla didn't flinch. Step after step, she walked into the dark blue nothingness. Someone else seemed to be walking towards her, but their footsteps were louder, heavier. It wasn't one person, she realized as a stretcher came into view. The four shadows carrying it she couldn't make out, but they stopped beside her. There was a small body lying on the stretcher, only partially covered by thin linen. The body was entirely charred, the dark bones clashing against the white cloth. However, it was the eyes that caused Tecla's jaw to drop. They were intact, and they were looking at her. Hands reached out for them, and she couldn't tell whether they were her hands or someone else's in her place, but she could feel the texture of the eyeball. It was hard and reminded her of one of those pickled vegetables that Lyzon would serve her for breakfast when she was little. Tecla's lips parted as she tried to say something, but all she felt were hands bringing the eyeball to her lips.

    Tecla's eyes snapped open, steamy air filling her lungs and she panted loudly as she tried to catch her breath. Her ears were ringing as her wide-open hazel eyes stared at the ceiling of the pantheon of the Mothers, with its spikes made of volcanic stone that threatened to rain down on her. She shrieked at the feeling of ice-cold sheets being wrapped around her naked body while those who watched cheered at the top of their lungs. Tecla's body shook as the Mothers covered her body and twisted her hair. They helped her sit up, their skinny arms wrapping around her waist. She caught the stare of the eldest Son of Ferngrunn, who nodded at her in silence, surrounded by his brothers and generals. They all wore the finest golden silks while their children sang a haunting melody that echoed through the temple. Mokr left his brother's side to stand closer to her as two Mothers carried a silver tray for her to use. There was a small vessel that looked like a teapot, and it seemed to have been made of porcelain. It was painted with representations of the Serpent curled around a large tree that reminded her of those umbrellas Lyzon would sometimes carry around when the sun was too hot in Strongshore. Three small cups were lined next to the pot, one empty, one stained with blue, and one stained with green. Tecla tried to stand up, but the Mother of Mothers walked around the platform and placed her thin fingers on Tecla's ankles.

  The Mother of Mothers stared into her eyes. She was so scrawny that the dark markings around her eyes and lips made her look inhuman. Her skin was wrinkled as well, but the Mother's hair was wavy and black. Not a single grey strand seemed to prove that she was older than dirt. Her long nails trailed up Tecla's legs, and the lady's body stiffened as she held her breath. From under the pale dress, no one could see it, but the Mother placed a fingertip between her inner lips and pressed hard against her flesh.

She stepped away as the room fell silent, and she turned around. "*Nraa mnonaa bigii,*" Tecla heard her say.

"She breeds," Mokr translated for her. "She is fertile," he continued as the Mother of Mothers spoke, making big gestures with her hands, which caused her dirty green robes to fly around her body. "Tonight," he said as his fawn eyes followed the woman's movements. "She who came from the South will drink the blood of the Deities, thus we shall know if the Heights graced us with their will."

The woman turned around to face Tecla, and her night eyes glanced at the tray while she spoke.

"Drink," Mokr translated again. "One sip for the Deities," he explained while the Mothers who held the tray poured the hot mixture into each cup. "One sip for the Sons and one sip for the Mothers."

Tecla reached out for the first cup with trembling hands. The moment the cup touched her lips, she remembered the terrible eyes she saw in her earlier dream. Or was it a dream? The liquid tasted bitter, although it smelled incredibly sweet. The blue one tasted slightly better, but she could still feel the bitterness on her palate. By the time she drank the last cup, Tecla felt like she was about to pass out if it weren't for the women holding her.

"Speak," Mokr interpreted once more. "You, who have drunk the Leaf of the Serpent, what do you see?"

Tecla's eyelids fluttered close and she arched her eyebrows in an attempt to keep her eyes open. She tried to focus on Mokr's voice, on Thaum's stare, and even on Remm's stoic expression. She looked at their matted locks, at the fur around their shoulders, but she couldn't see anything past it. She watched as the little children before her chanted again and she let go of the little strength she possessed.

Her body fell backward, and the Mothers laid her down softly as she shook feverishly. Tecla heard herself babble like a toddler who tried to learn how to speak, and all she saw was a blurry painting. She didn't recall the walls of the pantheon to be painted. They were black, and the arched windows pale green, but now she could see figures on them. Vivid green lights danced on the walls as she felt her hands lift the skull of the Serpent or a smaller version of it, and rest it on top of her head like a macabre crown. The skeleton of its body was trailing behind her, and all around her, bodies littered the ground. They were soldiers, she tried to say; dead soldiers littering the ground and the stairs of the towers. The sea level around the promontory was dangerously low, and shadows of winged beasts flew around her. Tecla closed her mouth when she heard Mokr's voice, and she understood that she had been talking. She had been telling them what she saw. However, there was another shadow she could see, but she couldn't name it. It was surrounded by a pool of blood and it wore colors that were neither hers nor the Sons'. She saw black, and leather, and crimson. It was looking at her but she couldn't look back at it. Tecla felt a weight in her left hand, and when she glanced down, a mesmerizing onyx stone shone in her hands.

"The Deities have spoken," Mokr's voice interrupted her vision. "War knocks at our doors," he translated as the Mother of Mothers raised her voice and terrorized the crowd. "But undefeated we shall be, for she who sits on Ferngrunn's throne will bring the light to the Dark Barrens and restore the Vale of the Gods."

"What is she talking about?" Tecla croaked out, leaning against one of the Mothers as she finally rose to her feet.

"She interprets the will of the Deities."

"She thinks this is a prophecy," Tecla whispered. "I don't think I saw anything about the Dark Barrens."

Mokr offered her a warm smile. "The Mother of Mothers is never wrong. What she sees happens or is happening right now." His stare dropped, and he told her in a hushed tone. "She said you are fertile."

Tecla nodded, her eyes darting around until she caught Mokr exchange a silent look with his eldest brother. Her face turned red nearly instantly. "Now?" she asked shamefully.

Mokr's smile was gone in an instant. "Here," he answered.

She felt the cold fabric around her arms and legs be removed and Tecla noticed how red her skin still was. It looked soft though, softer than it had ever been but she suspected it also had something to do with all the waxing she had been put through.

Her throat tightened at the feel of the light dress being torn from her body, exposing her to a large number of strangers, and holding her tears was hard. The act of sexual intercourse itself wasn't what scared her; it was the staring and the anticipation from unknown people that made her stomach churn. Tecla tried to focus on Thaum's eyes as the tall, muscular warrior came closer, but she failed. His light blue eyes were focused on her chest, it seemed, and one of his hands rested on her hip. He was so tanned, she thought, and she was so pale. She wasn't even sure of his age as he held her in his arms before depositing her body on the wooden platform again, with her facing him. He could have been older than Theliel for all she knew, but Mokr himself was younger than her, and he didn't look like a boy at all.

Thaum pushed her body a little further up, and some strands of her hair hung down, the wet ends dipping in the warm water. She watched in silence as he undid the front of his yellow britches, exposing a fully erect part of his body she never thought she would see, not in such circumstances. Tecla closed her eyes yet again when he grabbed her legs and pushed them against her chest, his most intimate parts sliding against hers. The handmaiden's words echoed in her mind; it wasn't just sexual intercourse, she remembered. She was to become pregnant after this. Tecla let out a choked sob. She didn't want to become pregnant. She didn't know anything about being pregnant.

What language would her child even speak? She wondered as Thaum parted her with his intrusion. Would she be allowed to raise her child, or would she suffer the same fate as Lady Voladea? Would marrying Thaum be the best option out of the three she had? Tears finally escaped her lidded eyes, running down the sides of her face. He pounded against her quite softly and slowly, as if to not hurt her, but she could hear the whispering and the chanting and even the cheering around them.

"Look me in the eyes," Thaum's raucous voice reached her ears.

Tecla tried, she truly did. But the last time she locked eyes with a man it didn't end the way she thought it would. Shaking her head, she curled her fingers around the back of her knees. Thaum's movements became more erratic and violent; she felt him hit every wall inside her, and the stinging pain she felt had her wondering if he ripped something. One of his hands gripped her breast, squeezing harshly, and she cried out, but her sounds were muffled next to his loud groans. Soon she was filled, and she felt him go limp halfway inside her body. Tecla didn't want to say it, but she hoped she would be with child right after. She couldn't imagine going through the same ceremony a second time, and with someone who seemed even less interested in her than the man above her.

The Mothers covered her body the moment Thaum stepped back. Tecla exhaled in short, small breaths. She didn't hope to be with child anymore. She hoped for death instead.

✳✳✳

The Red Road was entirely covered in snow. Past the southern gates of Silverholde, not many commoners were seen shoving the snow away and littering the path with salt. The skies were starting to clear up, with only a few clouds in the distance. He had packed the few belongings he had, only a few changes of clothes and some dried food he bought at Jehanel's Forum. His waterskin was heavy with water, and another dangled from the saddle, but that one was full of Noirmont wine, in case the nights became colder. Jascha's horse neighed as he pulled on the reins, aware of a presence that he didn't expect. He wasn't ready for any type of confrontation; he had decided to leave Silverholde and spend the remaining days of winter in the remote lands of Limemeadow. The city overlooking the Dancing Ocean was said to be warm the entire year, and it was still close to Wilderose, just in case. He surely hoped the woman in front of him wasn't trying to convince him otherwise.

Rosewillow looked warm under that thick ivory coat of hers, her hood pulled up and shading her eyes. She had no horse, and he wondered whether she planned on going anywhere on foot. The Red Road wasn't dangerous; he never heard anything about people being mugged or killed. The surveillants of the Regency often patrolled up and down, from Summerport to the Sand Towers, avoiding the Fog Lands in the best way they could. The woman looked oddly peaceful, and gone was the smirking face and the tempting look she often gave him. Jascha thought that maybe, for once, she was being herself. Whether that was a good sign or not he still had to find out.

"I heard what you did," she spoke, "for Mawde and her son. I went to say goodbye and she told me about the pension. She was heartbroken but her future seems a little less grim."

"I did nothing."

She chuckled, looking away for a moment. "Right," she whispered. "So, the Regency surveillants just happened to take a stroll in one of the most abandoned streets of the capital." Holding his cold gaze, she added, "I know you didn't visit Mawde yourself because of what you did to Rosaleah. I don't think you're the monster you try to be."

Jascha scrunched his nose, looking away. "Are we done here?"

"When I said you could come to talk to the Mastria, I meant it. I don't know what is going on with you but if it's truly related to the Rosencircle, you should—"

"You don't know what they do and why they do it, am I right?" he interrupted her, glaring at her face. "You talk a lot but none of the things you say truly make sense," he pointed out. "You were worried about my presence because what the Circle does is secret, is that correct?" Before she could answer, he went on, "You say I was never targeted by any of your activities, yet at the same time you believe my dead mother left the Rosencircle, which makes her a traitor of sorts. If I am no target now, what makes you believe I won't become one?

"Why are you so stupid, Willow?"

Her expression hardened, and she partially turned away. She licked her rosy lips, her green eyes darting around as she tried to form a proper sentence. "I just thought I could help you," she admitted. "You have tortured a good friend of mine and yet, here I am," she nearly growled. "Either I am stupid, as you said, or I am just trying to see past it—past her pain to consider yours. I believe what we do is right," she told him, taking a step towards him. "The search for the *Nakfèht* is real, but we don't harm people without a reason. The Mastria needs the Tear, and it's the only thing that matters."

"The Quiet Tear?" Jascha asked. "One of Aelneth's stones. The *Nakfèht* stole it from you," he reasoned out loud. "Is that how the story goes? The *Nakfèht* steals from the First Wardens and joins the Sarulites."

"It's more complicated than that," Rosewillow answered. "The Darling Mind, the Quiet Tear, and the Gifted Crosses were lost for many centuries after the great fire of Soleba. Some say they were scattered, others say they were destroyed, but we know it's nothing like that. The Mastria needs the Quiet Tear and the Darling Mind, but the first is more important. The Quiet Tear is the memory of this world. The only history that contains the truth," she admitted in a hushed tone. "The truth about Aelneth, the Oracle, the Rosencircle. The truth about everything."

Jascha shook his head at the revelation that brought him nowhere near the answers he needed for himself. "Killing people for the truth," he said sarcastically. "What a noble purpose."

Rosewillow narrowed her eyes at him, her lips curving up. "Is it? Do you feel noble when you do it?"

"Why now?" he asked. "You had centuries to find your cute jewelry," he said in a dismissive tone.

Rosewillow took a deep breath, and her face softened. "And it was in the moment the stars left the skies that the Oracle's eyes opened wide, black as the night, sucking in the light, that the seas were drained and birds rained down from their Heights," she recited quietly. "She will awake again and when she does, nothing will be able to stop her.

"There are things greater than us, Jascha," she told him as she walked away.

His black eyes watched as she walked down the Red Road, and for a brief moment, he thought of going back to Jamys' Yard, if only to bid farewell to Mawde and her little boy. It wasn't until Rosewillow disappeared down the road that he finally kicked his horse into a steady pace, riding South, until he found the Rippling Run and followed it in the direction of Limemeadow. His trust in Rosewillow was still null, but he had to admit she was persistent and sometimes right. The only other persistent woman he met was Rantha, but all he associated with the healer were nights of visions and weakness. He needed a break from everyone, a pause from it all. He hadn't had any sleepless night in a while now, and he only hoped it would be that way for a little longer. Jascha wasn't sure how long his body could endure it, he thought as the wind threatened to freeze his nose and eyelids. The last time he bled, he hadn't been able to rise to his feet for days and he stayed with Rantha for longer than he should have. Perhaps, the next time would be the last.

✳✳✳

"The walls of the Pavilion have been reinforced," the guard reported with a respectful nod.

Lord Angefort looked up from the stack of papers on his desk. "Good to hear. Are the others here?"

"Yes, my lord. Should I let them in?"

He nodded, grabbing his quill pen to sign one last document before the high-ranking members of the Regency entered. He normally didn't do this. As Chief Eleres once said, only the monarch could summon all the heads of the orders, and Lord Angefort was simply the Secretary of the Regency. However, he couldn't ignore the glaring facts that were presented to him, especially not now that Lord Lionhelm was dead and his master-at-arms formally requested a report on the Regency's elite forces. The silver lord leaned back into his wide, emerald chair, lacing his large fingers together as his brown eyes scanned the room. His observatory room was quite large as it was truly the antechamber of King Helias' bed-chambers, but only a few people knew that. Every order worked in their wing with their stairs and access to the gates, so no one ever visited him aside from a few guards or a physician, if need be. He had arranged his desk so it would face at least one of the tall windows, but the view was nowhere near spectacular. The backyards of the Pavilion were never properly taken care of, as only a few windows faced that way. They were covered in snow at the moment, and so Lord Angefort diverted his gaze.

  He never touched the paintings King Helias ordered to hang on the walls. He was constantly surrounded by the Rainiers, with their pale blonde hair and pewter eyes. Lord Angefort knew them by heart. He remembered on which side King Helias' mole was, how tall Princess Melisentia's cheekbones were, and how fat King Danyell was. He was still fascinated by the beauty of Princess Ailith and horrified by the number of parchments and old treaties signed by King Phorbas and framed next to his portrait. Everything around him was either silky or rough; the curtains, the rugs, the couches, but the common trait was always the color. Lord Angefort had come to hate emerald with a newfound passion. However, that hate never surpassed the one he harbored for King Helias.

  They entered the antechamber one by one. Grandmaster Rodbertus walked in first and stood before him in a composed manner. Sir Sybbyl Nobleleaf seemed way less accommodating, and Angefort could already tell that she wasn't pleased to be there. Sir Ferrand Nickletail walked in with his head held low and a messy folder in his arms. It was his fault if Lord Angefort had to do this, but not only. A stoic Saer Dunac joined shortly after, his eyes scanning his surroundings in repressed awe. Under any other circumstance, Lord Angefort would have smiled at the young Chief of the Surveillance. The guards were ready to close the doors when a short woman wobbled her way inside, earning all kinds of gasps and whispers from the others. Lord Angefort stood up slowly, folding his arms behind his back. He still wore black in Lord Lionhelm's memory and no one dared comment on it.

"Thank you for your time."

"What is this, Arther?" Matillis immediately barked. "Is King Helias finally dead too?" she asked tactlessly. "Is this why you had us go up and down all the stairs of the Pavilion when we could have been, you know, working, contrary to what you do," she complained, scratching her side.

"No, Grandmaster Matillis," Lord Angefort replied. "I would have freed the ravens if King Helias was dead."

"What then?" Sir Sybbyl asked, her blonde eyebrows knitted together. "This is the second time you summon such a meeting. And the first one didn't exactly go very well."

The secretary chewed on the inside of his cheek before clearing his throat. "The situation in the city is quite alarming. We've counted more dead bodies than in the last ten years. Famine, sickness, poverty in general. Several reports from the Surveillance have hinted at the fact that simple people seem to have less coin to spend which is in clear contradiction with the Treasure Council's reports. Trading has been bringing more riches than ever."

"Where are you going with this, if you don't mind my straightforwardness?" Grandmaster Rodbertus pressed, his fingers playing with his braided beard. "I've seen the guards, the soldiers, and the surveillants lined up to protect the Pavilion. Are we at risk? Of what exactly?"

Lord Angefort looked at Sir Ferrand, who paled. "Sir Ferrand."

The knight bowed his head, handing his laced folder to Sir Sybbyl so she could read it and pass it along to the others. "As you may know, Lord Theliel hasn't returned from Silverholde because of Lord Tithan Lionhelm's death. I have personally taken his duties as mine and needless to say, I was shocked. I am not easily shocked and I don't easily trust others but Lord Theliel has sworn to serve the Regency and his father was always our main support.

"The reports you will find in this folder are the reports Lord Theliel handed me. For many, many months. When Lord Angefort talked to me about the Surveillance's reports, I tried to understand," he went on with a shaky voice. "If the simple people don't have enough coin then perhaps, our taxes are not calculated properly. And if we can't collect the taxes then nothing else can go on. We can't possibly rely solely on Lord Lionhelm's support, on the Rain Lands' support. Their aid isn't supposed to be permanent. When the Regency was founded, we signed a treaty and it mentioned only one century of support until we managed on our own."

Matillis stuck out her chin as she raised on her tiptoes to peek at the folder Sir Sybbyl and Chief Dunac were reading with confused expressions.

"The simple people paid the correct taxes. The Regency received half of them," Sir Ferrand concluded.

"Half the money?" Grandmaster Rodbertus asked, his eyes widening slightly. "How is that possible? Don't you revise everything every moon?"

Sir Ferrand tilted his head to the side. "I used to, yes. Lord Theliel was in charge of the transcription of the tax reports from the other lands. Before he suddenly left the Regency, he asked me to give him more responsibilities, for he had been with us for over a decade, so I let him revise the Regency's books for the first three instances of tax collection. Needless to say, I don't expect Lord Theliel to be present on the day of the final revision," he whispered, looking at Lord Angefort with an ashamed expression.

When he didn't find the words to tell the others what the problem was, Lord Angefort offered him a smile. "What Sir Ferrand is trying to say is that he found forged seals from all over the Silver Lands in Lord Theliel's bed-chamber. Seals, types of paper, even wardrobe; items that we don't know how they came in the young lord's possession. Either way, the silvers are gone."

"But what is left?" Sir Sybbyl argued. "Surely a few months of… deceit cannot compromise our activities?"

"You are right, Sir Sybbyl," Lord Angefort conceded. "However, I am unsure if the new Lord of Strongshore will be as generous with his support as Lord Tithan was. And ending the year with half the money we need means heavy sacrifices. From us, from the people; I doubt they will react well, considering they are already either sick or violent," he told in honesty.

"Strongshore needs to do something," Sybbyl raised her voice. "It was Lord Theliel."

"And what do we tell them when they ask us what happened to the elite soldiers they sent us?" Lord Angefort retorted, raising his voice too. "Do you think the people of Silverholde is what matters the most to Lord Tiran? To Lady Voladea? To Lord Tylennald?" He felt his patience wither. "The moment Lord Tithan passed away was the moment we would collapse and I fear Lord Theliel knew it long before we did."

"What about the old man?" Matillis butted in. "King Helias. I know he's been sick his entire life, but surely his word matters more than some little Lionhelm doll."

Lord Angefort nodded, glancing at the double doors behind him. "The King," he breathed out, frowning and clearing his throat straight away. "When the Regency was founded, it was because King Helias couldn't rule anymore."

"We know that," Grandmaster Rodbertus pointed out. "We just—"

"He couldn't rule anymore and he left. He rode from Founder's Breach to Bane's Keep and no one saw him in public ever again," he stressed out. "That's what the people say, and that is what I can confirm. We signed the treaty, created the orders and the vaults, and everything the Regency needed to properly function. King Helias had fallen ill with the Violet Delusion, and he vowed to find a cure and return."

"Arther," Matillis said; her harsh tone dissolving. "Where is the monarch?"

Lord Angefort scanned the faces of the women and men who knew what he wanted to say out loud but still waited for him to voice it. Chuckling to himself in disbelief, Lord Angefort rounded his mahogany desk and placed his hands on the double door handles. He pushed them open with little effort, only to reveal the most distressing reality and the most well-kept secret he ever had the duty to guard.

The bed-chambers were empty. No furniture filled it, no art decorated the pale golden walls, not even a chandelier hung from the ceiling. The white, marbled floor reflected the dull ceiling, and the windows were coated with a thin layer of ice as the fireplace was lit only when the antechamber itself was too cold.

"This is…" He heard Rodbertus whisper in horror.

"King Helias was never here?" Chief Dunac asked, his light brown eyes scanning the bed-chambers.

Matillis came to stand next to Lord Angefort, her burly hand patting his forearm. "You were sworn to secrecy," she told him. "The problem is nothing can back our current dilemma."

"It's not a dilemma," Sir Sybbyl corrected angrily. "The Secretary of the Regency kept the truth about King Helias from all of us. The Head of the Treasure Council was incompetent enough to not see the difference between a real report and a forged one." When Sir Ferrand tried to argue, she raised a hand at him. "It is not a dilemma," she repeated. "It's war. That is what is going to happen, the moment word spreads. The overlords will wage war on us, and before them, the people of Silverholde will burn us alive not because we have wronged them but because they are hungry. And believe me, you would rather hope to be dead than face a crowd of starving commoners."

Lord Angefort nodded at her, a concerned expression marring his features. "Yes, Sir Sybbyl. This is why I called all of you. I'm sure together we can find our way out of this."

"Out of this?" the tall warrior asked, her eyes narrowing. "We are not running away from this."

"That is not what I meant."

"Guards," she called. The doors opened instantly, and two men stomped inside. "Arrest Lord Arther Angefort, the Secretary of the Regency, and Sir Ferrand Nickletail, the Head of the Treasure Council, for crimes against the realm."

There was a moment of silence and hesitation until one guard seized Sir Ferrand and the other moved towards Lord Angefort. They both readied their swords as the guards approached, glaring at Sir Sybbyl.

"I don't think you want a fight to occur here," Lord Angefort said, his right hand on the hilt of his broadsword.

Sir Sybbyl wasn't intimidated in the least. Unsheathing her weapon, she reminded him, "I can take down both you and Sir Ferrand. You will obey, now, my lord. I am the Suppressor of War and this is me honoring my pledge to the kingdom. You will both be judged for your actions and I think you'd prefer it to be us judging you and informing the people rather than having the latter decide about you."

Chapter XXXII

SAFE

They almost knocked him off his horse. As Goldsnout made his way past the northern gates of the capital, he couldn't recognize Silverholde and its people anymore. The last time he had been there, escorting Lord Jarvis to the Pavilion, the scene reminded him of a grim religious carving, with people tugging at everything and anything to escape the Pit of Torture. This was no different. Skinny hands grabbed the hem of his cloak, scratched the saddle of his horse, and Goldsnout found himself threatening the simple people with his sword, albeit reluctantly. They were starving, he could see that much. The few carts he saw around were full of rotten vegetables and he wondered where the other surveillants and guards were. There was no way he could ride to the headquarters with so many people begging him for mercy and food. A dripping, stinky tomato found its way to his cheek, and Goldsnout scrunched his nose, wiping his face with his forearm.

"Be damned!" he heard a man yell at him. "Traitors!"

"We want King Helias back!"

"Goldsnout," he heard a familiar voice call his name. "Over here."

He turned around and found Saer Dunac nod at him from the corner of the main street, escorted by a ridiculous number of soldiers who pointed their spears at whoever dared approach. Goldsnout recognized Dunac's uniform in a heartbeat. It was identical to Chief Eleres', and he could only conclude that the senior officer had been named Chief of the Surveillance. He silently rode in his direction, sheathing his weapon. The soldiers immediately shielded him as he was escorted in the direction of the Surveillance's headquarters, in the southern area of Silverholde.

"What is happening?" he promptly asked, lowering his head when he saw another simple man attempt to throw more waste at him.

"All surveillants are asked to guard the headquarters and be ready. You are quite late; we expected your return yesterday," Chief Dunac told him with a serious expression. "The Regency has lost more than half its income," he confessed. "That means no more pensions for the simple people who had a right to it because they tended to the Regency's buildings. No more salary, no more nothing. We can't afford any of it."

Goldsnout's hands tightened around the reins of his horse. "How did that happen?"

"It seems Lord Theliel Lionhelm had something to do with it, but it's Sir Ferrand Nickletail who is to blame. He and Lord Angefort have been arrested."

"Arrested?"

Dunac nodded. "Lord Angefort kept King Helias' absence a secret up until now. There are several reasons why the monarch's presence would have saved us from this situation but as of now, we need to retreat, lest it is us they will try to eat," he explained, glancing at the crowd who tried to follow them.

"What are we going to do?" Goldsnout asked, flabbergasted. "We can't let them starve. Surely, the lords will support the kingdom."

Chief Dunac shook his head. "I don't know, Goldsnout. Lord Tithan Lionhelm is dead, and I've learned about the loss of the elite forces he trained and sent to the Regency. That is why I was looking for you; I need to know what Chief Eleres was working on before he was killed. If we manage to get the Lionhelms back on our side, they might be more inclined to help us," he reasoned out loud. "Without them, this revolt could quickly turn into a war."

"I doubt this knowledge would help," Goldsnout said as the golden, pointy roof of the Surveillance's headquarters came into view. "The circumstances of the chief's death were… chaotic," he added, unsure about the words he used. "And quite frankly, losing another chief is not something I want to witness."

Saer Dunac smiled faintly at that, his light brown eyes glancing at Goldsnout. "We both know Chief Eleres lacked proper assessment. The man would only do what he thought was the right thing. I don't blame him for it," he told Goldsnout quietly. "But I don't intend on walking the same path as him. That is also why I was looking for you.

"You told me in Rainier's End that something was brewing. You have good instinct."

Had it been any other time, Goldsnout would have reveled in the praise he just received. But as they neared the gates of the headquarters, a familiar feeling filled his chest. Guilt. He had seen the rising violence and the hungry commoners in Rainier's End, and he didn't report on it. He didn't even mention it to Chief Eleres, and now the surveillants lined the battlements of the small, military fort. Goldsnout saw the cauldrons at their feet. They wouldn't hesitate to use them if anyone dared come close, but he didn't believe they would use the boiling water on the simple people.

"Archers!" he heard someone call from the gates.

Goldsnout turned around, and what he saw had him frozen in place. From behind the buildings that surrounded the headquarters, several surveillants charged on their horses towards them, and the gates were promptly shut, leaving some of the men who had escorted him and Dunac outside. Goldsnout hopped off his horse, mimicking the new chief as the latter dashed towards one of the commanders of the Regency's armies.

"Nock!" Dunac ordered, rushing up the stairs that led to the battlements.

"They are surveillants," Goldsnout protested right behind him, watching as hundreds of riders charged at the gates, right behind a group of men who carried a heavy battering ram. Other rebels shielded them the moment they saw the archers aim at their heads.

"They are against us," the chief corrected him. "Many guards, soldiers, and surveillants deserted the ranks the moment they heard the rumors. It is no surprise; the Regency has recruited both noblemen and simple people. Those whose families were affected by this situation didn't hesitate." Eyeing the commander beside him, Dunac nodded.

"Loose!" the commander ordered.

Goldsnout's watched with unblinking eyes as the arrows rained from the walls, killing many men on horseback. The less lucky fell to arrows that pierced their eyes, others saw their horses killed and the stumbling of the animals crushed them. The rebellious forces were cramped between the walls and the alleys, and Goldsnout wondered what these men were thinking as another volley claimed many lives. The walls vibrated, bringing him back to reality. The battering ram was hitting the gates steadily. One of the archers fell beside him and Goldsnout jumped slightly. A flaming arrow had pierced the man's arm.

"Lower the portcullis," Chief Dunac ordered the men below. "Now!"

They maneuvered it quickly, the grille made of a combination of wood and metal sliding down the grooves. The portcullis was halfway down when a strong hit from the battering ram caused a dent in the gates. Goldsnout kneeled as the enemy archers aimed at the battlements, and through a crack in the stone, he saw as more arrows were let loose and hit one of the spearmen who tried to lower the portcullis straight in the mouth.

"You stay here, Officer," Dunac ordered Goldsnout as he rushed downstairs. "Pour the water!"

Screams filled their surroundings instantly. Goldsnout's gloved fingers curled around the edge of the wall, watching in horror as the men below were burnt. Some roared their pain as they pushed the battering ram harder against the gates, effectively breaching them. They were his fellow surveillants, he repeated himself over and over again as he watched them fall to their knees either because of the defending archers or the cauldrons that were emptied on their heads. When did it come to this? He wanted to ask, watching as the spearmen that had been left outside when the gates were closed were being impaled against the walls. His incredulous stare traveled to the ranks at the back, and he could see even the simple people pick up the weapons of the fallen soldiers to charge at the entrance of the Surveillance's headquarters. And yet, despite the chaos around him, Goldsnout could only wonder whether the situation was similar in Rainier's End and if Rantha was safe.

***

She bled. Tecla hadn't told anyone, but she knew the handmaidens knew. They changed her bed when the sun rose, and the pale sheets were stained. She had watched the sunup for four hours on her balcony, enjoying the cool, salty breeze. Tecla liked her bed-chamber in the highest of the Sand Towers, and since the balcony had no doors, only light curtains, the ocean was always in view. It reminded her of Strongshore and the Tinted Bay, but there were no gardens for her to get lost in and for Fran to look after. Fran… Tecla had lost count and didn't know how many days had passed since she landed in the Sand Towers. It had to have been a few weeks at least, but she hadn't heard anything from home. It was as if everyone had forgotten about her.

The Mother of Mothers hadn't, though. She visited Tecla earlier, and the young lady figured that one of the handmaidens must have informed one of the Sons of Ferngrunn. The bony woman had touched her again, examining her breasts and checking her pulse as if Tecla were sick. The eldest handmaiden tried to explain to her in broken sentences that sometimes a woman could bleed even when she was pregnant, but it didn't seem to be Tecla's case. She was told that the Mother of Mothers was also the best healer in the Sand Towers and that it was always good to be examined by her. Tecla had her doubts, but voicing them wouldn't have made the woman leave. The lady was given ten days. In ten days, she would have to go back to Hvallatr and spread her legs again to try and conceive a child with Remm, the second of the Sons of Ferngrunn. Nothing disgusted her more, aside maybe from the clear liquid she was supposed to drink at that moment, the Leaf of the Serpent. She already knew it was bitter and foul, and she wasn't exactly in the mood for visions to take over her consciousness.

      Tecla sat next to Mokr and his brothers, who had invited her to what they called one of the six *mawkhta*; the days of drowning. The Sons of Ferngrunn and their generals, along with representatives of their banners such as the Nobleleafs and the Olborrs, gathered on the beach, close to the harbor but far enough as to not disrupt the traders who embarked and disembarked with goods from all over the known lands. The awaited entertainment days were spent watching staged naval battles that either featured ships no longer used or modified vessels to witness whether or not the inventions were viable or not. Tecla masked her boredom under a veil of tiredness as the monstrosity on the waves showed off its battened sails. They were of a vibrant warm color that clashed with the greenish hue of the wooden vessel. It seemed headed in the direction of the harbor until the second ship appeared. Shivers ran down her entire body, but Tecla didn't bother to rub her arms. Her sleeveless dress hugged her waist and the material was so light it even showed her nipples, but the people around her had already seen her bare, she thought. Surely, they could handle her chicken skin as she tried to figure out why the second ship was a Lionhelm one. The ship with battened sails seemed anchored as it slowed down entirely, while the Lionhelm galley moved quickly.

Tecla straightened her back in her uncomfortable iron seat, leaning slightly forward. "That can't be a real one," she pointed out. "We don't have warships so far north."

Thaum heard her, but his blue eyes were focused on the scene. "We built one like yours for this event," he replied with his heavy accent. "The Lionhelm fleet is the strongest of the Silver Lands, they say."

Tecla remained silent, glancing at Mokr, who smiled at her. She knew the Lionhelm captains never sent one galley at a time, not against a much larger ship; Tomas had forced her to read many books about warfare. The subject alone made her sleepy, but she remembered the content of those guides. She wasn't even sure her family's fleet even produced many galleys anymore, considering they needed hundreds of slaves to propel them, and her father wasn't that interested in the slave trade as far as she knew. Tomas also taught her that the captains had been discussing the creation of a brand-new type of warship, but apparently, there were a few setbacks regarding the materials and the ranged weapons meant to be mounted on the ships. Negotiations with the free cities of the Red Continent were mentioned, but Tomas never went further as he deemed the subject too complicated for a fourteen-year-old.

"I hope you don't see this as offensive," she heard Mokr say. "This is merely a show."

She nodded, but she knew he was lying. Thaum of Ferngrunn's behavior shifted since their first night together. Tecla imagined he thought she had rejected him, and knowing she wasn't pregnant with his child probably fueled his growing distaste for her. She knew he had done more than what was expected of him to please her; he learned her language and treated her kindly, but still, her heart wasn't in it. She did find him attractive enough, with his long, matted locks and bronze skin. Tecla felt like a cow meant to be mounted nonetheless.

The galley seemed ready to ram into the anchored ship when the latter fired a series of bolts at it. Tecla narrowed her eyes, ignoring the gasps and the stupor of the other spectators. The vessel with the rust-colored sails was now attached to the galley through massive rope darts that seemed to glow as if they were lubricated. The tightness around Tecla's mouth was a clear indication of her discomfort, and even though the ships were quite far from the shore, she could hear the cries of the rowing slaves who met their fate the moment the darts pierced the wood of their ship. From the ranged ship, flames erupted and danced all over the shiny black ropes until they reached the Lionhelm galley and set it on fire, burning the mast and the slaves on board. The arms emblazoned on the sails quickly burned away, and Tecla gritted her teeth as the lion heads turned to ashes.

Thaum said something in the ancient tongue as he clapped his hands together, receiving praise from his generals. "We can now cast fire without putting at risk our ship," he told her, unable to contain his pride. It was as though he had built the ship himself. "Rosewillow wood cannot burn."

It so appeared that it wasn't the fight between the two ships that interested him, but rather the effectiveness of the fire and the fireproof qualities of rosewillows. "Good," Tecla replied quietly, her hazel orbs meeting his glinting blue eyes. "I hope your men are immune to fire too."

He looked back at the burning ship, his smile never fading. "They are your men too. It is good that you came here instead of returning to the Regency," he quickly added before reverting to the use of the ancient tongue.

"The sister of one of my bannermen sent us an owl to tell us the Secretary of the Regency and the Head of the Treasure Council were arrested," Mokr flatly translated for her. "The capital is being wrecked on many fronts, and I have sent my armies to support the Suppressor of War. If your family decides to join us against the rotten regents, we will win back the stolen silvers with interests as well and can split some land. I have yet to learn more about the cause of the Regency's fall, but I will find out."

Tecla's heart sank at the possibility of Educator Tomas being harmed by a band of angry soldiers or violent commoners. Ironically, she hoped the conflict in Silverholde was the reason why she had yet to hear from anyone, just to feel less abandoned than she was.

✳✳✳

Theliel's cabin was rather small. It was located near the captain's, and the only window was above the headrest of his bed. He lied on the bouncy mattress with his right arm bent behind his head, and his fingers under the cushion clenched around the fabric as he was lost in his thoughts. There were a few owls on the ship, many trained to return to the major cities of the Silver Lands and the Red Continent. Only three knew how to fly back to the main island of the Zalejos Depths, and Captain Wulfscoe had advised him against the use of an owl to try and contact his sister Tecla. Over dinner in the crew's quarters, the Black Eagle told him that he had news from Strongshore. Lord Tithan's funeral had been a long procession from Strongshore to Summerport. The Holy Commander spoke kind words and recited verses from the Oracle's Memoir, and that alone upset Theliel, for his father was never a religious man. It appeared that Tesfira wasn't present during the ceremony, and no one mentioned seeing Tecla either. That knowledge coupled with the fact that his little sister never answered his message rang like an alarm in Theliel's brain. He doubted Voladea harmed the two women, but to think that she could have purposefully pushed them away wasn't a stretch. Wulfscoe also told him that Tithan Lionhelm's body remained visible for three days and three nights so that the simple people could pay their homages to their beloved overlord and place yellow daisies on his crystal coffin before cremation. The ocean surrounded the ship, but Theliel could still smell the scent of his father's favorite flowers just by thinking of a ceremony he was never able to attend.

 They had continued to enjoy dinner in relatively comfortable silence, with Sarkis doing most of the talking. His friend seemed thrilled but also very concerned about the improvised trip, and Theliel couldn't blame him. He had kept the truth from Sarkis on more than one occasion, for truth was a double-edged sword and Theliel wasn't sure who the weapon would swing at first. The gentle sway of the ship lulled Theliel into a comfortable and relaxed mood and his eyelids began to flutter close. Not having to wear his uniform and armor also made it easier for him to fall asleep. He had never felt freer.

 Lion's Glory suddenly shook, and he sat up instantly. He waited, thinking it was just a trick of the mind when it happened again. He heard the crew on the deck, and Captain Wulfscoe's orders. Theliel hoped it wasn't another ship attacking them; they were sailing without support.

 He ran out of the room and climbed the ladders, ignoring Sarkis as the man appeared behind him, pestering him with questions. It was so dark outside he couldn't see anything aside from a few faces where some crew members held torches. "What is happening?" Theliel asked one of the men loosening the ropes.

 "Haul up the spanker," Captain Wulfscoe's voice echoed. "Now, now, now!"

 Theliel ran in his direction but stopped near the railing when he thought he saw shapes ahead, silhouettes of construction on land or perhaps another ship. He narrowed his eyes to try and focus, but it was too dark for him. "Are we being attacked?"

Wulfscoe ignored him as a voice from below informed them, "Water in the hold! Water in the hold!"

"Good Gods," the captain whispered. "Find the damage, lads," he ordered. "Be quick and do not let more water flow in or we are doomed!" He couldn't see Theliel, but he knew the man was close.

"The hold?" Theliel repeated. "My silvers—"

"Worry not about the damned silvers," the captain chastised him before running towards the mizzen mast. The royal and top gallants were quivering, he could hear them. "Slack off the headsail sheets!"

Theliel followed him like a hound guarding the entrance of his home, but not without stumbling where he couldn't see his feet. "What happened, Captain? Answer me," he ordered, losing every ounce of patience he possessed.

"We need to move upwind," Wulfscoe informed him. "We are too close to the ruins of Driazon, and I'm afraid we already bumped into them if the ship wasn't damaged by a barrier island or a tied one. It's hard to see anything, and I didn't expect the wind to push us so fast towards the islands of the Zalejos Depths," he explained with a hint of contained panic in his voice.

Theliel swallowed hard, holding on to the base of the mizzen mast as the ship vibrated again. "It makes no sense. What about a lighthouse; why couldn't we anchor the ship earlier? Surely, there must have been better alternatives."

He couldn't see the irritation on the captain's face in the darkness that swallowed the night, but he could perfectly hear it in his voice. "The tribes of the islands don't build lighthouses. The last thing they want is for more lordlings to buy their children and their women. The goods we bring them are of use only for the tribe chiefs, but even they are reluctant to have us visit them. We are sons of the fays in their eyes." He chuckled. "I thought you were a well-educated man, Lord Theliel."

"And I thought you were a seasoned captain," was the Lionhelm's quick retort.

The loud noise that erupted as the main and mizzen masts were braced around was deafening to Theliel, who felt a hand on his upper arm. He could hear Sarkis' voice, but his words were muffled by the wind that filled the sails above their heads.

"Brace around the foremast," Captain Wulfscoe ordered, his words being repeated by the crew members who passed on the message.

"Are we sinking?" Sarkis pressed in a frightened tone. "By the Good Gods, we are, aren't we? I can feel it. I feel my clothes getting wetter."

"That's your piss, not the ship sinking," the captain bellowed. "Ease out the spanker!"

"Ease out," his men repeated.

Theliel winced as the first ray of sunlight appeared in the distance. Gone was the scent of daisies and the feel of the salty breeze on his skin. His hazel eyes watched in silent contentment as the horizon was filled with light, only to lift his eyebrows when he realized the horizon was truly an arch surrounded by more mountain arches that shielded a wild rainforest of a blue-green color. A golden waterfall poured from the tallest curve, possibly blocking the entrance to the inhabited areas of the islands. Theliel's heart pounded hard inside his chest. The rising sun tainted the skies with hues of red and orange that turned a clear shade of pale violet. Growing up, he heard the tales about the islands of the Zalejos Depths. He knew what they were supposed to look like but to witness their awakening at dawn was an entirely different story. The contrast between the dull greys of the silver coast and the colorful painting that came to life before his eyes was overwhelming, frightening even. This was what his father did, Theliel thought. His father spent most of his life on the waves and reached places like these. How could he not believe in something greater than humankind when golden waterfalls and shimmering clouds surrounded wild, untouched forests?

"The Enclave of Zalés," Captain Wulfscoe said. "The biggest of the three islands. The other two are hidden behind this massive one; Tagron's Refuge and the Haven of Ebajos," Pointing in the distance, he added. "And beyond them, the Phantom Chain, a series of small islands forbidden to man."

Sarkis stood next to the captain with his mouth wide open, letting out a series of interjections. The red-eyed, crowned eagle named Veadecta took its perch on Wulfscoe's extended arm, flapping its wings and nearly smacking the side of Sarkis' head. It called and whistled and the captain's amber eyes narrowed. Theliel watched the exchange in silence, wondering if the ebony man truly spoke the animal's language or if he had trained it to communicate specific things.

Veadecta took flight, and Captain Wulfscoe offered a thin smile to both Theliel and Sarkis. "The tribe chiefs are waiting for us, it seems. They expected our early arrival and they are not pleased."

"The bird told you that?" Sarkis sputtered.

"Why are they not?" Theliel asked instead, glancing in the direction of the golden waterfall. "We didn't come with ill intentions."

"We didn't," Wulfscoe agreed. "But many of his people who were sold to the Regency seem to have been killed. You wouldn't know anything about that, would you, my lord?"

"Why would I?" Theliel countered, shaking his head in disbelief. "I left the Regency quite some time ago."

"With their silvers."

Sarkis' eyes bulged out, rambling under his breath as he glanced back and forth between the two men.

Theliel's hands were balled into fists. "Their silvers," he repeated, chuckling. "The silvers my father kept donating would be a more appropriate description."

The captain folded his arms behind his back, walking closer to the mizzen mast and away from the younger men he was escorting. "It is not my place to judge, young lord, but you can't be surprised if we don't receive a warm welcome. Those people might have been bought but they were still considered family for the tribes of the islands."

Sarkis moved to stand right in front of Theliel, the shock on his face clearer than dawn. "Why did you steal from the Regency? What is wrong with you?"

"I didn't steal anything," Theliel answered in a deep voice through gritted teeth. "Do you think the Regency falls to pieces because part of their income was redirected? No, it falls to pieces because it is just a façade. Without Father, they have no authority, no sustain, no head figure.

"They don't have a monarch," he concluded. Sarkis paled, while Captain Wulfscoe remained impassible. "I found out a long time ago and I tried to tell Father. He never let me speak," he added, his voice filled with bitterness. "He couldn't care less."

"Or maybe he knew," the captain butted in tactlessly. "Maybe he knew and he thought you were competent enough to not let the Regency fall apart because some monarch most younger people have never seen didn't take his role seriously. How long were you a member of the Regency? A decade? No," he laughed softly. "More than a decade, is that right?"

"I thought it wasn't your place to judge?" Theliel retorted, tilting his head to the side. "What happened to that?"

"I am pointing out facts," Wulfscoe replied, his left hand toying with the hilt of his golden saber. "I have been at the service of the Lionhelms for many years. I know more about all of you than I would like to. Your move was a bold one, Lord Theliel," he conceded, nodding. "Just not a safe one. I hope it doesn't lead to repercussions your family will face instead of you."

624

Chapter XXXIII

Father's Land

Lord Tiran sat at the head of the Council of Steel's meeting table like a child prince sat on his king father's lap. His authority evaporated the moment the council room was filled. Councilors and lords took their seats in silence, sometimes exchanging looks that spoke volumes about their will to carry on with their duties under his rule. Lady Voladea stood beside her son Tylennald with a hand on his shoulder, and for the first time in her existence, she towered over those who swore fealty to her late husband. Her jaw was set tight and she still wore the black lace around her head to signal that she was still mourning. Was it for her son or her husband? Everyone in the room chose to believe what would be the most fitting. Through her cold demeanor, Tiran glimpsed the confidence and smugness that accompanied her every movement. Her dark brown dress flared around her lower body in a very angular shape, making her look more frightening than she was. She had yet to release Lady Gwethana, going against his wishes, but if the rumors about Silverholde and the Regency were true, she couldn't hold his mother prisoner for much longer.

The Surveyor of Summerport, Algar Irwine, cleared his throat before glancing at the other councilors. Neither Milefried nor Martus acknowledged him, focusing their attention on Lord Tiran, while Fantine stared unemotionally at the lords at the opposite end of the table. Lord Tylennald and Lord Lovel had little to do with the meeting of the Council of Steel; such meetings were usually private and only the Lord and Lady of Strongshore could attend them, but it seemed that wherever Lady Voladea went, either Lord Lovel or her son would follow.

"Dire news," Lady Lionhelm suddenly said, sliding a crumpled message on the table for the councilors and lords to read. "It appears that Silverholde is collapsing slowly. Lord Angefort is accused of crimes against the realm, and due to the friendship expressed between House Lionhelm and House Angefort, some dare say we, too, have conspired against the kingdom, especially since Theliel Lionhelm is said to have gone against the best interests of the Treasure Council," she explained in a flat yet concise manner. Lord Angefort is being held captive in his apartments at Rainier's Pavilion, and so is Sir Ferrand Nickletail.

"Guards, soldiers, and surveillants have abandoned their duties and are openly attacking those who didn't. It is my advice to this council that we take action immediately."

"I regret to say this," Fantine's deep voice filled the room, "but our best armies have been at the Regency's service. Judging by the lack of response, I assume they are either dead or in open rebellion. What does my lady mean by taking action?"

"War is not an option for us," Lady Voladea replied. "Not when we could simply disassociate our house from these criminals." She looked back at her grandson with interest. "May I suggest this to be proclaimed on the day of your investiture?"

Lord Lovel's blue eyes seemed to sparkle as he as well looked at Tiran, who was less than convinced. "How, Grandmother?" he asked. "Lord Angefort has already been imprisoned, and Theliel is missing."

"Lady Tecla was at the Regency with her brother before the silver vanished and the truth about our king was revealed," Lady Voladea went on, taking careful steps towards Tiran. "Who is to say she isn't involved as well?"

Whispers quickly filled the room, but the master-at-arms slammed her palm against the surface of the table to silence the councilors. "Lady Tecla is fourteen," she reminded them all.

"Old enough to be a woman," Lady Voladea replied sternly. "Old enough to make her own choices. We may not have her anymore, but we do have her most loyal servants who could very well be her and Theliel's accomplices," she reasoned out loud. "You will be Lord of Strongshore, Tiran," the grey woman continued, standing right next to him. "You can repudiate whoever you want and send a message to the traitors that would one day dare to return to your lands."

He scanned the faces of those who watched carefully. Uncle Tylennald was always composed. He wouldn't bat an eye even if someone suggested torture in front of him, or at least that was what Tiran thought. He never saw the man being shocked nor opposed to something his mother suggested. Lord Lovel, the calculating man who weaved his web of knowledge was silent. It was unusual and quite disturbing, almost as if he would have never imagined Voladea would urge an execution on a ceremony day. The councilors, on the other hand, were sheep; Surveyor Irwine was against executing simple people for someone else's crimes, but he wasn't about to voice his opinion. It was only the turmoil in his eyes that gave him away. Master-at-Arms Fantine was no different, and her lips quivered as if she was trying hard to not protest. The bald healer acted unfazed, and Tiran wouldn't have been surprised to see Martus nod at him.

Much to his surprise, Silver Master Milefried stood up, his head hunched forward and his eyes peeking at him. His eyes looked like they were about to roll out of their sockets. "I-I disagree, my lord. If you are going to execute a maid and a gardener, the simple people might rise against you."

Fantine was quick to stand up as well, a grateful expression replacing the anger that previously marked her features. "I am with Silver Master Milefried on this one," she spoke solemnly. "I doubt Lady Tecla and her most trusted people have anything to do with the actions of Lord Arther Angefort and Lord Theliel."

Tiran wet his thin, dry lips, and silently agreed with them. However, he knew this wasn't about innocence; Lady Voladea's suggestion was a straightforward political move. Disentangling Strongshore from the Regency and ruling out two potential heirs that could contest Lord Tylennald's position as Tiran's heir. Oh, how he wished he could spit it all out in front of everyone, Tiran thought. There was no other thought that brought him more joy; the humiliation of both his grandmother and uncle, but he had no one to back him. Lord Lovel was Tylennald's father-in-law and if Strongshore's elite fighters were truly dead, then Courtbridge would easily contrast him in battle. Edgemere was Tesfira's, and she only did what Tylennald told her to; not to mention that both Edgemere and Summerport seemed to be dealing with their problems. Mayor Silverworm hadn't come to pay his respects to Lord Tithan and Lord Thaesonwald, and Tiran overheard the Surveyor of Summerport talk to Lady Voladea about the obstruction of trade in many free cities of the Red Continent.

Tiran weighed his options many times but he always ended up with the same conclusion. He was alone and there was no support for him to gather. The only solace he could find was that with the Pavilion's downfall, there would be no reason to wait for the Regency to cast judgment on his mother's alleged crimes. Voladea and Tylennald and all the sharks of the Tinted Bay could have Strongshore if they so wanted, but they wouldn't have what was left of his family.

"You are relieved from your duties," Lord Tiran announced, looking straight into Fantine's blue eyes. "As you are," he added, glancing at Milefried. "Leave this instant," he ordered, ignoring the confusion and anger directed at him. "The investiture will take place tomorrow," he told Lady Voladea and the rest of the council while the guards escorted the former councilors out of the room. "I don't plan on taking two lives just to set an example," he quickly added. "Bring Lady Tecla's maid to Summerport. I also want my mother to be released," Tiran stated, earning a thin smile from his grandmother. "The Regency is no more. As the new Lord of Strongshore, I forgive her actions and demand that she is escorted back to Three Crosses, where she won't be of any harm to the southern lands."

"Spoken like a true lord," Lord Lovel commented, nodding his head.

Tiran wasn't flattered by his words. "Lord Riverguard, after tomorrow I expect you to return to Courtbridge in the company of Lady Wallysa and Lord Tylennald, to ensure that no rebel forces from Silverholde try and cross the Rough Rill. Their foolishness must be contained."

The blonde man bowed his head, his smile never leaving his face. "I will return to Courtbridge with my daughter, but if you don't mind me suggesting it, I think Lord Tylennald should lead a small garrison to Edgemere."

"Are you mad?" Lady Voladea interjected. "What for?"

"Let him speak," Lord Tiran commanded.

Lord Lovel stood up, raising his eyebrows at them, his grin widening. "We have yet to hear from Lady Tesfira, and I believe that it's in my kind lord's interest to quell the tension rising in the city-port as soon as possible. It would surely improve your reputation and show the people that you are the true heir of Lord Tithan, capable of making the right decision at a fair time."

The balding lord watched in silent approval as Healer Martus and Surveyor Irwine nodded their heads at Lord Lovel. Even his lady grandmother seemed to agree with the Lord of Courtbridge. Tiran wondered if she was narrowing his eyes because she was partly jealous of not having thought of such a plan herself.

"Do you agree?" he asked Lord Tylennald, who stood up as soon as he was talked to.

Tiran watched the man straighten his back and run a hand over the soft fur of his deep blue coat, fingers dancing over the family's arms finely embroidered on the large silver buttons. "If it so pleases my lord and nephew, I would gladly ride in your name to make sure Edgemere is under control and Lady Tesfira and her son as safe as they can be."

The lords and their councilors quickly scattered. Healer Martus was already in a conversation with Lady Voladea as they walked down the dark hallway, while the Surveyor of Summerport approached Lord Tiran to try and convince him not to proceed with the execution. As he opened the window adjacent to the shelves full of archive books, Lord Lovel knew both councilors were wasting their breaths, but the matters they cared about were none of his concern. The blonde lord inhaled the fresh air and rolled his shoulders as if his upper back ached. He knew Tylennald hadn't left, but he wasn't about to be the one to start conversing, not when his son-in-law's curiosity and impatience was palpable.

    At last, Tylennald brushed his lonely silver lock away from his eyes and talked, keeping a safe distance, as though he wished not to approach the Lord of Courtbridge. "If I wasn't entirely convinced that Hamley Silverworm poses no threat to us, I would assume you are sending me to battle in hopes I die."

    Lovel grinned at that, although Tylennald couldn't see it. "That would be a sinister plan of mine," he commented in amusement. "But I would never risk your life like that nor would I have you suffer such a pathetic end. Wallysa wouldn't forgive me and I hold my daughter's interests very dear."

    "Is that so?" Lord Tylennald asked, arching an elegant eyebrow and coming to stand right next to his father-in-law.

    "I've spent more time with you and Wallysa these past few moons than in my entire existence," the blue-eyed man told him, sounding almost nostalgic of times that never were. "I do not regret it one bit, I must admit. However, I have noticed something about you, Tylennald. Something that unsettles me greatly.

"You are too quiet and too eager to please others. You wish to please your lady mother, Wallysa, perhaps even me. And this trait of yours truly makes me believe that you did not attempt to forge Lord Tithan's will two decades ago."

Tylennald remained silent, his hazel orbs staring, his sharp mind calculating.

"Look at you," Lord Lovel went on, resting his large hand on his son-in-law's shoulder. "Of course, you wouldn't. How did a clever man such as your father believed you could? That is the question with its answer still pending. My guess is," he spoke, dropping his hand and pacing around the younger man, "Lord Theliel did it. Fake seals and fake notes were found in his chamber at the Regency, or so rumor has it."

Tylennald's expression shifted at that moment. His impassible look turned into a mixture of sadness and disappointment, and perhaps even resentment; Lord Lovel wasn't sure until the man spoke. "Theliel was always a problematic child," he said. "His perception of reality is different, but that didn't start showing until he was a boy of ten or eleven. It was the lying that came first when he was about nine. They were not big lies, mind you. If he pushed a stable boy off his favorite pony, he would say the little horse kicked the boy away. If he ate six eggs instead of five, he would say it was because one egg fell and he didn't want to pick it up from the floor. Father was spending a lot of time in the capital, preparing for the campaigns that would have him sail for the Zalejos Depths, and Theliel was left in my care. He was only one year younger than Terrel, and Elva still nursed. The boys were tight, like brothers.

"Theliel would stare at the wall or past his educator during lessons, only to suddenly ask questions that had little to do with the subject but a lot with our family. His playground was Father's observatory, his toys were Father's quill pens. I let him and I scolded Terrel when my son made fun of Theliel, who was never one to roll in the dirt and fight with wooden swords," Tylennald told the older lord, a scowl on his otherwise handsome face. "He called me his father many times, saying how ours was always cold to him and unwelcoming while I was kind and patient and younger. One day, though, I saw him. I saw him perfectly recreate Father's calligraphy. I told Father immediately, afraid that someone else would notice too and use it to their advantage."

Lord Lovel tilted his head slightly. "Like you would?"

"The Good Gods know of my innocence," Tylennald retorted firmly.

"Your mother, then. Someone must have known about the boy's… qualities."

"Lord Tithan was quick to come to the same conclusion as you. He shunned me and Mother, and when the will appeared in my possession, the weak connection between us and Father was broken entirely. Accusing a boy of nine or a grown man who was supposedly looking after him; what would you have chosen? What would you have done?"

Lord Lovel smiled politely. "I would have used the boy's talent to my advantage. It's not the correct thing to do, I know that. But sometimes doing the wrong thing saves you from being accused of it. Do not be afraid of collecting the loot others have stolen." His voice was deep and his tone hushed. "Sometimes great achievements are the results of one dishonorable act."

Tylennald shook his head, his light bangs swiping over his eyes. "That is one great line for a war declaration. I wanted to protect my family. I truly did, until it turned against me. My children left Strongshore when they came of age and thought they understood what happened. Nothing I could say would bring them back. Elva called me a weak, little man, and abandoned me. Terrel was ready to become a holy captain if it meant not having to be associated with me anymore. If it wasn't for Father's words and promises he would have done it instead of hiding behind the shelves of the athenaeum in Founder's Breach." His fists were shaking, almost as if he were ready to punch the stone wall next to him.

Lord Lovel's smile turned into a wide grin as he rounded the long table and took a seat, folding his hands on his lap. "War is the solution chosen by those with blunt minds. Tiran is one of those rulers who don't last long. Their hearts and bodies fail them under the pressure of duty and the weight of responsibility. Take pride in the upcoming victory in Edgemere, son of mine," he told Tylennald with ease. "Let the simple people look up to you. Hold their hands if you must. Cherish their gratitude."

Dark pools of hazel stared at him wondering if for once, the cynical lord who guarded the Rough Rill was on his side, or if he had always been, in his twisted way. No, Tylennald thought. Lord Lovel was on his own side and surely, securing Tylennald's position was securing his as well, for the blonde had no means of control over Tiran, similarly to Lady Voladea's lack of ability to talk sense into the unlikely heir. "You are confident about the simple people's distrust in Tiran," he whispered.

"I wouldn't call it distrust. The King Who Never Was, Prince Jamys, was a fool, history teaches us that. I stand by the belief the prince knew more than he let on. Build the men a temple and they will pray to the Good Gods, he is said to have told his father," Lord Lovel taught him. "Build the men shelters for their needs and they will pray to you."

Tylennald refrained from shaking his head. "However, Phorbas the Devoted succeeded, not Prince Jamys."

His father-in-law rose to his feet, holding the cushioned chair by the backrest to put it back in place. His fingers traced the fine wood, his rings making a soft noise against it. "When you are not the first in line to take over your father's land you make room for yourself." Their eyes met, speaking the words no one dared say, thoughts and realizations taking a life of their own as neither man voiced them.

Lord Lovel left the council meeting room before Tylennald could ask him the dreaded question about Thaesonwald. Never before had it occurred to him that his brother could have died from unnatural causes; accusing Lady Gwethana had been a painfully laughable masquerade, even he knew as much. Yet, the lord who dressed in purple had him thinking. Something about Lord Lovel's confidence convinced Tylennald that there was more to his argument than just a figure of speech. He leaned against the windowsill, gazing at the Great Gardens and watching the rays of dusk dance over the colorful trees that had lost nearly all their leaves to the cold weather and greedy wind. Strongshore felt like an unattainable height even for those who walked down its hallways and slept in the coziness and warmth of its beds. Tylennald was no stranger to the notion of inadequateness and yet, for the first time in his life, he thought that he wasn't too far from reaching the top.

✳✳✳

Tecla stumbled and fell to her knees despite being held up by her handmaidens. The climb up the tower to reach her bed-chamber was finally over, but her body couldn't take it anymore. She sobbed loudly, tears streaming down her cheeks as she were a babe pleading for milk. The eldest of the maids, Aalezon her name was, whispered something in her ear as she tried to pull the young lady up but failed miserably. Tecla's thighs were still shaking, and she could feel the sticky seed inside her escape the confines of her moon.

Remm of Ferngrunn had taken her body raw and fast earlier that night, in the publicity of the temple in Hvallatr. He had wished not to look upon her face, twisting her body around so he could penetrate her from behind. She could still feel the rough treatment, her flesh tearing and her insides bleeding as she was dry and unwilling. Tecla didn't try to contain her screams and the crowd around them wasn't as cheerful as they were when she shared the same intimate moment with Thaum. A part of her wondered if they thought the scene to be disturbing, or if they were simply bored with her antics. Remm surely was. When he was done, he pushed her body forward, away from him, and she dangerously dangled over the boiling green waters, her upper body clinging to the wooden platform while her lower back was propped up as if to make sure the seed would quicken inside her. The thought of it made her sick. With her luck, she thought, of all the Ferngrunns it would be Remm to impregnate her.

In the back of her mind, it was still her fault. Her fault for not telling her father what she wanted when she had the chance, her fault for being so uneducated about the culture of the Sand Towers and their rulers, her fault for being disliked by both her future husband and the woman she called mother for so many years. Her left hand reached for the pendant that hung low around her neck, and she clung to it for salvation. Her other hand slapped

Aalezon's arms away. Her bed-chamber was only a few paces away. She could get up on her own.

"Lady Tecla."

Mokr's voice was melodic and gentle, but she couldn't bring herself to look at him. Her eyes were probably swollen and redder than her face. It was an improper way of greeting her host and the only person who tried behaving like a human around her.

"Step back and turn around," the youngest Son of Ferngrunn ordered the handmaidens before he kneeled next to her, keeping a good distance as he wasn't allowed to touch her. Not yet. "Lady Tecla," he called again. "Do you wish me to summon a physician? We do have some who trained at the Regency's Observatory Vault."

"I don't need a physician," she mumbled. "I want to leave," she admitted to his face, lifting her head and blinking back the tears when her vision was foggy. "I-I don't think I can do this. I can't bed you if I'm not with child again; I don't want to. And I don't want to go through it again and again until I am round and broken and so defiled I can't even look at myself in the mirror," she cried, her arms quaking as she tried not to completely slump on the warm, brick floor. "Let me leave, please," she begged, sniffling and biting hard on her lower lip when she nearly begged again.

Mokr's face softened, or so she thought. His fawn eyes scanned her face when his hands couldn't touch her and wipe the tears away. His matted locks brushed his shoulders as he moved in hesitation, leaning in. "I can't, my lady," he whispered. She could hear the sadness in his voice, and it only made it worse for her. "It would be treachery. Things will improve, I promise," he quickly added, stiffening at the sight of her crying even harder.

"Will they?" Tecla defied him, her pleading look turning into a glare.

The young man ignored her outburst, choosing to help her to her feet instead. He offered her his forearm so she could push herself up without his hands touching her, and she reluctantly curled her small fingers around his bronze skin. He was more muscular than her fully grown brothers, she realized. Her knees were still weak, but what caught her off guard was the moment Mokr bent forward and placed a chaste kiss on her forehead. That had to be forbidden too, she thought, but he seemed not to care.

Her pain and her anger dissipated, even if only for a brief moment. Tecla was still convinced of her previous words, but she was glad that at least one person in the Sand Towers seemed to be on her side. Her sobbing quietened, and she offered him a small smile.

"Help Lady Tecla in her bath," he ordered the handmaidens before turning heels. "Let her rest for as long as she wishes on the morrow." He paused in his tracks and glanced behind him, "I heard a ship full of Limemeadow spices entered the harbor today. Perhaps, my lady wishes to visit the market when she is well."

Tecla inhaled deeply as she tried to regulate her breathing. "I would love to."

She entered the bed-chamber in silence, the three handmaidens quickly falling behind her. They were whispering to each other in a language she didn't understand, one that was probably from the islands they came from. The guards were watching her too through the lowered visors of their helmets, and she wondered if it was Mokr's attention that had them all staring at her, or if it was simply her disheveled look and pitiful pleading that made them lose any form of respect they might have initially had for her. Either way, the prospect of getting out of the tower not to watch ships sink or to spread her legs in front of strangers bettered her mood. The market she had yet to see and Limemeadow spices would remind her of her homeland. Of her father. The cooks in Strongshore always used such spices in their pies. They would turn the meat into golden and orange colors, and the hot bread would be yellow, but she still enjoyed it. Her mouth was already watering.

※※※

The floor was wet and smelly. Something dripped from the convex ceiling, and Lyzon hoped it was the water that washed down the dirt from the curvy figure of the castle. The cracks in the older parts of the Lionhelms' residence were not easy to repair, or so Fran used to tell her whenever he spoke with the builders who took care of the maintenance. Some tunnels were hard to access, and nobody paid them enough. The last part would be all Fran. She wondered how he was and if he shared a cell with anyone. He hoped it wasn't anyone dangerous; Lady Gwethana mentioned only petty crimes, but it wasn't as though the lady had seen the prisoners herself. As long as she didn't hear the gardener's voice, Lyzon figured he was no one's victim and that he fared better than she did. Lady Gwethana wasn't pleasant company.

The woman was foul and commanding. It had been some days since they swapped clothing and even more since the woman began teaching her everything she needed to know to make their identity swap as believable as possible until one of the two was out, preferably Lady Gwethana. Quite often, Lyzon would spot the older woman relieve herself without even bothering to sit up, drenching, and soiling the garments she wore. Lyzon preferred to use the pot the guards had thrown at them and would change only every three nights, but all in all, hygiene was the least of their worries. They were rarely handed food and water, and Lyzon found it harder every day to be able to stand. Even then, she lied on the cold floor, dressed in black and with her long mane clinging to her face like a second skin.

One of the guards finally left his spot near the stairs to talk to someone who didn't come down. She could only see their black boots. Lyzon wondered if it was still morning. Usually, the guards would leave when the cells went from cold to freezing. She watched as the guard nodded at the other person, and then proceeded to reach for the keys hooked around one of his large belt loops. The man quickly opened the cell she and Lady Gwethana shared, and her heart stopped beating.

She pretended to be fast asleep as the man's heavy steps thundered in her ears, causing her to jump.

"Come on, get on your feet," she heard him order Lady Gwethana. "Good Gods, you fucking smell of shit. Disgusting."

Lyzon's eyes cracked open, and she realized that the lady was still half-asleep. The guard didn't notice that he was addressing Lady Gwethana. She watched him mutter a couple of curses and leave the cell for a moment, coming back with what looked like a bag used to carry grain, only darker and shaped like a triangle. The guard forcefully grabbed Lady Gwethana by the arm, immediately covering her head and binding her wrists with an overused rope as he undeniably thought she was too weak to fight back. Lyzon's heart rate increased as a bad feeling crept inside her; this was not how things were meant to go. They were supposed to fake her death, and they hadn't even agreed on when to attempt it.

"Serell," the guard called. "Serell, take Lady Lionhelm."

Another guard appeared by the cell, and Lyzon panicked. They were taking her as well, but she wasn't Lady Gwethana. She knew how to play the part, at least in theory; she knew that the people of Three Crosses never emphasized the letter R when they spoke. She knew Gwethana Montel was the daughter of Lord Garit Montel and Lady Heleys née Woodgrip. She knew the lady had no siblings and never drank wine, only warm ginger juice with creeping laurel fruit extract. She also knew the woman birthed three children; Tiran, Perren, and a girl who passed away after six moons.

"Please, follow me, Lady Lionhelm," the guard named Serrel told Lyzon, offering her his gloved hand.

She ignored the fully armored man with his visor up, and her eyes widened at the sight of the real Lady Gwethana being dragged out of the cell and up the stairs when she could barely stand on her own. "I am cold," Lyzon panicked, wondering what would happen if she stood under the light of the nearest torch. Would they notice how dark her skin was? She was dirty and they didn't expect her to look as pale as the moonlight, but Lyzon was confident they would still notice the difference. "I request a shawl," she mustered. She almost pleaded for the shawl. Ladies didn't ask, Gwethana had told her.

The guard seemed hesitant, but eventually, he excused himself and grabbed the nearest cloak he could find. It was an old one, Lyzon noted. The men probably used it in case one of them was too cold on guard duty. It smelled of sweat and dirty rain, but everything in the keep smelled that way. She let the guard fasten the cloak around her shoulders, and Lyzon immediately covered her head with the hood, making sure it would drop as low as possible to cover her forehead and eyes.

Serrel offered her his arm as they neared the stairs, and the light that came from upstairs nearly blinded her. "This way, my lady. Your son has demanded you return to Three Crosses. In exile."

Lyzon didn't move. Her right foot was still on the first step, and she reminded herself not to look up and avoid the guard's stare. "In exile?" she repeated.

"Yes. You are allowed to stop by your summer residence first if you wish. A change of clothes might be appropriate."

"No," she immediately replied, regretting the urgency in her voice. "I refuse to stay any longer in a place where I was humiliated and accused without proof," she declared, keeping her voice steady and her tone strict.

"As you wish, my lady, although Lord Lionhelm will probably ask to see you first."

"He exiled me, didn't he?"

Lyzon nearly marveled at her performance but decided to take the guard's curt nod as her victory. She died to ask where they were taking the other Lyzon, but Gwethana taught her better. Never ask about the simple people, she said. And Lyzon didn't ask.

Chapter XXXIV

Promise

The fishermen of Limemeadow lived in tall towers rising from the sea in blocks of red, orange, and yellow stacked on top of each other like a game made for children who were still learning how to count. The blocks held their balance like dancers caught in a twirling trance, nets hanging from the windowsills and small boats attached to the wooden poles by the entrance of each tower. The highest steads even had balconies and little cupolas, though many were not properly taken care of, and little holes could be seen on some roofs. There came many ships, entering the harbor of the coastal city carrying goods from the southern lands and beyond. The air smelled of fresh fish, fried fish, and spicy bread. Silks and wool were sold by the Rippling Run, the lively marketplace hosting many stands while by the well at the entrance of the city, women and girls scrubbed their clothes and washed their hair. The sun was high in the sky and warmed those it touched with its rays.

　　Overlooking the streets and the Dancing Ocean, the stronghold of the Angeforts was of a humble size and surrounded by a wide channel dug. The castle shape resembled a crawling snake with its curvy defenses and narrow towers that spiraled upwards. The drawbridge was down as goods were brought to the lords in wide carts pulled by horses and mules but what made Limemeadow unique was certainly the pristine white of its stones and the deep mahogany of the covered battlements. The banners hanging from the gateways and the flags flapping on top of each turret displayed the Angeforts' crest, a shield and a helmet framed by silvery owl wings and feline fangs denting the equipment. A suitable choice for a house that was granted full lordship by the wishes of Tithan Lionhelm but was still deeply entangled with the southern lands, or so Jascha thought.

　　He dumped his dirty shirt that looked more grey than white in the bucket full of water and lye by the river. He stood with his upper body bare as the linen soaked, scratching the back of his head. He figured stopping by the barber would be a good idea. His straight black locks had grown way past his shoulders, and his cheeks were itchy where facial hair would grow untamed. Jascha stretched his arms above his head, kicking off his boots, and threw the puttees in the bucket where his shirt was soaking. He rolled the hem of his britches up until the fabric curled around his knees and dipped his feet in the water. It was slightly cold, but he was used to it. He watched with boredom in his eyes as two women ran in the river with their little children playing around them, their lower bodies drenched and their faces red with laughter. He didn't have time for simple moments, and the longer he stayed in Limemeadow, the more he was convinced that he should have gone straight for Wilderose. At the inn where he stayed, right by the quaint temple, he heard merchants talk about how they couldn't ride north anymore, too afraid of being mugged by the dangerously starved people of the capital. They said how trading with the coastal cities was safer and more profitable. They worried little about the arrest of Lord Angefort's brother, the Secretary of the Regency. He was deemed a traitor to both the realm and the Lionhelms. "The Good Gods have mercy on Lord Tithan's soul," the merchants would say, implying that the late lord had trusted the wrong people.

  Jascha was lying on the wet grass with his eyes half-open when a bulky figure hid the sun. He blinked, and the man who walked by was now sitting not too far from him, whistling as he mimicked Jascha and dipped his feet in the water. The man was older and tanned, a matted ponytail slapping against his back as the wind blew. Grey strands mixed with brown and the man was chewing on what smelled like wild plants. He reminded Jascha of Aalart if it wasn't for his large forehead and receding hairline.

  "Think your linen's ready for a rinse," the man told him. "If not, I can add some urine to that lye."

Jascha ignored him but sat up nonetheless to check if it was truly time to rinse and dry.

"You're not from here."

"Did you figure it out on your own?" Jascha rhetorically asked.

"I was just trying to have a conversation with ya. Name's Taf," he introduced himself, giving Jascha a yellow toothy grin.

"Jascha," he replied. "I'm from the Fog Lands."

"Ah." Taf chewed loudly. "A man who emerged from the clouds. Never met one before." His green eyes never left Jascha's face. "And where you come from, what do they say about the rest of the world?"

"I wouldn't know," the younger man replied. "Never had quite the chance to ask."

"You're pale. You sure look like an indoor lad. No reason for ya to mingle." Taf studied Jascha as if the northerner was a rare and wild animal. "Ya don't look half weak," he commented, scratching his round, dimpled chin. "I have a daughter of eleven, she bled already, ya know? If ya interested. She cooks divinely."

Jascha's eyebrows knitted together instantly as he tried not to make a face. "Eleven?" he wanted to repeat, settling instead for a vague answer. "I doubt she'd want that."

"What ya know?" Taf laughed loudly. "Ya don't seem bad. A man who takes the time to wash them feet must be clean in the head."

"I am a disease," Jascha replied calmly. "My dead mother told me that enough times as a promise I wouldn't forget. Trust a lady's word more than a man's foot."

The muscular man blinked at him before bursting into laughter again. The plants he chewed on caught in his throat, and Taf was soon coughing and spitting, his fist hitting his chest as he tried to gag the gummy plants out. "For the love of the Good Gods," he sputtered. "Well, that's no good thing to say for a momma," he commented. "Should've told her she passed on the disease."

Jascha should have felt offended. Taf's words immediately reminded him of the way his mother would scream and howl in the middle of the night, rolling down the stairs and clawing at the windows whenever he tried to fall asleep. Yet, no truer words had ever been spoken in his presence. He looked at Taf, his lips slightly curving up before the two of them laughed. Taf was still coughing, and it only caused more guffawing. Jascha felt tears prickling his eyes and he tilted his head backward, catching his breath. He wasn't sure when the last time he laughed at something was. He truly was about to die, he thought to himself. He couldn't even take what happened to him seriously.

"Shit, well, I must take my leave," Taf eventually said, rubbing his cheeks and kicking the air with his large feet in an attempt to dry them before grabbing his boots. "Come at the Marked Toad if you wish to eat the best fried fish in Limemeadow," he told Jascha. "We spend the night drinking and friendly brawling too."

"Friendly brawling?" Jascha repeated, raising an eyebrow.

"We just want to witness who is stronger. The man who wins beds the prettiest girl of the night. Women are feisty when they see how strong you can be. I swear the Rippling Run pools from between their legs after a good show," Taf explained with a depraved grin.

Jascha watched the man leave, the right side of his body slumping forward with each step. Taf probably hurt himself during one of his brawls or was born with a shorter leg, Jascha couldn't know for sure. He wasn't about to take up the man's offer when it came to the brawling part, but he never had fried fish. Stopping at Marked Toad sounded like a good kind of change, and Jascha decided he would spend some of his remaining silvers in a decent meal for once, instead of waiting for onion soup or purchasing fruit that was nowhere near ripe.

✳✳✳

"*Nekfihlè, nekfihlè,*" they called her as she walked past every stand in the sea market of the Sand Towers. Tecla was told it meant promise and that to the simple people and slaves of the northeastern coast, she was the embodiment of the promise the Deities made to Ferngrunn when he invoked their powers to defeat Alatros the Red.

Tecla rose after slumber much later than she usually did, her body still in pain. It was a bearable one, but still, she wondered if it would ever go away. Her long, wavy hair was curlier and looser, and the sun rays bleached it until it turned a blonde shade. She felt like a little girl again as she walked down the streets of the Sand Towers. She wore a pale blue dress with floppy sleeves that left her shoulders bare and the Darling Mind was braided around the crown of her head. She had a light breakfast that morning in the quiet company of Mokr and her handmaidens, a few guards following them around. She thought the walk outside the tower would be the highlight of her day until Mokr told her someone who claimed to be a friend of hers had come to visit her.

  Tecla had had high hopes. Her heart had beaten rather fast at the thought that her brother, or maybe even Lyzon or Fran had come for her. A familiar face was all she wanted to see. Instead, down the colorful and warm entrance hall of her new home was Lord Jarvis Angefort, clad in black and grey and wearing armor that bore the crest of his family. The young lord looked older than the last time she saw him, with lines around his baby blues and long brown hair framing his square face. He had offered to accompany her and Mokr and the train that followed them everywhere, and that was when Tecla realized that the Limemeadow ship that entered the harbor the previous day was Lord Angefort's.

  Mokr informed her in a casual yet anxious tone that his eldest brother broke his fast at dawn that day, for a long meeting would be held on the top floor of the shorter tower. They called it the Iron Conclave and only generals and commanders of the guard were allowed to participate. She would be allowed in there as well, Mokr said, once she married one of the Sons. Tecla had little interest in hearing about the Shields of the Towers and the leaders of horse archers. She imagined they discussed the Regency and its doom, knowing that one of the Sons of Ferngrunn's vassals was related to the Suppressor of War of the Regency, but if she had to choose a side, she would stand for the capital. The only way for Thaum's armies to reach Silverholde would be to sail for Limemeadow and take the Red Road, but she doubted such a plan was executable. The Lord of Limemeadow was Lord Arther's brother. Tecla often glanced back and forth between the two young men who escorted her. They rarely exchanged words, as they walked past the stands with vividly colored drapes meant to shield the merchants from the scorching heat. If there was any form of animosity brewing between the Sand Towers and Limemeadow, it would show, Tecla thought.

    When the silence became too heavy, she turned to the youngest Ferngrunn. "What did the Good Gods promise exactly? What is this *nekfihlè*?"

    "Where Hvallatr today stands was a mountain made of sizzling earth and fire," Mokr told her. "The Eye of the Iathienar. Ferngrunn had the means to hold Alatros' men off with his ten thousand mercenaries, but he wanted the odds to favor him. So, on the day that preceded the battle that would last three days and three nights, Ferngrunn offered his twelve daughters to the Deities and sacrificed them by pushing them into the Eye."

"Never was he to have daughters again," Lord Jarvis whispered. "For only strong warriors he would father."

Mokr nodded, stopping by a stand that offered honeyed cakes and glazed pork that stuck to one's fingers. "The Sons of Ferngrunn survived until now by raiding and taking slave women as their own. When the Rainiers became kings, we were often betrothed to ladies of the Rain Lands or Silverholde but the Deities promised us. Every Mother of Mothers repeated to us the day would come and a daughter will be born. The simple people have called *nekfihlè* every woman who wed a Son of Ferngrunn, hoping the day finally came."

He handed Tecla a honeyed cake that was shaped in a spiral. She bit into it, only to realize that the inside was spicy and burned the roof of her mouth. "Is this—"

"Winter lilac," Jarvis said, smiling at her. "The Sand Towers purchase all kinds of spices from us, because of the cakes they like to bake."

Mokr seemed to agree with him. "Strong flavors keep us alive in this heat."

Tecla noticed the way Mokr stared at Lord Jarvis as the latter bought himself a loaf of hot bread, speaking the ancient tongue flawlessly. She felt like an outsider more than she normally did, wondering why she had never been taught the language if her family planned on having her live in the Sand Towers. Her family, she repeated inwardly. No, her father would have never wanted it.

"You seem to know your way around here, Lord Jarvis," Mokr commented.

"I've been to the Sand Towers many times," Jarvis replied politely. "The bigger shipments are sent here, and my lord father insisted I learn all there is to know about your land, including the ancient language you speak. I often travel on those merchant ships," he said, nodding his chin in the direction of the harbor.

"I can't help but feel there is more to this unannounced visit."

Tecla's eyes widened so much she looked like a fish.

The young lord chuckled at that. "It was rude on my part," he admitted. "The Lionhelms and the Angeforts have been friends for many generations now. I intend on carrying the tradition. Lady Tecla left Strongshore before I could bid her farewell."

If Mokr was shocked to hear about her sudden departure, it didn't show. Accepting Lord Jarvis' words for what they were, the fawn-eyed man was about to speak when the marketplace quieted down, and all three of them turned around when the distinct sound of hooves reached their ears. There came Thaum of Ferngrunn on his Avoryon mount, followed by four of his generals armed with bows. They advanced at a moderate pace, spearmen following them closely, and the few guards that had been protecting Mokr and Tecla instantly saluted their leaders, but not before taking a few steps backward. The look on Thaum's face was far from the welcoming and otherwise warm expression he often displayed. He was frowning and his broad shoulders weren't relaxed as he clutched the leather handle of a hammer as big as his upper body. From the handle to the neck of the weapon, the Storm Serpent of the Sand Towers crawled like it was alive, and Tecla swore the head of the hammer was shimmering, a light blue aura clouded in red fading in the air. She had never seen Thaum wield his weapon, and the fact he did, coupled with the threatening stance he was taking, caused her legs to tremble. She felt Lord Jarvis' hand curl around her wrist, softly tugging her behind him while his other hand reached for the hilt of the sword strapped to his side. It looked like a one-handed sword, like those her older brothers carried in a fashion style rather than to make use of them, and she doubted Lord Jarvis' skills – if he possessed any – would save them from an attack.

Thaum spoke in the ancient tongue, and when Mokr didn't translate his sentences for her, Jarvis did.

"They say you touched her. The Shields say you touched her without permission. Has the witch bestowed her affections upon you?"

Mokr was already answering, but one of Thaum's generals dismounted, and Tecla's hands clutched Jarvis' brown cape.

"The man is no guest of ours," Lord Jarvis went on as Thaum spoke again. "His family has betrayed the Regency. The Sand Towers will not tolerate this insolence. The witch must learn her place, and so do you, little brother. Come now, all of you."

Tecla felt the urge to voice her thoughts at the many accusations, but the hammer was swinging menacingly, and even though neither Thaum nor his general wore any armor, their rippling muscles and sharp weapons were enough of a deterrent. Their matted blonde locks caressed the white, velvety fur around their shoulders, and she never thought death could look like a painting of war. Not for her.

"You have misunderstood my actions," Mokr finally said in the modern tongue. "Lady Tecla—"

"If you want to die like a lord wearing perfume and soft pants you can die now," Thaum interrupted him, hopping off his ivory horse and resting his hammer on his shoulder.

"Stop it," Tecla butted in, the panic in her voice betraying her sudden courage. "You have no right."

He ignored her altogether. "Mokr," he called. "Follow me. I will not choose violence against my kin if I can avoid it. The Mother of Mothers can judge you and them as well."

"I don't think so," Tecla heard Lord Jarvis whisper. He pulled her a little closer, his stare never leaving the eldest Son of Ferngrunn's face. "My lady, I beg you to follow everything I do."

Her eyebrows twitched as she tried to understand what he thought he was doing but he moved faster than she could process her own thoughts. Without even glancing at her, Lord Jarvis pushed her out of his way, unsheathing his sword to plant it swiftly in the back of a guard's knee, right where his flesh was unprotected. The man groaned and fell to his other knee, and soon an arrow was aimed at Jarvis' head. The horse archers were ready, Thaum himself stomping forward. Jarvis kicked the back of the injured guard, who rolled straight into Thaum's feet. Tecla screamed when another guard readied his spear behind her. Jarvis' sword was quickly nestled in the guard's throat, and before he grabbed Tecla's bicep, he raised his other plated arm when an arrow nearly found its way between his eyes. The arrowhead got stuck between the plate and the light chainmail he wore underneath, and he tugged Tecla down the street, running faster than she ever could.

  Her short legs tried to keep up with him, wincing when Jarvis purposefully bolted into the people curious enough to stop and peek at the action, standing on their tiptoes and craning their necks. Jarvis zigzagged between the stands of the marketplace and knocked some over, sending all kinds of fruit and other edible goods flying all over the place. Soon the street was filled with waste that slowed down Thaum's horse archers, but Jarvis didn't relent. Tecla's limb hurt from the way he pulled her left and right, wrapping an arm around her when she nearly stumbled over her dress.

  "My lady, we can't slow down now," he pressed between ragged breaths. "We need to hurry to the harbor."

  Tecla opened her mouth to retort when Lord Jarvis yelped, an arrow scratching his cheekbone as it missed. Ignoring the pain and the blood that poured down his face, the bold man dragged her down an alley and suddenly stopped, waiting for the horsemen to dash past them. Tecla found a brief moment of relief to catch her breath, hearing her heartbeat in her ears. She would be having a headache before it was all over.

"What—what do you think you're doing?" she croaked out. "They will find us and they will kill us. They have fast ships immune to fire and they know you came on that Limemeadow vessel," she reasoned while Jarvis inched his body towards the corner of the alley to see if they were all past their hiding spot.

"Good. Because I sold that ship the moment we entered the harbor. We are leaving on one of their trading vessels." He held her hand to his lips, kissing her knuckles. "Uncle told me Lord Lionhelm made you his heir in case Lord Tiran passed away without children of his own. Your place isn't here," he whispered. "You belong to Strongshore."

"You can't," Tecla retorted in a pleading tone. "The Good Gods know my lady mother doesn't want me there. Strongshore might be even more dangerous than here."

"Our ship is headed back to Limemeadow," Lord Jarvis reassured her. "My family will protect you. I promise you, Lady Tecla."

She wanted to believe it. She wanted to believe it with all she possessed. She was ready to sell her soul to the Pit of Torture if it meant keeping herself alive long enough to see her home again.

✸✸✸

The lower entrance of the keep was situated on a small cliff under the bigger promontory from which the imposing palace rose. It was surrounded by even smaller, rocky cliffs no man could reach, and from the platform built near the edge, one could see the tiny houses shaped around Strongshore by villagers who couldn't afford to live in Summerport or Edgemere or huntsmen who preferred the small forests that surrounded the Lionhelms' residence. A hole in the side of the keep let the dirty water of the palace sewers pour down the cliff and into the Dented Reef, releasing a foul stench that sickened all the people present. The sun would be setting soon, and Lord Tiran arched an eyebrow at the tiny crowd that gathered under the cliff. They were commoners who happened to have been near the beach, he realized. There was no way this execution would set an example, he thought bitterly. It should have taken place in Summerport, right before his investiture, but before he left, Lord Riverguard insisted that rumors were stronger than reality.

"You want the simple people to be divided," he said, perched on his brown stallion. "You want some to believe you to be merciful, and others to think you are ruthless. There can be two sides of a man, and a man dies quickly lest the simple people talk enough about him to keep him and his memory alive."

Aside from the guards meant to escort him to Summerport for the celebratory night, his audience consisted of a displeased Lady Voladea, who held a cloth close to her mouth and nose to block out the smells, his younger brother Perren, too distraught to understand why he was even there, and a headsman who went by the name of Betan. The man was short and fat, his face redder than cherries in the spring, with no hair on his head and his round chin bigger than his mouth. Tiran wondered when was the last time the man beheaded anyone. He hoped the ax was sharp and Betan's movements swift. The last thing he wanted to see was the headsman trying to separate the head from the body with the use of his heel where the steel didn't cut.

"People of Strongshore," Lord Tiran announced, his voice echoing in the distance. "Today is the day Strongshore becomes an independent kingdom once more." He looked at the few generals who had shown up behind his guards, then stared down at the people who sent curious glances his way. "The Regency has proved to be untrustworthy," he went on, clearing his throat when his voice broke. "And so have some members of our illustrious family.

"Lord Theliel Lionhelm stole from us and the Regency, and with Lady Tecla by his side the entire time, we have good reasons to believe she was involved as well. We intend to reassure you that Strongshore will keep looking after every single one of you and protect you from those who try to harm you in an attempt to dethrone us."

Lady Voladea turned around at the sound of the gates opening, a guard dragging the weak body of Lyzon to the elevated platform. The woman was dirty and barefoot, bugs crawling up her legs. The stench that accompanied her was strong enough to make her head reel. It was a blessing that her head was covered; she dared not to imagine what her hair looked like at that moment.

"Were the traitors to show at our gates, we know what justice awaits them," Tiran roared, earning himself loud cheers from women and men who surely didn't catch up with his speech. "Here stands one of their accomplices, Lady Tecla's most trusted servant."

Lady Voladea frowned, losing track of the feeble attempt of her grandson to sound convincing. The maid was wearing a couple of rings around her fingers, and that wasn't quite alright. She heard a muffled sound come from under the bag that covered the woman's head, but the guard kicked the back of her knees, and Lyzon was slammed face-first onto the floor. Her wrists were bound, her arms stretched before her, and she was trying to push herself up.

"Tiran," Voladea called.

"I, Tiran Lionhelm, Lord of Strongshore, future King of Drixia, Heir of the Reds and Potentate of the Salurites, sentence this woman to death."

"Tiran," his grandmother pressed, placing a hand on his elbow.

He shrugged her touch away, nodding at the headsman. He needed this to be over, Tiran thought as Betan positioned her on the chopping block. The woman protested, trying to jerk herself away until she felt the sharp weapon against her skin. It drew a small amount of blood, but it was enough to make her stay still. She was crying under that hood, they could hear it, and Lady Voladea grew more concerned. She called her grandson again, feeling that something wasn't right, but Betan lifted his ax, and with one blow, head and body were separated, blood spilling over the chopping block and pouring down the clear wood of the platform. The red stream dripped from the edge of the cliff as the body quivered for a moment.

Tiran didn't blink even as the body eventually stilled, his eyes catching the sight of the dead woman's hands. Green stones adorned her delicate fingers and he thought such hands could have never touched a dirty rag or washed linen every week. His thin lips parted as his stare trailed from the butchered body to the head that rolled away and out of the hood. Mouth agape and dark, glassy eyes directed at the darkening skies, Gwethana Lionhelm was dead. The crowd below seemed to ask for the head to be put on a spike for them to see, but Tiran only heard silence. He executed his mother.

Somewhere behind him, his grandmother seemed upset and even more distraught than his bawling brother, but as Tiran turned around to look at her, he couldn't find the words he wanted to hurt her with. A single tear escaped his eye, and he felt his shoulders weaken and his knees give way under his weight, but he remained strong. He had to remain strong.

Tiran let out a cry so raw the guards around him stepped back one pace, and he rushed towards the end of the cliff, where the ground was no more and only the sea embraced him after his neck snapped when his head met the sharp stones of the cliff shore, and his frail body rolled down. His bones cracked while he hoped that the blight waters would cleanse his soul.

666

Chapter XXXV

Lord of Strongshore

The winged sea-horse rising from the waters flew high in the skies as the riders escorting Lord Riverguard trotted in the direction of the gates of Founder's Breach. The western coast was visible from the Red Road, but it would take half a day, if not more, to reach it. From the high hills, Lord Lovel could see the endless fields of rice and grapes, the horses eating away, and the shepherds surrounded by their woollies. Grass still grew strong and green despite the winter season, and flowers of a pale rose color littered the way to Founder's Breach, the stronghold of knowledge, the city of a thousand elders, the middle ground for settling parties, the one place where treaties were signed and laws passed.

Founder's Breach was ruled by a council of five powerful lords, the wealthiest of them being Destrian Snowmantle, a man said to be too polite to claim a woman for himself. The last time Lord

Lovel had seen Snowmantle and his white bear crest was at Lady Tecla's feast. The man was aging quickly, far too quickly.

The walls of the city were not as tall as those typically seen in other seats of power, but Lord Riverguard knew the city was safer than most. A wide and tall mountain covered in snow could be seen behind the pointy roofs of the Wise Elders' home, and three towering aqueducts connected the stronghold to the mountain. The bridges carried the water to the city, but men could cross as well using the lower tiers of the aqueducts. It was said that the scholars of Founder's Breach often sent their trainees in the white mountain of the Windless Slope, to retrieve stones and carcasses, and to study the few tribes that survived after Warrior Queen Aelneth's conquest. Lord Riverguard's interest was never piqued by such research, but it seemed that many other lords were eager to fund such findings, for Founder's Breach rose tall and round, with intermingling baileys and long watchtowers of a light grey color with splashes of blue. Houses were carved into the wall and balconies protruded from the little cupolas on the upper stores. Crossbowmen patrolled the battlements and riders scouted past the mountains, yet not a horn was blown as Lord Riverguard and his men approached.

The gates were open when he crossed them, and the blonde lord noted how many homeless people dying of sickness and starvation sat by the side of the main road. Healers in floppy robes gave them food and builders constructed temporary shelters. They were people fleeing the capital and neighboring villages, Lovel realized. Founder's Breach couldn't welcome them all, but clearly, the Wise Elders were ready to try. However, that matter as well didn't catch the lord's attention. He wasn't about to waste more time than was necessary.

The athenaeum was located on the third upper bailey of the stronghold, and Lovel dismounted the moment he saw steep stairs curl around the walls. He knew Terrel Lionhelm was collecting dust with the rest of the manuscripts in the library, becoming an antique himself, and he also knew Terrel was aware of his presence. The young man was smart, and informed, much like Lovel, the difference being that Terrel wouldn't put his many talents to use. There were no guards by the entrance, only two young scholars with their heads shaved and sleeves large enough to hide a child in them, and they bowed in silence at the lord before they returned to their whispering. The silence was another detail that grated on Lovel's nerves. Everyone and everything around him was quiet and it seemed forbidden to look into someone's eyes directly. Even the doors of the athenaeum were left open, for the pushing and pulling would simply disrupt the scholars' concentration. Such were the lives of the pious, Lovel thought, not the lives of the curious, but who was he to contradict them?

His heels clicked against the glass floor that showed him his reflection, his deep purple cloak flowing around his body. His gloved fists were tense against his sides, and Lord Lovel walked in a straight line, paying little attention to the stairs above him that curved like upside-down bridges. Roots and branches rained down the walls and the pillars of the athenaeum, glowing a soft green and lighting the place better than any chandelier ever could. Lord Lovel could hear a ticking sound coming from above, and as he tilted his head backward, he saw that at the center of the ceiling, a round piece of machinery was working, gears grinding and scratching at the cupola. It had a golden hand that seemed to be moving, with an extended finger that pointed at the sun's position in the sky.

    Terrel Lionhelm didn't look up as his grandfather came forward. He leaned in closer as he tried to focus on his reading, but the clicking boots were making it hard for him to do so. That is why he preferred the flat sandals the Wise Elders wore. Lord Lovel rested a hand on the rectangular table made of crystal and framed by gold and sapphires. It had no feet, but asking about the table was the last thing on his mind. He watched Terrel work, scrunching his nose in displeasure. There was a certain roundness to the man's body, the result of years of hunching over books and sitting on cushioned chairs instead of training. Terrel was the only Lionhelm to have inherited Lovel's pale blonde hair, but the hazel eyes were Tylennald's. Terrel's face bore many scars due to smallpox when he was a child of six years of age, and his nose was rather flat, reminding Lovel of his wife's features.

    "Are you not going to greet your grandfather?" Lord Riverguard commented.

"Greetings, dear grandfather." Terrel's voice was calm and poised. "I expected you to come later. Many funeral invitations have been sent out. The Wise Elders call it the Red Winter. Once they butchered lions in the summer, now it seems the helms don't do well in the winter."

Lord Lovel frowned at that. "Two funerals are no butchery."

"Four," Terrel counted, lifting his head and staring into his grandfather's eyes. "Lady Gwethana was executed by mistake it seems, and my cousin disposed of his own life." He slid an open message in his grandfather's direction before focusing on his book full of calculations. "An owl arrived this morning."

Lovel licked his lips, letting out a small chuckle. "This makes my visit even more appropriate."

"I will not return to Strongshore," Terrel immediately said, wiping his nose with his loose white sleeve. "You are wasting your time here. Father can become Lord of Strongshore or King of Drixia, and whatever nonsense he wishes to become. I swore to the Wise Elders and I intend on staying here."

"You'd rather become a bald scholar than a prince? Is that what you are saying? The restoration of an ancient, independent kingdom must be more appealing than…" He paused, looking around. "This. Shelves full of paper-eating bugs and poor art."

"I'll take the shelves over Strongshore," the young man replied with boredom tainting his voice.

"Let me spare you the trouble of asking; I will not associate myself with the likes of those who convicted or banished their relatives. Theliel was a brother to me, I am glad he sought my help when he realized he too was done with the South."

"Boy, have you heard of what your brother has done to the Regency? Do you know Lady Gwethana murdered your uncle Thaesonwald?"

"Is there proof?" Terrel asked, turning the pages he was done examining. "The Regency laws are clear enough. No executions without trials."

"The Regency is falling," Lord Lovel pointed out, his fingers twitching against the cold table.

"Men can write down just laws and incorporate them into an unjust system. That, however, does not invalidate the laws you were bound to respect." Terrel glanced up, frowning at the silent man across from him. "You seem fairly calm about the outcome. Have you done it?" he asked. "Was it your doing? I can't comprehend why you'd want Father to become Lord of Strongshore. Do you wish to be the mind behind his ruling days? Even if you do become the man who holds the South, the name that will be written in history will still be the Lionhelms'. And what a history it will be."

Lord Riverguard inhaled deeply, forcing his shoulders to relax. "What do you mean by that?" he asked, his lips tight.

"You proclaim the independence of the South and restore the Kingdom of Drixia," Terrel reasoned, glancing up. "That is fair, for a time. The South is wealthy, with strong defenses and many ships guarding the bay. What happens after? What if the other lands reciprocate? Are we back to where we were before the Rainier dynasty, with centuries of war and rebellion?

"Do you and Father have what it takes to hold them all off?"

Lord Lovel didn't respond. The one person who was able to train a vanguard had been dismissed by Tiran Lionhelm, and the coin master left as well. He doubted Tylennald would find equally talented and capable individuals to replace Fantine and Milefried, for he wasn't certain such people even existed. At the same time, the other lands were past the Rough Rill, and not as militarily equipped nor wealthy enough to attempt to ride south. Terrel's reasoning was a coward's list of excuses.

"It wounds me to hear you have no faith in your blood, Terrel," the older man concluded, stepping back to circle the table and gaze at the few portraits that hung from the walls in between shelves. "Controlling the Lionhelms and their lands was never an ambition of mine," he told his grandson as he stopped in front of a large portrait of two women. It was right across from Terrel, and he could only guess why the young man chose to sit there. "But I won't deny it pleases me to think that my blood could flow in the veins of future kings of queens." He stared at the older woman in the painting. "Your sister?"

Terrel sat back, nodding. "Elva sent me this painting some years ago."

Lord Lovel smiled. Elva Lionhelm sat at a round desk, next to a vase full of yellow daisies with a couple of perfume bottles in front of her. Her bare arms were long and slender, and every feature of hers was her father's. Her chestnut hair was dark and long, cascading past her shoulders and covering the dress she wore. A golden circlet hugged her forehead with thin wings that looked that leaves on each side. Her hazels were so bright they seemed to burn the painting, just like the rouge on her lips accentuated her pale skin. Her cheekbones were tall and her nose strong, but it was the look on her face that froze Lord Lovel in place. There was an anger inside her that the painting delivered perfectly.

In her arms was a younger woman, a girl really, who wore black and crimson and smiled happily. For a moment, Lord Lovel thought Elva might have had a daughter, but the Lionhelms were easy to recognize, and the little bubbly girl shared none of Elva's traits. She wore a crown similar to Elva's, only it wasn't golden. It was pure iron with glinting rubies, and it made the girl's face look even narrower. She had long, straight hair so dark it was as if the black shone blue and grey, flattering the pale color of her eyes and the pink of her cheeks.

"Who is she?"

Terrel didn't let his emotions show as he stoically replied, "Elva's ward. She should be thirteen or fourteen by now. This painting's a little old."

"Does the ward have a name?"

"Why are you so interested, dear grandfather?" Terrel pressed, rising to his feet.

"Because the last time I saw a woman with hair this dark and eyes this pale, it was Lady Charlaine Rochelac, and I know for once that she had no daughters."

"Her name is Rohais."

"Only Rohais?" When Terrel didn't answer, Lord Lovel laughed lightly. "Well, will you allow your old grandfather to rest in Founder's Breach? I fear I won't make it to Courtbridge before sundown even if I were to leave now."

His grandson nodded, extending an arm. "Please, follow me. We break our fast after sunset, so you can join me and the Wise Elders before we lead you to the guest apartments on the fifth tier of Founder's Fort."

Lord Lovel blinked a couple of times. "You work on an empty stomach every day?"

"It is the only way to focus."

✶✶✶

"Open the gates!"

A gush of wind blew straight into Goldsnout's face as what remained of the gates was pulled open, allowing him, Chief Dunac, and a small garrison to exit the Surveillance's headquarters. Their losses had been minimal if they only counted the men taken down by the rebel forces. Those who perished due to the lack of food and wood for heating were hundreds, and they were amassed in the yard, left to rot when pyres couldn't be built in their honor. Goldsnout was covered in dirt, the bandage Old Martita had dressed his wound with long discarded, leaving the side of his face forever scarred. His beard had grown over the past days and his unruly red mane clung to his neck and shoulders. Saer Dunac looked worse than he did, with ashes from the flaming arrows tainting his armor and scratches marking his face from when he helped the soldiers push back against the battering ram and fight the surveillants who breached the gates. The fight ended up lasting for some nights, but ultimately the cold and the lack of food hit the rebels first.

    Opherus Goldsnout took hesitant steps past the walls of the headquarters, unfazed by the sight of survivors biting into the dead flesh of their fallen companions. He saw rats and stray dogs feed themselves as well, and cats chasing the mice and crawling charred bodies infected with flies and other bugs attracted by the gashes and dry blood that coated the fallen skin. The spearmen behind him advanced in a guarded stance, their feet digging in the mud. He should have been one of them, Goldsnout thought as he walked past the dead. The reason why he was alive was because Chief Dunac had personally looked for him, not for his safety but for his knowledge of Chief Eleres' work. Had he not been the privileged officer to walk beside the late chief, he would have been starving or left outside to be killed by the furious people, lest he joined them and be murdered by his companions.

"We should head to the northern encampment," Chief Dunac said. "We must find Sir Sybbyl Nobleleaf and know exactly how to proceed. Chaotic and unorganized fighting will only claim more lives than needed. We ought to find out what the other lords' stances are as well."

"Then why were we fighting them in the first place?" Goldsnout retorted, ignoring the looks he was receiving from the soldiers around them. "We shouldn't have fought back. Look at them. They would have retreated when the wind blew harsher."

"They were armed with the Regency's weapons," Dunac reminded him. "Do you think we would have come to terms had we let them in peacefully?"

Goldsnout didn't reply. They walked silently past the cadavers and some he even recognized. He felt cold, so cold he was sure his bones were freezing and slowly paralyzing his movements. There were horses on top of the dead, animals they had eventually thrown from the walls to crush those who tried to climb the defenses. It was all they could do once they ran out of arrows and no fire could be lit to boil the water from the well.

Something shifted next to them, and a silhouette moved behind a pile of bodies. One of the soldiers beside Dunac rushed to see, but before he could even assess the situation, his weapon was lodged into a boy's chest. Goldsnout ran towards him, pushing the soldier aside with his shoulder. A pair of brown eyes looked at him, filled with tears. The boy opened his mouth, but only blood came out. Goldsnout tightened his fists, glaring down at the soldier.

"Proud of yourself?" he hissed.

"I didn't know it was a boy!"

"Why did you attack then?"

"Enough," Chief Dunac quickly put an end to their fight. "Officer Goldsnout, if you think war is a fair game you have come to the wrong place. This soldier is here to protect us. It could have been a man hiding behind the pile with a lance or worse," he tried to reason. "I deeply regret the boy's death but it's better than starving, at this point."

"Are we killing them to show them mercy?" Goldsnout retorted. "Is that what you tell yourself now, Chief?"

Dunac's brown eyes turned a deeper color. "To the encampment, now. The Suppressor of War will give us the correct directives to follow."

Goldsnout wasn't about to keep quiet. He stuck out his chin, raising his voice. "Oh, I thought you were the Chief of the Surveillance. I thought our directives came from you and that our duty was to guard the simple people, keep the streets safe, bring criminals to justice."

"And how do we do that, Goldsnout?" Chief Dunac bit back, pressing his lips against his teeth. "How do we guard the people who hate us? How do we bring criminals to justice if those criminals are among our ranks?"

His words stung. They stung to the point Opherus could feel his veins throb and his eyes swell. If these were the new rules, he refused to follow them. Waiting for a general's orders was never part of the oath he swore to keep. Perhaps, he was a deserter as well, a rebel, an angry and starving surveillant, or maybe he was nothing. The Regency didn't exist anymore, or did it? Where were the powerful lords who carried on the King's message? Where was the wisdom that originated from over a thousand years of peaceful rule?

Goldsnout reached for the clasps on his shoulders, releasing the dirtied emerald cape and letting it fall behind him. Chief Dunac watched him with a bewildered, offended expression on his face. Goldsnout would have removed his chest plate too had he not needed it, for the owl of the Regency was engraved on it and nothing felt heavier than that crest.

"Opherus."

"I wish you luck, Saer Dunac. I will pray to the Oracle that She guides you through this war."

He didn't feel the blow until it hit him straight in the back of his head. Opherus let out a choked gasp, his eyes rolling in the back of his head as he fell forward, losing consciousness. Chief Dunac arched an eyebrow at the soldier that had been standing behind Goldsnout, the one the officer previously shoved.

"Enough of this," the soldier said. "Let's find Sir Nobleleaf. Let the rats eat him alive since he empathizes so much with dirt."

They walked past Opherus, whose body lied in the mud-stained snow. One of the soldiers even stepped on his back as they left him behind, probably wishing that the cold coupled with exhaustion took his miserable life.

✳✳✳

    They were met with little to no opposition. Tylennald Lionhelm sat straight on his horse, armored from head to toe. A thousand men, heavy cavalry and catapults, stood behind him in front of the small, E-shaped palace in Edgemere. The simple people fled the forum the moment they heard them march. Window shutters were closed and merchants scattered. Some children followed his army around out of curiosity, but they were promptly pulled back by their frightened mothers. Tylennald had been threatening the residence the entire day but never did he order the catapults to attack the frail walls. The palace was in a poor condition, with its dirty yellow color reminding him of some skin disease. Even from where he stood, Tylennald could see the shattered harbor that had yet to be repaired. The gardens of Edgemere were always said to have been beautiful enough to compete with the Great Gardens of Strongshore, and Tylennald witnessed the peak of their beauty when his sister Tesfira moved to Edgemere after her wedding. There once were tall peach trees and lush bushes of roses of every rainbow color, and a bright fountain at the center. Water would pour down the sides of the merman statue and short-haired white dogs would chase each other down the fruity mazes.

    As he looked at the dead branches and cracking leaves that littered the pathways, Tylennald didn't recognize Edgemere. It was abandoned and poorly maintained, and he was left to wonder if any help was still working inside the palace, for it was barely lit, the first and top floor a dark blur where shadows loomed over the windows. They were watching him and his men, they had been since they arrived. And they didn't seem to wish to come out.

Hamley Silverworm seemed to have a few loyal soldiers at his service; he could see them on the roof with their crossbows ready. They wouldn't be enough to stop his soldiers from barging inside the palace, but Tylennald didn't want any form of bloodshed. Tesfira and her son Deril were kept inside, and he feared that his actions could harm them.

A rider dashed behind him, calling his name. "Lord Tylennald, a message from Strongshore."

He turned around, worry creeping in the back of his mind. "What happened?"

"Lord Tiran… he…" The rider cleared his throat, finding himself at a loss for words. "You are the new Lord of Strongshore," he finally said. "Lord Tiran and Lady Gwethana are dead. You must return to Strongshore."

The news should have boosted his mood, but Tylennald only felt confused. Tiran's lordship was to be celebrated and instead, it was his death that was announced. Lord of Strongshore, Tylennald repeated inwardly. If that was true, he needed Silverworm to surrender the palace quickly. He needed to head back home and check on his lady mother, as well as summon his wife Wallysa. She had left with Lord Riverguard, the two of them parting ways at the Rough Rill, or so they had planned, but Courtbridge could wait, just as they had waited a lifetime for this moment to become a reality. His father would probably be livid at the news, but Tylennald found himself smiling, for the Good Gods were on his side.

He kicked his horse into a slow pace, stopping only when one of the crossbowmen on the roof aimed at his head. If he could be seen, then he could also be heard. "Release my sister, Hamley," he shouted, his voice echoing around. "We won't leave until you do, but we are not here to fight. We are family. Release my sister and nephew and no one will get hurt. As the new Lord of Strongshore, I command you to come out and relinquish your titles peacefully."

Tylennald was met with silence. He narrowed his eyes at one of the windows. Why no one replied was starting to unnerve him. They did listen, but they chose not to say anything.

"Hamley Silverworm," he shouted again, watching with wide eyes as drapes were flung over the balconies.

Endless silks that nearly grazed the ground flapped into the wind from where they were being hung, the deep burgundy color clashing with the pale walls. A silver rose was embroidered at the center of the banners, and Tylennald frowned, his lips curving down. It was the banner of the Rosenfields, and the Rosenfields were dead. His generals were coming closer, but he raised his hand to stop them. He knew they wanted to attack.

From the central balcony on the third floor of the palace, Hamley watched Tylennald with his oily hands plastered against the windows. He ignored the servants who bowed at him after releasing the banners, too busy muttering words inaudible to his wife and son. Tesfira held her son close, cradling his face despite him being taller than her. Her dark curls were frizzy around her body, and her grey dress didn't flatter her curvy shape as it looked like it had been worn for days from the way it was wrinkled around the sleeves and waistline. Deril sat in front of his uneaten meal in the dimly lit room while his mother stood beside him, sending careful glances at her husband.

Hamley jerked his hand as he tried to point at Tylennald outside. "Did you see? Did you see his face?" he marveled nervously. "He's Lord of Strongshore now, he said," he repeated with a high-pitched laugh.

Tesfira clung to her son. The stinky mutton meat was spoiled, but every night since she came back to Edgemere her husband would order the same meal to be served until they would finally eat it. Not tonight, the lady thought. Tylennald had come for her, and she would leave. Hamley couldn't hold her and Deril hostages, not when an army camped outside the gates. All she had to do was to remain calm, if only in appearance.

"What does he want? The madman," Hamley muttered, his body shaking as he paced in front of the balcony doors. "Does he have no children of his own to pester? Insolent maggot. I will never let him have my son. I won't let my son become the lord of the traitors."

"Please, my love," Tesfira forced herself to speak. "Let's go out and meet him. If he had ill intentions, he would have destroyed the place." She smiled at her son, who sneaked an arm around her waist as he tried to find comfort in her eyes. "We have been inside for quite some time," she went on, brushing Deril's black locks with her fingers. "Some fresh air—"

"Shut it, woman!" He broke a chair, the short burly man. He grabbed the broken feet, throwing the wood in the fireplace. "I have come too far; I have come too far."

Tesfira watched him hold his head in his hands, run his sweaty palms over his balding head. Hair fell as he repeated the motion enough times, and she grimaced. They had grown distant over the years but never before had she not recognized the man she married. The desperate man who seemed all too impatient for something wasn't Hamley. He stopped moving, covering his lips with shaky fingers as his eyes watered, staring into space. He padded across the room, coming in front of her to place a hand on her shoulder, and slid it up to her cheek. Tesfira released a breath she didn't know she was holding. He looked at her with a soft smile lighting his face. He had never looked at her that way after Deril was born.

"I have loved you," he whispered, before turning to face his son and kissed his forehead. "Pure love. But all that is pure in this world burns," he told his wife in content sorrow. "Spirits watch over us."

Spirits watched over them. Those were the Rosenfields' words, not theirs. Before she could ask him anything, the doors cracked open, and a pale woman clad in white nodded at Hamley. She held a helmet in her hands, and it wasn't long until she slid it over her head, covering her soft ginger locks and hiding her dark brown eyes. The color drained from Tesfira's face as she watched Hamley burst into a fit of laughter that mixed with distinct sobs. "Thank you," he would repeat even as the woman she had never seen before left.

"Thank you, Rosamund."

Flames hissed from the ground, rapidly clawing at everything, devouring the flowery rugs and the velvety curtains. The dining table made of gold was smoking, and the painted ceiling was coming off in fat chunks of the carbonized canvas. Tesfira screamed, rushing towards the door, Deril right behind her. He called for help when the doors wouldn't open, but Tesfira was already running for the balcony doors. She would jump, she would rather jump than burn alive, she told herself, only to be pushed against the floor by Hamley.

"Oh no, you won't," he snarled, straddling her body to keep her from moving.

Deril slammed his knee in his father's face, grabbing her mother to help her up. "We can't possibly jump," he told her, coughing when the smoke clouded his vision.

"We have to," his mother urged him, covering her mouth and nose with her sleeve. She coughed and choked.

The smoke was thick and dark, and she couldn't see Hamley anymore. She patted around until she found the handles of the balcony doors but they wouldn't open. She slammed her hands against the glass in desperation, crying and coughing at the same time until the glass smashed and she jumped. Deril had thrown one of the chairs at the double doors. He pushed his mother through the cracked opening, but the fabric of her dress was caught in shards. Tesfira yelped when the broken glass slashed the skin of her legs and arms, but at last, she could breathe. She fell to her knees on the balcony floor, blinking around to find Deril. Her boy emerged from the smoke through the same opening, and she breathed a sigh of relief.

She crawled on all fours to scream for help, but Tylennald's men were already forcing the gates of the palace. Tesfira stood up, her entire body shaking, reaching behind to find Deril's hand while her hopeful gaze focused on Tylennald.

A meat knife pierced her throat and Tesfira blinked, the metallic taste of her blood filling her mouth. She fell backward, her body landing on top of Deril's inanimate body. A pool of blood framed them like a mottled finish. All she saw was Hamley's teary stare over their bodies.

"Why do you always betray me?" he whispered. "Why do you always leave me?" he asked no one as the Edgemere residence burned down in the night, surrounded by blue embers that descended from the trees of the Wilderose forest like stars raining from the Heights.

Chapter XXXVI

SHORES OF SPIRITS

The War Council's meeting room was a pile of debris. Maps and pawns and tactical plans collected dust over the years, while the oldest parchments and records were moth-eaten or sometimes tossed in the fireplace along with broken chairs, painting frames, and whatever could be burnt other than wood. Sybbyl sat alone at the table, reading the message she received from her brother, Aslac Nobleleaf. He was just a boy in her eyes, but she knew he served the Sons of Ferngrunn fairly and faithfully. He wanted her back in the Sand Towers, Aslac wrote. The Sons of Ferngrunn would be riding to Silverholde soon, storming past Limemeadow and taking the city from the southern entrance. Sybbyl wasn't entirely sure when the note arrived; she had spent many days on patrol and giving orders to the few generals that remained, and only after the city was mostly emptied had she decided to catch up with the rest of her duties. It was complicated, to be the last one standing. Chief Dunac was young, freshly appointed, and she wasn't even sure he was still alive. She heard about the assault at the Surveillance's headquarters. Grandmaster Rodbertus had been evacuated alongside many educators and sent to Founder's Breach. Physicians had opted to stay in the capital to treat the ill and the injured. As for Mad Matillis, the woman was still secluded in her chamber and refused to come out. The knight doubted she would come out even with a fire going on. A fire would also probably not be sufficient to kill the hag.

The Suppressor of War was about to unseal another message when the door was opened. A guard bowed at her. "As you requested, we brought you Lord Angefort."

She didn't glance at the prisoner. She already knew how disheveled and tired he looked. She looked the same. "Thank you," she told the guard. "Sit, my lord."

Arther Angefort stepped forward, his eyes going blank as he took in the appearance of the War Council room. He had always known it to be the least maintained quarter of the Pavilion, a room as tall as it was narrow, hugging the highest watchtower of the castle which could be accessed through the stone steps that spiraled from the center of the chamber. It was rarely used, for the fireplace would cough smokes on the men who guarded the battlements, and peace had been a standard in the realm for many, many centuries. Lord Arther took a seat across from Sir Sybbyl, his baggy eyes glancing at the scrolls and the messages that had the knight's attention.

"Have you eaten?" she asked him, her thin lips pressed together as she read.

"Horsemeat and a very watery soup," he answered calmly. "My days as a prisoner aren't much different from what they used to be."

"I am glad," the short-haired woman replied, lifting her gaze. "Starving men is no goal of mine. But I am afraid the situation has escalated to the point no fair trial can be held for you and Sir Ferrand," she admitted. "Food is scarce. The soldiers and surveillants who left the Regency and abandoned their ranks have stolen weapons, food carts, silvers within their reach.

"We lost over a thousand men at the Surveillance, leaving only two hundred who are loyal to the Regency."

Lord Angefort hid his arms under his cloak as shivers coursed through his body. The watchtower was colder than his study. "The Regency's ranks count up to five thousand men," he recalled. "It's not much but it's more than most have. It should be enough."

"Food is scarce," Sir Sybbyl repeated. "You were a commander too; I know you know your numbers but I also know that you are aware of what a winter without provisions means. Half of our men have taken small boats up the Restless Channel to escape the city alongside civilians. They didn't care about King Helias; they didn't care about the Treasure Council. They cared about starvation, about their families. Most of them died trying to get away on the frozen waters," she informed him in a resentful tone. "Clawing at the ice when they can't even swim in armor and padded leather. The remaining half is here, split between rebels and faithful men. That's a little over two thousand soldiers." She threw the last message across the table and slumped back in her seat.

The silver lord frowned at the tiny crumpled scroll. The broken seal was House Lionhelm's. "Did my arrest bring you more trouble than any other decision you've made so far?" he boldly asked, running his gloved fingers through the shroud that covered his chin.

"The Sand Towers will attack Limemeadow, and they have enough ships to cause a lot of damage to the city and its walls," Sybbyl told him, looking away. Her thick blonde eyebrows were knitted together, and they didn't seem about to relax. "Their main armies are made of riders and spearmen; I am not sure if they bring a lot of siege weapons with them. The Lionhelms have publicly declared they don't support the Regency anymore and that they will execute the traitors who dare cross the borders of their independent kingdom." She spat the words like venom.

"The Kingdom of Drixia?" Lord Arther asked in surprise. "That is… dauntless."

"Stupid is the word," Sir Sybbyl retorted. "I reckon any little lord thinks he can build a kingdom when they have a vast fleet. Lord Tiran is dead," she told Angefort. "Lord Tylennald will succeed him. The man has no military knowledge that I know of but I wouldn't be surprised if they joined forces with the Sand Towers and come to slaughter us."

Unlikely, Angefort thought to himself. The moment his nephew told him about Lady Tecla's sudden leave, he asked Jarvis to find her and take her to Limemeadow. Lord Tithan wanted her to inherit Strongshore; Lord Angefort still had the will with him. If Jarvis found success in his mission, the Sand Towers wouldn't take Lady Tecla's abduction very well. From a tactical standpoint, going straight for Strongshore would be a mistake on their part. The naval forces of the South could take on any enemy; on the other hand, if the Sons of Ferngrunn captured the capital, they could stand a chance in the field. Strongshore's best fighters perished at the Rosenfield castle, Lord Angefort thought bitterly. They perished because of him. The guilt haunted him every night. He wished he told Tithan before; he wished he didn't agree to send Chief Eleres to Wilderose only to meet his demise. And as dishonorable as it sounded, Lord Angefort also chastised himself for having been blindly loyal to a king who never returned.

"Did Lord Tithan know?"

The question caught him off-guard. "Pardon?"

"Did he know about King Helias? Were you and he trying to take over the kingdom, the realm, or something else?" Sir Sybbyl asked. Her voice was soft for once, almost as if she wanted to believe in something else than her grim reality.

"He did," the old commander replied. "Every time our ruler was mentioned, he would find a way not to talk about him, as I did. They were friends, King Helias and Lord Tithan. Very good friends. King Helias had a dream about the kingdom's ideals and he wanted them to be shared by all in perpetuity," Lord Arther explained, resting his elbows on the table. "Lord Tithan drafted the Regency's system, mirroring his own Council of Steel. He believed that power had to be split and that everyone needed to be represented; women, men, the rich, and the poor."

Sybbyl smiled faintly at that. "Can't say he was wrong," she croaked out. "Do you have any idea if King Helias is still alive? He must be over eighty by now."

He took in a deep breath, raising both black eyebrows, and shrugged. "I don't know, Sir Sybbyl. His lasts words to us were that he would find a cure and not let the Violet Delusion consume him but whether he made it safely to the Rain Lands or not, we never knew."

"I don't know where to send you, Lord Arther," the warrior told him in honesty, their eyes meeting briefly. "If I send you back to your family, I commit treason, although the Regency is no more, let's be honest. And if you make it to Limemeadow, the Sons of Ferngrunn could capture you. I can't have you ride south because the Lionhelms have made it clear as to what awaits those who betrayed them, whether they are friends or family."

"I appreciate the fact that you don't wish to see me dead."

Sir Sybbyl stood up, not bothering to gather the scrolls and messages, leaving them scattered over the dirty table. "I will stay here, my lord. Come what may."

He mimicked her actions but extended an arm for her to grasp his hand. "So shall I."

✳✳✳

Tecla's body couldn't stop shaking.

She had been granted a small cabin; the small vessel of the Sand Towers being pushed at full speed by the wintry winds. Lord Jarvis told her the Good Gods backed them, for they wouldn't have to sail against the wind and they would arrive in Limemeadow before they expected. Tecla, however, wasn't as confident as the young lord.

They boarded the ship quietly after sundown, but not before Jarvis got rid of the plates that bore his crest and displayed the winged defender of the Angeforts. He kept his attire bland and neutral, with padded leather covering his upper body, and offered Tecla his warmer cloak. The fur wasn't thick enough for the winter, but Limemeadow wasn't Silverholde, and according to him, they would safely disembark. Tecla thought about his words as she snuggled into the brown cloak, sitting next to the porthole with her knees bent. She hugged her legs to try and stop shivering, but she failed miserably. She left Mokr to face his brother's rage although the boy tried to be as kind as he could to her. Tecla feared for Mokr's life, but hers was more important, Lord Jarvis said. Her thoughts and worries wouldn't quit haunting her, even as she tried to eat, wash up, and sleep. The ship sailed fast, but she imagined the Sons of Ferngrunn were right behind them, gliding just as rapidly.

Outside the porthole, she saw the flashing light of a lighthouse. They had been at sea for some days now, but Tecla didn't count. The moon shone brightly in the skies after sundown, and she didn't expect the escape to last as long as the time spent traveling from Strongshore to the Sand Towers. Limemeadow was much closer to the northern lands, only a few days away from the capital itself.

There was a distinct knock on her door, and she didn't have the time to allow anyone in. Lord Jarvis bowed deeply, and she saw him carrying a pair of heavy boots. "Forgive me for the intrusion. We will soon reach the harbor, but may I suggest we land on a smaller boat?" She knew it wasn't a question. "You might want to remove the sandals, my lady," he quickly added, handing her the warm shoes. "It is snowing lightly."

"Thank you, Lord Jarvis," Tecla whispered, following his advice. "Why the smaller boat? Is the sea level too low?"

He wasn't good at hiding his emotions. The worry that filled his blue eyes confirmed her own. "I am afraid the Sons of Ferngrunn have sent their fleet after us. Either they realized we were not on the merchant ship I arrived on, or the captain of that vessel gave us away. It matters not," he quickly said, offering his hand. "We will not risk your life on this ship."

Tecla held his hand, following him in silence as they ascended the ladder that connected her quarters to the main deck. The sun was still not ready to set it seemed, but the skies were already tainted by purple and orange hues. A pinnace was already being lowered on the forepart of the deck, the crew members waiting for her and Lord Jarvis. She didn't listen as the young man exchanged a few words with the captain of the merchant ship. She dreaded the news they could have shared. She didn't want to hear about scouting or anything that could have confirmed that Thaum and his men were about to get her, for she doubted she would survive if they managed to capture her. She sat in silence, her head and half her face covered by the hood of Jarvis' cloak. Every sway and every jump, and even the screeching of the ropes had Tecla's heart jumping out of her chest.

    Aside from Lord Jarvis and herself, six other men rode on the boat, grasping the oars they would use for propulsion. They were well paid for their silence, as Lord Jarvis wasted no time before he handed a bag of silvers to each one of them. That money alone would last them a year, Tecla figured. They rowed in synched precision, and Tecla's lips parted in anticipation as she watched the grey, dusty sand of Limemeadow come into view. She could even see the Angefort's stronghold in the distance, with its white walls reflecting the sunlight. The sight of the castle should have quelled her anxiety, but Tecla couldn't find it in her to convince herself that staying with the Angeforts would ensure her safety. Her family should have kept her safe too, and they were the main reason for her predicament.

Three distinct shots could be heard before the sound of wood breaking filled Tecla's ears. She screamed immediately, covering her ears and shutting her eyes before she forced herself to look behind. A much wider warship pierced the merchant vessel she had traveled on with gigantic rope darts, and Tecla found it hard to breathe. She had seen it before. The battened sails, the green hue of the ship, and the fire that emerged from it to engulf the other one; she had been right all along. The Sons of Ferngrunn had managed to catch up with them in no time.

"Faster! Faster, now!" Lord Jarvis ordered the men who executed longer strokes with the blades of the oars.

Tecla's hands curled around the edge of the bench she sat on, only to be suddenly tugged upwards by Jarvis, who then pushed her straight into the cold, salty water. She swallowed a bit, her eyes stingy as she came to the surface, the young lord right behind her. Another pinnace was right behind theirs, advancing fast, three archers making quick work of the rowers as their throats and chests were pierced from behind.

She felt Jarvis reprimand her for her slowness and state of shock, but more water filled her throat as she opened her mouth. He slid an arm around her body, swimming towards the beach. Her cloak was heavy with water, and she was afraid of drowning faster than a babe. How Jarvis managed to swim while fully clothed was a mystery to her. Perhaps, he was more willing to live than her. Tecla's feet came in contact with something, and soon her knees were covered in sand. Her light dress hiked up her legs, and between coughing and heaving, she managed to pull it back down. The blue-eyed man above her hoisted her up, pushing her in the direction of the thin woods ahead.

"Go now, Lady Tecla," he urged her. "Run fast, as fast as you can," he told her, gripping her upper arm until it became red.

"What about you? I don't even know where to go," she protested, her tears already filling with tears.

"The southeastern gates of the city are past these woods. I beg you to go, now."

Her panicked expression morphed into one of regret as she understood why he couldn't escort her anymore. An arrow had pierced his shin between the moment they jumped off the boat and made it to the beach. The salty water added to his pain, and he had lost a good amount of blood swimming. Her hazel orbs looked past him, and she saw the archers finish off the rowers they didn't kill with one shot. They would soon land as well, but they wouldn't kill her and Jarvis with a swift move. Tecla took in the sight of the ship with warm, battened sails burning down the merchants and their goods, glared at the twin hammers carved into the archers' chest plate, and held Jarvis' hands.

"I am not leaving you behind," she told him fiercely. "You have protected me in the memory of our families' friendship. I can't let some ranged cowards kill you."

"I don't plan on dying, my lady," Jarvis said, offering her a warm, yet sad smile. He grasped the hilt of his one-handed sword and kissed her knuckles. "I will just give them a hard time."

Tecla broke into a run, but her clothes were heavy with water, and she quickly stumbled forward, her feet stumbling over a mixture of rocks, shells and even the hem of her dress got in the way. Something sharp and pointy hit the side of her thigh, and as the arrow embedded itself in the ground, she told herself she didn't want to die. She had been thinking about her death to the Sons of Ferngrunn for a while now, but this was the first time it almost became a reality. The young woman gathered the little strength she still possessed, ignoring the cries of those who were falling under Jarvis' sword. Jarvis' own sounds made her heart sink, and she bolted into the thin woods. The pendant braided with her hair was freely slapping against her back, and Tecla snatched it immediately, afraid of losing it. Grandmaster Matillis told her to get rid of it some moons ago, but the Darling Mind was a gift of her lord father, and she wouldn't dispose of it nor let it fall while she attempted to save herself.

The sun was close to setting, but Tecla sobbed away while running, trying not to think of the looming darkness or the warm blood running down her left leg. No more sounds were coming from the beach, but something wasn't quite right. She slowed down, looking around, her eyes unblinking. She swallowed hard, a small whine escaping her lips. She couldn't see the walls of the city. She had probably run in the wrong direction, Tecla thought, her feet slowing down until she merely walked. She wished she could scream if that didn't mean giving away her location. She slid down the trunk of a tree, one that was as slim as her, and she pressed a hand to her chest to try and slow down the beating of her heart. Breathing was difficult, and she wanted to pass away from the fear that consumed her.

A gush of wind was quickly followed by the startling noise of an arrow hitting the tree right next to the one she leaned against, and she yelped. She covered her lips instantly, calling herself all kinds of names, before running away. Galloping sounds became louder than her panting, and Tecla knew it was over.

She saw the white mount before she identified the rider, but it mattered not. Thaum of Ferngrunn had found her, dashing on his Avoryon horse, and Tecla wished she had stayed with Jarvis. Perhaps, arrows would be better than having her head smashed by Thaum's hammer.

✳✳✳

His mouth was still full of sticky, salty oil as he exited the Marked Toad and tied his bag on Arora's saddle. Jascha ran his tongue over his teeth, the taste of fried fish was still very present. He had to admit that the tavern across the owl post served fine food. It was messy and smelly; his hair carried the scent of grease, but he welcomed the change after months of watery soups and pieces of dry, salted meat. He threw his leg over the saddle, ignoring the judging stare he earned from Taf, who leaned against the doorframe of the entrance.

"Ya should stay, fun is about to start, lad."

Jascha's black eyes glanced at the reddening skies. "I don't think so," he replied.

"Took ya quite some days to show up, and now ya leave without a good fight, and a great fuck."

Jascha shook his head at the older man, raising an eyebrow at the way Taf shifted his weight on his long leg. "I sleep early," he said in a light tone.

"The creases and the black shadows under your eyes suggest otherwise."

He had nothing to say about that part. Jascha had spent most of his time in Limemeadow trying to get himself clean and sharpen his blades between visits to places he had only heard of. The oldest temple of Limemeadow was called the Shores of Spirits, but the tall pillar it once was had been reduced to a broken tower with etched figures and faces on every side. They were so dusty it was hard to understand what they represented, and the only part he recognized was the one where a winged beast that looked like the Iathienar without talons fought a serpent twice its size but what caught his attention in the first place were the women's statues by the gates of the temple. They were all naked with their faces shielded by golden masks, and while the clay and the stones of the ruined temple withered away with each passing day, the gold of the masks remained intact. Jascha had wanted to ask the

Angels of Steel that guarded the place how they managed to not have hail scratch down the masks on the least fortunate of days, or how the old wars hadn't destroyed the site, but the Angels were mute, and no holy captain had been in sight since he arrived in the coastal city. Only an old, balding woman tried to warn him while he watched with curious eyes, telling him to leave, for the place was haunted by the spirits of the dead, the fays and their kin and their enemies. Jascha paid no attention to her warning, but he was sure he heard whispers and even music coming from inside the pillar. Entering was forbidden.

Taf was right about his lack of sleep; ever since he stopped at the Shores of Spirit and circled the broken arches surrounding the pillar, the whispers had followed him into his dreams. He saw sarcophagi under the sand and chains that bound them to the arches, and the statue of a person clad in furs and wearing a helmet resided inside the pillar he never entered. The barber who cut his hair and shaved his short beard said the Shores of Spirits was built by Warrior Queen Vaethnil of Old Drixia after her mother passed away to appease the fays of Soleba. Jascha had taken it as his cue to leave Limemeadow, for it seemed that Wilderose was a recurring answer to his questions.

He nodded at the tall man with one leg shorter than the other, wondering how Taf could even brawl properly with half a limb. "Thank you for the meal," Jascha said.

The echoing, loud sound of a horn being blown covered Taf's answer, and they both looked in the direction of the watchtowers. The city bells were rung from every corner, and black, thick smoke emerged from the harbor.

"A fire?" the tavern owner wondered out loud.

"An attack," Jascha corrected him as he saw a surveillant dash past them in the direction of the southern gates, the closest entrance from the harbor.

He couldn't stay trapped in Limemeadow, he told himself as he kicked Arora into a quick pace. He was right behind the surveillant who screamed at the top of his lungs to close the gates, and the iron bars were almost clasped together when Jascha made it past the entrance. The surveillant was yelling at him, he could hear it, but Jascha only glanced back to make sure he wasn't being followed. The surveillant meant well, in his mind, but Jascha decided that very morning he wouldn't spend another day without answers. He rushed past the merchants and the simple people who ran in the direction of the gates before they were locked, paying no attention to those he ran over and those who avoided him by throwing themselves to the side. The Red Road reconnected with the coastal streets past the thin woods that separated the beach from the outskirts of Limemeadow, and Jascha leaned forward as his horse sprinted.

The smell of smoke was heavy in the woods, and he was sure at least a portion of the forest would catch fire. He saw burning ships and boats in the distance as he glanced to his right but he couldn't quite see the sails of the vessels to understand where they came from and what they could want. Not that it mattered much to him.

Echoes of hooves stomping over the fallen leaves reached his ears and Jascha narrowed his eyes. Something flew past him, and he let out a groan, nearly losing his balance. Something had scratched past his cheek, and when a droplet of blood fell on his mount's white coat, Jascha pulled on the reins of his horse to slow down. An arrow embedded itself in the tree next to him, but he couldn't see who shot it as the skies were darker and the moon peeked behind clouds. Jascha pressed his lips together, his right hand coming to unsheathe the longer blade strapped on his back, the one with the fanged pommel. He saw another rider in the distance and a silhouette than ran in his direction, and Jascha twisted his body as to crouch on the saddle, coming to a nearly standing position on Arora's back while avoiding the lower branches of the skinny trees.

"There you are," he whispered as he saw the archer ready to shoot, but the man seemed surprised to see him.

Jascha launched himself aiming his blade at the archer's neck. The two of them fell to the ground, rolling in the snow as the archer's horse fled while his slowed and stopped a few paces ahead. Jascha watched as the dark undertones of his steel were coated with blood and the archer's head came off, rolling until it hit the base of a trunk. He blinked, recoiling when he saw the man's bow and the twin hammers above the arrow rest. Jascha rose to his feet, sheathing his weapon and glancing in the direction the archer had come from. It wasn't from the beach but the northern parts of the woods, meaning whoever attacked the city had landed before the city bells rang.

A light whimper interrupted his thoughts, and when he turned around fully, he saw a girl crawl away from a tree. She looked at him with wide-open, hazel orbs. It was the girl from the athenaeum, he realized. She was dirty, and drenched, with a light cloak that did a poor job at covering the nearly transparent dress she wore. Jascha averted his eyes, grabbing the reins of his horse before he hopped on. The fear on the girl's face was the clear indication that the archer had been after her.

"More will come," he told her, narrowing his eyes in the distance. "The city closed the gates already."

Tecla came to stand in front of him, readjusting Lord Jarvis' cloak. She didn't say anything as she stared into the horse's deep blue eyes, and flinched when the man who decapitated one of Thaum's soldiers extended a hand.

Jascha gave her a look full of annoyance. "Do you plan on staying here? I don't have all night, and I doubt you'll stumble across someone else before they find you." When she hesitated, he noted the way she eyed the saddle. It had no lower pommel.

"I don't know how to ride on that," Tecla whispered meekly, her cheeks turning redder than they already were from the chase. She took his hand nonetheless, nearly falling off the moment she threw her left leg over the saddle. "Sorry," she whispered, holding onto the front arch.

Jascha was tempted to have a jab at ladies and their sidesaddles, but instead, he scooted backward to put more space between the two of them. The girl was small enough to fit without having to double ride with one person squeezing the cantle, but as Arora flew in the direction of the Red Road, he wondered what he was doing. He had to reach Wilderose, he couldn't be looking after girls who had a bounty dangling over their heads.

Something warm dripped over his leg, and Jascha glared down. "You're bleeding," he commented. "Hold that wound," he ordered her. "If they have dogs, they'll find you in no time."

Tecla paled. She hurriedly tried to tear a piece of her skirt, nearly losing her balance when her hands let go of the saddle pommel, and the man behind her made a sound. She felt him reach for something, and soon a small bag fell in front of her. He said nothing, but the horse slowed down, and she fished for any piece of linen she could find inside the leather bag. She was surprised to find a clean shirt and with a bite, she quickly tore a sleeve to press it against her open wound. She had to take care of that before it worsened, but the white mount was already going faster.

She wanted to thank him, whoever he was, but nothing came out other than a simple introduction. "I am Tecla Lionhelm."

Jascha exhaled loudly, almost in boredom. "I know," he whispered, his breath hot against her ear.

It smelled of something sweet and fried. She was hungry.

Chapter XXXVII

A Sense of Peace

The Red Road was cluttered with fishermen, merchants, and even villeins who fled Limemeadow the moment the fire spread from the harbor to the main residential areas of the city. The clear path led north, in the direction of the capital, but elders and children alike strayed from it to follow the Rough Rill, hoping to reach Founder's Breach in the West before the winter and the fever claimed their lives.

Jascha's horse came to a stop; it was dark all around them, only the stars and the torches held by the vagrants lighted the road. He wanted to ride in the direction of the Rough Rill only to cross Courtbridge before dawn, but there were surveillants and Angels of Steel down the road. They looked very alike when surrounded by the shadows, only the Swords of the Faith wore armors of very light color and matching golden capes, while the surveillants proudly flaunted the emerald of their uniforms. One man sitting by a handcart full of caged owls called for people's attention as they walked past him, repeating the same words over and over again, his stare blank and his lips chapped.

"Rough Rill straight ahead," he said, ringing a small bell. "Drixia has risen."

Jascha followed the pace of the other travelers, but they frequently halted whilst all he wanted was to get past them. He couldn't, not with all the soldiers around to guard the path; it seemed the slowness was due to a holy captain serving warm soup to every person who left the Red Road to venture around the forests and abandoned villages that stood between Courtbridge and Founder's Breach.

Tecla was snoring lightly, her face hidden by the hood of her cloak. She was slumped into his chest as if he were a chair, and she almost dropped the piece of linen she pressed against the wound in her thigh. Jascha was left with one hand holding the reins and the other pushing the cloth against the gash. It probably stopped bleeding, but the lighting wasn't enough for him to properly check. She jumped at once, smelling the chicken soup. She let out a chirpy yawn, tired eyes glancing around, and a large bowl was handed to her.

He recognized the holy captain instantly. "Chadras," he spoke.

The sandy-haired man smiled fondly at him but not before bowing respectfully. "Jascha. It's good to see you're well. Are you going home?"

The holy captain spoke with him, but his eyes were focused on the young woman who gulped down the soup. Jascha wondered if the middle-aged man recognized her or was simply curious, but either way, he couldn't waste too much time in pleasantries. "I wished to cross Courtbridge," he answered. "What are you doing here?"

The holy captain nodded his chin at the cauldrons around him. "We took the provisions from the Temple of Phorbas. We wish to help those in need during the exode."

"Aren't there more people to help in the capital?" Jascha countered, his thoughts immediately directed at Mawde and her little child in Jamys' Yard, although he had little to no hope for them.

"There are not so many people left to help," the holy captain whispered, his shoulders slumping. "Those we can help we try to direct to Founder's Breach. Their gates are open. Courtbridge, on the other hand, is locked. And the drawbridges to cross the Rough Rill and head south are raised," Captain Chadras revealed.

Jascha could feel Tecla's back stiffen, and he pushed the bowl closer to her face. The least she spoke the better. "The South is no longer accessible," he reworded the man's information.

"The Kingdom of Drixia sent owls all over the continent to inform the other lords they are now an independent kingdom and that they had no part in the Regency's downfall. They stated their… disappointment after the betrayal of Lord Arther Angefort, Sir Ferrand Nickletail, and Lord Theliel Lionhelm, considering the years the South spent supporting the Regency, on a personal and economical level.

"Their borders are closed, yes," the holy captain concluded.

Jascha's jaw tightened, and he diverted his glare from Chadras' face. He should have left long before, he reasoned inwardly. He didn't think the Lionhelms would close their borders, and the only other way to access Wilderose was to board a ship in Limemeadow and enter Edgemere, but it looked like that option as well seemed unachievable. His fists were so tight that his knuckles were probably turning white under his gloves.

"Who is the King of Drixia now?" Tecla's soft voice broke the silence around him.

"I hear Lord Tylennald's coronation will soon take place."

She watched as the holy captain glanced at the man with the bell. He was from the owl post, she realized. It was official, then. Something had happened to Lord Tiran, and although Jarvis said she was her father's heir, it was too late. Lady Voladea's favorite ruled over Strongshore and Tecla chuckled bitterly. Perhaps, Lord Jarvis too died in vain.

"I suggest you head home," Captain Chadras told Jascha while he handed a bowl of soup to the old woman behind them. "Circle Silverholde and go home."

Tecla handed the empty bowl to the captain, who offered Jascha some food, which the younger man turned down. He hurried his horse in the direction of Silverholde, following the Red Road.

Both blank and curious stares were sent his way as the Defenders of the Faith watched him ride uphill. He kept the pace rather slow, finding it hard to dash away from Limemeadow when a girl who couldn't ride without a sidesaddle sat in front of him. She would probably fall off at some point and break her neck, not to mention he was a little tired as well. It would take them a little over a day to reach the outskirts of the capital if they didn't stop too often. He wasn't sure if this girl was used to riding.

As though she read his mind, Tecla asked, "Are we stopping soon?"

"As soon as we get a little further away from the Rippling Run," Jascha answered. "I don't plan on sleeping next to a freezing river."

She nodded, but he didn't notice. "I haven't thanked you," Tecla said, ashamed of her lack of manners. "Jascha, is that right? Thank you for not leaving me to die," she went on, laughing lightly at herself. "You don't have to carry me around."

Jascha glanced at the skies when he wanted to roll his eyes. She was a rambler.

"I mean, I got the part where I couldn't get home but—"

"Get off then," he spat.

"What?"

"I never understood people like you," he sighed out. "You say I don't have to do anything for you, but from what I see you can't go anywhere on your own. Just be quiet."

Tecla frowned, clasping the pommel of the saddle and straightening her back. It was only then that she realized he was still pressing the soft linen against her thigh, and her anger evaporated. She remained silent as she gently pushed his hand away to check if the bleeding had stopped, and she grabbed the dirtied piece of his shirt sleeve to bandage her thigh. It was tricky not to fall from the horse as she lifted her leg a little, but thankfully, Jascha didn't scold her when she leaned in a bit to not lose her balance.

"That needs to be cauterized," she heard him say.

As much as she agreed, she didn't want to take care of the wound. It would be more pain for her to endure, and at that point, she couldn't help but wonder why she bothered trying to survive. It so appeared that aside from Lord Jarvis, and perhaps this stranger, not many people cared for her well-being. Lyzon did, she reminded herself. She still hoped Lyzon was alive. And Fran. And Tomas. It was stupid of her but she fantasized about the day she could live a simple life in a small village, surrounded by the people who cared. All she wanted was to see them again. The hut they would share wouldn't have to be too big either; she just wanted a field full of yellow daisies surrounding the house. And maybe a peach tree.

"Do you know any scary story?"

Jascha's eyebrows shot up. "What?"

"Whenever I rode with my brother, we would tell each other scary stories. To pass the time." She sounded nostalgic, as well as a little childish, recalling times that never were.

"Is this the same brother who dismantled the Regency?"

Tecla chose to ignore that bit. She preferred giving Theliel the benefit of the doubt until she met him again. After what her family did to her, she wouldn't put it past them to pin lies on Theliel as well. "So," she cleared her throat. "Do you know any stories?"

Silence.

"Theliel told me about this crazy night when he and Lord Angefort stopped at the castle of the Rosenfields, right beneath Wilderose," she began, drumming her fingers against the saddle and occasionally petting Arora's fur. "It was just them and some of the greatest warriors of the South. Well, they shared a pleasant dinner filled with laughter and rumors about other knights and lords, until someone knocked on the doors of the great hall.

"But there was no one behind the doors," Tecla told him, lowering her voice. "And then, arrows rained from the battlements, killing dozens of warriors, but no one could see who was shooting at them.

"Corpses crawled from the portcullis and out of the well, and fire consumed the great hall. Theliel saw the rotting corpses of little girls who screamed for help, and brides reduced to skeleton figures, and by the time it was over, less than twenty men survived."

Jascha made a noise in the back of his throat. "Made-up."

Tecla ignored his comment, clapping her hands. "Oh, and I forgot. Before that, deep in the forest, they saw a man butchered by unseen criminals. Butchered, they said, for his limbs had been torn from his body, tree roots piercing his hands, his feet, curling around his spine until they reached his neck and snapped it."

She peeked behind to gauge a reaction from him, but Jascha sat completely still, his breathing even. Tecla looked away; boredom was written all over her face. She couldn't believe any part of the tale frightened him a least a little; she had been terrorized when Theliel told her. Then again, with the way Jascha had flown from his horse to the archer hunting her, she imagined he had had his share of bloody scenes.

The truth was that the description of that man's death felt too familiar to Jascha. He could feel the gripping pain around his bones right after she mentioned it, and his mind was already trying to find a way to reach that forest although the borders wouldn't be easy to cross. He was ready to raze down cities to reach Wilderose and Jascha's frustration upon realizing he had wasted precious days in Limemeadow culminated at that moment.

"Your turn," he heard her say. "It's your turn to tell a scary story," Tecla elaborated.

"No stories," Jascha replied. His throat felt sore all of sudden.

"Just one," she pressed, staring ahead when she caught a glimpse of a night owl perched on a high branch. A part of Tecla wondered if there were any other animals around at night, at least in the area they traveled around. She hoped none of those ate human flesh.

Jascha moved behind her, and she felt his chest press a little closer to her back. "I killed a woman," he spoke without difficulty. "I stabbed her flesh a dozen times until I saw her lungs and her insides went limp. It was relieving."

Tecla's faint smile disappeared, and her fingers stopped drumming. She felt her stomach churn at the mention of the woman's insides, and her left hand rested on her tummy. Could it be that the Sons of Ferngrunn weren't the worst men she had ever met? She felt Jascha's hand on hers, pressing into her stomach.

"No more stories," he breathed against her face before gripping the reins with both hands again.

❇❇❇

He wasn't dead, Goldsnout thought as his eyes fluttered open. He was surrounded by people who whispered and others who sounded in pain, groaning, and grunting. The ceiling was nothing more than the roof of a tent full of tiny holes, and water dripped down the wooden poles that kept it up. He could hear the crows chant outside as if they beckoned the sick to die quickly so they could, at last, feed themselves.

Goldsnout was lying on a wobbly bed, and he felt a tight bandage around his head. The pulsating pain inside his skull was bearable, and he figured he had been out for quite some days. He felt stitches on his arms and legs, and someone had left some water and bread on the small table next to his bed. He sat up slowly, exhaling loudly when his back cracked. Being in the same position for days and nights without waking up had weakened him more than any injury. He sighed in relief as he spotted his armor and his broadsword by the bed. The last thing he remembered was Chief Dunac's face, but he wasn't entirely sure what they had been discussing before his mind went blank. He had intended to leave, and that appeared to be that.

A large, round man with a massive belly wobbled in his direction, his vivid green robes hurting Goldsnout's eyes. The man kneeled awkwardly beside him, dipping a towel in some warm water before taking Goldsnout's hands to clean them. "You are finally awake," the big man spoke. "It has been days; we thought you'd never recover."

The young officer eyed the man's purple turban and his fat nose. Every part of his face moved whenever he talked. "Where am I?"

"Healing camp. Behind Maugre's Arena," the man replied. "We are the physicians and educators who decided to not leave the capital. My name is Tomas," he added with a bright smile. "I used to be an educator. And you?"

Goldsnout took the towel from him, feeling a little uncomfortable when an older man washed him as if he were a babe. He wiped his forearms clean, careful not to go over the stitches too much. "I was an officer. A surveillant," he replied. "I left the ranks. I think."

"There is no shame in that," Tomas told him, huffing and coughing as he stood up. "Do you have any family to return to?"

Goldsnout's lips parted, letting out a sound that was neither a chuckle nor a groan. His neck was tense and his eyes watery. The first person who came to mind was his mother, a woman too old and too kind, and he wondered if she was still alive. He was worried that even Limemeadow, the city of spices and trade with a harbor full of thin, colored silks and men who fried everything they found, suffered from the famine and desolation that claimed Silverholde. He feared the surveillants had abandoned their ranks in every other land, stolen goods and coin, and put the heads of those who opposed them on spikes. His mother now lived in a small house by the watermill; she didn't even have a real door but a simple fabric covering the entrance of her place like curtains decorated a window.

And then, there was Rantha. He thought about her too, constantly. He hoped nobody stormed Rainier's End, and that if they had, she would be doing what Tomas did; take care of those who somehow survived. He knew it was what made Rantha feel privileged; to ensure that others survived and lived the best of their lives. She let her wishes die for others to accomplish theirs, and Goldsnout couldn't imagine what it would feel like to run to her and find out his hopes were only whims.

"I do," he eventually replied, dipping the towel in the water to rinse it. "I am not sure if I can go and see them."

His lime eyes met Tomas' warm stare. The former educator sighed loudly, pointing at the trays of food resting between the rows of stretchers and improvised beds. "I will get you something to fill your stomach. The gates of the city are closed, I am afraid," he admitted. "But I've heard some of the bravest decide to let their bodies being carried away by the rivers. I would simply climb the walls, but I am a bit too heavy."

Tomas' laughter filled the tent, and Goldsnout found himself smiling. It was nowhere near a grin nor a display of happiness, but the tanned educator's words gave him a little hope. He too would rather climb the walls instead of attempting to swim or row his way out, but he was covered in bruises and severely famished. He doubted he would be able to move before a few days, and even then, he wasn't convinced he could climb the walls without anybody hearing him groan or shooting an arrow at him in the middle of the night, thinking he was an intruder and not someone who was simply unwilling to die in a graveyard he didn't belong to.

Goldsnout slurped his broth almost in silence, his void stare trailing past his bed to watch those who did beg to die. They had amputated limbs; others had gone blind or were burned to such an extent they couldn't move anymore. Probably some of them had met the same fate as those the Surveillance condemned with liters of boiling water. They had fought against the Regency, and the Regency healed them, just as he had fought for the Regency and decided to abandon it.

"Any owls around here?" he asked Tomas the moment the man handed him another piece of bread to give his meal a semblance of flavor. "I would like to send a message."

The educator shook his head, the smile never leaving his plump lips. "The owl post is closed and the messengers have left the city. Sir Sybbyl Nobleleaf ordered that any man, woman, or child who can leave the capital does so."

"So, with your authorization, I could leave," Goldsnout reasoned.

"You were one of them," Tomas pointed out. "I am fairly sure it's treason in your case."

"Well," Goldsnout said, splitting the piece of bread to hand half to the educator. "Make sure I can climb those walls then." They shared a quiet laugh along with the loaf, and the red-haired man added, "I have a woman to marry, and a mother to take care of."

"May the Oracle and Her Angels grant your wishes and fill your heart with peace."

✹✹✹

The fire they used to warm themselves was small and quiet, and with so many trees surrounding them, it looked like a small ember about to die. Jascha's horse was tied to a branch and dozed standing. She had seen him chew on dry meat after he threw his bag at the bottom of a tree to use it as a cushion, but he wasn't about to lie down and sleep. He was heating the steel of his short blade over the fire, and Tecla wished he had simply slammed her head against something, anything. She didn't want to feel it. She didn't want to see it.

"Bite this," he told her, throwing a branch at her as though she was a bitch.

She whimpered. "Does it have to be a branch?" she argued with no real intention of fighting. Talking calmed her nerves. She had been surrounded by so many people who didn't speak the modern tongue that it was liberating to finally say anything.

Jascha ignored her question. "Lift the dress," he ordered, his voice a little lower than before.

Tecla did as he told her, and soon her injured thigh was exposed. The wound was nasty, she thought as she let the dirty fabric of her pale dress pool around her upper thigh. It was red and brown and black, and she swore she saw a fly crawl from that hole. She briefly glanced at Jascha, whose eyes were solely focused on the wound, and she saw the way he scrunched his nose in mild disgust.

"If you need to scream or pass out, just do so," he advised her. "No point fighting it."

His black pools looked into hers, and he repeated, "Bite the stick."

Tecla closed her eyes and shoved the piece of wood between her teeth. She didn't immediately feel the pain as the hot blade was pressed against her flesh. It stung like a hard pinch until she felt her skin on fire, and strangled screams made it past her lips, her legs trembled violently, and she squirmed in place as her left hand dug into the dirt while the other arm reached out to push Jascha away. She felt him grab her wrist and pin it down, nearly twisting her arm. She was so weak in comparison that one pull of his felt like a heavy punch.

"It's over," she heard him say in a tone that didn't match his brute force.

He reached for his bag by the roots of the tree that protruded from the ground and took what remained of his clean shirt. He tore another piece with precision using his teeth and carefully wrapped it around her leg, making the bandage tight but still quite loose to allow normal blood flow. She watched with nearly fascinated eyes as he eventually threw what remained of his clothing inside the bag and pulled down her dress. He was mindful of his fingertips, and Tecla never felt Jascha's skin brush against hers. Not that she particularly wanted to, she thought to herself.

Caught up in her thoughts, Tecla was unprepared when a thick and heavy cloak fell on top of her, covering her body entirely. She swam to find a way out as if she were trapped under endless sheets, and when she finally managed to breathe again, most of her hair was covering her face in a messy shroud. She pushed her mane back, flushed and annoyed, and she glared at the man across the fire, who crossed his arms over his chest as he sat against the trunk, his sheathed blades in his arms.

"You need to cover yourself or the fever will get you before the Sons of Ferngrunn do," Jascha told her, closing his eyes. "Are they after you because of your brother and the Regency?"

Tecla lowered her gaze, wrapping herself in his comfortable cloak. It smelled of woods and fish and rain, and she liked it. She felt oddly at ease. "They could think I'm responsible for that too but that's not why they attacked Limemeadow," she replied. "They feel betrayed by the Regency, and they will march to the capital, I'm sure. They want my head because they believe I bewitched the youngest brother while I was still being… matched."

Jascha opened his left eye. "Matched?"

"I didn't do anything," she protested. "It was a misunderstanding."

"So, they took turns," he said out loud, causing her to feel deeply ashamed, unrightfully so. "Typical dogs," Jascha sneered. "One of them touched you before it was his time."

"Wait, you—" Tecla swallowed before she choked on her saliva. "You know about their tradition?" How could she not be aware of their practices but a simple man could? Did the Sons of Ferngrunn have a reputation or was it common knowledge she just happened to skip? Tecla wanted to hit something, hard, but she was surrounded by snow and mud, and the trunks of the trees would shatter her hand.

"Why would you choose them without knowing anything about their rules?" he asked her back, closing his eyes again. "Are you demented?"

"I didn't choose anyone. My moth—my father's wife chose for me. She didn't bother informing me," Tecla retorted, forcing herself to lie down by the fire. "She's not my mother," she whispered in a neutral tone that surprised even her.

"Can I… Can I ask you where we are going?" she asked, pressing her little fists under her chin.

"South was the plan but it seems neither of us has been graced with fortune," he muttered, his voice heavy with sleep.

Tecla let him rest, wondering how he wasn't freezing to death with only padded leather and regular garments covering his body. She realized that she wasn't sleepy nor tired, as she had rested during the ride, whilst he hadn't. Jascha's face looked far more relaxed, and one recent scratch marred his right cheek where the archer who was after her hit him. Tecla thought she had been very lucky, between Lord Jarvis and this kind, albeit rude person who looked after her despite knowing only her name. She guessed it was her name that brought her both good and bad fortune, and while she worried about her uncertain future and wondered whether Jascha had truly stabbed a woman a dozen times, Tecla fell into a soundless sleep right before dawn.

Chapter XXXVIII

The Quiet Tear

It was the year sixty-three after the Creation, but as the forty royal guards pointed their swords at the ceiling of the throne room, the Court of Drixia sang the beginning of the first year after the Collapse. Voladea Lionhelm had abandoned the title of Lady of Strongshore in favor of Queen Mother, but she was granted only a seat of honor beneath the throne. As the pride of her life walked carefully down the aisle that led to the throne, she watched with a veil over her face and a hefty weight on her chest. This was the moment she had always dreamed of but never thought possible. What it cost her and her family was not a fair price, that much she knew, but she had lived enough to see her son crowned king. She found solace in it, even if for only a moment between shallow breaths.

Tylennald's footsteps echoed through the once audience chamber, now restored to its former use and purpose. His shoes were ivory-colored with silver decorating the heels and the tips, the swirling patterns complicated enough to make one's head reel. His coat was shimmering cobalt with white fur grazing the hem and hugging his broad shoulders. On the back of the cape that topped his coat, the three lion heads that hissed at each other with snake-like tongues were crowned and gathered around the blade of a sword bigger than them. Tylennald didn't lower his gaze as he covered thousands of years of history painted at his feet while he advanced. He knew it by heart, just as everyone else who was born and raised in the South. There was no mystery to be unraveled between the snowy hills of the Avoryon and the path made of blood, dirt, and torture down the map of the continent. And so, he walked past the unconquered towers and the hostile black mountains that could no longer be seen through the fog. He found the cradle of peace and its pavilion, the shores of the dead and its lighthouse, but the vastest of lands was his only, past the Rough Rill and draining the seas. Wallysa walked behind him in a dress that mimicked his attire and jewels heavier than her. She held her head high but was escorted by no one. There should have been her firstborn by her side, and her daughter behind her, and their children if they had any. They would have been followed by Tesfira and her family, Theliel and Tecla, and their other relatives would have gathered around the cushioned chair as painted as the marbled floor. They would all have been reunited under the words of their family, carved with precision above their heads. Formed from many, now as one; but Tylennald found he was the only one.

    The throne had been modified to erase the emerald and the gold of the Regency that his father once commissioned, and where the backrest arched, a silver lion skull had been forged to frame the king's head as he sat. Tylennald turned around, his face cold and his hair brushed back. He sat down, the Holy Commander appearing next to him to place the blessed family sword on his lap. It was a weapon Lord Tithan himself refused to bring along whenever he left Strongshore. The steel shone like the stars in the night, a bright glimmer of blue and gold, with the fuller part of the blade being the most colored. The grip was made of quiet tears, black and mysterious, like the rocks found at the bottom of the Rough Rill. The pommel was a lion's mouth, and the rain guard a lion's claw. They said the sword, Silencer, had been forged from Alatros the Red's weapons, a mixture of blunt ends and bastard iron that only magic and Iathienar bones could hold together.

    "Tylennald, son of Tithan, Heir of the Reds and Potentate of the Salurites," the Holy Commander began, detaching the skull mounted on the backrest of the throne, "on this day, you become the King of Drixia and those who oppose you shall meet their end. Their bodies will fall and their heads will be cut off; their skulls will be piled and melted until from many, they become one."

    The teeth of the lion's skull bit Tylennald's forehead when the crown was lowered and the Holy Commander kneeled beside him. The royal guards cheered and the southern knights bowed; their ladies bowed and the servants brought black wine and honeyed turkey, but one man was louder than all the others, and his voice bounced from wall to wall.

"Praised be the King of Drixia!"

And praised he was, Voladea thought behind her layers of black. Acclaimed he would be as the beasts crawled back in their foggy dens and the snakes drowned in their seas of sand. His hazels looked at her and her body tensed. Gone was the respect that once filled his eyes and warmed her chest, replaced by a calculating mind and a remorseful heart. Tylennald's square cheeks and bold nose were framed by a strong forehead and a clean jaw. He had always looked a lot like his father to the point they could have been brothers, and now that he looked at her the way Tithan used to, Voladea felt like the outsider she had always been all over again. Tylennald blamed her for Tesfira's death, and he put his half-sister's life above the counsel of his mother. He had no idea to what extent she pushed herself to ensure his position.

"He will be a great king," she heard Healer Martus whisper beside her, bowing his head in respect.

"Tylennald will be," Voladea agreed, her dry lips breaking as she opened her mouth to speak. "For a time, perhaps a generation, unless his head weighs more than the crown."

"That is no untroubled thought."

"I have committed all kinds of misdemeanors to see him where he is," Voladea whispered, her voice breaking. "And my reward is to be treated as furniture."

Martus placed a comforting hand on her elbow. "Grief changes men, but they always come back to their senses."

"Even when they are absolute monarchs?" she asked, wishing not to hear his answer as she turned heels and quietly left the room.

Her black attire disappeared between the shadows and her absence wasn't noted.

✳✳✳

The cold water soothed her scalp while the warm sun rays dried her dress over her body. Tecla lied upside down on the river bank, soaking her hair in hopes of cleaning it. She woke up when the sun was already high in the sky, and Jascha was nowhere to be found. Her first thought was that he ended up abandoning her to her fate, but then she saw his horse and his bag, and she figured he went to find something to eat or needed some time alone. She understood he wasn't a talkative person. They traveled more the day before, and he drove his horse fast through the mist until the Rippling Run crossed paths with another river and they stopped for the night. Tecla's hair was reduced to a tangled and dirty mess, and as soon as she was alone, she dipped her feet in the Restless Channel, and then her entire body, leaving her light cloak along with Jascha's on a nearby branch. She had shaken the dirt off them, but she felt dirtier than her clothes were.

Tecla thought she was glad that no one seemed to be passing by, for the nearly transparent dress covered very little. She toyed with her pendant, letting the stream wash away the salt and the dust. She sat up slowly, shivering when a light breeze caressed her skin and fought with her fingers to untangle the knots. Her hair was even matted in some places, and she figured she would have to chop some locks if she didn't find a way to comb her hair. She turned around to walk in the direction of the tree where she had left her boots and cloak, only to find Jascha sitting by the fire, roasting what looked like a little less than ten squirrels.

She made no sound as she wore Jarvis' cloak again and slid the boots over her ankles. She handed Jascha his cloak; it was a warm sunny day even though the winter was far from over. He shrugged it off. His eyes were fixed on her chest, or so she thought until her face was redder than berries and she realized it was the pendant he was staring at.

Tecla sat next to him. "My father gifted me this when I was born, but I rarely wore it. The necklace is long and I was always too small. My maid eventually came up with the idea of braiding it into my hair," she babbled away until she was handed a slightly burnt squirrel.

"The Darling Mind," Jascha whispered, grabbing some food as well. "Looks smaller than I thought."

She tilted her head, a slight smile adorning her lips. "You sure know a lot of things for a simple man," she told him. "But yes, it is smaller than it should be. I was told the other half was lost." Tecla nibbled at her food, glancing at the pendant that dangled from her neck and rested on her lap. The meat was tasteless, but it was better than eating dirt.

"I've been taught how to read," Jascha replied.

The right side of his mouth slightly curved up; it wasn't quite a smile, but it was a change from his usual demeanor around her.

"There is a…" He paused, wiping his mouth with his fingers. "There is a place, not too far from here. A shelter, if you will. In case you want to stay somewhere safe."

Tecla frowned, her mouth forming a small pout while she thought about it. "Is it, though? Safe, I mean."

"I am not sure." He rested his elbows on his bent knees, leaning closer to the fire. "There are some abandoned stables and huntsmen's huts before Rainier's End; we could get there before sunset if we leave soon. I'd rather have a roof over my head tonight," Jascha informed her. "A snowstorm approaches."

Her hazel eyes glanced at the clear sky, and she sent him a dubious look. "How do you know?"

"Arora knows. She's been in a mood all morning."

Her stare trailed back to the mare that dozed in the shade of the tree, and she dared not question his words. She figured some people had a special connection with their animals; Theliel too had a strong relationship with his first horse, she remembered. Tecla had been jealous of it as well, and she pestered their father so he would allow her to adopt and raise a pet of her own, but he always refused. Father said animals who couldn't run free were miserable. Tecla could still hear his voice as he lectured her about the Red Summer when the Reds of Vaethnil battled the Reds of her brother Rhofros and to distinguish themselves, Vaethnil's sons wore their beasts as protection, caring very little about the lions going extinct. Tecla rebutted often that she needed no lion, even a small forest cat would suffice, but none of her wishes was ever granted. It all sounded silly to her now. The thought of Strongshore alone felt foreign and lost as if eons had passed since she left home. Soon she would be fifteen years of age, a grown woman most would say, and she felt less of a child as well. All the little things that frightened her had vanished from her mind, but all that positively intimidated her or made her curious was whisked away as well. Perhaps, this was what Lady Voladea meant when she said it was time to become an adult.

  Tecla had never gone outside Silverholde before. She had traveled along the Red Road with Theliel, but they had been headed to the southern gates of the city and followed the street that climbed to the Pavilion without really stopping anywhere. By the time it was sundown, Jascha halted his horse between a hilly valley and a forest so dark and thick it made Wilderose look like a clearing. There was not a single trace of people living nearby, and the huts were empty, just as

Jascha told her. The huntsmen had nothing to hunt in this area since the Violet Delusion, and they as well perished a long time ago. Still, she heard crows, and where crows went death could be found, which meant that at some point something did live. The wind blew harshly, messing her hair and lifting her dress. Tecla hugged herself, pushing her way inside the little hut that smelled of mold while Jascha tied his horse inside the stable.

  Her fingertips traced the windowsill and she peeked through the broken glass. She saw a well in the yard, but something had been growing inside for many years as she saw roots and branches and things that even moved come out of it. She shivered, looking away. The fireplace didn't look like it could be used, but she wasn't sure. She had never lighted a fire before. Lyzon took care of that, always, and now Jascha did. She sat by the spent fireplace, waiting and hoping that there were no mice or someone's bones lurking in the other corners of the room.

  Jascha slammed the door behind him but remained still by the frame. One of his hands gripped the hilt of the dagger strapped to his side, and he seemed to be listening closely. Tecla's heart started beating rapidly at the mere thought that the Sons of Ferngrunn had caught up with them, and she crawled closer, making no noise. She heard the voices of two, maybe three men. They spoke the modern tongue, and that in itself was a relief. They couldn't be Thaum's men, she told herself. Their accent was as heavy as their words were crude. Tecla stood up carefully, hidden between the corner of the wall and Jascha's shoulder. She tried to say something, but he placed two fingers over her lips like a silent command to remain quiet.

"That was kind of easy," a man who walked by the hut said. She heard a splash of water, and she figured he was cleaning himself by the stream.

"That village was full of old men and sickly children; what did you expect?" another man commented.

Jascha made a noise, and Tecla instantly tried to hold him as he fell to his knees. She didn't know what was happening, although her first thoughts were that he was sick and she instantly blamed herself for wearing his cloak so often; the constant changes in temperature probably caused his stomach to feel iffy. Or maybe it was the fever. She kneeled beside him, trying to see his face in the darkness, but she couldn't.

He coughed, and something spilled over her. "Good Gods," she whispered, raising a hand. "You are bleeding," she noted, panicking faster than when Jarvis had dragged her across the marketplace to escape from the Sand Towers. "What is wrong?" Tecla pressed, shaking his shoulders. "What do I do?"

Jascha didn't reply. His head lolled backward, and Tecla threw her arms around his shoulders to avoid him bumping straight into the wall. His forehead rested between her neck and shoulder. She had to think of something. His body spasmed and he sounded like he was choking on something.

There wasn't a part of her body that didn't shake as she tried to lift him. She slid the scabbard of his twin swords off his back and put it down as quietly as possible. Next, she pressed her own back against the wall and let the man lie down, resting his head on her lap and forcing his body to the side. She wasn't sure this would help, but at least he breathed now.

The three men outside still guffawed outside, and Tecla unsheathed the smaller blade Jascha carried around. She couldn't even see how big it was and what edge was sharp, but it calmed her to hold it. Just in case, she thought. Just in case they came in.

"Well, they had fine women," the first man said. "That little healer kid. Marie, Marel, or something. Truly fine," he went on, making high-pitched, lewd sounds. "And she kept saying no as if she didn't enjoy it."

Tecla tasted the bile in her throat. Was this how Thaum and Remm talked about her too? "No," she whispered. It couldn't be. It hadn't been the same, she repeated to herself. The rogues outside had wanted to hurt the woman they talked about; she wished to think at least Thaum's intention was different. It could have been a lie she told herself, but it helped her steady her breathing.

"Please," she begged no one. "No noise," she told both herself and the man who was still very much in pain.

At last, the men left, mentioning a big snowstorm ahead, and Tecla let out a loud sigh, dropping the light sword. She broke into tears, failing to understand why, but knowing deep inside that she had hit the bottom. Those men had awakened all kinds of memories inside her, and she softly slammed the back of her head against the wall. She wanted to sleep, she wanted to forget. She wanted it to end.

One of her hands was entangled in Jascha's long black hair and as he opened his eyes, he felt as if he had slept for a decade. The metallic taste of blood was still fresh in his mouth, and he groaned, rolling off her lap. He saw the starless sky through the broken window, and he realized he had been out for quite some time. The sun hadn't set yet when he felt his ears ring and his chest tighten. It was odd, he thought as he tried to stretch his legs on the floor. In the past, he would have been out for days and bleeding until he forgot what he saw. This time he couldn't quite remember either, but he was awake, and his head was reeling as if it was still happening. But it wasn't. He smelled smoke and heard loud prayers, and he thought he saw banners flapping in the wind, but nothing else was clear enough.

Tecla moved beside him, and she was probably trying to see his face. "What happened?" she asked quietly.

He chose not to answer. "Are they gone?" Jascha asked instead. He knew they were, but he didn't want to tell her anything. Talking about it would anger him, and for once he didn't feel the rage bubble inside him. He didn't want that to change so soon.

"They are."

"Get some rest then," he told her, closing his eyes and toying with the hilt of his dagger. He unsheathed the weapon only a bit before letting it slide back inside its protection, the slight noise lulling him to sleep and evening his breathing. The problem was the girl's sniffling. "What is it?" he grumbled.

"Nothing," Tecla muttered, inching her body away.

"Horseshit," he commented dryly. "Are you cold?"

She didn't respond straight away. She wasn't exactly warm, but that wasn't the reason she was upset. Still, she preferred not to tell him the truth; he wasn't very straightforward either, so in Tecla's eyes they could both mind their own. "I guess," she whispered back, fingering the light material of her brown cloak. When riding Jascha always wore his bear fur, and he hadn't handed it to her earlier when they dismounted.

The young lady heard the rustling of clothes and she felt the soft fur graze her cheek. "Take half," he ordered her. "I don't feel quite well," he admitted in a lower voice. He sounded weak.

Tecla rolled inside the open cloak until her face met his shoulder, and she stiffened. Jascha was still making that maddening sound with his dagger, and she guessed he hadn't even noticed she bumped in a little too close. She closed her eyes, listening to her breathing. One of her hands wiped the tears away, and when she didn't hear the scratching sound of steel anymore, she thought Jascha to have fallen asleep. But his fingers touched the skin between her lips and her left cheek, and she lifted her head to catch a glimpse of his face.

"Can you stop?" It didn't sound like a real question.

He moved again, and his hand dropped. Tecla slid up the floor, narrowing her eyes to see his face. He lied flat on his back, and her lips parted. She wanted to say something, but nothing felt alright. Jascha propped himself on his elbow, and she could feel his glare directed at her. She rested a hand on his wrist and inched herself closer. He seemed to flinch under her touch, and that felt like a blow aimed at her stomach. Her breath fell on his chin, and she heard him swallow.

"I ask you not to," he said. It was neither a plea nor an order, and his voice sounded more pained than anything.

Tecla wanted to ask why, but the word died in her throat. She leaned in instead until her lips found his. It was only that, one kiss and one breath they shared. She tasted salty from her tears, while his were the lips of a bloodied corpse. Jascha's hand gripped the side of her neck, and he shared another breath with her, pushing her against the floor as his tongue lapped at her lips. Her leg sneaked up his side, mimicking the way her arm was curled around his shoulders, her tongue pressing against his. He snapped out of it, tearing himself away from her, but not quite letting go of her body.

She was sprawled there, her hair reaching out in all directions, her dress hiking dangerously high, and even her necklace was caught in a knot between her locks and the ties of her mantle. Jascha could see her face despite the darkness, light hues often escaping the pendant she wore. Tecla's fingers found the hem of his shirt, tugging him towards her. She looked at him without fear nor disgust. He grabbed her wrist, tearing a piece of dead skin from his lips, and tried to disentangle his legs from hers. She was faster than him, however, cradling his body against hers. She didn't try to kiss him again, preferring to press her fingers around his spine in a simple embrace.

  Jascha lowered her on the floor again, his hand sliding under her dress and past the bandage around her thigh. He found her round hip and the crook of her waist. He traced her skin as if he could still feel the corset she wore for years. Her ribs were narrow and her skin dry. One move and he could break her bones, but she didn't seem afraid of death. Tecla breathed against his earlobe, planting her nails in his shoulders when his hand traveled down again, around her belly button, and up her stomach until he could squeeze her breasts. They weren't exactly big, not in his hand at least, and she wondered if that was a problem.

  It wasn't, as he grabbed her firmly, one arm around her upper body and his explorative hand pushing her legs apart. They both lied on their sides, facing each other under a faint green light, and she moaned in his mouth. His thumb found a place even she had never touched. It was like a small switch, and every stroke made her squirm. Two other fingers pushed inside, coated with wetness and gripped by her muscles. He bit her lips then, pressing his fingertips against every spot he could find, every bump and every line. His movements were slow and barely noticeable, but Tecla's hips jerked forward, and he removed his hand to undo his britches. She didn't even feel it as he entered her, her mind foggy and her mouth ravaged. The hand that was coated in her juices found her bottom cheek, spreading her further, and one wet finger rested at her back entrance. She yelped against his mouth, feeling his nails plant themselves in her skin, and his finger tease a place she didn't know could be teased.

    He panted against her lips, ever so releasing her tongue, and bucked his hips against hers fast. Jascha noticed the way she kept her eyes closed all along, but he too had a hard time keeping his open. She pushed him then, rolling their bodies on top of the fur, and she straddled his body. Her dress barely covered her, and her cloak had been discarded somewhere behind her. One of his hands tugged at the front of the flimsy fabric, revealing her hardened nipples for him to bite, and lick, and suck. Something hot and wet pooled between their joined bodies, and he glanced at her face. Red cheeks and swollen lips. Half-lidded eyes peered at him. His hands curled around her waist, slamming her body down on his to hear more sounds erupt from her throat. He felt himself stretch inside her and Jascha sat up, fisting her hair. Tecla's head lolled to the side, her cheek resting against his forehead until she licked his lips and looked at him.

    He released a breath he didn't know he was holding, and she vanished from his sight. He sat naked on his bed; the crimson sheets covered by black pelted fur. The canopy was dusty and the furniture in his room was ruined. He remembered. There had been fire after his parents fought, right there, in his bed-chamber. His mother had pulled the black curtains, ripped them off, and thrown them in the fireplace. She had pulled her hair out too, the long black locks falling out of the updo and littering the stone floor. She couldn't bear the sight of her hair around her feet, and so she had pushed the rugs, and the chairs, and the tiny round table he played at—everything was to burn.

    Jascha could feel her arms around him too. He felt small. He was small. Her grey-blue eyes stared straight ahead as she climbed the large, curved stairs that led to his father's bed-chamber. She was clenching her jaw and the little black hat she wore to hide just how much she hurt her scalp also covered her forehead. He felt sorrow invade his mind as he took in his mother's appearance. Her small, pointed nose, her rosy lips, and her slender arms; how long had it been since she cradled him like that?

    The door was pushed open and he heard his parents scream again. He saw his old, weakened father left to starve. He wore long, high-waist pants and an elegant coat that flared past his waist like a double tail. His clothes too were black and shiny, but the old man's eyes were filled with anger and desperation. His unruly grey hair went past his shoulders, and he tried to take Jascha away.

    "Not the boy, Karleen," he shouted at Jascha's mother. "Not my boy." His northwestern accent was thick and not pleasant to hear, especially when he butchered Jascha's mother's name, yet in the little boy's memory, the accent was associated with playdays. He liked playdays.

She shoved him out of her way, but not before snatching a strand of grey hair. Jascha watched her kiss it and let it catch fire from the nearest wall torch. Jascha heard himself cry, high-pitched, deep sobs filling the hallways of the ancestral home.

"No, Father," his mother hissed. "It has to be him."

Jascha remembered the way he tore his eyes away as the kind old man he knew as his parent burned. The servants had remained silent, even that girl he played with when she wasn't cleaning the floors didn't say anything. "Irry, Irry," he called, earning only a slap from his mother as they abandoned their home and hopped on a carriage followed by wagons. All he had wanted to do that day was to play with Irry and her straw dolls.

His chest was hurting as though a horde galloped over his body and crushed his bones. It was night then, and the starless skies reminded him of the ceiling of his room. Black, infinite, and cold. He couldn't hear the singing of the striges nor any other sound though. No wild animal seemed to inhabit the forest. He lied down, unmoving, unflinching. His mother was there, Jascha was sure of it. He couldn't see her, but he could recognize her touch. For the first time, his mother's touch hurt him. It was horrible, he thought as she pressed something inside his chest, something that cut through his skin like wild cats scratched down trees. His body shook violently and he heard himself cry again. He sobbed until he felt too weak, and the smell of charred skin nauseated him.

He must have done something that greatly upset that woman named Karleen who looked less and less like his mother. Jascha was not allowed to leave his bed-chambers, which he now shared with his father.

"Lord Larcel," the servants who brought them food would greet the charred corpse whose eyes looked right back at them. Jascha only wanted to cry as he ate alone. One day, he decided this Lord Larcel wasn't his father, for the playdays would always be the same and the pile of bones never moved one of his wooden soldiers. He turned the chair to have Lord Larcel look outside the window, although the fog was so thick Jascha doubted the lord was entertained.

Jascha could feel tears stream down his cheeks. The little wooden soldiers had been removed, and it was that day again. He had relived that day countless times now. It was the music box on the vanity, her mother's reflection, fancy and smiling. "The first, the last, the only boy. Can that be?" he heard her sing. It was the day of his eleventh birthday. She needed him to be awake, for he was a man now. "A weak, disgusting man," she would say in front of her handmaids. "A disease," she would repeat while she lowered her body on his, writhing and biting his jawline.

Someone who shouldn't have been allowed to exist, he thought. She hated him, truly; she blamed him for many things, and he never really understood why, but the biggest disappointment for Karleen was the day he heard the cries in her room. Jascha had been used to the groans and the moans. He had seen her smile and snarl. She had brushed his hair and pushed him down the stairs. Those cries were different, and a sandy-haired man knelt beside him. The maids rushed in and out of his mother's bed-chamber, buckets full of blood and dirty linens. Jascha was handed a little creature that moved in his arms. It was no bigger than the dolls he played with when he was allowed to see Irry. The man with kind eyes told him he was allowed to choose a name, for his mother slept, and he wasn't sure when she would open her eyes.

"I don't know," Jascha echoed the little boy's words.

The animate doll was taken away from him rapidly. Karleen beat him for days when she finally rose from her slumber. Not a girl, she screamed at the top of her lungs. Not a girl. They would take her away, and then they would realize she had stolen from them, she told him. Jascha had no idea who she talked about. His ribs were broken and he had trouble breathing, but finally, his mother collapsed, and her scrawny body was taken as well.

They locked her away, with only a few healers coming to check on the fog that had touched her. They came every day until they fell ill as well, and only the man with kind eyes returned. He was with another man, Jascha could see it now. The stranger was tall and lean, wearing garments that reminded him of his father's attire, but the tailcoat was pure emerald. Pewter eyes looked at him, and the stranger with wavy, platinum hair offered him a warm smile. It made him cry, for the man held the little doll in his arms.

"This is what she wanted. The girl wouldn't be safe," the sandy-haired man said.

"It was always our agreement," the other man replied. His knuckles brushed against the moving doll's face and Jascha wanted to pull on the blanket that hid the toy from him. "You are a serene girl, aren't you, Rohais? Or do you prefer Julischa?"

Jascha's eyes burned as the man walked away and all he could do was furiously pound against the locked doors of the mother's bedchamber. The doors quaked so hard the handles shaped in the canine beast of his lands nearly came to life. He called his mother's name, begging her to open the doors and let him in. He wanted his wooden soldiers back, and the doll too, and the real Lord Larcel, and to be able to smell her perfume again.

The pain was too unbearable as the pounding threatened to make his head explode. His hands patted around, gripping the first object they found. The boy needed to stop. The screaming was insupportable too. He needed it all to stop. He aimed at the boy's back, planting his dagger into his flesh, and he was left with silence, and the distinct smell of something burning.

Jascha looked down, and his hand was tainted. Half his dagger was embedded into naked skin, and where his scar had once been on his chest was now a deep gash that smelled and smoked. He stopped breathing as his eyes looked back into

Tecla's and he watched the way her hazel orbs once stained with blue sucked in the black of his irises. She held something in her hand, a wide onyx-colored stone that had come right out of his burnt chest. It was shaped just like Tecla's stone, only he could see his reflection in it. His eyes were now grey-blue, just like his mother's had been, and the ringing in his ears disappeared.

The woman coughed and whined in his arms, glancing back and forth between the Quiet Tear in her hand and his dagger in her stomach.

"No," he whispered, dread filling his voice. "No, no, no," he repeated, laying her down with care as her eyes darted around. "I have to find… I have to… What did I do?" he whispered to himself, fisting his hair. He couldn't let her die, not like that, he told himself.

"What did I do?"

Chapter XXXIX

Moondust

The three knocks thundered against the wooden door so hard that Rantha thought the wall would come down as well. "Open the fucking door," came the harsh command. "Rantha, open the door!"

Rantha wearily walked towards the door and heard Zurzon exit one of the rooms upstairs. They exchanged a worried look, one that said opening the door was a mistake, but she couldn't help it. They would probably break in either way. She hoped she was wrong as she gripped the handle and pulled. She had sent both Sanson and Maryell away the moment fires erupted around Rainier's End and the surveillants left the city to either march on the capital or flee for their safety. They weren't the main problem though; Rantha had preferred to send both her apprentices to their respective families the moment food became scarce and merchants no longer entered the city. Many people fell ill over the winter due to the lack of provisions, and with diseases came the vultures, and the mice, and those who couldn't move stayed in the confines of their houses until they no longer could bear it and tried to find something to eat, belongings to sell.

    She and Zurzon had treated some who had come in either injured or poisoned from eating rotten flesh, and they all died. The family from Three Crosses was still upstairs, and she would guard the shelter at night while Zurzon looked after them. Rantha glanced at the shovel by the door she kept in case someone decided to target the Illusion Shelter. It was still dirty from the last body she buried in the yard. She wished she could build pyres for all of them.

    Rantha opened the door, her face relaxing for a moment. She raised her eyebrows and her full lips parted. She pushed back the green shawl that covered her curls and stared at the man who stood in the snow with a pleading look.

    "Help me, please."

    Her lips moved, but no sound came out. She cleared her throat. "Jascha? Is that… Is that you?"

    The face was his, and so his hair, but gone were the midnight pools, replaced by smokey azure eyes. The hard contours of his face seemed blurred as if he had stepped out of a painting, and he was crying. In his arms was a woman with a dagger in her stomach, and Rantha recognized the weapon instantly. The man who stood at the door was indeed Jascha. The light chestnut-haired girl seemed to be breathing, but with difficulty.

Rantha's expression quickly changed. It was his dagger, and Opherus had been clear with her. She shouldn't let him in. The ire she had witnessed before came back stronger than ever, and Jascha pushed her out of the way, barking at her like a feral hound.

"Just let me in."

She heard the stairs cracking under Zurzon's weight, and soon the tanned man narrowed his almond eyes at the woman Jascha carried. The words they exchanged were lost on Rantha the moment she noticed the bloodied bandage around the woman's thigh. Sweet Yenny was on her mind, the way she had been injured and how she fell out the window and smashed her head.

Rantha's slender fingers curled around Zurzon's shoulder, and she nodded at him so he would take the girl. Peares and his family stayed upstairs, and previously Rantha hadn't wanted to risk anyone's life by having them stay in a nearby room with open wounds, however, Irryelda seemed to be plagued mostly after sundown and not as frequently as before. They could still hear her moans and one-sided conversations, but Rantha was focused only on one thing; getting Jascha out of her house.

"You need to leave now. You can't stay here," she told him, mustering the courage to send him away.

He turned around to fully face her, his fists clenching and unclenching. "Who do you think you are?"

"Who do you think you are?" she snapped right back at him. "You think you can barge in here after the way you left? After what you've called me? And what about her," Rantha breathed out, pointing in the direction of the stairs. "What did you do?"

Jascha tilted his head in an animalistic manner. She was sure he would have snapped her neck if she wasn't about to take care of the girl.

"Oh, go on," she gauged him, pushing him away. "Act offended and dangerous." She turned heels to look after the girl he brought in, but not without warning him. "But get out of here."

She bolted away from him, rearranging the rag around her shoulders to properly cover her hair. In the kitchens, she dipped her hands in a cauldron full of hot water to make sure she was clean. She rushed upstairs and pushed the door open with a hip movement. Zurzon seemed already at work. He removed the two cloaks the girl had been wearing and let them on the floor and tore the dress she wore to cover her body with clean linen. Rantha studied her face for a moment, but she didn't look like anyone she had seen before. She had to be a wealthy lady, however, for around her neck a blue-green pendant shone brighter than Rantha's oil lamps and she seemed to be clutching another precious stone in her hand.

Had Jascha tried to steal from her? No, that sounded ludicrous. The healer knew he carried enough silvers with him, and if he had wanted the girl's jewels, he wouldn't have brought her to the shelter. If he had meant any harm, he wouldn't have brought her to the shelter, Rantha mentally corrected herself. Perhaps, she had misjudged the situation. Still, it was his dagger in the young woman's stomach.

      Rantha sat across from Zurzon, clean gauzes in her hands. She watched him extract the dagger with a steady hand to respect the way it had pierced the girl's skin and dropped it on the end table where his other tools were. Rantha pressed the gauzes into the wound immediately, applying enough pressure while Zurzon wet the young woman's lips with some Dreamer's Root juice to ease the pain. The older healer replaced the gauzes several times until the bleeding became less violent, and the two of them proceeded with cleaning the wound. It wasn't too deep, she realized in relief. The extent of the damage could be controlled, and no major blood vessel seemed to have been slashed.

      "I've got this, Rantha," she heard Zurzon whisper. "Could you get her some clothes? I think it's better if you're the one to dress her."

      She nodded, smiling faintly. She picked the woman's clothes from the floor. The bloodied dress had to be thrown away, Rantha decided. The front was torn and it was ruined in several spots, not to mention it was too soft and too light of a piece of clothing to be worn in the winter. She threw it in a corner. She would wash it and use it as a cleaning rag some other time. The lighter cloak needed to be doubled, for that one too, was too light for the season. Rantha's brown eyes glanced at the sleeping woman and wondered where she came from for her to be wearing these clothes and survive. Rantha balled the brown mantle under her arm and shook the heavier one. It was Jascha's, she recognized the fabric. She had cleaned it before.

Something fell from an outer pocket, and Rantha sighed. She had been holding the cloak upside down. She bent and grabbed the half-crumpled paper, and she felt her strength leave her. The furs fell from her arms as she recognized Yenny's calligraphy and the blue ink she used whenever they studied together. Opherus had been right all along.

"Zurzon, please dress her yourself when you're done," she spoke seriously.

Rantha padded across the small room, folding the drawing and sliding it in the pocket of her skirt. She closed the door behind her; the hinges screeched a bit, but it wasn't enough to alarm the family resting in the room at the far end of the corridor. The shelter was rather quiet, she thought as she came to the top of the stairs. Jascha hadn't left at all. He sat with his head in his hands, his body leaning against the top newel like a scolded child. Somehow, she still found herself empathizing with him. She stood beside him, watching the way his shoulders slumped and his chest heaved.

He sensed her presence, for he wiped his face with his hands and rose to his feet without ever looking at her. "So," he croaked out.

"She will recover," Rantha told him. "What happened to you?" she asked, sounding worried when she was truly furious. "Talk to me."

Jascha turned his head in her direction, his azure stare the mirror of a thousand emotions he never felt until that day. "I healed," he voiced out incredulously.

Rantha nodded, her lower lip quivering. She wished she felt relieved for his sake, but the injustice of it all was too heavy. He had healed, but he was still the man who took Yenny from her, wasn't he? Her fingers tightened around the wrinkled paper in her pocket, and finally, she handed it to him. "I found this," she told him bluntly. "Did you do it? Did you push Yenny out of that window?" she asked quietly, yet resentfully. "What else did you do to her?"

He shook his head lightly, a pained chuckle filling their ears. "I don't think you could ever understand."

"I understand she tried to help you, as I have. As the girl with a bleeding stomach has." She took a step closer, trying to have him look at her. "I understand," Rantha contradicted him again. "I understand you brought her here because it wasn't your intention to hurt her. Tell me it wasn't your intention to hurt Yenny either."

Jascha's eyes never left hers. She waited for a yes that never came while the floor was quickly filled by a woman's cries and incomprehensible sentences muffled by bawling. Rantha let the tears run down her cheeks with the next blink of her eyes. She tossed the drawing, paying no attention when it flew over the stairs and fell somewhere on the lower floor.

"I wish it was you." She punched his chest; her movements fragile. "I wish it was you," she repeated.

He grasped her wrist, and it sent her over the edge.

"Leave," she growled at him. "I will not let you in there," she told him, waving at the door that led to Tecla. "You have done enough."

Jascha's hand clenched her limb so tightly it cut off the circulation. "Move, Rantha," he ordered her in the voice she finally recognized, the one filled with disgust. When she didn't budge, he shoved her against the nearest wall to walk towards the room, but she was quick.

Rantha leaped at him, her fingers tugging at his jacket to stop him. She tried pushing him out of her way, but the opposite happened. He seized her forearms and spun around, bending her shoulder at an awkward angle, and she screamed out of pain. They wobbled backward, and she wouldn't let go of him despite the fact he heard her bones pop. Jascha made a sound in the back of his throat and shoved her forcefully, causing Rantha to stumble on the hem of her dress. Her heel slipped against the floor nosing, and she rolled backward down the stairs, releasing a cry of panic. Her head hit the wall string, her teeth collided with the riser of the stairs, and Jascha froze in place when he saw her smash her face against the split landing. The wood cracked, but she kept falling down the narrow tread, and when it was over, she no longer moved. Her neck was bent at an impossible angle, and her wide-open eyes stared at the ceiling.

The door opened behind him, and he heard Rantha's apprentice mutter something at his back. Jascha didn't acknowledge his presence until

Zurzon's hands were on his shoulders, but Jascha flared his nostrils and walked backward until the two of them collided with the door frame. Zurzon let out a pained scream as his spine hit the corner of the wooden frame and Jascha quickly rushed to the end table where his dirty dagger was. He heard humming coming from an adjacent room, followed by the hushing and shushing of someone else. He knew that tune. He had always known that tune.

"Dark and steady, Loveleen walks,
"She has not seen daybreak yet.
"Loveleen tell me where he is,
"I know my boy surely lives."

✳✳✳

Tecla could still feel her ribs break. She could feel every blow the woman aimed at the little boy, hear every word hissed in his face, and even feel the woman's flesh against her own as she forced her body on the child. Tecla felt sick, the shivers and the emotions that coursed through her body as if they were truly part of her life wouldn't stop. They poured on her in quick, endless succession, and from the relentless pounding on the doors with the crest of the feral beast, she found herself covered in snow. Her ears were filled with screams that vibrated in her throat but weren't hers. She felt another body straddling her. She heard a song, and the flesh of her back was exposed. She felt the air pierce her body as though she were a mere ghost.

"Loveleen you have sent him to his tomb."
"You said you didn't know the song."

Tecla turned around, only to see Jascha's face. He looked paler and blood had splashed all over his clothes. She looked in the black of his eyes, only to see more pairs of eyes. She stared at a girl with green eyes who smiled and drew and screamed, and then she saw the tears of one not as fair. She smelled the scent of soups and tarts that mixed with blood, heard the hammers of a forge, and the singing of little children playing in the open and running towards her. Tecla felt nails pinning her limbs and the iron bite at her skin, marking her like an animal. She felt the blood spill from where it shouldn't, from her ears to the space between her bottom cheeks. Everything was dark around her until she saw Jascha again, but he was with another; one taller and fuller, with vivid emerald eyes she had seen before. Her stare stung like a hot needle under her skin and her vision faded again.

Footsteps shook her from her reverie, and she found herself between the shelves of Danyell's Athenaeum. She saw herself between books but didn't hear the words she already knew.

"What do you have?"

"Stones and Songs of Aelneth," Tecla answered.

Her eyelids fluttered open, and she saw two people hunched over her body. She couldn't focus on their features, but one had hair just like Lyzon's. Tecla smiled. She had only been dreaming. It had all been a dream, and she was back home. Almond eyes glanced at her and that look alone sent her somewhere she had never been before. She saw golden waterfalls and mountains shaped like arches. People spoke a melodic language she didn't understand, and a group of children and young adults swam in an ocean so deep Tecla could see the darkening blue of the depths. The man who looked at her seemed much younger, and his hair was shorter. His arm was extended in the direction of a little girl who swam naked on her back and laughed loudly. She was tanned too, with thick black hair and feline eyes.

"Lyzon," she heard the man call the little girl in a worried tone.

"Lyzon?" Tecla whispered.

He said something after, but Tecla didn't understand their foreign words. The little Lyzon swam closer to the beach and wrapped herself in a light towel.

"Please, dress her yourself once you're done," another woman spoke.

Tecla looked around and saw a brown woman with a squeezed paper in her hands. She was beautiful, Tecla thought. The woman had little dimples around her mouth and eyes big enough to swallow the moon with one stare.

Her face stuck in her mind even after the woman left, and she watched as another woman walked around a small keep, not even half the size of Strongshore's keep. She looked a lot like the beauty who just left, but small differences were enough of an indication that at best, they were related.

"Mama. Mama."

"Stop playing in the yard, Rantha," the woman scolded a child Tecla couldn't see. "Sir Loys wants to see you."

The girl ran with flowers in her arms, her body disappearing in the field of golden, blue, and white roses until she reached a massive tree with branches and leaves that formed one big, colorful umbrella. Two men argued while they shielded themselves from the sun, but Rantha didn't seem to notice. She ran faster and laughed even louder, squirming as she stumbled and rolled forward.

"Loys, I can't possibly remain here. Your sister Eloisa was clear about this. She will tell her lord husband and they will claim Bane's Keep as theirs the moment word spreads."

"What Lovel Riverguard wants is none of my concern. Stay, Thierry. We are far from Courtbridge. And I don't need the castle, I don't need anything."

The man named Thierry shook his head, and politely bowed before turning heels and never looking back.

Tecla felt something warm engulf her, and when she finally woke up, she realized her stomach was bandaged. Her thigh had been taken care of too; she could feel the stitches. But most importantly, someone slid a thick shirt over her head and warm puttees up her legs. She wore a skirt as well, one loose enough for her midsection to be examined.

Zurzon averted his eyes and he smiled at her. He was at the door, looking like he was leaving. "Stay still, my lady," she heard him say. "It's best if you rest. It's nothing serious."

Tecla lied back down but she could hear the voices outside. It was Jascha and the previous woman, Rantha. Her voice was breaking. Their sounds were loud enough to make the walls vibrate. Their fighting seemed to have woken up someone else as Tecla heard haunting wails and hushed voices that reminded her of gargles. There was a scream followed by a loud thud, and Tecla held her breath. She couldn't stay still.

She pushed herself up, groaning when the pain in her stomach pulsated through her body. She leaned against the night table then the wall, taking steps so small she wasn't sure she would make it outside.

She heard another thud, and this time Zurzon's voice reached her ears. "What do you think you're doing? I'm going to kill…" The rest of his sentence was muffled.

Tecla was almost at the door of the tiny room when she saw Jascha barge in with the man who just dressed her wound. She heard someone sing behind the wall she leaned against, and Jascha looked panicked, as his hands trembled and his steps carried urgency and despair that weighed even on her. He took three long strides to reach her, and before he said anything, he retrieved his dagger from Zurzon's tray and grabbed his cloak that was still on the floor. He quickly wrapped it around her body, avoiding her stare.

The almond-eyed man wouldn't allow them to leave, she realized as he pushed himself towards

Jascha, who stepped out of his charge and locked his arm around the slightly shorter man, who coughed and gasped for air.

"I would have thanked you; I would have," Jascha breathed in his ear, his icy stare locking with Tecla's.

She was frightened, he could tell, as his dagger sheathed itself in Zurzon's lower back once, twice, and enough times to have the floor coated in blood. The healer's body fell to the ground, and the thud had Tecla jump slightly, but she didn't look away. Jascha walked up to her, lifting her with ease. He was still breathing hard, and her forehead was pressed against his chin, his lips only a kiss away from her skin.

Tecla tightened her hands around the black stone she wouldn't let go of while they went downstairs. Her hazel eyes flecked with blue and tainted with black watched in silent dismay the way Rantha lied on the ground, lifeless, and soon they were outside. He put her down on a small cart full of rubbish and straw that didn't belong to either of them. Jascha tied it to his mount using ropes around Arora's body and neck, and it wasn't long until he hopped on and had them leave like thieves.

Her eyes never trailed away until the shelter disappeared from her sight. There was a time where she would have cried relentlessly. She stared down at the Quiet Tear, reveling in its glossy hue. Such times were lost, she thought. They no longer belonged to her; she did not belong to herself.

✳✳✳

Tomas was right. The only way out of the capital was to climb up the walls, but Goldsnout found the perfect timing to do it. He remembered the shifts of the surveillants, and sometimes even he had to patrol at night either with Gulmont or Longspire. It was before Chief Eleres decided he would be the officer to train under him and thankfully, the shifts hadn't changed. The surveillants and the guards had separate meeting points in every area, but Melisentia's Opera stretched a little further compared to the other main parts of the capital, and so Goldsnout found a window to make the climb while it took more time for the assigned men to exchange their reports and return to their spots. He remembered telling Chief Eleres how that kind of system couldn't work and that it would have been far better for the replacement to arrive directly to the spot assigned to them before the previous guards left, but the chief had argued that reports would be lost by the time they'd be sent to the meeting points and then back to the Surveillance's headquarters. Eleres had always been too attached to his pieces of paper to see what would have been more practical, but at that moment, Goldsnout was glad. At least, he could climb up and down without hurrying too much. He didn't want one of his stitched wounds to snap open, despite the fact they were mostly superficial.

Traveling without a horse wasn't easy. It was much slower, but Goldsnout figured it was a good way of getting his strength back. He would be walking only two days; Rainier's End wasn't that far, and he had grown accustomed to the heavy snow. Educator Tomas had given him a couple of loaves of spicy bread so he wouldn't starve until he reached the little town before the Fog Lands. He found shelter between rows of dead trees and forgotten houses; his mind clouded by thoughts fueled by the rumors he heard around Silverholde. They said Limemeadow was being sieged, sometimes they said it was razed. Others said neither rumor was true and that the Sand Towers were riding in the direction of the capital. Tomas had talked a lot about the Drixians, or so they liked to be called lately, mentioning how disappointed he was to hear that the dungeons had been emptied and the prisoners sold as slaves. The word alone was dreadful; it always reminded Goldsnout of how Rantha would undermine herself calling herself a slave.

  Not for long, he chanted in his head. Soon, he would convince her to leave Rainier's End before it was too late. They would find a way past the fog to reach the Rain Lands, or they could try and see if the harbor of Founder's Breach was still in use, if the westerners hadn't closed their gates. They didn't have to stay in the inland towns until a lord, a warrior or a king decided to lay waste to cities and villages. They would manage, and he would write to his mother, hoping that if she didn't respond it was because she had already left the city. Goldsnout woke up with high hopes as the snowstorm quieted down and Rainier's End came into view.

His boots dug into the mud with every step he took. He covered his freckled pink face with the sash around his neck, shielding his eyes with his forearm as the wind sent fat snowflakes in them. He reached the central inn, the initial dread that pooled in his belly spreading through his entire body. Most houses had been burned down, and piles of dead bodies cluttered the streets. Those who seemed alive still either cried or shoved their hands inside the pockets of those who left them, in hopes to find something they could sell, or eat, or both. His thoughts went to Sir Loys Rosenbane, but soon he found the little house behind the inn no longer existed, and his heart sank. He should've told Rantha the truth, he thought with remorse. She had cared for that man, and he had cared about her.

Goldsnout hurried, trying to ignore the massacre around him as he walked in the direction of the outskirts, closer to the Rippling Run. Rantha had to be well; she was hardly a target of muggers and bandits or even soldiers going rogue. She healed people and possessed nothing; she even shared her home with two other grown men.

He reached the Illusion Shelter like a man looking for water in the Dark Barrens. Some lights were on, and from outside Goldsnout could almost see the ghost of the Illusion Lodge, where Rantha said Sir Loys once hosted gatherings, although the taller floors no longer existed. Only Bane's Keep could be seen far behind, its silhouette the only memory of times he never lived. Goldsnout heard screaming inside, or was it chanting? Perhaps,

Rantha's patient was awake, the one touched by the fog.

    The door was open, and he tentatively knocked, but his hopes left him. There she was, the woman he made so many promises to, lying on the floor, completely still. "Rantha," he called, hoping to hear her say something.

    He kneeled beside her, his hands shaking above her head as though his touch would break her more than she already was. Her once bright, warm eyes were wide and void of any emotion or thought, and he couldn't feel her breath on his skin. He lifted her body slowly, hugging her close.

    "Rantha?" he tried again. Her arms were completely limp. Goldsnout broke into tears, his body moving back and forth. "Please," he begged no one. "Wake up. Rantha, say something; you can't—you can't be gone."

    His large arms engulfed her, pressing her face against his chest. His hands found her curly tresses, brushing, and tugging gently. Opherus' lips kissed her forehead and her cheeks. Her lips were cold, and salty as if she had been crying before leaving this world. He still talked to her, hoping she would hear him. Hoping she would forgive him.

    "I should have come sooner," the redhead said, sniffling when his nose was too runny. "I should have left that shithole long ago. You deserved better than me," he chastised himself, fingers tracing her broken neck. "I should have taken you far away from this, but I never insisted. I wanted you to do what gave you a purpose," he told her blank face.

He closed her eyes and rested her head under his chin. Goldsnout lied down too; her body was heavy, but void of any soul. He wanted to die as well; he wanted the ceiling to crumble on top of him along with the skies and the moon. And its dust. She was his, and she was no more.

Epilogue

The woods were thicker around the Restless Channel, or perhaps they seemed that way because the night sky was entirely covered by a thick, dark cloud Tecla had only seen from very far away when she landed in the Sand Towers. The air was frigid, and she couldn't feel her toes inside her boots. The pain in her stomach was still lacerating, and she tried her best not to move. She watched Jascha's back tense as he drove Arora into the forest with ease, as though he already knew his way. She wondered how he could see anything. She didn't even know how long they had been traveling since they left the town called Rainier's End. It could have been hours, but it felt like days.

"Stop the cart," she told him bluntly. Surprisingly, he did.

Jascha dismounted in silence. His nose was red from the cold but he wasn't even shivering. She didn't expect him to suffer from the cold when he callously stabbed a man. She wasn't sure he had it in him to feel much, not when she recalled everything she had seen from his past. He came from a dark place and Tecla thought that even if he disappeared on the other side of the known lands, he would still be in that dark place he was raised in.

He stood next to her and helped her sit up, but Tecla wanted to stand. She wanted to feel the blood flow down her legs, lest she would freeze. Her hair was full of straw. She scratched her scalp, but her nails raked down her skin and she winced. Her flecked eyes rested on the hilt of his dagger. She could still hear Zurzon's flesh tear and his blood splash over his feet.

"Why?" she asked him simply. "Why would you use them?"

Jascha's grey-blue eyes turned a darker shade. "Half of that was an accident."

"Only half."

"What do you want from me?" he rebutted. "Do you want me to tell you I regret it all? What would it change? What would it bring you?" he insisted until his toes touched hers and he loomed over her, his words cutting like the edge of a headsman's ax.

"I don't want anything from you," Tecla answered in a flat tone. "What I want is irrelevant and unattainable. I wanted to go home," she admitted, nodding her head. "I wanted to see those who have wronged me fall from their pedestal. I wanted to see my friends again, and my brother, and be the person I used to be but that is not possible." She lowered her gaze. "I know what you are. I've seen it."

"Have you?" Jascha echoed. His hand found hers, and he stared at the rock nestled against her palm. "You can take it all back," he told her. "If that's what you want."

"It's not funny," Tecla said bitterly, taking a step back. "Tylennald Lionhelm sits on my father's chair thanks to the blood of others. Those who know it are either dead or captured. And those who don't know it want me either dead or captured. I could maybe hire an army from a foreign land but what do I pay them with?" she reasoned, a dejected smile on her chapped lips.

Jascha's shoulders relaxed, and again he stepped forward. "You can have mine," he offered. She laughed and cried at the same time, thinking he was mad. "Three hundred thousand men," he went on. "I don't know how many striges are fully grown by now but maybe a hundred are."

She stood still, taking in his words. She knew those numbers. She had studied those numbers.

"Riders, infantrymen, crossbowmen, halberdiers," he went on stoically. "That woman you say you've seen," Jascha pointed out, his voice faltering, "was Charlaine Rochelac. And the man you've seen was her father, and my father too, Larcel Silenteye. I am the only one left.

"Their men, their weapons. You can take them."

Tecla couldn't believe the words he spoke. She licked her lips, looking at him wearily. "Are you …"

"Sóley Jascha Rochelac," he finished for her, saying his name with shame rather than pride.

Tecla's heart nearly jumped out of her chest, not with excitement, but rather in apprehension. "You're speaking the truth," she stated, although she had meant it as a question. "You're offering your house's forces to me, but what do you want in return?"

"Nothing," Jascha answered. "Everything," he breathed out when she lifted her eyebrows at him. "You."

Her. She wanted to take it all, even if it meant doing exactly what Tylennald did; build something spilling the blood of others. She wanted to brutally march south, and she wanted to see a dozen daggers up Lady Voladea's throat, but it didn't feel quite right. Her father had wanted a peaceful rule for the Silver Lands, one that would last long after kings and queens passed away, one where cities prospered without any family having to send their children to war, or at least that was what she believed.

Jascha didn't say anything to convince her further, standing in front of her like a statue made of marble. She couldn't erase the blood on his hands from her mind. The fresh memory lingered between them like an impassable wall and yet, she could still see the other side of him, feel his hand pressing the cloth against her wound when she fell asleep.

Tecla stretched her arms and her hands held his. She could have danced down the murky road, like the fays danced with death, for his were hands that took lives without second thoughts. His was a world where what stood between him and what he wanted needed to disappear. Her hands released his, and she slid her arms around his body, her head resting against his chest. Jascha wrapped only an arm around her shoulders, inching her towards the cart so she could lie down again. Maybe one day she would be what stood between him and what he wanted, and she would have to disappear.

Appendix

The Regency

"One right, our fatherland."

The Regency is an institution founded by King Helias Rainier before he retired from his functions after reportedly falling ill.

The founding of the Regency took place in Founder's Breach, where a treaty was signed by the overlords of the Silver Lands, resetting the royal calendar.

The Regency resides in Rainier's Pavilion, in the capital of the Silver Continent, Silverholde.

Several orders form the Regency and are led by women and men appointed by King Helias or named by their predecessors:
- Lord Arther Angefort, Secretary of the Regency;
- Grandmaster Rodbertus of Three Crosses, Head of the Observatory Vault;
- Sir Sybbyl Nobleleaf, Suppresser of War;
- Sir Ferrand Nickletail, Head of the Treasure Council;
- Chief Thierry Eleres, Head of the Surveillance;

- Grandmaster Matillis, Head of the Occult Vault until it was closed.

Notable members of the Regency are Theliel Lionhelm, a member of the Treasure Council, Opherus Goldsnout, an officer of the Surveillance, and Tomas of Silverholde, an educator of the Observatory Vault.

House Lionhelm

"Formed from many, now as one."

House Lionhelm is an ancient house of the South, said to be blood-related to the descendants of Alatros the Red, the warrior who conquered most of the territories of the Silver Continent and founded the Kingdom of Drixia after an equally successful conquest across the Tinted Bay.

They reside in Strongshore and rule over its neighboring cities, Edgemere and Summerport.

They have ties to every other noble family of the continent either by marriage or other peaceful agreements.

The current headmasters of House Lionhelm:
- Tithan Lionhelm, born from the marriage between Theliel and Tecla Lionhelm, both deceased, a man of eighty-three years of age;
- Voladea Lionhelm née Terraward, his wife, a woman of seventy years of age.

Their children:

- Thaesonwald Lionhelm, a man of fifty-seven years of age,
- Tylennald Lionhelm, a man of forty-eight years of age;
- Tesfira Lionhelm, a woman of thirty-six years of age;
- Theliel Lionhelm, a man of twenty-nine years of age;
- Tecla Lionhelm, a woman of fourteen years of age.

Their relatives:
- Lady Gwethana Lionhelm née Montel, Thaesonwald's wife, and their two legitimate sons, Tiran and Perren Lionhelm;
- Lady Wallysa Lionhelm née Riverguard, Tylennald's wife, and their two legitimate children, Terrel and Elva Lionhelm;
- Hamley Silverworm, Tesfira's husband, and their only son, Deril Lionhelm, a man of twenty-four years of age.

Strongshore's Council of Steel looks after the daily matters of the South, and each member is named by the headmasters of House Lionhelm:
- Fantine of Glimmerforest, Master-at-Arms;
- Milefried of Summerport, Silver Master;
- Martus of Summerport, Noble Healer;
- Hamley Silverworm, Mayor of Edgemere;
- Algar Irwine, Surveyor of Summerport;

- The Holy Commander of Oracle Hill, Protector of the Faith.

The vassals of House Lionhelm once included the Dawnshields of Everspring, the Sunhorns of Bouldershell, the Terrawards of Summerport, the Rosenfields of Wilderose, and the Angeforts of Limemeadow; however, most of these houses perished due to the Violet Delusion.

House Rochelac

"At once our enemies rest."

The Rochelacs are a family as ancient as House Lionhelm, and they claim to descend from Rohdron the Skeleton, an inhuman being of the tall black mountains.

They reside in Noirmont, the tallest of black mountains, inside a castle carved in the stone, and rule over the surrounding Fog Lands including the town of Three Crosses, where a monstrous beast plagues the simple people and the village of Beggar's Pool.

For centuries, they were involved in the Crimson Crystal Wars to expand their empire from the inland toward the coasts.

Their fate remains unknown since the purple fog engulfed their lands, and their people often suffer from a mysterious illness named the Violet Delusion.

Their current family tree is speculated upon, for Charlaine Rochelac, daughter of Loveleen Rochelac and Larcel Silenteye, is said to be deceased and to have left a son to rule in her place.

The vassals of the Rochelacs include the Montels of Three Crosses and they are the only ones known to have survived the Violet Delusion.

House Rosenfield

"Spirits watch over us."

Rising on lands often disputed between the descendants of Alatros the Red and the First Wardens of the continent, House Rosenfield was a minor house of the South that became a vassal of House Lionhelm during the Crimson Crystal Wars.

Their castle stands between the wooded meadow of Wilderose and the Rough Rill, and the surrounding lands have been abandoned by the villeins of the Rosenfields to trade in the city-port of Edgemere.

The last known heir of House Rosenfield was Frederyc Rosenfield, a knight who left his position as Holy Commander of the Oracle's Angels of Steel for unknown reasons.

From his union with an unnamed lady, Sir Frederyc had three daughters: Breonna, Reanna, and Deanna. They are said to have been massacred by their father, and the haunting tales of their deaths are still told in every corner of the Silver Lands.

House Riverguard

"To the skies, we rise."

Standing strong between Wilderose and Silverholde, House Riverguard holds Courtbridge, surveilling the Rough Rill and the Red Road.

The castle-city once had walls that stretched from the East to the West to prevent the crossing of the river, but such walls are no more than ruins.

Despite the reputation of turncoats, the Riverguards maintain a firm hold on their lands and are deeply invested in the matters of the South.

The headmasters of House Riverguard are:
- Lovel Riverguard;
- Eloisa Riverguard née Rosenbane.

Their children:
- Wallysa Riverguard, married to Tylennald Lionhelm;
- Meryld Riverguard, betrothed to Arther Angefort.

Sons of Ferngrunn

"Grow strong, die free."

The Sons of Ferngrunn are the most ancient tribe of the North, claiming to be of the blood of Ferngrunn, a warrior of the Avoryon Hills who moved to the northeastern coast to found the Sand Towers.

The history of the Sand Towers and the Sons of Ferngrunn is old and shrouded by mystery but many agree on saying that Ferngrunn was the one warrior able to defeat Alatros the Red during his conquest of the South thanks to a pact he made with the Deities.

The towers the Sons of Ferngrunn live in allow them to watch over the holy city of Hvallatr, the only city between the coast and the Dark Barrens that separate them from the Fog Lands of the Rochelacs.

The current Sons of Ferngrunn in charge of the Sand Towers are Thaum, Remm, and Mokr. They boast a vast navy and strong military but they have remained peaceful throughout the centuries.

Notable vassals of the Sons of Ferngrunn are House Nobleleaf and House Olborr.

House Rosenbane

"Risen to the Heights."

Born from the legitimization of a bastard branch of House Rosenfield, House Rosenbane left the South in favor of the capital. King Maucolyn Rainier granted them lordship over the lands between Silverholde and the Fog Lands, and for centuries the Rosenbanes were in charge of the keep where the worst criminals were sent.

They resided in Bane's Keep until the knight appointed to it fell ill and allegedly died to the Violet Delusion and the town where the castle still stands was renamed Rainier's End, the small settlement being the last location where King Helias Rainier was seen in public.

The last known Rosenbanes are Sir Loys, and his older sister Lady Eloisa, who married Lord Lovel Riverguard.

Sir Loys was respected for opening the Illusion Shelter, a place that welcomes the ill and the injured after a good part of his Illusion Lodge was burned.

Healers Rantha and Zurzon worked for Sir Loys since they were little and until his death.

CPSIA information can be obtained
at www.ICGtesting.com
Printed in the USA
BVHW031727030221
599298BV00001B/4